MISTRY, Rohinton

Family matters

by the same author

TALES FROM FIROZSHA BAAG
SUCH A LONG JOURNEY
A FINE BALANCE

ROHINTON MISTRY

Family Matters

faber and faber

First published in 2002
by Faber and Faber Limited
3 Queen Square London WC1N 3AU
Paperback edition first published in 2003
This paperback edition published in 2006

Typeset by Faber and Faber Ltd
Printed in England by Mackays of Chatham, plc

The right of [Rohinton Mistry] to be [identified as author of] his work
has been ass[erted in accordance with Section 77 of the Copyright,]
[Designs and Patents Act 1988]

Excerpt from [ ] © 1935
(Renewed) b[ ] [for the world, exclu]ding the
US, China, J[apan, Okinawa controlled by Warner Chappell] Music
Ltd. All r[ights reserved. Used by permission of Warner] Bros.
[Publications US Inc., Miami, FL. 33014]

Excerpt from 'One Day When We Were Young' by Oscar
Hammerstein II and Dimitri Tiomkine. Copyright © 1938. All rights
for the world, excluding the US, China, Japan, Okinawa controlled
by Warner Chappell Music Ltd. All rights reserved. Used by permission of Warner Bros. Publications US Inc., Miami, FL. 33014

A CIP record for this book
is available from the British Library

ISBN 978–0–571–23055–6
ISBN 0–571–23055–5

2 4 6 8 10 9 7 5 3 1

For Freny

A SPLASH OF LIGHT from the late-afternoon sun lingered at the foot of Nariman's bed as he ended his nap and looked towards the clock. It was almost six. He glanced down where the warm patch had lured his toes. Knurled and twisted, rendered birdlike by age, they luxuriated in the sun's comfort. His eyes fell shut again.

By and by, the scrap of sunshine drifted from his feet, and he felt a vague pang of abandonment. He looked at the clock again: gone past six now. With some difficulty he rose to prepare for his evening walk. In the bathroom, while he slapped cold water on his face and gargled, he heard his stepson and stepdaughter over the sound of the tap.

"Please don't go, Pappa, we beseech you," said Jal through the door, then grimaced and adjusted his hearing aid, for the words had echoed deafeningly in his own ear. The device was an early model; a metal case the size of a matchbox was clipped to his shirt pocket and wired to the earpiece. It had been a reluctant acquisition four years ago, when Jal had turned forty-five, but he was not yet used to its vagaries.

"There, that's better," he said to himself, before becoming loud again: "Now, Pappa, is it too much to ask? Please stay home, for your own good."

"Why is this door shut that we have to shout?" said Coomy. "Open it, Jal."

She was two years younger than her brother, her tone sharper than his, playing the scold to his peacemaker. Thin like him, but sturdier, she had taken after their mother, with few curves to soften the lines and angles. During her girlhood, relatives would scrutinize her and remark sadly that a father's love was sunshine and fresh water without which a daughter could not bloom; a stepfather, they said, was quite useless in this regard. Once, they were careless and spoke in her hearing. Their words had incandesced painfully in her mind, and she had fled to her room to weep for her dead father.

Jal tried the bathroom door; it was locked. He scratched his thick wavy hair before knocking gently. The inquiry failed to elicit a response.

Coomy took over. "How many times have I told you, Pappa? Don't lock the door! If you fall or faint inside, how will we get you out? Follow the rules!"

Nariman rinsed the lather from his hands and reached for the towel. Coomy had missed her vocation, he felt. She should have been a headmistress, enacting rules for hapless schoolgirls, making them miserable. Instead, here she was, plaguing him with rules to govern every aspect of his shrunken life. Besides the prohibition against locked doors, he was required to announce his intention to use the WC. In the morning he was not to get out of bed till she came to get him. A bath was possible only twice a week when she undertook its choreography, with Jal enlisted as stage manager to stand by and ensure his safety. There were more rules regarding his meals, his clothes, his dentures, his use of the radiogram, and in charitable moments Nariman accepted what they never tired of repeating: that it was all for his own good.

He dried his face while she continued to rattle the knob. "Pappa! Are you okay? I'm going to call a locksmith and have all the locks removed, I'm warning you!"

His trembling hands took a few moments to slide the towel back on the rod. He opened the door. "Hello, waiting for me?"

"You'll drive me crazy," said Coomy. "My heart is going dhuk-dhuk, wondering if you collapsed or something."

"Never mind, Pappa is fine," said Jal soothingly. "And that's the main thing."

Smiling, Nariman stepped out of the bathroom and hitched up his trousers. The belt took longer; shaking fingers kept

2

missing the buckle pin. He followed the gentle slant of sunlight from the bed to the window, delighting in its galaxies of dust, the dancing motes locked in their inscrutable orbits. Traffic noise had begun its evening assault on the neighbourhood. He wondered why it no longer offended him.

"Stop dreaming, Pappa," said Coomy. "Please pay attention to what we say."

Nariman thought he smelled the benign fragrance of earth after rain; he could almost taste it on his tongue. He looked outside. Yes, water was dripping to the pavement. In a straight drip. Not rain, then, but the neighbour's window boxes.

"Even with my healthy legs, Pappa, walking is a hazard," said Jal, continuing the daily fuss over his stepfather's outing. "And lawlessness is the one certainty in the streets of Bombay. Easier to find a gold nugget on the footpath than a tola of courtesy. How can you take any pleasure in a walk?"

Socks. Nariman decided he needed socks, and went to the dresser. Looking for a pair in the shallow drawer, he spoke into it, "What you say is true, Jal. But the sources of pleasure are many. Ditches, potholes, traffic cannot extinguish all the joys of life." His hand with its birdwing tremble continued to search. Then he gave up and stuffed bare feet into shoes.

"Shoes without socks? Like a Pathan?" said Coomy. "And see how your hands are shaking? You can't even tie the laces."

"Yes, you could help me."

"Happily – if you were going somewhere important like the doctor, or fire-temple for Mamma's prayers. But I won't encourage foolishness. How many people with Parkinson's do what you do?"

"I'm not going trekking in Nepal. A little stroll down the lane, that's all."

Relenting, Coomy knelt at her stepfather's feet and tied his laces as she did every evening. "First week of August, monsoon in fury, and you want a little stroll."

He went to the window and pointed at the sky. "Look, the rain has stopped."

3

"A stubborn child, that's what you are," she complained. "Should be punished like a child. No dinner for disobedience, hanh?"

With her cooking that would be a prize, not a punishment, he thought.

"Did you hear him, Jal? The older he gets, the more insulting he is!"

Nariman realized he'd said it aloud. "I must confess, Jal, your sister frightens me. She can even hear my thoughts."

Jal could hear only a garble of noise, confounded by the earpiece that augmented Coomy's strong voice while neglecting his stepfather's murmurings. Readjusting the volume control, he lifted his right index finger like an umpire giving a batsman out, and returned to the last topic his ears had picked up. "I agree with you, Pappa, the sources of pleasure are many. Our minds contain worlds enough to amuse us for an eternity. Plus you have your books and record player and radio. Why leave the flat at all? It's like heaven in here. This building isn't called Chateau Felicity for nothing. I would lock out the hell of the outside world and spend all my days indoors."

"You couldn't," said Nariman. "Hell has ways of permeating heaven's membrane." He began softly, "'Heaven, I'm in heaven,'" which irritated Coomy even more, and he stopped humming. "Just think back to the Babri Mosque riots."

"You're right," conceded Jal. "Sometimes hell does seep through."

"You're agreeing with his silly example?" said Coomy indignantly. "The riots were in the streets, not indoors."

"I think Pappa is referring to the old Parsi couple who died in their bedroom," said Jal.

"You remember that, don't you, Coomy?" said Nariman. "The goondas who assumed Muslims were hiding in Dalal Estate and set fire to it?"

"Yes, yes, my memory is better than yours. And that was a coincidence – pure bad luck. How often does a mosque in

4

Ayodhya turn people into savages in Bombay? Once in a blue moon."

"True," said Nariman. "The odds are in our favour." He resisted the urge to hum "Blue Moon."

"Just last week in Firozsha Baag an old lady was beaten and robbed," said Jal. "Inside her own flat. Poor thing is barely clinging to life at Parsi General."

"Which side are you on?" asked Coomy, exasperated. "Are you arguing Pappa should go for a walk? Are you saying the world has not become a dangerous place?"

"Oh, it has," Nariman answered for Jal. "Especially indoors."

She clenched her fists and stormed out. He blew on his glasses and polished them slowly with a handkerchief. His fading eyesight, tiresome dentures, trembling limbs, stooped posture, and shuffling gait were almost ready for their vesperal routine.

With his umbrella, which he used as walking stick, Nariman Vakeel emerged from Chateau Felicity. The bustling life was like air for starving lungs, after the stale emptiness of the flat.

He went to the lane where the vegetable vendors congregated. Their baskets and boxes, overflowing with greens and legumes and fruits and tubers, transformed the corner into a garden. French beans, sweet potatoes, coriander, green chilies, cabbages, cauliflowers bloomed under the street lights, hallowing the dusk with their colour and fragrance. From time to time, he bent down to touch. Voluptuous onions and glistening tomatoes enticed his fingers; the purple brinjals and earthy carrots were irresistible. The subjivalas knew he wasn't going to buy anything, but they did not mind, and he liked to think they understood why he came.

In the flower stall two men sat like musicians, weaving strands of marigold, garlands of jasmine and lily and rose, their fingers picking, plucking, knotting, playing a floral melody. Nariman imagined the progress of the works they performed: to supplicate deities in temples, honour the photo-frames of someone's ancestors, adorn the hair of wives and mothers and daughters.

The bhel-puri stall was a sculptured landscape with its golden pyramid of sev, the little snow mountains of mumra, hillocks of puris, and, in among their valleys, in aluminium containers, pools of green and brown and red chutneys.

A man selling bananas strolled up and down the street. The bunches were stacked high and heavy upon his outstretched arm: a balancing and strong-man act rolled into one.

It was all magical as a circus, felt Nariman, and reassuring, like a magic show.

On the eve of his seventy-ninth birthday, he came home with abrasions on his elbow and forearm, and a limp. He had fallen while crossing the lane outside Chateau Felicity.

Coomy opened the door and screamed, "My God! Come quick, Jal! Pappa is bleeding!"

"Where?" asked Nariman, surprised. The elbow scrape had left a small smear on his shirt. "This? You call this bleeding?" He shook his head with a slight chuckle.

"How can you laugh, Pappa?" said Jal, full of reproach. "We are dying of anxiety over your injuries."

"Don't exaggerate. I tripped on something and twisted my foot a little, that's all."

Coomy soaked a ball of cotton wool in Dettol to wipe the scrapes clean, and the arm, smarting under the antiseptic, pulled back. She flinched in empathy, blowing on it. "Sorry, Pappa. Better?"

He nodded while her gentle fingers patted the raw places, then covered them with sticking plaster. "Now we should give thanks to God," she said, putting away the first-aid box. "You know how serious it could have been? Imagine if you had tripped in the middle of the main road, right in the traffic."

"Oh!" Jal covered his face with his hands. "I can't even think of it."

6

"One thing is certain," said Coomy. "From now on you will not go out."

"I agree," said Jal.

"Stop being idiotic, you two."

"And what about you, Pappa?" said Coomy. "Tomorrow you'll complete seventy-nine years, and still you don't act responsibly. No appreciation for Jal and me, or the things we do for you."

Nariman sat, trying to maintain a dignified silence. His hands were shaking wretchedly, defying all the effort of his will to keep them steady in his lap. The tremor in his legs was growing too, making his knees bounce like some pervert jiggling his thighs. He tried to remember: had he taken his medication after lunch?

"Listen to me," he said, tired of waiting for calm to return to his limbs. "In my youth, my parents controlled me and destroyed those years. Thanks to them, I married your mother and wrecked my middle years. Now you want to torment my old age. I won't allow it."

"Such lies!" flared Coomy. "You ruined Mamma's life, and mine, and Jal's. I will not tolerate a word against her."

"Please don't get upset," Jal tried to calm his sister, furiously caressing the arm of his chair. "I'm sure what happened today is a warning for Pappa."

"But will he learn from it?" she glowered at her stepfather. "Or will he go out and break his bones and put the burden of his fractures on my head?"

"No, no, he'll be good. He will stay at home and read and relax and listen to music and—"

"I want to hear him say that."

Nariman held his peace, having spent the time usefully in unbuckling his belt. He now commenced the task of untying his shoelaces.

"If you don't like what we're saying, ask your daughter's opinion when she comes tomorrow," said Coomy. "Your own flesh and blood, not like Jal and me, second class."

7

"That is unnecessary," said Nariman.

"Look," said Jal, "Roxana is coming with her family for Pappa's birthday party. Let's not have any quarrel tomorrow."

"Why quarrel?" said Coomy. "We will just have a sensible discussion, like grown-ups."

Though Roxana was their half-sister, Jal and Coomy's love for her had been full and complete from the moment she was born. At fourteen and twelve, they were not prey to the complicated feelings of jealousy, neglect, rivalry, or even hatred, which newborns evoke in siblings closer in age.

Or perhaps Jal and Coomy were grateful for Roxana because she filled the void left by their own father's death, four years earlier. Their father had been sickly through most of their childhood. And during brief stretches when his lungs did not confine him to bed, he was still weak, seldom able to get through the day unassisted. His chronic pleurisy was the symptom of a more serious pulmonary disease, its two dreaded initials never mentioned among friends and relatives. Just a little water in the lungs, was how Palonji's illness was described.

And Palonji, to alleviate his family's anxiety, made a running joke out of this coded description. If Jal, always full of mischief as a child, did something silly, it was due to a little water in his head. "You must plug your ears when you wash your hair," his father teased. Clumsy hands meant the person was a real water-fingers. And if little Coomy cried, her father said, "My lovely daughter does not cry, it's just a little water in the eyes," which would promptly make her smile.

Palonji Contractor's courage and his determination to keep up his family's spirits were heroic, but the end, when it came, was devastating for Jal and Coomy. And three years after his death, when their mother remarried, they were stiff towards the stranger, awkward in their dealings with him. They insisted on addressing Nariman Vakeel as New Pappa.

The word stung like a pebble each time it was hurled to his face. He made light of it at first, laughing it off: "That's all – just New Pappa? Why not a longer title? How about Brand New Improved Pappa?"

But his choice of adjectives was infelicitous; Jal told him coldly that no one could be an improvement on their real father. It took a few weeks for their mother to convince her children that it would make her very happy if they dropped the New. Jal and Coomy agreed; they were maturing rapidly, far too rapidly. They told their mother they would use whatever word she wanted. Merely calling him Pappa, they said, did not make him one.

Nariman wondered what he had let himself in for by marrying Yasmin Contractor. Neither had come together for love – it was an arranged marriage. She had taken the step for security, for her son and daughter.

And he, when he looked back on it all, across the wasteland of their lives, despaired at how he could have been so feeble-minded, so spineless, to have allowed it to happen.

But a year after the marriage, into their lives had come the little miracle. Roxana was born, and with the quantities of affection lavished on the baby, it was inevitable that the warmth of it should touch them all. Love for their little Roxana rescued them from their swamp of rancour; unhappiness was thwarted for the time being.

❧

Six o'clock approached, and Nariman began to get ready for his birthday dinner. He had been waiting eagerly for this evening, to see Roxana and her family. And as he dressed, that enchanting time of his daughter's birth filled his mind.

The rain started again after having let up most of the day. A new shirt, Jal and Coomy's gift, was waiting on the dresser. He removed it from its cellophane wrap and grimaced, feeling the starched fabric. No doubt, it would bite him all evening.

The things one had to endure for one's birthday. There were perfectly good shirts in his dresser, soft and comfortable, that would outlast him.

Over the thrumming of the rain a hammer commenced its noise somewhere in the building while he fumbled with the tight new buttons. No one considered the problems of the old and the frail, the way they packaged shirts for sale with impregnable plastic wrappers, pins stuck in all the trickiest places, cardboard inserts jammed hard under the collar.

He smiled as he thought about Roxana, her husband, and their two sons. He'd never imagined, delighting in her as a tiny baby, that one day she would be grown up and have her own children. He wondered if all fathers marvelled like him.

And if she could have remained that little baby for a while longer? Perhaps that one period of his wedded life when he'd been truly happy might have lasted longer too. If only we could have the impossible, he thought, we could vanquish unhappiness. But that was not how things worked in the world. The joyous family time had been short. Much too short.

He remembered the moment when Jal had taken the baby in his arms. How thrilled he had been as she clutched at his finger. "What a grip she has, Pappa!" Then Coomy had clamoured to hold her sister. "Look, she's blowing bubbles, just like my ring!" she had exclaimed in delight, referring to the soap-bubble kit she had bought at a fun-fair.

But Jal and Coomy's devotion to Roxana – even that had come to an end, felt Nariman, after she married and left to live in the flat he had procured by paying an enormous pugree. That was the time when they first began throwing at him the "flesh and blood" phrase, accusing him of partiality.

If at least the childhood bond, when relations were not tainted by "half" or "step" combinations because hyphens were meaningless to them then – if at least that had endured, it would have offered some consolation, something good salvaged from those miserable years. But this, too, was denied him. Naturally. Only a rotten ending could come out of such a rotten beginning.

And what was the beginning, he wondered. The day he met his darling Lucy, the woman he should have married? But that was not a rotten day, it was the most beautiful of mornings. Or was it later, when he renounced Lucy? Or when he agreed to marry Yasmin Contractor? Or that Sunday evening when his parents and their friends first broached the idea – when he should have raged and exploded, stamped out the notion, told them to mind their own damned business, go to hell?

Thirty-six years had passed since. And still he remembered the Sunday evening, the hebdomadal get-together of his parents' circle of friends. In this very drawing-room, where the furniture was still the same, the walls carried the same paint, and all their voices still echoed from that Sunday evening.

Much rejoicing had erupted when his parents announced that their only son, after years of refusing to end his ill-considered liaison with that Goan woman, refusing to meet decent Parsi girls, refusing to marry someone respectable – that their beloved Nari had finally listened to reason and agreed to settle down.

He could hear every word on the balcony where he sat alone. As usual, Soli Bamboat, his parents' oldest friend, semi-retired and still a very influential lawyer, was the first to respond. "Three cheers for Nari!" he shouted. "Heep-heep-heep!" and the rest answered, "Hooray!"

Soli Bamboat's vocal machinery, despite a lifetime's struggle with the treachery of English vowels, was frequently undone by them. His speech had been a source of great puzzlement and entertainment for Nariman in childhood.

Counting his parents, there were ten Sunday-evening regulars. No, nine, he corrected himself, for Mr. Burdy's wife, Shirin, had died the year before, following a swift illness. After the mourning, Mr. Burdy had reappeared at the Sunday gatherings and, in Nariman's opinion, tackled the part of widower with admirable diligence. A tasty pakora or someone's special homemade chutney would make him sigh dutifully, "Oh how my Shirin would have enjoyed it." After laughing at a funny anecdote he would at once add, "In humour my Shirin was number one – always the first to appreciate a joke." But he never seemed comfortable in this role and, a few months later, decided to try the jovial born-again bachelor. The group accepted the change, giving its approval tacitly; Shirin was no longer mentioned on Sunday evenings.

So much for love and loyalty and remembering, thought Nariman. Meanwhile, the group responded thrice to Soli's heep-heep-heep before commencing with an assortment of individual cheers and good wishes for his parents.

"Congratulations, Marzi!" said Mr. Kotwal to his father. "After eleven years of battle you win!"

"Better late than never," said Mr. Burdy. "But fortune always favours the bold. Remember, the fruits of patience are sweet, and all's well that ends well."

"Stop, Mr. Proverb, enough," said Soli. "Save a few for the rest of us."

Curious about their comments, Nariman shifted his chair on the balcony so he could observe them without being seen. Now Mrs. Unvala began professing that she had always had faith in the boy to make the right choice in the end, and her husband, Dara, nodded vigorously. Their opinions were offered as a team; the group called him the Silent Partner.

Then Soli entered the balcony, and Nariman pretended to be engrossed in a book. "Hey, Nari! Why are you alone? Come and join the circle, you seely boy."

"Later, Soli Uncle, I want to finish this chapter."

"No, no, Nari, we nid you now," he said, taking the book away. "What's the rush, the words won't vaneesh from the page." Seizing his arm, he pulled him into the drawing-room, into the centre of the gathering.

They thumped his back, shook his hand, hugged him while he cringed and wished he hadn't stayed home that evening. But he knew he would have to face them at some point. He heard Soli Uncle's wife, Nargesh Aunty, ask his mother, "Tell me, Jeroo, is it sincere? Has he really given up that Lucy Braganza?"

"Oh yes," said his mother. "Yes, he has given us his word."

Now Mrs. Kotwal scuttled across the room, pinched his cheek, and said, "When the naughty boy at last becomes a good boy, it's a double delight."

He felt like reminding her he was forty-two years old. Then Nargesh Aunty beckoned from her seat on the sofa. She was the most softspoken of the group and usually drowned by its din. She patted the place beside her and bade him sit. Taking his hand in hers, which was shrivelled from burns in a kitchen accident during her youth, she whispered, "No happiness is more lasting than the happiness that you get from fulfilling your parents' wishes. Remember that, Nari."

Her voice came to him from a great distance, and he had neither will nor energy for argument. He was remembering the week before, when he and Lucy had watched the tide go out at Breach Candy. Some children were dragging a little net in pools of water among the rocks, searching for sea life forgotten by the amnesiac waves. As he watched them splash and yell, he thought about the eleven years he and Lucy had struggled to create a world for themselves. A cocoon, she used to call it. A cocoon was what they needed, she said, into which they could retreat, and after their families had forgotten their existence, they would emerge like two glistening butterflies and fly away together . . .

The memory made him weaken for an instant – was he making the right decision? . . . Yes. He was. They had been ground down by their families. Exhausted by the strain of it. He reminded himself how hopeless it was now – Lucy and he had even reached the point where scarcely an evening went by that they did not quarrel about something or the other. What was the purpose in continuing, letting it all crumble in useless bickering?

Then, while the children nearby squealed with excitement at a creature caught in their net, Lucy tried one last time to *convince him: they could turn their backs on everyone, walk away from the suffocating world of family tyrannies, from the guilt and blackmail that parents specialized in. They could start their own life together, just the two of them.*

Struggling to maintain his resolve, he told her they had discussed it all before, their families would hound them, no matter what. The only way to do this was to end it quickly.

Fine, she said, no use talking any more, and walked away from him. He found himself alone beside the sea.

And now, as his parents and their friends discussed his future while sipping Scotch and soda, he felt he was eavesdropping on strangers. They were delightedly conducting their "round-table conference," as they called it, planning his married life, having as much fun as though it was their whist drive or housie evening.

"There is one problem," said Mr. Burdy. "We have indeed shut the stable door before the horse bolted, but we must provide a substitute mare."

"What did he say?" asked Nargesh Aunty.

"Mr. Proverb believes the bridegroom is ready, but we nid to find heem a bride."

"Don't you think," she said timidly, "that love-marriage would be better than arranged?"

"Of course," said his father. "You think we haven't encouraged it? But our Nari seems incapable of falling in love with a Parsi girl. Now it's up to us to find a match."

"And that will be a challenge, mark my words," said Mr. Kotwal. "You can look as far from Bombay as you like. You can try from Calcutta to Karachi. But when they make inquiries, they will find out about Nari's lufroo with that ferangi woman."

"Impossible to hide it," agreed Mrs. Unvala. "We'll have to compromise."

"Oh I'm sure Nari will find a lovely wife," said his mother loyally. "The cream of the crop."

"I think we'll have to forget about the cream of the crop,"

said Mr. Burdy. "As you sow, so shall you reap. You cannot plough the stubble of the crop one day, and expect cream the next."

They laughed, and their jokes became cruder. Soli said something insulting about ferangis who wiped their arses with paper instead of washing hygienically.

The detachment with which Nariman had been listening evaporated. "How sorry I feel for you all," he said, unable to choke back his disgust. "You've grown old without growing wise."

His chair scrooped as he pushed it away and returned to the balcony. He picked up his book, staring blankly at the pages. There was a light breeze coming in from the sea. Inside, he could hear his parents apologizing, that the poor boy was distraught because the breakup was still fresh. It infuriated him that they would presume to know how he felt.

"Prince Charming didn't appreciate our humour," said Mr. Burdy. "But there was no need to insult us."

"I think he was just quoting from a book," said Mr. Kotwal.

"My big mistake," said his father, "was books. Too many books. Modern ideas have filled Nari's head. He never learned to preserve that fine balance between tradition and modernness."

"Time weal pass and he'll become normal again," said Soli. "Don't worry, prosid one step at a time."

"Exactly," said Mr. Burdy. "Act in haste, repent at leisure. Remember, slow and steady always wins the race."

Disregarding their own advice, in a matter of days his parents' friends arranged an introduction for him. "You will meet Yasmin Contractor, a widow with two children," they told him. "And that's the best you can expect, mister, with your history."

Either this widow, they explained, or a defective woman – the choice was his. What sort of defect? he asked, curious. Oh, could be cock-eyed, or deaf, or one leg shorter than the other, they said breezily; or might be someone sickly, with a

weak lung, or problems in the child-bearing department – it
depended on who was available. If that was his preference,
they would make inquiries and prepare a list for him.

"No one is denying you are handsome and well educated.
Your past is your handicap – those wasted years, which have
thrown you beyond the threshold of forty. But don't worry,
everything has been considered: personality, family back-
ground, cooking and housekeeping skills. Yes, the widow is
our number-one choice. She will make you a good wife."

Like an invalid steered by doctors and nurses, he drifted
through the process, suppressing his doubts and misgivings,
ready to believe that the traditional ways were the best. He
became the husband of Yasmin Contractor, and formally
adopted her children, Jal and Coomy. But they kept their
father's name. To change it to Vakeel would be like rewriting
history, suggested his new wife. The simile appealed to his
academic soul; he acquiesced.

And that, perhaps, was my first mistake, thought Nariman,
still struggling with the buttons on his birthday gift. How had
Jal and Coomy felt, as children, having a different name from
the rest of the family? Had they resented it? Felt left out? He
should have considered their perspective before agreeing with
Yasmin. He should have tried to make up for the loss they had
suffered with their father's death, tried to give them the normal childhood they had missed, taken them on excursions, on
picnics, played games with them, tried to be a friend to them
. . . and perhaps things might have turned out differently. But
the knack of thinking like a child, empathizing, were skills he
had not learned then. Nowadays it was so much easier.

Defeated by the buttons, he put the shirt aside and started
for the WC. His stomach was rumbling ominously. He tried
to remember what he had eaten, as he went down the long
passageway to the back of the flat. It was the only toilet of the
three that still worked.

16

Each step was an effort of concentration, while his shaking hand sought support from the wall that was covered with large pictures hung high along its length. His forefathers brooded in their dark frames, their stern expressions and severe mouths looking down on him during his frequent trips to the WC. He often worried about reaching the toilet in time. But this unhappy flat, he felt, at least justified the gloomy style of portrait photography. To his eyes, the ancestral countenances grew increasingly cheerless with each passing day.

He shot the bolt in the door and sat, grateful that the sole surviving toilet had a commode. He couldn't imagine how he would have managed to squat in either of the other two.

Down at the other end of the passageway, Coomy was calling into his room to hurry, that Roxana's family would soon be here. Her steps approached the WC, and she tried to open the door.

"Who's inside?"

"Me."

"I should have known from the stink!"

When he returned to his room she was waiting. The hammer was still going, somewhere in the building.

"You broke the rule, Pappa, you went without telling me."

"Sorry. I forgot."

"I need to do number one, I could have gone first. Now I must sit in your smell." She paused. "Never mind, get dressed. They'll arrive any minute and blame me for not having you ready."

He held out the new shirt, his distal tremor making it seem as though he were shaking a flag. "The buttons are difficult."

It was a long-sleeved shirt, and she helped him with it. He inquired about the source of the persistent hammering.

"Edul Munshi downstairs, who else," she said, fastening the cuffs. "Only one maniac handyman lives in Chateau Felicity."

The doorbell rang as she buttoned the front. Nariman's face lit up: Roxana and Yezad and Murad and Jehangir, at last! His eager fingers tried to help with the shirt.

She brushed them aside and raced through the last few buttons, skipping a couple at the end, flustered about things still to be done in the kitchen. The Chenoy family always had to come on time, she grumbled, even in a heavy downpour.

2

JAL LET THE FAMILY IN and ran with their umbrellas and raincoats to the bathroom to prevent a puddle by the door. He returned with a cloth, mopping the trail of water. After everyone finished wiping their rain-shoes on the mat, he led them to the drawing-room.

"That's a big shower you got caught in."

"Yes," said Roxana, "and these two naughty boys forgot their caps. Look at their hair, soaking wet. Can I borrow a towel, Jal?"

"Sure." Settling them in the threadbare sofas and chairs, he needlessly moved a couple of side tables, picked up cushions only to replace them in the same spot, and turned on a lamp. He inquired anxiously if the light was bothering their eyes.

"Not at all," Yezad assured him.

Jal's usual jitteriness obscured his pleasure at seeing them. He excused himself, saying Coomy needed help in the kitchen.

"The towel, Jal," Roxana reminded him. "Before these two little saitaans catch a chill."

"Oh yes, sorry." He dashed off and returned with apologies for the delay.

She threw the towel over Jehangir's head, rubbing vigorously so that his shoulders shook. He decided to exaggerate the effect, letting his arms and hips shake in a wild dance.

"Stand still, you clown," said his mother. She ran her fingers through his hair to check. "There. Your turn, Murad."

"I'll do it myself," said Murad, not about to relinquish the sovereignty acquired recently, on turning thirteen.

His mother passed him the towel, then opened her purse to find a comb. Jehangir waited patiently while she restored the parting on the left and slicked back the rest. "Now you look less like a ruffian."

Murad took the comb next, and went to the showcase at the other end of the drawing-room. Squinting into the glass front, he styled his hair to his own satisfaction, without a parting.

Roxana put away the comb and warned the boys to behave themselves, not annoy Aunty and Uncle. Yezad delivered a caution as well, adding under his breath that of course it was hard to predict what might annoy those two – the only certain way was to say nothing and do nothing.

"This evening pretend you are two statues," he said.

Murad and Jehangir laughed.

"I'm serious. There'll be a prize for the best statue."

"What's the prize?"

"A surprise."

They froze immediately, to see who could sit still without blinking for the most time. But it wasn't long before Murad's statue came to life and began exploring the room. He wandered to the window and peered out under the curtains, then tried to open them. He yanked with both hands to slide the rings. The rod and drapery came tumbling.

"See what you've done? Sit down at once!" said his mother through clenched teeth to appear fierce, though she knew she was hopeless at it. "You're older than Jehangir, you're supposed to set a good example."

Murad picked up the rod and began threading it through the rings. As he got one panel on, the second slipped off at the other end.

"You heard Mummy," said Yezad. "Leave it."

"I'm just putting it back for Aunty."

Yezad uncrossed his legs and moved to the edge of the sofa, as though to rise. "Sit down, I said."

Seeing the flash of anger in his father's eyes, Jehangir tensed, hoping his brother wouldn't be defiant. They were both well acquainted with Daddy's temper.

Murad returned to his chair, pouting and scowling. But as quickly as it had appeared, his father's anger melted. "Now let's hope your Aunty doesn't explode."

Roxana was certain the noise would bring Coomy to investigate. But no one came until Nariman, his new shirt tucked unevenly into his trousers, appeared in the doorway.

"Happy birthday, Grandpa," chorused the boys. Jehangir was first off the sofa this time, running to Nariman as he shuffled towards his chair.

"Stop!" Roxana checked her son's exuberance. "Let Grandpa sit first, you'll knock him over."

She wondered if her father's feet were dragging more than the last time they met; he was definitely more stooped. The doctor had warned them, symptoms would be aggravated when the Parkinsonism began making rapid gains. Funny choice of word, she thought, "gains," as though the wretched disease was a stock on the share bazaar in which Jal dabbled.

Lowering himself into the chair, Nariman lost control and fell into it heavily. He smiled at the anxious faces.

Jehangir hugged and kissed him, holding his chin and squeezing gently, enjoying the rubbery jujubelike feel and the tiny stubble dotting it like sugar. His grandfather laughed and bowed his head for the next part of the ritual: the stroking of his bald head.

This special greeting had evolved a few years ago when he had affectionately grabbed the boys' chins, and they had grabbed his right back. Fascinated by its texture, they had explored other features of their grandfather's physiognomy and found that his glabrous pate, hard and smooth and shiny, sang a delicious counterpoint to the jujube chin.

Murad approached and held out his hand, feeling too old now to indulge in childish chin squeezing. Nariman shook it, then drew him close for a hug.

"Show us your teeth, Grandpa," said Jehangir.

Nariman obliged, letting his dentures protrude briefly before sucking them in.

"Again!"

"Stop bothering," said Yezad. "This boy of mine is becoming a rascal-and-a-half. Many happy returns, chief." He shook his father-in-law's hand heartily and patted him on the shoulder.

Finally, Roxana embraced him, saying it was good to see him looking so well. "God bless you, Pappa, may we keep coming for many, many years."

"At least till one hundred," said Yezad.

"Yes, Grandpa, you must hit a century," said Murad. "Like Sachin Tendulkar against Australia."

"Easily," said Jehangir. "Only twenty-one to go."

"Good arithmetic," chuckled Nariman. "But I've had more than my fair share of birthdays."

"Don't say that, Pappa," said Roxana, and a little frown knit her brow. She sat on the sofa adjacent to his chair.

Jal, who had returned in the meantime, adjusted his hearing aid; it gave him more trouble when there were several speakers in the room. "What? What did Murad say about hen curry?"

"Century," said Roxana, repeating for him all the things he had missed, while he smiled and nodded. Then Coomy called out, and he hurried back to the kitchen.

"How many more birthdays for your century?" Nariman asked Jehangir. "Ninety-two, I think?"

"No, Grandpa, that was last year. Now only ninety-one."

"And for Murad?"

"Just eighty-seven."

"Excellent. Soon you'll be young men with many girl-friends. I hope you'll invite me to your wedding." His spirits were rising with each passing minute. The joy and laughter and youth they brought was an antidote to the sombreness enveloping his flat, the hours when he felt the very walls and ceilings were encrusted with the distress of unhappy decades. The furniture too, of teak and rosewood, the huge armoires and four-poster beds looming darkly, glum hulks waiting for

22

some dreaded end, seemed once again welcoming and hospitable. And that long row of family portraits in the passageway – today their dour grimaces seemed comical.

Roxana asked, keeping to a whisper, "Things okay with Jal and Coomy?"

"The usual theatrics and keech-keech, that's all," said Nariman. "Most of the time—"

He fell silent as Coomy, carrying a bowl of potato chips, entered with a loud hello to everyone. The collapsed curtains drew her eyes at once, but before her outrage became words Roxana apologized, "This naughty boy pulled the whole thing down. He's going to get a solid punishment."

Pre-empted, Coomy was magnanimous. "Never mind, Jal will fix it later. I just hope no shameless mavaalis try to peer into our house."

"But we're on the third floor, Aunty," said Jehangir.

"So? You think mavaalis are only at street level? They could be in the building opposite. They could be with a telescope in that skyscraper a mile away."

Puzzled, Jal asked, "Who's in the skyscraper?"

"Just switch it off," advised Coomy. "We're not discussing anything important."

"Let him listen!" said Roxana indignantly. "He wants to enjoy the conversation."

"And who will pay for new batteries? Do you know how expensive they are, how quickly that little box eats them up?"

"But it's a necessity, like medicine."

"Calling it a necessity doesn't magically produce money for it," said Coomy, and recited the prices of items she thought were necessities: onions, potatoes, bread, butter, cooking gas.

"You should budget for every expense," said Roxana. "Keep separate envelopes."

"Thank you very much, I also studied home economics in school. Envelopes are no use without money to put in them."

"You're right," said Yezad to conclude the argument. "We all have the same problem."

"Rubbish," snapped Coomy. "You don't have the problem of looking after Pappa, with all his expenses."

Roxana wanted to snap back that Pappa's pension paid for everything. But Yezad gave her a little sign – the silly disagreement over batteries was turning into a major fight – and changed the subject: "By the way, Coomy, what's that non-stop hammering?"

"Idiot Edul Munshi, who else."

"Now he'd be thrilled to fix your curtains," teased Yezad.

Jal retreated in mock horror. "Please, anyone but Edul. Unless you want the house to tumble on our heads."

They laughed, for Edul Munshi who lived one floor below fancied himself a talented handyman. Signs of his incompetence were evident on his front door: the nameplate hung crookedly, and the hasp didn't quite meet its staple. He was famous in the building for his fine set of tools, and notorious for his willingness to share them – by playing his cards right, he was able to follow them into someone else's fixing and repairing. And this meant the world to him, since there was very little he could do nowadays in his own flat; Mrs. Munshi had decided there was a limit to how much of their home her husband should be allowed to ruin.

"I wonder who is the buckro trapped this time in Edul's tool box," said Yezad.

They laughed again, and Nariman looked around with satisfaction, glad the fight had been avoided. "Come, let's have a drink."

"Just wait five more minutes," said Coomy. "My coals are ready for loban, the sun has gone down."

She left the room to return with the silver thurible, walking in a haze of white smoke. Her head was now covered with a white mulmul scarf.

The fragrance of frankincense delighted Roxana, for ritual and religion meant more to her than it ever had to Yezad. After her mother's sudden death, her training had been taken over by the Contractor side of the family, and Nariman's

24

heavy conscience had refused them nothing. They had taught her the prayers, performed her navjote, taken her to the fire-temple for every holy day.

Later on, in married life, she missed these observances. Yezad did not believe in them, he said going to fire-temple on Navroze and Khordad Sal was enough for him, and loban smoke was merely one way to get rid of mosquitoes.

The silver thurible in Coomy's hand, which had belonged to Mamma, filled Roxana's senses with reverence and child-hood memories. She awaited her turn as Coomy offered it to each person for obeisance.

Yezad, being nearest, was first, and he clasped his hands in a perfunctory manner.

"Cover your head," whispered Roxana in her husband's ear.

"Sorry," he murmured, and put one hand over his hair, moving the other through the smoke towards himself. Murad and Jehangir grinned to see their father's clumsiness.

After everyone had finished, Coomy made a circuit of the drawing-room, the smoke lazily tracing her path. The solemn expression with which she floated about amused the boys.

"Your aunty is a very pious woman," said Yezad when she left the room, and struggled to hold back his laughter.

"Indeed," said Nariman. "She has a direct line to the Almighty."

"Stop it, you two," said Roxana, annoyed. She wanted to savour the moment; for her, loban smoke was like angels and fareshtas floating through the house.

Coomy pushed back the white mulmul scarf from her head and announced it was time for drinks. "What about you, Murad and Jehangir? Fanta or Thums-Up? Or," she said, opening her eyes wide to convey the delight of a special treat, "my own homemade raspberry sarbut – that's what I'm having."

The boys were familiar with their aunt's anaemic concoction, pale pink, sugary, and flavourless. "I'll have that later," said Murad. "Fanta for now."

"Same for me, Aunty," said Jehangir.

Jal offered to look after the adult drinks, and began making Scotch and sodas for Yezad, Nariman, and himself. Roxana requested the rejected raspberry sarbut and Coomy's face brightened.

"Martyr," whispered Yezad in his wife's ear, letting his lips brush the lobe.

Nariman noticed, and smiled with pleasure. He delighted in his daughter's happiness, the bond she shared with Yezad. He had often seen them communicate with subtle signals invisible to the world.

He overruled her choice of sarbut. "On my birthday? You must have something stronger."

"No, Pappa, it goes straight to my head and then down to my legs."

"But he's right, Roxie," said Yezad. "Today is special."

Jehangir and Murad added their voices to the demand: "Yes, Mummy, you must have liquor today!" They liked the slight tipsiness that overcame their mother once or twice a year, erasing her look of perpetual worry.

Sighing, she consented to rum and Thums-Up as though undertaking a difficult task. "Listen, Jal, very little rum, lots of Thums-Up," she instructed, then sat back, anticipating the drink with pleasure.

Still Fanta-less and propelled by boredom, Murad went to the showcase, which had pride of place in the drawing-room. Jehangir followed. This cabinet was a magnet whenever they visited, made more powerful by their uncle and aunt's interdiction against touching anything.

Roxana watched them with growing concern. Nariman moved his hand through the air as though patting his daughter's arm to assure her that it was all right.

"But, Pappa, you have no idea what a chaavat Murad is.

And his brother as well, when they're together. Otherwise, Jehangir will sit still for hours, reading or making his jigsaw puzzles."

She nudged Yezad to keep a sharp eye on the two. "The last thing we want is them fooling around with the shrine."

"Shrine" was their secret word for the clutter of knick-knacks, toys, and glassware that packed the shelves of the cabinet venerated by Jal and Coomy. Their sacred icons included a clown with ears that waggled when his stomach was squeezed, a white fluffy dog with a bobbing head, tiny replicas of vintage cars, and a battery-operated Elvis who would soundlessly strum his guitar. At one time, the Elvis doll could also sing a verse of "Wooden Heart," but, as Jal liked explaining to visitors, something had gone wrong with the mechanism on the very day in August that the King had died.

When they acquired a new toy, they would demonstrate it proudly, then perform its solemn installation behind glass. All that was missing in this ritual, according to Yezad, was incense, flowers, and the chanting of prayers. He dismissed Nariman's explanation that Jal and Coomy's sickly father and their unhappy childhood was the reason for the shrine. There were lots of deprived children, said Yezad, and they didn't all grow up into toy fanatics.

Besides the toys, the showcase held some silver cups, prizes Jal and Coomy had won long ago at school. Little tags on the trophies recorded their achievements: Jal Palonji Contractor, 3rd Prize, Three-Legged Race, 1954; Coomy Palonji Contractor, 2nd Prize, Lemon-and-Spoon Race, 1956; and many more. They had not kept all their prizes, just the ones for which their father had been present on Sports Day to cheer them on.

There were also two watches, much too small for their wrists now, and two fountain pens, presented to them on their navjote by their father, almost forty years ago. The ceremony had been arranged hurriedly on the advice of the family dustoorji, when it seemed Palonji did not have much longer to live. The children had yet to commit to memory all

27

the requisite prayers, but the dustoorji said he would overlook that deficiency: better for the father to witness the navjote, even if the initiates were a few verses short, so he could die secure in the knowledge that his progeny had been properly welcomed into the Zoroastrian fold.

Bored with looking through the glass, Murad decided to open the cabinet doors. Roxana alerted Yezad, who warned their son not to touch anything.

"The glass is dusty, I can't see."

He glanced over the assortment of items, ignoring the vases, silver cups, a plastic gondola with gondolier, the Air-India maharaja perched atop the nose of a jumbo jet, an Eiffel Tower. Two grinning monkeys at the centre of the display had snared his curiosity.

One was equipped with a drum and sticks, while the other clutched in its paws a bottle labelled Booze; both had keys in their backs. Standing so as to shield his hands, Murad began winding the drummer. Jehangir the accomplice provided additional cover.

But the telltale clockwork betrayed them. The sound, to Coomy's ears, was as familiar as the breath of a cherished infant. She abandoned the drinks and rushed to her beloved cabinet.

"Very bad of you, Murad, very bad," she said, managing a spurious calm before the distress slipped out and made her shrill. "I've told you a thousand times, don't touch the showcase!"

"Put it back at once," said his mother.

Murad ignored the command and kept winding. "I'm not doing anything wrong."

"You heard Mummy," said Yezad.

"Hand the monkey to Jal Uncle, you wicked boy!" said Coomy, frantic now. "He'll work it for you."

"But I want to do it."

Yezad rose. Time to give in, decided Murad. Before he could relinquish the toy, however, Coomy slapped his cheek.

28

For a moment it seemed to Roxana that Yezad would strike Murad and Coomy. She jumped off the sofa and dragged her son by his arm into a chair, then restrained her husband with a firm touch on his shoulder. To Coomy she said sharply that if any hitting was required, his parents were right there to complain to.

"I have to complain? Here you are, watching the boy misbehave! If you did your duty, I wouldn't need to raise my hand."

"That's a joke-and-a-half," said Yezad. "Children wanting to play with toys is not misbehaviour."

"Go ahead, defend him. That's how children become bad."

"You see, Murad dikra," said Jal, wincing, a finger to his ear, "the mechanism is delicate. One extra turn and the spring could break. Then my drummer would be silent, like my Elvis."

He finished winding and placed the monkey on the table. Its arms began moving up and down, the sticks striking the drum with a feeble tap each time. "Wonderful, isn't it? I'll start the other fellow as well." And the monkey with the Booze bottle now raised it to his mouth, lowered it, repeated the sequence. "I tell you, these two are great. You never tire of watching them."

The boys took no interest. The pleasure of winding the toys, setting them in motion, was what they had sought.

"Ungrateful children, turning their backs on the monkeys," said Coomy.

"Enough now, Coomy," said Nariman. "Let's forget it."

But a tide of grievance had risen in her veins. She said she would not forget it – maybe that was the way he dealt with problems. No wonder he had ruined his own life, and everyone else's. No wonder he had carried on shamelessly with that Lucy Braganza, and destroyed Mamma's life and . . .

Nariman looked at the others, raising his hands in a helpless apology, and Roxana tried to stem the outburst. "From where to where are you jumping, Coomy? Why drag up all that? In front of the children? And what's the connection with the monkeys?"

"Don't interfere between Pappa and me. If you want to see the connection, think a little."

Six lives he, a father in name only, had drenched with unhappiness, she continued, and she would never forgive that, especially his disgraceful behaviour with his mistress after marriage. What character of woman – not woman, witch – would do such things? And if she wanted to die in that manner, then why hadn't she done them all a favour and—

"Coomy, we must show Roxie the new doll you got," interrupted Jal. "Look, it's a Japanese doll, Roxie."

He was partly successful; Coomy lowered her voice, but kept muttering. Dutiful admiration from Roxana for the pretty kimono, the rich colours, and the pure gold threads in it, made her roll to a stop. She pointed out the little parasol, which was her favourite detail, even more than the sweet little slippers.

Then the toys were shut away in the cabinet. Having made up for her children's sins at the shrine, Roxana sat again beside her father, thankful that peace had been restored.

Three Scotch and sodas, two Fantas, one rum with Thums-Up, and Coomy's homemade sarbut were finally ready. They drank a toast to Nariman, after which he proposed they drink to the health of the four monkeys.

"Four?" asked Jal.

"Two of Coomy's and two of Roxie's."

They laughed, and Coomy smiled sportingly. Nariman asked the boys how things were shaping up at St. Xavier's since the start of the new school year. "Do you like your new classes?"

"They're not new any more, Grandpa," said Jehangir. "School reopened a long time ago: eleventh of June. Almost two months ago."

"That long?" smiled Nariman, remembering his own childhood when time behaved with the same good sense instead of tearing past insensitively as it did now, whole days and weeks gone in the blink of an eye. "And how are your teachers?"

"Fine," the two answered together.

"Tell Grandpa what Teacher has made you," Roxana prompted.

"I'm a Homework Monitor," said Jehangir, elaborating that there were three of them in the class and they had to check if the students had completed the previous day's homework.

"And what happens when someone hasn't?" asked Nariman.

"I have to tell Miss Alvarez, and the boy gets a zero."

"And do you?"

"Of course," said Jehangir, while his mother made a face to protest the question.

"What if the boy is your friend? Do you still tell Teacher?"

"My friends always do their homework."

"Smart answer," said Jal.

"Well, whose son?" asked Yezad, and they laughed.

"Now if this Homework Monitoring system was a Government of India scheme," said Jal, "rich boys wouldn't do homework, and offer bribes to the teachers."

Yezad made a noise between laughing and snorting. "And the principal would threaten to sack the teachers unless he got a percentage."

"Stop corrupting the children," said Roxana.

"Corruption is in the air we breathe. This nation specializes in turning honest people into crooks. Right, chief?"

"The answer, unfortunately, is yes."

"The country has gone to the dogs. And not well-bred dogs either, but pariahs."

"Maybe the BJP and Shiv Sena coalition will improve things," said Jal. "We should give them a chance."

Yezad laughed. "If a poisonous snake was in front of you,

31

would you give it a chance? Those two parties encouraged the Hindutva extremists to destroy the Babri Mosque."

"Yes, but that was—"

"And what about all the hatred of minorities that Shiv Sena has spread for the last thirty years." He paused to take a long swallow of his Scotch and soda.

"Daddy, did you know, Shiv Sena is going to have a Michael Jackson concert," said Murad.

"That's right," said Jal. "I saw it in the newspaper. And Shiv Sena will pocket millions – they've obtained tax-free status by classifying it as a cultural event of national significance."

"Well," said Yezad. "Michael Jackson's crotch-clutching and his shiny codpiece must be vital to the nation. I'm surprised the Senapati doesn't find him anti-anything, not even anti-good taste. Otherwise, the crackpot accuses people left and right of being anti-this or anti-that. South Indians are anti-Bombay, Valentine's Day is anti-Hindustan, film stars born before 1947 in the Pakistani part of Punjab are traitors to the country."

"I suppose," said Nariman, "if the Senapati gets gas after eating karela, the gourd will be declared an anti-Indian vegetable."

"Let's hope his langoti doesn't give him a groin rash," said Jal. "Or all underwear might be banned."

They laughed, and Yezad made himself another Scotch and soda. "Frankly, I don't care who the government is, and what they do. I've given up on a saviour. Always turns out to be a real saviour-and-a-half."

"Daddy, why do you say 'and-a-half' for everything?" asked Jehangir.

"Because the half is the most important part."

Jehangir didn't understand, but laughed anyway. He was happy to see his father holding forth.

"Let's talk about something else," said Roxana. "Politics is very boring."

"You're right," said Yezad. "So, chief, what did you think of the World Cup?"

Nariman shook his head. "I don't approve of these coloured uniforms they wear. Cricket is white flannels. Fixed overs and rushing to finish a match in one day is not cricket."

"The worst part is the fanaticism," said Yezad. "Every time India and Pakistan play, it's like another war in Kashmir."

"I thought you were going to stop talking politics."

"Sorry, Roxie. So, chief, when will you open your present?"

"Right now."

The boys ran to the hall table for the gift. They laid the long, narrow package in Nariman's lap, where it rocked to the palpitations of his legs.

"Can you guess what it is, Grandpa?"

"A rifle? A sword?"

They shook their heads.

"A long rolling pin, to make very big chapatis?"

"Wrong again, Grandpa."

"I give up."

Roxana said to wait for Coomy, who called out from the dining room to go ahead and open it, she couldn't stop what she was doing. To remind them she was in the background, getting things ready for dinner, she allowed plates and dishes to clatter from time to time.

Roxana watched her father tackle the wrapping paper, and nudged Murad to help him. She asked if the new medicine was an improvement.

"Much better, look," Nariman held out a trembling hand. "Steady as a rock. Relatively speaking." As the padding of crumpled paper fell away, a walking stick stood revealed. "It's beautiful," he said, running his fingers along the gleaming surface.

"Pure walnut, chief."

"And look, Grandpa, we put this special rubber cap on the end, so it won't slip."

33

"Perfect," said Nariman. He passed the stick to Jal, who admired it, tapping the floor with a flourish.

Coomy came in and, halfway into the room, stopped in her tracks. "I can't believe my eyes."

"What is it, wrong colour?" asked Roxana, for her sister was superstitious about such things.

"Think for a moment," said Coomy. "What are you giving, and to whom? A walking stick. To Pappa."

"He likes to take walks," said Yezad. "It'll be useful."

"We don't want him to take walks! He has osteoporosis, Parkinson's disease, hypotension – a walking medical dictionary!"

"And you want to install me on the bookshelf. But I won't stay cooped indoors twenty-four hours a day."

"I agree with you, chief. A person could go crazy."

"Oh, you agree? And do you know what happened yesterday? I didn't want to say it on Pappa's birthday, but now I will. No, Jal will. Tell them, Jal."

He cleared his throat, adjusted his hearing aid, and said in a mild voice that the night before Pappa had had an accident.

"Nonsense," said Nariman. "I stumbled and twisted my foot, that's all." He pulled up his sleeve to show the band-aid. "This is the enormous wound they are worried about."

Yezad's laughter and Roxana's relieved smile made Coomy feel helpless. "Please listen to me," she pleaded. "Next time Pappa might not be so lucky. It's no joke at his age, going out alone."

"Maybe you should go together, a walk will be healthy for everyone," said Roxana.

"You want to injure all of us in one shot?" Coomy turned to her brother, "Again you've become quiet. Must I do the arguing and seem like the bad person always?"

"It's his hearing aid," said Yezad. "Makes it difficult to participate. You know, Jal, nowadays with advanced technology, the new gadgets are very powerful. And so small, you hardly notice them."

34

"Forget it," said Coomy. "If he can't hear with this big one, how will he manage with a tiny one?"

"The streets are a death trap," began Jal. "Footpaths are dug up, pedestrians have to compete with traffic, dozens of fatalities daily. We told Pappa to stroll around the flat for exercise, it's big enough. For fresh air he can use the balcony. Why risk life and limb on those murderous pavements?"

"I think you are overreacting," said Yezad. "I agree you have to walk cautiously, not rely on traffic signals. But it's still a civilized city."

"Is that so?" said Coomy. "In that case, why were you trying to leave for Canada?"

Yezad didn't like being reminded of it. "That was years ago. And not just because of traffic and pavements."

Then Coomy said that since, in their opinion, there was nothing wrong with Pappa's walks, she wouldn't worry herself about it. But if, God forbid, something terrible happened, she and Jal would deliver him straightaway to the Chenoy residence.

"The chief is welcome," said Yezad. "Just make sure you bring us one of your extra rooms. We live in a two-room flat, not a seven-room palace like this one."

"Laugh all you like, but I am serious." There would be no other choice, she declared – an ayah or nurse would be unaffordable, and a nursing home out of the question. "Jal will tell you how hopeless the share bazaar is, Mamma's investments make barely enough to let us eat dar-chaaval. And you know better than anyone, Pappa used up all his money to pay for your flat."

"But this lovely place is for you," said Roxana. "Why do you keep envying us?"

"Lovely place? A haunted house, fallen to rack and ruin! Look at these walls, not a coat of whitewash in thirty years! What we will do if the roof leaks or the last remaining toilet breaks, I don't know. To think we could all have lived happily together, right here, one family. But you insisted on leaving us."

35

"Now wait," said Nariman, "don't blame her. It was my decision."

"Why are we discussing ancient history?" asked Roxana. "All because you don't like Pappa's birthday gift?"

"The walking stick is a sign of how inconsiderate you've become. Never were you like this, not till you got married and left. Now you have no concern for how we live or die. And that hurts me!"

She turned away to dab at her eyes. Roxana watched for a few moments, feeling awful, then put her arm around her. "Come on, Coomy, don't be silly. Every day I think of you and Jal and Pappa. Please stop crying."

She led her to the sofa, sitting her down between Yezad and herself. Sniffing, Coomy complained that she still hadn't heard a word about the shirt she and Jal gave Pappa.

"It's a lovely shirt," Roxana assured her.

"They complimented me on it when they came," her father covered for her. "You were still in the kitchen."

"Look, chief," said Yezad. "How about a jigsaw puzzle instead of the walking stick? I'm sure Jehangir would be happy to give you one of his. Or some of his Famous Five books."

"On one condition," said Nariman. "Every evening Coomy and Jal must read aloud to me about an adventure."

"You'll be the Famous Three," said Jehangir, at which everyone laughed, including Coomy.

She called them to the table and offered the usual apology for its inadequacy: she'd done her best, but what with the shortages, and the prices in the market, and the good quality stuff being exported, it was so difficult to cook a decent dinner.

"It smells fantastic," said Yezad.

"Yum-yum," said Murad, as his aunt pointed him to one of the two chairs at the end. Jehangir tried to make a break for a place closer to their grandfather, but she thwarted him, putting him next to his brother.

With everyone seated, Nariman inquired why the good dishes were not laid out. Coomy clutched her forehead.

"Each year you ask the same question, Pappa. What if something breaks or chips?"

"She's right, Pappa," said Roxana. "We don't use them in our house either."

"Be that as it may, tonight I want the fine china."

Jehangir repeated the phrase softly to himself, be that as it may, relishing the combination of words. His father whispered that Grandpa's English was the best in the family.

"Don't be difficult, Pappa, please!" pleaded Coomy. "If something cracks, how will we ever replace it? The whole set will be spoiled."

"We'll have to risk that. Life will go on. Locked away unused, eventually it will age and crack in the sideboard. What use is that? Better to enjoy it."

"Fine," said Coomy. She unlocked the cabinet and took one dinner plate from the stack. "Happy? You eat from that."

"I want the full set. Dinner plates and side plates for everyone, the big rice platter, the serving bowls."

"But the food is already served. You want me to empty it? And wash twice? I'm sorry, I cannot do that."

"In that case, you'll have to eat without me."

He tried to leave the table amid general protest, while Coomy, close to tears, appealed to the others. She said this kind of cranky behaviour was what she had to put up with all the time.

"You know, chief, in my experience food tastes better in ordinary dishes," said Yezad. "Good ones distract you with their elegance."

Jehangir and Murad said their plates were beautiful, and offered to exchange with Grandpa, holding them up to display the Peter Pan scenes painted on them. Jal mumbled something about eating from banana leaves and following the fine old traditions. Roxana promised to arrange another dinner for her father, served in the good dishes, if he started eating now. But Nariman could not be persuaded.

"What's the use," said Coomy. "I surrender."

"Don't worry, it won't take long," whispered Roxana as they brought out the bone china. "And I'll help you with washing."

Jal, Yezad, and the boys were shooed away from the table. The place settings were removed and replaced, the food transferred into the Royal Doulton, and everyone called back.

"Thank you, Coomy," said Nariman. "The table looks splendid."

"Don't mention it," she said, gritting her teeth and serving him first. He enjoyed fish heads, and she spent a moment to locate the two pomfret heads lurking in the paatiyo's depths.

As the dishes travelled around the table, if something clanged or was set down heavily, Coomy flinched. The journey of the large rice platter was the most trying. When the spoon slipped from Murad's fingers, striking against the edge, she cried out, "Careful!"

"The dhandar-paatiyo is delicious," said Roxana, and her praise lit up Coomy's face.

"Quite hot, though," noted Jal.

"Paatiyo has to be hot, or it doesn't deserve the name of paatiyo," said Yezad, his napkin patting away the chili-driven moisture on his brow. He suggested putting on the ceiling fan.

"No, no," said Coomy. "Pappa will get a cold."

"In this weather?" said Nariman. "Heat stroke, more likely."

"Fine. I'm not going to argue." She rose and turned on the switch.

There were sighs of appreciation as the air began to move. But the fan, unused for months, had collected layers of dust on its blades. Little grey clouds were soon swirling over their heads.

"Look," pointed Murad, first to notice the impending disaster.

"Quick, protect the food!" said Coomy, shielding her plate by leaning over it.

"Duck for cover!" shouted Jehangir.

"Hit the dirt!" yelled Murad.

"Actually, the dirt is about to hit us," said Nariman. "What have you two been reading? Cowboy comics?"

Meanwhile, everyone copied Coomy, bending over their plates as Jal sprang to the fan switch.

"Nobody move till the dust settles," said Roxana.

"How are you managing, chief?"

"Quite well," said Nariman. "Bent is a natural posture for me. And I'm enjoying a close look at my dinner. The pomfret has a baleful countenance."

"Maybe some dust fell in its eyes," said Yezad, and the boys laughed as their grandfather sang to his fish heads, Dust Gets in Your Eyes.

Coomy burst into tears. "Are you happy now with your fan? You ruined the dinner on which I wore out my backbone in the kitchen!"

Roxana said nothing was ruined, everything was perfect, the dust had been foiled by the prompt action. "I can't wait to eat more of this delicious dhandar-paatiyo."

Looking up and around, Jal announced that the air was safe again. So they raised their heads and, to comfort Coomy, resumed with busy noises. The clatter of cutlery was the only sound at the table.

Then the whine of a power tool tore through the quiet, and Coomy flung down her napkin. Enough was enough, a little hammering was one thing – this kind of unearthly screeching at night was beyond tolerance.

She stuck her head out the window: "Mr. Munshi! Stop that noise! Hai, Edul Munshi! It's Pappa's birthday dinner! Have some consideration and stop your idiotic noise at once!"

The tool ceased, and she returned to the table, frowning at her plate. Jal said that Edul's wife, Manizeh, was a good woman – it was probably she who made him stop.

"Give credit where credit is due," said Nariman. "Coomy knows how to get results."

They finished eating without further interruptions. The cutlery fell silent; no one could be persuaded to another helping.

Roxana asked the boys to carry the plates to the kitchen, and before Murad could protest, Jehangir slid off his chair to collect them. He knew Mummy was being nice to Coomy Aunty, and also trying to show off, that her sons were good boys.

Nariman excused himself, something was stuck in his dentures. Jehangir followed him to the bathroom and watched him pop them out for a scrub.

"You know, Grandpa, I wish my teeth could also be removed. Would be easier to brush them, reach all the tricky places."

Nariman laughed gummily, sniffed the plates to check for odours, then reinserted them in his mouth.

After a dessert of falooda, everyone trooped to the balcony. It had stopped raining, and the air smelled clean. They slapped one another's backs to dust off their clothes, Jehangir taking the opportunity to thump Murad harder than the dusting warranted. The earlier unpleasantness faded into the background. Edul Munshi's hammer was thudding again, but softer now in deference to the late hour.

"Chalo, time to go home," said Roxana. "Tomorrow is a school day."

"Be that as it may," said Jehangir, "let's stay a little longer." He beamed, thrilled that he'd been able to use the phrase.

Laughing, his grandfather ruffled his hair. "Yes, sit for a while."

"You don't know this boy," said Yezad. "Tomorrow morning he will be glued to his bed – head is aching and stomach is hurting and bum is paining."

"We'll come back soon," said Roxana, and kissed her father's cheek.

The sad look of loneliness returned to Nariman's face, as Jal fetched the raincoats and umbrellas from the bathroom.

Securing the front door against the night, Coomy said that each time the Chenoy family visited, she felt exhausted, as though a whirlwind or a vantolio had passed through.

"That's strange," said Nariman. "To me it feels like a fresh breeze has stirred the stale air."

"You never miss a chance to snub me, do you?"

"It's not a snub, Coomy," said Jal wearily, "just a difference of opinion."

THEY WERE THE ONLY ONES at the bus stop, where a large puddle had collected on the broken pavement. The wet road was glossy black in the street light, shimmering and hissing under the wheels of passing traffic.

"Pappa talked very little tonight," said Roxana.

"Except when he wanted to bug Coomy," chuckled Yezad. Lowering his voice, he added that Dr. Tarapore had warned them about the symptom.

Jehangir asked who Lucy was, and his mother said she used to be a friend of Grandpa's.

"Girlfriend," said Murad, smirking, and she told him not to be silly. But Jehangir persisted with the topic, wanting to know why Coomy Aunty was so angry about Lucy.

"You'll know when you're older."

"There's nothing to hide," objected Yezad. "Might as well tell him."

Reluctantly, Roxana explained that Grandpa had wanted to marry Lucy, but couldn't, because she was not a Parsi. So he married Uncle and Aunty's mother. "Who was also my mother, I was born to her."

For Jehangir, the answer did not explain his aunt's anger. He asked if there was a law against marrying someone who wasn't a Parsi. His father said yes, the law of bigotry, and his mother said exasperatedly that he was confusing the child.

Then Yezad helped to change the subject, teasing Roxana that if she hadn't married him, she'd still be playing with toys in her father's house. The boys pretended to wind each other up. They mimicked the robotic drinking and drumming of the monkeys.

"Poor Jal and Coomy," she said. "So sad."

"Why?" asked Jehangir.

"Because they never got married, they don't have a family like us."

"And it always feels gloomy in their house," said Murad.

Two men unsteady on their feet approached the bus stop and stood behind the Chenoys. Laughing and continuing their noisy argument, their breath heavy with liquor, one gave the other a shove, making him stagger against Roxana.

"Sorry, sorry, sorry!" he giggled.

Yezad began edging towards the drunks to interpose himself between their boisterousness and his family. But when his manoeuvre was complete, they noticed the change.

"Bhaisahab, I already said sorry to your wife!"

"Yes, it's okay."

"Don't be scared, let her stand next to us!"

"It's fine," murmured Yezad.

"Aray, bavaji, we are not bad people! Little bit of bevda we drank, now we are feeling happy, so happy, so happy!"

"Good," said Yezad. "Happiness is good."

Ignore them, Roxana mouthed the words silently.

Then one of the men began singing "Choli Kay Peechhay Kya Hai." He sang it with an exaggerated leer, and the crude question in the song, directed at Roxana, made her stiffen, fearful about Yezad's reaction.

She said, with silent lips again, Just ignore them, Yezdaa.

Murad and Jehangir, who understood the popular lyric's double entendre, took their mother's hand in a confusion of shame and anger.

Their father waited a little, then turned to the drunks. "Shut up," he said quietly.

"Don't threaten us, bhaisahab, don't spoil our happy mood! What's wrong, you don't like Hindi film songs?"

"Not that one." He kept his tone even, to contrast with their intoxicated braying. "You want to know what's behind the blouse? I'll show you what's behind my fist."

"Stop it, Yezad!"

"Stop it, Yezad!" they shrieked in falsetto, and stumbled about, hysterical with laughter, clutching each other for balance. "Don't tingle-tangle with us, bavaji! We are Shiv Sena people, we are invincible!"

To Roxana's relief a bus rattled into view, route number 132: theirs. The drunks did not get on.

"Bye-bye, bye-bye!" they waved, as the bus carried the Chenoys away. Another shriek of "Stop it, Yezad!" was followed by drunken laughter floating in the dark.

After he bought their tickets, she chided him about his two Scotches, they had clouded his judgement. And he was setting a bad example for the children, they would also be tempted to fight in school.

"Daddy and Murad and I could have given them a solid pasting," said Jehangir.

"See what I mean? You shouldn't react to such loafers. Especially two together."

"Two drunks are two half-men. Besides, when I'm angry I get very strong." Then, in her ear, "And when I'm aroused I become very long."

"Yezad!" she blushed.

"I'd have straightened them out with my karate chop. I used to break bricks with it."

She knew he could, she'd witnessed it a long time ago, when they were still unmarried. They had been strolling near the Hanging Gardens late one evening, past a deserted construction site, where the watchman dozed in a secluded corner. There was a stack of fresh bricks awaiting the mason. Let me show you something, said Yezad with all the confidence of youth out courting. He formed a trestle of two bricks, placed a third across them, and broke it with a blow of his hand. Show-off, she exclaimed, then was sceptical: You must have picked a cracked one. Okay, you select. She did, and he broke that one too.

She looked at him, smiling at the memory. "You were young then. Your hand has become soft now."

44

"Still hard enough to break their necks."

Murad said he had never seen Daddy chop a brick in two, and his brother said, Yes, Daddy, yes, please show us, which annoyed their mother. "Are there any bricks in this bus?" To Yezad she repeated, "Ignoring low-class drunkards is the only way."

"Some things can't be ignored. Maybe Jal is right, Bombay is an uncivilized jungle now."

"You should try again for Canada, Daddy," said Jehangir.

"No. They don't need a sporting goods salesman. You try, when you're older. Study useful things – computers, M.B.A., and they'll welcome you. Not useless things like me, history and literature and philosophy."

As the bus approached the Sandhurst Bridge turn to Hughes Road, the boys pushed their faces closer to the window. They were about to pass their father's childhood home.

"There it is," said Jehangir, "my building!" as Jehangir Mansion came into view.

They laughed, and the boys stared at the ground-floor flat where their father had spent his youth. They tried hard to get a glimpse through its windows, as if that would tell them more about their father, about his life before he was Daddy. But some of the rooms were dark, and curtains on the others concealed the secrets of the flat.

"Can we go in one day?"

He shook his head. "You know it was sold. There are strangers living in my house now."

The bus completed the turn, and the boys craned their necks to keep Jehangir Mansion in sight. The ensuing silence was touched with sadness.

"I wish you had kept on living there after marrying Mummy," said Jehangir. "Then Murad and I could also be there now."

"Don't you like Pleasant Villa? Such a nice home?"

"This looks nicer," said Murad. "It has a private compound where we could play."

"Yes," said Yezad. A wistful look passed over his face as he remembered childhood years, and friends, and cricket in the compound. "But there wasn't room for everyone in that house."

"And Daddy's three sisters didn't like me," added Roxana.

"Now," protested Yezad, then let her continue, for he was the one always saying no need to keep secrets from the children.

Youngest among the four, Yezad had been the recipient of his sisters' unrelenting adoration. It was a fierce and jealous love, the three doting on their baby brother with a zeal that verged on the maniacal. In childhood, such a love posed few problems; it was considered cute and charming. During the teenage years, he was their guardian, their knight-at-arms. Many were the fights he got into when schoolboy teasing and off-colour remarks happened to include his sisters. In college, it was more serious; during his first year he thrashed two louts who were harassing his youngest sister in a part of the back field.

Then other girls became part of his circle of friends at college, and his sisters' fierce love turned oppressive, the first hint of trouble ahead. That women who were nothing but strangers should presume to share their brother's attention was unthinkable. Their reactions ranged from indignation to anger to bitterness; Yezad often had to choose between peace at home and an evening out with friends.

"And when Daddy and I got engaged, it was too much for them," said Roxana. "They treated me so rudely, they wouldn't take part in any of the wedding ceremonies. I was stealing their baby. No matter who Daddy married, they would have treated her the same. Isn't that right, Daddy?" She patted Yezad's hand, and he nodded.

"Maybe if you had stayed, they would have become friendlier," said Murad.

Yezad shook his head. "You don't know your aunties, it would have meant years of fights and quarrels. When Grandpa gave us Pleasant Villa, that was the best thing for us."

Jehangir said he always wondered why they had only Jal Uncle and Coomy Aunty, whereas his friends had so many uncles and aunties. "We never go to see the others."

Then Yezad said they had learned enough family history for one evening, what with all the things Coomy Aunty was upset about, and now this discussion about his sisters. And Jehangir said he was going to write a big fat book when he grew up, called The Complete History of the Chenoy and Vakeel Families.

"As long as you say only nice things about us," said his mother.

"No," said Yezad. "As long as he tells the truth."

THERE WAS NO KNOCKING, no doorbell, only a muffled thud, making the hairs on the back of Coomy's neck stand on end. She kept her head inside her newspaper, but racing through her mind were recent reports of daylight robbery, thieves forcing their way into homes, killing occupants, looting flats.

She and Jal were alone. Nariman, taking the opportunity of a lull in the rain, had ventured out for a short walk. The monsoon had been unrelenting for the last fortnight, and he had refused to pass up this fine evening.

The sound came again, louder, so that Jal heard it too. "Shall I go?" he asked.

"Wait by the window – in case you have to shout for help."

She approached the door on tiptoe to look through the peephole. Anything suspicious and she could withdraw, pretend no one was home. There was urgent shouting in Hindi to open quickly. First one voice, then another: "Darvaja kholo! Jaldi kholo! Koi gharmay hai kya?"

She retreated, gathered her courage, went forward again. Dreading she might see what she saw in bad dreams, she looked. And she knew, in that instant, that it was the other nightmare, the one concerning her stepfather, upon which the curtain was rising.

From the arms of two men hung Nariman, a helpless dead weight. One was carrying him at the knees; the other had passed his arms under the shoulders, fingers interlaced over Nariman's chest. The man gripping the knees was hitting the door with his bare foot, producing that muffled thud.

When Coomy flung the door open in mid-kick, he almost lost his balance. Nariman's birthday gift was hooked onto the man's shirt-front. Its weight made the button strain at the hole.

"Jal! Jal, come quick!"

The two men were panting, and sweat poured off their faces. They smelled terrible, thought Coomy, recognizing them from the ration shop, where they carried bags of grain home for customers, their muscles for hire. Mustn't be strong ghatis, she felt, if the weight of one medium-built old man tired them.

"What are you waiting for?" said Jal, frantic. "Chalo, bring him in! Nahin, don't put him on the floor! Sofa ki ooper rakho! Wait, maybe inside on the palung is better." He led them to Nariman's room. "Theek hai, gently, that's good."

The four of them stood around the bed and looked at Nariman. His eyes remained closed, his breathing laborious.

"What happened?"

"He fell into a khadda and we pulled him out," said the man with the walking stick dangling at his chest. Exhaustion made him succinct. He lifted his shirt-tail and wiped his face.

"The stick, Jal, the stick," whispered Coomy. Her brother understood her concern – the sweat would soil it – and plucked it off the shirt.

"It was a khadda dug by the telephone company," said the second man. "The old sahab's leg is hurt."

Nariman groaned, "My ankle . . . it may be broken."

They were relieved that he had regained consciousness. The sound of his voice made Coomy feel it was all right now to scold a little. "Every day we warned you about the danger, Pappa. Are you pleased with yourself?"

"Sorry," said Nariman feebly. "Wasn't on purpose."

"These fellows are waiting," whispered Jal. "We should give them something."

She consulted her stepfather: how far had the ghatis carried him? She wanted to calculate the amount by applying the ration-shop standard of payment. But hovering on the edge of consciousness, Nariman was not precise.

"Just give them a decent bakshis and let them go," said Jal. "They haven't delivered a sack of wheat, it's Pappa they rescued from a ditch."

She disagreed; what difference did it make, in terms of labour, whether they were lifting Pappa or a gunny of rice or furniture? Load and distance were the main thing. "And just because Pappa is hurt doesn't mean money grows on trees."

She had a better idea: the ghatis could carry Pappa across the road to Dr. Fitter's house. "Remember how obliging he was for Mamma? He took care of death certificates and everything, from beginning to end. I'm sure he'll help us with Pappa."

"You're not thinking straight, Coomy. That was more than thirty years ago. Dr. Fitter is an old man now, he has closed his practice."

"Retirement doesn't mean his medical knowledge evaporates from his head. He could at least tell us how serious it is, whether to go to hospital."

They argued back and forth till Jal said the men should wait while he went to inquire. If Dr. Fitter was willing, he could just as easily examine Pappa here, not put him through the agony of being manhandled across the road.

The doctor didn't recognize Jal, and seemed annoyed at being disturbed at dinnertime. But when Nariman Vakeel's name was mentioned, he remembered the long-ago incident at once, and asked him to step inside.

"How can I forget such a tragedy?" He hesitated. "So unfortunate for you and your two poor little sisters . . ."

"It's Pappa," interrupted Jal, "he's hurt his ankle," and elaborated on the circumstances.

"Whenever your father leaves in the evening, I watch him from my window. He suffers from Parkinson's, doesn't he?"

Jal nodded.

"Hmmph," the doctor grunted. "I could tell from the way

he takes his steps." He paused, becoming angry. "You people have no sense, letting a man of his age, in his condition, go out alone? Of course he'll fall and hurt himself."

"We told Pappa, but he just won't listen, he says he enjoys his walks."

"So one of you cannot go with him? To hold his hand, support him?" He glared reproachfully, and Jal, unable to meet the accusing eye, stared at the doctor's slippers. "Now the damage is done, what do you want me to do?"

"If you could please take a look," pleaded Jal, "see if it's broken . . ."

"A look? Who do you think I am, Superman? I didn't have X-ray vision in my youth, and I certainly don't have it now."

"Yes, Doctor, but if you could just—"

"Just-bust nothing! Don't waste time, take him to hospital right away! Poor fellow must be in pain. Go!" And he pointed to the door, out of which Jal hurried, glad to get away.

Dr. Fitter secured the latch and went to grumble to Mrs. Fitter in the kitchen that Parsi men of today were useless, dithering idiots, the race had deteriorated. "When you think of our forefathers, the industrialists and shipbuilders who established the foundation of modern India, the philanthropists who gave us our hospitals and schools and libraries and baags, what lustre they brought to our community and the nation. And this incompetent fellow cannot look after his father. Can't make a simple decision about taking him to hospital for an X-ray."

"Yes, yes," said Mrs. Fitter impatiently. "Now tell me, Shapurji, do you want your egg on the kheema or on the side?"

"On the side. Is it any wonder they predict nothing but doom and gloom for the community? Demographics show we'll be extinct in fifty years. Maybe it's the best thing. What's the use of having spineless weaklings walking around, Parsi in name only."

He kept complaining, pacing between kitchen and dining

room, till Mrs. Fitter told him to sit. She brought the dinner to the table and served him a generous helping. The aroma of her masala mince, and the egg beaming with its round yellow eye, cheered him up at once.

"Whatever's going to happen will happen," he said after chewing and swallowing his first morsel. "In the meantime, eat, drink, and be merry. Absolutely delicious kheema, Tehmi."

Dr. Fitter's lack of cooperation outraged Coomy, and she was not convinced by the sense of urgency Jal carried back with him. "If it's that serious, why didn't he come to help? Before we rush to hospital we should call Pappa's regular doctor."

"But even Tarapore will need an X-ray. We'll end up paying for his visit here, and then again in hospital."

Eventually, they agreed to go to Parsi General. The two men put Nariman, who was semi-conscious again, in the back seat of a taxi, and she rode in front with the driver. Whenever the wheels hit a bump in the road or went through a pothole, Nariman groaned in pain.

"Nearly there, Pappa," said Coomy, reaching over her seat to take his hand.

His fingers clutched hers like a frightened child's. She almost snatched her hand back, but the impulse passed, and she left her hand in his. After a moment, she gave his fingers a comforting squeeze. Through the rear window she could see the second taxi in which Jal was following with the ghatis.

❧

The X-rays were studied and Dr. Tarapore consulted with a specialist, for the fracture was complicated by osteoporosis and Parkinsonism. Surgery was ruled out. Nariman's left leg was encased in plaster of Paris from his thigh down to his toes.

The assistant who performed the task wore glasses that speckled with white dots as he proceeded. He kept up a constant stream of chatter, hoping to distract the old man from his pain. "How did this misfortune happen, sir?"

"I slipped into a trench."

"You are having difficulty with your bifocals, I think?"

"My spectacles can't be blamed. There was no barrier around the trench."

"That is so shameful." The assistant, whose name was Rangarajan, paused to check the consistency of the plaster in its receptacle. "Yes, pavements have become a serious peril. Every few feet, dangerous obstacles are threatening life and limb of the citizenry."

Nariman thought the chap would get on well with Jal and Coomy, he shared their phobia of pavements.

Then Mr. Rangarajan chuckled, "With so much daily practice, we could all become gold medallists in the obstacle race, we Bombayites. Or should I say, Mumbaikars."

He lowered his voice, but only half-jokingly, "These days you never can tell who might be a Shiv Sena fanatic, or a member of their Name Police. It is my understanding that some Shiv Sainiks have infiltrated the GPO, subjecting innocent letters and postcards to incineration if the address reads Bombay instead of Mumbai."

He started to layer the paste, wetting it as necessary to ensure gradual induration. "May I please inquire about something, Professor Vakeel?"

Nariman nodded. He was enjoying the touch of archaism in the educated South Indian's diction, and grateful for his garrulity.

Mr. Rangarajan asked if he had any friends or colleagues in foreign countries who might help him find a job, because he was trying to emigrate. He had sent applications to several countries including U.S.A., Canada, Australia, England, New Zealand. "Even Russia. Although after the collapse of the Soviet Union, welcome for Indians is not as warm as before. In the old days there was love between us – how many Russian boy-babies were named Jawahar, girl-babies named

Indira. Nowadays, I don't think any Russians are naming their children Narasimha or Atal Behari."

"Nowadays," said Nariman, "they probably name their children Pepsi or Wrangler."

Mr. Rangarajan laughed and wiped up a stray dab of plaster. "The age when great leaders flowered among us is gone. We have a terrible drought."

"The problem is worldwide," said Nariman. "Look at U.S.A., U.K., Canada – they all have nincompoops for leaders."

"Nincompoops," repeated Mr. Rangarajan. "That is too good, Professor Vakeel, I must remember the word. But it's more tragic for us, in my opinion. This five-thousand-year-old civilization, nine hundred million people, cannot produce one great leader? How much we need a Mahatma these days."

"All we get instead are micro-mini atmas," said Nariman.

Mr. Rangarajan giggled endearingly, scraping the bottom of the plaster container. He returned to the topic that had engendered this digression. "I used to work in a Kuwaiti hospital. But after Gulf War everyone was kicked out. George Bush killed the Iraqis, and killed our jobs. Now my main objective is to go somewhere else for better prospects. And U.S. is best."

And what about his soul's prospects, thought Nariman. Would they improve in a foreign land?

When Mr. Rangarajan finished, his hands and arms and apron were as white as a pastry chef's. Nariman was wheeled away on a gurney to his bed in the male ward.

Later in the day, the doctor came to see him again.

"How are you feeling, Professor Vakeel?" he asked, taking his pulse as he spoke.

"My wrist is fine. The problem is in my ankle."

Dr. Tarapore smiled with pleasure, the vintage Vakeel sarcasm was undiminished even in pain. And that was a good sign. The doctor, who was in his early forties, had been Nariman Vakeel's student long before the latter became his patient. Compulsory English courses that science students were force-fed during their first two years at college had brought them together.

But seeing Professor Vakeel in the stark hospital surroundings last night had left him unsettled. Running through his mind this morning was a welter of feelings – nostalgia, sorrow, regret for lost time, lost opportunities – and he was unable to understand the pathology of these human phenomena.

Also running relentlessly through the successful doctor's mind were lines from "The Rime of the Ancient Mariner." And the confused man of medicine gave vent to the poem that Nariman used to teach the science students: "'It is an ancient Mariner, / And he stoppeth one of three. / By thy long grey beard and glittering eye, / Now wherefore stopp'st thou me?'"

Nariman frowned. He noticed for the first time that Tarapore's longish hair was unusual for a doctor – on an advertising executive it would have been normal, he felt.

The wardboy went past, distracting them with the rattling trolley that he pushed among the beds. He was a young man who did his work in a dynamic manner. The washed urinals were placed under the beds with a forcefulness that declared his urge to establish order. His counterpart in the female ward was not called wardgirl or wardmaid, but ayah. Ayah, looking after children, thought Nariman. That's what the old and the sick were in this place.

Dr. Tarapore finished taking the pulse and made a note in his chart before continuing the poem, "'He holds him with his skinny hand—'"

"Excuse me, Doctor. Why are you reciting Coleridge? Your prognosis about my fracture would be infinitely more welcome."

Dr. Tarapore grinned like a schoolboy. "For some reason I was thinking of your class, sir, in college. I loved your lectures, I still remember the 'Ancient Mariner,' and 'Christabel.' And all the stories of E. M. Forster that we studied from *The Celestial Omnibus*."

"Stop bluffing. I have Parkinson's, not Alzheimer's, I remember those classes too: the room packed with a hundred and fifty science rowdies, hooting and whistling, wallowing in their puerile antics to impress the ten girls in the class."

Dr. Tarapore blushed. "That was the university's fault – not counting English marks for the final average, only attendance. The fellows didn't care. But I promise you, sir, I never took part in that hooliganism."

Nariman raised one eyebrow, and his ex-student modified the disavowal: "Maybe I whistled once or twice. Without enthusiasm."

He was silent after his confession, feeling he was gushing. He went on with his work, putting the stethoscope to his ears, making notes in Nariman's file, taking the blood pressure. But what he really wanted from his old professor were some words of wisdom about life.

He tried again. "Sir, the 'Ancient Mariner' has brought back the happiest years of my life, my years in college." He paused, added, "My youth," and immediately regretted it.

Doctor has a sensitive conscience, thought Nariman. Over a quarter-century and still feeling guilty for misbehaving in class. Or was this chit-chat part of his bedside manner?

He decided to abjure his cynicism. "What year were you in my class?"

"In First Year Science – in 1969."

"So you are in your forties now."

Dr. Tarapore nodded.

"And you dare speak about youth as though you'd lost it?"

"Actually, sir," said Dr. Tarapore, "I do feel old when I—"

"Hah. And how do you think I feel when former students talk to me about their youth? 'Let the dead Past bury its dead,'" he said to close the topic.

"'Act – act in the living Present!'" completed Dr. Tarapore, and awaited kudos for recognizing the quote.

"Excellent. So let us follow Longfellow's advice. Tell me when you will return my ankle to me."

Sufficiently inspired, the student strapped on the years he had shed. Dr. Tarapore was restored to the bedside, tapping on the hard, white plaster of Paris carapace and pronouncing, "The cast is sound."

His action seemed frivolous to Nariman. "Of course it's sound – there's enough cement here to resurface my flat. Your plasterer got carried away."

Dr. Tarapore laughed. "The tarsus is one of the most troublesome group of bones, especially at your age. We must give it sufficient support, shield the metatarsus, immobilize the leg. We have to be extra careful because of Parkinsonism. We'll take another X-ray in four weeks, but you can probably be discharged tomorrow."

He shook hands and left to speak with Jal and Coomy in the corridor, to give instructions about Nariman's care.

During the two days at Parsi General, Jal gave up his daily session at the share bazaar to spend the hours with his stepfather. Coomy too stayed the entire day at the hospital. Nariman was touched, and urged them to go home, relax, there was very little they could do here.

"It's okay, Pappa, we'll keep you company."

He asked if Roxana and Yezad had been informed.

"We decided not to worry them right now," said Coomy.

Then, to amuse him, they related Edul Munshi's visit to their flat, who had overheard someone in the building talking about the accident. The only words he had caught were "Nariman Vakeel" and "broken," but that was enough to make him hurry over with his tool box, offering his services.

"Wait till you hear what Coomy told him!"

"'Sure, Edul,' I said, 'we'll be very grateful for the repair. Only thing is, you have to go to Parsi General.' He was puzzled: 'Why Parsi General?' 'Because Pappa is there,' I said. 'So?' he asked. 'The broken item is Pappa's ankle,' I said."

"You should have seen his face, Pappa," said Jal.

"I had no idea he was that desperate," chuckled Nariman.

His dinner arrived, and they helped him with the tray, sharing his custard because he didn't want any and it seemed a shame to waste good food. They put the tray outside for collection and said good night.

He did not mind being alone. The wardboy on the night shift was an older man, much older than the dynamic day fellow. Early sixties at least, thought Nariman, and wondered if his shaking hands were also due to Parkinson's, or something else. He made up for the imperfection of his hands with the perfection of his smile. A smile of enlightenment, thought Nariman, so like Voltaire's in old age, in the portrait that graced the frontispiece in his copy of *Candide*.

And how did one acquire such enlightenment, he wondered, here, in a grim ward, collecting faeces and urine from the beds of the lame and the halt and the diseased? Or were these the necessary conditions? For learning that young or old, rich or poor, we all stank at the other end?

Nariman wanted to draw him into conversation, but hesitated each time he came by. The aging wardboy asked him how he was feeling, did he need anything, were the pillows comfortable.

Then he smiled – and Nariman felt as though they had just concluded a long and heartfelt exchange of ideas.

Next day Mr. Rangarajan returned to inspect his handiwork. For the most part, the cast had set uniformly, without weaknesses. But there were two places where he wanted to apply more plaster. "Better to be on the safe side than the sorry side."

Concerned about Nariman's haggard appearance, he tried to regale his patient with more stories and anecdotes from his working life. "This is a really good hospital, Professor Vakeel, a five-star hotel compared to some. After my unforeseen departure from Kuwait, I came back to our motherland and got a job at a government hospital in Indore. What a truly dreadful place. Rats running everywhere, and nobody getting upset about it."

"Must have been just before the plague outbreak."

"Oh yes. Two terrible things happened while I was there. One patient's toes were chewed up. Then, a newborn was eaten by rats – partially, but fatally."

Nariman shook his head.

"And rats were not the only problem," continued Mr. Rangarajan. "There was one man with his leg in a full cast, even bigger than yours. He was complaining that the leg was burning, driving him crazy. All day like a madman he was screaming, begging for help. The doctors thought he was being fussy. Finally, he couldn't bear it any more and jumped out of the window. When they removed the cast from his corpse, they found his flesh raw, crawling with bedbugs."

Nariman shuddered. He was glad Mr. Rangarajan had finished his work and was packing up his implements.

Dr. Tarapore saw Nariman once more, on the eve of his discharge. This time he did not recite any poetry, but had another word with Jal and Coomy, reiterating the do's and don't's: "Please see that my dear professor gives his ankle complete rest – not an ounce of weight for four weeks."

"Yes, doctor, we'll make sure," said Coomy. "Pappa will be good now, I think he has learnt his lesson. Haven't you, Pappa?"

Nariman would not dignify her question with an answer. Dr. Tarapore said with a smile that silence was consent.

Later in the evening the dynamic wardboy requested a letter of reference. He cautioned it was against hospital rules, so please to keep it a secret.

Nariman wrote on hospital stationery procured by the resourceful fellow that Mr. Yadav was a diligent worker who exuded genuine concern for patients, and was meticulous in his duties; it had been a pleasure to make his acquaintance; and he wished Mr. Yadav well in his future endeavours.

He examined the page when he finished, curious about his wobbly handwriting. The letters grew progressively smaller from beginning to end, he hadn't been able to control their size. This was something new – another symptom of Parkinsonism, he assumed.

The wardboy was overwhelmed without having read a word. He took his benefactor's trembling hand in both of his, reluctant to let go.

On the morning of Nariman's departure, Mr. Rangarajan stopped by to wish him good luck. But the elderly wardboy from the night shift was nowhere around, and Nariman was disappointed not to learn his name. Never mind, he would remember him as an incarnation of Voltaire.

Then it was time to go home. Jal rode with him in the ambulance. Soon after emerging from the hospital gates, they came to a standstill near the main intersection where a political procession was making its way.

"What party is it?" asked Nariman.

"Who knows. It's hard to read the banners from here. BJP, JD, CP, VHP, BSP, doesn't matter, they're all the same. Did you sleep well last night?"

Nariman responded with a vague gesture of his hand. They waited for the traffic to start moving again.

NARIMAN EXPECTED TO FIND the door open and Coomy waiting by it with a tray of flowers, vermilion, and a husked coconut. Instead, Jal used his latchkey. The ambulancemen followed him inside with the stretcher. There was no ceremonial tray, no one to perform the aachhu-michhu.

"Coomy isn't home?"

Jal shook his head. "At fire-temple. For Mamma's prayers."

Of course. It was the death anniversary. He had forgotten.

"And then she's going to buy some things for you – bedpan, basin, all that stuff."

The Parsi traditions around birthdays, navjotes, weddings, arrivals, departures normally earned Nariman's indulgence. He had never set great store by rituals. But the absence of the silver tray hit him keenly.

"When will she be back?"

"Soon. You don't have to go to the bathroom right away, do you? Have a nap, I'll put some music on for you."

Glad to be in his own bed, Nariman nodded off while the Schubert quintet played in the drawing-room, till voices trying to keep low disturbed him a short time later.

"A commode?" said Jal, as the taxi driver put it down with a thump in the hallway. At Coomy's beseeching, the man had carried the box up in the lift for her, but the meagre tip disgusted him.

"If I wanted to work for a coolie's salary, I wouldn't drive a taxi," he muttered as he left.

"Thank you, bhai, thank you very, very much," said Coomy, pretending she hadn't heard, and shut the door. "How is Pappa?"

"Sleeping. But you were supposed to buy a bedpan."

She began unwrapping the smaller parcel, which was an enamel wash basin, and placed it beside the covered wooden box with four stumpy legs. "I felt this would be better than a bedpan."

"What do you mean, better? Doctor said a month in bed. The foot must not touch the floor."

"Listen. I was in the shop, looking at bedpans, and I began to imagine the . . . the . . . procedure. What it would be like to place it under Pappa, and when he was done, to remove it, and clean him, and wash it, and . . . Don't make me say everything. You know what I mean. The whole thing is embarrassing."

So she had decided a commode would be more decorous, Pappa could sit right beside the bed, relieve himself more easily. "All we do is empty out the pot."

"But Doctor said the bones will take months to heal if we're careless."

"We are not making Pappa walk to the WC or anything. Let's try it out, see how he feels."

They carried the commode to their stepfather's room, and he pretended to be awakened by their presence. "Oh, Coomy, you're back. What's that, a new night table for me?"

She laughed. "No, Pappa, it's a lovely commode, look," and she opened the lid.

"We thought it would be more comfortable than a bedpan," said Jal. "Don't you think?"

"Whatever is most convenient for you is fine with me. I'm such a burden already."

"Don't worry, Pappa, we'll manage. It's only for four weeks." Jal dragged the box closer, positioning it by the bed. "Feel like going?"

Nariman nodded. They raised him by his arms to a sitting position. Next came the trickier part: to help him stand and make a quarter-turn for the commode. They reminded him to take the strain on his right foot, leave the left aloft, then hoisted him.

To lift an almost dead weight vertically was more difficult

than they had expected. And as soon as Nariman was upright, his broken ankle sank to the floor.

"Don't put it down!" yelled Jal in panic.

"I can't help it, the plaster is too heavy." He stifled a moan as they half-carried and half-pulled him till he was in position. They knew his pain from the sharp intake of breath and stiffening of the body. They began to lower him.

"Wait!" cried Coomy. "The pyjama isn't untied."

Summoning his last vestige of strength, Jal held on with one hand and yanked the drawstring. The fabric clung, refusing to slide down. He wiggled his hips against his stepfather's till the pyjama bottom dropped around the ankles.

After seating him they stood back, breathing hard. Sweat had broken on Nariman's forehead, his eyes were closed. His bladder was taking a while to function.

"Are you okay, Pappa?"

He nodded. Then a muffled ringing from the aluminium pot made them exchange looks of triumph and relief.

"Take your time," said Jal. "No rush, do it all – number one, number two, everything."

His bowels did feel heavy, but the pain had left him no energy to effect an evacuation. "I've finished."

Coomy knelt at his feet and slipped off the pyjamas. To get him back in bed they struggled and panted through the earlier motions in reverse, crying out at one point, for they were losing their balance, almost tumbling in a heap with him.

"There," said Jal, "it's done," and straightened his back. "What we need is a system, a method to make it smooth."

"Yes," whispered Nariman, "we do."

Averting her eyes, Coomy eased out the crumpled sheet that was trapped beneath his buttocks and pulled it over him. "Our biggest error was not taking off the pyjama first. For four weeks you will be a nudist, okay, Pappa?"

He hardly heard her through the pain. She and Jal forced hearty laughter to cheer him up, as she shut the commode lid and they left the room.

"What about the pot?" asked Jal.

"Later, it's only a quarter-full." Out of earshot she said that despite her joke, it was very disconcerting for her to look on Pappa's nakedness.

"Why? He's an old man, Coomy."

"That's not the point. I was already eleven years old when he became our stepfather. It was not like a baby growing up with her real father. I feel I'm looking at a naked stranger."

"But there's no difference," argued Jal, suspicious that she was trying to foist the toilet duties on him. "It's exactly what you would have seen on our father."

Further discussion was useless, she declared – Jal was a male, and would never be able to understand how she felt.

With the help of a painkiller the throbbing in Nariman's ankle subsided. He tried to sleep again but something didn't feel right. It wasn't the cast, something else, more subtle, that he couldn't quite identify.

He shifted his shoulders, adjusted the pillow, pulled his collar straight. He gripped the top edge of the sheet covering him and shook it, making it billow to fall back evenly upon him. And its breath upon his naked thighs, as it settled, revealed the source of his discomfort: his missing pyjama bottom.

He remembered now, Coomy had removed it while he was on the commode. Felt odd, lying in bed without it. Not something he was used to. As though he had lost the top layer of his skin.

He considered calling out, asking for it. But Coomy would be annoyed. And it did make things easier to leave it off.

Like mother, like daughter, he thought, reminded of the time when Yasmin had deprived him of his pyjamas. His pyjamas, and a lot more.

From room to room, cupboard to cupboard he wandered, looking for something to wear. But there wasn't a scrap

Yasmin had overlooked while he was having his bath; he had only his towel, and she refused all his appeals.

"Come, Coomy – you too, Jal," he cajoled the children when their mother was sterilizing Roxana's feeding bottle in the kitchen. "Tell me now, where did Mamma hide my clothes?"

"I don't know," said Jal, in response to his stepfather's pestering. Coomy signalled her refusal by putting a finger on her lips, warning her brother to keep his big mouth shut too.

Clever move on Yasmin's part, he thought, feeling no resentment for her – what right did he have to resent? He was the one behaving unreasonably; she had been the model of patience and understanding on so many evenings, tolerating the farce. For farce was what it would have seemed to her and to their neighbours in Chateau Felicity: the sight of Lucy on the pavement, staring up at the window where he stood. And then, when his remorse would drag him downstairs, to have to observe the two of them together, no doubt looking like a lovesick couple.

Poor Yasmin, he thought as he scoured the house, searching for a shirt, underwear, anything. And poor Lucy, holding her twilight vigils for him . . . to what purpose?

His mind wandered back over the time since their parting at Breach Candy. Those four months before his marriage to Yasmin, before Lucy had started to seek him out. The wedding preparations had kept him busy, and the new family looming on his horizon had occupied his mind. The hustle and bustle of his parents' Sunday group, their constant visits with advice and tips for the wedding day – it had all helped to suppress thoughts of Lucy. But he realized later that Lucy would have had no such distraction – she would have been quite lost. And after the festivities, he had learned from a mutual acquaintance that she was not doing well – she had abandoned her M.A., she did not have a job, and was still living at the YWCA. The news had concerned him, for he had hoped she would make up with her parents and return home.

Roughly three months after his marriage, as he was leaving work one afternoon, there she was outside the college. Just a coincidence, he had thought.

There was awkwardness in their exchanges – How are you, fine thank you. Then she asked, "Did you have a good wedding?"

He mumbled yes, thanks, and she asked another question: "So how's married life? Have you found fulfilment yet?"

Now he felt a slight sense of alarm, also an urge to reassure her, to say that things would turn out well for her too. But he uttered a few pleasantries and made his escape, trying to keep his confusion at bay.

From this time, her pursuit had begun in earnest. And there was no reasoning with her. She telephoned him at work, at home, wrote letters, even waited at the college gate for him on some days. He told her what she was doing made no sense, when they had decided months ago that it was best to end it.

"You decided," she said. "I thought it was a mistake. I still do. I still believe you love me. Admit it. I know that something is still possible between us."

"Come now, Lucy, let's not be naive again. We were naive once before. Thinking we could change our parents, change the ways of the world. What you're saying is completely—"

"Oh, Nari, you're still not being honest with yourself." Her voice was pleading.

"Please. I have no energy to go through all that again. And please, Lucy, for your sake and mine, stop following me." He tried to convince her that he wished her the best in life. But he had responsibilities now, a wife, two children, things could never again be as they were.

She stared at him, unmoving. And, for a moment, he saw the woman he had known, her eyes alive. He put out his hand, touched her arm, then turned homeward.

But her words remained with him. His emotions were in turmoil. Doubts about the decision at Breach Candy, buried deep beneath layers of rational argument, were surfacing again.

Could it be she was right? . . . The only solution was to stay away from her.

From then on, if he saw her standing by the college gate he would circle around the building and take the back entrance. But the relief at having managed to evade her was invariably mingled with the heaviness of loss.

And how supportive Yasmin had been after the wedding, through those two years of pursuit, advising him to be firm without being harsh, reminding him the unfortunate woman had endured a profound disappointment. She even helped him rehearse little speeches to make to Lucy, a judicious mixture of reason and sternness. But he never delivered them – when the moment arrived, he invariably felt that he had hurt Lucy enough.

Then the evening visits began. To Yasmin, they did not pose a threat at first, or even an inconvenience – the answer was simple. "Just ignore her," she said. "There are dozens of people on the footpath – she is one more. When she gets tired, she'll go home."

But Lucy on the footpath brought back the past with a force that left him shaken. Holding the window bars, he waited, while Yasmin asked him was he feeling unwell, was something wrong?

"Nothing," he mumbled, unable to explain that the sight of Lucy, standing motionless, her face turned towards his window, had accomplished what he had dreaded – filled him with a torrent of memories from their early days together. First, her family forbidding her to go out with him. Then her brothers warning her that they would beat up her boyfriend if they caught them together. That was when Lucy had threatened to kill herself, should they harm him.

Would she have, he wondered? Her parents had taken it seriously enough. Soon after, they as good as imprisoned her at home.

And he had found himself standing outside, gazing up at her window, while her brothers emerged and stared at him, *trying to intimidate him, softly uttering menacing words. He remembered how comforting it was to be able to see Lucy's face. All through that monsoon, even when rain was pelting in, she never shut her window. And he never sought shelter, holding his open umbrella at a suitable tilt, getting wet but making sure that their faces were not hidden from each other.*

Now Lucy, every time she appeared, reminded him of his need during those long-ago days. And each time, despite his feeling of uneasiness, he could resist her eyes for no more than a few minutes before going downstairs.

His reaction puzzled Yasmin. She insisted that he was causing harm to the distraught woman by indulging her in this manner. Her patience was also wearing thin, and an unpleasantness had entered their arguments. Strange, she said, that a professor of English should be incapable of delivering a simple, straightforward message – perhaps he enjoyed ogling the poor woman every evening.

The morning that his clothes disappeared, his indignation gradually made way for a sense of relief. His wife's action had awakened him to the ludicrousness of his predicament; it had given him time to think.

By and by, he telephoned the college to say he was indisposed, and cancelled his lectures. He waited till noon and appealed to Yasmin once more.

"No," she said, "you'll get your clothes at dinnertime."

"Do you want me to sit naked at the table for lunch?"

"I don't mind."

He sat with his damp towel around him and they ate an omelette in silence. He did not ask her again, spending the rest of the day in bed with a book.

At six-thirty, when Lucy appeared, he stood at the window and they were joined by their eyes. Then he moved away, and picked up his book again. Minutes later, unable to concentrate, he slammed it down and went to Yasmin.

"I've got the message," he assured her. "I promise you, today is the last time. I'll tell her that even if she stands on the

68

footpath for twenty-four hours, she won't get me downstairs again."

Yasmin said she had heard his promises before, which was why she had taken charge of matters. What she was doing, she said, was for everyone's benefit.

At seven, he went to the door in his state of undress. He opened it, and took a step outside. The children watched him in amused horror. He saw Coomy giggle and whisper something in Jal's ear.

"Go if you have the guts," said Yasmin with a little smile. "You're not getting your clothes back."

"If that's the way you want it." He began descending the stairs, and she ran after him.

"Have you gone stark-raving mad? I know you don't care for me, but what about the world? What about the children? And our baby?"

He continued calmly on his way, crossed the road, and joined Lucy on the footpath. Without any greeting, he told her this was their final meeting. He would not abet her in wasting her life. He would stay away from now on. But as he reminded her of her sense of dignity and self-respect, he felt he was uttering platitudes that were persuading neither one.

She waited till he stopped talking. "I love your outfit, Nari."

He smiled in spite of himself.

Then, with mischief in her eyes, she made as if to pull the towel off, and he jumped backwards.

She laughed at his panic and offered him her hand. He took it. She covered it with her left, grasping tight so he couldn't withdraw it.

Her behaviour was disgraceful, he continued, she must not loiter here any longer. Yes, she'd made her point about staring at the window, but to keep it up for so long was absurd. He repeated that this was the last time he had come downstairs to see her. This time, he meant it.

She listened in silence, caressing the back of his hand.

He finished speaking and gently extricated his hand: "Bye, Lucy. And good luck."

As he started back, some children on the ground floor of Chateau Felicity began yelling from the window, "Hai, naryal-paanivala! What price is your naryal?"

He nodded at them and their teasing, he knew his garb was strikingly similar to the knee-length loongi worn by the beach-side vendors of coconut water. When he was back upstairs, Yasmin threw the cupboard key at him.

"I'm sorry," he said. "I had no choice. But it's over now."

"Yes," she said softly, "it is over," while Jal and Coomy, who were sitting beside her, glared at him.

Four more times that day they helped him to the commode, and reached the end of their stamina. Towards evening he fell into a troubled slumber. Grateful for the respite, they sat on the balcony.

As the street lights came on, Jal said he was no longer young, he did not have the strength for this kind of labour. "My hernia and appendix, and God knows what else down there, will explode at this rate."

"What about me, my back is in pieces."

"I think you made a big mistake."

"What?"

"With the commode. Bedpan would have been much easier."

"Rubbish. The only mistake was to let the urine sit collecting in the pot."

For time had deepened the malodour. Holding her nose after the fourth usage, she had emptied the pot in the WC, swished some water around to rinse, and put it back in the commode.

They could not rest long on the balcony. Soon it was the dinner hour, and they pushed extra pillows behind Nariman to let him sit up.

"Too high," he said, and Jal removed one.

Now it was too low, he needed something in between, but did not dare say it. He ate little, anxious to lie down again.

"Did you like it?"

"Delicious, thank you."

Coomy held the basin under his chin while Jal waited with soap and water. Nariman washed his mouth, had a quick little gargle, and blew his nose. Little gobs of mucus floated in the shallow water; Coomy looked away. Then a light spray fell upon her fingers along the rim.

"Oh God!" she recoiled. Jal put aside the soap and water to take the basin. She fled to wash her hands.

The seagreen snot. The nosetightening snot, thought Nariman.

"What?" asked Jal.

"Nothing." More accurately, he thought, the colour was jade.

In preparation for bedtime Jal placed a copper frying pan and spoon on the night table. "If you need something, use this to wake us."

He demonstrated, and Coomy put her hands over her ears. "Louder than Edul Munshi's hammer," she said. "The whole building will run to your bedside."

Like the ones before, this feeble attempt at humour was a failure. Then, as though on cue, the hammering began again in the flat under them.

"The fellow is shameless," she said. "Even a sick man is not allowed to rest."

"I forgot my teeth," said Nariman, letting his dentures protrude to remind her.

She fetched the glass from the bathroom and held it under his mouth.

"That water has not been changed," he sucked the teeth back in.

"I'll change it tomorrow, I'm exhausted."

He released his dentures into the stale water. There was a slight splash, and they sank to the bottom, grinning silently.

Three times during the night they were summoned by the spoon and frying pan. And the final gong was for the bowel movement they had been encouraging all day. They helped their stepfather onto the commode and the stench filled the room.

Jal pushed open the window and turned the ceiling fan to FAST. Prescriptions and papers on the dresser were sent fluttering into a corner. Nariman shivered in the sudden draft.

Cleaning him was something they had not considered clearly. Placing a pail of water and a mug beside the commode, they hoped his left hand could wash himself as usual.

The normal way, however, was unmanageable for him. Immobilized by the plaster mass, he did not have the strength to manipulate on the commode.

Still, no harm in trying, they suggested. Jal wished they had thought of purchasing toilet paper, it would have been easier for Pappa.

"But I have some," said Coomy. "I bought a few rolls last year during the water shortage. Luckily, we never had to use them." She ran to fetch one from the storage cabinet at the end of the hallway, and tore off several panels.

Gripping the paper carefully, Nariman made a valiant effort to wipe himself. He pivoted on one buttock to reach behind, and almost fell off the commode.

"Forget it," said Jal, scared by the narrow escape. He put his hands under his stepfather's armpits and eased him off the seat. "Hurry, I can't hold him for long."

Coomy conducted a few cursory passes with paper, gagging in the process. "It's done."

They resumed positions to get him back in bed. Nariman clenched his jaw; pain had filled his eyes again. They saw the tears as they wished him good night.

"The pot," Jal reminded her.

"Your turn. I emptied it last time."

"That was number one, it doesn't count. And this commode was your idea."

"So if the shit was in a bedpan you'd be happy to handle it?"

He grabbed the pot and stormed off to the WC. She followed him there and back, saying it was just the first day but already she couldn't take any more, and they better find a solution instead of fighting.

"We'll discuss it tomorrow," he said testily, dropping the pot into the seat. "It's three a.m. and I am dead."

"You were not lifting him alone. My plight is the same."

There was no attempt to keep their voices low. The fan was still at fast, making the bedsheet flap busily where it hung over the side.

"Before you go," said Nariman.

"What?"

"Could you please turn the fan down?"

Jal rotated the knob to SLOW, and the flapping sheet settled into gentle swaying.

4

AT SEVEN A.M., the doorbell invaded Coomy's sleep, and
she woke resentfully from a lovely dream. She was dancing in the ballroom of the Taj Hotel, a band was playing old-
time favourites: "Fly Me to the Moon," "Tea For Two" in
Latin rhythm, "Green, Green Grass of Home." Gliding through
a foxtrot in her partner's expert arms, she raised her eyes
upwards and saw the chandeliers, the crystals glittering like
precious jewels. She could smell the cakes and sandwiches and
coffee being readied in the ballroom's antechamber. But she
never saw the face of her partner, all she knew was his mas-
terly hand on her back, guiding her without a misstep.

The doorbell made her groan and turn to a fresh area where
the sheet was cooler. She waited, hoping Jal would go to the
door. The house remained still. Then the ringing tore through
the quiet again.

She jumped out of the four-poster bed, her heart beating
fast, and let in the servant for her three hours of cleaning.

"Listen, Phoola, sweep my room first," she instructed. "I
have a headache, I'm going back to sleep."

She watched Phoola leave her chappals by the door and pad
soundlessly through the darkened flat. Her presence was slight,
and went unnoticed. But when illness or indisposition kept her
away, she was seen everywhere: in the dirty cups and saucers,
upon the dusty furniture, in the sheets of unmade beds.

Coomy lay down again as Phoola returned from the
kitchen with the short whisk broom, hunched and wrinkle-
faced, looking much older than her fifty-three years. She
moved with quick, small steps, knees permanently bent, her
bright green sari hitched high and tucked into the waist.

She lowered herself to her haunches, and the careless whispers between broom and floor reached Coomy's ears. Her eyelids opened a crack. For a moment she thought she was back in her dream where things had changed drastically: her dance partner had altered into a green, froglike creature, moving low across the floor with a gliding-swaying combination.

The broom grew loud, swooshing and rustling in a special display of industry, particularly under the bed, and Phoola's head even bumped against the slats a few times. Coomy knew it was for her benefit. She was glad to see her finish and go on to Jal's room. Nothing would disturb him, she knew, he would snore through the sweeping, she could hear him all the way here in her room.

She turned again to her interrupted dream, and the vague yearnings it had provoked. It made her think about the dance classes she and Jal used to attend in their teens. Pappa had paid for their lessons . . . so generous despite everything that had happened with Mamma and Lucy, never grudging them a thing. And sometimes they took little Roxie along, she loved to sit in a corner and watch them practise . . .

"Bai," said Phoola from the doorway.

"What, what?" Coomy turned, making the bed creak in sympathy. "I told you to leave when the work is finished."

"The work is not finished, bai. The work can't be finished."

Coomy threw off the sheet and sat up to look at the servant gone crazy. "I don't understand what you are saying."

"Come see for yourself, bai."

The fetor was ripe as they reached the room. Nariman had closed his eyes again, pretending to be asleep.

"But how can it smell?" whispered Coomy, more to herself than to Phoola. "Jal emptied it last night."

Had her lazy brother been sloppy, had he left something stinky behind in the commode? Holding her nose, she lifted the lid; the container was spotless.

Nariman decided: he would open his eyes and come clean. He smiled the next instant, amused by the thought – clean was a state much to be desired in his present condition.

"I'm sorry, Coomy, I assumed it was just gas and . . . I tried to pass it . . ."

"Oh God!"

She fled the room, followed by Phoola, who seemed pleased with the dramatic effect of her discovery. "You see, bai? I cannot work in that smell. I am not a mahetrani who cleans toilets and goo-mooter."

"Yes, Phoola, you—"

"Just give me my salary, I will leave now. There is lots of work available in other houses, without a smell that turns my nose into a sewer."

"Okay, Phoola, forget sweeping today, just scrub the pots and pans. There is no smell in the kitchen."

"Bai, it is best if I leave. I will come tomorrow for my money."

Coomy followed Phoola to the door, trying to mollify her without success. When the front door closed she was certain another one was opening, on the calamity of servantless days, and she felt crushed. She went to wake Jal.

"Get up!" she shook him by the shoulder. "See what Pappa has done!"

He fumbled for his slippers. "Am I not allowed even two hours' sleep?"

She ignored the protest and dragged him to Nariman's room. The smell made comment unnecessary. He leaned against the door frame, shoulders sagging, all optimism spent.

"And to top it off," said Coomy, almost in tears, "when I found him in his mess he was smiling. Smiling! As though this is something funny!"

"No, Coomy, you misunderstand," said Nariman, and hastened to explain the accidental pun that had amused him. "Now you see why I smiled?"

"Enough, please, I see what I see."

For a moment Jal too, like his sister, was defeated. The fouled bed was the last straw. His Waterloo, he thought, feeling not a flicker of amusement at his own pun, too disheartened to say it aloud. The time for attempts at humour was long past.

To set about the clean-up, they needed Nariman off the bed and temporarily on the commode, but he pleaded that the ankle was hurting too much. "I don't mind the smell, the damp is very slight. Please leave me on this mattress."

"Impossible," said Jal. "It will only get worse, the stuffing will rot. And God knows what it will do to your skin. Ready, Coomy? One, two, three, up—"

Nariman cried out softly, like a forgotten door moaning in the wind.

They took away the soiled sheets and surveyed the mess. Coomy said it would have been less severe if only she had remembered the rubber sheet. "We still have it. I should have put it under him, the way Mamma used to do for Roxana when she was a baby."

"The mattress must be removed," said Jal. "We'll give him the one from Mamma's room."

It was hung over the balcony railing and given a brief wash, then left in the sun, while Jal muttered it was obvious: this extra trouble was the result of the commode.

"What do you mean?"

"Pappa's pain is so intense when he gets up for the commode, he preferred taking a chance with his gas."

"I don't believe it. A little bit might slip out with gas, not such a huge puddle."

The next instant, she broke down weeping, saying it was too much for her, she no longer knew what to do, how to take care of Pappa, and now with Phoola gone, the burden of the housework was on her head as well. Looking after Pappa had been hard enough when he was not bedridden, and the things she had to deal with, the spatters in the toilet bowl, the mess in the bathroom sink, his dentures staring at her every morning and every night.

"No one has helped me all this time, not you, not Roxana, not Yezad. Now . . . I don't know . . . it's so depressing, and difficult . . ."

Her sobbing frightened Jal. She was supposed to be the

solid pillar, he the crumbling type. He tried to correct the reversal right away.

"You're just tired, Coomy," he soothed her. "Come, sit down." He took her hand and led her to the sofa. "This work is new to us, and new for Pappa too. But it will get easier as we get used to it."

She listened gratefully to his comforting words; they were restoring her. She agreed to go to the commode shop tomorrow morning. "I'll get a bedpan in exchange."

He suggested she stop by the Chenoy place too, tell Roxana about the accident. Perhaps she and Yezad would be of some help if they knew.

She dismissed the idea. The help they'd give would be no help – just useless advice and criticism. She didn't want a rush of Chenoys here, spending evening after evening telling her how to nurse Pappa, especially that Yezad. Besides, she had no energy to be their hostess, offering tea and cold drinks between bedpan and basin.

❧

Jal missed another morning at the share bazaar. He spent the time praying Pappa would hold tight till Coomy returned. And when she did, he welcomed the bedpan and urinal as though they were the vessels of salvation.

But the optimism mustered around these new utensils was a meagre thing, ending abruptly at their first trial. While the back-breaking labour of lifting Nariman to the commode was eliminated, the rest remained as repelling as before.

It was ridiculous, said Coomy, that with so much technology, scientists and engineers still hadn't invented a less disgusting thing than a bedpan. "Who needs mobile phones and Internet and all that rubbish? How about a high-tech gadget for doing number two in bed?"

They continued to cope, poorly, with the excretions and secretions of their stepfather's body, moving from revulsion to pity to anger, and back to revulsion. They were bewildered, and indignant, that a human creature of blood and bone, so efficient in good health, could suddenly become so messy. Neither Nariman's age nor his previous illnesses had served to warn them. Sometimes they took it personally, as though their stepfather had reduced himself to this state to harass them. And by nightfall, the air was again fraught with tension, thick with reproaches spoken and silent.

They took him his dinner on a tray and handed him his dentures in the glass. "Can you do one thing for me?" asked Nariman.

"We're doing everything we can for you," said Coomy.

"Yes," he smiled appeasingly. "My dentures are smelling, I haven't been able to clean them for five days."

Snatching the glass from him, she went to the bathroom, gritting her teeth. She poured out the water, taking care that his teeth did not tip out, and threw in a few flakes of laundry soap, filled fresh water, swirled. She rinsed twice and returned, pleased to have managed without touching.

Nariman slipped the dentures gratefully into his mouth. Then his face turned bitter as he tasted the detergent.

"What's wrong?" asked Jal.

"Nothing. Thank you for cleaning them. By the way, does Roxana know about me yet?"

"What do you think?" said Coomy. "Have I had one free moment since you went and broke your bones? I apologize if your lordship is not happy with the service."

"Please don't be upset, Coomy," he pleaded. "I'm sorry, I wasn't thinking."

Sleep was yet to come and salve his pain, but he let silence answer the "Good night, Pappa" that ventured from the hallway. A hand snaked around the door frame, groping for the switch, and the light went off.

Nariman blessed the darkness. He squirmed, feeling sticky

all over, and tried to scratch his back, starving for a rub of talcum powder. Since his return from the hospital, neither Jal
nor Coomy had thought about changing his clothes. Or
offered him a wet towel, never mind a sponge bath. They
would, if he asked, but he did not want to risk their clumsy
hands.

Raising his right shoulder off the bed allowed the ceiling
fan's slow breath upon his sweaty back. He gazed at the
window, its glass luminous in the street light. The bars,
standing stark, were oddly comforting. Old friends, he
knew them well, keeping him company in the hours he had
spent holding them while looking out the window, waiting
for Lucy. And the flaking paint, which sometimes he flicked
off the bars with his fingernail . . . like the flakes of dandruff
that he flicked, when he was younger, when he had hair. His
floc-flicking fingernail . . . flicking the floc . . . and the frock
Lucy wore . . . the clarinet frock he called it, because, he told
her, it made her look slim as a clarinet . . . when they were
young . . .

"'One day when we were young,'" he half-hummed, half-
imagined the words of the song, "'one wonderful morning in
May. You told me, you love me, when we were young one
day . . .'"

Their song, his and Lucy's, ever since they had seen the *The
Great Waltz*. He remembered the Sunday-evening show at
Metro cinema. The day he had named the yellow dress . . . and
after the film he said she was as gorgeous as Miliza Korjus.
They strolled to the Cooperage maidaan, found a bench, far
from the crowds gathered around the military band playing
energetic marches. He and Lucy were sheltered from the
bandstand by trees and bushes.

He walked his fingers along the row of large yellow buttons, up and down the front, gently pushing each one – playing the clarinet, he said. She laughed, teasing, that he wasn't
depressing the proper keys. He thought the remark a challenge. They kissed, his fingers undid the buttons and stroked

her cleavage, slid inside the brassière to her nipples. She sighed with pleasure, and he murmured in her ear that he had found the right keys. But fingers were not enough, a clarinet needed a mouth to play it, he said, let me demonstrate my embouchure, and tried to undo the brassière by reaching behind. No, not here, she said. So his mouth nuzzled what it could reach, they would leave the full clarinet concerto for another time . . .

An ambulance howled past the building, its flashing beacon throwing a chaotic brilliance across the window. For an instant, the bars seemed bathed in daylight. Then the window glass regained the soft street lamp radiance that he was used to staring at.

There was a breeze outside, he could hear it rustle in the branches of the tree. Shadows played on the pane. Leaves, moving like the claws of a nocturnal beast.

Suddenly he was shivering. He wished the fan were off, but dared not call for help. He pulled the sheet tight about him. Once again he was gripped in the knowledge of his helplessness. What would happen to him now? Weeks left to go, and he was at their mercy for everything. Already they were fed up with the work, with him, with his being alive.

No, that was uncharitable, they were doing their best. He checked the clock: hours to sunrise. On the window the patterns had changed, the leaf silhouettes formed a gaping maw. He closed his eyes, feeling a sob rising in his chest. It wouldn't do to let them hear.

∼

"The strain is killing me, my back is shattered," said Coomy, as she sat on the balcony with Jal. "We don't go to bed tonight without deciding about Pappa."

"I agree," said Jal. "Let's hire an ayah."

"Impossible. There's no money."

"You always say that."

"See for yourself. Check the bank book. The hospital bill has eaten up the dividends we had saved."

There was a commotion in the street, and they stopped talking as some men ran past on the pavement below, followed by a crowd shouting after them. It was hard to tell what was going on. Coomy said it looked like people chasing thieves, maybe pickpockets. Jal thought it was just some boisterous tomfoolery. The street soon resumed its normal state of busyness.

"There is so little in my life," said Coomy. "Home and market, market and home. I can't even go to fire-temple."

"You're not the only one. My work is also interrupted."

"You call that work? Visiting the share bazaar every morning and gossiping."

"If I didn't look after Mamma's investments carefully, there wouldn't be a paisa in this house."

"And if you got a real job, there would be money to pay for an ayah or wardboy."

They were back where they started, hurt and angry, their reasoning clouded by fatigue and frustration as they gazed over the balcony railing at the never-ending streams of traffic. Then, pausing in their argument, they agreed tacitly to a truce.

"I don't want to be disgusted with Pappa while he lies helpless in bed," said Coomy. "But I can't help hating him."

"You don't hate him," said Jal, scared by the word's power. "You hate the work. We just have to try our best to do our duty. Even as a stepfather, he was always kind to us, we mustn't forget that."

After talking late into the night they rose to go to bed, still without a solution. Passing their stepfather's room, they heard a peculiar sound from within.

"Did you hear that?"

"I'm not sure." Jal stopped to adjust his earpiece. Now he, too, heard the whimper. They stood outside the door, and there was no mistaking it: he was crying.

"What shall we do?" asked Coomy, tears of empathy rising in her own eyes.

"Go to him, of course."

Without switching on the light, they entered the room and tiptoed to the bedside. "Pappa," she stroked his shoulder gently. "We thought we heard you . . . are you okay?"

Nariman was grateful the room had been left dark. He stirred to acknowledge their presence. "Yes, fine."

"Is it the pain?" asked Jal. "Would you like another pill?"

"I'm all right. You two need rest, go to bed now." And he made a kissing sound.

"Good night, Pappa."

They kissed the darkness too and retreated, worried about this new development.

Over the next few days they found him weeping again, sometimes in the afternoon during his nap, though most often at night. They decided to inform his physician.

∾

Nariman questioned Dr. Tarapore's presence and the necessity of the thorough examination.

"I thought I'd mentioned it in hospital," bluffed the doctor. "A check-up, a week after you went home. To make sure everything's going the way it should."

"Is it?"

"Absolutely. And the pain is under control?"

"The first two days were bad," said Nariman, and Coomy held her breath – would there be a complaint about the commode?

"But that's only natural," he continued. "I took four painkillers a day. Now just one, at night, does the job."

"Excellent," said the doctor. "Excellent."

But the change a week had wrought in the professor's appearance worried him. His condition was unexplainable by a broken ankle. Taking Jal and Coomy outside the room, Dr. Tarapore told them they needed to raise his spirits.

"Depression is not uncommon during illness, but in old people it can be severe. Don't let him see you worrying, be bright and optimistic around him, talk of cheerful things, happy memories. Laughter and joviality are as important as his medications."

The doctor also reminded them to pay attention to his back, to prevent bedsores. He recommended daily washing with sponge or towel, use of a good talcum powder, and frequent changes of position by propping him up with pillows. Once the skin was broken or the tissue ulcerated, he warned, it would be torture for the professor, and quite unpleasant for them to deal with.

Coomy said it was easy for Dr. Tarapore to go on about being cheerful, he didn't have a lifetime of misery to deal with. "Happy memories, he says. But how can you manufacture them at this stage in life?"

"We could talk about Roxie, when she was a baby," suggested Jal. "Pappa was very happy then. We were all happy, Mamma too."

"How long can we use one topic?"

He shrugged. "What worries me most is the harm we could do because we don't know proper nursing. You heard what Doctor said about hygiene. It's a huge responsibility."

"Which Roxana and Yezad don't have to share. And that's not right, I've been saying it all along."

"But you're the one who doesn't want to inform them."

"What good is informing? As long as Pappa is here, they are escaping the burden."

He shook his head, not knowing which way to turn. "You know, I shouted at Pappa last night and felt so ashamed afterwards. Sometimes, from frustration, I think up horrible solutions. Sleeping pills to keep him quiet. Anti-diarrhoea medicine, to block him up for a few days."

He worried the mole under his right ear. "Isn't there a saying that when God sends us difficulties, He also sends strength and wisdom to deal with them?"

She said strength and wisdom were reserved for those who behaved courageously, stood up for their rights. "And we've never done that, have we?"

"What do you mean?"

"Think – why is there no money for an ayah? Because we let Pappa spend all his savings on Roxana. Our problems started from that. Thank God for the money Mamma was able to leave us." Once again her anger was revived. "If Mamma was alive, such injustice would never have happened. How I hate them all!"

"Don't say that, she's our sister. And Pappa did give us this flat. Now we must do our share."

"I don't owe Pappa anything. He didn't change my diaper or wash my bum, and I don't have to clean his shit either."

"How could he? You were eleven years old when he married Mamma." Despite the grim moment, he could not help laughing.

Coomy smiled weakly. "I just don't think I should be the one having to do all this for him."

"Anyway, that's not the main problem," said Jal. "Even if we become a pair of Florence Nightingales and take first-class care of Pappa's body, how do we provide laughter and joviality? They don't come out of a medicine bottle. What if he really dies of depression?"

Coomy put her finger across her lips; an idea was gathering shape inside her head. "Whenever Pappa meets Roxie's family, he's in a good mood. He and Yezad are always laughing and enjoying."

"So?"

"He should be with them, for the bright and cheerful atmosphere Doctor prescribed."

"That's absurd," said Jal. "Yes, Pappa and Yezad get along well. Doesn't mean he wants his father-in-law for several weeks in those two tiny rooms."

"And how about what Roxie wants? If Doctor says it's a question of life or death, surely Yezad has no business to say no."

They argued one side, then the other, till they managed to convince themselves Roxana would take him in without a murmur, grateful to them for giving her the opportunity. "In fact," said Coomy, "I'm sure she'll be annoyed that for one week we didn't let her know."

❧

Helping his stepfather with tea and toast for breakfast, Jal said there was an idea to consider: "A short visit to Pleasant Villa, to help you recuperate."

Nariman nodded, and said the tea needed sugar in it.

"I put a whole spoon," said Coomy.

"It doesn't taste sweet."

She added more, reminding him sugar was no longer available on the ration card. "At market prices, we need to cut down."

"What do you think of the idea, Pappa?" asked Jal.

"I think Roxie's flat will be fun for you," said Coomy, "with Yezad and the boys for company. Your recovery will be faster – happy mind means healthy body. The weeks will fly."

They waited anxiously for him to speak.

"It's good to see the smiles returning to your gloomy faces," he said at last. "They were beginning to look like those portraits in the passageway."

"Well, Pappa," said Jal, "worrying about you doesn't leave us much time for smiling. Watching you in pain, unable to entertain you in any way, we feel terrible."

There was a longer silence. Suppose I say no, thought Nariman, and give them good reasons – they could still have

86

their way. Suppose I say, This flat is my home, and I put it in your names because I did not differentiate between you and Roxana. Would you now throw me out in my helplessness? They would probably laugh that I was getting dramatic.

"Lying in bed, here or there, is all the same to me. But it will be difficult for them, in such a small flat."

"Small?" said Coomy. "By Bombay standards it's huge! You know very well that in chawls and colonies, families of eight, nine, ten live in one room."

He studied their anxious faces again. "If Roxana and Yezad agree, I have no objection. Speak to them first."

"What a thing to say, Pappa," said Coomy. "Of course they will agree. Why do you think we haven't told Roxie so far about your fracture? Because she would have insisted on looking after you – she would have fought with us to take you to Pleasant Villa. And we wanted to spare her the trouble."

So it was decided. Lame humour and close attention to inconsequential matters kept the façade from crumbling as preparations were made for the transfer. A suitcase was taken down from top of the cupboard and dusted. Coomy gathered clothes in her arms and brought them to the bedside for approval.

Nariman said yes without looking. She seems cheerful, he thought, as though preparing for a holiday.

Jal asked if he wanted to take any books. He replied he wasn't sure.

"Tell us later, we can bring you whatever you like." He put Nariman's safety razor, shaving soap, and brush in a plastic bag and handed it to Coomy for the suitcase.

She tucked it under the shirts. "You should grow a beard, Pappa, forget the razor. A philosopher like you needs a beard."

"Yes," said Jal. "A Socratic beard."

Nariman smiled. They were trying so hard.

"Anything else to pack?"

He shook his head. If he had a photograph of Lucy, he would have asked them to include it. But they had all been burnt, every single one, by Yasmin. Over red hot coals, in the same silver thurible that she used for loban during her evening prayers.

Perhaps that hadn't been such a bad thing. It had made him rely on memory. Lucy's image was beyond burning.

∾

To help with the journey, Coomy gave him an extra painkiller next morning while she went through a mental checklist, wondering if she had missed anything. "Jal, did you pack the glass in which Pappa keeps his dentures?"

"It does not matter," said Nariman. "Roxana won't grudge me a tumbler to soak my thirty-two."

"If something is missing we can take it later," said Jal to curb her excitement, which was embarrassing him.

"I better make sure or Roxana will say I don't look after you." She hurried to the bathroom. The glass she detested was on the shelf. She shook out the drops of water and put it in a brown paper bag. "Okay, Pappa, all set now."

"The ambulance is here," announced Jal at the window.

Poor children, thought Nariman, it was difficult for them to disguise their eagerness. And he couldn't blame them. The blame lay with the ones thirty-six years ago, the marriage arrangers, the wilful manufacturers of misery. He could still hear his parents' voices after the wedding benediction, Now you are settled in life, and we can die in peace. Which they had, a year later. They had survived long enough to perform their duty but not to witness the misfortune it would foster.

Two men in ill-fitting white uniforms and floppy leather chap-pals entered with a stretcher. The driver made Jal sign an invoice with the job starting time, and the destination address was confirmed.

The ambulancemen moved Nariman to one side of the bed

to make room for the stretcher. They slid him expertly onto it and tucked in the sheet, advising him it was best to keep his eyes closed. They emerged from the bedroom, carefully negotiating the turn through the door, with Jal and Coomy following behind.

As they marched down the passageway, Nariman opened his eyes. From his supine position he saw the glum portraits of his forefathers on the walls. Strange, how their eyes looked at him – as though they were the living and he the dead.

The slight up-and-down motion of the stretcher, like a boat bobbing on the sea, made his ancestors seem to nod. Nodding to concur with his fate, with his departure from this flat.

He wondered if he was seeing the familiar faces for the last time. He wanted to tell the ambulancemen to make a tour of each room so he could examine everything, fix it in his mind before the door closed behind him.

5

ADIATONIC SCALE executed in perfect legato drifted upwards from the ground floor of Pleasant Villa. How sweet a simple do re mi can sound, thought Roxana on the third floor, humming along with the violin.

The octave was completed, and she called out from the kitchen, "Get ready, Jehangir, the water's hot!"

The violin pursued the major scale into the next key. He ignored his mother, absorbed by the jigsaw piece in his hand. To locate its place in the world of his puzzle was all he wanted at the moment.

"Almost boiling now, Jehangir. And so am I, I'm warning you."

"It's not my turn today."

"Don't try your tricks – Murad had his bath yesterday. Hurry, the water is turning to useless steam!"

A shadow fell upon the incomplete Lake Como. He looked up and saw his father standing over him. "You can't hear Mummy? Go at once, don't make her shout."

Roxana felt tender towards her husband. She could never predict if he was going to side with the children or support her.

Jehangir relinquished the jigsaw, and Yezad took over. "Your son is completely addicted. The way he concentrates, you'd think he was looking for his own place in the world."

He picked up the blue piece that had defied Jehangir and tried it in various parts of Lake Como before giving up. "Not yet time to fit this piece. You have to build some more."

"I know," said Jehangir, pulling his towel off the line that stretched across the front room between his bed and Murad's.

On rainy days, when washing couldn't be hung on the balcony, the line became a fragrant curtain of wet clothes, and he preferred the room like that, in two compartments. Then he pretended to be one of the Famous Five, or the Five Find-Outers, who all had their own rooms and lived in England where everything was beautiful. His imagination transported the clothes-curtained room to the English countryside, into a house with a lovely garden where robins sang and roses bloomed, and to which he could return after having an adventure or solving a mystery. How perfectly he would fit in that world, he thought.

His school uniform was in the pile of clothes stacked on the clothes horse. The towel was damp with the monsoon's humid breath. As far as he was concerned, the bath time would be better spent piecing together more of Lake Como, its tranquil shores, its blue skies . . .

Murad demanded a bath as well, and Roxana said she had enough on her hands in the morning without his new nonsense. "First, even alternate days was too much for you. Now you want it daily."

"Your boy is growing up," said Yezad, "and growing sensible. For that we should celebrate, Roxie."

"Please use her correct name, my mother is not a cinema house," said Jehangir, imitating his grandfather's tone, for he knew it would amuse Daddy.

"Listen to him – making fun of Grandpa. Next time meet the chief, you're in trouble, you rascal." Then he p hands around Roxana's face. "I can see the whole w these eyes. Better than any cinema."

The ground-floor violin continued its practice, di major scales like sunbeams. Jehangir and Murad made them happy when their parents were this v the darker days filled with shouting and figh more often than they cared to remember.

"Can you see *Jurassic Park* in Mummy' Murad.

"No *Jurassic Park* and no dinosaurs," said his father. "But I can see *Love Is a Many Splendoured Thing*."

They laughed again, and Roxana said that was enough gayla-gaanda for one morning, these three lazys would be late if they didn't look sharp. "Come on, push your bed in," she told Murad. "Breakfast is coming."

Grumbling that he was the only one among his friends who still hadn't seen *Jurassic Park*, he slid his low cot under the settee that was Jehangir's bed. It disappeared from sight with a protesting groan. The dining table, flush against the wall, was pulled into the newly created space. Now there was just enough room around it for four chairs.

Jehangir wondered whether he would ever feel about bathing as Murad did. Daddy was the only one with the privilege of bathing every day because he had to go to work and meet customers. He followed a careful ritual with soap and talcum powder and pomade. He had a Turkish towel, soft and fluffy. The rest of them had coarse plain ones.

He had once asked Mummy why that was. She said Daddy worked so hard at the Bombay Sporting Goods Emporium, and had such a difficult job, anything special she could do to pamper him, she would. It was very important that he left the house each morning feeling tip-top, she said. She often asked Daddy, Are you happy, Yezdaa, is everything okay? This question Mummy asked Murad and him too, she wanted happiness for all of them, needed to check it constantly. And he always answered yes, even when he was feeling very sad.

A nagging doubt brought him back to the jigsaw puzzle for another look. "Murad can have my turn," he tried again. "I don't need it today."

"Don't need?" His mother lifted his arm and sniffed under [i]t. "You stink like a goat."

"Ah, the armpit test," said his father. "From Mummy's [fa]ce, looks like you failed."

"Be that as it may, you should also sniff Murad," said [Jeh]angir. "See who smells worse."

92

"Time you learned a new phrase," said his father. "We should visit Grandpa again."

"It's your turn today, and that's final," said his mother. "If Murad wants a daily bath he must get out of bed before the tap goes dry. At six, like me."

When no one was looking Jehangir checked his own armpit, and smelt the usual interesting odour. The water was boiling now; his mother took a rag in each hand and lifted the pot off the stove.

"Out of my way," she called repeatedly, like a ship's horn in a fog, "move aside, move aside," staggering to the bathroom in a cloud of steam, where she emptied the vessel in the bucket half filled with cold water. Her great fear was colliding and scalding someone in the morning bustle. She wouldn't let Yezad carry the hot water either, God forbid, if he burnt himself and was laid up, they would . . .

But she refused to allow herself to complete that thought. "Scrub yourself properly, don't forget to use the soap, and – now where are you off to?"

"Toilet."

"Again? Hurry, the water will get cold. And Yezdaa, the clock in the kitchen has stopped."

"Can I wind it, Daddy?" asked Murad.

"I've told you a hundred times how special that clock is, and how delicate. You'll wind it when you're older."

Murad muttered that everything had to wait till he was older, and at this rate there would be so much piled up for him to do, there would be no time for it all.

Dissatisfied with the knot, Jehangir pulled the Nehru House tie off his neck, smoothed the creases, and made another attempt. He tried a new type that he had learned at school, a bulbous variation on the samosa, called the pakora knot.

"Stop playing with the tie and eat your food," said Roxana. "Bath, breakfast, uniform – constantly I've to be after this boy."

Halfway through the buttered toast, his stomach felt wobbly again. He tried to slip away unnoticed, to avoid the cross-examination he knew would follow.

But his mother was keeping count. "Third one? What's wrong? And your brother has sneezed seven times since he woke up."

He shrugged and continued to the WC while his father teased her about her score-card. Passing by the shelves with the kitchen supplies, Jehangir ran his fingers over the glazed surfaces of the three earthen jars. The large, dark brown one, shaped like an amphora, held the ration-shop rice; the ochre cylindrical jar was filled with ration-shop wheat; and the smallest one, reddish brown, squat, and stout, contained the expensive basmati rice, reserved for special days like Pateti and Navroze and birthdays.

He loved the feel of these bunnees, his fingers forever trying to steal the cool from their glaze. No matter what month of the year, calm and unruffled they sat like three gods in that ill-lit passage. During mango season the fruit was hidden in rice, where it ripened to gold, much better than in straw. And the grain felt silky, trickling over his burrowing fingers when he tried to find the fruit again to see if it was ready for eating.

The chain needed several tugs before the tank yielded its cleansing cascade. Alerted by the flush, Roxana waited for him to pass the kitchen.

"Maybe you should stay home today," she said, frowning.

He did not touch the jars, or anything else, on the way back. It was his mother's strict rule: after the toilet, hands had to be washed immediately, with soap, twice, before they could participate again in the world outside the WC.

The distant violin was now weaving mist and melancholy in minor scales. Jehangir's third trip had condensed a cloud of worry upon Roxana's face. Still frowning, she returned to the pan to scramble two eggs for her husband's breakfast. She wanted him to give up eggs, or at least cut down, have them on alternate days.

"Please listen to me, Yezad, it's not good for you," she started for the umpteenth time. "There is so much in magazines and on TV about cholesterol and heart trouble."

"All fads and fashions, Roxie. My father and my grandfather lived to eighty-two and ninety-one. Ate eggs every morning till the day they died."

Then, mimicking a raucous waiter in a crowded Irani restaurant, he recited, "Fried, scrambled, akoori, omelette!" He made these words loud and guttural, deliberately mispronouncing omelette as armlet, which made Murad laugh and choke on his tea.

Jehangir smiled gratefully at his father. The week before, when his mother had pleaded the same thing, the response had been very different: "Good, the sooner I die of heart trouble, the better. You'll be free to marry a rich man." Then, Jehangir's eyes had filled with tears, Mummy-Daddy were fighting about money, as usual, because it was not enough to pay for everything, and he had gone to stand on the balcony by himself.

He sniffed his twice-washed fingers to make sure they carried the soap fragrance: sometimes his mother demanded proof. But her inquiry now was about the stomach, not hands; she wanted to know if it was runny all three times, and was there any mucus.

He hated these bowel questions, they embarrassed him, made him feel like an infant in diapers. Ignoring them was impossible, Mummy would keep pestering. Best to get them over with quick answers.

"Second and third time runny, no mucus," he said in a monotone, and rejoined the breakfast table.

Murad decided there wasn't enough butter on his toast. He went to the refrigerator for the dish hidden behind the bread and milk. With the door open, the mechanical clanks and knocks from its innards sounded louder.

"What are you looking for?" asked Roxana.

"Butter."

"You have enough. That packet has to last till Sunday. And get away from the fridge before you catch a chill."

"Don't worry so much, Roxie," said Yezad. "The way you treat your sons, you'll have to change their names to Namby and Pamby."

She said making fun of her was easy, but without her alertness God knew what calamities would befall Jehangir with his weak stomach, and Murad with his tonsils that swelled like balloons at the slightest cold. And besides, she was the one who had to stay up all night holding their heads while they vomited, putting damp kerchiefs of eau de cologne on their fevered brows: "You never have to worry, I always make sure you sleep. And I am stuck with the problem of paying for doctor. Why don't you do the budgeting, you'll find out how little money there is, how difficult to buy both food and medicine."

Jehangir listened, feeling depressed. The morning, which had started so nicely, was turning into a fight. Then, to his relief, his father took his mother's arm and squeezed it.

"You're right, Roxana, prevention is better than cure. But our Jehangla has too many absent days this term. His ground-floor disturbances will create top-floor deficiencies."

Jehangir wondered if he'd get to miss school today. He preferred his father's pet name for him to his mother's because hers was Jehangoo, too much like goo-goo gaa-gaa baby talk.

His father turned to him. "Well, rascal, what have you eaten this time?"

"Nothing, I'm fine." He knew Daddy was referring to the occasion when forbidden green mangoes had been consumed with friends at school.

"Why do you want to stay home? They have toilets in school."

Jehangir stopped chewing; the masticated bits gathered at the front of his mouth in a rush of saliva, and his buttered toast threatened to redeposit itself in his plate. The lavatory at school was disgusting, it stank like railway-station toilets. The boys called it the bog. The first time he heard it, he was puzzled by the word. He had looked it up in Daddy's dictionary, and found more than one meaning. Slang for lavatory, it said; also, wet spongy ground. He imagined wet spongy ground, imagined putting his foot in it, and agreed "bog" was the perfect word.

He didn't have to answer his father's question; his mother did: "It's risky for Jehangoo to eat canteen food today. He must stay home, I'll make soup-chaaval for him."

The soup of boiled mutton ladled over white rice was Jehangir's favourite. He looked forward to a cosy day: reading in the comfort of Mummy and Daddy's big bed, making his Lake Como jigsaw puzzle, lunch, a little afternoon sleep, more reading.

"So what will you do at home?" asked his father.

"He'll rest, and do some lessons," his mother answered.

"And read the Famous Five," added Jehangir.

Yezad shook his head in exasperation. "I don't know why they still keep that rubbish in the school library."

"But Enid Blyton is fun for children," said Roxana. "It doesn't do any harm."

Yezad said it did immense harm, it encouraged children to grow up without attachment to the place where they belonged, made them hate themselves for being who they were, created confusion about their identity. He said he had read the same books when he was small, and they had made him yearn to become a little Englishman of a type that even England did not have.

❧

Unheralded by a siren, the ambulance waded through the traffic swamping the lane and sputtered to a halt at the entrance of Pleasant Villa. Meanwhile, Roxana finished attending to her pressure cooker. French beans for dinner in the first compartment, mutton soup for Jehangir's lunch in the second, plain white rice in the third. The weighted valve was perched upon the vent. She watched it jiggle to the song of steam, then went to hang out the washing on the balcony.

In the years immediately after it was built, four-storeyed Pleasant Villa was indeed a pleasant place to live. But rent control and the landlord's determined neglect had reduced it to the state of most buildings in Bombay, with crumbling plaster, perforated water tanks, and broken drain pipes. Its exterior, once peach in colour, now resembled the outcome of an emetic. Electrical wiring had badly deteriorated, made a meal of by sewer rats. And the wrought-iron balcony railings, the building's finest feature, were also being eaten, by corrosion.

On the balcony, Roxana thought again of Yezad. She had waved to him from up here when he left for work – their goodbyes always consisted of a kiss at the door plus a wave from the balcony – and her little outburst was quite forgotten. But it still worried her, his refusal to get his cholesterol checked, or to cut down on eggs.

Like a bad omen, the white animal bulk of the ambulance caught her eye. Wet garments heavy in her hands, she glanced over the railing. The sun was back after three days of cloud and rain. Her ears remained alert to hissing from the kitchen: the cooker was building up a good head of steam. She began pegging the washing to the line.

One by one she shook out the wet clothes, enjoying the fine cold spray that flew when she snapped them, and imagined with pleasure the fragrant sunshine her arms would hold in the evening while taking in the dry things. She remembered when Jehangir was four or five, he had hugged her as she was bringing in the washing, buried his face in it and said, "You smell like the sun, Mummy."

He didn't do that any more, hug so spontaneously, nor did Murad. Nowadays it was more stiff, mandated by the occasion. Part of growing up, she thought sadly. Then the cooker released a burst of steam, a shriek that made her hasten to the kitchen.

This mid-morning blast punctuated the continuing practice session of Roxana's ground-floor neighbour. The scales had ended some time ago, and Daisy Ichhaporia's fingers were now limbering up with double-stopping exercises that ascended Pleasant Villa muscularly from balcony to balcony, crossing paths with the steam whistle.

"Fair exchange," said Daisy Ichhaporia once, when Roxana had apologized for the daily nuisance. "My noise for yours." She played first violin in the Bombay Symphony Orchestra.

"Oh but I love to hear you practice. It's just like going to a concert."

"That's very sweet of you," Daisy had smiled graciously at the compliment and, in return, had shared with Roxana her knowledge about the perils of pressure cooking, perils with which she claimed first-hand acquaintance. She had spoken of explosions and fires, of lunches and dinners that went rocketing in defiance of gravity. She had a stockpile of stories about gastronomy gone awry, which she narrated with gusto: of someone's papayta-noo-gose that had detonated, sending the potatoes flying like little cannonballs to mash against the ceiling, the chunks of meat shredded like shrapnel, and of so-and-so's prawn curry that had turned into modern art upon the kitchen walls, worth putting a frame around, art that could satisfy at least four out of five senses. And the super-hot temperatures of pressure cooking made it impossible to clean up the mess, for the food welded to the plaster. Only a hammer and chisel could pry it off, said Daisy.

Roxana had had the privilege of viewing some ceiling stains in Daisy's kitchen, which, the latter swore, were the remains of pork vindaloo. "The day it happened," said the violinist, "I sold my pressure cooker for scrap metal."

Roxana might have followed suit had the warnings come from someone other than a violinist who reputedly practised at home with her clothes off. During BSO performances she was clothed, of course – in a long black skirt, a black, long-sleeved blouse, and a string of pearls that just barely reached her bosom.

It was well known that Daisy Ichhaporia, in her heart of hearts, wanted to be a world-famous virtuoso. In Pleasant Villa they joked that she indulged in nude practice sessions to seduce the devil, make him appear and grant her satanic control over the instrument so she could play like a female Paganini. Daisy-ninny, they called her, behind her back.

Roxana herself had never seen Daisy in anything less than a robust brassière and serviceable knickers, of a cut so generous they might as well have been blouse and skirt. The violinist had explained the occasional disrobing, that it got too hot while practising fully clothed because of the passion she poured into the music, passion which made her perspire so profusely that the salt-laden effusions dripping from brow and chin and neck threatened the health of her valuable instrument.

Sometimes, lost in rehearsing, Daisy forgot to draw her curtains as dusk fell and lights came on. Then a small crowd would gather outside the window to watch the bajavala woman. Eventually, someone from Pleasant Villa would bang on her door to draw her attention, the curtain would shut, the fans disperse.

The violinist's absentmindedness was uppermost in Roxana's mind when exploding pressure cookers had been discussed. She rather enjoyed the sense of danger with which Daisy's descriptions had endowed the mundane appliance; she liked being the mistress who put the demon of steam into harness. It would be silly to take Daisy too seriously.

But it would be injudicious to ignore her entirely. Thus her curiosity about the ambulance took second place to the cooker's warning whistle.

༄

A recrudescence of doubt made Jal hesitate at the building entrance. What would happen afterwards, after Pappa came home again, how would it be between them? And between

Roxana and them? How much bitterness was all this going to create?

He tried to look on the bright side – at least he could resume his mornings at the share bazaar.

"Go on, hurry," said Coomy. "Talk to Roxie."

He looked up at the Chenoy balcony and saw clothes drying on the line. "I have a feeling we are about to do a horrible thing."

"That's because we are such sensitive people. We need more sense and less sensitivity. Isn't our plan the best choice for Pappa?"

"I hope so. But you come with me, I don't want to go upstairs alone."

"Stop worrying, Yezad is at work, and she'll agree immediately." Her words denoted confidence, though her tone shared his misgivings. "If I come up, will Pappa be all right, alone with the ambulancemen?"

"You think they'll run off with him?"

In the lobby a dirty, faded cardboard sign hung upon the lift: OUT OF ORDER. Coomy grumbled that she couldn't remember the last time they had been able to use it, and it was tragic that for a flat in this broken-down building, Pappa had spent all his savings.

"Looks too small for the stretcher anyway," said Jal, peering between the bars into the tiny cubicle, dusty and cobwebbed.

Taking the stairs gave them time to rehearse their strategy. He was to describe the events, starting with the fall and ending with the doctor's warning. She would join in if he forgot something; her trump card would be held in reserve.

They were out of breath as they reached the top. His hand went to the doorbell, but she made him desist till they stopped panting. After a minute she nodded her assent; he rang; they waited.

"Hallo," said Roxana. "What a surprise." More than surprise, she felt a vague anxiety. It had been years since her brother and sister had just dropped by.

"Can we come in?" asked Coomy.

"Of course." She stepped aside to make way. "Everything all right? Pappa okay?"

"Fine, fine."

She had to excuse herself, the pressure cooker was calling again. On her way back from the kitchen she told Jehangir, snuggled in bed, to come and greet them.

"There's a very important matter to discuss," began Jal, after she sat down.

"Shouldn't Yezad also be present?"

"Preferably, yes, but it's urgent. You see, a week ago, Pappa had an accident."

Roxana's hand flew to her face as he described the evening, the ghatis lifting Nariman out of the ditch and carrying him home, the taxis to Parsi General, the X-ray, the plastering of the broken ankle. She was in tears as she imagined the harrowing hours for her father.

Coomy put an arm around her, stroking her hair, while Jal explained that Pappa was slipping into depression, according to Dr. Tarapore, and it was hindering his recovery. Roxana's tears turned to anger.

"Why didn't you let me know at once? All of us would have come to keep him company. Why did you wait so long?"

"We didn't want to worry you," said Coomy. "And frankly, there hasn't been one spare minute."

"But the bad days are over now," said Jal. "We are here now, and Pappa needs your help. Let's concentrate on that."

"Of course," said Roxana. "Yezad and I and the children will visit him every evening."

Coomy shook her head. "That's no good. He'll be happy when you arrive, depressed when you leave. Up and down like a yo-yo he will go, even worse off."

"The scariest time for him is in the night," said Jal. "After midnight he weeps the most – so intensely, it wakes us up."

"Don't cry," said Coomy, kissing Roxana's cheek. "There's an easy solution. If Pappa stays here for a few weeks, in your happy, homely atmosphere, he'll soon be smiling again."

"How lovely that would be." She paused to wipe her eyes with her fingers, then dried the fingers on her skirt. "How I wish I could do that."

"Why can't you?"

"You have to ask? Don't you see the size of this flat?"

"I'm sure you can make space if you try."

Roxana considered in silence. "You're right. Let's look around and find a place for Pappa."

She began pointing out the few items that filled up the small room, explaining their function as though they were arcane museum pieces: "The daytime settee, on which you two are sitting, is Jehangir's bed at night. Under it, Murad's cot. There," she lifted a corner of the counterpane.

"Nice and low, comes out at night, slides back in the morning. Next to it, one armchair, and a Formica teapoy, which Murad moves aside when he pulls out his bed. And our huge dining table for two, with four chairs. Shall we go to the back room now, where Yezad and I sleep?"

Feeling uncomfortable, Jal demurred, that there was really no need, they had no business poking and prying.

"Not at all," said Roxana. "You're family, you are helping."

The sight of Jehangir in bed surprised them, as though they had not bargained for a witness. "No school for you?" exclaimed Coomy.

"Upset stomach," said Roxana. His uncle and aunt patted his shoulder, told him to get well soon and not eat too many mangoes.

Besides the small double bed, there were two cupboards and two clothes horses. A little desk and chair were squeezed into the corner by the bed, where the boys did their homework. She showed the furniture like a tourist guide presenting the sights.

"Any suggestions?"

Jal was apologetic. "It wouldn't be right for us to reorganize your home. You should decide."

"You think so? Wait, there's still the kitchen, the bathroom, the toilet to inspect. And don't forget the passage by the WC – could be a place there, near the rice and wheat and sugar and kerosene."

"Listen, Roxana, you can stop being silly now," said Coomy.

"What about you two? You keep Pappa's accident a secret for the whole week, then you come suddenly in the middle of the day when Yezad is at work—"

"Why do you need Yezad? This is your house, your father's money paid for it. Besides, you already have Yezad's permission."

"What?"

"Remember Pappa's birthday? The walking stick you gave him? That day I said to you and Yezad, if Pappa has an accident on one of his walks, I will bring him straight to Pleasant Villa. And with his big mouth Yezad said sure, welcome any time. Now how welcome is your attitude?"

"Aren't you ashamed to say that? You know I would do anything for Pappa. But to twist a joke like that?"

"Everything is jokes for you and Yezad," said Coomy. "You are experts at laughing and having fun."

"That's exactly why Pappa needs to be here," pleaded Jal. "Yezad's talent for laughter is the medicine for Pappa."

"It won't be a laughing matter if the depression finishes him," said Coomy darkly. "Dr. Tarapore told us, with old people depression kills before illness or injury. And it will be on your heads. Your laughing heads."

"Please, no fighting," said Jal. "Let's discuss calmly."

"Well," said Coomy, "there's nothing left to discuss, thank you very much." The time was right to play her trump card. "We'll just have to turn the ambulance around."

Roxana ran confusedly to the balcony, froze to the railing for a moment, and ran inside again. "That ambulance – you mean Pappa is in it? You left him alone in his condition?"

His mother's sobs got Jehangir out of bed. A big loop of his pyjama string was showing. He tucked it away and went to the front room to stand beside her, slipping his hand in hers, fixing his uncle and aunt with what he hoped was a reproachful stare.

"Don't overreact, Roxie, Pappa is very comfortable, we paid for a top-notch ambulance," said Coomy. "Sit down for a minute."

Tears blurring her eyes, Roxana shook her hand free of Jehangir's and started down the stairs at full speed. Descending with more caution, Jal called frantically to please slow down.

"All we need is for you to break your ankle!" shouted Coomy.

Jehangir shut the door after them and went to the balcony. On the third floor directly opposite, the green parrot in its cage was shuffling and swaying dementedly from side to side. He whistled to it, inspecting the rooms he could see into. Other people's homes always seemed happier, more fun than his own.

He looked down at the waiting ambulance. A few neighbours had gathered on the pavement, including Villie Cardmaster from next door, whom Daddy called the Matka Queen because everyone went to her for advice about which Matka numbers to play. Mummy said Matka was a bad thing; she thought it terrible that a woman should not only gamble openly, but encourage others. She didn't like Villie Aunty very much.

He saw his mother emerge from the building and run past the little group. He saw Villie Aunty's arm go out as though to reassure her. His mother ignored it, wrenched open the rear door of the ambulance, and disappeared inside.

Kneeling beside the stretcher, Roxana held her father's hand and stroked his head.

"Don't worry, my child. I'm all right."

She bent her head to kiss him. His pungent odour repelled

her, but she fought the impulse to move away. She wondered how well they had been looking after him.

"This idea was not mine," he whispered. "They promised to talk to you and Yezad before bringing me."

"I know, Pappa." She stroked his lightly stubbled chin and gave it a gentle squeeze.

He smiled. "You too? What is it with my chin?"

She squeezed again. "Sometimes our children teach us nice things."

Meanwhile, Jal and Coomy had arrived on the ground floor, where the gathering of neighbours was temporarily distracted by a stranger in the lobby whom they had surprised in the act of noting down names from the building directory. His furtive manner made them suspicious. Confronted, he said he was working for a company that conducted market surveys, then slipped away.

Rubbish, they declared after he'd gone, he didn't look like a market surveyor. Villie Cardmaster said he was most likely from Shiv Sena, listing names and addresses – that's how they had singled out Muslim homes during the Babri Mosque riots. Probably planning ahead for next time.

"Chalo," said Coomy to the ambulancemen, loud enough to be heard inside the ambulance. "Take a U-turn, there is no space here for the patient."

Roxana jumped out from the back. "Wait," she said to the driver. "Please take him to the third floor."

"Are you sure?" asked Coomy. "Have you decided where to put Pappa?"

Roxana snapped at the men who were looking at Coomy for confirmation, "Come on, hurry."

Coomy nodded at them, pointing upstairs. Then one attendant climbed in, the other grasped the handles at the tail end, and the stretcher emerged from the vehicle. Nariman covered his eyes, squinting against the bright sky.

"Sorry for the delay, Pappa," said Jal. "We gave Roxie a scare, because it was a total surprise."

"She had every right to be scared," said Coomy generously. "But there is not the slightest need to worry, Pappa is fine. See, Roxie?" She lifted the sheet to show her the cast. The hovering neighbours came closer with sympathetic murmurs.

"Upstairs, double-quick," said Jal. "Before these ambulancevalas fall asleep. If they drop Pappa, it will be like Humpty Dumpty."

He chuckled alone. Like a policeman directing traffic, he gestured to the men and they moved forward, noisy in their floppy chappals. Their steps were heavy on the stone stairs, the leather delivering a sharp slap with each footfall.

On the landing halfway to the first floor, they discovered it was not wide enough for the stretcher to turn. They tried squeezing through by tilting the stretcher, and Nariman clutched hard at the sides as he shifted sharply.

"Aray, watch it!" shouted Jal from behind. "You want to throw the patient down the stairs?"

An argument broke out, the ambulancemen saying that the only way to continue was to pass the stretcher over the banister with the help of Jal and the women. Roxana thought this was extremely dangerous, and pleaded with Coomy to return home with Pappa, promising to spend every other night there to look after him, relieve her of the duties.

But the stretcher was hoisted high, the pass made over the banister, and the manoeuvre completed. It was repeated twice more to reach the third floor. Jehangir was waiting at the door to receive them.

"Move, dikra," said Coomy. "Make way for the men."

"Is Grandpa okay?"

"Yes," she assured him with a pat on the head. "Go on, ask Grandpa, he can talk perfectly. Only his ankle is broken. Now, Roxie, where do you want to put Pappa? You must choose before these fellows leave, we can't shift him later."

"Pappa will take Jehangir's bed – the settee. Okay, Jehangir?"

"Sure." He thought Grandpa looked very small on the

stretcher, and was relieved to see him smile and whisper thanks. "You're welcome, Grandpa."

"My suitcase and bedpan are still downstairs," said Nariman, addressing no one in particular.

"I'll fetch them," said Coomy, anxious to be out of the way.

The ambulancemen had difficulty getting Nariman onto the settee. It was narrower than a bed, and there was no room to position the stretcher for a smooth transfer. They had to leave it on the floor and lift him over.

"Aah!" he cried, and Roxana's hand sprang to her mouth. She shouted to be more careful.

Jal paid the men and saw them to the door. He pulled up a chair next to the settee and took Nariman's hand, stroking it comfortingly. "Hope it wasn't too strenuous, Pappa. You know, Roxie, he is a brave soldier, not once has he groaned or moaned in all these days."

"Not so brave. I groaned quite a lot with the commode."

Roxana wanted to know what was this commode business, if Pappa was not to move from his bed?

Breathless, Coomy entered with the suitcase and the newspaper-wrapped package of urinal and bedpan, cursing the broken lift. She was miffed by the question she overheard: "What do you think, we did it to torture Pappa? We were hoping commode would be more comfortable for him."

"It was a mistake," said Jal. "Mistakes happen when you don't know."

Before leaving, they explained the medicines for Parkinson's disease, osteoporosis, and hypotension. Roxana decided to write down the dosage and frequency for the various pills and drops.

"It's okay, I know it by heart," said Nariman.

Coomy took her aside and whispered not to rely on him. "He forgets, and sometimes gets mixed up with his words."

They said goodbye with good cheer, Jal joking that in three weeks they would organize a race between Pappa and

Jehangir. "We'll have to give Pappa a good handicap, or Jehangir will stand no chance."

Coomy said it would be lonely in the big flat without him. "Come home soon, Pappa." She kissed his cheek, then waved from the doorway.

❧

The first thing was to air out the room, said Coomy upon returning to Chateau Felicity. She felt the smell had reached every part of the house, including the kitchen.

"How could it?" Jal tried to reason. "It's not that strong."

"Maybe you're losing your smelling power, along with your hearing. You should ask Doctor to check." She opened the windows and doors of all seven rooms, and turned on every fan, dusty or not. Dust would be dealt with later.

"How strange," she said, after an hour or more had elapsed. "I still smell it – even in Mamma's room, so far from Pappa's."

"Probably stuck in your head. More psychological than real."

"If I can smell it and it bothers me, does it matter where it is?"

"Yes. If it's in your head, nothing will get rid of it. Like the damned spot on Lady Macbeth's hand, remember? All the perfumes of Arabia, all your swabbing and scrubbing and mopping and scouring will not remove it."

She told him the smell was irritating enough without his silly comments. "You sound like Pappa, so gloomy and theatrical. Come on, help me with the work."

They spent the afternoon giving Nariman's room a thorough cleaning. His bed linen was left to soak in a bucket of suds, the waterproof rubber sheet in another. The window curtains were taken down. Everything in the room – the night table, chest of drawers, cupboard, window frame, door, ceiling light-shade and bulb – all of it was wiped down with Dettol solution and dried.

When evening came Jal said he had had enough. He sat in the twilit drawing-room while she worked on.

Around eight, she came in to ask if eggs-on-potatoes would be okay for dinner. The room was almost in full darkness.

"I'm not hungry, just make enough for yourself."

But she didn't want any either. "I know, let's have my rasp-berry sarbut. We're too tired to eat, a drink will be good for us." She reached for the light switch on the way out. He requested her to leave it off.

Back with the drinks, she thought she heard her brother sighing in the dark. She put the tray down and turned on a table lamp. "Jal? What's wrong?"

He shook his head.

She sat across him and gave him a glass. "Come on, drink, it will refresh you. It's the strain of these last few days, I feel the same way."

He shook his head again. "What have we done, Coomy?"

"Nothing, we haven't done anything. Stop being a sissy-baby."

But she was feeling equally wretched. By sheer force of will she swallowed a sip, then said, "It had to be done. We had no choice."

She ran out of words and switched off the table lamp.

6

AFTER HER FURY against Jal and Coomy had abated, Roxana began to worry about Yezad. He enjoyed Pappa's company and sense of humour, sure, but family get-togethers only occurred at modest intervals, lasted a few hours, nothing so demanding like three weeks of bed-bound convalescence.

"Hope Yezad won't mind," said Nariman.

"He won't." Could Pappa really read her thoughts, as he used to claim when she was a child? She moistened his face with a wet towel and dried it.

"Grandpa, you smell like Murad does after playing cricket," said Jehangir, wrinkling his nose.

"Don't be rude," said his mother.

Nariman smiled. "I've been clean bowled. Or maybe it was leg before wicket."

She apologized that there was not enough water for a full sponge bath, and promised to save a bucket for tomorrow.

"I told you this morning, don't force me to take a bath," said Jehangir.

"Oh, so you knew Grandpa was coming? Boy is getting too smart, Pappa. Good thing you're here to straighten him out. Come on, you, stop laughing, get the talcum for Grandpa."

He was back in an instant with the tin of Cinthol powder, watching as his mother eased off the stale shirt and sudra. Grandpa's skin hung loose on his arms and abdomen. On his chest it formed two pouches, shrivelled breasts. Two little balloons from which all air had escaped. The hair on them like wisps of white thread.

Roxana crumpled the sudra to wipe the sweat from her father's back and armpits. She shook powder from the tin and rubbed briskly, again lamenting the lack of water. Then she fished a clean sudra and shirt from the jumble in the suitcase and helped him into them.

"Thank you. I feel fresh as a daisy."

"You won't say that if you meet our ground-floor Daisy, Pappa, the way she sweats when practising violin." She took the smelly clothes from the room, setting them aside in a pail for tomorrow's laundry. "Chalo, lunchtime. I've made some light soup-chaaval for Jehangoo's upset tummy, you can share that."

She filled a plate for her son and called him to the table; her father's helping was in a bowl. "Easier for you, Pappa. I'll hold it if you like."

He put his hands out to receive the food, and rested its weight on his stomach. The cornflower patterned bowl rose and fell with his breathing.

"It moves like a boat, Grandpa," observed Jehangir. "Your stomach is making waves for it."

"So long as no one gets seasick," said Nariman, barely avoiding a spill as he raised a spoonful to his lips.

"Did Coomy forget your medicine this morning?" asked Roxana.

"I took my pill," he murmured, surrendering the bowl and spoon. "It's been a lot of exertion for one day, that's all. Tomorrow will be fine."

Jehangir came and stood by the settee. After watching for a moment, he said he wanted to feed Grandpa.

"It's not a game. Eat your lunch before it gets cold."

He polished off the rice and soup in his plate and was back at the bedside. "Now can I?"

Nariman made a small gesture with his head for Roxana to let him.

She handed over the food. "But I'm warning you, be careful, Grandpa's just put on a clean shirt."

"Yes, Mummy."

"And don't try to stuff his mouth, the way you do yours."

"Yes, Mummy," he sighed with weary exasperation. "I know Grandpa chews slowly, I've seen his teeth."

The unhung washing was waiting on the balcony. She shook out the clothes, fretting about the wrinkles already settled in the fabric, and kept glancing inside the room to make sure Jehangoo was behaving himself. The balcony door framed the scene: nine-year-old happily feeding seventy-nine.

And then it struck her like a revelation – of what, she could not say. Hidden by the screen of damp clothes, she watched, clutching Yezad's shirt in her hands. She felt she was witnessing something almost sacred, and her eyes refused to relinquish the precious moment, for she knew instinctively that it would become a memory to cherish, to recall in difficult times when she needed strength.

Jehangir filled the spoon again and raised it to his grandfather's lips. A grain of rice strayed, lingering at the corner of his mouth. Jehangir took the napkin to gently retrieve it before it fell.

And for a brief instant, Roxana felt she understood the meaning of it all, of birth and life and death. My son, she thought, my father, and the food I cooked . . . A lump came to her throat; she swallowed.

Then all that was left of the moment were the tears in her eyes. She wiped them away, surprised, smiling, for she did not know when they had sprung, or why. There was contentment on Pappa's face, and a look of importance on Jehangoo's, relishing the responsibility of his task. And both had a sparkle of mischief in their eyes.

"Just a little bit left, Grandpa. Let's do an aeroplane."

"Okay, but careful."

"First of all, Biggles is climbing into the plane," said Jehangir, filling up the spoon. "Now the cockpit is closed." He started revving and announced the chocks were off, they were ready for take-off. The spoon taxied several times round the bowl and was airborne. After a straight ascent it began to swoop and swerve, banking sharply and looping the loop.

"Prepare for landing, Grandpa."

Nariman opened his mouth wide. The spoon entered, he clamped down on it, and the food was safely unloaded.

"Last one now," said Jehangir, scraping the bowl clean. "Ready?" This time the aerial acrobatics were more ambitious. "Bombs away!"

Rice spilled down Nariman's chin and throat and collar. Roxana rushed in from the balcony, still clutching Yezad's crumpled shirt. "I warned you! Not for five minutes can you behave yourself!"

"My fault," chuckled Nariman. "I didn't open properly."

"Don't encourage the boy, Pappa, he'll go from bad to worse. You should be strict with him." She asked if he wanted the basin for a gargle – he was meticulous about his dentures after every meal. From the way he declined, she knew that he was trying to save her the extra work.

"What's next on the agenda?" he asked Jehangir. "You fed me lunch, I could help with your homework."

"My lessons are not on the agenda," he laughed, delighting in the new word. "Mummy's big bed is on the agenda, I'll lie in it and read my book."

"You could read here, aloud, so I can enjoy as well."

Jehangir hesitated; reading aloud was something he did twice a year only, for the Reading and Recitation exam. "I've already finished three chapters. And you won't like it, it's just a children's story, Enid Blyton."

"No matter, you can continue with chapter four. If I'm bored, I'll tell you, I promise."

So Jehangir and Nariman learned in chapter four that George, for some defiance in the earlier pages, was now sulking in her room where she had been sent by her father, who, to make things more difficult, insisted on calling her Georgina ("She hates her name," he interrupted to tell his grandfather, "she's a tomboy"). Julian, Dick, and Anne, who were visiting for the hols ("they're George's cousins," he explained quickly), felt that Uncle Quentin was being rather beastly to poor old George. And how rotten for her not to be out with them, walking along the shore, especially since the weather was simply topping, and the sea was such a smashing shade of blue that morning ("Cerulean," said Grandpa, "like the sky," and Jehangir repeated, "Cerulean") while Timmy, whose gorgeous tail just wouldn't stop wagging, ran beside them, having a jolly old time examining every rock and shell, barking in fright at a frightened crab and making them all laugh, only it wasn't much fun laughing without good old George and . . .

His mother touched him lightly on the shoulder. He looked up. She put a finger to her lips and pointed to the settee: Grandpa was asleep.

Her father and her son were still sleeping when she lit the stove and made tea at three-thirty, dropping the leaves directly into the kettle of boiling water. Afternoon tea did not merit the teapot and cosy she used in the morning. And when she thought about her routine, crystallized into domestic perfection over the years, she found it odd because morning was the hectic time – the leisurely ritual would have better suited the afternoon.

But it was worth the trouble for Yezad's sake; he loved mornings. He loved the breakfast hour, the radio playing, and the bustle in the flat and building, and in the street below where the vendors sang out their wares, alert to summoning customers who gained their attention by clapping or producing that special staccato hiss. Sometimes Yezad imitated the vendors' songs and chants, and then the boys competed to see who could do better.

She listened for the vendors too, waiting to run downstairs with her purse. Some in the building kept a basket and rope ready by their window, to lower with money and haul back up with their change and their potatoes, onions, mutton, bread, whatever they needed. Roxana did not use the system, too public for her liking. As Yezad joked, this now was real window-shopping: by keeping an eye on the basket-on-a-rope commerce, you could tell who was eating what on any given day.

Yezad was always laughing and joking in the morning, chatting with the boys, telling them little stories. Just yesterday he'd told them the one about old Mr. Engineer, who had lived all his life in Pleasant Villa, and had died recently. "Remember his special rope-trick, Roxie?"

She nodded, while Jehangir and Murad pleaded to hear it. The bath water had not reached a boil, so Yezad narrated Mr. Engineer's escapade from many years ago, when he had fallen on hard times: every morning, when it was time for the eggman to arrive, Mr. Engineer would wait by his second-storey window. From the balcony above him, the third-floor basket would hurtle towards the pavement, then ascend slowly with its fragile cargo. As it was rising past Mr. Engineer's window, an unseen hand would emerge, snatch an egg, and carry it off to the kitchen for breakfast. When the basket reached its destination, they would shout from the third floor at the eggman below: Hai, mua eedavala! Dozen means twelve, not eleven! The eggman would stand firm for a while, argue, then capitulate and send up one more egg.

One morning, the culprit was finally observed with his hand in the basket. Caught egg-handed, said Yezad, and the upstairs neighbours confronted Mr. Engineer with reluctance, embarrassed by the whole business. Unabashed, Mr. Engineer said, Who am I to reject what God sends floating to my window?

Jehangir and Murad laughed loudest at this point in the story, laughter filled with admiration and fellow-feeling, while their father concluded, "Ever since, the entire building has called it Mr. Engineer's Famous Rope-Trick."

Murad said it reminded him of another story that Daddy had told them, about the king named Sisyphus who was punished in Hades. "I think Mr. Engineer is like Sisyphus."

"How?" challenged his brother. "Mr. Engineer didn't have to push a big rock up the hill, over and over."

"It feels like that," insisted Murad, but uncertain how to explain his feeling. "The basket going down every day, then going up, and poor Mr. Engineer with no money, standing there to steal his egg – it's just like a punishment, day after day. It's sad."

"I know what you mean," said his father. "If you think about it, in a way we are all like Sisyphus."

There was silence while they thought about it. Then Jehangir, nodding gravely, said he understood. "It's like homework. Every day I finish my lessons, and next day there is more homework. It never ends."

They laughed. "But Mr. Engineer's story has a happy ending," said Yezad. "A few days after he was caught, his doorbell rang in the morning, and when he opened, no one was there. Only a brown paper bag upon the floor. Inside it, one egg. This kindness happened twice a week, and continued till the day he died."

"Why only twice a week?" asked Murad. "Why not one egg every day?"

"Who knows," said Yezad.

Roxana, with a meaningful look in his direction, said whoever it was probably didn't want to give the old man high cholesterol. Yezad pretended not to hear.

Meanwhile, the boys started a list of food they wished would float past their window: muffins, porridge, kippers, scones, steak and kidney pie, potted meat, dumplings. Their father said if they ever tasted this insipid foreign stuff instead of merely reading about it in those blighted Blyton books, they would realize how amazing was their mother's curry-rice and khichri-saas and pumpkin buryani and dhansak. What they needed was an Indian Blyton, to fascinate them with their own reality.

Then the announcer on the radio said it was time for one of yester-year's golden hits, and Engelbert Humperdinck came on. Yezad and the boys sang along with the refrain, "'Just three little words: I love you!'"

Roxana smiled, waiting till the song ended before sending Murad and Jehangir off to get ready for school.

But that was yesterday morning. And how things had changed this afternoon, she thought, pouring a cup for herself, leaving the kettle on the stove. Later, around six, she would boil fresh water for Yezad's tea. His evening cup was not at all like the morning. In the evening she saw the bruises inflicted by the working day. The love she felt for him then was like a hurt, as he told her about the clients he had had to deal with, obnoxious because they controlled large budgets and knew they could be rude with impunity, invariably angling for kickbacks from the money they spent to purchase sports equipment for the schools or colleges or corporations they represented. And he had to swallow his disgust, let them know tactfully that the proprietor, Mr. Kapur, did not allow it . . .

Anger and frustration would fill his face as he sipped the tea. Sometimes he drank from the cup; more often he poured a little in the saucer and stared into it, as though the answers he needed lay in its unfathomable depths. She was afraid to touch him with words, silence was all he could bear. And she understood, in some small way, what it was to be him who tried so hard for the family he loved. All she could do was wait for night to fall and restore him in the alembic of sleep.

So in the morning he was ready again, armed with optimism. She watched him return to the fray, knowing how it would end in the evening, and knowing that he knew it too, and yet he persevered. Then she felt her husband was as brave and strong as any Rustam or Sohrab, her hero, whose mundane exploits deserved to be recorded in his very own Shah-Nama, his Yezad-Nama, and she thanked fate, God, fortune, whoever was in charge.

She feared about how Pappa's arrival would affect their morning. No matter what, she had to preserve its rhythm for

Yezad. Yes, she was determined: not a hair of the routine that gave him so much joy would be allowed to change.

Halfway through Roxana's second cup, Jehangir and Nariman awoke, roused by Murad's doorbell. She opened the door and squeezed his arm as he rushed past, not risking a rebuff by detaining him for a hug. He flung his school bag under the desk and went to the front room.

"Hi, Grandpa," he said, as though to find him lying on the settee was quite normal.

"Don't you want to know why he's here?"

He listened while she told about the accident, and thought a bit. "Since Grandpa is visiting, I'll sleep on the balcony, Jehangir can have the cot."

"No, I'll sleep on the balcony," said his brother.

"What?" said Nariman. "Both of you want to flee the room? Do I smell so bad?"

They protested it wasn't that – sleeping on the balcony was an adventure for them, where they could see the stars and the clouds.

"We'll decide after Daddy comes home," said Roxana, unwrapping the bedpan and urinal. She examined them and took them to wash. People have different standards of cleanliness, she thought, fuming anew at Jal and Coomy.

"What are those?" asked Jehangir, as his mother returned and slipped the utensils under the settee.

"They are for Grandpa."

"For what?"

"That's his soo-soo bottle," pointed Murad, "and that's for number two."

Jehangir made a sceptical face. "What's it really for, Mummy?"

"What Murad said. Grandpa cannot walk to the toilet."

Jehangir made another face and said chhee, but it was more a matter of form than actual revulsion.

At six-thirty, the boys heard their father at the door and raced to open it.

"Daddy! Can I make a tent and sleep on the balcony?" shouted Jehangir before Murad could turn the latch.

"No, Daddy, it was my idea, you can ask Mummy!"

The excited reception pleased Yezad. "At least let me put a foot inside. Say hi to your tired father before making demands."

"Hi," they said in unison. "Can I sleep on the balcony?"

He shut the door, sliding home the security bolt. "Roxie, what's this crazy plan your sons have?"

He entered the front room and stopped. "Hello? Chief? Is that you?" He puzzled about it: came to visit, of course – but all by himself? And why lie on the settee? Feeling unwell, maybe.

The plaster cast that would have offered a hint was concealed by the sheet. Not to seem taken aback, he smiled and went to shake hands while Jehangir insisted that since Grandpa was in his bed, he should be the one to get the balcony. Murad argued that he was older, he would be safer there, Jehangir might get up in the night and fall over the railing.

"Quiet, or I'll give you each a big dhamaylo," said their mother. "Balcony, balcony, balcony! Is that all? Before I can even tell Daddy about Grandpa?"

Drying her hands upon her skirt, she approached the settee. "You won't believe it, Yezad, when you hear how badly Jal and Coomy have behaved."

"They tried their best, my dear," said Nariman softly. "Don't be angry with your brother and sister."

"Half-brother and half-sister, Pappa, let's be accurate."

"You never thought this way when you were children," he said sadly.

"And they never acted this way."

"Will someone please tell me what happened?"

She related the events of the morning and the past week. Yezad's head was shaking when she finished.

"I must say, chief, I have to agree those two have behaved badly. I'd use much stronger words. Turning up like thieves, leaving you in the ambulance, blackmailing Roxana."

"They couldn't cope," said Nariman. "This was a way out. For successful dumping, advance notice is unadvisable. Remember that, both of you, when you want to return me to Chateau Felicity."

"That's not funny, Pappa. Where is their sense of decency?"

"I wonder what would happen if you demanded to go back," said Yezad. "It's your home, after all. You should put your foot down, chief, just to see what they do."

"If I could put my foot down, everything would be fine," said Nariman with a wry smile. "How can you force people? Can caring and concern be made compulsory? Either it resides in the heart, or nowhere."

"Still, it's infuriating – they've pushed you out of your comfortable flat into this cramped little space."

Nariman shook his head. "That huge flat is empty as a Himalayan cave for me, this feels like a palace. But it will be difficult for you."

"You're welcome to stay, chief – your house, after all."

Nariman turned his face away. "Never say that, please. Notwithstanding my barging in today, this flat is yours and Roxana's. Your wedding gift. It ill behooves anyone to suggest, after fifteen years, that I am attempting to commandeer these premises."

The stiff and formal turn of Nariman's diction told Yezad he had offended him. "Sorry, chief, didn't mean that."

"We'll manage fine, Pappa," said Roxana. "Three weeks will fly before we know it."

"Exactly," said Yezad. "And Murad and Jehangir will help their mother with the extra work. You promise, boys? We'll soon have the chief good as new."

Jehangir pulled the urinal and bedpan out from under the cot. "That's Grandpa's soo-soo bottle," he explained to his father, "and that's for kakka."

"Don't touch those things," said Yezad, suddenly angry. "Wash your hands at once."

With Roxana's and Nariman's worried eyes following him, he stalked out to the balcony where he stood till she announced dinner was ready.

∾

Jehangir claimed he was expert now at feeding Grandpa, and helped him with the French beans. Yezad remarked that the chief not only had his private nursing home but also his own butler – what more could he want?

Nariman wondered if resentment was concealed behind the words. "I'm truly blessed to have such a family. Makes up for all other deficiencies."

"We should decide about the bedding," said Roxana. The kitchen was not an option, she felt, mice and cockroaches persisted despite the poison she spread regularly. The passage between kitchen and WC would be unhygienic. And the floor near the front door had a perpetual damp patch whose origins had yet to be traced. Which left the balcony.

"Yippee!" said Jehangir. "Simply smashing! I'll make a tent and have a midnight feast in it."

"Sorry," said Murad, "Squadron Leader Bigglesworth needs it for a base to conduct secret operations."

"Only one way to settle this," said Yezad. "You'll have to share. Grandpa is here for three weeks – let's say twenty days. So ten days each."

Their father tossed a coin to see who would be first. Murad called tails and won. The two thin mattresses on the cot parted company: one remained behind for Jehangir, the other went outside, upon a plastic sheet.

"Hope it rains heavily," said Murad. "It will be just like the

Biggles adventure when his Hurricane crash-landed in Sumatra in the middle of a storm."

"Silly boy!" scolded his mother. "Pray to God it remains dry! What will we do if your mattress is soaked? Once again your medicine bottles that we can't afford will rule my life."

Yezad tried to placate her fears: there was very little chance of rain tonight, tomorrow he would rig something up on the balcony for protection. But she was not willing to take the risk.

"It's only the beginning of September. If Murad falls sick it will be impossible for me, now that I have Pappa to look after." She threatened to sleep on the balcony herself if it wasn't one hundred per cent rainproof.

Now Murad worried his adventure was about to slip out of his grasp. "It's okay, Mummy," he reassured her. "Daddy and I will dress the balcony in a raincoat and gumboots and cap."

Rummaging among the shelves outside the kitchen, they found two small plastic sheets, enough to cover the spaces in the wrought-iron railings but nothing large enough to make a roof.

"Ask Villie," suggested Yezad to Roxana. "She might lend us a tarpaulin or something."

"You go. I can't stand her, with her dear and darling, and her gambling."

Villie Cardmaster, or the Matka Queen, as Yezad called her, was about his age, and lived with her mother in the next flat. She had taken to professing preference for her single state, declaring she had no use for a groaning-moaning fellow keeping her up all night with his demands. Sometimes, though, she looked wistfully at men, as though sizing them up for herself.

Her days were occupied with housework and caring for her ailing mother, who had shrunk to the size of a six-year-old. Villie was able to lift her without much effort as she took her from the bed to the bathroom, and to her easy chair on the balcony, or to the dining table, carrying her around like a wrinkled doll.

Any spare time that Villie squeezed out of her day was devoted to analyzing dreams. She assigned numeric values to objects and events from a dream, which were then used to play Matka. The illegal numbers game was the thread upon which the beads of her hours were strung. She interrogated friends, neighbours, neighbours' servants, and those who shared their dreams were rewarded with the fruits of her analysis. She had a little Matka flutter almost every day, placing the bets when she went for her daily shopping to the bunya, who was also a bookie.

"Hallo, Yezadji!" she exclaimed, delighted to have a visitor. She used the honorific suffix with every male, regardless of age or station.

"Sorry to bother you, Villie."

"What use are neighbours if you can't bother them? Come in, my dear, bother me all you want."

He followed her smelly housecoated figure inside. The full-length garment, loose and buttoned along the front, disguised her form efficiently. She wore it from one bath to the next, which meant three or four days. She slept in it, cooked in it, and conducted her daily shopping in it, the last with a significant modification: she wrapped a sari over the housecoat, draping it rather uniquely – half-a-dozen safety pins held it in place, for there was no petticoat waistband into which it could be tucked. She called the housecoat her all-purpose gown.

He realized why the flirting depressed him: it was the gulf between her coquettish words and slovenly appearance. Without too many details he explained why he had come, but Villie had seen the ambulance in the morning and heard the row.

"I understand, Yezadji," she said with a wink. "In-law troubles make the strongest into helpless kittens. Come, let's see what we can find."

She led the way, expressing regret for Nariman's predicament. His tragic life, she called it, and recounted some of the sordid details. Her familiarity with the facts did not surprise

Yezad – there were many in the Parsi community who could recall the scandal with Villie's mix of sympathy and satisfaction.

She stopped before an old dresser crammed with odds and ends. "Make yourself at home, my darling, look freely through these drawers."

Noticing his reluctance, she knelt to help him get started. "By the way, I have a strong Matka number for tonight. A dream so powerful, so numerically forceful I haven't had in months."

"Good luck, Villie, hope you crack it."

Despite his lack of curiosity, she dramatically lowered her voice to preserve the dream's numinous power and continued, with reverent cadence, "A cat is what I saw. A cat beside a large saucer of milk."

"And it discussed numbers with you?"

With a pitying smile she pulled things out of the drawers for his inspection. "The message of cat and saucer was so strong, Yezadji, there was no need for discussion."

"So the two of you communicated by telepathy?"

Villie shook her head. "The cat was sitting up straight, looking at me. Her head and body formed a perfect eight. And on her left side, the saucer of milk, round, like a zero. So tomorrow's number is eighty."

He was not through with teasing. "But, Villie, did you dream in English or Gujarati?"

"I'm not sure. What's the difference?"

"Huge difference. Gujarati number eight" – he drew it in the air with his finger – "does not look like a cat sitting up straight."

"Big joker you are, Yezadji." She laughed, but the seed of doubt was planted.

They found some squares of oilskin and a four-by-six section of canvas, not sufficient to roof the balcony. Then, from the last drawer, he pulled out a large leathery sheet that was packed inside a shopping bag. "What's this?"

"Oh, the old tablecloth. For our family dining table."

"Must be huge."

"It is. It was. So huge, sixteen could sit comfortably."

They each took hold of an end; the layers, stuck together, separated with a sound like fabric rending. As the dark green rexine unfolded, Villie let her memories unfold with it.

"Such happy times, Yezadji, we had around this tablecloth. Every Sunday afternoon, the whole family together, for dhansak lunch. Bavaji was fanatic about it – curry-rice okay for Saturday, but try to cook anything except dhansak on Sunday and heaven help you. So Maiji never argued. And at one o'clock uncles, aunties, cousins would arrive and start chattering as though we hadn't met for months."

Yezad thought about the balcony waiting to be fixed, but he did not have the heart to interrupt. Villie's face was aglow with happiness.

"Always Bavaji made me sit at his right hand, and my brother, Dali, at his left. And for Sunday lunch the rexine tablecloth was topped with another, of Belgian lace. Bavaji did not allow knick-knacks or vases upon it, saying it was a crime to cover up a work of art.

"How lovely those days were, Yezadji. Wait a minute, let me show you something."

She returned with a framed photograph: a family of four, posed formally at one end of a long dining table. Mother, father, two well-behaved children, the boy scrubbed and shining in short trousers, shirt, and tie, the little girl in her ribbon-bedecked frock of pink organza.

"My seventh birthday – which fell on a Sunday. Very special." She sighed. "Why is it that when we grow up, suddenly the happy days are behind us?"

Yezad had no answer. "What happened to that dining table?"

"My brother took it to his new flat when he got married."

"Does he have big Sunday lunches, family tradition?"

Villie twisted her mouth in answer. "He destroyed the table. It wouldn't fit through his front door, so he got a carpenter to turn it into a sectional table. God knows what junglee wood he used for framing, but in two years it was eaten to bits by white ants."

She stroked the cloth and began folding. Yezad helped, wondering about the workings of a fate that had transformed Villie from the sweet little pink-frocked girl, sitting at her father's right hand for Sunday dhansak, to the dream-obsessed, Matka-besotted woman with a rancid smell. What cruel trajectory had led from there to here?

She did not replace the tablecloth in its bag. "I'm sure this will be large enough to cover the balcony."

Yezad was startled. "Don't you want to save such an important memento?"

"Memento-femento I don't believe in. A big tablecloth without a big table, without guests to sit and laugh and talk, is no use. Cover the balcony before your little boy catches a chill."

"Thanks, Villie."

She pushed the odds and ends back into the drawers and slammed them shut. "You know, Yezadji, you're right. If my dream was in Gujarati, I'd use a different method: the sound of the word. Cat would become bilaari – bey number for bilaari. Combined with zero for saucer, I should bet twenty. And you too, my dear, put some money on twenty and eighty, safe in both languages. You'll win enough to build a pukka room on your balcony."

He said no need, he wanted to keep it as a balcony, the situation was temporary.

"That means nothing," said Villie, seeing him to the door. "Everything is temporary, Yezadji. Life itself is temporary."

Wasn't it typical of that woman, said Roxana, to keep a man chatting for as long as possible with her dear-darling nonsense. And when she heard that Villie had shown him a photo, she asked what kind of new perversion was that woman up to, wasn't Matka enough for her?

"It was a family photo, when she was seven," said Yezad, which made Roxana feel foolish, and then guilty about taking the tablecloth, as he told the story behind it, repeating Villie's sad remembrances. "You know, she's not a bad person. Just a little weird. And she offered to get your shopping from the bunya, she goes every morning."

He spread the rexine on the balcony and made holes at suitable distances along the edges, feeling a twinge at each perforation. He would buy metal eyelets tomorrow at the Bora's hardware shop, reinforce the raw punctures, make it strong as tarpaulin. With short lengths of rope through each hole, he fastened the sheet to the balcony railing.

Murad began equipping his rexine tent for the night. He took his toy binoculars, compass, and weapons: a paper knife and water pistol. He wanted to keep a candle and matches as well in his emergency hideout, deep in the darkest recesses of the Sumatran jungle, but his mother refused.

"Mummy is right," said Yezad. "It won't be very pleasant if you burn down Pleasant Villa."

"Ha, ha, very funny. Mummy always imagines horrible things."

"Speaking of imagining, chief, what's this about being depressed? Are Jal and Coomy imagining it? I can't believe it of a philosopher like you."

"Depression is a red herring," said Nariman. "I think a lot about the past, it's true. But at my age, the past is more present than the here and now. And there is not much percentage in the future."

"You've got many years left with us, Pappa."

"I wonder why Dr. Tarapore thought it was depression," said Yezad.

"The quack misdiagnosed based on what Coomy and Jal said. He has yet to learn not everything can be explained clinically. 'The heart has its reasons which reason knows nothing of.'"

"That's lovely," said Roxana. "Shakespeare?"

"Pascal."

She repeated the words to herself, silently, The heart has its reasons . . .

Lying on his cot, Jehangir listened, attentive to the adults' conversation, wondering what depression felt like. Was it the sad feeling when it kept raining for many days? He watched, envious, as Murad prepared for his night on the balcony. Then he heard Grandpa ask in a timid voice for the soo-soo bottle.

"I'll get it for you," he said, jumping off the cot.

His father crossed the room in two violent strides and stood in his path. "What did I say about that bottle?"

Jehangir froze. He thought his father was going to hit him. He sounded angriest when his voice was so scarily quiet.

"Answer me. What did I tell you?"

Cowering, he replied, "Not to touch those things."

"So why did you try to get it?"

"I forgot," he said, his voice tiny. "I wanted to help."

Next moment the anger disappeared, and his father's hand was on his shoulder. "You don't have to help with this, Jehangla."

His father nudged him towards the cot. He watched his mother pick up the soo-soo bottle. She lifted the sheet and put Grandpa's soosoti into it. It was small, not much bigger than his. But Grandpa's balls were huge. Like onions in a sock, even bigger than Daddy's, which he had seen many times when Daddy came out of the bathroom and took the towel off to put on his clothes. His own were like little marbles. He wondered if the size and weight of Grandpa's made it uncomfortable.

"Lie down, Jehangla," said Daddy. "You don't have to look at everything. Good night."

Then Mummy brought the basin for Grandpa to gargle and clean his mouth before going to sleep. He made that funny move with his jaw to push out his teeth. They slid into the glass, into their watery bed, before Jehangir closed his eyes.

With her head next to Yezad's on the pillow, Roxana thanked him for being so understanding.

He suggested it might be best to hire a hospital ayah, running herself ragged was not the answer. "We'll make Jal and Coomy pay the cost. Tell them it's our condition for accommodating Pappa."

"After the way they behaved, I don't want a thing from them. I don't want to see their faces for three weeks, till Pappa is on his feet."

She assured him it wouldn't be difficult, with a little patience and understanding. Then she described how bad Pappa smelled when he'd arrived. "All it took was a napkin and water, and talcum, but Jal and Coomy hadn't bothered. And you saw the stubble on his poor face – they packed his razor in the bag. As if he can do it himself."

"We'll call a barber. But three weeks, and that's it. I will accept no excuses from those two rascals."

"Oh I'm not going to let them push Pappa from his house for longer than that. Just watch me, I'll straighten them out."

She came closer, hugged him, and kissed the ear into which she'd been whispering, nibbling it. He sighed. His fingers reached for the hem of her nightdress and pulled it up around her hips as she raised her bottom slightly. His hand moved under the soft fabric. She said better wait a little, the boys were asleep but she was not sure about Pappa.

Nariman opened his eyes and wished Lucy's large, sad eyes would stop haunting him. Turning his head, he looked for the familiar bars on his window, and saw his grandson's cot instead. He was not in Chateau Felicity. He must stay quiet tonight, muzzle his memories, must not disturb Roxana and Yezad, and the children sleeping close by.

Drowsy from the painkiller, he drifted on a cloud resembling slumber. Among the murmurs from the back room the word "ayah" caught his ear . . . and memory began its torments again. Lucy accepting employment as an ayah in Chateau Felicity – to be closer to him, she'd said. And the work was no hardship, she assured him, it was a great comfort to live and sleep in the same building.

Even before she became a servant, heartache had etched lines of fatigue on her face, making it gaunt. Domestic drudgery was now worsening it. How outrageous, he thought, that she would do this to herself, go to such absurd lengths just to retaliate, to make his life miserable because he had refused to meet her on the footpath any more.

Her employers were the ground-floor Arjanis. They knew who she was – they had often seen Lucy with him. The ground-floor Gestapo, he would joke with Lucy during the years when they were still going out, for Mr. and Mrs. Arjani were always at their window, keeping an eye on the comings and goings in Chateau Felicity. And later, they would watch her on those evenings when she stood like a lost child on the pavement, staring up at his window.

But hiring her as an ayah for their grandchildren, he realized, was an act of vengeance. Years earlier, around the time he had met Lucy, Mr. Arjani had been sued by Nariman's father for libel, and this was the reprisal, it became clear now.

Such a monumental waste of time and energy the lawsuit had been, he thought, as he remembered the religious controversy that had fuelled the feud. A priest had performed a navjote ceremony for the son of a Parsi mother and non-Parsi father – an absolute taboo for the conservative factions. The event had ignited one of those periods of debate and polemics and bickering that infected the Reformists and the Orthodox from time to time, like the flu.

So his father, famous for his letters to the editor, wrote one condemning the priest: that for the misguided dustoor in question, the sacred investiture ceremony of sudra and kusti had no more significance than tying an ordinary string around one's waist, given the cavalier way he was bestowing it on all and sundry; that it was renegades like him who would destroy this three-thousand-year-old religion; that Zoroastrianism had survived many setbacks in its venerable history, but what the Arab armies had failed to achieve in A.D. 652, priests like him would accomplish; the purity of this unique and ancient Persian community, the very plinth and foundation of its survival, was being compromised. Ignorance may be bliss, he wrote; however, the ignorance of mischief-making priests was anything but – it was poison for the Parsi community.

Though the bombastic tone of his father's rhetoric was amusing, it had left Nariman shaking his head in despair. The Jam-e-Jamshed dedicated a special box each morning to the controversy. And each morning his father sat back and enjoyed the letters, for and against, instigated by his missive, his face lighting up with satisfaction when he opened the paper over breakfast and read choice bits aloud to his family.

Invariably, his father would find a way to connect the controversy with Lucy. He would cite examples in it to illustrate why intermarriage was forbidden. Extracts from the correspondence would be presented as unshakeable arguments for prohibiting relationships between Parsi and non-Parsi.

Nariman tried to use the openings offered by the breakfast discourses. He pleaded with his father to invite Lucy to lunch or tea, talk to her before making his mind up. But his father refused – it would be unfair, he said, to raise the poor girl's hopes. Sometimes, his mother suggested timidly that there was no harm in finding out what kind of person she was. His father said she might be a wonderful person, as gracious and charming as the Queen of England, but she was still unsuitable for his son because she was not a Zoroastrian, case closed.

How naive, to have kept hoping his father would change his mind, or that a passive stance would avoid unpleasantness, improve the chances for Lucy and himself. He had underestimated his father's stamina, his willingness to trade familial happiness for narrow beliefs.

Then Mr. Arjani's scathing letter appeared in the newspaper, and his father's morning entertainment ended abruptly. Coming from the ground-floor neighbour, it felt like an attack from a traitor in his own camp. And though he had decided at the outset that he would restrict himself to just one letter, taking the high road thereafter and ignoring the yip-yap of the rabble, he lifted his pen to fire a second salvo.

He called Mr. Arjani a prime example of the substandard mind whose cogitations were clearly worthless, unable to grasp the simplest tenets of the religion and the supreme significance of the navjote. Mr. Arjani's views, he wrote, did not deserve the dignity of debate.

Mr. Arjani joined the battle with vigour. The exchange became ever more vitriolic, ending with the letter that took them to court. In it, Mr. Vakeel was accused of being a rabid racist who, in his maniacal quest for purity, wouldn't think twice about eliminating the spouses and offspring of intermarriage.

His father was advised by his Sunday-evening group that it was time to sue for defamation of character. Mr. Arjani was offered the chance to withdraw his statements and apologize. He refused. A group of Reformists financed the defence and, though they lost, were pleased with the ensuing publicity.

His father gave a party to celebrate the victory. The Sunday-evening group presented him with the page from the Jam-e-Jamshed, framed behind glass, featuring the full retraction and apology.

They were behaving as though they'd won a cricket match, thought Nariman. For them, the ruling was a validation of their beliefs rather than a technicality of libel law. While the case was before the court, his emotions had been mixed. He didn't want his father to lose; at the same time, he had hoped that if those bigoted ideas were scrutinized in public, his father might recognize them for what they were.

But there had been no such redemption. And now, ten years later, with his parents dead, he had to watch Lucy become the instrument of the Arjanis' confused vengeance. Mr. Arjani bragged to everyone in Chateau Felicity – hiring Marazban Vakeel's son's girlfriend as an ayah was a fine revenge. To see the drama that Professor Vakeel and Lucy put on was first-class fun. Poetic justice, he said, far superior to the justice of law courts.

If only Mr. Arjani had thought a little. If only he'd realized that his late father, with his narrow views, would have agreed with his old enemy that Lucy was better suited to be an ayah than his daughter-in-law anyway.

But Lucy's decision flabbergasted Nariman. He asked her if she was doing it for the money. He would help her, no need to humiliate herself, he would find her an office job.

Smiling, she shook her head. "Don't you understand why I am here? You're on the third floor, I am on the ground floor, and it comforts me."

He warned her that for all the good that would do, they might as well be in different cities – he was going to keep his word, he would not see her any more. "You're wasting your time, slaving for a pittance."

She smiled. "I never even notice the work. And the three children are very sweet. You know how much I love children. Remember the plans we made, Nari? Six little ones we want-ed, and the names we picked—"

"Please, Lucy, don't do this to me!" he walked away in anger.

But then, every morning, as he left for work, he saw her take the three Arjani children to school. He heard Mr. Arjani shouting instructions to her from the window, to carry the children's school bags because the books were too heavy for their little shoulders. "I don't want my grandchildren deformed by humps," he said.

Nariman watched Lucy struggle with the three bags. Not many mornings passed before he went to relieve her of their weight, walking with her to the children's school.

At noon, Lucy had to deliver the children's lunches. Depending on his lecture schedule, he would be there to help with the hot tiffin boxes and the basket of crockery and the Thermoses filled with cold drinks. Mr. Arjani boasted that he now had two servants for the price of one.

Nariman, his conscience heavy, knew his wife was watching it all from upstairs. He knew that what he was doing was utterly unfair to Yasmin. When he returned from work, he found Jal and Coomy beside their mother, trying to console her. They would not look at him. They no longer came to wish him good night before going to bed.

And Yasmin asked what she had done to deserve such treatment. Why was he torturing her? Why had he married her if he cared so much for Lucy?

"I care for her only as a human being – to make her end her madness."

"You said you had ended it, that time when she used to stare at our window in the evening. Why should I believe you now?"

"Please understand, without speaking to her, how will I convince her to give up this awkward situation?"

"She's not going to listen. Don't you see she's making a fool of you? Trying to make you feel guilty?"

"Perhaps I am," he said, and wished he hadn't, for Yasmin began to lose her temper.

"Forget about me. You've already ruined my life. Think of yourself, how it hurts your reputation at university, and how it will affect the way people talk about our little Roxana. She will carry her father's shame."

"There is nothing shameful about my behaviour," he said quietly. "I consider it an honourable way of conducting myself, under the circumstances."

"A strange idea of honour! First you marry me, then throw me aside. Now you sniff like a dog after her. And what about her family, why are they letting her abuse herself this way?"

"Her family has disowned her, you know that."

After enduring the mortification for months, Yasmin issued
an ultimatum: she would take Roxana and leave if he did not
stop being the ayah's assistant. He had one week to decide.

"What good will it do?" he tried to reason. "There will be
hardship for you and our child."

"You have the gall to talk about hardship? What do I have
now? Comfort and happiness?"

As the week drew to a close, he requested her not to make
a bad situation worse. She said he'd regret the day he was
born if he didn't heed her warning. She had had enough, she
was going to stand up for her rights, if not as wife then at least
as mother.

"You can't go," he pleaded, a note of hysteria entering his
voice for the first time. "I need my darling Roxana, you will
not take her from me . . ."

Roxana and Yezad stood in the dark, peering into the front
room. It had distinctly sounded like Pappa was calling her.

"Must have had a dream," said Yezad.

They waited a few moments, then went back to bed, agreeing not to mention it in the morning. It would only make him
feel foolish. Better to keep his spirits up. Whatever was bothering him would recede of its own accord.

7

THE NINE-ELEVEN LEFT THE STATION as Yezad arrived at the platform. He fought his way onto the nine-seventeen; the train moved out with men running alongside.

Grabbing an overhead railing, he chose to stay near the exit – too far in would mean a return struggle at Marine Lines. He squeezed himself nearer one of the fans, though, to minimize his own sweating and the smell of armpits around him.

These tactical manoeuvres were performed by instinct, the instinct for survival in the urban jungle, he used to joke with college friends – instead of tree branches, you swung from railings inside trains and buses, hung from bars outside them. Tarzan comics and the novels of Edgar Rice Burroughs were more instructive than he or his teachers had imagined.

His dream for an end to this apeman commute had led him to apply for immigration to Canada. He wanted clean cities, clean air, plenty of water, trains with seats for everyone, where people stood in line at bus stops and said please, after you, thank you. Not just the land of milk and honey, also the land of deodorant and toiletry.

But his fantasy about that new life in a new land had finished quickly, Canada was done with. And he assuaged his disappointment by keeping track of problems in the land of excess and superfluity, as he now called it: unemployment, violent crime, homelessness, language laws of Quebec. Not much difference between there and here, he would think: we have beggars in Bombay, they have people freezing to death on Toronto streets; instead of high- and low-caste fighting, racism and police shootings; separatists in Kashmir, separatists in Quebec – why migrate from the frying pan into the fire?

Of course, there were times when he wished his application had been successful. That immigration officer, bastard racist, he thought, I'll never forget his name. If I'd been accepted, Jal and Coomy would have been forced to look after the chief – they couldn't have driven him in an ambulance to Canada.

Ten days of Nariman's three weeks' bedrest had elapsed. Almost halfway there. But it troubled him to see Roxana struggling to cope, pretending everything was normal. He thought about their quarrel that morning; and later, she had stopped him for an extra kiss before he left for work. They had held each other on the landing, first checking Villie Cardmaster's peephole – the smallest noise could summon her eye. The sense of lurking danger made the kiss sweeter. But Roxana didn't know that since Nariman came to stay he'd been late for work every day, it would have given her one more thing to worry about.

At Marine Lines station the crowd trying to get on met the avalanche of alighting passengers. He pushed himself clear, glancing at his watch – nine-thirty already – and mopped his face. The air was a gigantic wet sponge. He thrust the damp handkerchief into his pocket and waited to cross the road.

Being manager of the Bombay Sporting Goods Emporium meant he had to unlock the shop door by nine-thirty to let in the peon who swept and swabbed the entrance and the front steps, made tea, and dusted the glass cases displaying cricket bats, stumps, caps, footballs, badminton racquets, and other samples from their stock. Then the peon, Husain, would remove padlocks from the security shutters that covered the two large windows. Clanking and rattling, the steel would roll up, revealing plate glass behind which sat more sports equipment. Now Husain would take his cloth and give the glass a quick shine. By ten o'clock they would be open for business.

It was an eight-minute walk to the shop, and Yezad increased his pace. Husain would be waiting: his kholi in Jogeshwari, rented on a twelve-hour basis, had to be vacated at seven a.m., when the other renter arrived from his factory night shift. So he killed time near the shop, aware that he was more fortunate than those who rented eight-hour rooms.

Yezad's haste was not for Husain's benefit, who was content to sit on the step, chew his first paan of the day, watch the world go by. The proprietor sometimes appeared early at the shop, and to be seen coming late made Yezad feel like a schoolboy.

Six shops down from the Bombay Sporting Goods Emporium was the Jai Hind Book Mart (Texts For Schools & Colleges – Reference Books Our Specialty, stated its signboard). It, too, opened for business at ten. Vilas Rane sat outside, leaning against the locked doors, a clipboard and writing paper in his lap. He raised his hand in greeting.

Yezad nodded, waving back, and hurried on.

"No need to rush, Mr. Kapur hasn't come yet."

"Oh, good."

When he reached the shop, Husain rose from his haunches and salaamed. Yezad unlocked the door and tossed his briefcase in his chair before returning to Vilas. "Busy? Lots of scribbling?"

"Nothing so far," said Vilas, holding up the clipboard to reveal the blank page.

Besides his job as a salesman at the Book Mart, Vilas had a sideline. He was a writer of letters for those who couldn't, who poured out, into his willing ear, their thoughts, feelings, concerns, their very hearts, which he transformed into words upon paper at the nominal rate of three rupees per page. The language could be one of three: Hindi, Marathi, or Gujarati, depending on the clients, mainly labourers come to the city from distant villages to work at the docks or on construction sites. A scribe-written letter was their only link with their families.

Sometimes, a client on a tight budget became silent when Vilas Rane's pen had filled up the affordable number of pages. If it was a ramble, with the main substance already committed to paper, Vilas wound up the letter. But there were occasions when a customer, describing something crucial, in a voice fraught with emotion, would choke back the words because he had run out of money. Then Vilas would take what was offered and ask the man to continue at no charge till his heart had been lightened, while his pen turned the outpourings into narrative, into something tangible that the customer could carry to the post office and see off on its long journey to his family.

"You'll never be a good businessman," Yezad chided him. "Do you think Bombay Sporting would last if Mr. Kapur gave away cricket bats for free?"

"What to do, I'm human," said Vilas. "Nothing is more cruel than a letter cut short for lack of money. It's like death – one moment the words flowing, next moment silence, the thought unfinished, the love unconveyed, the anguish unexpressed. How can I let that happen? Sometimes, my clients receive this type of truncated letter from their village. I read it to them. And suddenly, in mid-sentence – it ends. The pain it causes is unbearable. I'll never do something so unkind."

Vilas Rane's sideline as a scribe had started accidentally, when a cleaner was hired to work at the Book Mart. One morning while dusting the shelves and stacks, he said to Vilas, "Isn't life a funny thing, Raneji. Here I am with books all day. I feel them in my hands, and smell them, sometimes even dream about them. And yet, not a single word can I read."

The observation touched Vilas more profoundly than the periodic governmental laments and platitudes about illiteracy in the country. "So you want to learn to read?" he asked the cleaner, whose name was Suresh.

"No, no, no," he said bashfully. "My brain is not willing to learn something so difficult. No, all I want is for you to write a letter for me."

After the shop had closed, the two sat on the steps and Vilas prepared to scribble a quick paragraph. Between the salutation: "My dear Pitaji and Mataji" and the leave-taking: "Your obedient son," he filled five pages.

Three weeks later came a reply, the first letter Suresh had ever received. He held his breath, watching as his benefactor took a sandalwood letter opener from the counter display and slit the envelope.

"Only one page," observed Suresh sadly.

"Don't be disappointed," said Vilas. "A letter is like perfume. You don't apply a whole bottle. Just one dab will fill your senses. Words are the same – a few are sufficient."

Suresh was sceptical as Vilas began to read the scrawl of the village scribe. There were invocations for success and good wishes for health and prosperity. But the rest was devoted to conveying the family's happiness at listening to Suresh's letter. Such a beautiful letter, they said, it is like being with you in the city, sharing your life, taking the train to your book shop, watching you work. And we hear your voice in every line, so wonderful is the effect of the words.

Suresh was glowing with pride as the letter ended. "One page only," said Vilas. "And see how much pleasure it has given you?"

The cleaner began telling neighbours in his chawl about the marvellous letter-writer who had transported his thoughts and feelings to his family. And it was not long before Vilas's scribal services were formalized into a full-fledged sideline. On the steps of Jai Hind Book Mart his clients gazed in wistful wonder at his penmanship, like the hungry on a feast to which they had no hope of being invited.

From time to time, Yezad tried convincing him to charge more. But Vilas said higher rates would mean fewer letters; besides, he had come to regard this as a form of social work. If he didn't do it, his clients might turn for help to a Shiv Sena shakha where they would be exposed to vicious communal propaganda, might even get recruited in their sticks-and-stones method of political persuasion, their fine art of scoring debating points by breaking opposition bones.

"But let me be honest. More than anything else, I enjoy the letter-writing."

"More than your acting group?" asked Yezad, for Vilas used to speak with great passion about his amateur drama society.

"That hobby is gone. There are some new members who think they know everything. They conduct workshops and discuss theories. Not my cup of tea."

But his satisfaction from letter-writing grew more profound with time. He heard all about his clients' lives: the birth of a child; a family quarrel about money; a wife left behind in the village who was sleeping with the sarpanch; a sick father who had died because the nearest hospital was two days' travel on kutcha roads; a brother injured in a farm accident who had recovered and was home again.

And Vilas, writing and reading the ongoing drama of family matters, the endless tragedy and comedy, realized that collectively, the letters formed a pattern only he was privileged to see. He let the mail flow through his consciousness, allowing the episodes to fall into place of their own accord, like bits of coloured glass in a kaleidoscope. He felt that chance events, random cruelty, unexplainable kindness, meaningless disaster, unexpected generosity could, together, form a design that was otherwise invisible. If it were possible to read letters for all of humanity, compose an infinity of responses on their behalf, he would have a God's-eye view of the world, and be able to understand it.

"Best of all," he told Yezad, "it gives me so many ready-made families. I share their lives, like an uncle or grandfather who knows everything about everyone. Isn't that a wonderful reward?"

"I'm having enough trouble with one family. If you're not busy, write a letter for me."

"Sure," said Vilas. "To whom? God?"

"To my brother- and sister-in-law. Those bastards are making my life miserable. Two of them with nothing to do all day in their huge house. He wastes his time at the share bazaar, she at the fire-temple. And they can't even look after their poor father. My wife has to slave instead. No room to move in the flat, and every night his bad dreams wake us up."

Vilas urged patience, reminding him that in ten more days his father-in-law would return home and life would return to normal.

"Thank you for the obvious advice," said Yezad. "Where do you get such wisdom?"

"Through my sideline. I write letters, therefore I am."

"Ah, of course. See you later, Monsieur Rane," said Yezad, and started back for the shop.

At the Bombay Sporting Goods Emporium, the steel shutters were still down, the litter in front of the shop not picked up. The shop was dark. Yezad switched on the lights. Nothing had been dusted, the tea hadn't been made.

"Husain! Where are you? Sahab will be here any minute!"

He found the peon sitting on the floor in a corner of the storage area. Hugging his knees, which were drawn up to his chin, he was gazing at the wall. He looked up with a wan smile when Yezad approached.

"Chalo, Husain, start working."

Husain returned his gaze to the wall and murmured, "Sorry, sahab, today I don't feel able."

Yezad sighed, studying the grizzled fellow in his khaki shirt and trousers. The collar was frayed, the knees worn thin. Time to order replacement uniforms for him. Though it was not really a uniform; Mr. Kapur provided two sets of the outfit periodically, to help Husain out.

He wondered whether to try and persuade the peon to rise, or leave him for Mr. Kapur. Husain had been hired at Bombay Sporting almost three years ago, several months after the Babri Mosque riots, at the urging of the Ekta Samiti, which was asking businesses to help rehabilitate riot victims. On the days that Husain was incapable of working, Mr. Kapur was the one who nursed his battered emotions till he was ready to resume his duties.

Whenever Yezad found himself getting annoyed by Husain, he would remind himself about the peon's story, about the burning chawls in Antop Hill, goondas setting people on fire . . . Husain and his Muslim neighbours watching as their chawl went up in flames, wondering where his wife and three sons were . . . and then four burning figures tumbling down the steps of the building, their smoking hands beating at the flames . . . while the goondas sprinkled more kerosene from their cans over Husain's family . . .

In the dark storage area, Yezad shuddered. "What about chai, Husain," he tried to draw him into conversation. "Don't you want a cup this morning?"

"Chai, no chai, all the same, sahab."

Yezad wondered why, on these days of black depression, Husain came to the shop to sit in the corner. Mr. Kapur had assured him he would not lose any wages if he was unwell. But perhaps on such days, more than ever, Husain needed the company of those he trusted.

The telephone rang. Husain did not move from his corner. At the best of times he was reluctant to pick up the receiver with its gaping mouth. The instrument scared him, its power to carry disembodied voices making him wary of sending his own into it, to end up who knew where.

Yezad answered on the fifth ring; it was Mr. Kapur.

"Hello, Yezad. Sorry, were you with a client?"

"No – with Husain. He's sitting in the back today."

"Aray, poor fellow. Another one of his bad days? Okay, just let him relax."

"And your invoices to be delivered?"

"Tomorrow, Yezad. Or day after, doesn't matter." Mr. Kapur was about to hang up, then stopped himself, "I won't be in till afternoon, maybe three o'clock. Something urgent – tell you later. And please keep an eye on Husain, okay? Bye."

Yezad put the receiver in its cradle and set about lighting the display cases, tidying, hurrying with the work. It was almost time for his ten-thirty appointment. No end to the

144

unfairness in his life, he thought, manager doing the peon's work.

While he was winding up the steel shutters, the client arrived. Mr. Malpani of Alliance Corporation stopped by the door, checked his watch, then stared at the long steel handle in Yezad's hands.

"Good morning, Mr. Chenoy, you got a promotion, it seems," he said, and laughed at his own joke.

Yezad smiled politely, thinking Mr. Malpani looked more like a mongoose each time he saw him. The furtive eyes on his small face darted around the shop as though searching for something to ridicule. He led him to his desk, offered him a chair, and excused himself while he went to the bathroom to wash a spot of grease from his hand.

When he returned, Mr. Malpani was peering at papers on the desk. He did not bother to stop till Yezad walked right by him and sat in his own chair.

"So everything is ready, Mr. Chenoy?"

Nodding, Yezad opened the file and began going over the particulars of the contract. He detested the man, had done so ever since the time he had hinted, in his oily manner, how they could both make a little extra on the side if Yezad played the game. The only reason Yezad still had the account for the sports club was because Mr. Kapur was friends with Alliance's managing director.

"Looks fine," said Mr. Malpani. "Except for one thing."

Aware of what was coming, Yezad feigned ignorance.

"You have once again made no provision for stomach puja," said Mr. Malpani with his yelping laugh. "Every time I am telling you, you should add some extra. Little bit for your stomach, little bit for mine, and everybody is happy. You are still not learning the proper way to do business."

Yezad smiled as though it was nothing but a joke. "Thank you very much for coming, Mr. Malpani. As usual, it's a pleasure doing business with you."

They shook hands and he walked the man to the door. He

felt like washing his hands again. Such an unappetizing experience, first thing in the morning. But he should have expected it, the way the day had begun. Nothing went well unless it started well. His mind turned again to the quarrel . . .

For the past ten mornings, Roxana's first thought on waking was to preserve the routine for him. He could sense it. She kissed his back and got out of bed, filled water for the day, brushed her teeth.

His turn was next in the bathroom while she made tea, went into the front room, opened the curtains, woke the boys. Jehangir had to be shaken by the shoulder, but Murad was up, reading in the tent. She asked Nariman if he needed anything.

"No hurry," he answered as usual. "I have no train to catch."

She brought the teapot to the table and covered it with the cosy. Pouring for Yezad, she told him how she had surprised Murad reading by the morning light.

Then, noticing Nariman's restlessness, she asked him again. It seemed wrong that he should wait with a full bladder while they, barely six feet away, drank tea and ate toast and butter and eggs. She insisted on giving him the urinal.

"You mustn't pretend, Pappa. Holding it in is not healthy."

When he was done, she tucked the urinal under the settee because Jehangir was still in the toilet.

"It's very unsanitary to leave it sitting on the floor," said Yezad, offended.

She ran without comment to the kitchen to fetch the boiling bath water for Murad, who was already in the bathroom, refilled the vessel, put it back on the stove for Yezad's bath, then got the basin and towel for her father.

"I could have carried the tapayli to Murad," said Yezad. "Why don't you let me help?"

"If you burn yourself, who'll bring home the salary?"

He watched as she gave her father his mouthwash. Nariman gargled, and a thread of saliva hung from his lips; stretched to the limit, it broke, clinging to his chin.

Yezad looked away to keep his mind on his breakfast.

146

Another bite and he pushed the plate aside, the egg half-eaten, while she rushed past with the basin and wet towel. The dirty water swished and threatened to splash over the rim. He flinched, shrinking backwards in his chair. "Better slow down. So much non-stop dancing will put you in the *Guinness Book of Records* or flat on your back."

"I'm fine, don't worry," said Roxana.

"How can I not? Have you looked at yourself in the mirror?"

"I've no time for mirrors."

"You should take a moment, see what the strain has done to your face."

"Does it matter? My face is no longer my fortune."

Her remark pained him, he wanted to hold her, assure her she was as lovely as ever. Instead, he turned to Nariman. "Your daughter always has smart answers. Tell her what you think. Go on, tell her truthfully."

Nariman squirmed. "There's some truth in each point of view."

"Please, no diplomacy – just be honest. See the hollows in her cheeks, she looks like a famine victim from Orissa!"

Nariman gave in and said what Yezad wanted to hear. "He's right, Roxana, you should slow down, I keep asking you not to hurry for my sake."

"You think it's fair, Pappa?" she said, handing him his dentures. "Should other people decide how and when to do the work if I'm the one who has to manage it all?" She grabbed some things from the table and stamped out, calling to Murad in the bathroom not to waste time.

"I've upset her," said Nariman.

"It had to be said – she'll kill herself at this rate."

Yezad drew the plate towards him again and tackled the congealed egg. He mopped up what remained of the yolk with his last piece of toast and cut the white, now gone rubbery.

Jehangir, returning to the front room, watched his father swallow the pieces. "Finished, Daddy?"

He nodded, adding, "Good boy," as his son stacked plates, saucers, and cups, and set off to the kitchen with the load.

Nariman attempted to mend the mood: "He is a wonderful child."

"So is Murad," said Yezad quickly, putting his father-in-law on the defensive, then regretting it. He hated himself for the habit he seemed to have of making uncomfortable the people he loved.

Jehangir came back from the kitchen and opened one of his jigsaw boxes. He made no attempt to build the picture, picking up pieces at random, tracing their squiggly contours with a finger.

"What are you doing?" asked his father.

"Nothing," he spoke into the box.

"Put on your uniform. You want to make Mummy shout at you? She has enough to do."

He continued his desultory examination till Yezad yanked the box away and slammed the lid on. "Don't make me angry."

Jehangir looked up, and now his father saw the tears in his eyes. "What's the matter, Jehangla?"

He liked it when his father called him that. His brother was only called Murad. Sometimes it seemed unfair – there should have been a name to make Murad feel special too.

"Are you unwell, Jehangla?" His father felt his forehead, bending so his face was beside his son's.

Jehangir smelled the tea on his father's breath. He shook his head and rubbed one eye. "Mummy is crying in the kitchen."

"You know why?"

"I asked her, but she won't say."

"Go, get ready for school. Mummy will be all right, trust me." He squeezed his son's shoulder and went to the kitchen.

Jehangir's ears accompanied his father. Next moment he heard his mother sobbing, and his lower lip began to quiver. He rose, drawn towards the sound.

"Let them be alone," said his grandfather. He pulled in his sheet to make space on the settee. "Sit, tell me what's wrong."

148

He allowed his grandfather to hold his hand. "I feel sad when they fight," he whispered. "I want them to be happy, and nice to each other."

"It's difficult for them right now. Once I am gone, things will be better."

"But they both like you. Why should it be difficult if you are here?"

"Liking has nothing to do with it. People have their own lives, it's not helpful when something disturbs those lives."

"You are so quiet, Grandpa, you don't disturb anybody." He looked at the hand holding his, the veins like cords, and felt the slight tremble in it travel into his own. "I'll miss you when you go back to Jal Uncle and Coomy Aunty."

"I'll miss you too. But we have ten more days together. And afterwards, you can visit me. Agreed? Now you must get dressed."

Jehangir slid off the settee and rubbed his grandfather's chin, which had a larger bite to it than usual. On the way to the clothes horse he made a detour and peeked cautiously into the kitchen. His mother was in his father's arms. She still had tears in her eyes. But she was smiling.

He wondered what magic passed between grown-ups, that they could go from shouting to crying to smiling in such a short time. Whatever it was, he was grateful for its existence, and went to change in the back room.

M R. KAPUR'S FIRST THOUGHT on arriving at the shop was about Husain. "Did he go for his pao-bhaji lunch?"

Yezad shook his head. "I took him some tea. He left it after one or two sips."

"Poor fellow," said Mr. Kapur, hitting a backhand in an imaginary tennis game. He was always wielding invisible bats and racquets, kicking footballs, dribbling with a hockey stick, particularly when he had something on his mind.

He hurried to the storage area, cursing under his breath the bastards who had destroyed Husain's life and the lives of thousands like him. His arm swung, hitting backhands, fore-hands, smacking goondas as though they were tennis balls, sending them all to perdition.

"How are you, Husain miyan?" He crouched beside him in the dark corner and patted his shoulder. "You'll have some tea?" He took his elbow and made him rise, bringing him to the front of the shop, into the afternoon light.

Yezad made three cups of tea and carried them to the counter. "Chalo, Husain, we'll all drink together."

The peon thanked him and received his cup. Mr. Kapur pointed out things in the street, saying look at the colour of that car, and what a big truck, and there goes so-and-so from the Jai Hind Book Mart. He entertained Husain as he would a sick child.

Yezad too made a contribution to the effort. No matter how often he watched Mr. Kapur during these times of crises, he was touched by his employer's gentleness as he went about mending the cracks in Husain's broken life.

When Yezad had started at the shop fifteen years ago, he'd assumed a formal employer-employee relationship, but Mr.

Kapur had soon redefined it, making him a friend and confidant, someone to grumble at or with. He insisted that Yezad give up the habit of calling him by his surname. They compromised: during business hours he was Mr. Kapur; after closing time, Vikram.

Besides their abhorrence for the Shiv Sena and its narrow parochial ways, they shared a lament for the city they felt was slowly dying, being destroyed by goonda raj and mafia dons, as the newspapers put it, "in an unholy nexus of politicians, criminals, and police."

Vikram Kapur had arrived in the city in his mother's arms, six months old. He told Yezad, whenever there was an opportunity to refer to the story of his life, "My family was forced to abandon everything and flee Punjab in 1947. Thanks, of course, to the brave British, who abandoned their responsibilities and fled India."

Sometimes, when Mr. Kapur spoke about 1947 and Partition, Yezad felt that Punjabi migrants of a certain age were like Indian authors writing about that period, whether in realist novels of corpse-filled trains or in the magic-realist midnight muddles, all repeating the same catalogue of horrors about slaughter and burning, rape and mutilation, foetuses torn out of wombs, genitals stuffed in the mouths of the castrated.

But Yezad's silent criticism was always followed by remorse. He knew they had to keep telling their story, just like Jews had to theirs, about the Holocaust, writing and remembering and having nightmares about the concentration camps and gas chambers and ovens, about the evil committed by ordinary people, by friends and neighbours, the evil that, decades later, was still incomprehensible. What choice was there, except to speak about it, again and again, and yet again?

"So there was no choice for us," Mr. Kapur would say. "We had to run. And we came here. But Bombay treated us well. My father started over, with zero, and became prosperous. Only city in the world where this is possible."

And because of his background, he claimed his love for Bombay was special, far exceeding what a born-and-bred Bombayite could feel. "It's the difference between being born into a religion and converting to it," he said. "The convert takes nothing for granted. He chooses, thus his commitment is superior. What I feel for Bombay you will never know. It's like the pure love for a beautiful woman, gratitude for her existence, and devotion to her living presence. If Bombay were a creature of flesh and blood, with my blood type, Rh negative – and very often I think she is – then I would give her a transfusion down to my last drop, to save her life."

At times, Yezad thought the proprietor's passion for Bombay verged on the fanatical. But he also understood that he was pouring into it his yearning for his family's past in Punjab, lost to him forever. And Bombay, perhaps by default, had become the recipient of his devotion.

So Mr. Kapur collected books about the city, old photographs, postcards, posters, and shared everything with Yezad, all the little-known facts about its history or geography that he uncovered during his researches.

"You know why I was late today? Let me show you." He sat Husain down on the steps where he could watch the road, to keep him from going back to his dark corner in the storage room. Wielding an imaginary cricket bat, he went behind his desk and made a sound with his mouth: pock! of willow and ball connecting. Then, with a magician's flourish, he produced two photographs out of his attaché case.

"I had to rush to buy these from a private collection. Before the dealers got there." He slid one across to Yezad.

Great way of running a business, thought Yezad. A proprietor who races off to buy photographs, a peon periodically unable to work. He wondered what would happen here without him. He examined the print: the foreground showed a canopy of trees; beyond it, a row of graceful bungalows. In the background, behind the residences, was a maidaan and more foliage.

"Seems like a charming place."

"Guess where it is?"

Had to be long-ago Bombay, Yezad knew, to be in his boss's collection. He scrutinized it again, seeking a clue to the location. "Resembles a European city more than Bombay."

Mr. Kapur laughed. "If I said this is your chaotic Marine Lines station, would you believe it?"

"That's a photo-and-a-half. How many years ago?"

"Roughly 1930s. Those are military bungalows, just before they were demolished, when the army got new reclaimed land in Colaba cantonment."

"What a change – just sixty years."

"Look," Mr. Kapur pointed at the picture, "if you follow this side of the road, you come to Sonapur cremation and burial grounds. And your station stands here. Before the reclamation, at high tide Back Bay would cover the place where the railway tracks now run."

Yezad began to see the present-day Marine Lines in the old photo. It had a strange effect on him, as though he were living in two time zones, six decades apart. But it was a pleasant, reassuring feeling.

He relinquished the print, placing it carefully on the desk. "That must be valuable."

"Beyond money," said Mr. Kapur. "These are my beautiful Bombay's baby pictures. Priceless. Her time of innocence. Now look at the other one."

Yezad's brow wrinkled as he studied it – the place had a vague familiarity about it.

"Follow me," said Mr. Kapur. They went outside to the pavement, where he pointed towards the corner, at Metro cinema, then held up the print in Yezad's line of vision.

"That's it! Dhobi Talao junction, before Metro was built!"

"Correct," beamed Mr. Kapur.

Husain rose from the steps, curious to see what it was that they found so exciting. Mr. Kapur welcomed him: "Ao, Husain, dekho, very interesting."

But the faded black-and-white photograph contained nothing to amuse the peon. He studied it to humour his employer and returned to the step.

Yezad's eyes moved from the print to the junction where six roads converged, and back to the print, willing the cinema to disappear with the picture's aid. "What are these low structures in the photo?"

"I went to the Asiatic Society library and did some research. This plot of land was acquired by the Metro Goldwyn Corporation in 1936, on a lease for ninety-nine years, at one rupee per year. What you see in the photo are the stables of the Royal Air Force."

"Why would the Air Force need stables?"

"For their horses."

"Very funny. Okay, so why would they need horses?"

"To wheel the planes out of the hangars, to haul heavy machinery – mix of high tech and low. Like it still is – last week, the phone company was laying state-of-the-art fibre-optic cable near my house, but the ditch was being dug with pickaxes and spades, the rubble carried away in baskets on women's heads."

They went inside, and Mr. Kapur turned to the news of the day. He did not bury himself only in the city's past, he also burrowed in the complicated morass of contemporary politics, following every turn, every new abomination perpetrated by the government, which, he said, hurt him as though his own flesh had been wounded.

"So now the bastards are going to shut down the Srikrishna Commission."

"Which one is that? For the terrorist bombs?"

"Yes, as well as the Babri Mosque riots. Everything was on the point of being exposed: Shiv Sena involvement in looting and burning, police helping rioters, withholding assistance in Muslim localities."

"Don't get excited, Mr. Kapur," cautioned Yezad. "You know what your doctor said about blood pressure."

As Mr. Kapur took a deep breath and fell silent, Husain

became agitated: "Is true, sahab, yes! Police so – so bud-maash!"

"Hanh, Husain, wohto sutch baat hai," agreed Mr. Kapur, changing to Hindi to make it easier for the peon, who could follow their English conversation only up to a point.

Husain switched languages too, and became more eloquent: "Sahab, in those riots the police were behaving like gangsters. In Muslim mohallas they were shooting their guns at innocent people. Houses were burning, neighbours came out to throw water. And the police? Firing bullets like target practice. These guardians of the law were murdering everybody! And my poor wife and children . . . I couldn't even recognize them . . ." His voice was a sob now and he stopped speaking.

"Hahn, Husain, it was shameful," said Mr. Kapur, writhing in his chair. "More than three years have passed, and still no justice. Shiv Sena polluted the police. And now Shiv Sena has become the government."

Still sobbing, Husain said he would bring them more tea, but Yezad offered to get it instead. Mr. Kapur motioned to him to wait: it would be good for Husain, who found the brewing of tea, the serving and drinking of it, always a therapeutic pursuit.

The peon soon returned with steaming cups. "Shukriya, Husain miyan," said Mr. Kapur. "You have some? Good."

Then he turned to Yezad. "Am I silly to be so disgusted by these evil men? Aren't you outraged by it all?"

"I am a born-and-bred Bombayvala. That automatically inoculates me against attacks of outrage."

Just before closing time, Yezad handed over the cash payments for the day, the ones for which no invoices or receipts had been issued. Mr. Kapur asked him to stay for a drink.

"How are you feeling, Husain? Beer laayega?" The peon nodded, and received money for the errand.

"Two bottles of Kingfisher. Jaldi, hanh, before they turn warm in your hands." Husain laughed, promising to keep his hands cool, and set off for Merwan Irani's beer bar at the corner.

"Well," said Yezad, "I finalized the contract for Alliance Corporation this morning."

"Excellent. Come, let's sit in my office."

Tiny though it was, the cubby-hole was air-conditioned, and Yezad was always happy to be invited in. He watched Mr. Kapur go to the large, hard-shell suitcase in the corner and, with his back to him, dial its combination lock. The money from the cash transactions went inside.

This daily routine had startled Yezad when Mr. Kapur had first explained it to him with a dollop of flattery, saying it was a blessing to have a Parsi employee: "I don't need to worry about cash sticking to the lining of your trousers. If only there were more communities like yours."

Yezad had been embarrassed. "I'm sure we have our share of crooks and good-for-nothing loafers."

"Oh, don't be modest, the Parsi reputation for honesty is well known. And even if it's a myth – there is no myth without truth, no smoke without fire."

As a new employee, Yezad hadn't pursued it further, more concerned about the implications of tax evasion, wondering if Mr. Kapur realized he was praising his employee's honesty in the same breath as he was instructing him to be dishonest. Of course, the proprietor had justified the suitcase by calling it his pension plan, a "non-standard business practice" that everyone was forced to follow, thanks to the government's absurd tax laws.

Now Mr. Kapur locked the suitcase and put out two glasses to await the beer. Yezad came back to the new contract, the size of the order, estimates about net profit – the figures were ready at the tip of his tongue. He was hoping Mr. Kapur would be impressed, which would give him an opening to discuss improvement in his commission from the deal. Anything extra would help, with Nariman to look after.

But Mr. Kapur was not interested in talking shop. "We do that all day. Bombay Sporting is now closed for the night."

Meanwhile, Husain returned with the Kingfishers and opened the tall bottles, pouring carefully, for he knew sahab did not like too much foam.

Smiling at his glass, Mr. Kapur took a long draught and topped it up. He examined the bottle, still a quarter full, and held it out in Husain's direction. "Want it?"

"Yes, sahab," said the peon, reinforcing the response with a circular nod.

"After you finish drinking, you can go home. I'll lock up."

Husain gurgled it down before them. "Very nice," he said, eyeing the other bottle.

"Want more?" asked Yezad. He, too, was rewarded with a circular nod.

"Now you won't get drunk, will you, and come late to work tomorrow?" joked Mr. Kapur.

"Aray, sahab," he laughed, "only a little baby will get drunk in this much beer. An old fool like me has to drink six full ones." He drained the bottle, thanked them both, and left.

They sat in silence for a while. Mr. Kapur reclined in his chair and put his feet up on the low filing cabinet. "Something I need your opinion about."

"Sure."

"You know how I'm always talking about Bombay – how much it means to me, how much it has given me. You've heard my family story."

"Yes, many times."

Mr. Kapur took a deep breath. "I want to run in the next municipal election."

Yezad stared at him, feeling that combination of affection and exasperation which Mr. Kapur often evoked in him. "Why?"

"I just told you – because Bombay is everything to me. No use complaining about crooks destroying it if—"

"I mean, what good will it do? You always say politics is filthy, soiling everything it touches."

"That's no excuse any more." Mr. Kapur took a swallow and put his glass down. "If the woman you love is being molested, will you do nothing just because you are outnumbered? No, you'll defend her, end up beaten and bloody, maybe dead, and God knows how much it will help her. But you'll still intervene."

"Yes, but that's a personal—"

"Same thing. My beloved Bombay is being raped."

Yezad knew there was no arguing with him when he spoke of the city in these flesh-and-blood terms. "Okay, let's say you run. Which party would you choose?"

"No party. Independent."

"How effective would you be?"

"I already answered that: it doesn't matter. I cannot stand by and watch the thugs."

"What about Bombay Sporting?"

"You can take my place. All the suppliers and major buyers know you. And of course I'll make it worth your while."

The proposal made Yezad contemplate the possibility with new interest. The increment would help Roxana, things would no longer be so tight at the end of each month . . .

He was almost ready to support the crazy idea. Then he felt ashamed of his selfishness. "That's not the point. Isn't it your duty to look after your father's legacy? Doesn't your Bhagavad-Gita tell you to let nothing interfere with duty?"

"That's a good one, Yezad," he smiled. "So how shall I define my duty? Definitions are the last refuge of the scoundrel, but I really feel my father would be happy with my decision." He emptied his glass. "Wish I hadn't sent Husain home, he could have got us more beer."

"Have mine, I've a lot left."

"Are you sure?"

"If you don't mind it from my glass."

Mr. Kapur slid his glass over. "You see how we two are sitting here, sharing? That's how people have lived in Bombay. That's why Bombay has survived floods, disease, plague, water shortage, bursting drains and sewers, all the population pressures. In her heart there is room for everyone who wants to make a home here."

Right, thought Yezad, fourteen million people, half of them living in slums, eating and shitting in places not fit for animals. Nice way of sharing the gift of Bombay. But none of this would have any effect on Vikram Kapur launched in poetic flight.

"You see, Yezad, Bombay endures because it gives and it receives. Within this warp and weft is woven the special texture of its social fabric, the spirit of tolerance, acceptance, generosity. Anywhere else in the world, in those so-called civilized places like England and America, such terrible conditions would lead to revolution."

Which might not be a bad thing, thought Yezad.

"From now on," said Mr. Kapur, "in this shop we will celebrate all festivals: Divali, Christmas, Id, your Parsi Navroze, Baisakhi, Buddha Jayanti, Ganesh Chaturthi, everything. We'll decorate the windows, put up appropriate greetings with lights and all. We are going to be a mini-Bombay, an example to our neighbourhood. I made this decision after an amazing thing I saw last week."

He drank what he had accepted from Yezad's glass. "Last week, I parked my car near Grant Road station and bought a platform ticket. To watch the trains and passengers. Just felt like it."

He paused for another swallow, and continued, "I never travel by train, I see how crowded they are when I drive past the tracks. But from the platform that day I saw something new. A train was leaving, completely packed, and the men running alongside gave up. All except one. I kept my eyes on him, because the platform was coming to an end.

"Suddenly, he raised his arms. And people on the train reached out and grabbed them. What were they doing, he would be dragged and killed, I thought! A moment later, they had lifted him off the platform. Now his feet were dangling outside the compartment, and I almost screamed to stop the train. His feet pedalled the air. They found a tiny spot on the edge, slipped off, found it again.

"There he was, hanging, his life literally in the hands of strangers. And he had put it there. He had trusted them. More arms reached out and held him tight in their embrace. It was a miracle – suddenly he was completely safe. So safe, I wondered if I had overreacted to the earlier danger. But no, his position had been truly perilous for a few seconds.

"I waited on the platform to see more trains. It was then I realized that what I had witnessed was not a miracle. It happened over and over: hands reaching out to help, as though it were perfectly normal, a routine commuter procedure.

"Whose hands were they, and whose hands were they grasping? Hindu, Muslim, Dalit, Parsi, Christian? No one knew and no one cared. Fellow passengers, that's all they were. And I stood there on the platform for a long time, Yezad, my eyes filled with tears of joy, because what I saw told me there was still hope for this great city."

Yezad nodded quietly. What Mr. Kapur had described, he saw every day – a mundane sight in the daily grind. But Mr. Kapur had revealed an aspect of it he had not seen, and it made him wonder what else he had missed.

"Now you understand why I want to act before it's too late," continued Mr. Kapur. "This beautiful city of seven islands, this jewel by the Arabian Sea, this reclaimed land, this ocean gift transformed into ground beneath our feet, this enigma of cosmopolitanism where races and religions live side by side and cheek by jowl in peace and harmony, this diamond of diversity, this generous goddess who embraces the poor and the hungry and the huddled masses, this Urbs Prima in Indis, this dear, dear city now languishes – I don't exaggerate – like a patient in intensive care, Yezad, my friend, put there by small, selfish men who would destroy it because their coarseness cannot bear something so grand, so fine."

Yezad was silent, admiring Mr. Kapur's ability to adapt

Shakespeare. Nariman would enjoy it, he would repeat it for him tonight. "Bravo," he exclaimed. "If you can do that in Hindi and Marathi as well, you'll win the election." He offered him his hand.

"So I can count on your vote?"

"For the last seven or eight years, I haven't voted in any election – not local, not national. But for you, I will vote early, and I will vote often."

They laughed, and rose to lock up the shop.

❧

The boys had taken to spending some time each day after school at their grandfather's bedside. Murad discovered that Grandpa in his youth used to make model aeroplanes. He began discussing biplanes and monoplanes from the First World War with him. They compared the Fokker D.VII and the Spad, the elegant Sopwith Camel, and the deadly Fokker Eindecker, while Jehangir listened.

"I think the Camel is Biggles's favourite," said Murad. "But he also flies the Spitfire and Hurricane. Did you have them in your collection?"

"No," said Nariman. "They are Second World War. Unlike me, Biggles is ageless. By the time the balsa-wood models came on the market I was much older, there was no time for my hobby."

He shifted, trying to adjust his pillow, and the boys did it for him. "Thank you. Now, speaking of time, isn't it time for your homework?"

"You haven't told me a story yet, Grandpa," complained Jehangir. "You keep talking about aeroplanes with Murad."

So Nariman continued from the day before with tales about his childhood friend Nauzer, whose parents had had a veritable menagerie of birds and dogs. Though it was not a huge flat, just four rooms, they had been crazy about animals, and had a golden retriever, two Pomeranians, and three Sydney

Silkies. Jehangir's eyes shone as his imagination embraced such a lively household.

"Then there was a big cage with lovebirds, and finches that sang," said Nariman. "And a parrot named Tehmuras. But he had his own private cage, which he went into at night. During the day he roamed free."

"He didn't try to fly away?"

"Never, he loved it there, and the dogs loved him, especially the golden retriever, Cleopatra. She let Tehmuras walk all over her, perch on her back, even on her head. Sometimes he would sit between her paws and rest his beak next to her nose."

Jehangir sought details about the birds' colouring, the dogs' diets, and their sleeping arrangements. "Did Tehmuras talk?"

"Tehmuras was an African grey parrot, he was brilliant. You see, Nauzer's mother was very strict, she made him do his homework every evening. So the parrot learned to say, 'Nauzer! Time for lessons, Nauzer!' in the mother's voice. As soon as my friend came home from school Tehmuras would start repeating that. And Nauzer threatened to make a special little muzzle, to silence Tehmuras."

Jehangir laughed anxiously. "Was he serious?"

"It was a joke. Nauzer loved all living creatures, even the snails we found in the school garden in the monsoon."

"Did he have a cat?"

"No. No cats. Parsi families never keep cats. They consider them bad luck, because cats hate water, they never take a bath."

"Sound familiar, Jehangoo?" said his mother as she came in from the kitchen. "Maybe you were a cat in a previous life."

"Cats stay clean by licking themselves," said Jehangir. "I read it in a book, it's very hygienic."

"Yes," said Nariman. "But beliefs are more powerful than facts. Like our belief in spiders and cocks."

"I've never heard of that."

"Well, Parsis don't kill spiders, and they only eat the female chicken, never a cock – you must know that, from the story of Zuhaak the Evil One."

"No, I don't."

"Of course you do," said his mother. "I told it to you when you were learning the prayers for your navjote. We read many stories from the Shah-Nama – about King Jamsheed, about Rustam and Sohrab. And the one about King Gustasp's favourite horse becoming lame, how our prophet Zarathustra cured it by passing his hand over the hocks and fetlocks."

"I remember those, but not the one about Zuhaak."

"Pappa, I think he just wants to hear it from you."

"No, really, I don't know that story."

"Well," said Nariman, "a very long time ago, thousands of years ago, there lived an evil king whose name was Zuhaak. Out of Zuhaak's shoulders grew two immense serpents, ugly and smelly, that had to be fed every morning with the brains of two young men. For more than nine hundred years Zuhaak ruled, and brought indescribable misery upon the people, devouring their sons day after day. The people prayed for deliverance; the centuries passed; and finally, the great hero Faridoon arrived to confront Zuhaak. This evil monster had murdered Faridoon's father, and Faridoon was seeking vengeance. They met in hand-to-hand combat. It was a terrible fight, a fight that lasted days and weeks. Sometimes it seemed Faridoon was winning, sometimes Zuhaak. But in the end Faridoon overpowered him and tied him in huge chains. Unimaginably strong chains, that no file could cut or hammer smash. And when Zuhaak was rendered helpless, the good angel Sarosh instructed Faridoon to bury him deep inside Mount Damavand. Thus, the universe was saved."

"And the spider and the cock?"

"They are the ones who protect us in Faridoon's absence. The evil Zuhaak with his snake shoulders is still alive, and very strong. With his supernatural strength, he struggles and rages all night long in the bowels of Mount Damavand, trying to free himself. Early in the morning, while it is still dark and the sun has not yet risen, when Zuhaak has almost succeeded in bursting his chains, the cock crows and warns the world that the Evil One will be loose again in the universe. Then the good angel Sarosh at once sends out the spider to spin its web and mend the chains that Zuhaak is about to break. Thus the world is safe again. The cock and the spider keep it safe for us, one day at a time."

Jehangir nodded. "So if people ate up all the cocks and killed all the spiders, there would be no one to help us fight all the evil."

"Exactly. My friend Nauzer loved this story. He would sit for hours gazing at a spider spinning its web. Especially outdoors, in sunshine after rain, with drops like jewels caught in the gossamer."

Jehangir began scrutinizing the ceiling, walls, and corners of the room, looking for a web. He wanted to see for himself how beautiful it might be.

Murad began to laugh. "My brother is a crackpot, Grandpa. Now he'll worry about Zuhaak and start protecting spiders."

"I'm not a crackpot. I know there isn't any Zuhaak. It's just a story, like Santa Claus."

"They're both real," said Murad. "And Zuhaak will catch you if you sleep on the balcony."

"You're saying that because you want to steal my turn tomorrow."

"I think you're right, Jehangir," chuckled his grandfather. "But even if Zuhaak were real, he wouldn't bother you. He'd be busy with things like diseases and famines, wars and cyclones."

The room did not reveal any spiders. Jehangir made his mother promise: next time she found a web, she would let him look at it first.

"And when your leg is all right, Grandpa, can we go to meet your friend's dogs and birds?"

"But that was a long time ago, Jehangir, those pets are" – he paused, making a sorrowful gesture with his hand – "are gone."

He saw Jehangir's reluctance to accept that the pets were dead, and continued with more directness, "I remember when Cleopatra died. My SSC exams were only a week away. But I went with Nauzer and his parents to bury her. A friend of theirs who had a cottage in Bandra said they were welcome to use the back garden, so we went in a taxi. It was a rainy day. We had to try many taxis before one agreed, and even then, the driver refused to allow a dead dog on the seat. We put Cleopatra in the boot, wrapped in a sheet. Nauzer and I carried her. The sheet got wet and muddy. That was the first time I saw Nauzer crying."

The sorrow from sixty-two years ago, of the burial of a dog he'd never seen, arced across time and touched Jehangir. Aching with grief, he asked, "Did you and Nauzer dig the hole?"

"No, the gardener had it ready. It was next to a lemon tree. Then Nauzer's mother wanted to see Cleopatra one more time, and Nauzer unfolded the wet sheet. I think that was a mistake. The beautiful golden-brown coat was dirty and yellow, the hair in knots and tangles. We quickly put back the sheet and buried her."

Elbows on his knees, face cupped in his hands, Jehangir sat gazing at the floor. He had run out of questions.

"You see, having a dog is not easy," said his mother. "It's not just laughing and playing with the dog. You have to be prepared for the sadness when it dies."

"I know that." He turned to his grandfather again. "But your friend might have new pets, we could go and see those."

Nariman shook his head. "My friend Nauzer – he died two years ago."

A cloud passed over Jehangir's face. "How old was he?"

"Seventy-six."

He counted: Grandpa was seventy-nine; if his friend was still alive, he would be seventy-eight. One year younger than Grandpa. And yet the friend was dead.

He felt his hands go cold and tears start to stab his eyes.

The arithmetic was threatening his grandfather's life, he wished he could forget the cruel numbers. He rose abruptly and went to the balcony.

Roxana mimed for her father, drawing a line with her finger from her eye down along her cheek. Murad pretended to be unaffected, more grown-up.

Nariman waited for a while before calling, "Jehangir, do you know the story of Faridoon's life after he defeated Zuhaak?"

"No."

"It's about Salim, Tur, and Iraj, the three sons of Faridoon. Don't you want to hear the end?"

"Yes," he answered, but stayed on the balcony because his eyes were still wet. Gazing down at the blurred pavement, he saw his father appear in the lane, striding homewards.

Yezad used his latchkey, disappointed that Jehangir was not at the door, and asked Roxana why her son was standing on the balcony. She hushed him, it would embarrass Jehangoo if he heard, he'd been crying because of a story Pappa had told, which had made him sad.

"Jehangla! Come here, talk to me."

Jehangir gave a final wipe to his eyes and went in with a weak smile.

Yezad took his hand. "Now what story is this, chief? Why are you making my son cry? When I tell stories, it makes everyone laugh." He went on giving Nariman a mock scolding, but his annoyance tinged with jealousy was unmistakable.

Jehangir wrenched his hand out of his father's. "Don't be angry with Grandpa," he said, aware that the tears he had got rid of had returned to his eyes.

"Okay, then I'll be angry with you. Tears before I leave for work, tears when I come home!"

Jehangir's shoulders shook with silent sobs as he went to the balcony again.

Turning to enter the back room, Yezad walked into wet clothes on hangers suspended in the doorway. In a rage he tore the clammy shirts from his face and flung them aside. "Is this a place to dry the washing?"

"There's no space on the balcony because of the tent," said Roxana softly, determined to stay calm. "Where can I dry them?"

"Take them to Chateau Felicity. Your bloody brother and sister can dry them in their seven rooms."

She gathered up the clothes from the floor, shook them out, hung them up again. "Tea, Yezdaa?"

He did not answer. She made it anyway, and asked him how it was at work.

"How do you think? Look at this – grease on my shirt. I had to do the peon's work, open the bloody shutters."

"I'll wash it in Surf, the stain will disappear."

"And what about your father's gloomy face? Now he's making Jehangir gloomy as well. Doesn't anybody know how to smile or laugh?"

"Shh, Pappa will hear! You used to call it his philosopher's face, now it's gloomy just because he's staying here?"

In the front room, Murad asked his grandfather to start the next story, the one about Faridoon's three sons. Nariman shook his head, afraid Yezad might take it as competition. "Later. Come, do your homework now."

Roxana brought the tea to the dining table and sent both boys to their desk. She gathered up the washing from the chairs, to spread out later, after Yezad went to bed.

He saw her arms full of damp clothes. "Leave them, I only need one chair," he tried to make amends.

While he drank his tea she sat with him and chatted about how Villie Cardmaster had bought onions and salt for her this morning from the bunya. "You were right, she really is quite nice."

"Ask her for a Matka tip. If we win big, we can hire a hospital ayah."

"I will starve before I gamble, or let you gamble."

"Calm down, I wasn't serious." He watched his father-in-law's hands trying to rest but thrashing about in the region of his chest, as though he were beating it.

Murad came and sat with them. "You know, Grandpa," he said, "you should play the bongoes."

"And why is that?"

"The way your fingers move, you'll be good at it." He attempted his idea on a chair, making his fingers tremble like his grandfather's to see if they could produce a thrum.

"Don't be a clown," said Yezad. "It's not funny."

He made him return to his lessons in the back room, told him to follow his younger brother's example. Jehangir heard the peace-offering and smiled into his book.

8

ANXIETY ABOUT THE IMPENDING verdict wakened Nariman with a jittery stomach. Three weeks had passed, and Dr. Tarapore was to visit today to pronounce upon the ankle.

So far, Nariman had managed to hold off each morning till everyone finished tea and breakfast, and left for school and work. He took pride in sparing them his smell; but his bowels were letting him down this last day.

"I'm sorry," he whispered to Roxana, "I don't dare delay, or it will be a bigger mess."

"Don't be silly, Pappa, if you need the bedpan you must have it." She made sure its edges were dry, as he turned slightly to one side to let her position it.

Yezad was silent until the smell began to fill the room. He felt his gorge rise. Pushing his plate from him, he fled into the back room, and she followed.

"Such a stink with my breakfast," he said, not caring to lower his voice. "You couldn't wait a few more minutes."

"I could, but Pappa couldn't. Haven't you noticed, all these days, not once has he done number two till you left the house?"

"Why not the same today? Or does he want to give me a sample before leaving?"

"Stop being disgusting!" She walked away to the front room where the boys were teasing Nariman.

"Chhee, Grandpa!" said Jehangir. "It's an atom bomb!"

Murad said more like a hydrogen bomb. Yezad shouted from the back room to get out, it was not hygienic to eat in there.

"Millions of people live in the gutters of Bombay!" Roxana shouted back. "Eating and sleeping next to drains and ditches! This whole city stinks like a sewer! And you are worried about Pappa's bedpan? How stupid can you be!"

"See that, chief? She calls me stupid because of you. Is that fair?"

"My daughter calls everyone stupid," observed Nariman softly. "Including me."

Jehangir was scared that another fight was beginning, like the one about Grandpa's soo-soo bottle a few days ago. "I have a new joke, Daddy," he said. "Can I tell you?"

"Later."

"Please, Daddy, it's very funny."

"All right," he said grouchily.

"Once upon a time, some tourists were in Vienna, and they went to the Beethoven museum where—"

"That's a stale joke," scoffed Murad. "Everyone knows about Beethoven's last movement. I have a new one."

"I don't want any filthy jokes," warned his mother.

"But mine isn't filthy. Just listen to it: Some tourists were in Vienna in the Beethoven museum and—"

"You're copy-catting mine!" protested Jehangir.

"Let me finish, it's completely different, okay? So the tourists went into a room where there was an open coffin with a body in it, all rotting and green, worms crawling out of it. The frowning face had a wide forehead and untidy hair, just like Beethoven's. Next to the coffin was a music stand with the manuscript of the *Fifth Symphony*. The tourists were upset, they asked the guide what was going on. He told them to be patient and watch the exhibit carefully. So they waited. Soon, the corpse raised a hand out of the coffin and erased a bar of music. A few seconds later, the hand came up again and erased another bar. The tourists were shocked, they asked the guide, Isn't this the body of Ludwig van Beethoven, why isn't he buried in the ground? The guide said, Please be calm, mein damen und herren. Ja, this is Beethoven the composer, ja, he is dead. And now he is slowly de-composing."

Everyone laughed, and Roxana said she didn't know where

the boys picked up these things. Jehangir sensed he had been upstaged by Murad, but didn't mind. Together they had averted a fight between Mummy-Daddy. Amid their clowning and teasing, she cleared away the bedpan.

Before leaving for work, Yezad stopped beside Nariman's bed. "Good luck, chief, when Dr. Tarapore comes."

"Thanks, Yezad."

Roxana waited at the door to kiss him. "Sorry I shouted," he said in her ear. "You know how I am about smells." She closed her eyes as his arm pressed her against him.

"Can you do me a favour, Yezdaa? Ask the corner barber to come now for Pappa's shave, before Doctor gets here."

"Sure." He started down the stairs, then stopped. "If Jal and Coomy visit, don't let them bully you in Doctor's presence, don't agree to anything."

"Knowing them, they've forgotten the check-up is today," she said, reassuring him with a flying kiss.

༄

For Jal and Coomy, the three weeks were ending as they had begun, in squabble and confusion, fretting and arguing, feeling guilty about what they had done, lacking the strength to put it right. They were ashamed of visiting their sister, and not all their toys and knick-knacks in the showcase could distract them from their torment.

More than the present, the future worried Coomy. Even if Pappa's ankle mended, letting him move around a little, it wouldn't be long before he was bedridden again. Dr. Tarapore had warned that Parkinson's would incapacitate him. The kind of nursing it would require terrified her. She and Jal had really made a valiant effort, she felt – what was the use of denying your limitations? "And if Roxana had any decency, she would keep her father for longer."

"What?" exclaimed Jal in disbelief. "In that tiny flat? This is Pappa's house."

"I can't have him back, please don't force me. I haven't even found a servant to replace Phoola, the sweeping and swabbing is breaking my back. For days I've begged you to find a way out. Not one suggestion have you offered."

Which was not surprising, since Jal wanted to accept the inevitable, bring Pappa home. "Be reasonable, Coomy. We said three weeks, we must keep our word. If Roxana can look after him, so can we."

"We? You run off every morning to the share bazaar. And three weeks does not balance the fifteen years I've looked after him. If you're feeling noble, stay home and nurse Pappa. Otherwise, use your head and think of something. Time is running out, the doctor comes today."

But he had no suggestions when they set off at six-thirty, and endured her in silence till they arrived at Pleasant Villa.

Dusk had fallen, and the stairwell was half-dark. Jal tried to locate the switch in the lobby. He blundered into the wrong corner, into cobwebs, and retreated, clawing at his face to get the strands off. They began climbing in the gloom.

As they rounded the first landing, the lights went on. They heard someone on the flight below, taking the steps two at a time. "They're in a hurry, let them pass," whispered Jal.

"We're first," said Coomy. "Whoever it is will wait. Always you let people take advantage."

❧

Behind them, Yezad was closing the gap. How like a long-married couple they were, he thought, rather than brother and sister. "Coomy's right, Jal," he called over the banister. "You must stand up for yourself."

"Oh! Yezad!" said Coomy. "Sorry, didn't know it was you."

"Not at all, you have as much claim to the stairs as me. So how are you both? Come to take Pappa home?"

Layering care and concern over her panic, she said, "We missed him. I hope doctor says he is all right now."

"Oh, he's been all right for three weeks, hasn't he?"

She suffered the dart without response. They reached the top floor and he used his latchkey, calling out to warn Roxana, "Hello! Look who I found on the stairs!"

Greetings were exchanged, familial niceties completed, and they stood at their stepfather's bedside.

"You seem much better than three weeks ago, Pappa," said Coomy. "This visit has been good for you."

"And a lovely shave as well," said Jal. "See those pink cheeks. Going on a date, Pappa?"

"Yes, with destiny."

"But you're still lying down," said Coomy, staying in the lighter vein. "I thought Doctor might have taken you for a trial walk."

"And I thought you might have forgotten where you left me."

"What a thing to say, Pappa. I was just telling Yezad how much Jal and I missed you. Come, Roxie, don't make us worry – what did Doctor say?"

"What's the rush, relax, have some tea first," said Yezad, though he too was anxious to know. And Jal, smiling, moved towards the dining table.

"Love to, but we are in a hurry," said Coomy, before her brother could sit. "We want to go to fire-temple to offer thanks for Pappa's recovery."

"Good, I'll go with you," said Nariman, "and then we'll head for home."

"That's lovely," said Coomy, her smile a rictus of dismay. "That means Doctor gave the okay to get up? Have you tried out your crutches?"

"Oh Pappa, stop teasing her," said Roxana. She wished she could have shared the news alone with Yezad first, Dr. Tarapore's explanation about the pills for Parkinson's disease and its main ingredient, L-dopa, and the side effects. Dr. Tarapore had said they were not to worry, disconcerting though it may be if her father rambled incoherently. Stopping the pills would mean losing complete control of his limbs.

She didn't want to spout all this before Jal and Coomy, and stuck to the ankle. "Doctor told Pappa to wait till next week to get up. He removed some plaster today, look."

She lifted the sheet – the cast, which used to encase his leg from the thigh downwards, and the entire foot, was somewhat reduced at both ends. His toes were exposed, and the knee.

Coomy began to sense a reprieve. "That must feel more comfortable for Pappa."

"So what happens now?" asked Yezad. "This week, I mean?"

"Doctor needs Pappa at Parsi General for an X-ray in eight days. This week is up to us."

"Excuse me, it's up to me," said Nariman. "And I want to go home now."

"Really, Pappa, how insensitive," said Coomy. "You want to offend poor Roxie and Yezad? This is home as well, isn't it?" Meeting with silence, she continued, "You can come back with us now, Pappa. But that means calling one ambulance to take you from here to Chateau Felicity, a second ambulance next week to take you to hospital for X-ray. Then a third one to take you home again."

"Don't worry, we'll share the expense," said Yezad.

"It's not the money," she protested. "It's the risk, each time those junglee ambulancevalas grab Pappa and throw him on their stretcher. God forbid, if they twist something, imagine the pain and suffering, and prolonging of his recovery."

Everyone paused while this dire forecast hung in the air. Then, to her surprise, Coomy received support from an unexpected source.

"She's right, chief. You should stay on, it's just eight more days."

Roxana looked gratefully at her husband while Coomy tried not to appear too relieved. "Is there enough medicine for a week?" she asked. "Or shall I get more?"

They began counting the pills, and one fell to the floor. Coomy bent to her knees to retrieve it. The delay she wanted was hers, she thought, but the inevitable had merely been postponed by a week. After that, what?

As she hunted for the fallen pill, she noticed the plaster removed by Dr. Tarapore. The bits lay on a sheet of newspaper under the teapoy, fragments large and small, some of them still holding the curve of Nariman's leg.

And suddenly it came to her. There was the solution – staring her in the face.

"Yes, the medicine is enough for ten days," announced Roxana, finishing the count.

"Good," said Coomy. "And Pappa will be home before then. Oh look, there's the pill, under the chair."

She picked it up, then they said goodbye, making arrangements to meet at Parsi General in a week.

∽

"Don't you appreciate the beauty of it?" Coomy asked, still trying a week later to convince Jal. "Isn't it amazing that the plaster from his own leg gave me the answer to our problem?"

"But it's so deceitful, so destructive, so extreme," he tried yet again to dissuade her.

"You have another idea? Are you willing to do his bedpan and toilet from tomorrow?"

"But he's getting better."

"Don't fool yourself. Pappa will never get better."

"How will we live with this on our conscience?"

"We'll get used to it. I'm sure conscience is easier to look after than Pappa. To be honest, I cannot bear the thought of him back – in this four-week gap, I have been remembering Mamma, and everything else, more sharply."

"I remember Mamma and her unhappiness too. But isn't it time to forgive?"

"Did Mamma have time to forgive him before she died, is what I'd like to know!"

"We can't really be sure what happened," said Jal wearily.

"You can think what you like – there is no doubt in my mind. You and I were both in the room when Mamma and Pappa had their last fight. We both heard Mamma's words before she went up to the terrace."

He sighed. "The more time passes, the more I feel there is no sense blaming anyone – it was just a sad, unhappy mess. Sometimes, life is like that."

"Stop the philosophy and do what needs doing. Go to Edul Munshi."

"Okay, don't yell, I'm going," said Jal, and trudged down the stairs. She was always dredging up the past, he felt. It was abnormal, harbouring so much anger after thirty years. And now she was using the past to justify keeping Pappa away, unable to overcome her revulsion for the smelly sick-room chores. Like himself. If only some of the share prices would go up, they could hire a hospital ayah, solve the problem peacefully . . . instead of this crazy plan of hers . . .

He prepared himself for meeting Edul Munshi and broaching the subject. He thought about Edul's wife – poor Manizeh, he knew she rued the day when Edul had stopped at a second-hand book stall and, among the books and magazines spread out on the footpath, come upon an American journal devoted to the do-it-yourselfer. Edul still told people the story of how he had found his calling, and preached the virtues of handiness to anyone who would listen.

"You know why America is a great country? Because they believe in do-it-yourself. And we are poor and backward because we don't. Now I understand what Gandhiji meant when he taught svavlumban. With his doctrine of self-reliance, Mahatmaji was the first genuine Indian do-it-yourselfer. His vision is true, DIY is the only way to save this country."

He had embarked confidently upon this new path, and learned the handyman style of personifying the tools he worked with. He even had his own song, sung to the tune of "Candyman": "The handyman can 'cause he fixes it with love and makes it work all right."

Arriving at the Munshi flat, Jal stood at the door with its crooked nameplate and rang the doorbell. Since Edul had been fixing it, the pushbutton had to be jiggled and coaxed before it responded with an unpleasant jangling.

Manizeh opened the door. "Edoo! Upstairs Jal is here!"

Jal waited, offering up a smile filled with sympathy. In the beginning, Manizeh had been so pleased with her husband's hobby, bragging to the building about his wonderful tools and gadgets. The things they could do left you gasping in amazement, she told her neighbours. But as time went on, she saw the devastation those same instruments could wreak.

Edul's first project had been the installation of wooden shelves in the kitchen. After days of work during which everyone, including the servant, watched with awe, Edul proclaimed, using what he presumed was an American accent, "Okay, Manizeh, these babies are ready. Load 'em up."

She placed three tins, one on each of the shelves, and stood back to admire the effect. Seconds later, the shelves crashed to the floor.

Edul was mortified. How could his expensive, shiny tools betray him? He picked out the screws and brackets from the debris, blew off the plaster dust, and examined them with a dazed anger.

His broken heart mended in a few days, and he tackled the job again, the shelves staying up this time. But there were gaping holes in the wall plaster. And the patching he accomplished left the surface uneven as the wall of a mountain cave. Manizeh assured him it was fine, that for modern decor, interior designers recommended textured walls.

Next, Edul had taken on a dripping tap and turned the leak into a flood. Struggling through the Sunday morning, he did change the washer, addressing it as the slippery swine. But to open and shut the tap required the full strength of both hands.

After a series of small jobs that he managed to convert into progressively larger disasters, Manizeh took control of her husband's hobby. The rules were clear: Edul had to submit all his projects for her prior approval.

Invariably overambitious, they were always refused. His dreams of installing new flooring, performing a bathroom renovation, constructing built-in closets fell by the wayside. Occasionally, when she was certain it wouldn't leave ruin in its wake, he was allowed to undertake something modest such as hanging a picture frame.

For work on a larger scale, Edul had to satisfy his cravings away from home. He often tried to convince people to borrow his tools, which came with his services. Unfortunately, most of his friends and neighbours had grown aware of the hidden cost of the loan, and were not inclined to pay it.

But Jal was optimistic as he waited for Edul to appear. Not much harm could come of asking for a simple hammer, he thought.

"How are you, Edul?"

"Champion, Jal. You?"

"Fine. Doorbell not working?"

Edul tried it, pushing the button this way and that till brief contact produced the unpleasant jangling. Manizeh grimaced.

"Just needs a few more adjustments," he reassured her.

Learning that Jal wanted to borrow a hammer, he began to salivate. "Tell me what you're doing. The right tool for every job – that's the handyman's motto. I have three types of hammer: claw, ball-peen, and bricklayer's."

"My gosh, Edul, you're really well equipped."

"A few basic tools," he said modestly. "It's not how many, but how well you use them. So what's the job?"

Jal hesitated. His lie shouldn't be too interesting or Edul would jump right in. "Shoes."

"Shoes?"

"Yes, some nails in my heels have popped out."

"Sure. Step inside, we'll bang them in."

"Not these, my other pair. At home. Coomy's as well, we're both having heel trouble."

178

"Okay, I'll come with you."

"And handle my dirty shoes?" said Jal. "Can't insult you like that."

"Don't worry, Jal my son, we handymen are used to all kinds of dirt."

Jal had to think fast or he would soon be climbing upstairs with the handyman in tow. "Can I be honest, Edul? We need your help later – a more difficult job. So let me do this alone, or Coomy will feel over-obligated and won't ask for that favour."

Edul's eyes grew large. "What's the difficult job?"

"A window." Fairly safe choice, thought Jal, there was bound to be at least one problem window if he came demanding to examine it. He decided he must get away now, the chap was quite worked up. "Could I have the hammer?"

"Sure. This one's right for your job." He showed Jal how to use the claw to remove the nails. "Always best to throw the old buggers out and put in new ones. Take my pliers as well, in case the claw doesn't grip. And this iron block should fit inside the shoe, like a last."

Thus equipped, Jal climbed the stairs to his flat. It had been relatively easy. And Edul did seem knowledgeable. Perhaps people complained too much of his shortcomings; exaggeration, after all, was a human tendency.

He fiddled with his hearing aid, pretending he couldn't hear Coomy scolding him for taking so long with Edul. He followed her into their stepfather's room, where she placed a tall stool on the bed and told him to climb up.

"It wobbles."

"I'll hold it."

He hesitated again. "What a mess it will make. Shouldn't we cover the furniture, Pappa's nice things?"

"For once, use your head. A mess is exactly what we need."

He put one foot on the stool, then the other, and remained in a squat till he was sure of his balance. "Ready?" he asked.

She was gripping its legs. "Yes, yes, ready."

"I'm going to stand up now."

"Shall I clap?"

"Hold the stool tight!" He stood, and steadied himself, checking if he could touch the ceiling. Yes. He rested the fingertips of his left hand against the smooth surface, and immediately felt more stable.

"Go on, begin."

Sighing, he swung the hammer. It landed with a half-hearted thud, raining bits of plaster upon the bed and in Coomy's hair. "I just thought of something – what if someone hears the noise?"

"Who, the crows? Only the roof is above us."

He continued, creating holes and cracks in the ceiling. Some sections crumbled readily, others resisted. He paused to give his shoulder a rest, and moved to places that were less damaged, following her directions.

"Isn't that enough?"

"Keep going. Dr. Tarapore removed more plaster from Pappa's leg."

Finally she asked him to come down and give his opinion. "Does it look genuine?"

From below, the ceiling appeared worse than when his face had been close to it. He felt sick as he surveyed the wreck, and nodded.

"Good, we can work on the other side."

The stool was placed upon the dresser, he climbed onto it, and did as he was told. From Nariman's room they went to Roxana's old bedroom, then to each of theirs.

The ceiling in their mother's room was left intact. Jal wondered if it might not seem suspicious. Coomy said no, it wouldn't, because everyone knew that God worked in mysterious ways. She went to the bathroom for a bucket of water and a mug.

"Is this necessary?" he asked. "It already looks realistic."

"There have to be water marks. What if Yezad wants to check the damage? Every detail of our story should be solid." She began throwing water towards the ceiling, but instead of hitting the target most of it splashed down upon her. "You'll have to get on the stool again."

Jal soaked the broken areas, being liberal with the water as she suggested: if the furniture and floor got wet, it would look more natural.

Then it was time to clean themselves up, wash the plaster out of their hair, and rehearse how to break the news of this misfortune tomorrow at Parsi General.

D R. TARAPORE SMILED at the X-ray with satisfaction; the bones had healed well. "Quite remarkable, Professor, at your age, with osteoporosis."

He instructed Nariman in some simple exercises to be performed sitting down: wriggling the toes, flexing the foot, placing it flat on the ground and raising the heel. Walking would be restricted to a few steps each day on crutches, for the next four weeks. "Walking, my dear Professor," he said, "is not a means of taking you from point A to point B. If the crutches are difficult, just stay in bed. But don't neglect the exercises."

Roxana wished Coomy was there to hear this, she worried Pappa would exert more than he should, once he went home. Then it was off in a wheelchair to Mr. Rangarajan the plasterer.

"What a pleasure to meet Professor Vakeel's youngest," said Mr. Rangarajan, shaking hands with Roxana. "And are you following in your esteemed father's footsteps, as educator and broadener of minds?"

She shook her head. "I'm just a housewife."

"Just?" Mr. Rangarajan was aghast. "What are you saying, dear lady? Housewifery is a most important calling, requiring umpteen talents. Without housewife there is no home; without home, no family. And without family, nothing else matters, everything from top to bottom falls apart or descends into chaos. Which is basically the malady of the West. Would you not agree, Professor Vakeel?"

"I don't think they have a monopoly," said Nariman. "We do quite well here too when it comes to creating miserable families."

Mr. Rangarajan laughed. He drew Roxana's attention to the manner of tying the tensor bandage. "Basically, it's a figure eight. Please, check the tension I am employing."

While Roxana was observing the technique, Jal and Coomy arrived in a flurry of movement and expression, as though they had travelled great distances under inclement conditions. "Such a relief to find you, Pappa. We asked for Dr. Tarapore, but the receptionist said you had left already."

"What's wrong?" asked Roxana.

"Too much," she whispered. "I'll tell you in a minute."

"Now that everyone is assembled," announced Mr. Rangarajan, "I will start the bandage at the very beginning."

"I wonder how long this gadhayro will take," said Coomy in Gujarati.

Embarrassed, Nariman intervened, "We mustn't detain you any longer, Mr. Rangarajan, your other patients are waiting. Thank you very much for your help."

"But it is no trouble—"

"Thank you, bye-bye," said Coomy.

For a moment, Mr. Rangarajan looked offended. But he recovered his poise, wished the professor a speedy recovery, and left.

They pushed Nariman's wheelchair into the corridor, parking it by a bench near the window. "You won't believe our bad luck," said Jal, "when we tell you what happened last night."

"The big water tank on the terrace burst," said Coomy, "and the ceiling collapsed." She described the roar that had awakened them, and then bits of plaster falling on their beds, which was fortunate, for they were able to jump out before the water soaked in and larger pieces came crashing down.

"Some were the size of footballs. I must say, Pappa, God is watching after you. If you were in your bed last night, a big chunk could have cracked your head. Maybe your broken ankle, and moving to Pleasant Villa, was God's way of protecting you."

"Luckily, there was not too much water," said Jal, uncomfortable with casting God in a supporting role in their deceitful drama. "The tank must have been only half full."

"Both of us shifted to Mamma's room," added Coomy. "It's undamaged. The only safe place."

"Strange," said Nariman. "It's right next to yours."

"Who knows," said Jal. "Maybe the terrace is uneven and the water couldn't flow that way. Or Mamma's ceiling might be stronger."

"God works in mysterious ways," declared Coomy.

Nariman said there was no need to waste time in theological discussions – best to go home, get things back to normal, a broken ceiling did not bother him.

The idea was declared absurd in a chorus of disapproval: there could be structural problems, something else might collapse; besides, Jal and Coomy were able-bodied, they could run at the first sign of crumbling, but Pappa would be trapped.

"I'm willing to take the risk," said Nariman.

Eventually, Roxana convinced her father to return to Pleasant Villa for a few more days, while the damage was assessed. Coomy promised to send Pappa's pension to help with his expenses.

"I hate putting you and Yezad through more difficulty," said Nariman.

"Don't be silly, Pappa, it's not your fault," said Roxana.

"An act of God is no one's fault," said Coomy.

As they set off for the ambulance, Jal pushing the wheelchair, Nariman observed that Coomy was getting into the bad habit of burdening God with altogether too much responsibility: "And that is good for neither God nor us."

❧

In the evening Yezad heard the news about the ceiling without emotion. He'd had a hunch Jal and Coomy would not be taking the chief back with them today.

Roxana protested they were scarcely to be blamed for the water tank. "As Coomy said, it's an act of God."

"Yes, and His act is mainly in her behalf, isn't it? Must be all her visits to fire-temple and her sandalwood bribes. I might have some influence too if I went more often."

"That would be so nice, Yezdaa," she said eagerly. "And you could take the boys with you, light a deevo—"

"I was just being funny," he interrupted, and her face fell.

They helped Nariman up, the crutches were put in place, and, with Yezad's support, he took his first steps. Slowly, they covered the four feet between the settee and the chair. He sat down, wincing with the effort, and the boys clapped.

"One small step for Grandpa's foot, one giant leap for Grandpa," said Murad.

"Exactly," he panted.

"So how was it, chief?"

"All right."

"Any pain?" asked Roxana, having seen him wince.

"A little. But that's to be expected." He remained in the chair till dinnertime, when they pushed him closer to the table so he could eat with them.

Roxana had made dhandar-paatiyo to celebrate her father's first steps, though it bothered her that it was without fish. For a small pair of pomfrets the machhivala had demanded a hundred and thirty rupees. Ninety she could have managed, scrimping on other things, but the rogue had refused to budge – why should he, people were lined up to buy at his price, the obscene wealth there was in Bombay these days. So here it was, a fishless dhandar-paatiyo, an incomplete celebration. She began to lay the table.

"I notice you never use my mother's good dishes that I gave you on your wedding," said her father.

"Naturally, Pappa, they're so precious, so old and delicate."

"Is that a reason to keep them locked up? I am old and delicate, and Jal and Coomy wanted to keep me locked up. You can't live like that. Use the dishes."

"How will I ever replace something so valuable if it breaks?"

"Human beings break, and you cannot replace them either. Are dishes more important? All you can do is enjoy the memories."

"There's my philosopher," said Yezad. "You tell her, chief."

"Don't encourage Pappa. Such inauspicious words when we're celebrating his recovery."

"Not inauspicious," said her father gently. "There's only one way to defeat the sorrow and sadness of life – with laughter and rejoicing. Bring out the good dishes, put on your good clothes, no sense hoarding them. Where is the cut-glass vase and the rose bowl from your wedding? The porcelain shepherdess with her lamb? Bring them all out, Roxana, and enjoy them."

"You're being silly, Pappa. Like on your birthday – making Coomy do double work with your demands."

The reminder blotted the smile from Nariman's face. What an age it seemed since that evening two months ago. When he was still able to stand, dress himself, go to the toilet, go for a walk. Before his fall, before the nightmare with Coomy and Jal and the commode, the days in bed with his stinking body, frightened and shivering.

Roxana at once regretted her words; their effect on her father was painful to observe, and she looked to Yezad for help. He shifted uncomfortably in his chair.

Then Jehangir cleared his throat like a grown-up about to make an important announcement: "Be that as it may, the good plates are on the agenda."

Nariman laughed, and Yezad said it was about time this little brown parrot learned some new expressions from Grandpa. Murad pretended to train him: Jehangoo sweetie, pretty Jehangoo. The good dishes were brought out from the lower section of Yezad's cupboard, the rose bowl took the centre of the dining table, and the porcelain shepherdess was assigned the teapoy to graze her charges.

Through dinner, Yezad's thoughts kept turning to the days ahead. The morning stress, the overcrowding, the smelly front room – all of it would continue. And providing for one more person, when every rupee was budgeted, meant a shortfall of twenty-five per cent in Roxana's food envelopes. Not to mention things like soap and washing and dhobi.

"About your pension, chief," said Yezad. "How much remains after buying medicines for the month?"

"To be honest, I don't know. Coomy runs the house. I gave her power of attorney for my accounts a long time ago."

"And what about the ceilings? I should take a look, see how bad the damage is."

"As far as I am concerned," said Nariman, "the damage is irrelevant. Broken plaster is no calamity."

Yezad nodded; to voice his money worries now would not help, better to keep a calm, patient demeanour for Roxana's sake. "We can manage for another week or so."

When the medication ran out and Roxana went to purchase the next lot, she discovered that what Coomy had given her as her father's pension did not cover even the cost of the pills. There had to be some mistake, she thought, perhaps Coomy had sent a partial amount.

The chemist's bill was paid by making up the difference from housekeeping money. To compensate, she bought bread but not butter, and a small tin of cooking oil instead of the more economical large one. Tea, sugar, rice could wait till next week. And dinner would be meatless, just cauliflower with potatoes.

She placed the pill bottles on the side table next to her father. He inquired if the money had been enough, and she nodded, convinced that Coomy and Jal would soon show up with the balance. To Yezad too, when he asked during dinner, she said, "It's okay for now."

In the days that followed, her frugalities began to be noticed. At breakfast, Murad grumbled there was no butter

187

on his toast, and Jehangir said his tea was bitter, it needed more sugar.

Yezad didn't like their fuss. "You boys are spoilt. Be thankful you at least have toast to eat and tea to drink. You know how many millions in the world would be happy to have what you have?"

Towards the end of the week, Nariman found it harder to hide the pain in his ankle when he stood on crutches. He had remained silent because the three little steps he took went far in sustaining everyone's hope.

Then one evening, as he tried to stand, the agony in his ankle made him scream out, the crutches slipped, and he fell back upon the settee.

Throwing aside his newspaper, Yezad rushed to him. Roxana ran in from the kitchen. Once they determined he was safe, they grilled him about the scream. He tried to pass it off as a sudden twinge, but she saw through it and pried the secret out.

"That bloody Tarapore," said Yezad. "The quack-and-a-half was in a hurry."

Nariman shook his head. "To be fair, we were all relieved when he said I could get up."

"Don't defend him, chief. If this was America, we could sue him for millions."

But Dr. Tarapore was duly consulted again, and was quite forthcoming about the setback. The X-ray had not lied, the cracks had mended, but calcium deficiency and porous bones had allowed hairline fractures to reopen.

The full regimen of bed-care was back in force.

At least once a day Roxana sat with her envelopes to pore over the contents, debating if she should transfer a few rupees from the one marked Milk & Tea into the one for Butter & Bread, or from Meat into Rice & Sugar. Jehangir sat with her, asking the price of a slab of Amul butter, a packet of tea, a kilo of mutton, while working out sums in his head and making suggestions.

Lost in anxiety, she discussed the finances with him till she realized what she was doing. "That's enough, Jehangoo, money is not your worry. Daddy and I can look after it."

"Yes," he started, "but Daddy will . . . ," and though he trailed off, she understood his fear.

A fortnight passed since the ceilings had collapsed. Jal and Coomy were nowhere in sight, and Yezad refused to call on them, saying he didn't want any favours from those two.

"May I make a suggestion?" urged Nariman. "Arguments between you and Roxana will not solve the problem. The pension payment notwithstanding, my expenses have remained unmet. Hence, my instructions are to make a withdrawal from my savings account. My money, which I earned by the sweat of my brow. Simple as that. In short, the question of favours does not arise."

"I feel awkward," said Yezad, "to announce we've come to collect Pappa's money. If they had any decency, they would have brought it to us."

"I have an idea," said Jehangir. "You can say you came for Grandpa's walking stick, the one we gave him on his birthday."

Yezad chuckled, patted his son's shoulder, and said that was exactly what they would do.

9

YEZAD AND ROXANA walked across the debris covering the drawing-room floor, stepping gingerly over the plaster chunks. Jal hurried to brush off the plaster powder from two armchairs. He thumped the cushions, and coughed in the rising dust.

Coomy crunched her way into the room. He began tidying a third chair, but she touched his elbow to indicate she would stand. So he remained standing too, behind her, while she grumbled that the sun had set, the coals for loban were ready, and she was just about to start praying the Aiwisruthrem Geh.

"Very sorry," said Yezad, "we had no intention of jumping the queue between you and God."

"Don't make fun of sacred matters," said Roxana, as Jal chuckled. She explained why they had come, setting Coomy's head shaking in exasperation.

"What nerve Pappa has. How long will you indulge his nonsense? Remember his birthday dinner, and my prediction? Everyone made fun of me. Now you must think I'm a prophet."

She went to her stepfather's room and fetched the birthday gift. "Barely hobbling on his crutches, and he demands his walking stick. Such madness."

Yezad switched to the more important subject. "What about these ceilings, Jal? I thought they'd be fixed by now."

"We got someone to check," Coomy answered for her brother. "They wanted to charge too much."

"And the landlord?"

"Hah. We'd have to go to court to make him repair it. And Pappa doesn't have the twenty years the case would take. Anyway, another contractor will come."

"Another?" Yezad attempted to keep the mood light. "Already two in our midst – Jal Contractor and Coomy Contractor."

This amused Jal, but he took his cue from Coomy's unbending sternness.

"By the way," said Roxana, "I bought Pappa's medicines. The money wasn't enough."

"I know that," said Coomy. "I used to buy them every month."

Roxana waited for her to continue. But there was nothing else. "Could I . . . could I have the rest of the pension?"

Coomy gave a short laugh. "That was it. All of it."

"Are you sure?" asked Yezad.

"What are you implying? I'm robbing Pappa?" She rushed from the room and returned with a bank book.

"Oh Coomy," said Roxana, "he doesn't need to see it. It was just an expression of his surprise."

"Sounded like an expression of insult to me!" She threw the book in his lap.

"No, Coomy, please don't take it like that," Roxana tried again. "As you know, it's very difficult looking after Pappa – the expenses."

"The work too," said Yezad. "Don't be so modest." He turned to Jal, "It's a job-and-a-half. Her exhaustion at the end of the day worries me."

"Remember the ground-floor Arjanis?" said Coomy. "Hired a full-time nurse for their father, and she gave him bedsores. Roxie gets so much satisfaction from serving her aged parent. Ask her, if you don't believe me."

"I do," agreed Roxana. "If at least the medicines were covered by his pension, I could manage the rest. Government should be ashamed of itself, the amount it pays."

"If government had a sense of shame, lots of problems would disappear," said Jal.

"Yes," said Roxana. "So, can you give me the difference from Pappa's savings account?"

Coomy offered her short laugh again. "There's no such thing."

"But Pappa said the money from fixed deposits—"

"Pappa's brain is soft as a pickled mango. You listen to his bak-bakaat, then come to accuse me? I wonder how firm is your brain."

Roxana looked at Jal to see if he would speak up; he was playing again with his hearing aid. "Abuse me if you like," she said. "For Pappa, show a little respect. He's a problem now, but after your father died, you were fed and clothed thanks to him."

"And thanks to him, also, for killing my mother."

"Don't talk rubbish! And she was my mother too!"

"And mine," added Jal, in a voice pleading for peace.

"Yes, yes, our little sister knows that," said Coomy. "What she doesn't know is, month after month we've made up the difference for Pappa's medicines, his food, his clothes, dhobi, everything. We have more than repaid him. We have subsidized him all these years. Out of the goodness of our hearts, Jal and I looked after him. Not for anyone's praise or thanks."

"Or because you live in his house and will inherit it," said Yezad, as a bolt of disapproval flew from Roxana's eyes.

"Oh, Mr. Clever thinks he knows everything," said Coomy. "Coming here with his are-you-sure and the-rest-of-the-money and what-not. Let me tell you about this house, Roxie, now that your husband—"

"Please let's not fight," said Jal.

"Don't interrupt! He started it, now he'll hear the truth! You know, fifteen years ago, when Pappa bought your flat for you? He also went to the landlord of Chateau Felicity and put this flat jointly in Jal's name and mine." She surveyed their stunned faces with a look of triumph.

"What a fool," muttered Yezad.

"You heard that?" she pounced. "This ungrateful man called Pappa a fool."

"I heard," said Roxana. "And even when Yezad calls him a fool, it has more affection than all your words of concern."

"Go ahead, defend him! Do what you like! But don't dictate to me in my house! For that's what it is, mine and Jal's. And we will repair the ceiling at our convenience, unless you have money for it. Pappa will return when we want him to."

"So that's it?" said Yezad softly. "You're kicking him out of his own flat?"

"Don't twist my words! No one kicked him out, Dr. Tarapore said his depression needed—"

"We know all about that," said Yezad, clenching the walking stick and rising. "So what shall we tell the chief?"

"Please tell him," said Jal, "we'll get the house fixed as soon as possible, so he can come back."

Because her brother's rage was a rare thing, Coomy watched in silence for a while. It was as though the order of nature had broken at last.

"What was the point?" he screamed, pacing wildly about the room. "Why did you force me to get Edul's hammer? Why did you destroy the ceilings? You could have told them weeks ago we were kicking Pappa out!"

"I wanted Pappa to stay away, but in a civilized manner," she said quietly. "Without fighting, or ruining family relationships."

"Why should you care? Family does not matter to you! You keep nursing your bitterness instead of nursing Pappa. I've begged you for thirty years to let it go, to forgive, to look for peace."

He started pacing again, raising his arms to the ceiling, shaking them in despair. "Look around, look at what you've achieved."

She looked, hoping to calm him by doing his bidding, and saw the dust and plaster everywhere. She raised her eyes and saw the mutilated ceiling. She shuddered. For the first time since the hammer blows, her heart sank.

"Don't turn away! You said you wanted a ruin, so feast

your eyes! Happy? Ruined house, and ruined relations with our one and only sister."

Then his voice lost its hysterical edge, suddenly subdued by sorrow. Exhausted, he sank into a chair and covered his face.

She sat too, watching him, thinking of all that he'd said, thinking of Roxana . . . their little doll . . . how they had loved her when she was born, how crazy they were about her, carrying her everywhere, taking her wherever they went, Marine Drive, cinema, Hanging Gardens . . . and how much she had adored them, in those childhood years . . .

What remained now of all that love? Exhaustion washed over her too and tears came to her eyes.

Hearing her sniff, Jal lifted his face out of his hands. "What's wrong?"

"Nothing." Then she began to weep. No one gave a thought to her feelings, she whispered, the unkind things they said to her, and Yezad accusing her of stealing from Pappa, after all that she had done for Pappa, for so many years . . .

❧

Yezad leaned the walking stick in the corner by the settee and asked his father-in-law about his finances. The questions were simple and direct, but Nariman seemed confused, unable to provide any helpful information.

"What were you saying about your savings account?"

"I can't remember."

"According to Coomy you have no money. No house, either."

His blunt way of putting it distressed Roxana. "Don't worry, Pappa, you know how stupidly she talks sometimes."

"I, for one, have had enough of her insults," said Yezad. "We're never going there again. Not unless she apologizes. I forbid you to visit them."

"That means punishing poor Jal as well," she pleaded. "He hasn't ever uttered one rude word to us."

"If he fiddled less with his hearing aid and showed more gumption, he could make his sister behave herself."

"Please don't quarrel," entreated Nariman. "Tell me what Coomy said to annoy you."

They told him. "So is it true?"

He gave a little smile. "It may be."

"If you put the flat in their names, you should know."

"It was many years ago. The poor children, hurt so much already. I think I may have signed something."

"Very foolish of you."

"I don't understand."

"It's very simple – you have no legal claim to that flat now. Not unless you go to court and fight."

Nariman turned his face to the wall and composed himself before speaking. "Not to have me around must be a pleasant holiday for them. But are you suggesting I've been thrown out for good?"

"Only one way to check: ring their doorbell, see if they'll take you in," said Yezad.

"Don't worry, Pappa, they're just delaying. They want you back fully recovered – to make it easier for themselves."

She went to warm the dinner, and Yezad followed her. The recalcitrant stove resisted the spark. Switching off the gas cylinder, he took the lighter from her and cleaned the burner, saying they had to find a way to outwit Coomy and Jal. "That's what this has become, a battle of wits."

"But if they have no intention of taking Pappa back . . ."

The burner lit with a whoosh of flame. "Nothing doing. If they play this game, so will we. They kick him into our house, we find a way to kick him back into theirs."

"Pappa is not a football. I won't behave like them."

"You don't have to, I'll do it." He kept tinkering with the gas lighter, making sparks with the flint.

She grabbed it from his hand and slammed it on the table. "I'll tell you right now – if you force Pappa out, you may as well throw me out at the same time."

The ultimatum left him silent for a few moments. "So that's it? That's all I mean to you, your family means to you?"

"And what's Pappa if not family?"

Considering it worthless to argue the definition, he left the kitchen and sat at the dining table, playing with the toaster, pressing the lever down and releasing it, over and over. What a muddle life had become, he thought, wishing Mr. Kapur would get on with his campaign planning, the election was only three months away. The promised promotion would at least solve the money troubles.

"The spring will get spoiled, Daddy," said Jehangir.

Yezad sighed and pushed the toaster away, as Roxana carried the steaming pot to the table, cut the loaf of bread, and divided the slices among the five of them. The odd one left over she placed in Yezad's plate, then called the boys.

"What's for dinner?" asked Murad.

"Irish stew." She spooned onions, potatoes, and gravy into his plate.

He examined the serving. "Where's the mutton?"

"Good question," said Yezad. "Probably grazing in Ireland." He dipped a piece of bread in the gravy and started eating.

Watching his father, Jehangir followed suit, and declared the stew was delicious. It made his mother smile as she filled the remaining plates.

She came to her father's bowl, and he said, at the first spoonful, "Thanks, that's enough."

"What's the matter, chief? Don't like our meatless dishes? Better eat some, or you'll upset your little Roxie."

"Please, Pappa is already feeling bad, okay?"

"He might feel worse. Soon it could be bread and water."

"Stop it! How can you be so mean?"

Nariman raised his hand. "Whatever Yezad wants to say, I deserve to hear. You are suffering on account of my short-sightedness. It was stupid of me to sign over the flat." He mashed a bit of potato and continued softly into his bowl, "To so many classes I taught *Lear*, learning nothing myself.

What kind of teacher is that, as foolish at the end of his life as at the beginning?"

"What is *Lear*?" asked Jehangir.

Nariman swallowed the potato. "It's the name of a king who made many mistakes."

"You are not to blame for Jal and Coomy's behaviour, Pappa. What you did is proof of your kind and trusting nature."

"Kindness and trust don't put a roof over your head," said Yezad.

"Don't worry," said Nariman. "This Lear will go home again. I know Coomy – she'll let me return when she's ready."

They ate in silence for a while. Then Murad asked if there was more bread.

"You got your share," said his mother.

"But I have some gravy left in my plate."

She passed him one of her slices, and his father pointed at him. "Give it back to Mummy," he commanded, and held out one of his own.

"No, we cannot deprive Daddy," she said. "He has to go to work, bring home the salary."

"And Mummy needs her strength to bring the bedpan." He tossed his slice into Murad's plate beside the one she had placed.

Murad left the table without touching either slice, and his mother said at this rate no one would miss the mutton, the children's stomachs would fill up with their father's childish displays.

He waited till the boys cleared the table, then put on his shoes.

"Where are you going?" asked Roxana.

"Nowhere special."

The door slammed. Her hand covering her mouth, she stared at the rose pattern in the tablecloth. In fifteen years of marriage it was the first time he had behaved like this.

"Don't be distressed," said Nariman. "The poor man is sunk in worries. Probably gone for a little walk, to clear his head. It always used to help me."

"Oh Pappa, how does it help to say nasty things, lose his temper?"

"What else can he do? He is not a saint – none of us is."

She took the hand he held out to her. In so much pain himself, she thought, and he still comforts me.

The boys hurried to the balcony to watch their father emerge from the building and cross the road. They waited for him to turn and wave, but he disappeared round the bend.

"He went towards the bazaar, Mummy," reported Murad.

"Did he . . . wave?"

"Yes," said Jehangir quickly.

Gaining the corner, Yezad could observe his sons on the balcony without being seen himself. Their anxious faces distressed him. How much pleasure he used to get from seeing their healthy appetites. The last few weeks had erased all that . . . and Roxie taking smaller helpings every day, to leave something in the pot, but the boys weren't fooled by it . . . The first time, Murad had hesitated, though Jehangla had quickly refused, signalling to his brother. Now they always said they were stuffed, forcing her to take her share. Murad must have been really hungry tonight, to have asked for more bread . . .

The thought bore through Yezad's mind like an auger. He checked the balcony again. Certain no one was watching, he recrossed the road in a dangerous weave through traffic and ducked into the Pleasant Villa entrance. He crept up the stairs to the third floor, tiptoeing past his own door to Villie Cardmaster's, and knocked.

It opened at once.

"Hallo, my dear Yezadji!" she boomed. "What brings—"

"Shh!" He entered and pushed the door shut behind him. Her usual odour, like the smell of Belgaum ghee gone slightly off, made him want to step back. "Roxana mustn't know I'm here."

She giggled. "What are you planning, my dear?"

"I need a favour."

"Speak, Yezadji."

"How's the Matka these days?"

"Up and down. My own dreams are reliable. With others I lose money. Trouble is, my sleep isn't what it used to be."

She put a stray lock of hair in place and straightened her crumpled collar. "But why this sudden interest in Matka?"

"Just temporary . . ." he hesitated. "To make some extra money. For a surprise. For Roxana."

"Oh, you two lovebirds!"

"How about today, any suggestion?"

"My dream was so solid last night, the numbers are guaranteed today."

"What did you see?"

Her eyes grew bashful. "It was very personal." Realizing that he wasn't going to insist, she said, "I might as well tell you – I'm not responsible for what happens in dreams, am I? You see, I was shopping at Grant Road for a bra. And I stopped at a stall with a good selection. The fellow asked me what size, and I said my usual, 34A."

Yezad started feeling uncomfortable; she continued, "The shopkeeper shook his head and stared at my chest. Such a rude fellow. With a dirty smile, he said, 'Madam, you are not 34A. I've been in this line for many years, one look at your lovely form and I can tell – you are 36C.'"

Despite himself, Yezad took a quick look: Villie's chest was the same as ever, shapeless under her dowdy housecoat.

"'Stop staring,' I said to the mavaali, 'I know my own chest, I have worn 34A for years now, and I am not a blossoming schoolgirl.' 'Just try it on, madam,' he said, 'then tell me.' 'Are you crazy?' I said. 'Try it standing here on the pavement?' 'No, take it home, madam, trust me – breasts and brassières are my business, my livelihood. You will be very happy with 36C. Bring it back if it doesn't fit, I will refund full purchase price plus ten per cent for inconvenience.'

"So I brought it home. And would you believe it? The fellow was right, 36C fit me like my own skin!"

Now she abandoned the dramatic stance and tone adopted to act out the dream. "You follow, Yezadji? Today's Matka is thirty-six – three for opening, six for closing."

Yezad took out his wallet and gave her ten rupees. "Can you put this on thirty-six for me?"

"What time is it? Oh dear, I'll have to hurry."

She ran into the next room and came back with a faded yellow chiffon sari, proceeding to wrap it over the housecoat. "Now where are my safety pins? Help me with them, Yezadji. Shoulder, waist, here at the back. And this one I'll pin over my stomach. There. Thank you, my dear."

"You're welcome."

She examined herself in the mirror, front and profile, and was satisfied. "If I'm in time, you'll get eight hundred and ten rupees for your ten."

"When do we know the result?"

"Closing is declared at twelve o'clock. You'll come?"

"I'll wait for morning. Good night." Over his shoulder he added, "Sweet dreams."

∿

Two hours after the lights were switched off, Jehangir was still tossing, unable to fall asleep. The boards under the mattress creaked with every move. He worried his mother might come to check. Haunted by the unhappiness that had appeared like an ugly creature to live in their home, he clenched his fists and tried hard not to cry.

He thought about his father's anger – not the flash that would blaze now and again, like thunder and lightning, then clear, and bring back a smile like sunshine. This dull rage, constant over days, was different.

The last few weeks puzzled him. It was quarrels and sarcastic comments all the time. Gone away completely was his parents' tenderness, and the happy looks they used to exchange in secret (not secret from him, though, he saw everything). The pleasant whispers and soft laughter from their bed at night would put him to sleep like a lullaby, assuring him all was right with his world. Now it was falling part. Angry hisses and harsh mutterings from their room made him cry in the dark.

If only he could earn some money for Mummy-Daddy. Like the Famous Five and the Secret Seven, who did chores and went on errands. They didn't even need the money for something important like he did, they just bought liquorice and humbugs. And ice cream, which they called ices. It was all so unfair, his life was never going to be fun like theirs, none of them had a sick Grandpa who needed lots of expensive medicines. The fighting between Mummy and Daddy was all Grandpa's fault.

Jehangir looked across at the settee and wondered if his grandfather was asleep or his eyes were just closed. He could hear him breathe, the tremble of his limbs had abated. His medicine bottles were on the table. Jehangir had made it his duty to bring the pills to his grandfather with a glass of water. Sometimes Grandpa choked, and Jehangir flinched in empathy as the pills were coughed out, then wiped the water sputtering down his chin and neck, coaxing him to take a deep breath ("in and out, Grandpa, in and out") and try again, slowly, with more water.

What did Grandpa think about, alone all day in bed, never complaining? Jal Uncle and Coomy Aunty's unkindness? Maybe he worried about where he would go if Daddy got fed up and told him to leave. Poor Grandpa, so old and weak, and all the pains in his body that made him wince and moan, though he kept it hidden (but not from him, for he saw everything).

Jehangir began crying again, his brief resentment turning to sorrow. He had heard Dr. Tarapore talk to Mummy in secret, that Grandpa would get worse, there was no cure, it would be harder and harder for him to use his arms and legs. "Locomotion will be increasingly difficult," the doctor had said.

His tears caused the darkness to become blurry. He hadn't realized nighttime could be just as vivid as daytime, and as liable to distortion. Maybe he could earn some money by offering to work for Villie Aunty, any small jobs. And for Daisy Aunty downstairs. Murad might go with him. The two of them together could do big jobs and earn even more.

In the cradle of this comforting thought, he fell asleep at last. He dreamt that Grandpa was on his crutches, swinging along briskly, and everyone was applauding him. But then he began to slow down, something was wrong with one of the pair. When he got to the kitchen he discovered that the upper half of the crutch had turned into a huge joint of mutton. Daddy took the big knife from the drawer and started sharpening it, to cut the meat and cook it, but Mummy said no, how would Pappa be able to walk without it? And soon there was another terrible fight, shouting and yelling, till Grandpa said it was okay, he could manage. Relinquishing the mutton joint for Daddy and Murad, whose mouth was watering, Grandpa demonstrated with the single crutch and almost crashed to the floor. Mummy screamed at Daddy that he was going to kill her poor father in his greed for mutton; besides, so much red meat would increase his cholesterol and leave her a widow with two young boys to look after . . .

Jehangir woke with a start. He sat up, and the cot gave out a loud creak.

"What's wrong?" whispered Nariman.

"Your crutch, Grandpa, I had a dream it was spoilt . . ."

"My crutch is all right. Come, hold my hand and sleep."

Jehangir groped across the space between the settee and the cot to take his grandfather's hand, and was soon sound asleep. He did not dream again that night.

"WAIT," CALLED ROXANA, and ran to the door for the bye-bye kiss, but her husband had already disappeared down the stairs. Yet another morning, she thought, which had failed to work its healing magic on him.

Yezad reached the second-floor landing, heard the door close, and waited. Now with the sunlight bathing the stair-case, he felt he had been very foolish last night. Giving Villie ten rupees to bet on her dream bra size – money as good as thrown in the dustbin.

Through the stairwell soared Daisy Ichhaporia's violin music, accompanying his return to the third floor. He knocked, Villie's eye came to the peephole, he put his finger to his lips. She opened and beckoned him inside. Her house-coated figure was swaying romantically to the violin, which made him thankful that the music was part of a sedate second movement, not something wild and fiery like a czardas.

Still moving with the melody, she thrust her hand down her front and extracted a roll of notes. Grabbing his wrist, she smacked the money into his palm. "There you are, my dear. Eight hundred and ten rupees. Count it, go on."

He stared at it, incredulous. Then he greedily unrolled the notes still warm from her bosom. "This is fantastic. Beginner's luck, I guess."

"What do you mean, beginner?" she was indignant. "I've been dreaming since I was a little girl."

He walked to the station feeling depressed despite the win, thinking about Villie's lonely, stunted life. But her size 36C had certainly delivered the Matka. Coincidence? Or had she predicted the future? And if dreams could do that . . . no more worry and anxiety. The worst news, foreknown, would lose its sting. Of course, the pleasure of any good news would diminish as well. But that was a price he was willing to pay.

Tonight, he would secretly distribute a hundred rupees in Roxana's envelopes. Then another hundred the next week, and the next . . . and if she noticed, he'd say, Surprise! Extra commission from Mr. Kapur.

∽

On the way to the Irani restaurant for their afternoon tea break, Vilas pointed to Mr. Kapur's Divali display: "Very dramatic." Cardboard cutouts of Ram and Sita stood in a circle of oil lamps. Prone at their feet was the ten-headed, twenty-armed demon king Ravan.

"Looks like Ram and Sita are visiting the raakshas in hospital," said Yezad.

"Mr. Kapur didn't have it last year, did he?"

"No. But he's decided to celebrate every festival from now on. He's looking forward to Christmas. Watch out for even more dramatic windows."

"Speaking of drama," said Vilas, "two chaps from my amateur society are dropping by to say hello."

In the restaurant he and Yezad skirted a mess of spills and overturned chairs by the entrance. Behind the counter stood Merwan Irani, huge and rotund at the open till. He was sorting notes into their denominations. His florid countenance, shiny with sweat, turned to greet them.

"What happened here?" asked Yezad. "Fight?"

Merwan Irani explained that a scuffle had broken out with a customer: "Saalo maaderchod came in like a king, sat down, and ordered tea with bun-muskaa, extra butter and all. With loud busy teeth, batchar-batchar, the bastard ate everything, happy as a goat in a garbage dump, and gurgled down his tea. When he got the bill he said, Sorry, no money. My waiter thought he was joking. But the bhonsrino kept refusing to pay."

That was when the waiter pushed him and the fight began. Eventually, three waiters held the man down while Merwan himself went through the man's pockets. "But I found nothing except a snot-filled handkerchief. Absolute karko, not one paiso. He said he had no money, but was hungry – just imagine the maaderchod's courage."

"At least he was honest," said Vilas.

"Aray, bugger the mother of honesty! Half this country is hungry. If they all behave like this chootiya, how will I survive? I gave him one solid backhand chamaat."

He raised his hand to demonstrate, and they glanced at the beefy palm, the pudgy fingers like sausages, and felt pity for the poor victim.

"No point calling police," continued Merwan. "They would just thrash him and let him go." But he had had a word of advice for the man before sending him on his way: it would be wiser to steal an apple or banana in the bazaar and run away.

The man said that was what he usually did, but today being the tenth anniversary of his college graduation, he'd felt a yearning for tea and bun-muskaa, which he and his friends used to enjoy in those happy days. Then he tucked his shirt neatly back into his pants, combed his hair, tied his shoelaces, and shook hands with Merwan. They had parted quite amicably.

"What makes me sad is that a college graduate cannot find a job," said Merwan.

"Very common," said Vilas. "Ordinary B.A. or B.Sc. is no good," said Vilas. "Only ones making money are computer people."

"I've heard about highway robbery, home invasion, break-and-enter," said Merwan. "Never seen a tea and bun-muskaa burglary. What times have come."

They laughed and went to their table in the rear. At the kitchen door the waiter held up two fingers to confirm their usual two cups; they nodded. Just then, Vilas's friends appeared at the entrance. He waved them over, and raised four fingers for the waiter as he introduced Gautam and Bhaskar to Yezad.

They shook hands and pulled up chairs. Bhaskar wore round, steel-rimmed Gandhi glasses, and both had khadi satchels slung over their shoulders. The satchels were as voguishly patched as their jeans, and gashes in the homespun revealed tantalizing glimpses of the books and magazines within, while scrupulous rips in the denim exposed selected areas of skin.

The tea arrived. "My treat today," said Yezad, and turned to the waiter, "Suno, bhai, four mutton patties and one plate wafers."

Vilas brought his face closer to whisper, "Why are you spending? You've got money problems, with your father-in-law."

"It's okay, I won some cash in Matka today."

"Really? I didn't know you played Matka."

"My first time. This Matka Queen lives next door, she is a powerful dreamer. She put the bet for me."

"Beginner's luck," said Vilas. "Save the money and don't play any more."

Gautam said for most people Matka was a harmless bit of fun, like buying a lottery ticket. "Basically, however, it's a criminal scourge that has Bombay helpless in its grip."

The waiter returned with the order of patties and wafers. Yezad chuckled. "Come on. You make it sound like the Cosa Nostra is running Bombay."

"Basically, Cosa Nostra are babes in the wood, compared with these Bombay gangs," said Gautam. "With all due respect, you have no idea what you are talking about."

"Excuse me," said Yezad, taken aback by this fusillade from someone he'd just met.

Bhaskar intervened, "You see, we're journalists, and Gautam did a story recently about Matka. An in-depth analysis about the politician-criminal-police nexus. Shiv Sena was also mentioned in his article, and they didn't like it. Last week, some of their goondas caught him outside the office."

"They blackened my face," said Gautam matter-of-factly, biting into one of the mutton patties.

"What did they do, abuse and threaten?" asked Vilas.

"I was not speaking in metaphor."

"You mean they actually . . . ?"

"Yes." Gautam described how a dozen of them had accosted him, screaming that journalists who maligned the Shiv Sena and blackened its good name by printing lies would receive the same treatment. The men twisted his arms behind him and grabbed his hair to keep him still. They had a tin of Cherry Blossom black shoe polish, and applied it to his face and ears and neck, even ruining his shirt in the process.

"Gautam looked like Al Jolson when they finished," said Bhaskar, and Yezad and Vilas laughed.

"It's not a laughing matter," glared the journalist. "My eyes and skin were burning, I had to rush to a doctor. And to remove all the polish took so much scrubbing, my face is still sore."

"Those people are absolutely lawless," said Yezad. He thought he could see a black spot beside the Adam's apple, and wondered if it was a bit of leftover Cherry Blossom or just a skin blemish.

"I bet you," said Vilas, "whichever shakha those Shiv Sainiks came from, the police chowki in their neighbourhood knows exactly who they are."

"One thing is certain," said Bhaskar, "the article hit a nerve. People think it's not so bad when Shiv Sena extorts money from rich businessmen – 'donations' for their 'charity' work. But Matka also finances Shiv Sena machinery. And Matka money paid for the plastic explosives with which the terrorists blew up the stock exchange. You see the paradox? The enemies of the nation, and political parties that claim to be defenders of the nation, all rely on the same source."

"Problem is," said Vilas, "so do millions of ordinary people. The numbers they bet each night give them reason to wake up next morning. In some ways Matka is Bombay and Bombay is Matka."

"Sounds profound but makes no sense," said Gautam. "Those who play it should know they're supporting a criminal enterprise."

"I guess this was my first and last time," said Yezad.

As Gautam nodded approval, raising his patty for another bite, Vilas arrested his wrist: "Matka money is paying for that."

"I know. But wasting it won't prevent illegal activity. In fact, throwing away something so delicious will compound the felony."

They laughed, and munched the crisp wafers. Then Bhaskar said it had been a long time since Vilas had written for their amateur drama society, and surely there was plenty of raw material collected in the course of his scribal work.

"Actually, I read a letter this morning which could be a full-length tragedy," said Vilas. "Came from the man's village in Uttar Pradesh. It was regarding his younger brother."

He summarized the contents penned by the village scribe: the younger brother had been spending time with a girl from a higher caste, and this had annoyed people in the village, especially the girl's relatives. Both had been told to stop. As a warning, some men from the girl's family had assaulted the young man, which only made the couple more defiant.

One evening the two were found in each other's arms. The men tore the lovers apart, beat them, pulled out their hair, ripped their clothes off. An urgent meeting of the village panchayat was called. The couple, bruised and bleeding, was brought before them.

The boy's family said if their son had committed a crime, the police could register a complaint. The girl's family argued it was a village matter, requiring the traditional punishment. The panchayat agreed. A decision was rendered in minutes: hanging, for both, after slicing off their ears and noses.

The boy's father went on his knees before the panchayat and wept for mercy, suggesting a compromise: remove the ears and nose, but let his son live. They said no, the offence was too serious, leniency would only encourage more bad behaviour from youngsters.

In the eyes of the panchayat, both families were aggrieved parties. Thus, the girl's father had the privilege of hacking off the boy's ears and nose; the boy's father was offered the girl's face to disfigure. He refused, so the girl's father performed his daughter's amputations as well, prior to the hanging.

"A very sad story," said Gautam. "But it wouldn't be suitable for us."

"Why not?"

"We need urban themes. Basically, our mandate is to awaken the urban poor to their plight."

"And there are problems with this story," said Bhaskar. "If it's a tragedy, who is the tragic hero, what is his fatal flaw, his hamartia? And what about the audience, what form will their catharsis take? These questions have to be considered."

Vilas rolled his eyes at Yezad. "Look, the audience will feel compassion for the two young people, and outrage towards the barbarians and the caste system. Isn't that enough?"

The journalists shook their heads with wise smiles.

"Wouldn't work, trust me," said Bhaskar. "We want you to write something about Shiv Sena. They are our greatest urban menace."

"But don't mention them directly," said Gautam. "Or they'll burn down the hall where we meet."

"Try an allegorical style," said Bhaskar. "Perhaps write in the form of a fable."

Yezad played with the salt-cellar, sliding it about the table. "What about the boy's parents? They must have gone to the police."

Already irritated by the two journalists, Vilas pounced upon Yezad: "You sound like a foreign tourist talking about law and order, and democracy. You know perfectly well in this country how things—"

"You're right," said Yezad, feeling foolish. "It's just that when you hear such terrible things . . ."

"Yes," said Vilas. "When people feel helpless, they say things to make themselves feel better. Or they deny the injustice."

"Isolated incidents, they call them," said Gautam.

"Exactly," said Bhaskar. "They say that our nation has made so much progress – satellite TV, they say, Internet, e-mail, best software designers in the world."

Gautam chuckled. "Hamaara Bharat Mahaan, they repeat like that government slogan," and they laughed.

"Let me give you an example," said Vilas. "A while back, I read a novel about the Emergency. A big book, full of horrors, real as life. But also full of life, and the laughter and dignity of ordinary people. One hundred per cent honest – made me laugh and cry as I read it. But some reviewers said no, no, things were not that bad. Especially foreign critics. You know how they come here for two weeks and become experts. One poor woman whose name I can't remember made such a hash of it, she had to be a bit pagal, defending Indira, defending the Sanjay sterilization scheme, defending the entire Emergency – you felt sorry for her even though she was a big professor at some big university in England. What to do? People are afraid to accept the truth. As T. S. Eliot wrote, 'Human kind cannot bear very much reality.'"

He looked at his watch, started at the time, and gulped down his tea. He and Yezad rose to return to work.

"Nice meeting you, Yezad," said the two young men. "Keep in touch, Vilas, write something for us, promise?"

While Yezad was settling the bill, from the kitchen came a loud crash of crockery. Voices began yelling in a cacophony of blame. Merwan Irani flung the change at him, locked the till, and scampered to the rear as fast as his bulk would permit, his massive hands and forearms hanging motionless at his side.

Like a moving mutton stall, thought Yezad.

"Poor fellow," said Vilas. "He's not having a happy day." Outside, he continued, "You see what I mean about these actors? Too pseudo for me. They become blind to real life with their intellectualizing. Stanislavsky-this and Strasberg-that, and Brechtian alienation is all they talk about."

Still unsettled by the story of the hanged couple, Yezad asked if he had written a reply for the client. Vilas shook his head, the poor man was in shock. "I tried to return the reading fee he had paid in advance. How could I take money and give such news? But he did not want to cheapen his brother's death, he said, by hearing it for free. He wanted to go back to his village, avenge his brother. Poor fellow. How to tell him life is not an Amitabh Bachchan movie? That justice is a mirage?"

"What did you advise?"

"To write to his family, to share his grief and anger. What else?" Vilas sighed. "It's one thing to read about this type of incident in a newspaper, but can you imagine the man sitting next to me, both of us unsuspecting, and I open the letter containing the murder of his younger brother?"

"Like a doctor whose patient is terminal," said Yezad.

"Worse. The doctor can at least prepare his patient and the family. But when I am handed a letter, I don't know what is in it. My eyes see the words, my mouth utters them, and there is nothing I can do except keep reading."

"You could pause and first offer some comfort: sorry, it's bad news, please brace yourself. Warn him like a doctor."

"There's a big difference, Yezad. When a doctor does it, he is not violating the Hippocratic oath. In fact, kindness and compassion is a good doctor's obligation. But were I to soften the news, break it gradually, it would be a betrayal of trust."

"Oh, come on – kindness is betrayal?"

Trying to make him understand, Vilas spoke with great fervour: "When a client places a letter in my hands, it's a sacred trust. I pledge to read the words for him in the way they would be consumed by his own eyes – if he could read. That's the inviolable contract: not one word added or omitted or delayed."

"You're taking it too seriously. At most, it's like a little white lie."

"Some things can only be taken seriously!" Vilas's voice rose, and people passing assumed the two were quarrelling. "Little white lies are as pernicious as big black lies. When they mix together, a great greyness of ambiguity descends, society is cast adrift in an amoral sea, and corruption and rot and decay start to flourish. Such is the time we are now passing through. Everything is disintegrating because details are neglected and nothing is regarded seriously."

Out of breath, Vilas realized he was overwrought. "Sorry, Yezad, you must think I'm obsessed with my letters. You have enough problems of your own without listening to my extended family tragedies."

"It's okay, they make my problems small by contrast."

"Yes, but only for now. Once evening comes and you go home to your father-in-law's agony, your struggling wife, and your children without the things you want for them, your burdens will become huge again. The suffering world will be no comfort."

"Thanks, that's very cheering."

"So will you play Matka again?"

Yezad frowned, and shrugged. "I would prefer not to. If my salary goes up, I don't need the Matka Queen."

"You just need patience, my friend. Patience is within you, rupees are without you. And you are without rupees." He laughed. "Good one, hanh?"

"Very funny. Within or without, intelligent people should know how to make money when they need it."

"But you are not qualified, in this culture of crookedness."

"Why not?"

"Because of your upbringing, your belief in integrity and fair play."

"You sound like Mr. Kapur, his nonsense about Parsi honesty."

"Not nonsense. Myths create the reality. Point is, there was a time when living according to certain myths served your community well. With the present state of society, those same myths can make misfits of men. Even the British knew when to observe their myth of 'not cricket, old chap' and when to hit below the belt, kick you in the balls, poke you in the eyes."

They laughed, and Vilas continued, "Of course, now they'll have to invent a new expression because cricket itself is not cricket – just another crooked business, with bookies and bribes and match-fixers who break the cricket-loving hearts of us subcontinentals."

"So you're advising me to become crooked as well?"

Vilas smiled and shook his head. "You won't be able to. Try it if you like – you'll always be a cricketer."

All the cricket talk made Yezad think of the times when he and Nariman used to go to the first-class fixtures at Wankhede Stadium. A genuine fan, the chief, didn't miss a single Test or the Ranji Trophy. Such a treat to sit with him, listen to him describe the greats of the past, the giants he'd seen in action at the old Brabourne Stadium, people like Lala Amarnath and C. K. Nayadu and Vijay Merchant and Polly Umrigar . . .

The memories of those days filled Yezad with a deep sadness – Nariman was now lying helpless in bed. And not even his own bed.

How time passed and changed things. For himself too, the years were slipping away – nothing but the interminable tedium of one pointless day after another . . . was this all his life was ever going to be? Forty-three, and what had he accomplished? Couldn't even get to bloody Canada for a fresh start . . . and the children growing up so fast – what did he have to offer them? Nothing.

He said goodbye to Vilas, entered the shop, and returned to his chair. Slouching over the desk, his chin in his hand, he gazed out the window at the traffic in its usual, vicious snarl, the cars and buses venting aggression along with their exhaust fumes as they made their crawling way towards Dhobi Talao junction.

He was glad when Husain came up and distracted him, asking if he'd like some chai.

10

After brooding over it for two days, Jehangir shared his plan with his brother on the way to school.

Murad said first of all the neighbours wouldn't give them any jobs, and even if they did, they would pay so little, it would make no difference to Mummy-Daddy's money problems.

"How do you know how much they will pay?"

"Because. Haven't you heard them arguing with servants, and the way they treat them?"

"They wouldn't do that with us."

"They'd be worse, because we're children."

Jehangir suggested another scheme: selling their storybooks to friends at school.

"Where do you get these brainwaves? We'll make hardly anything – much less than what they cost. Mummy-Daddy will get angry for wasting their money. Anyway, we need hundreds and hundreds of rupees for Grandpa."

They parted at the school gate, and Murad disappeared in the sea of beige uniforms that covered the quadrangle. Dejected, Jehangir lingered by himself, racking his brains for a solution till the first bell rang, then trudged up the stairs, weighed down as much by his worries as by his school bag. Someone came bounding up behind him and thumped his back.

"Hi, Milind."

"Match today," said Milind. "I hope you remembered. Catholics versus non-Catholics." He brandished his cricket bat, which was the non-Catholic bat; the other team would bring its own. And the stumps, represented by chalk lines on a tree in the playground, would be ecumenical.

Milind's trouser pocket bulged with a tennis ball for the match. Cricket balls were prohibited, considered too hard and dangerous for the playground. He recited the names on the Catholic and non-Catholic teams, keeping his voice to a whisper; St. Xavier's did not approve of such divisions in the student body, not even for cricket.

At the start of the school year the matter was addressed during assembly. "Many years ago," said Father D'Silva, "when the game was becoming widely known in our country, the Bombay Pentangular Tournament was inaugurated, in which teams of Hindus, Muslims, Parsis, and Europeans, plus a fifth one, called the Rest, played for the championship. But it was a cause of great sadness for Mahatma Gandhi. He said that in work and in play, we, the children of Mother India, must be as one family in order to free her from the chains in which she was enslaved. He grieved and fasted, met with team captains and coaches, impressed them with his knowledge of batting, bowling, and field placements, and convinced them of the need for team spirit and unity. Under his guidance the Pentangular was abolished – there would be no more cricket based on religious or ethnic divisions.

"Remember, boys, in this great school of ours we strive to follow the advice of the Father of Our Nation. We must not think of ourselves as Catholic or non-Catholic, for we are all children of this gracious and loving Alma Mater who makes no distinction of caste or creed."

Attentive during assembly, the students promptly forgot Father D'Silva's exhortations on the playground. As far as they were concerned, there was nothing sectarian about their game, and their method was one way to organize the teams. Last week it was Vegetarians versus Non-Vegetarians. They had also played Oiled Hair versus Un-Oiled, and Starched Uniforms versus Un-Starched. Nonetheless, the school was always on its guard against the slightest whiff of communalism, and especially so after the Babri Mosque riots.

Thus Milind was careful not to disturb the secular corridor where Father D'Silva was always on the prowl, and whispered the teams in his friend's ear. Jehangir liked the names on the Catholic team: Henry, George, Francis, William, Philip. They sounded like the names in Enid Blyton's stories. Although the surnames were D'Souza and Fernandes and D'Mello, not at all like the surnames of the Famous Five or the Five Find-Outers. He wished he could change his own name. Jehangir, Jehangla, Jehangoo. Could be shortened to Jehan. Which was a lot like John. John Chenoy. He liked the sound of it, drawing him one step closer to the lovely world of those books.

"We'll start the match in the short recess," said Milind, who was captain of Non-Catholics. "I'll put Rajesh in the extras and get you in the team."

"I'm not feeling well," said Jehangir.

"Come on, yaar, you never play with us."

The second bell rang. Anxious to get to his seat, Jehangir promised to join them if he felt better by short recess. Unlike his brother, he was not keen on sports. He followed the cricket scores and listened to commentaries, but that was all.

The third bell tolled the start of the school day, the peals escorting Miss Helen Alvarez into her classroom. Sixty-one pairs of shoes shuffled, desks creaked, and benches groaned as the class rose: "Good mor-ning, Tea-cher!"

"Good morning, boys. Please take your seats."

Once more the shuffle and rumble swept the room as they did her bidding. Most of them had lost their hearts to her, for Helen Alvarez was pretty, and fragrant with perfume. A petite Goan in her twenties, she had prominent cheekbones and a button nose. She was always smartly dressed, wore high heels, and kept in step with fashion. This year, because hemlines were rising, the boys' pulses also rose quite often, especially when she ascended the two steps to the platform, settled in her chair, and crossed her incredibly smooth legs.

The straight-backed chair had a cane seat. If Miss Alvarez stood up after sitting for a few minutes, the pattern of the weave was impressed upon her tight skirt. This made the boys feel she was sharing an intimate secret with them. They wondered if the geometric design went deep enough to leave its imprint on her lovely bum.

Jehangir feasted his eyes shyly on Miss Alvarez's charms. He adored her, and it upset him when some of the fellows, latching on to her first name, likened her to the Helen of the old Hindi movies, the actress in revealing outfits, with whom they were familiar because of the videos their parents rented to indulge their 1960s nostalgia. The Hindi-movie Helen was always cast as the vamp, the seductress who performed sexy cabaret numbers to entice the hero away from his one true love. Though the hero sometimes faltered, he always renounced Helen before the movie ended, returning safely to the arms of his virginal heroine.

For Jehangir, however, Helen the teacher was the virginal heroine. He felt angry when the boys spoke of Miss Alvarez in crude ways. But he held his tongue, or life at school would have become intolerable with teasing. To be one of the three Homework Monitors appointed by Miss Alvarez was difficult enough.

Homework Monitoring was Miss Alvarez's pet project, her system of having assignments checked by the pupils' peers. The goal, she said, was to inculcate the qualities of trust, honesty, and integrity in her students. She told them the classroom was a miniature model of society and the nation. Like any society, it must have its institutions of law and order, its police and judiciary. And it could be a just and prosperous society only when the citizens and the guardians of law and order respected and trusted one another.

"If you are good citizens of my classroom," said Miss Alvarez, "you will be good citizens of India." She believed this was the way to fight the backwardness and rot and corruption in the country: classroom by classroom.

Back in June, as she was explaining her homework system at the start of the school year, Jehangir had been deeply moved, for he related her words to the things he overheard when Daddy and Grandpa and Jal Uncle discussed politics: about poor people in a village in Bihar who'd died of hunger because money for food and irrigation went straight into the pockets of corrupt district officials; about the four hundred and fifty children crushed to death while attending a school function because the contractor who built the hall had cheated on the cement; and about the dozens who were burnt alive in a fire at a cinema without a sprinkler system because the owner had bribed the safety inspector to give him a false certificate.

Yes, thought Jehangir earnestly, his heart beating with ardour and enthusiasm, yes, he would help Miss Alvarez fight corruption and save lives, he would make things better for everyone in the country. He resolved to be the best Homework Monitor possible, hard-working and impartial and scrupulous.

The thoroughness with which he approached his duties at once made him unpopular with the habitual offenders. They badgered him for leniency, they cajoled and intimidated, promised friendship and threatened enmity. Resisting them endlessly was hard. Sometimes he wavered: would it hurt to let Arvind off for getting the East India Company's dates wrong, to overlook Vasant's incomplete arithmetic, to ignore Anthony's muddled précis?

Then he would glance at Miss Alvarez on the platform with her kind eyes and silken legs, and, like the hero of Helen's Hindi movies, his sinews would be stiffened afresh, the vamp of temptation shaken off. Summoning up the blood, he would make an honest entry in the Homework Register.

Now five months into the school year, he was more at ease with his role, inured to his classmates' blandishments and insults. It was poetry homework day, and next in line was Ashok's desk. He sat beside him, made him shut the book and recite.

"Hey, sala Jehangir," he was softly menacing, "be nice to me, I'm warning you."

Miss Alvarez called Ashok a Perpetual Problem, and periodically sent notes to his parents. They owned textile showrooms, a Maruti dealership, and three petrol pumps, and regarded the teacher's notes with grave concern, but Ashok's punishments at home did not improve his performance in class.

"Ready?" asked Jehangir.

"'Break, Break, Break' by Lord Alfred Tennyson," said Ashok.

"Alfred, Lord Tennyson."

"How can that be, yaar? Alfred is his name, the surname is Tennyson. Do you say Jehangir Mr. Chenoy or Mr. Jehangir Chenoy?"

Jehangir decided to let it pass. Miss Alvarez had decreed that sixteen lines of the poem be memorized; the poet's name wasn't part of the homework, strictly speaking.

Ashok started, "'Break, break, break, break—'"

"Only three breaks."

"Ya, ya, I know. The extra break is for your head, if you act smart." He sniggered at his cleverness in covering the error. "I'm warning you, don't count that as a mistake, it was a joke."

Jehangir gave him the benefit of the doubt.

"'Break, break, break,'" Ashok started again. "'On thy cold—'" he paused, "wait, don't tell me, I know it. 'On thy cold, grey stones, O Sea! And I' – umm – it's something about my tongue, my tongue something something—"

"Give up?"

Ashok refused; Miss Alvarez's rule permitted three prompts, and he didn't want one so early in the poem. He gave his head a vigorous scratching, started again, and stalled at the same place, glowering at the Homework Monitor: "What's the line?"

"'And I would that my tongue could utter—'"

"I knew it, I said tongue. 'And I would that my tongue could utter,'" clearing his throat, he went for the stanza's last line: "'The thoughts that arise.' Okay? Second verse?"

"First one isn't complete."

"What? 'The thoughts that arise' – that's the last line."

"'The thoughts that arise in me.' Second mistake."

Ashok wrung his hands and pleaded to let it go, but Jehangir would not relent.

The next quatrain went at breakneck speed: "'O, well for the fisherman's boy, / That he shouts with his sister at play! / O, well for the sailor lad, / That he sings in his boat on the bay!'"

"Good," said Jehangir, hoping the Perpetual Problem would make it this time.

"'And the stately ships go on, / To their heaven under the hill.'"

"Haven, not heaven."

"What's the difference? Heaven, haven, same thing, yaar. Please don't," he begged, as the Homework Register was opened. "Please, I'll get into big trouble with my parents."

Jehangir prepared to make the entry. "I can't help it, Miss Alvarez said—"

"Wait a second." Ashok put his hand in his pocket and fished something out. "Here," he pulled Jehangir's hand under the desk.

It was ten rupees. Jehangir shoved the note back as though it had burned his palm.

"It's for you," pleaded Ashok. "Just mark me correct."

Jehangir refused.

Ashok visited his pocket again and added another note to the first. He thrust them both at the Homework Monitor.

Twenty rupees! This time, Jehangir paused to examine the money before pushing back the crumpled notes. "No."

"Keep it, yaar, it's a gift. No one will know. I won't even tell my best friends." He pressed the cash on him again.

Jehangir hesitated. "You'll tell Vijay and Rajesh," he said, knowing the three were inseparable.

"Not even them."

He looked once more at Ashok's money. A small packet of

butter. Or mutton for one meal. Or a week of eggs for Daddy's breakfast. That's what he was holding in his hand.

His heart pounding, he put a tick beside Ashok's name and pocketed the money. His head swam with the enormity of what he had just done.

By the end of the school day the weight of the clandestine transaction had quite disappeared, replaced by another burden: spending the money. If he bought food, they would ask how he had paid for it. Giving the money to Mummy meant the same problem. He could say he found it in the quadrangle. But they would insist he turn it over to Brother Navarro in the Lost Property Office.

On the bus he touched the cash in his pocket. Once he figured out a way to use it, things would heal between Mummy and Daddy. He could add to this money by doing chores for Villie Aunty. Never mind if Murad didn't want to join in the plan.

Gazing out the bus window, he dreamt of happiness returning to their home. Then the bus turned the traffic circle, and on the footpath he saw someone exactly like his brother. His eyes lost him in the crowd, found him again, confirmed it was Murad. Why was he walking home? What had he done with his bus fare?

He kept wondering till the bus neared Pleasant Villa and stopped at the corner. He jumped off, his hand returning over and over to his pocket, fascinated by the power contained in pieces of paper. His confidence surged. He would go to Villie Aunty right now.

He knocked on her door.

"Hallo, my little Jehangirji, what a surprise. How are you?"

"Fine, Aunty."

"Any good dreams lately?"

He thought about the mutton-crutch dream. "No, Aunty."

"Does your mummy want something from the bazaar?"

"No, I was wondering . . . is there any work I can do for you, Aunty? You can pay me for it."

She clapped her hands with delight. "Tell me, does your mummy know you are doing this?"

"It's a secret."

She looked at him fondly. "Look, my dear, you can help, but I can't give you money. If your parents found out, they would say I was making a servant of their son."

"I wouldn't tell them," he protested.

"Helping people is good, my darling, but not for money."

Murad was right, she wanted to cheat him, make him work for free. "Thank you, Aunty," he muttered, and left.

Stupid Villie Aunty. And stupid Enid Blyton too. From now on, he wasn't going to believe a word in her books. And those silly Famous Five – he didn't need them for inspiration. He knew what to do, he'd make things better for Mummy and Daddy, all by himself. But he still preferred the sound of John Chenoy.

TOWARDS CLOSING TIME Mr. Kapur invited Yezad into his tiny office where the air-conditioner was at full blast, its roar blanketing them from the city outside. Must be how it feels in a jet plane, thought Yezad – removed from everything, far from the real world.

On the desk were three photographs in cellophane sleeves. Mr. Kapur turned them face down as Yezad entered. "I've a surprise for you."

"Those?" He reached for the black-and-white pictures.

"Hang on, you must see them in the right order. This one first."

Yezad broke into a grin. "Hey, it's a shot of Hughes Road. Where I grew up."

"Why do you think I brought it? And for your info, the name was changed to Sitaram Patkar Marg years ago."

"It'll always be Hughes Road for me."

Mr. Kapur smiled approvingly, and Yezad continued, "I can describe every detail here. This building – it's Jehangir Mansion, my parents moved there when they got married. I bet you the photo was taken from Sandhurst Bridge, from the roof of Dadajee Dhackjee. And opposite Jehangir Mansion is Sukh Sagar. Look, the Bush Radio signboard is also visible."

He paused. "Can't be a very old photo – looks the same as today."

"It's recent," said Mr. Kapur. "About 1990. Important for my collection, though, in the context of the other two."

He waited for him to hand it back so they could proceed to the next one. But Yezad continued to drink it all in. "Amazing, how a photo shows you things your eyes forgot to see."

"Especially in a familiar place," said Mr. Kapur. "The lens is our third eye."

The photograph, conjuring up the street for Yezad, let him hear the traffic, smell the meaty smoke that always hung outside the Sizzler, taste the bhel-puri. He could feel the tension in the picture's monsoon sky, the grey clouds reminding him of the many times he would get caught without a raincoat while coming back from college (only sissies wore raincoats, was the wisdom then), stepping off the number 83 bus outside Sukh Sagar, running across the road, home to Jehangir Mansion, soaked to the skin in less than a minute, and his mother scolding him for leaving behind the raincoat she had folded and placed with his books . . .

"Look at this one now," said Mr. Kapur.

Yezad let the first picture go. And a lump filled his throat as soon as he laid eyes on the next one. It was still Hughes Road, but pristine, from a simpler time. The photographer must have stood at the other end of Jehangir Mansion, outside Madon Chemists; the intersection of Hughes Road and Sandhurst Bridge was now the focal point. The light suggested early morning. Not a car in sight, the road deserted except for a handcart. Three lone figures stood on the footpath, mysterious, like seers or soothsayers prophesying the explosion of population in Bombay's future.

He swallowed to clear his throat. "When I was very small, this is how quiet the street was." He coughed. "What year is it?"

"From the Buick sign outside Metro Motors, I'd guess late 1940s," said Mr. Kapur. "Maybe five years before you were born?"

"That's around the time my parents got married," said Yezad. "So this is the street they saw after their wedding."

In the dawn light, the buildings and trees waited like childhood friends to whisk him back. And the old street lamps, strung over the centre of the road. He'd forgotten how charming they were, almost ornamental, unlike the towering steel of the new lights. He kept gazing into the photograph, and a little boy appeared with his father outside Madon Chemists . . . and when the school bus rolled into view his father gave him a final hug before parting for the day . . . Then it was late afternoon, the bus brought him back hungry for his tea, eager to play in the compound before homework time commenced . . . and there was his mother at the bus stop, to take his hand, take him safely across the road where half-a-dozen cars might pass every so often . . .

He ran his fingers over his eyes, and the ghosts receded. "It's like magic, this picture. Capturing time . . ."

"Last one," said Mr. Kapur, passing it across the desk.

Yezad was almost afraid to take it. But he looked, and was relieved – just some scenery. He wondered why Mr. Kapur was showing him a photo of coconut trees growing alongside a road. Then he saw the cast-iron railing, and his eyes widened.

He recognized the intricate railing that hugged the curve of Sandhurst Bridge where Hughes Road joined it. But there was no Jehangir Mansion, no Sukh Sagar, no Metro Motors. Where these buildings would later stand, there were coconut palms, some arching over the road, some growing straight to the sky. And beyond them, the sea.

He shivered, unable to understand his emotions – the picture, empty of his beloved landmarks, should have meant nothing more than a scenic postcard.

"You're feeling cold," said Mr. Kapur, and went around his desk to the air-conditioner. There was a click; the roar disappeared. The silence seemed eternal in its suddenness, vast, empty as space.

Yezad asked softly what year it was in this picture.

Turning from the control panel, Mr. Kapur put his hand on his shoulder. "It's 1908. The year Hughes Road was constructed."

Yezad nodded, not trusting his voice. He tried to blink the blurring image into focus.

"This is terrible," said Mr. Kapur. "I brought the photos to cheer you up because you've been looking depressed lately." He threatened to take them away if they were upsetting him.

"I'm not upset, they're amazing pictures, it's just that . . ."

"I know, I'm only joking." He patted Yezad's shoulder and returned to his chair.

"This railing," said Yezad, "it's not very clear in the photo."

Mr. Kapur took a magnifying glass out of his drawer. "A beautiful example of cast-iron workmanship. Very ornate. I like the standards rising like minarets at each span."

Yezad pored over the prints through the lens, crossing the breadth of Jehangir Mansion, stone by stone, pointing out details for Mr. Kapur. "Before the road-widening, this wall used to be much farther away from the building. So we had a nice big compound."

And the boys who lived in the building were the kings of the compound, driving the ground-floor tenants to despair with their games and noise. Usually it was cricket, which reached a frenzy when England or Australia were visiting for a Test series. But in 1960, during the Rome Olympics, they had abandoned cricket for a while and all of them pretended to be Milkha Singh running the four hundred metres. They'd measured the compound to calculate the number of laps required, and wished they had long hair like the Sikh's, which they could tie in a topknot, and a beard whose wisps could flutter as they blazed around the track like the Flying Sardar.

Mr. Kapur laughed to hear how some of them had tried, without much success, to simulate Milkha Singh's topknot: stuffing kerchiefs with paper and fixing them with rubber bands to their heads. But the bands kept snapping off when they ran.

Yezad began to indicate the various flats, who lived where, then stopped. "I'm boring you with all this stuff."

"On the contrary," said Mr. Kapur, who seemed to be relishing the flood of memories released by his photographs. "It sounds like Jehangir Mansion was a Parsi Baag."

"It wasn't. This ground-floor flat had a Muslim family. Shahrukh's family. His father drove a taxi, and sometimes he would pack six or seven of us in his Hillman and take us to school."

"And Shahrukh was also part of your crowd?"

"Oh yes, absolutely. But," he admitted after a pause, "you know how boys fight. And if sometimes there was an argument – whether someone was l.b.w., for example – when Shahrukh disagreed, we used to say to him, go to Pakistan if you don't like it. And we teased him about his circumcision, calling him an ABC, you know, Adha Boolla Catayla."

Yezad shook his head with remorse. "When I dream about my childhood, I wake up wishing I could find Shahrukh, tell him I'm sorry. The sad part was, later the family did go away, to Pakistan, where they had relatives. We all felt guilty afterwards."

He put down the photograph and picked up the earliest one again, when the street was only palm trees. "You said this was 19-what?"

"1908."

"It's like seeing the first morning of Hughes Road," he said reverently. "And this perfect railing – it fascinated me. How I loved to touch its circles, its volutes and spheres. Whenever I was out with my father, he let me climb on the parapet where the railing was bolted. I loved to swing along hugging the railing, and he kept his arm ready near my waist, just in case, till we came to the end where I jumped down to the footpath. We did the same on the way home. To see the railing was to know you were home. From Opera House, nearing the corner, there it was to greet you as the bridge was crested."

"Why was the railing so important?"

"I don't know," said Yezad. "Maybe it was the only thing of beauty in our lives. I remember, on some nights, we'd be awakened by clinking noises, a thief trying to steal a piece of it, to sell for scrap metal. All over the building lights would go on, heads would lean out of windows, shouting and screaming. The poor thief would run like hell to commit an easier robbery."

The clanking sound of descending steel shutters reached the office. Husain was getting ready to shut the shop.

Yezad put the prints on the desk and returned the magnifying glass. "You know, in these pictures you've shown me my loss."

"I'm sorry, Yezad, I—"

"No, I'm grateful." The photographs had made him aware how much the street and the buildings meant to him. Like an extended family that he'd taken for granted and ignored, assuming it would always be there. But buildings and roads and spaces were as fragile as human beings, you had to cherish them while you had them.

"Do you realize," said Mr. Kapur, "in the fifteen years I've known you, this is the first time you've talked about your life, your childhood?"

"Oh, I've been going on and on," said Yezad, embarrassed.

"Only fair. Otherwise it's always me and my family history."

"But yours is more interesting."

"Everyone underestimates their own life. Funny thing is, in the end, all our stories – your life, my life, old Husain's life, they're the same. In fact, no matter where you go in the world, there is only one important story: of youth, and loss, and yearning for redemption. So we tell the same story, over and over. Just the details are different."

He reached for the air-conditioner. "Very warm again in here, isn't it?"

"Yes, but you should cut back. The electricity bill is getting bigger each month."

Mr. Kapur chuckled and moved away from the panel. "That's what I like about you, Yezad – you're careful with my money."

He lifted his hands over his head and swung them forward, sinking an invisible basketball. He put away the photographs after checking that the cellophane sleeves were sealed. "From three pictures, so many memories. And this can happen with every single photo – each one conceals volumes. All you need is the right pair of eyes," he made the gesture of turning a key, "to unlock the magic."

They left the cubicle and came into the half-darkened shop where Husain waited by the door. The steel shutters were padlocked. Ram, Sita, and the recumbent Ravan looked forlorn in the unlit store window.

"I'm convinced of one thing now," said Mr. Kapur. "You love this city as much as I do. If not more. I hope you understand why I want to run in the upcoming municipal election."

Yezad nodded. "So you're going ahead?"

"Absolutely. I've made pukka plans. Soon I'll be organizing full-time, plotting strategy. All my most influential friends are supporting me. And I've drafted a sort of manifesto – I'll e-mail it to you. I need your opinion."

"I don't have a computer."

"No? I'll print it out for you. And I've got lots of ideas for the actual campaign."

He described one of them: instead of the banal exercise of handing out pamphlets, he would take along a team of helpers in a van equipped with tea and snacks – a tea-stall on wheels, complete with folding chairs and stools. In each block, they would set up in entranceways, courtyards, compounds, under staircases, wherever there was space. Then he would invite residents to chat with him while taking refreshments.

"It will be neighbour meeting neighbour over a cup of tea, the community rediscovering human bonds, participating in a healthy airing of ideas and dreams and visions."

"Sounds great," said Yezad. "And as far as Bombay Sporting is concerned, you can rely on me."

"I intend to. Let's discuss that soon – your new responsibilities and the remuneration to match." He added conspiratorially, "Don't forget my special suitcase, that will also be in your charge. It must finance my campaign."

They laughed, and Husain smiled as he locked the door, as though it made him happy just to be close to their mirth. With a salaam he handed over the keys, and they said good night.

Yezad felt at peace with the world, more calm than he had been in weeks. Strange, that the photographs that had agitated him so much should have this effect. Perhaps it had been a positive sort of agitation, as with medicine bottles that needed shaking.

At the station he let the clutch of sweaty humanity bear him on its tide into the train. Gripping the overhead bar, he thought of Jehangir Mansion and Hughes Road. How dear were the memories now, of his childhood home. The place had not been much in his mind; by the time the family had left for good the building was so run down, the foundation turned by rats into a labyrinth of burrows, they were glad to see the last of it. And yet, it must have had a hold on him all along.

He pictured Mr. Kapur's photos of the building, the street, the railing. He liked him more than ever; understood him better, for sure. His election run would work out well for both of them.

Lost in a cloud of optimism, he almost missed his station, jumping off as the train began to pull out. He started whistling.

Roxana hurried from the kitchen to shush him, Pappa had had a terrible day, mustn't have slept last night, had been in and out of slumber all morning and afternoon, muttering things to himself.

While they waited by the door, Nariman began to murmur, "Lucy, my love, my sweet clarinet, I'll play sweet music upon you . . ."

Roxana raised her brows and put a hand over her mouth, deciding she needed to get the boys out of hearing. Strange that Pappa's hands were still, but his mind was not. Murad could remain on the balcony; Jehangir would have to leave the dining table with his books and sit in the back room.

"There is more space here," said Jehangir, intent on listening to every word of Grandpa's, puzzling to make sense.

"Do what I say," whispered his mother. "We need the table for dinner." She shut the adjoining door and he sulked at being cut off from Grandpa's secrets.

"Come live with me and be my love," said Nariman. "And we will all the pleasures prove . . ."

She brought the plates to the table and asked, "Pappa? Will you eat dinner?"

He groaned, and Yezad said not to bother him if he was feeling a bit off today, better to let him rest, keep his stomach light.

She nodded. "By the way, Yezdaa, the clock needs winding."

On the balcony, Murad heard his mother's words. He came inside feigning nonchalance, walked past his parents, and sneaked into the kitchen where he put a stool near the wall and climbed up. He opened the clock's glass door. His fingers groped in the place under the pendulum for the shining chrome key, and inserted it.

The creak of the winding spring reached Yezad's ears as he was going by on his way to the WC. "What do you think you're doing?"

"The clock had stopped," said Murad.

Without a word he lifted his son off the stool and dragged him to Roxana in the back room.

"I'm going to kill him," he said quietly. "Right here, in front of you, I'm going to kill him."

"Stay calm, Yezdaa!" she pleaded. "Tell me what he did."

"He was winding the clock."

She flinched; it would be difficult to save Murad from a thrashing if that was his crime. "Let's ask him why he did it when he knows he shouldn't. Tell us, Murad."

Murad kept a defiant silence. Jehangir watched from the desk in the corner, petrified.

Roxana tried again: "You know that clock is very special for Daddy. Why did you do it? Please tell me."

Murad hesitated. "I wanted to help Daddy. He's always tired in the evening."

"Clever excuse," said Yezad. "But it won't do. Of the dozens of things he can help with, he picks the one thing he shouldn't."

Roxana preferred to accept the reason at face value if the punishment could be averted. "That's nice of you, Murad. Say sorry to Daddy anyway, you did something wrong. You know how precious the clock is, you've heard the story."

"Which one is that?" asked Jehangir.

"Don't try your tricks, Jehangla."

"No, really, Daddy, I don't remember it."

"It's possible," said Roxana. "He was very young when you told it." She knew the story would be a good way to calm Yezad.

"I've forgotten it completely," said Jehangir, even more earnest.

"The clock used to hang in Daddy's home in Jehangir Mansion," began Roxana. "In the kitchen. It was a gift to his father from his bank chairman, for his bravery."

Yezad corrected her: "The engraving says, 'In gratitude for an exemplary display of courage and honesty in the course of duty.'" Then he took over the story, as she hoped he would.

"My father was the chief cashier. Once a week he would carry cash between his branch and the head office, accompanied by an armed guard. It was the system, those days. And the incident occurred during the final months of the Second World War."

"How old were you?" asked Jehangir.

"I wasn't even born then. But my father was making his weekly trip in a taxi with the guard, Duleep Singh. Suddenly, they heard a terrifying explosion, like the whole city had blown up. And death and destruction began raining from the sky. The explosions continued, no one knew what was happening. People in the streets thought that enemy bombers had arrived over Bombay. Hundreds lay dead in minutes. And my father's taxi driver was so scared, he stopped the car, jumped out, and ran, screaming 'Bhaago, sahab, bhaago!' Then Duleep Singh also panicked, forgot his rifle in the taxi, and took off.

"So there was my father, left alone with a case containing five lakh rupees, and no transport, no protection, chaos in the streets.

"All the terrible possibilities began going through his mind. If some bad elements knew he was carrying this fortune in cash, they could kill him and no one would ever know. Or the explosions could finish him – there were hundreds whose bodies were never found. If that happened, the bank might think he took advantage of the situation and disappeared with the cash. This was what he feared most, the loss of his good name."

"Couldn't he hide in a shop or a building?" asked Murad.

"Shops, houses, everyone had locked their doors. They thought the enemy was invading. The only thing my father could do was to try to reach head office. He kept praying Yatha Ahu Varyo, and walked on.

"Moving cautiously, sheltering under porticos and door-ways, he arrived at head office hours later. There, too, the doors were locked. He knocked and hammered and shouted till the watchman approached. Recognizing my father who came every week, he let him in at once."

"But what were the explosions?" asked Jehangir.

"I'm coming to that. You see, because it was wartime, two British ammunition ships had docked in the harbour. There was an accident, those ships exploded, and the ammunition bombarded the city. It was only later that people understood the extent of the destruction, the thousands who were killed.

"And in the bank, they realized how brave my father had been, how determined and, above all, honest. When the clock was presented at the bank's annual function, the chairman made a speech praising my father's courage. He said that just as the clock would tell the time accurately, so would Mr. Chenoy's act tell accurately about honesty."

Yezad paused. "When your grandfather was in danger of being killed, what concerned him most was not the loss of his life, but the loss of his good name. He always said, when he finished telling me the story, 'Remember, people can take everything away from you, but they cannot rob you of your decency. Not if you want to keep it. You alone can do that, by your actions.'"

"Let the words of Daddy's father stick in your mind forever," said Roxana. "Understood?"

"Yes, Mummy," said Jehangir.

"And what about you, Murad?"

He nodded.

The flat was quiet, and it was over an hour since everyone had gone to bed when Nariman started to talk. Roxana prayed he would fall silent before Yezad was disturbed.

Then her father raised his voice. "You disgrace the role of fatherhood! When you call the woman I love a whore, when you call this house a raanwada just because I invite her here, I despair for you!"

Yezad jumped out of bed. "Did he say raanwada?"

Roxana shushed him. "I think he's arguing with his father about Lucy."

"What kind of language is this, for a small boy to hear."

"Don't worry, Jehangir is asleep."

"Did you check?"

She got out of bed and crept to the door. She looked, and smiled: her son seemed safe in the arms of peaceful slumber.

"Who knows what else your father will scream out?

Nariman Vakeel's life would make a good novel, but it's not a bedtime story for a child."

He lay on his back, grumbling it would take him ages to fall asleep now. She put her hand on his chest and played with the hair, caressing and soothing him like a child.

Nariman lapsed again into soft murmurs. Jehangir listened with his head propped up on an elbow. He was glad he'd been able to shut his eyes before Mummy saw him awake. He didn't want to miss what Grandpa said, it was the only way he would ever learn anything. Every time he asked Mummy-Daddy a question, they told him not to be curious about grown-up people's problems.

"Come down from the ledge, my love," he heard Grandpa say in a begging voice. "Please, Lucy, that's not a good place to sing. Come down, my darling, stand beside me, and I will sing with you . . ."

Grandpa was getting very upset now: "I'm frightened, Lucy, please step down, my love . . . ," and Jehangir was afraid he would become loud and wake Daddy again. He wondered if he should hold Grandpa's hand, the way Grandpa had held his the other night, maybe that would comfort him.

But after pleading for a few minutes, Grandpa began to hum his song, "One Day When We Were Young." So Lucy must have listened to him. Lowering his elbow, Jehangir let his head touch the pillow. He fell asleep to the soft singing, puzzling about what ledge it was that Grandpa's girlfriend was standing on, and why was Grandpa so scared of it?

11

J EHANGIR STUDIED HIS REFLECTION and wondered if anything about his appearance had changed. He knew stories
in which guilty secrets were revealed in physical manifesta-
tions – skin breaking out in boils, nails turning black, voice
getting hoarse, hair falling out.

The twenty rupees had sat hidden in his pocket for days
while he agonized. How to use the money without getting into
trouble? Thankfully, the face that stared back at him from the
mirrored door of his father's cupboard seemed normal.

Then he heard a violent blast from the kitchen – much louder than the pressure cooker's usual whistle. He ran to see. His
mother told him to stand back, it was too dangerous to go near
the stove. She herself stood frozen, a few feet away from the
beast spouting steam and food through its valve. The first powerful gush had left its mark on the wall and ceiling.

He watched from the passage, fascinated by the cooker.
Then, through its hissing and gurgling came the sound of the
doorbell. His mother didn't seem to have heard it ring, so he
went, looked through the peephole, and opened. Daisy Aunty
marched briskly past him into the kitchen.

"Put off the stove," she said, and his mother jumped at the
voice.

"Daisy!"

"Put off the stove," repeated Daisy Aunty, then decided to
do it herself. She grabbed a kitchen cloth and wrapped it over
her hand for protection. With the other hand shielding her
face, she bent low and crept closer to the stove.

Like a cowboy trying to get the drop on a rustler, he
thought. Then she reached out and put off the gas with a

quick turn of the knob. The fastest knob in the West, he decided.

"Now a bucket of cold water," she said, still very businesslike, and poured it over the cooker. The beast was subdued.

"Thank you," said his mother, limp with relief. "I don't know how it happened, I'm always so careful, the weight was on the valve, everything was fine, and I was with Pappa."

"It happens," said Daisy Aunty. "Soon as I heard that fortissimo trumpet, I knew your cooker had exploded." She stepped back to survey the results. "Looks like a Jackson Pollock."

"What?" asked his mother.

She pointed to the wall. "Modern art. What was in the cooker?"

"Yellow dal, and a tomato gravy."

"Nice colours," she said, admiring the combination.

Jehangir returned to the back room, to the mirror, where he had been examining his face. He opened the cupboard door, and the inside drawer, where Mummy kept her envelopes. What if he slipped his twenty rupees in them, without saying anything? She would find the money, think it was from Daddy's salary, and just spend it.

She was still with Daisy Aunty in the kitchen, cleaning the mess. Neither Murad nor Daddy were home. And Grandpa was asleep. Now was the time.

He reached for the familiar envelopes that he handled on paydays, sitting with Mummy while she divided the salary. She would let him count the cash when the bank notes were new, and he enjoyed their crisp smell. If they were old notes, she was more cautious – you never knew who else had touched them, how hygienic were their hands, did they wash twice with soap after going to the toilet?

He leafed through the envelopes and read their labels: Butter & Bread, Gas Cylinder, Ghee, Rice & Sugar, Milk & Tea, Water & Electricity, Meat . . . on and on they went, flooding his head with their demands. All he had was twenty rupees. How worn and crumpled the envelopes were, the flaps tearing at the fold. He could remember three years ago when they were sparkling white. Mummy-Daddy had been talking for days about something called an increment. He asked what it meant. "More money," she said happily. Then Daddy said that with inflation it would buy less, and he asked what inflation was. "A monster that dines on our future," said Daddy, explaining about rising prices and purchasing power. But Mummy was hopeful, she was going to make up a new budget, with a new set of envelopes for good luck.

Now they were old and smudgy, and didn't seem to hold any luck. There were so many of them, so much more money was needed to make a real difference. Where to put the twenty rupees, where would it do the most good? He had to decide quickly, Mummy and Daisy Aunty would soon finish in the kitchen.

He flipped through and stopped at Butter & Bread. Yesterday morning Daddy had said, "Dry toast again, thanks to your family." And Mummy replied, "I haven't seen your family being much help in fifteen years," which made Daddy angrier. "At least they don't treat our home like a hospital," he said.

They had begun fighting again, Mummy reminding him how halkat his three sisters had been just before the wedding, they hadn't allowed him one chair or bed or cupboard from the family flat though he was entitled to his share of the furniture. Not one broken stick had they given him from Jehangir Mansion, and it was a wonder he could take his clothes and shoes with him. And Daddy said that if she was going to bring up his family history, he could do the same about hers, only hers was too terrible to utter in front of the children.

Mummy said had it not been for his sisters, they could have settled in his house, Grandpa wouldn't have spent all his money, he'd still be master of his destiny. But Grandpa had sacrificed everything for them, he had said not to start a new life in quarrel and bitterness.

"So just remember," said Mummy, "my family didn't create our problem."

Daddy had pointed at Grandpa on the settee. "What do you think this is? Let me tell you, I didn't marry you for the honour and privilege of nursing your father."

Remembering his parents' harsh exchanges, Jehangir stood frozen with the money in his hand. Everything felt heavy inside his chest, the way his head did when he had a headache. He wondered if this was what a heartache felt like. Was there a pill for a heartache?

Noise in the kitchen alerted him; he decided: Butter & Bread was the best choice. He slipped in the twenty rupees, replacing the envelopes just as his mother came down the passage. Daisy Aunty was inquiring about Grandpa, and they went into the front room.

"Look who's here, Pappa – Daisy Ichhaporia."

His grandfather looked blank for a moment, then his face became bright: "The violinist."

"Very good!" they said, and Jehangir thought it sounded like the praise from Mummy when his exam marks were good.

"And where is the violin?" asked his grandfather.

"Oh Pappa," his mother laughed, "Daisy came to help me in the kitchen, not to play a concert."

"'If music be the food of love, play on, give me excess of it,'" he whispered to Daisy's delight. "You should go nowhere without your violin."

"Why don't you tell her, Pappa, how much you enjoy her music? You know, Daisy, whenever he hears you practise, he is in heaven, you should see his face."

Taking her aside, she said the music was a blessing on days when Pappa was having a bad time – the moment her violin started, he grew calmer, as though he had taken a dose of medicine.

"How interesting," said Daisy. "Some time ago I read a book about music therapy. It prescribed specific compositions for things like migraine, high or low blood pressure, stomach cramps. I don't remember exactly, but Bach was the one prescribed most often, especially certain fugues from the *Well-Tempered Clavier*. Wait, I'll be back in a minute."

She returned with the violin and started a lively piece that filled the room with its energy. Smiling, Nariman closed his eyes to listen, and Roxana gestured to Daisy, indicating his pleasure.

The music swerved and circled, and Jehangir thought that was how it must feel racing along in an open motor car on an empty road, lots of birds flying above, sun shining, small white clouds floating in the sky. The piece ended with a flourish of the bow.

"Bravo," said Nariman, and tried to clap but there wasn't much sound. The others made up for it. "I used to have a 78 rpm of Heifetz performing it," he continued. "Sarasate's *Zapateado*, isn't it?"

She nodded, pleased that he knew the piece.

"What does Zapa . . . the name mean?" asked Jehangir.

"Za-pa-te-a-do," his grandfather repeated. "A dance in which you stamp your feet. From 'zapato,' which means shoe in Spanish."

Jehangir preferred his own interpretation of birds and clouds and a motor car. He echoed the word, "Zapato – sounds a lot like sapat."

"Correct. That's because Gujarati and Spanish both belong to the same Indo-European family."

Daisy began to play Mendelssohn's *On Wings of Song* and they fell silent. Jehangir thought this time the music was more tender, pouring so sweetly out of the violin he could almost taste it. It reminded him of honey pouring from a spoon in delicate golden threads. When he had a sore throat, his mother mixed honey with lemon juice to make the throat smooth.

Daisy finished the piece, and they clapped again. She began putting the violin away. "Is that all?" said Nariman. "You can just as well practice here today."

"You don't want to listen to all my rubbish, Professor Vakeel."

He convinced her that he did. But her sheet music and stand were downstairs, so she played a few more pieces from memory, then returned the violin to its case, promising to come the next day if he really wanted.

"Promise me one more thing."

"Certainly."

"Promise me that when I'm dying, you'll come to play for me."

Daisy said she was sure he had many years ahead of him.

"The number of years is not the issue. I want your violin to fill my ears when my breath is leaving me – whenever that may be. Is that a promise?"

He held out his hand to her. She hesitated, but was unable to refuse him. Her hand clasped his, to seal the pact: "Promise," she said.

Roxana was frowning now, and Jehangir was very distressed, as though her agreeing to his grandfather's request would hasten the sad moment.

MISS ALVAREZ MADE A LITTLE SPEECH in praise of the Homework Monitors and her class. Jehangir was convinced she would see guilt in his eyes, and was afraid of meeting hers. He picked a spot on the blackboard to focus his gaze.

"Boys, I want you to know there is improvement in the marks of those who were not doing well at the start of the year; even the Perpetual Problems are working harder. Do you know why? Because you want the respect of your classmates. I am so proud of you. Thank you, keep it up, and congratulations to everyone."

Then Miss Alvarez crossed her class-electrifying legs and began marking test papers while her Homework Monitors went about their task. It was a quiz on dates of the Mughal Empire: ten questions for each student.

Moving from desk to desk, Jehangir was preoccupied with what would happen when he came to Ashok. A week had passed since the last time. Would he offer money again? The fear of getting caught by Miss Alvarez sat in the pit of his stomach.

Long before it was Ashok's turn, the brown paper cover on his history textbook was damp from the sweat of his palms. He wiped them on his shirt sleeves, but they grew moist again in seconds. He kept his fingers away from the centre, trying not to streak the ink where Daddy had written on the brown paper cover:

Jehangir Chenoy
Standard IV A
History

Daddy's handwriting was perfect as pearls. That was how Mummy praised it, and the letters were all joined together by the lustre of royal blue ink. She encouraged him to try and write as beautifully. It was too late for Murad, his handwriting crawled like bedbugs all over the page, she said at the start of each school year, when they brown-papered their books and sat with Daddy at the dining table while he wrote out their names, classes, and subjects. It was the best part of going back to school after the May vacation. Jehangir loved the fresh gloss of the brown paper, the smell of new books, the thrill of his name flowing from the nib of Daddy's fountain pen. And he could tell that Daddy enjoyed it too from the important look on his face. Sometimes Daddy joked that the process of learning couldn't begin till the books bore the student's name, for the knowledge inside them wouldn't know whose brain to travel into.

And now, Daddy's beautiful pearls were in danger of being smudged by the sweat of his wickedness. Dragging the burden of guilt and fear behind him, Jehangir reached the source of his anxiety.

He commenced the homework questions about the Mughal Empire, ignoring the wink Ashok gave him. The ease with which he could maintain a dignified distance, as though they were not handcuffed by a nasty secret, now surprised him.

"What year did Babur become king of Farghana?"

"1947," grinned Ashok, and put his hand in his pocket.

"The First Battle of Panipat was fought in—?"

"1947." He pulled out a twenty-rupee note and Jehangir put his hand under the desk.

"Humayun became Emperor in—?"

"1947."

Jehangir pocketed the note as they went through the questions. Ten times Ashok answered 1947. He got a mark of nine out of ten in the Homework Register.

Jehangir moved on, his palms perfectly dry, wiped clean by confidence. How simple it had been. All that fear for nothing, he thought, and took his place to test Vijay.

Vijay and Ashok, along with Rajesh, spent the short recess together, sat together for lunch in the long recess, and travelled home together. Vijay's mother loved coconut oil, so his hair was always shining. When the class had played the Oiled Hair versus Un-Oiled cricket match, Vijay wanted to be captain because his was the oiliest.

Jehangir commenced the ten questions while Vijay struggled to come up with answers, pressing upon his temples with his fingers as though to squeeze out the correct words. He had soon used up his quota of three errors.

"Sorry," said Jehangir, and opened the Homework Register.

"Okay," sighed Vijay, and whispered to put his hand under the desk.

"What for?"

"Chal yaar, don't pretend. I know the price – twenty rupees."

Heart pounding, Jehangir refused to take the money. That swine Ashok! He'd betrayed him! And after promising not to tell anyone. "I have to mark you failed."

"Okay. Just see what happens."

"What can happen?" he tried bravado.

"First I'll rub my hair all over your textbook. Then I'll tell Teacher you're taking money."

"She won't believe you."

"Ashok will come with me, he'll say he paid you."

As he crumbled under the threat, Vijay slipped the money into the history text.

A corner of the note stuck out. Terrified it would be seen, Jehangir stuffed it into his pocket. He entered eight out of ten for Vijay in the Homework Register.

A few desks later he came to Rajesh and, from the big grin on his face, knew what to expect without a word being spoken. They went through the routine of the history quiz, and Jehangir pocketed another twenty.

❦

From then on, along with Ashok and Vijay, Rajesh made up the trio that supplied him with sixty rupees each week. This ability to get money without effort, something for nothing, filled him with wonder, and a sense of power.

Before long, he took it for granted: his due. He resented it if one of the three got the homework right (usually Rajesh, who worked harder and was not rich like the others). And when he slipped the smaller amount in his mother's envelopes, he felt he was letting her down.

Then he found a way to control the outcome. Miss Alvarez gave the Homework Monitors a suggested list of questions for each assignment, but they were free to make up their own. She trusted their good judgement, she reminded them.

In geography, he first asked Rajesh from Miss Alvarez's list, but they were too easy and he got them right. Time to bowl a googly. He combed the textbook for obscure facts: "State the total annual volume of flow from all the rivers in India."

"What?" said Rajesh, incredulous. "That's not a fair question!"

Jehangir dismissed the protest with a cold silence, and revealed the answer. "1,680,000,000,000 cubic metres per year."

"Bastard."

Fishing for two more errors, Jehangir assaulted him with similar questions of a numerical nature.

"This is supposed to be geography homework, not arithmetic!" sputtered Rajesh. He glared at him with hatred and handed over twenty rupees. "Just wait, I'll show you."

Smiling, Jehangir pocketed the money and continued down the row to the next boy.

HASTE MADE HIM SHUT the inside drawer noisily after he had slipped the sixty rupees into various envelopes. His mother heard it in the kitchen, and caught him at the open cupboard door.

"What are you doing?"

He thought quickly. "I wanted to look at Daddy's letters, the Canadian ones." She'd believe this, he'd always loved hearing his father tell the story about the application and interview.

"You shouldn't touch his shelf. Anyway, you found the letters?"

"No. I didn't want to mix up his things."

She nodded approval for his sound decision. "Ask him when he comes home, if he's in a good mood." Then, stroking his cheek, she brought her face close to his. "What's wrong, Jehangoo?"

"Nothing."

"Are you happy?"

He nodded.

"Come, your tea is ready. Why is Murad so late again? How does he miss the bus and you don't?"

"I go full speed down the stairs and run to the bus stop." He wasn't going to reveal that his brother had lately been walking. Murad must have a good reason for saving the bus fare – maybe he, too, wanted to help their parents.

But Murad was home before long. And his mother didn't ask again, for his father also arrived soon afterwards and said "Unbelievable" as he unlatched the door.

She wondered what could have annoyed him the moment he stepped inside. "Is something wrong, Yezdaa?" she asked timidly.

246

"For the first time in weeks, something is right."

Her anxiety melted into a smile. "What is it?"

"See if you can guess. Here's a hint – I didn't climb three floors to get home today."

"What did you do, fly up?" said Roxana, and Jehangir laughed, relieved at the way they were talking.

"Yes, I did," said Yezad. "I flew up in a cage."

"The lift is working!" shouted Murad.

"After eight years. Can you believe it, chief?"

"Good news, indeed," said Nariman. "The miracle of modern technology has returned to Pleasant Villa."

They laughed, and Jehangir, feeling exuberant, said, "Three cheers for the good old lift!" He was happy that his father was happy this evening. "Hip-hip-hooray!"

"Sounds like you read that in Enid Blyton," said Yezad, while Roxana told them all to sit at the table, the food was ready.

Dinner began. The dish consisted of potatoes, boiled, sliced, and fried with onions, chopped green chilies, and cumin seed. She knew the preparation was incomplete, cooked without the final layer of four eggs beaten to a froth. As she was serving, she became concerned that the meal looked much too plain.

"Very tasty," said Yezad. "Green chilies are magic."

Jehangir nodded in grateful agreement. "Daddy, can I change my name to John? As a short form?"

"Did you hear that, Roxie? Your son wants to become a Christian."

"No, I'll still be a Parsi, just my name will be slightly different."

"Listen, Jehangla, your Christian friends have Christian names. Your Hindu friends have Hindu names. You are a Parsi so you have a Persian name. Be proud of it, it's not to be thrown out like an old shoe."

"An old zapato," said Jehangir.

"Not that we can afford to throw out anything these days."

The unpleasant subject of money was coming close again, worried Jehangir, and he stopped chewing. His mother asked if he didn't like the dinner.

"It's very tasty," he said, picking up speed.

"Did you tell Daddy what you were doing in the cupboard?"

The question turned Jehangir dumb with fear. He was barely able to shake his head.

"What were you up to, rascal?"

"He wanted to see your letters," said his mother. "All your Canada correspondence."

Relief rolled over Jehangir. Like waves of water, he thought. He knew that his mother brought it up because, like him, she wanted to extend Daddy's good mood for as long as possible.

When they had finished eating, he asked his father to tell the story.

∾

The immigration story used to have two parts: dream and reality. But over the years the dream – of prosperity, house, car, CD player, computer, clean air, snow, lakes, mountains, abundance – had been renounced, since it was never going to come true. That part of the story had shrunk to almost nothing. To compensate, the other part had grown, and was now the entire story, beginning with the letter Yezad had written to the Canadian High Commission about his desire to emigrate with his family, which, at the time, consisted of Roxana and three-year-old Murad.

"You've heard it all before," said Yezad, as Jehangir kept badgering him.

"Yes, but you've never read us the letter, Daddy."

"I think I have."

"I, for one, would love to hear it, Yezad," said Nariman.

"Oh, all right." He went to the cupboard and, while rummaging for the correspondence, took the opportunity to insert the remainder of his Matka winnings in five envelopes at random. In the front room he opened the package of letters and found the one they wanted to hear.

Pulling out a sheaf of pages, he explained that years ago, when he was writing to the Canadian High Commission, he had decided that because his qualifications were limited – he was not an engineer, nurse, technician, or anyone in high demand – his letter would have to accomplish what degrees and diplomas normally would. It should make the High Commissioner sit up and take notice that here was an applicant worthy of Canada. Words had power to sway, words had accomplished mighty things, they had won wars. Surely the language of Churchill and Shakespeare and Milton, ignited with a careful mix of reason and passion, could win him a mere immigration visa.

So he had written a paean to Canada, its awe-inspiring geography, its people, its place in the world, and the munificence of Canada's multicultural policy, a policy that in the beauty of its wisdom did not demand the jettisoning of the old before letting them share in the new. He had written that much had been made about the American dream and its melting pot, which, in his opinion, was more a nightmare: a crude image better suited to a sulphurous description of hellfire and brimstone than to a promised land. No, the mosaic vision of the Canadian dream was far superior – a mosaic demanded imagination and patience and artistry, an aesthetic lacking in the brutality of a fiery cauldron.

He paused. "It all sounds so pompous now."

"Go on, Daddy," said Jehangir. "It's a letter and-a half."

Yezad laughed, turned to the next page, and read aloud: "The generosity of the Canadian dream makes room for everyone, for a multitude of languages and cultures and peoples. In Canada's willingness to define and redefine itself continually, on the basis of inclusion, lies its greatness, its promise, its hope.

"My family and I would like to share in this dream. We believe in its nobility, and wish to spend our lives in a society that dedicates itself to becoming a light unto the world.

"I have a dream that one day soon my family will depart this place of disaffection forever, and will live where the values of compassion are paramount, where the creed of selfishness is caged and exterminated, where compromise is preferred to confrontation, and the flower of harmony is cultivated.

"Most of all, I have a dream that one day soon my wife, my son, and I will be able to lift our heads towards the Canadian sky and sing 'O Canada' with all our hearts."

The letter ended with details of the usual practical nature, which Yezad skipped over. "God," he said. "Did I really write all this naive nonsense?"

"Well," said Nariman, "it's very good for what it was meant to achieve. Sufficient unto the day—"

"Would you believe, I spent six weeks of hard labour in composing it, drafting and redrafting, agonizing over the commas, adding one, removing another, before mailing it to New Delhi. Then there was three months of silence from the bloody High Commission. I wondered if I'd said something to offend them. The echo of that Martin Luther King speech – perhaps they were upset I had quoted an American hero in the process of applying to Canada. Maybe I should have done more research, found a Canadian quote. Or maybe I had written too harshly about the American melting pot, which could have gone against me, marking me as a radical, an America-hater or -baiter who might be trouble. Perhaps there was a slight note of disloyalty to India? That was something I wanted to avoid.

"Finally a response came. Guess what, chief – a two-line form letter, saying an application was enclosed, with instructions regarding its completion. Look, here's the photocopy."

"I still can't believe it," said Roxana. "How could those people have ignored a letter like that?"

"Bureaucracy," said Nariman. "The wa wa worst enemy of humankind."

"True," said Yezad, exchanging glances with Roxana – she had heard it too, the falter in her father's speech. "So I filled out the application form, but my hopes were low by this time. If I could not impress them with my letter, what was left to influence their decision? Nothing.

"Imagine the surprise when six months later they requested an interview. Once again, I became enthusiastic, because the High Commission never interviewed applicants unless they were likely to be accepted. And the whole family was invited, not just me."

"I still remember what we wore that day," said Roxana. "Daddy had on his dark blue double-breasted suit, I put on the mauve skirt and jacket I used to have. For Murad we bought a very sweet bow tie. We took a taxi so we wouldn't get all sweaty."

"Yes," said Yezad. "When we reached there, the reception-ist said the Immigration Officer, Mr. Mazobashi, would be calling us in shortly. We sat on a sofa in the waiting area. The room was full of families dressed up like us – as though we were a wedding party. Some women were wearing kilos of gold jewellery. How ridiculous, when I think of it now. But at that moment, all I could think of was the Immigration Officer's name: Mazobashi.

"I was thrilled. This was the beauty of Canada, I felt, that Mazobashi could be as Canadian as any other name. Chenoy, for example. Then a voice called out in the hallway: the Chenoy family. Like a doctor calling the next patient into the examining room. And when I saw the man, I didn't think it was the Immigration Officer – the fellow was dressed like a chaprassi, in a crumpled kurta-type shirt hanging over his pants, feet in Kolhapuri chappals, filthy toenails.

"But we went in to the office, and he slid into the big arm-chair behind the desk. On the desk was a brass nameplate: M. M. Mazobashi. So this shabbily dressed man was going to conduct the interview. Was this how little he thought of us? Then I decided to suspend my judgement. Perhaps

Canadians were even more casual than Americans."

"Going native is what the British used to call it," said Nariman.

"Right," said Yezad. "Mr. Mazobashi opened our file without asking us to sit. There was only one chair, I nudged Roxana to take it. He noticed, and said, 'Yeah, sure, go ahead,' pointing to another chair in the corner.

"When we were seated he said, 'Aren't you people feeling hot in your suits and jackets?' and I smiled, 'No, sir, the AC is working most efficiently.'"

"Actually," said Roxana, interrupting the story, "the office was freezing, I wished I'd taken my nylon scarf. And I was worried Murad might catch a chill. That man must have seen me shiver. He was so abrupt, 'Whatsamatter, too cold for you? And you want to live in Canada?' Such an uncultured fellow, I didn't like him from the first minute."

"Anyway," said Yezad, "he suddenly left the office, and came back with a glass of water. I thought he was showing some courtesy at last, but he poured it into a little plant on his desk. 'How far is Canada, do you know?' he asked me without warning. I said it would depend on which part of Canada, the figure could increase by almost six thousand kilometres if he meant the West Coast."

"Good point," said Nariman.

And Jehangir was pleased, for Daddy had scored over the mean Mr. Mazobashi. "Is this when you told him he was a rude man?"

"No, not yet. He opened the file again, lit a cigarette, studied his nails, asked why we wanted to go to Canada. I repeated some sentences from my long letter, and ended by saying something I shouldn't have – that we wanted to go for the same reasons his family went.

"He sneered at me: 'My family was born in Canada.' I kept quiet. He now asked me the first relevant question of the interview: 'You sell sports equipment, it says here. Tell me more about that.'

"I began answering, but he cut me off. 'Okay, okay, that's enough about cricket and badminton and table tennis. You plan to sell sports equipment in Canada?'

"'Yes, but I'm willing to do any job if—'

"'Well, tell me something about Canadian sports. How many players on an ice hockey team?'

"'Eleven?'

"'Wrong. How many periods in a game?'

"'Two?'

"'Wrong. What's a power play? Do you know what it means to deke? What's an icing penalty? Tell me the difference between the CFL and the NFL. How many franchises in the NHL? How is lacrosse played?'

"He was firing questions at me like a machine gun. 'You Indians,' he said finally. 'You're so naive. You want to go and freeze your butts in a country you understand nothing about, just to make a pile of money. Well, thanks for your interest in Canada, we'll let you know.'"

Jehangir waited – he knew the good part was coming.

"He was expecting us to meekly rise and leave," said Yezad. "But I stayed in my chair. 'Excuse me, sir, may I say something?' He said, 'Sure, but make it snappy, I've got more of you people to interview.' And I said, 'Oh yes, I'll certainly be snappy.'

"I leaned forward in my chair. 'You, sir, are a rude and ignorant man, a disgrace to your office and country. You have sat here abusing us, abusing Indians and India, one of the many countries your government drains of its brainpower, the brainpower that is responsible for your growth and prosperity. Instead of having the grace to thank us, you spew your prejudices and your bigoted ideas. You, whose people suffered racism and xenophobia in Canada, where they were Canadian citizens, put in camps like prisoners of war – you, sir, might be expected, more than anyone else, to understand and embody the more enlightened Canadian ideals of multiculturalism. But if you are anything to go by, then Canada is a gigantic hoax.'"

"Bravo," said Nariman, while Murad and Jehangir clapped proudly.

"Yes, I made quite a speech. It's been so many years, I can't remember it all."

"You said something about the flag that stood behind his desk," prompted Roxana, "about the leaf."

"Oh yes, I said it was a wonder the red maple leaf on the flag was still flying, that it had not withered with shame and fallen off, from being forced to share his office."

"Perfect," said Nariman.

"My research was thorough before I applied. Vilas, my book-shop friend, had lent me a novel called *Obasan*. And another book, called *The Enemy That Never Was*. Plus some others, about building the national railroad, the Klondike gold rush, confederation in 1867. In fact, I think I was better informed about Canada than many people born there. Except for Canadian sporting events. And this man was turning me down."

Nariman shook his head sadly. "We always assume that people who suffer atrocities acquire a greater than average capacity for compassion. But there is no such guarantee. Anyway, I'm glad you did not emigrate."

"So must Jal and Coomy, chief. An ambulance from Bombay to Canada would have been too expensive."

"I'm glad you did not," repeated Nariman, "because I think emigration is an enormous mistake. The biggest anyone can make in their life. The loss of home leaves a hole that never fills."

His father-in-law's words brought a lump to his throat, reminding him of Mr. Kapur's photographs of Jehangir Mansion and Hughes Road. His lost home. That feeling returned, of grief and emptiness, and a strange calm.

He inserted the various forms and letters back inside the large envelope, along with all his clippings of news items concerning Canada, collected over the last twelve years. He knew even more about the country now than he had done when facing Mr. Mazobashi. The sting of rejection had created a thirst in him to better understand the rejector.

He took the envelope back to the cupboard, then stopped. Why had he saved all this? He knew why – he had clung to the idea of applying again some day, of succeeding.

He sat upon the bed and shook out the large envelope. The letters, forms, photocopies, news clippings fluttered out in a heap. He began ripping them up.

The sound of tearing brought Roxana to the back room. "What are you doing?" she asked, horrified.

"Getting rid of garbage."

For a second she thought of rescuing the documents. Then she understood: Yezad was right, it was not worth keeping.

She joined him on the bed, cross-legged, and began tearing. It felt good. They looked up from the pile, smiling, and their eyes met.

When everything had been shredded into a mound of paper petals, he reached over it to pull her closer to him. He put his arms around her, cradling her head on his chest.

On the balcony, Murad told Jehangir he had an idea for Daddy: why didn't he complain to the government in Canada that Mr. Mazobashi was rude and unfair during the interview?

"Because," said Jehangir wisely. "Governments never help ordinary people."

"You're thinking of India," said Murad. "It's not like that in foreign countries. I'm going to suggest it to Daddy."

"Wait," said Jehangir. "Don't go now, Mummy-Daddy are kissing."

12

THE BURSHANE MAN REMOVED the empty cylinder from under the stove while Roxana kept watch: leave him alone and he might pocket a spoon, or a bottle of masala from the shelf. She sniffed – a trace of gas from the disconnected hose had smudged the air.

The fresh cylinder rumbled into place; the man knelt to fasten the hose, then lit the burner to test the flow. The flame was a clean blue. With a grunt he hoisted the empty cylinder to his shoulder, and was escorted out.

As she hurried to fetch the money, a glance at the invoice made her pause – another increase in price. She had half a mind to tell the fellow to take it back. Kerosene for the old Primus would be cheaper. But the nipple was probably blocked, the pump stiff. And she still had to cook for tonight.

Riffling through the envelopes to find the one marked Gas Cylinder, she noticed money in Butter & Bread. Twenty rupees? Impossible – they'd been without butter for days.

The Electricity envelope passed under her fingers, and she felt something in it – she looked: forty-five rupees. But the bill had been settled on the third of the month.

She paid the Burshane man and returned to the cupboard to examine all the envelopes. According to her calculations, they contained an extra hundred and eighty rupees.

That evening, she told Yezad about it. "There's some gotaalo in my accounts," she confessed cautiously, fearing he might think her incompetent. "I've checked over and over."

"Maybe Mr. Kapur made a mistake in my pay packet. But why worry if it's more money? Just spend it where we are short."

He smiled inwardly, though a bit puzzled himself – he'd added a hundred and twenty.

In the days that followed, he kept hoping for, and, in a strange way, almost dreaded, Villie's next powerful dream, the temptation it would hold. Every time he left home, she waylaid him on their third-floor landing or on the stairs, and plied him with her "hot tips," as she called them. Sometimes, when her explanations seemed to make sense, he'd be appalled at himself: how could he see logic in poor Villie's numeric nonsense? He hated being so weak as to clutch at her fantasies.

Then he thought of the powerful brassière dream – explain that, if it was all bunkum. Perhaps Villie had some natural affinity for the science of statistical probability. Like Shakuntala Devi, and all those mathematical prodigies, who could multiply twelve-digit numbers in their minds, give you the answer in less time than it took you to use a calculator. Whatever the reason, Villie's formula seemed to work.

Torn between the real world and the hope dangled by Villie's realm of numbers, he decided to let destiny choose for him. If he got the promotion at Bombay Sporting, he'd have nothing more to do with Matka. But Mr. Kapur had become silent on the subject. Should he remind him? Better still, why not just ask him for a raise? Surely he deserved it, the amount of work he had taken on lately – no need to wait for the election campaign . . .

As the days went by and he awaited destiny's edict, he placed the occasional small bet (to keep in touch, he told himself), winning and losing just enough to preserve, for the next powerful number, the kitty he had saved from the size 36C dream. He soon began to feel like an expert, and a discussion about dreams and numbers had the same air about it as people describing a day at the office. The sense of excitement that accompanied the bets, especially that tense moment just before he heard the Matka result, the warm flush he felt, which could turn to elation or loss – that, too, was something he was starting to enjoy. And every time his kitty grew, he skimmed off a few rupees to slip into Roxana's envelopes.

"More errors, Yezdaa," she said whenever the extra amounts surfaced. Her cheerful announcement made it clear she was willing to play along. She assumed he was earning extra commissions; slipping them into her envelopes was just his way of saying they would not quarrel any more.

Several weeks after his first windfall, Villie flung her door open as he returned from work. "Good news, Yezadji."

Restraining his hand that was reaching behind for his wallet, she said, "How excited you're getting, my dear. At least hear the dream before you take it out."

Was it underwear again, he wondered, withdrawing the notes he had carefully tucked beneath the coin compartment. The last of his winnings. He counted them and wished for more, to make this a much bigger bet. If only he could get his hands on some cash right now. "I really should just give you my money and go, Villie."

"Won't take ten seconds, Yezadji, it's short and sweet."

He shuffled his feet, and she added, "You were in it."

"Oh yes?"

"The simplest dream I've ever had. So simple, most people would forget on waking. You and me, in my kitchen, eating chocolate."

"That's it?"

"I told you it was short and sweet." She giggled. "Maybe I should say long and sweet – it was a big Cadbury bar we were sharing. I took a bite, then you took a bite. Our mouths were watering, the chocolate all sticky—"

"I'm sure you've worked out the correct numbers," he interrupted. "You're the expert, you don't need me."

"In my dream I needed you," she smiled coyly. "You were the one who brought the Cadbury bar."

"Me?"

"Yes, you unwrapped it yourself, showed me how big it was, counting the pieces before giving it to me."

"And?"

"Eighteen pieces," she whispered seductively. "Eighteen, my darling, is our number."

They shook hands, wishing each other luck before he escaped home.

For the rest of the evening Yezad's distractedness made Roxana fear that he was slipping into his bad mood again. And to think the last few weeks had been so pleasant. What was it that made him change so completely?

She had been planning to tell him about Murad coming home late every day, so he could take their son to task. But it could wait for a better time. She resolved to keep out of his way, attempt no conversation.

The boys were confined to their desk in the back room. They worked away busily to present a pleasing picture for their father while he had his tea. And after he finished, Jehangir announced with importance that he had to write an essay titled Why I Think India Is a Great Country.

"Will you help me, Daddy?" he asked, hoping it would please him.

"Come to me when your teacher gives an essay about why India is a hopeless country."

The remark provoked Roxana into forgetting her resolution. "That's such a cruel thing to say to a little boy."

"The truth is cruel sometimes. You can help him with the lies. Or Professor Vakeel will invent some facts."

"With pleasure," said Nariman.

Jehangir looked to his mother for permission. She nodded, and he sat at the dining table. "Okay, Grandpa, I'm ready."

From his chair in the corner, Yezad observed his son's intense concentration, and the pleasure written all over Nariman's pain-filled face. What had his life become, that he no longer had the patience to sit beside his own son and help with an essay?

He couldn't bear to watch, and got up. Colliding with the teapoy, he turned into the back room and sent Murad out of it. He tried to fasten the door that always stayed open. Swollen from disuse, he had to wrestle with it to work the bolt.

The sound of it shooting into place worried Roxana. She waited for a minute, then stood with her ear to the door.

There was only silence. Not even footsteps. He had been so restless this evening, so strange in his demeanour. "Yezad?" She knocked on the door.

He did not answer.

"Yezad, are you all right?"

She kept knocking, calling out his name. Panic pushed her to kicking and banging. "Please, Yezad! Please unlock the door!"

It opened suddenly and she lurched forward. His arm prevented her from advancing farther. "Are you going to stop your hysteria? Or shall I tie up your arms and legs?"

He slammed the door. Stunned, she kept staring at it for a few seconds before turning away. She sat down at the dining table with Jehangir, who had stopped writing.

"Go on with your essay," she said weakly. "Daddy is just upset about something."

"I wonder if all is well at work," said Nariman.

"How would I know? He tells me nothing, he's behaving like a complete stranger," she whispered.

Jehangir edged off his chair and buried his face in her shoulder. She kissed his hair.

"He won't tie you up," he sobbed.

"Of course he won't."

"He just said it because he's angry," said Murad.

❧

Yezad lay on the bed, ashamed of his behaviour, telling himself he had no choice – how could he proceed without locking the back room? And he was doing it to benefit his family, wasn't he? Except that he still was not sure if he had made the right decision. He rose and paced the room, clenching and unclenching his fists, before striding purposefully to the cupboard.

He took out the envelopes. Many of them were empty, the bills paid at the start of the month. From those that still held cash, he began removing it: Butter & Bread, Milk & Tea, Rice & Sugar . . .

As he pulled out the notes, he felt for a moment that he was snatching away the very food named on the envelopes. He told himself not to be fanciful – tomorrow he would replace it a hundredfold.

But why, then, did he feel like a thief? If only he could share the strategy with Roxana – but she'd never agree. Apart from her hatred of gambling, she'd say the risk was too great.

A rough count told him there were just over seven hundred rupees. Stuffing the money in his wallet, he returned the empty envelopes to the cupboard and went to unlock the back room.

With his hand upon the bolt, he hesitated again. This was it: if Villie's dream did not—

His fingers wrenched back the bolt with a crash. He came out as if nothing had happened, and kept walking to the front door.

"Please, Yezad," appealed Roxana. "Tell me what's wrong, where are you going?"

"For a walk."

He got in the lift, slammed shut the collapsibles to announce his departure, and descended to the lobby. After lingering there for a while, he started up the stairs.

His footfall on the stone steps echoed in the empty hallway. On the second floor he heard laughter, and paused. The happy voices of children floated out, a little girl squealing with delight about something, the mother's voice calling them to dinner . . .

He wanted to flee the sounds. Their familiarity chafed him, reminding him of what it was that had escaped from his own tiny flat, once just as happy and warm and loving . . .

It would be again, he told himself. As soon as he had wrenched the control of circumstances into his own hands. He continued up the stairs and knocked at Villie's door.

He skipped greetings and niceties. "Quick, make one more trip to your bunya." His wallet was ready in his hand, and he pulled out the stack of notes. "Bet this for me."

Taken aback by his abruptness, Villie maintained her own pleasant manner. "With pleasure. But are you sure, my dear? So much?"

"That's not your business. Just go before betting closes."

She took the money without another word, hurt that her Matka comrade could speak this way to her. It was not in the spirit of the game.

Around nine o'clock he wondered if the opening had been declared. Leaning on the balcony railing, he waited, wishing for a breeze. November, and still no relief – it might as well be May, considering the heat. What would the opening be? One. Had to be.

At nine-thirty he said he was going out.

"Again?" Roxana's fatigue made it more statement than question.

He saw the look she exchanged with her father. "You have rules and quotas for me? Like Coomy's rules for him?"

"You're more like Coomy, the stupid things you say."

"That's a joke-and-a-half. You watch every move I make, asking a dozen questions if I say I'm going for a walk—"

"Go where you want! Walk, run, crawl, I don't know what you are up to, and I don't care!"

He got into the lift and made his angry noise with the

collapsibles. Repeating his earlier charade, minutes later he padded up the stairs and knocked.

"Well?" he demanded.

Villie smiled. "My dear, one is the opening."

She saw the relief in his face, and wanted to give him a way out. "It's not too late to cancel your closing, if you don't trust my dream. Lalubhai will do it as a favour to me."

He did not answer.

"You'll still get your winnings for the opening number."

He calculated: a total of seven hundred and eighty-five rupees had been bet. Which meant he had already won nine times seven hundred and eighty-five rupees. He took a moment to work it out in his head: seven thousand and sixty-five.

Fantastic, he thought, just grab it and—

But if he let it all turn on the closing, and eight came up, he would get that amount multiplied by nine, he would get – "Pencil, Villie?" He scribbled the sum on her front door. The answer awed him: sixty-three thousand, five hundred and eighty-five.

Enough to pay for everything. Even to repair the ceilings in Coomy and Jal's flat.

"If you want to cancel, I must go right away," her voice broke through his calculations.

"No," he ordered, "let it stand." Then he became conscious of the tone he was using. "Sorry, Villie, too much stress for me."

"I understand," she said, and patted his shoulder.

Pushing down on the mattress with his hand, Yezad flipped over on to his back. The violent movement rocked the head-board. Breathing hard, he muttered that the room was boiling hot. His feet scrabbled away at the sheet to pull it down, and he dried his clammy palms against his pyjamas. Moments later he pulled the sheet up again, shivering, his sweat running cold.

He turned towards the alarm clock, and got up on his elbow. Such a loud ticking, he thought, no wonder it was keeping him awake. The numbers no longer glowed in the dark as they did when it was new.

Squinting, he leaned closer: half past midnight. Matka had closed.

Roxana tried to soothe her husband by putting her arm over him, but he tensed in her embrace. Despairing, she released him, asking herself if the end of their marriage was approaching, now that even her touch repulsed him.

At last his squirming and writhing began to wind down; she sensed he was falling asleep. His legs kicked the darkness a few times before settling with his knees drawn up to his stomach.

Then, from the front room came the sound of her father talking in his sleep. He was not agitated tonight, it sounded like contented murmurings, and she was glad for him, but she still worried about Yezad being awakened. Oh Pappa, she wished silently, please not too loud, Pappa.

They had been to a matinée. The Magnificent Ambersons, *which was showing at the Regal. Afterwards, he and Lucy went for a stroll along Cuffe Parade. This was the routine of their early years: cinema in the afternoon, a long walk, then dinner at a restaurant like Volga or Parisian. But the film had left them pensive, thinking about pride and arrogance, about downfall and disgrace. The sea was rough, the high wind making it difficult to talk as it whipped their voices and hair and clothes.*

They found a bench in a sheltered spot. Now the smell of rain was in the early-evening air. The vendors of coconut water, sugar cane, peanuts had all disappeared. Only a little girl selling flowers was still there, scurrying up as soon as she spied them. "Chamayli, sahab? Chamayli for memsahab?" she pleaded in a high-pitched voice.

He bought a strand of jasmine and tried to fix it in Lucy's hair. But she was not used to wearing flowers. She took them off, wrapping them round her wrist. He raised it to sniff the fragrance. "Jasmine wrist and rose-petal hand," he said.

He kissed her palm, then began licking her fingers, one by one. A few minutes later he said, "Why are we wasting time here? My parents will have left by now."

She was reluctant to go home with him, afraid of being surprised. But he assured her that his father and mother would be at Sammy and Jini Kotwal's annual whist drive and dinner, which never ended before one in the morning; there was no chance of running into them. "And even if we do – well, you have to meet them at some time."

It started to rain, and they took a taxi. The traffic became slower, the horns louder. The windshield wiper kept jamming, and the driver had to reach outside to get it going with a nudge. He had a towel on the front seat for his soaking arm.

When the taxi arrived at Chateau Felicity, the ground-floor neighbour, Mr. Arjani, was at his window, enjoying the downpour. "Hello, Nari!" he hailed him, adding pointedly, "Your parents are out, I saw them leave half an hour ago."

Nariman nodded, and as they passed his door he could be heard sharing the news excitedly with Mrs. Arjani, that the Vakeel boy was bringing home a brand-new girlfriend. Nariman glanced at Lucy's face while waiting for the lift. "Pathetic, aren't they," he whispered.

Upstairs, he put on the security chain so the door couldn't be opened, just in case. She asked, Wouldn't it better to lock the door to his room instead?

"My room doesn't lock. And they would walk right in, even if it were shut."

"Oh God," she cringed at the thought. "Is this worth it?"

"Yes," he whispered, nibbling her ear, lifting her hair to kiss her neck.

"You should cover up your ancestors' portraits," she said as they went down the long passageway to his bedroom.

"They're all scowling at me."

"They were never loved by an angel."

She sat on the bed to take off her shoes. He drew the curtains, and the dusk-laden room grew dark except for a scribble of light at the overlapping panels. He switched on the table lamp. They started to undress, and when she was down to her underclothes she pointed shyly to the light: "Turn it off."

"I need to see you – all of you. Please."

"Why?"

"To let all my senses worship you."

She paused, and continued to unbutton, pleased by his answer but complaining she could never win an argument with him. Standing behind her, he undid her brassière, then sniffed the back of her neck. He raised her arm and sniffed under it. She laughed. "What are you doing?"

"Worshipping with my nose." He stood before her, buried his face between her breasts, and inhaled. Kneeling, he hooked his fingers in the elastic waistband of her underpants and slid them to her ankles. She stepped out of them and waited. Still kneeling, he leaned forward and rubbed his nose in her hair. Her hands held his head to keep it there a moment longer.

In bed, with his ear upon her chest, he listened to her heartbeat. He kissed her, tasted her tongue, then her ears, and her nipples. Lower, he licked her navel, then meandered below . . .

The doorbell rang. The sound travelled savagely through the silent flat, pursued by a cluster of aggressive knocks. They sat up in bed, their pleasure already in tatters. Nariman decided to ignore the noise – whoever it was would go away concluding no one was home.

But the knocking and the bell continued. Thinking he heard his father's roar, he stepped into the hallway to listen. Yes, it was him. They rushed to put their clothes on. Lucy hurried to the drawing-room, straightening her hair as she went. After a cursory glance at his own person in the hall mirror, he unchained the door.

His mother's face was colourless, as though she were going to faint. His father was supporting her on one side, Soli Bamboat on the other. He took over from Soli, and asked what was wrong.

"My usual," said his mother, her voice coming in a gasp. She tried to smile. "Blood pressure dropped suddenly again."

With his mother's weight on his shoulder, they went down the passageway to his parents' room. He helped to take her shoes off. After she was safely in bed he left the room with his father.

Now his father lost his temper. "And may I ask what is going on here? Your mother is ill, I bring her home and find we are locked out of our own house! While she staggers on the doorstep!"

"I'm sorry, I wasn't expecting you so early." He detected the evening's liquor on his father's breath, and Soli's too.

"That's no excuse!" his father thundered. "Why must you—"

Then through the drawing-room door he spotted Lucy. "So this is the reason!"

"Yes," said Nariman quietly. "I had to put the chain on, you don't respect my privacy."

"Bay-sharam! What kind of unnatural son seeks privacy from his own parents? Unless he is planning filthy behaviour?" He gestured towards Lucy on the sofa, who was staring out the window, away from them.

"Shh, Marzi, poor Jeroo is slipping, you'll wake her up," said Soli, the vowels confounding him as usual. "Let's have some piss and quiet. We can deescuss all this later when she is filling better."

"Later? Already it's too late! This son of mine has turned my house into a raanwada, bringing his whore over here! It's the kind of immorality that's destroying the Parsi community!"

Nariman crossed the room to take Lucy's hand and lead her out of the flat. They didn't wait for the lift, in case his father opened the door to shout more abuse.

Not until they had put two flights between them could he feel safe. They stopped in the silence of the stairwell. "I'm sorry, Lucy. And I'm ashamed of my father's behaviour."

"It's not your fault," she said, keeping her composure although her voice trembled. "Just bad luck."

They smiled and shared a long kiss, sheltered by the bend in the stairs. After seeing her off in a taxi, he returned upstairs.

Retreating to his room would not help – his father would follow him there. So he waited, ignoring the flood of words, till a pause prompted him to speak.

"I have only one thing to say. When you call the woman I love a whore, and our home a raanwada because I invite her here, you disgrace the role of father. And I despair for you."

"Oh Nari, Nari!" intervened Soli. "You must never spick to your father like that, no matter what the risen."

"My son has never respected me like a father. Here is the proof, Soli, you just heard him."

The accusations and bitter recriminations continued, with Soli trying to make peace between them. He cajoled and scolded alternately. "Come, Marzi. Forgive and forget. Enough, Nari, not another word."

There was silence now, and Soli took the opportunity to philosophize: "Boys weal be boys, Marzi. Better that he has all his fun and froleek now. Afterwards, find a nice Parsi gull and settle down. Right, Nari? No hanky-panky after marriage."

He seemed determined to pursue his humorous approach to mending the rift: "So tell me, Nari. This gull-friend of yours – will she have to tell her padre in confession what you two deed today?"

He ignored his father's friend, who guffawed and continued, "I have it on good eenformation that these padres make the gulls tell all the juicy details – was he touching you, were you touching him, did he put it een?"

Soli laughed again, his belly heaving, and his father chuckled. They cautioned each other about disturbing Jeroo. Then Soli

*began teasing Nariman for his lack of humour, and Nariman
snapped that he had found nothing remotely funny in his puerile
remarks . . .*

About to go to her father's bedside, Roxana remembered
Yezad's tortured sleep and restrained herself. Her father's
mumbled fragments persisted in the darkness. Yezad's arm
slammed the headboard. Had he heard Pappa too? Or was it
the demons in his own head?

Her father continued in a subdued way, not the angry blast
from before. She heard Jehangir make soft kissing sounds to
comfort him, and her heart filled with a strange, painful happiness. What a beautiful boy, God bless him, so dependable,
so grown-up, who could tell from his behaviour he was just
nine . . .

She lay with her eyes open, listening. Pappa's suffering she
could guess at. But she would have given anything to understand Yezad's hell. If he wouldn't confide in her during their
waking hours, she wished he could at least talk in his sleep,
give her some hint of what was eating him.

～

Their eyes, with dark circles under them, met over their
teacups. She looked wretched, thought Yezad, with her haggard face and slumped shoulders, and it lacerated his heart.

But his doubts had been routed by the morning light. Soon
he would be able to tell her the truth, explain his actions. With
the stack of sixty-three thousand and whatever-it-was rupees
in his hands, forgiveness would be easy to secure.

He left before nine, following the usual drill to get to
Villie's door. Would she have collected the winnings from the
bookie? He resolved to take the money to Roxana straight
away and end her misery. He'd be late for work, but it
wouldn't kill Mr. Kapur to unlock the shop himself.

He knocked. No answer. He knocked louder. Nothing. Where was the silly woman – she knew how anxious he was. Maybe this was her revenge for his rudeness last night. But he had apologized. Perhaps she was at the bunya even now, counting his money – such a large sum, taking more time.

He knocked again, and fished for his handkerchief to wipe his sweat. His thumb, moistened with a little spit, laboured to erase the calculations he had scribbled on Villie's door. The pencilled numbers became a leaden smudge. He knocked once more, then gave up and started for work.

Time crawled. He remembered the snail Jehangir had brought home from the school garden, inspired by his grandfather's stories of the animal-lover. It had crawled about on the balcony – whatever had happened to it? . . . This day was moving slower than the snail, it would never be closing time.

But the hour did come when the shop closed. He ran to the station and fought his way into the first train to arrive.

His feet flew along the pavement to Pleasant Villa. Too exhausted for circumspection, he took the lift to the third floor, ascending through the evening smells of dinners being cooked in Pleasant Villa. His mouth watered . . . mutton chops frying somewhere. He didn't care who saw him at Villie's, it was all going to turn out well, in a few moments he would put the money in Roxie's hands.

While he imagined their happy reconciliation, the door opened. Instead of the jovial Matka Queen, before him stood a stricken woman, her demeanour pleading for consolation.

"Yezadji!" she wailed softly. "What a sad, sad day for me!"

His first thought was a death in the family – her ailing mother. "I'm so sorry, Villie. What happened?"

"You haven't heard? Where were you all day?"

"At work."

"So? All Bombay knows about it. Every lane and every gully is buzzing with no other talk – police have shut Matka down."

"When?"

"Early this morning." She said that at midnight, as usual, she had stood by her window for first-floor Sampat to stop under the lamppost and tell her the closing. "He held up eight fingers."

Yes, he thought. Yes, my troubles are over.

Without reacting to his relieved intake of breath, she continued, "Police raids started a few hours later. Our own poor Lalubhai was arrested around four-thirty."

"But this has happened before, no? A big shor-shaar closes Matka for a few days, then everything calms down and it starts again."

"Not this time." Those previous raids were pre-arranged among the Matka chiefs, police, and politicians, she said, only some small bookies ever went to jail. Last night was a surprise to everyone. "And this time they have smashed Matka completely. All day I have spent at Lalubhai's shop, with his sons, who are trying to get bail for him."

She said the police were arresting people from top to bottom – big bookies and small, kingpins and little safety pins. Rumour was that since those terrorist bombs had blown up the stock exchange and shattered Bombay, they had to do something about Matka. Even the crookedest politician didn't want Bombay to be the next Beirut.

"No Matka, no Lalubhai, nothing left for me. What will I do with my dreams?"

"Never mind, Villie." He made a feeble attempt at consoling her, nudging playfully with his elbow. "Your powerful dream came true. You finished with a bang. Like a cricketer's century in his final innings before retirement."

"You know, Yezadji, when I heard about the raids, you were first in my thoughts. I wish you had let me cancel your bet."

His hands went cold. "The result was eighteen! That's what we played – eighteen pieces of Cadbury chocolate!" His voice had risen, he realized, and he lowered it. "The raid was not till after midnight, the number was already declared."

"So? Everything is confiscated. Lalubhai's sons don't have one paisa left."

"Surely . . . ," he tried, and was dumb. Then he clutched at words weak as straws: "Surely a receipt, a record . . . something to show? To prove . . . ?"

"Think before speaking. Matka is illegal – how can there be receipts and account books? And if there was, where would you take it? Police station? You want to join Lalubhai in his jail cell?"

Without another word, he dragged his feet out of her flat and into his own.

In the back room, Yezad sat on the bed to remove his shoes. He called to Roxana, and Jehangir came as well.

Yezad told him to go: "I've to talk to Mummy in private."

His son looked at her, and she nodded. Yezad shut the door after him and got the envelopes out of the cupboard.

"Sit," he said, and put the envelopes in her lap. She began checking inside them, and fear flooded her face.

"Yes, they're empty," he said dully. "All of them. I took the money."

Starting with his first secret Matka wager weeks ago, he told her everything. She began to seethe, but her anger was soon subdued by worry, by the sound of his voice that was drained lifeless. She almost wished he was raging again.

She set the empty envelopes aside and moved closer till their shoulders touched. At once he leaned towards her, and she put her arm around him.

He promised to replace the money with an advance from Mr. Kapur against future commissions – schools and colleges would soon be ordering new equipment, the loss would be easily made up. As for Villie, he never wanted to talk to her again, she and her powerful dreams could go to hell . . .

As he unburdened himself, Roxana blessed their good fortune that they were past the middle of November – the major expenses, school fees, electricity had already been paid.

O N HIS WAY TO WORK Yezad noticed that Christmas decorations had appeared in many shop windows. Till last week their Divali displays were up. Now it was cotton wool and plastic holly and tinsel.

This would be the morning to ask Mr. Kapur for the advance, he resolved. And an increment – he needed it now, more than ever. Mr. Kapur was bound to be in a great mood, his new Christmas display was arriving. For days, he'd been as excited as a child.

But it was curious, thought Yezad, that Shiv Sena hadn't yet made Santa Claus a political issue, considering the tantrums thrown by their mobs over Valentine's Day. Since coming to power they'd been in a constant fit of censorship and persecution. Top of the list were Muslims, their favourite scapegoat as usual, he felt. Then the Sena had destroyed the work of famous Indian artists, deeming it disrespectful towards Hindu gods and goddesses. Men's magazines, endangering Indian morals with nudity and sex and vulgarity, had their offices set on fire. And women weren't allowed to work in bars and discos after eight o'clock because it was against Indian family values.

What a joke of a government. Clowns and crooks. Or clownish crooks. Santa Claus with mask and machine gun would be a fitting Christmas decoration for the Shiv Sena. Or any other party, for that matter.

He acknowledged Husain's greeting and unlocked the shop door, wondering what Christmas trappings Mr. Kapur had planned. Usually, the window was left to Husain: a basic string of lights, a silver star, a Season's Greetings sign in letters of red and green, their serifs and descenders sporting snowflakes and icicles. When done, a beaming Husain would invite Mr. Kapur and Yezad to admire his perennial master-piece.

But this year Mr. Kapur had been hinting at something grand: "Wait and see, our new display will be the talk of the town. It's coming soon, Yezad. Are you in the Christmas spirit?"

If he only knew what was happening at home, thought Yezad, and how precarious his financial position. He hoped they weren't in for anything too garish or religious – there were enough mangers, Jesuses, Marys, Josephs, Santa Clauses, and flashing lights all over the city already.

A honking at the kerb summoned Husain to unload the car. Yezad followed, and found a grinning Mr. Kapur waiting by the open trunk. "I went to my carpenter's shop to pick it up personally because—"

He broke off to caution the peon: "Aray Husain, sambhaa-lo! Bahut delicate hai, na."

At once Husain showed extreme concern and cradled the packages like babies. He took them inside the shop, one by one, and deposited them gently on the counter, as though tucking them to sleep in their cribs. Mr. Kapur started unwrapping.

"Are you ready? Tan-tan-tana!" he sang a fanfare and ripped off the paper.

Revealed in all its antlered splendour was a reindeer dressed in cricketer's whites, a peak cap squeezed between the horns. The two-dimensional plywood figure, about eighteen inches high, was fitted with a base so it could stand on its hind legs. There were five such reindeer, each in a slightly different pose, plus the wicket-keeping reindeer, tougher-looking than the others, with an intimidating glint in its eyes – one mistake and it would whip your bails off.

"Fielding side," said Mr. Kapur. "So? What do you think?"

"Fantastic," said Yezad mechanically. His mind, preoccupied with money matters, was calculating the best possible moment to make the appeal.

Then he realized that Mr. Kapur was eyeing him curiously, and he began to show more interest. "Fantastic," he repeated. "But why not a full team?"

"Our window isn't big enough for eleven. I've got one more in here, though."

Mr. Kapur unwrapped the last package, the biggest, and lifted out a Santa Claus with his bat ready to drive the ball to the square leg boundary. He was not in whites, having retained his red uniform; his pads and gloves were red too. Nariman would never approve, thought Yezad.

"Chalo, Husain, make room in the window," said Mr. Kapur excitedly. "Let's set it all up. Oh, wait, I forgot to show you the most important thing."

His hand disappeared inside his attaché case and emerged with a small, specially modified electric motor. He connected the device behind Santa's shoulder, on the unpainted side, and switched it on. The bat began to rise stiffly, as though the joints were plagued by acute rheumatism. When the plywood arms were almost vertical, the bat paused, then started its painful swing downwards.

"All the way for four runs!" said Husain.

They laughed and began arranging the display, arguing lightheartedly about the field-placing. "We'll take turns," said Mr. Kapur. "Tomorrow you be in charge of the fielders."

Next came what he called the accessories: the plywood stumps, artificial turf for the wicket, white tape to mark the creases. And there was the usual holly and cotton wool to toss around.

"Cricket at the North Pole," said Mr. Kapur, beaming with pleasure. "First time in the history of the MCC."

Watching him, Yezad thought his boss looked like a little boy playing with a mechanical Santa. Was this a man preparing to run for election? He was on his hands and knees now, crawling among the turf and tinsel, moving it here, scattering it there, till things were to his satisfaction.

No, thought Yezad with a smile, impossible to see him in politics.

"Come on, Mr. Chenoy, stop smiling and help me with these decorations."

Yezad entered the window to join in hanging up the baubles and miniature stockings. He yearned for the return of the ambitious entrepreneur bent on growth and expansion. If Mr. Kapur had any sense, he would put him in charge right away, regardless of election plans. He'd perform wonders with Bombay Sporting, he'd be able to—

"Hey, Yezad, it just occurred to me. I could rent a Santa Claus outfit, distribute sweets to customers."

"You're not serious."

"Would be fun, no?"

No, thought Yezad, but Mr. Kapur was keen on it. And now was the time to make the loan request, while he was merry as the man whose red clothes he wanted to wear.

"I need a favour, Mr. Kapur," he began, continuing in a confidential whisper: unforeseen circumstances, urgent expenses.

"Sure. Just make out the advance, I'll sign it."

"Thanks, Mr. Kapur." That was easy, he thought with relief. "By the way, how are the campaign plans for the election?"

"Superb. Lots of support from friends and neighbours."

"You know you can rely on me to run the shop."

"I'm counting on it."

"And you know, Mr. Kapur, I was thinking – no need to wait, I can take on more responsibility right away, to relieve you. You'll have more time for your planning, as well as for these Christmas celebrations."

"Thanks, Yezad. But I think I can manage for now. When campaigning begins full-time, of course you'll be in charge."

"Maybe we should finalize—"

"Sahab!" called Husain urgently from the pavement; he had been scrutinizing the window from outside.

"What?" asked Mr. Kapur, and hurried to the door. Cursing the interruption, Yezad followed.

"Sahab, big problem! There is bat, wicket, fielders, wicket-keeper. Sub kootch hai. But no ball only."

Mr. Kapur slapped him on the back with affection. "See, Yezad, how sharp is my Husain miyan. Even you didn't notice the ball was missing."

"So where is it?"

Still being crafted, he said, and it would arrive in a few days. He warned them to stay ready for another fabulous surprise.

13

B EFORE THE END-OF-DAY PRAYER, Miss Alvarez called Jehangir to her desk. He could smell her perfume as she handed him an envelope. Knees unsteady, he returned to his seat and slipped it into his school bag.

The Catholic boys closed their eyes and made the sign of the cross, a few others imitated them indifferently, the rest put their hands together. The class began chanting, "We give Thee thanks, Almighty God . . ."

Jehangir trembled, forgetting the words he repeated every day. He was sure the note could be about one thing only. Teacher had said, Please give this to your parents. He'd heard sadness in her voice. Yes, Teacher, he'd mumbled.

But he didn't give it to his mother on getting home. He waited, and was glad he did, for his father was in a good mood, which meant now she would be happy too, and things would be easier with the note. It frightened him to think what might have happened if Daddy had been like he was that day when he threatened to tie Mummy up. He pushed the sealed envelope at him.

"What's this?"

"From Miss Alvarez."

"Why?"

"Open it, Yezdaa, you'll find out," said his mother, prompting him as one would a child. "Probably Jehangoo has come first again in a test or something."

He turned to the balcony to hide his face as his father tore open the envelope and read aloud:

"Dear Mr. and Mrs. Chenoy,
I would be grateful if either one of you would be able

to see me tomorrow. Besides regular class hours from
8.30 a.m. to 4.30 p.m., I will also be available for an hour
before assembly.

Please accept my apologies for the inconvenience.

Yours sincerely,

Helen Alvarez

(Std. IV A)"

"Why is she calling us, Jehangoo?" asked his mother.

"I don't know."

"Are you hiding something?"

"No."

"So will you go?" asked Yezad.

"How can I? Who'll stay with Pappa?"

Sighing, he told Jehangir to let Miss Alvarez know he
would be there tomorrow at four-thirty.

In the empty classroom Miss Alvarez's high heels echoed
sharply as she descended the platform and shook hands. "I'm
sorry to make you come all the way, Mr. Chenoy, but it's
quite a serious matter."

Her appearance reassured him: how serious a matter could
he possibly hear about from one who looked so pretty? He
thought of his own school days – they hadn't invented such
lovely teachers then. His time at St. Xavier's was filled with
fierce masters named Mr. Lobo and Mr. Mascarenhas and
Mr. Monteiro, big-moustached disciplinarians. Nothing
resembling a Helen Alvarez.

Jehangir lingered in the corridor outside, and she called him
in. "I still find it hard to believe that my best student was
involved with those other boys," she started reluctantly.

Yezad smiled, wondering what sort of mischief the youngsters had been up to, part of him pleased that Jehangla was in
it with his peers. No sense being goody-goody all the time.
Childhood, boyhood wasn't complete if the rascals didn't get

into trouble. He'd been the same, during his own years in this school . . .

And the classrooms had hardly changed. Rows of empty desks stretched behind Miss Alvarez, he could see them over her shoulder. That schoolboy smell of sweat and youthfulness and foodstuffs was in the air, ammoniac, mingled with traces of ink, snacktime biscuits, lunchtime sandwiches, puri-bhaji, ragdaa patties. Permeating everything, occupying the room as solidly as the furniture, a timeless smell . . .

Suddenly, Yezad's own youth was upon him. Memory began to populate the empty benches with faces from the past. Those happy days, when a week of school was a lifetime, rich and complete; in a week, strangers might become dear friends, battles could be lost and won, whole kingdoms acquired, for time worked differently then. How slowly the seasons changed then – from one monsoon to another seemed an eternity, the skies pouring endless rain, the only bright spot the chance of a holi-day if the roads got flooded. And when that happened, you were always warned to stay away from the kerb, keep to the inside of the footpath, because drain covers could be missing – stolen and sold for scrap – and every year children were swept away in the sewers. The buses and cars, half-submerged, looked like strange boats navigating an inland sea. And it was an adventure to wade through the perils of waist-high water, through the murk and floating rubbish, pretending it was the Amazon where the anaconda lurked. Performing feats of unimaginable bravery, you reached higher ground, finding civi-lization when you arrived home to hot tea and a snack and a holiday . . .

"So you see, Mr. Chenoy, it's my most important project," said Miss Alvarez.

His name pulled him back into the present – she was talk-ing about Homework Monitoring. He remembered Jehangir explaining it at Nariman's birthday party. Barely four months ago . . . seemed so much longer . . .

He faked a concerned nod: "It sounds very interesting."

"And I had such high hopes for the class. But now I have to suspend the project. You see, three boys who didn't do their homework gave money to the Monitor to get good marks."

Jehangir scrutinized his father's shoes, his own, and Miss Alvarez's, which revealed her toes, each crowned with a lovely little ruby. Then the tears made his eyes blurry, and the rubies became one long crimson smear.

Meanwhile, Yezad tut-tutted and shook his head to show disapproval. He wondered what was Jehangla's role. Not the bribing, he had no money; besides, his homework was always done, and he was a Homework Monitor—

The incipient thought froze in his mind. "Did you catch the three?"

"Yes. Also the Monitor who took the money." And as she spoke, her arm went up and embraced her pupil's shoulders; she was able to make it a gesture of identification and protection.

Yezad's eyebrows rose as he looked at his son, then at Miss Alvarez.

She nodded sadly.

"I don't know what to say." The classroom smell nauseated him now as he looked again at Jehangir for explanation. But Jehangir's eyes were still studiously examining footwear.

"I was just as shocked when I found out," said Miss Alvarez. "Not by those three, they're such duffers." She blushed at her word. "I mean, they're hopeless in their studies because they don't care, they come from rich families, parents who think money will get them everything in life. But Jehangir was my golden boy."

She swallowed. "When I discovered that every week he was taking sixty rupees, twenty from each of the three, I was so upset, I—"

Sixty. She had said sixty. Yezad stopped listening. Sixty was the difference between what he put in the envelopes and what Roxie found.

"—and I wanted to lay a firm foundation for my boys, make honesty a permanent part of their character. So they would be able, as adults, to resist the corruption in our society. Especially those who might enter politics or the IAS. Instead, that very evil has already infected my classroom. How will things ever get better for our country?"

Yezad mumbled how sorry he was, and promised to make sure Jehangir learned his lesson from the incident.

"This morning I woke up feeling I should give up teaching," said Miss Alvarez. "What's the use, I asked myself, if my best pupil can be tempted into doing wrong."

"You must never give up, Miss Alvarez. You are a wonderful teacher, Jehangir has told us all about you, and how much he likes you. He says you are the best teacher he's ever had."

Now Jehangir began to cry, silently first, then with sobs that made his shoulders convulse. "I'm sorry, Teacher," he whispered.

She smiled. "I think I will keep on teaching. And I hope you will learn from this big mistake."

Yezad assured her nothing like it would ever happen again, he gave her his personal assurance. She said she wished all parents were as cooperative, and thanked him for coming.

∿

The wait was agonizing. He wanted them to punish him quickly, get angry with him. Instead, his father kept squeezing his shoulder, saying things like, It's okay, Jehangla, don't worry, and his mother pressed him to her side and said my poor child, he frets just like a grown-up. It was her fault, she insisted, for letting him see the envelopes, she was to blame for his finding out how little money there was.

That was all – no scolding or slaps. And it left him feeling horrible.

Then they began bickering between themselves, laying the blame where it wouldn't quite fit. To listen to them hurt each other because of what he had done was going to be his punishment, Jehangir realized.

282

"See what your disgraceful half-sister and -brother have done," said Yezad. "A child of nine has to take part in bribery and corruption."

"Don't exaggerate," said Roxana. "Some bad boys offered Jehangoo money, and he accepted it to help his family, end of story. No need to twist it and turn it and make it into something ugly."

"But it is ugly. And there's only one way to explain it. The same corruption that pollutes this country is right here, in your own family, in Jal and Coomy's shameless trickery and betrayal. Think of the example they have set. Is it any wonder Jehangla took the bribe?"

"Do you know what nonsense you are talking? Can you hear yourself? Our son did not take money to buy bubble gum or ice cream for himself. He did it to help his parents with food, and with his Grandpa's medicines."

"So it's all my fault. Because I cannot provide enough to run this deluxe nursing home for your father."

"I didn't say that."

Then Yezad said if ten years ago he could have looked into the future, he would never have given up on his Canadian dream. He would have tried again and again, that racist immigration officer could not have blocked his way forever. And they would all be living happily right now in Toronto, breathing the pure Rocky Mountain air instead of the noxious fumes of this dying city, rotting with pollution and garbage and corruption.

And Roxana said did he think Canada was a land of living saints? And so far as she knew, the Rocky Mountains were still in Alberta, unless the government had quietly shifted them to Ontario one night.

The slip embarrassed Yezad, and he said very good, full marks in geography, and now he wanted to talk no more about this, he would go to the balcony for some peace and quiet. No, not balcony, he corrected himself, they didn't have one any more, they had a jhopadpatti.

"Why do you say needlessly nasty things?" she appealed. "Why must you call the children's tent, something they enjoy, a jhopadpatti?"

"Just look at it: Villie's smelly old plastic tablecloth. Go to any slum, you'll find plastic is the building material. What can I call this but a jhopadpatti?"

"Call it what you like, I've no time to argue. I still have to go to market, buy potatoes, cook dinner."

"What were you doing all afternoon?"

"Ballroom dancing! What do you think? Pappa needed a sponge bath. You know how long that takes? And changing the sheets with him in the bed? If I don't do it you complain about smell."

"The room is still smelling. Non-stop he farts. What do you feed him?"

"Same thing I feed you. But his stomach doesn't work as well. You'll see when you get old."

"Now put a curse on me."

"Why is it a curse? You're never getting old? Murad! Jehangir! Open your books. I want to see your homework finished when I get back."

On the balcony Yezad saw Roxana emerge from the building with her basket, his eyes following her the way hers used to follow him when he left for work every morning, when they still would wave to each other. She stepped off the footpath and he almost shouted, Wait! There are cars coming!

But she had seen them, and stepped back up to the kerb. He sighed with relief. She watched for a break in the stream of traffic, then rushed across. She moved with the awkward scurry of an exhausted person, and it hurt him to watch. Her shoulders looked so stooped from up here. His darling Roxana. Slowly her loveliness was being erased by the burden upon her, and he couldn't protect her from it. Why, in his thoughts, did he feel nothing but love for her, yet, when she

284

was before him, quarrel and animosity came out of his mouth, as though she were the enemy?

Time passed as he stood on the balcony and saw the clouds assume the colour of the evening. The setting sun was painting copper edges around them. He looked at the chaos of television cables and radio antennae and electrical connections and telephone lines spread out against the sky. Fitting, he thought, for a city that was chaos personified. This mad confusion of wires, criss-crossing between buildings, haphazardly spanning the road, looping crazily around trees, climbing drunkenly to rooftops – this mad confusion seemed to have trapped the neighbourhood in its web.

"Bottle, please," called Nariman from inside.

Yezad straightened from the railing he was leaning on, and turned his head. A ragged flight of crows cawed through the tangle in the sky. He waited; Nariman called again.

Should he? It was not his job, he had made it clear to Roxana – at least this one thing he would be firm about . . . and she would be home shortly, in any case.

The twilight was crowded now with birds racing against the evening and bats welcoming the darkness. He watched them flutter back and forth, baffled within the hurdle of wires.

"Please, I need my bottle."

The words drifted rudderless through the room. Moments later, Jehangir approached his father timidly on the balcony. "Daddy, I think Grandpa wants to do soo-soo."

"Yes, I heard. Mummy will be back soon," said Yezad, and made him return to his books.

Nariman appealed again, louder now. "The bottle, please! I'm bloated . . ." His tired voice trailed away and was silent for a while, then started once more.

Roxana heard the plea from the front room as soon as her foot was in the door. "Is everyone gone deaf?" she demanded. "Poor Pappa needs to do soo-soo!"

"What did you want me to do?" asked Yezad.

"Give him the bottle, what else! Play cricket with him?" she said, picking up the urinal.

He shook his head.

"I've never asked you to help me! Can't you at least help Pappa when I'm out?"

He shook his head again. "I told you the day the chief came here, I warned the boys also – no touching the bedpan or bottle."

"What is so bad about the bottle? I keep it clean and hygienic!" She said perhaps he should try to remember the teachings of Gandhiji, that there was nothing nobler than the service of the weak, the old, the unfortunate.

He told her not to bring Gandhiji into it, not one thing he taught had worked for India. "He gave away Pakistan and left the country with problems."

"You sound like those RSS fanatics, trying to blame a saint. Instead of getting upset about the bottle, be glad our children can learn about old age, about caring – it will prepare them for life, make them better human beings."

"First they should learn about fun and happiness, and enjoy their youth. Lots of time to learn about sickness and dying."

"No time like the present. It's a chance to practise kindness every day, like Daisy practises her violin. If they learn kindness, happiness will follow. And one day, when we are old and helpless, they'll not turn their backs on us."

Yezad said he hoped the day would never come when they placed such a heavy load on their sons. He would make sure to arrange their affairs more wisely, so they wouldn't end up without a rupee to their name when they were old.

THE CROWS WERE CAWING, the parrot screeched across the road, the vendors sang on the pavement, breakfast was almost ready. Murad had finished his bath, and was putting on his uniform in the back room. But Jehangir refused to open his eyes till his father, shaking his shoulder, said he would be late for school.

"I'm not feeling well."

"What's wrong?"

"Stomach's hurting."

"Are you sure? Not because of Miss Alvarez?"

"No, it's really hurting."

"Miss Alvarez is a very kind teacher, you'll be all right."

While his father went to bathe, Jehangir took out his Lake Como jigsaw puzzle, and tried pleading with his mother. She was more sympathetic. "Didn't you sleep, Jehangoo? Such dark circles under your eyes."

"His conscience kept him awake," yelled Yezad from the bathroom as he undressed. "Which is good, it means it's in working condition." He continued to call out encouragement over the clatter of mug against pail, and the splashing water.

But Jehangir stopped listening. He wanted to escape into the Lake Como puzzle. Its familiar landscape was far less complicated than his real world. One thousand, two hundred and seventy-two pieces, the lid declared, making it his most difficult jigsaw. The colours moved in gradations so subtle that the blue of the sky melted into the lake (cerulean, he remembered Grandpa's word) and the deep dark greens could be tree foliage or part of the dense shrubbery hugging the hills. Their reluctance to yield their secrets was their charm. He treasured his fragments in the cardboard box.

And when the lake began to emerge, and the path along its shore, he would be gone – into the puzzle, walking alongside the peasant girl who led, by its muzzle, a donkey pulling the jingling cart piled high with hay, down the road that curved and disappeared into the wooded hills. Piece by piece he would build his refuge, enjoy the lake breeze and golden sunlight on his face, feel the lush grass under his feet, smell the fragrance in the air . . .

The last was the most elusive, he'd discovered. There were no pieces to fit together to make a fragrance. It was nowhere in the landscape, and everywhere.

He had to imagine the fresh air that would linger over the path inside the jigsaw puzzle. And birdsong – where there was fresh air, instinct told him, there was bound to be birdsong. Not the raucous cawing of scavenger crows, but birdsong like his father's whistling, bold and sweet. His father's whistling, that could banish unhappiness, even the memory of unhappiness. His father's whistle was invincible, it floated over him like a cheerful umbrella, and when he held his hand and they walked under it, the world was safe and wonderful. Jehangir loved him then, and didn't want to be anyone but his father's son, not even if he could have switched places with one of the Famous Five . . .

Across the road, the parrot screeched again. He began throwing the pieces back into the box, it was hopeless, the jigsaw was not working for him.

His father came into the front room with his towel around him and a finger in his ear, trying to dislodge the water blocking it. "Tell me, Jehangla, how many days can you stay home to avoid Miss Alvarez?"

"I told you my stomach hurts." He could smell the scent of Cinthol soap on his father's skin.

"It will stop hurting if you go to school. Trust me. Ignore those bad boys, do your lessons as always, and you'll be fine."

Water dripped from his father's head onto the lid of the jigsaw puzzle. Jehangir moved it out of the way. His father went into the back room to put on his pants, returning with the towel over his head to dry his hair.

"You're a first-class student, Jehangla, you have nothing to be afraid of." He left the damp towel around his neck and placed his arm over Jehangir's shoulder. "You know what your name means?"

He shook his head.

"It means 'conqueror of the world.'"

Jehangir was impressed. He looked up and smiled weakly at his father. The scattered curls of his chest hair were still damp.

"A stomach ache cannot stop the conqueror of the world." His father patted his back and told him to get dressed.

Murad came into the front room with his school tie slung loose around his collar. "What does my name mean?" he asked.

"You are a boon, a blessing," said his father.

"And Mummy's name?"

"Roxana means the dawn."

"And yours?"

"Guardian angel. Come here, let me fix your tie."

Jehangir wondered about these names as he watched his father make the knot, while Murad kept asking for more meanings. Grandpa's was especially complicated, from the Shah-Nama story, and Daddy tried to remember the lineage of the hero, Rustam, whether Nariman was the great- or the great-great-grandfather. Then Grandpa, who'd just woken up, told them the answer: great-grandfather.

Their names taken together, thought Jehangir, made the perfect family: they were blessed, they possessed the whole world, they had their own guardian angel, and Mummy's dawn light shone upon all of them. Yet Mummy and Daddy were fighting and unhappy . . .

"—and though you might not know it now, these are your

289

happy days, your school days," said Daddy, talking to both of them. "Before you know it, they'll slip through your fingers. And when you're older you'll remember them with longing, you'll yearn for them to return. But they won't. So grab them now and enjoy them."

Jehangir wanted to believe his father, but first the world that had fallen apart had to be pieced together again. He wished it was like making a jigsaw puzzle – open the box, reconstruct Grandpa's flat in Chateau Felicity, fix Grandpa's bones, patch up the quarrel with Coomy Aunty and Jal Uncle. And most important of all, piece together the lovely mornings of story and laughter and joking, which seemed to have disappeared so completely.

～

Yezad saw the boys off to school with extra hugs. At the door, he kissed their foreheads. Then he returned to the dining table.

He sat there dreaming, picturing his sons in the doorway where they had just waved goodbye. Growing up so fast. Seemed like yesterday Murad was starting kindergarten and Jehangir was crawling in diapers. And look at them now. To think he had created them, he and Roxie, these two beautiful sons of theirs.

Then he sternly reminded himself: every dog and cat could reproduce, he had not invented the process or done something unique. It was this kind of sloppy thinking that made population control impossible in this country.

But his sense of wonder returned despite his very sensible view of the subject. And, lost in his thoughts, he began whistling softly "Sunrise, Sunset."

Roxana recognized the tune and came to sit beside him. He stopped, and she stroked his arm. "What are you thinking, Yezdaa?"

"Nothing important."

"Tell me."

He sighed. "I was watching the boys get ready, thinking they looked so handsome in their uniforms."

She smiled.

"And I was remembering the years when they were small, how I'd carry them in my arms and on my shoulders, and the games we played. I could never do that now. And then I thought of that song. The one when Tevye and his wife are at their daughter's wedding – you remember the film?"

Roxana nodded. "She marries the tailor."

"Yes. And Tevye is watching the ceremony, he looks in wonder at his grown-up child and the bridegroom. And that made me think, one day Murad and Jehangir will be married, we'll be watching the ceremony. And afterwards we'll be old, and alone."

"Don't be silly, Yezdaa. They'll always be our sons."

"No. They'll be their wives' husbands."

"I've never heard you so sentimental before," she said. "What's the matter with you, these days?"

He remained silent. Then he drew her close and put his arm around her.

Mr. KAPUR CIRCLED the parcel like a little boy fighting the temptation to open his gift before the appointed hour. Inside was the special ball for the Christmas window. He and Yezad awaited the peon's return from an errand.

"Husain will be disappointed if we do it without him," said Mr. Kapur, playing a forward defensive stroke with his imaginary bat.

Absorbed in his thoughts, Yezad nodded without listening. He had made his decision: before the day was over, he would again attempt to pin Mr. Kapur down, ask him when he was going to start campaigning full-time. Extract some commitment from him.

"You're really enjoying this Christmas tamasha, aren't you?" he tried as an opener.

"You know my policy: in our cosmopolitan shop, we honour all festivals, they all celebrate our human and divine natures. More the merrier." Smiling his cheerful, humanity-embracing smile, Mr. Kapur stood beside the window, looking out into the road over Santa Claus's shoulder. He nodded at passersby, waved at the pao-bhajivala, yelled out good morning to an acquaintance.

"Your policy is absolutely correct," said Yezad. "This city is a miracle of tolerance. And it must stay that way."

"You're starting to sound like me," said Mr. Kapur, amused by the earnest tone.

"Well, I've been listening to you for fifteen years," said Yezad, and they laughed.

"Look, there's Husain." They waved to hurry him on. And to entertain them, the peon affected a run like a toddler on unsteady feet. "Chalo, miyan, the special ball has come."

Mr. Kapur tore away the protective padding and held up the custom-designed prop. Made of a round light bulb, it was the bright red colour of a new cricket ball, with rows of stitches painted along its circumference to resemble the seam.

"So? What do you think?"

"I think it's brilliant," said Yezad. He'd use this new ball like a pace bowler exploiting the shine, he thought. He'd try yorkers, googlies, full tosses, whatever it took to get Mr. Kapur's wicket.

"Wait till you see it in action – even more brilliant than it looks." Mr. Kapur rummaged in the packaging for the cord and socket. "It's synchronized with the motor for Santa's arm – every time the bat approaches the ball, it lights up."

"Good, let's connect it." The sooner it got working, the better – then the boss would be at his mellowest, ready to be generous when they discussed the terms.

Mr. Kapur had brought a spool of transparent thread from his wife's sewing basket. He unravelled a length and tied the end to the socket, to suspend it from the ceiling.

"I'll go up the ladder," volunteered Yezad. "It's a very delicate job. Too close, and the bat will smash the bulb. Too far and it won't look realistic."

From the top of the ladder he let the bulb descend to within a foot of the floor, steadying his hand against the ceiling. "How's that?"

"Little lower," said Mr. Kapur. "I want it to appear like it's going to connect with the sweet spot."

Yezad allowed two more inches of thread to slip between his fingers. "This window is going to attract hordes of people. We'll need a special havaldar for crowd control."

"I hope so. Little bit to the left."

"You know, Mr. Kapur, you should take this opportunity to publicize your own name in the display. A sign saying, Compliments of the Season, from Vikram Kapur, Proprietor."

"No, that would look cheap."

Yezad tried again to ease into the topic. "At least put a campaign slogan in the window: A Vote For Vikram Kapur Is a Vote

For Santa Claus. Or: Hit a Sixer, Vote Vikram Kapur."

"Good one, Yezad," he attempted a laugh. "But there isn't going to be an election."

Yezad heard the note of unease. He moved the string more to the left, and forward, following the guiding hand below. "Of course there is."

"Not for me. I don't think I'm going to run."

The transparent string escaped Yezad's fingers. The bulb fell to the floor and shattered.

"Oh no!" Mr. Kapur jumped back to avoid the glass.

Yezad's hands were shaking as he came down the ladder. Apologizing, he heard his own voice as though it was a stranger's. "But why not, Mr. Kapur?"

"You dropped the ball! Oh Yezad, Yezad, Yezad!"

"I'm sorry, Mr. Kapur. But please tell me—"

"Now I'll have to order another one." He walked off in disgust. "It'll take three or four days to come."

"You're not listening to me, Vikram. I'm asking you why not."

Mr. Kapur looked at him, then turned and faced the window again. "For five days Santa Claus has been swatting air with his bat," he grumbled. "Five days I waited for that ball."

Distressed as Yezad was, he knew Mr. Kapur needed to be pacified. "Maybe we can put in a regular bulb for the time being," he suggested.

"That will look more ridiculous," muttered Mr. Kapur. But after moping for a while, he agreed to try it. Husain went to fetch a spare bulb from the storage room.

"I don't understand," ventured Yezad. "With all your plans and preparations, the manifesto you told me you wrote, now why are you changing your mind?"

"Lots of reasons. It's . . . it's too complicated. I think it's unrealistic of me to hope to—"

He broke off and looked away, but Yezad could see the sheepish expression reflected in the window glass. "It's too dangerous. My wife made a good point: she said elections these days are nothing better than fights between gangsters. And after thinking about it, I have to agree with her. Besides, she's worried about my blood pressure."

Toying with the bulb socket, he seemed to want to explain further, when Husain returned, dragging a broom behind him and waving a sixty-watt bulb. "Look, sahab, I found it!"

Mr. Kapur appeared relieved at the interruption; he busied himself in the window. The peon swept up the bits of red glass that were scattered around like drops of blood. The cotton wool and tinsel and holly, shaken out, dislodged more droplets. When they were through, Mr. Kapur inserted the bulb in the socket and started the motor.

The bat descended, the light came on; the bat rose, the bulb went off. Husain cheered like a spectator in the stands at Wankhede Stadium, to try and make his employer smile. But the substitute bulb's thin yellow light had jaundiced the mood.

How could Mr. Kapur let him down in such an offhand manner, despaired Yezad. Wife said no! Was that any kind of explanation?

For the rest of the day he struggled with a sense of hopelessness. He felt anger and betrayal, till calmer moments prevailed and he saw how irrational he was being – Mr. Kapur knew nothing really about his difficulties.

Perhaps he needed to confide in Mr. Kapur, tell him why his decision not to run was such a profound disappointment – that he had pinned all his hopes on the promotion. He would have to swallow his pride and confess that it had become impossible to make ends meet on his salary: two children, school expenses, prices rising month by month . . . and now, to add to that, sick father-in-law who'd been kicked out by his stepson and stepdaughter, no room in my tiny flat, and no money for medicines, plus bedpan stinking in the front room . . . causing quarrels with my wife, but I feel obligated to him because he bought the flat for us when we got married . . .

Yezad put a hand to his forehead. No, the entire story was too messy. Much too messy to tell someone who was ultimately a stranger when it came to revealing all these personal family matters.

Through the afternoon, he watched the spasmodic Santa struggling with arthritic shoulders. Every once in a while the little motor malfunctioned; then the bulb blinked rapidly and the bat made little tremulous up-and-down movements. Like Santa has Parkinson's, he thought.

Husain ran to fetch Mr. Kapur, who in turn ran to reset the switch. After an adjustment, Mr. Kapur issued a stylish thumbs-up signal and returned to his office. The bat resumed normal operation.

The slow strobe of the light bulb began to cast a hypnotic spell over Yezad as the hours wore one. He felt immobilized, like the reindeer in their fielding positions, and the frozen wicket-keeper, ever ready to stump Captain Claus and yell "Howzat?" to the invisible umpire.

But the challenge was never sounded. And the longer Yezad gazed at the idiotic tableau, the more depressed he became. Nothing made sense.

Suddenly, his life seemed to him as meagre as poor Villie Cardmaster's – going from the lovely little pink-frocked girl in the birthday photo, eyes shining with innocent hope, to the woman she now was . . .

He tore his eyes away from the mesmeric Santa and watched Husain instead. The peon stopped frequently to adjust a shred of cotton wool, a plastic leaf, a strand of tinsel.

Yezad envied his ability to delight in simple things. What was his secret? Husain's life, ravaged by the nightmare of his family's murder, was still able to find pleasure in all this tawdry paraphernalia.

Like Mr. Kapur, who emerged from his office, smiled forgivingly at Yezad, and went to the window display where he stood grinning for a few moments before returning to his desk.

14

WHILE ROXANA WAITED for the lift in the foyer of Chateau Felicity, she heard a car by the entrance, followed by a clatter and rattle and crash. It was Edul Munshi with his tool box.

In no mood for his handyman chit-chat, she hoped the lift would rescue her before he came in. This visit to Jal and Coomy, this attempt to sort things out with them, had heightened her anxiety. She needed to find a way of bringing Pappa back, the strain on Yezad was too much now – behaving so strangely, these last few days . . .

"Oh, look who's here," said Edul behind her. "Haven't seen you in months, Roxana. How are you?"

"I'm fine. And you?"

"Champion. Just came from helping a friend with a shaky leg." He added, "His dining table."

"Is it all right now?" she asked politely, and Edul launched into a full account of the repair, of how his friend Cavus liked taking shortcuts, wanting to drive in two quick screws, but he had convinced him to take the leg right off, do it the proper way, so it was as solid as Mount Everest when he had finished.

"Manizeh is a lucky woman to have such a talented husband," said Roxana.

He blushed with modesty. "I do a little bit here and there. By the way, haven't seen your brother or sister lately. How's your pappa?"

"Much the same. Doctor says we cannot really hope for improvement in Parkinson's."

Edul shook his head sympathetically as the lift arrived and they got in. "What a complicated thing the human body is. If only there were do-it-yourself tools for when it goes wrong."

"We have doctors."

"Never trust professionals. Not in renovations and not in sickness. It's a long time since I saw your pappa being taken by ambulance. Has he returned?"

"He's at my place. Upstairs the ceiling needs to be fixed."

His eyes lit up. "No one told me about the problem."

"Coomy is looking after it." Roxana lunged for the button as they came to his floor, but was too late.

He made a don't-worry gesture with his hand. "To get a contractor who is honest, knowledgeable, and affordable is very hard. Three minimum requirements. Maybe I should talk to Coomy."

"That would be helpful." Advice from a third party might embarrass Coomy into acting, she thought.

"I can recommend someone completely honest, extremely knowledgeable, who will work for very little. In fact, for just material cost."

She knew what was coming but played along. "Sounds hard to believe."

He smiled. "If I may say so myself, it's myself I am talking about."

The lift stopped and he pushed the door open for her. She tried to imagine the scenario, should he be unleashed in Pappa's flat – like placing a straight razor in a monkey's hand.

"Wouldn't be fair," she said, "taking advantage of you."

"Where's the question of taking advantage? I'm volunteering. You know me, I enjoy it, it's my hobby. I enjoy the happiness I bring to people's hearts when something broken is made whole again."

The lift bell clamoured through the shaft; someone was summoning it to the ground floor. "Thanks, Edul, but we can't ask you to do such a big job. The ceilings are badly damaged."

He ignored the person downstairs who was yelling now to shut the doors so the lift could return to the foyer. "Big job or small job, the secret is to proceed methodically. Measure twice, cut once, is the handyman's motto. Think the problem through, visualize the solution. Like playing chess. It's a special knack some people have."

He continued to describe his virtues for the job, but she wasn't listening – it had just occurred to her: the ceilings were already in a pitiful state, they didn't need protecting from Edul. No matter how unskilled, he couldn't make them worse.

And suddenly, it didn't seem such a bad idea: he could clean up the mess, perform some rough patching, make the ceilings safe. Gouges and cracks would still show, so what? It was for free, and at least Pappa could go home.

But first Coomy needed to be convinced. "If you're confident," she said, "I can tell Jal and Coomy of your kind offer."

"Cent per cent confident," he assured her.

The screamer on the ground floor had gone silent, having abandoned all hope of getting the lift to descend. Edul asked if he should go upstairs with her. "I could size up the job right now, do a rough estimate on materials."

"Better if I talk to them first. Imposing on you for such a huge favour will be their decision."

"Not at all," he said, getting back in the lift. "Renovation, for me, is never an imposition." The lift started down, but his voice floated up, "It is my source of satisfaction."

"Coomy! It's Roxie come to visit!" Jal announced jubilantly. "Come, Roxie, come!" he took her hands and drew her inside, giving her a long hug. Joy and relief filled his eyes, that the estrangement was not going to be permanent. "Why is Yezad not with you?"

"Still at work." She saw the way his face was lit – as though she had flicked a switch – and was touched by the welcome.

"Coomy!" he called again. "Where are you, Roxie has come!"

"Shushum hmm hmm!" admonished Coomy from her room to indicate she was praying, then showed herself in the passageway for a moment, her head covered in white mulmul.

"Oh, sorry," said Jal.

She came to the drawing-room a few minutes later. "Why so excited, like the Queen of England has arrived?"

"No, no, not Armeen and Hoshang – our Roxie!"

Coomy tapped the hearing aid in his pocket. "Is it empty again?" The two women put their hands lightly on one another's shoulders; their cheeks touched.

"How is Pappa?" asked Coomy.

"The same. He keeps asking about the flat, if repairs have started. I keep saying soon, Pappa, soon. He's very sad, he understands I don't have a real answer."

Jal's face mirrored his uneasy conscience. He wrung his hands and touched the earpiece, appealing silently to Coomy.

"Your gadget is giving you trouble," she said. "Go, buy new batteries. I'll tell you Roxie's news later."

"No, it's fine." He stopped fidgeting.

"Pappa has good days and bad," continued Roxana. "What makes it worse is that his pills finish before the next pension comes."

"I wish we could help you with more money," said Coomy. "But Pappa's account is empty. And share bazaar is very bad these days – Jal can tell you."

"So enough of my troubles," said Roxana. "Tell me about yourself. How are you both?"

"As you see: sunk in our misfortune, in plaster and dust."

"Still trying to find a contractor," murmured Jal.

"No further collapse?" asked Roxana. "Everything safe? Good." Then she curbed her tongue; sarcasm wouldn't help her mission of reconciliation. "That reminds me. Guess who I met downstairs. It was so lucky – Edul Munshi."

"You call that lucky?" said Coomy. "Only people who are cursed run into the fellow," and Jal laughed, glad it was becoming more amicable.

"I know what you mean," said Roxana. "But he asked about your ceiling and offered to fix it, free of charge."

"Of course he would," said Coomy. "He would pay to work in someone's flat, he's so desperate. His wife won't let him touch a thing in the house."

"He's not a handyman, he's a clown," chuckled Jal. "He should take his tools and join the circus."

"My reaction was the same. Then I began to think: none of us has the money for a contractor. If he can at least apply new plaster, it will be an improvement."

"No, the man is a menace," declared Coomy. "When he changes a light bulb, the whole building has a power failure. And you want to him to work for us?"

Roxana shrugged. "It's your choice."

The earlier tension began creeping back into the room. Then, to her surprise, Jal spoke up, "I like the idea. What's the harm in letting Edul—"

Coomy turned sharply, and he fell silent, waiting to be told off. But the argument never materialized.

Yes, thought Coomy, let Edul do the work. What could be better than having the idiot make a bigger mess of things? With his penchant for prolonging every job to prolong his own pleasure, Pappa's return could be delayed indefinitely. She wouldn't need to invent excuses.

Edul would be the perfect, unwitting accomplice.

M R. KAPUR HELD UP A FINGER to object, and pointed at his watch. "See the time? No more 'Mister.'" He peered into Yezad's face. "For two days now, you look so depressed. What's wrong?"

Yezad shrugged. "I guess because of everything that we've talked about . . . and those old photos, and . . . you made a convert of me. I really believe a good man like you should be in politics. Otherwise, only crooks and scoundrels reign over us."

"Isn't this funny," said Mr. Kapur with a sad smile. "We've completely reversed – I sound like you, you sound like me." He sighed. "Wish I had a choice."

"We always have a choice."

"But family comes first, Yezad, you understand that. Family service before public service, my wife reminded me. And besides my blood pressure, there's the suitcase money – I agree with her, we shouldn't spend it on the election."

He took Yezad by the arm and led him to his office. "Don't be so disappointed. It seemed like a good idea, once. Now it's finished – we have to accept that."

"You said it was your duty."

"Oh yes. Mine, and every good citizen's. I'm not special. But I've come to realize, duty is worthless in this case."

"Meaning?"

"Think about it – pure duty is unconcerned with outcome. Even if I become a municipal councillor, fight the good fight, what do I have at the end? The satisfaction of knowing I've done my duty. As far as Bombay is concerned, nothing changes. Nobody can turn back the clock."

Yezad listened in disbelief. Mr. Kapur's complete about-face was hard to take.

"So," continued Mr. Kapur. "Nothing left now except to talk of graves, of worms and epitaphs. Let us sit upon these chairs and tell sad stories of the death of cities."

Yezad said nothing. If the boss wanted to babble, he'd have to do it without the benefit of response or reaction.

Then Mr. Kapur made a lame attempt at humour. "You know my problem? I am one who loves Bombay not wisely, but too well. And I think I make my wife jealous. She doesn't want another beauty competing with her."

Intense irritation now made Yezad break his resolve of silence. "Don't you have any Indian sources to quote, for a change?"

The acid in the retort dripped away harmlessly; the mere fact that Yezad had decided to speak delighted Mr. Kapur. "That's a basic problem with our education, yours and mine. Anyway, Shakespeare is like Bombay. In them both, you can find whatever you need – they contain the universe."

Seething inwardly, Yezad studied his watch. "If you don't mind, I'll make a move."

Mr. Kapur locked his desk. "I hope you're not still angry."

"What right do I have to be angry? It's your life, your wife, your decision."

Mr. Kapur picked up his attaché case and switched off the lights. "Have you noticed, Yezad, I took your advice? I'm not using the air-conditioner. From now on, I'll accept whatever Bombay offers: heat, humidity, sea-breeze, typhoon."

"I've been following this philosophy for years. Of course, it's easy for me, I can't afford air-conditioning."

"You don't need it. We Indians have our own built-in cooling system – chilies and garam masala make us sweat, the breeze evaporates the sweat, and we are cool."

Yezad smiled weakly.

Mr. Kapur made one last attempt to placate him. "Think of this, Yezad: we'll always have the photographs. Our city is preserved in them. And the record will remain for those who come after us. They will know that once there was a time, here, in this shining city by the sea, when we had a tropical Camelot, a golden place where races and religions lived in peace and amity . . ."

Yezad stopped listening, again feeling exasperation and, in spite of himself, affection, which the man's passions and contradictions provoked. He was certain that, in two months, when the election was over, Mr. Kapur would regret not making the attempt. Or he might change his mind again in the next few days, and decide to run – who could tell where Mr. Kapur was concerned.

As they walked to the door, Yezad saw him gazing fondly at his Christmas display. Someone should tell him he was too young to slip into second childhood. He needed a jolt of some sort, something drastic, to shake him out of this daze of self-satisfaction.

All along the street, establishments seemed to have taken their cue from the Bombay Sporting Goods Emporium. The Jai Hind Book Mart featured a barefoot Santa in padmasana, an English translation of the Bhagavad-Gita open in his lap; perched upon his nose were half-moon reading glasses. Rasoi Stainless Steel had an aproned Santa stirring a large cooking utensil. The Bhagat Opticals Santa wore stylish reflector sunglasses.

Every shop had to have one, thought Yezad wearily, they were no longer content with a Christmas tree, a star, an angel. The men's clothing store had one with shirts and ties draped over his outstretched arms. The shoe store's held a stack of shoeboxes. Mercifully, the sari shop had refrained from a six-yard spree of cross-dressing.

The whole exercise was tedious, devoid of wit (the Book Mart excepted, thanks to Vilas's imagination). For once, a Shiv Sena agitation would be welcome, against this nonsense. Where were those goondas when needed, why weren't they rampaging down the street, smashing these crass displays?

Perhaps that was the type of stimulant Mr. Kapur needed. If his fielders were de-antlered, the blinking bulb silenced, the annoying white-bearded batsman drawn and quartered by the Sena's storm troopers, it might bring back his fighting spirit. What a salutary shock for him, if Shiv Sena came to his doorstep . . .

Outside the shuttered Book Mart, Vilas hailed Yezad from his perch. He patted the step and made room for him to sit.

"No, it's late," said Yezad, kneading his neck muscles, trying to ease the stiffness.

"You look upset. Something wrong?"

"Mr. Kapur – you know about his election plans, he was so committed before. Now it's a complete reversal. He told me his wife said no."

Vilas laughed. "How sweet. A henpecked Punjabi must be a rare thing."

"I don't know what's happening to him. And my promotion has vanished."

While they talked, a labourer with an empty basket approached the bookstore, halting at a respectful distance. In readiness for the scribe, he pulled out a letter from within his head-cushioning turban and attempted to smooth the crumples.

"Your customer," said Yezad, relinquishing the step.

The pain was stuck between the shoulder blades like a knife. He rubbed the neck muscles again and again, turned his head left-right, left-right, then up and down. Instead of walking straight to Marine Lines station, he took the longer way around Dhobitalao, down Princess Street – time to think. His breath was short and shallow, he was almost panting. Breathe in over five steps, he told himself, out for the next eight. In for five, out for eight . . .

A blast of diesel fumes made him cough. Bloody pollution. This was no city for deep breathing. Not unless he managed to slip into Mr. Kapur's old photographs. In the old Hughes Road . . . And talking to Vilas had only agitated him again. Easy for Vilas to say be patient, find a way to motivate Mr. Kapur, while here he was beside himself with worry.

A motorcyclist puttered by wearing a breathing mask. Soon everybody would need one, the way things were going – but wouldn't it be great if there were a mask to filter out the world's problems . . .

"Sahibji," said a voice.

He turned around: it was the man in the sandalwood shop outside Wadiaji fire-temple. Yezad realized he was just passing its gates.

"Sahibji," said the man again, pausing in his task of sorting the sandalwood sticks by size. "Sukhad? It's genuine Malbari."

He wore a prayer cap of black velvet, observed Yezad, the type his father used to wear. Declining the sandalwood, he continued on his way.

A few steps later he hesitated, returned to the gates, and entered the compound. It was empty except for two bicycles chained to a post. Probably for the chasnivalas, he thought, delivering chasni to families who had requested prayers. Ages since he had partaken of a chasni . . . almost forgotten what paapri and malido tasted like . . .

He stopped at the doors of the fire-temple, knowing he was bareheaded. He could use his handkerchief if he . . . No – he had no intention of entering.

The light inside was poor, but he could see the long verandalike space with its stone floor, the ablutions area with its stone parapet. At the far end, a lone figure was drying his hands and face before starting his kusti prayers.

Now the man pulled out his sudra and shirt so they hung over his trousers. He reached under the shirt to his kusti and began untying the knots as he prayed. He unwound it from around his waist, then raised it to touch his forehead.

And that slight gesture in the dim light brought back the words of the prayer Yezad hadn't recited in years . . . Ahura

306

mazda khodai, az hama gunah, patet pashemanum . . . he let it run through his mind, feeling a sense of deep satisfaction that he could still remember it. Then the man formed two loops with the kusti and lifted it to his brow again. Yezad knew he had reached the manashni, gavashni, kunashni section, in preparation for retying the sacred cord . . .

And watching the solitary figure, the veranda in his mind began to fill with the happy crowds he would see when he came here as a boy, with his parents, on Navroze and Khordad Sal, everyone in their colourful New Year finery, clutching sticks of sandalwood, thronging the parapet, eager to grab the silver karasio to wash their hands, complete their devotions, get on with the day's festivities. The women who wore saris, like Yezad's mother, had easy access to their kustis, but the ones who had to raise their skirts to untie the knots flocked to the privacy partition. They were the modern women, looked upon disapprovingly by the orthodox who believed that once a girl began menstruating she had no business wearing a frock. Some men would cast surreptitious glances towards the frosted-glass screens, hoping the light would show them more than a blurred silhouette. Many a time he heard some grandmother complain that mua mavalis couldn't behave themselves even in the atash-behram on an auspicious day, the louts deserved to be flogged.

After the kusti prayers, the family would venture farther into the fire-temple through the main hall. Inside, the crowd was equally thick. The closer you came to the sanctum, the warmer it grew, the fire blazing high, brighter than on any other day of the year, for the silver trays were overflowing with sandalwood offerings. You had to wait your turn to kneel before the sanctum and bow your head to the ground.

And after the fire-temple, there would be visits to relatives, sweets to be distributed, sumptuous meals to be eaten. And in the evening, to the theatre for an Adi Marzban farce or his variety entertainment show, chock full of Parsi jokes and skits and songs . . .

The solitary worshipper finished his kusti, climbed up the steps from the veranda past the fluted columns, and disappeared within the inner recesses. The washing area was desolate now.

How tranquil it seemed inside where the man had gone, thought Yezad, cool and dark. Roxana was right, it was a real oasis in the midst of this big, mad city.

He heard a shuffle of feet from the hallway to the left, the slap of sapats, and before he could retreat a tall, thin figure in white was standing next to him. The dustoorji was wearing his full prayer garb, the robes fragrant with sandalwood smoke. The smell brought a wistful smile to Yezad's face.

The dustoorji smiled back. "Sahibji," he said, raising his right hand to his forehead, and paused, bringing his head forward as though to better observe this Parsi lingering outside. His pupils were reduced to sharp points by his thick glasses.

Yezad felt they were boring into him like drill bits, but was unable to look away. The long white beard made the thin face even longer.

The dustoorji spoke again, "Is it a cap you need?"

"No, no, thank you," said Yezad, flustered. "Not today . . . I'm getting late." Turning on his heels, he fled to the train station.

The boys were alone in the back room when he got home. He asked them where their mother was.

"She went out, Daddy."

"I can see that. I asked where."

"She didn't tell us."

He went to the kitchen and put the kettle on for himself. Nariman's voice, requesting his bottle, drifted softly in from the front room.

Jehangir came hurrying to the kitchen. "I think Grandpa wants to do soo-soo."

Though his son's concern touched him, he was firm. "We went through this last week, didn't we?"

"Yes, Daddy, but I think he wants to do it very badly."

"Listen, Jehangla, I promised myself when your grandfather was thrust into our lives – I will never touch the bottle or the bedpan. And neither will you."

Jehangir looked puzzled while his father was saying all this. There was sadness in his father's voice. He tried again, explaining that the bed might get wet.

"That's not your concern. Do your homework."

His shoulders drooped as he went back exhaling heavily. He heard his grandfather call out again, "Please, it cannot wait. Ultimately . . . it will issue forth . . . ," before lapsing into a whimper.

Yezad finished making his tea, stirring his grievances into it. After a sip from the saucer he gulped the rest down and made a face. Not as good as Roxana's.

He returned his empty cup and saucer to the kitchen, peeked in the back room where the boys were doing homework, and went to the balcony to lean over the railing. Was he becoming one of those pathetic men who were models of geniality everywhere except in their own homes, where they were bullies?

No, he refused to believe it. His very life, the one he'd been leading till a few months ago, had been kidnapped. Roxana's family had stolen his peace and contentment. And till he could regain it, he would have to face the squalor within these four walls, in this place that used to be his sanctuary from the brutal city.

He should have sat in the fire-temple instead of coming back. Back to this wretched front room, this nauseating sickroom. Not that it would have done much good – couldn't live in the fire-temple permanently. This mess would always be waiting for him.

Jehangir found it impossible to pay attention to his homework; the sounds from the settee were anguishing him. He knew how uncomfortable it was when you wanted to do soo-soo, and couldn't. He had had to suffer once when Miss Alvarez had given a test and no one was allowed to go to the bathroom. But at least he'd been able to run as soon as the bell rang. Poor Grandpa had to lie there waiting, not knowing when he would get to do it. And why was Daddy so stubborn about the bottle? Jehangir always understood intuitively what was upsetting him, but this time it was as though he had picked a reason at random.

"Go and ask again," he urged his brother.

"I don't know what's your problem," said Murad. "Mummy told us to call Villie Aunty. She told us she had arranged it all."

"But what will she think when she sees Daddy is home? It's not fair, he should give Grandpa the bottle."

"In your dreams."

Nariman moaned again, and Jehangir couldn't bear it any longer. Ashamed to fetch Villie Aunty, he put down his pencil and went to the settee, ignoring Murad's frantic warnings.

Grandpa hadn't had a sponge bath for three days, he smelled like the hamper when it was full of dirty clothes for the dhobi. He took the bony trembling hand, braced himself, and pulled as hard as he could to help his grandfather to a sitting position. Mummy always made him sit up for soo-soo, she said it was good for his joints to get some movement.

The urinal crouched like a smooth white animal under the settee. He picked it up and guided Grandpa into its mouth, carefully, or the edge would hurt. It was like that game-stall at a mela, he thought, where you had to pass a small loop clear along a metal wire; if it touched, a buzzer went off and you lost. Sometimes Grandpa said ouch, if Mummy was in a hurry.

They waited. Nothing happened. Grandpa looked helplessly into his face, frowned in concentration, and let out an aggressive groan, almost like a growl.

Then Jehangir made the hissing sound his mother used, to help things along. "Soosss," he said. "Soo-soo-soo-soo sssss!"

His father heard the sibilating prompts and came in from the balcony. "What do you think you're doing?"

"Grandpa wanted to do soo-soo very badly," he mumbled, as the translucent plastic acquired a yellow wash and started to fill. Nervous about his father, he found it difficult to hold steady.

Then the trickle faded, became a drip, stopped. Jehangir gave a little shake, the way he had seen Mummy do it. As he withdrew the urinal, a few drops dribbled on the bed. He thrust it forward again, but it was too late. The final drop, lingering at the foreskin's tip, was all he managed to catch.

15

EVENING AFTER EVENING, between seven and nine, Edul chipped away at the plaster from his wobbly portable scaffold made of two stepladders linked by a plank.

Jal adjusted the plastic sheets that shrouded the furniture, then stood in the doorway to keep an eye on the ceiling. From time to time he interjected that this spot looked fine, Edul should move on, or that area was undamaged, no need to mess it up.

In response, Edul offered gems from his handyman's book of proverbs: "Preparing is three-quarters of repairing, Jal my son. I have to check the wood lath behind the plaster, make sure it's not rotten. If you hurry, you'll spoil your curry." Then he rapped on the intact plaster with his knuckles and acknowledged the sound with knowing nods. "Hear that? See what I mean?"

Jal manipulated his earpiece to listen, so he could dispute the sound. He cocked his head and asked Edul to tap the plaster again.

But her brother's efforts at speeding the job along worried Coomy. Interrupting her evening prayers, she called him to the kitchen and told him to stop nagging the man. "Edul will get fed up and leave. You do want Pappa back, don't you?"

Jal muttered that he had wanted him back three months ago. He couldn't understand, he said, why she had made Edul start in the drawing-room instead of Pappa's bedroom.

"I want Edul to practise in the drawing-room, learn from his mistakes. We can't make Pappa the guinea pig."

So Edul's assault on the plaster continued. Through the dreary evenings the hammer continued its endless tattoo. Like misfortune banging on the door, thought Jal. And all the while, he worried about Roxana and Yezad, about how impossible things must be in their tiny flat.

Occasionally, the handyman livened up the proceedings with a distraction. One evening, they heard two crashes, followed by Edul's bellowing. They rushed in to see him with his hands over his face, screaming that plaster had got into his eyes.

"Let me look," said Coomy, but he would not move his fingers. She told Jal to hold down his wrists while she pried apart the upper and lower lids and blew twice in each eye.

Edul blinked, rubbed his eyes, and wiped them dry. "You're a genius, Coomy."

"I learned it from my father. My real father, Palonji – Jal was always getting sand in his eyes when we went to Chowpatty, such a mischievous boy."

Then she reminisced about those visits to the beach, with the set of bucket, spade, sieve, and watering can that their father had bought them, and the castles they would make, especially Jal, who was very talented at it, and the pride their father would feel when other families stopped to admire. "He always said Jal would be a master builder, live up to the name of Contractor."

Edul laughed. "This Jal?" Retrieving the hammer and chisel from the floor, he sprinted up the ladder again.

On another evening, a piercing howl rent the gloom. They did not run, having grown accustomed to Edul's crises; they walked wearily to the drawing-room, and found him sucking his thumb.

"Gardeners have green thumbs, handymen have black-and-blue ones," he said, attempting a hearty laugh. "Occupational hazard."

"Hammers are slippery things," said Jal, sorry for him.

"Not at all, my hammer is first class," said Edul, too honest to seize the excuse. "A good handyman never blames his tools." The thumb disappeared again into his mouth.

"How is it?" asked Coomy. "Want to put ice on it?"

"Champion," he answered, but took the ice all the same. After sliding it around the thumb for a while, he popped the cube in his mouth and crunched it down.

A fortnight after Edul started work, Jal secretly withdrew five hundred rupees from the bank. Secretly for the time being, he knew, for Coomy would find out. But he didn't care.

Late that evening he went to Pleasant Villa, and heard music coming from the flat. Inside, he was surprised to see a violinist at the foot of Pappa's settee. Roxana detained him in the hallway: would he mind not greeting Pappa – he had been in great distress for the last twenty-four hours and was at last on the verge of sleep.

"I'll stay in the back room," said Jal.

She returned to sit by her father. Moisture trickled from the corner of his eyes. She dried it with a napkin while Daisy finished the allemande from a Bach *Partita* and waited with the bow poised over the strings like a question mark – more music?

Roxana indicated silence, and they withdrew quietly. Yezad introduced Daisy to Jal in the back room. "My brother-in-law."

"That was a beautiful piece," he said, shaking her hand. "Thank you so much for playing for Pappa."

"No thanks necessary," said Daisy. "It's a pleasure." She reminded Roxana to send Jehangir tomorrow, should she be needed.

"Such a lovely lady," said Jal after she left. "Is she married?"

"No," said Yezad with a mischievous smile. "Shall we fix you up?"

"No," Jal blushed. "Just wondering. And how's Pappa?"

"Worse, I think," said Roxana, and told him about the trouble he had begun having with his speech.

The response saddened him, and he went on tiptoe to look into the front room. "He's become so thin since the last time. Skin and bones, as though his flesh has melted away."

"Doctor said it's rapid atrophy of the muscles. Come, sit." She indicated the bed, and asked for news from Chateau Felicity.

Half-leaning and half-sitting at the foot of the bed, he played with a corner of the sheet and said Coomy was okay, everything was fine. Then, unable to countenance his lie, he unburdened himself in a rush of emotion.

"Everything is a mess, I don't know what to do any more. That idiot Edul, thock thock thock he's banging away at the ceiling day after day. And Coomy refuses to tell him to hurry, she insists it won't be safe if he rushes."

"She has a point," said Roxana charitably.

"And we know what the point is," said Yezad.

"I was hoping he would finish plastering in a few days and Pappa could come home," said Jal. "At this rate another month or two will go by, with that fool and his hammer."

"Not much we can do," said Yezad.

"But it's not fair, in this tiny place. And poor Roxie with such a lot to do. Plus the medicines and expenses, and . . ." He pulled out the envelope with five hundred rupees. Unsure who to hand it to, he concentrated on straightening the crumpled edges. "I . . . this is for . . ."

Roxana opened the envelope, and let Yezad see inside. "Does Coomy know about this?" she asked gently, not wanting to offend her brother.

"It's my money as much as hers. I don't need her permission, I can give Pappa a gift if I want."

Yezad smiled his approval but could well imagine what lay in store for Jal. He held the envelope out towards him. "Are you sure? Coomy might get a little upset."

Jal hesitated, and twisted his earlobe. "I don't care," he said, his sense of self-esteem healthier than it had been in months. "What is she going to do, throw me out of the house as well? If I had a choice, I would myself leave."

The unexpected declaration surprised Yezad and Roxana. They exchanged looks. "Did something happen with Coomy?"

"No, nothing special. Just the usual – I have no brains, I'm useless, I'm interfering. And I'm fed up of listening to her thirty-year-old anger." He paused. "If you had a huge flat like Chateau Felicity, I would come and live with you." Looking at Yezad, he added quickly, "Only if I was welcome, of course."

"If I had a huge flat, I would insist on you living with us," said Yezad.

"I could even help Roxie take care of Pappa. My share of the money could contribute for expenses. How nice that would be."

He got up to leave, and they assured him he was welcome to visit as often as he wanted. Smiling gratefully, he entered the front room again on tiptoe, and approached the settee.

His stepfather's eyes were shut, but his lips were moving. Jal watched in sadness, imagining the relentless memories haunting his sleep. He stood there for a few moments, his fingertips lightly resting on Nariman's shoulder.

Rain had fallen earlier, everything was wet on the rooftop terrace. When he reached there, taking the stairs two at a time, his heart thudding like a hammer against his chest, Lucy was still standing on the parapet.

"'One day when we were young, one wonderful morning in May,'" she sang, gazing towards the horizon, not looking down at the evening traffic, or the crowd that was gathered below to see what might happen next.

It was Mr. Arjani from the ground floor who had sent someone to inform him of this fearful turn of events. At first, he'd refused to believe the messenger – if Mr. Arjani had been vindictive enough to hire Lucy as an ayah, he wouldn't put it past him to attempt a joke as cruel as this.

But he had gone to the window to check. Yasmin and the children huddled around him. What they could see was the hullabaloo in the street, people on the pavement looking up, pointing, shouting, cars stopping in mid-traffic, drivers cran-

ing their necks. There was no doubt now in his mind, Mr. Arjani was not playing a joke, something was happening on the rooftop.

As Nariman had got ready to run to the terrace, Yasmin asked him to think twice before starting another nonsensical drama with this woman. Mr. Arjani should deal with it, if he insisted on keeping her as his ayah – it was not her husband's responsibility.

"But I do feel responsible," he said – for the past, for the eleven years he had gone out with her, but also for driving her, in part, to this act of desperation. "Wouldn't it have been better if you'd just let me keep walking to school with her?"

"And for how long? Till the Arjani brats graduate? You should have put a stop to it months ago, when she first came here, staring at our window! But you indulged her, so she went further! And now this!"

Jal and Coomy, at the other end of the drawing-room, were watching him resentfully from the corners of their eyes. He knew what they were thinking – here he was, being mean to their mother again, making her cry. They had grown used to their parents' fights, he thought sadly. Grown used to seeing their mother's anger, and what they probably thought of as their stepfather's callous goading of her. He wished he could explain that he meant her no unhappiness. That he felt as helpless in all this as they did.

Suddenly, Coomy screamed, "Stop it, Pappa! You can't go to the terrace!" Her mother hushed her, gave her a kiss, then sent her and Jal to their rooms to do their school work.

"This is not the time to debate and regurgitate the past," he pleaded with Yasmin. "The situation is too precarious."

"If it's precarious, there's nothing you can do. The woman requires professional help in a mental hospital."

"Maybe you're right. But before they can take her there, she needs to come down."

"She will when she's tired. How long can she stand on the ledge and sing?"

317

"Or she might tire, get dizzy, and fall. Do you want an unhappy woman's death on our conscience?"

Yasmin agreed reluctantly to let him go.

On the stairs that led to the roof, he could hear Lucy's voice. He reached the terrace and saw her on the parapet. Her hair was loose over her shoulders, the way she used to wear it before. She looked slender in the evening light, young again. She seemed happy again, silhouetted against the grey sky, swaying in waltz tempo.

Then he shuddered; his step on the wet flagstones reminded him the ledge she was standing on would be just as slick. There was no time to waste.

His father's old foe was hiding with his son behind the large water tank. They beckoned him over. Mr. Arjani indicated with broad gestures the need to avoid any sudden sound. He whispered that they had tried to reason with her, but their attempts had only appeared to annoy her, and they had retreated.

"We must hurry – God forbid if her foot slips and she plummets to the ground. Poor woman doesn't deserve that. And can you imagine the aggravation of a police case?"

Nariman swallowed his disgust and ignored the remark. He looked cautiously around the water tank.

"How do you think we should tackle this?" asked the old man's son.

"Best if you both left the terrace," said Nariman.

They were glad to tiptoe away. Mr. Arjani whispered his gratitude to him before going, something about forgiving and forgetting.

Once he was alone with Lucy, he joined in the singing, "'When songs of spring were sung—'"

She heard his voice, and hers fell silent. She turned around on the ledge, away from the street, and scanned the terrace. She spotted him by the water tank. "Hello, Nari."

Her smile, softly reproaching, stabbed his heart. "How are you, Lucy?"

"I've missed you."

"I've missed you too."

A thin sheet of rainwater near the ledge held her image within its mirror. Then the reflection moved, as she took a step to one side. He skipped a breath.

"I no longer see you in the morning, Nari, when I take the children to school. Or in the afternoon."

"Because I go to work."

A slight breeze passed over the terrace, skimming the rainwater. Lucy shimmered in the ruffled mirror. She began singing again. He remained silent.

"Why don't you sing with me? Is something wrong with me?"

"Oh, Lucy, you're still as gorgeous as Miliza Korjus."

A radiant smile lit her face. "It's been so long, Nari, since we went to the cinema."

"Come down, Lucy, and we'll sing together, I promise."

She sang on.

"Please, Lucy, that's not a good place to sing. Step down, my love, stand beside me."

Abruptly she held out her hand, and he helped her off the parapet. Her palm felt rough against his; he cursed her employer for what he had done to her. Then he led her down the stairs from the terrace into the building, and she sang all the way to the ground floor.

At the door of the Arjani flat she turned and waved to him, as though he was just seeing her home after an evening out. Before the door could shut, she gave him a flying kiss. To soothe the twinge in his heart, he quickly returned it.

The Arjanis hailed him as a hero, but he brushed aside the profusion of thanks. They assured him they would get in touch with her family, take appropriate steps to help her. He was relieved the incident had ended safely.

A few days passed. He rang the ground-floor doorbell to inquire what progress they had made.

Mr. Arjani welcomed him in and renewed his thanks. "You will be pleased to know Lucy is absolutely normal again."

"That's good," said Nariman. "But what she did that day was not normal, she needs a doctor."

"Oh, come on, Nari, everyone is allowed one mistake." It wouldn't be fair, said Mr. Arjani, to lock her up in a lunatic asylum for her silly drama – after all, most women did strange, inexplicable things at some point in their lives, didn't they, what with their complicated periods and menopauses, and all those types of female problems. Why, his own lady wife, God bless her, after fifty-two happy years of marriage, sometimes behaved in ways that left him baffled. Besides, there were no complaints about Lucy's work, she looked after his grandchildren lovingly, cooked and cleaned. If they were to take her to a doctor and reveal what she'd done, he was almost certain to have her committed. "As far as I'm concerned," said Mr. Arjani, "that would be an abuse of power."

There were times when Nariman felt like seizing the initiative and getting medical attention for Lucy. But it was hard to predict the outcome. He was well aware of the inhuman conditions in government hospitals, the cagelike rooms where mental patients were locked up. Unless there was a family on the outside, looking after the patient's interest, it was a life sentence. How could he deliver Lucy to such a fate?

But he kept reminding Mr. Arjani of his responsibility. His words grew sharper, till Mr. Arjani told him he had no business interfering in someone else's household.

"I am compelled to," said Nariman. "Your conscience is calloused enough to feel nothing."

"Look who's talking about conscience! Mr. Model Husband himself!"

Yezad tried for a while to follow the train of Nariman's murmurs, then turned upon his side towards Roxana and remarked that it had been good to see Jal this evening, to see he'd found a bit of backbone at last. "I only wish it had been sooner. Maybe then the chief might not have been thrown out of his own house."

"Who knows," said Roxana. "Some things only happen when they are ready."

"No, it's up to us to make happen what we want."

He put his arm over her, deciding the time had come to follow his own advice.

T HE STREET WAS YET to brew its morning congestion of
traffic and fumes as Yezad arrived outside Jai Hind Book
Mart. He felt a change was in the air, perhaps cooler
December weather, at last on its way to relieve the heat.

A client who was leaving with a freshly written letter bent
to touch Vilas's feet in gratitude: money alone was inade-
quate, said the man, for the precious service. Vilas shooed him
off. "If you do that I'll never write for you again."

"Sorry, Raneji, very sorry," the man said, hands joined and
raised to his forehead.

Vilas sent him on with a forgiving wave, and gave Yezad
the gist of the matter: a family was selling one of their daughters. Aged fourteen, she was to wed a sixty-year-old widower.
"Says he wants a wife, but the whole village knows he's buying a slave. And the family is doing it for the usual reason –
can't afford to feed everyone. The fellow who was here, the
girl's older brother, wants his parents to wait, he'll send more
money soon."

Bleary-eyed, Yezad listened impatiently, worn out by
Vilas's accounts of his clients' wretched lives. He felt he had
no more stamina for grief or misery. "Look, I've found a solution," he broke into Vilas's story, and described his plan for
motivating Mr. Kapur.

"Now this is where you come in. Go to your local Shiv Sena
shakha and make a complaint about these Santa Clauses taking over Marine Lines and Dhobi Talao. Tell them about this
foreign invasion, instigate them to take action." He glanced
sideways at Vilas doodling on his writing pad. "Why are you
shaking your head?"

"I don't have any influence at the shakha."

"You can complain as a loyal Maharashtrian, a patriotic Indian, a faithful Hindu."

"I am none of these."

"You could pretend."

"Okay, let's say I do. The shakha pramukh still wouldn't start a riot. That only happens under direct orders from the top."

"You could at least suggest it."

"You're not thinking straight," sighed Vilas.

"What do you mean? You were the one who said Mr. Kapur needed motivation."

"Not like this. Never disturb the sleeping snake, nor tease the crouching tiger."

"I can do without your proverbs."

They sat in silence for a while, watching the traffic, the vendors, the schoolchildren hurrying by with satchels and water bottles.

"I used to enjoy Christmas in the old days," said Yezad. "But just look at those asinine windows. Leaving aside my personal problem, Shiv Sena would be doing us a favour. Killing two birds with one stone."

Vilas sighed again. "When Shiv Sena comes, it will bring more than one stone. It will spread such terror, we'll all be trembling like your father-in-law."

"I wish you'd stop exaggerating," snapped Yezad. He rose, dusted off his pant seat, and descended the steps.

"Won't you hear a suggestion from me before you go?" Vilas patted the place beside him and Yezad sat again. "Your plan, in principle, is quite good. The only problem is involvement of Shiv Sena. We need to replace that hazardous element with something benign."

"Meaning?"

"You remember my two friends you met a couple of months ago? Gautam and Bhaskar, the actors?"

"Yes."

"I can ask them to act as Shiv Sainiks. They'll be thrilled to do it, they're always looking for new projects."

"That's your suggestion? A riot consisting of two actors?"

"Have patience, let me explain." Meanwhile, another client arrived and greeted Vilas with a namaskaar. He asked the man to wait, then lowered his voice to describe what he had in mind.

Yezad was sceptical.

"It will work, believe me," persisted Vilas. "We'll succeed with the power of words. Gautam and Bhaskar are excellent actors."

"How can they be more effective than the real Shiv Sena?"

"With real Shiv Sena, you'll have people rampaging like wild animals, glass shattering, smell of smoke and fire, goondas with sticks and bricks. Forget it, Yezad, it's too dangerous. In any case, Mr. Kapur is the type of person better swayed by words, not a display of brute force – don't you think?"

Yezad had to get back to Bombay Sporting, so they agreed to meet in the evening, discuss the plan, put something down on paper. Yezad vacated the step for Vilas's next customer.

TWO DAYS LATER, Mr. Kapur went for his scheduled blood pressure check-up after lunchtime. Then a few minutes later Husain left on his errands. Good, thought Yezad, the afternoon was unfolding as they had planned.

Pacing the length of the store, he once again reviewed in his mind what he would say on Mr. Kapur's return. His eye caught the flash of the annoying red bulb; he switched off the motor.

He walked himself through the scene, practising, improvising, running over the description of the imaginary visitors, their mannerisms. Mustn't be too exact, Vilas and he had discussed that. People taken by surprise, scared, usually had trouble recollecting accurately, they said things like: Oh, he was wearing a green shirt . . . no, maybe grey . . . or greyish green . . . They rambled, they speculated, and he needed to remember that in his performance.

So he spent an hour in rehearsal till Mr. Kapur entered the shop with a ho-ho-ho, as he had been doing for the last few days. He inquired about the stationary Santa Claus.

"Stuck again. I turned it off."

Mr. Kapur went into the window, flipped the switch, and saw the bat through half-a-dozen repetitions. "Works okay now."

Questioned about his blood pressure, he said the doctor wanted him to continue the same pills and avoid getting agitated. He pottered about the window, moving the fielders into new positions. Passersby stopped to look, and he smiled and nodded genially at them. "I guess nothing exciting, in my absence?"

Yezad raised a tense face. "Someone paid us a visit," he said softly, and swallowed.

"Yes?"

"Two men. From Shiv Sena."

"Hah." Mr. Kapur waved his hand in a dismissive gesture, keeping an eye on the rising and falling bat. "I hope you threw their pamphlets or whatever in the dustbin."

"They weren't distributing pamphlets."

Mr. Kapur turned his back on the window and paid more attention. "What did they want?"

"They said they were from the tax department."

Mr. Kapur frowned. "But you said Shiv Sena."

"They didn't mention it at first."

"So the buggers were rude to you, hanh?"

Yezad shook his head. "They wished me good afternoon, called me sir. Made it scarier, actually, when I knew who it was. I said the shop hadn't received any tax notification. With a big smile they told me they were not government people, but special Shiv Sena tax department. And they wanted to discuss a small problem."

"Hah."

Yezad paused; his voice, uttering the words he'd practised, sounded strange to his ears. Was it convincing Mr. Kapur? Under cover of the desk, he wiped his palms against his trousered knees and continued, "They were informing all shops, hotels, any business with Bombay in its name, that they had to change it to Mumbai within thirty days. Or pay a fine."

"What did you say?"

"I asked if the government had passed a law about this. They said no need for a law, it was new Shiv Sena policy."

"The swine. And?"

"I said I was just an employee, the proprietor was out. Now one of them got angry: First you say you are in charge, suddenly you are just employee – giving us double talk?

"I thought he was going to hit me. But I kept calm. If you were sales tax or income tax inspectors, I could help you, I said, but this is a special matter."

"What did they look like? Goondas? Muscleman types?"

"Ordinary Maharashtrians, clerks. Skinny, with oily hair. And one had a thin moustache. Or did they both? – Can't remember."

Mr. Kapur nodded. "I can imagine them exactly."

The comment made Yezad more confident. The deeper he went into the story, the more his characters acquired the solidity of flesh and blood. He recognized their potential instinctively, letting them grow was easy. A little supervision was all that was needed, like a parent or puppeteer.

"Funny thing is, even though they looked harmless, they intimidated me. Their tone, their voices clearly said they had the power. They knew I was scared of them."

The slightly amused expression receded from Mr. Kapur's face. He had accepted the gravity of the situation, thought Yezad.

"Did they give you their names?"

"Yes. Balaji something . . . Deshpande, I think. And Gopinath Sawant. Wait a sec – maybe Balaji Sawant and Gopinath Deshpande? Anyway, they said the change was easy, they had forms I should sign. I said I couldn't."

"That must have made them extremely happy."

"Balaji began shouting. I said how can I do a name change without the owner's permission, a name is very significant, success or failure depends on it. Gopinath whispered in Balaji's ear and he said we understand your problem, we can issue a special exemption. Requires down payment of thirty thousand rupees, plus five thousand every month for as long as you want to keep Bombay."

"Bastards! Extortion!"

"Or we must change to Mumbai Sporting Goods Emporium."

"No!" Mr. Kapur banged his hand on the glass counter.

The genuine anger produced by his fabricated story startled and pleased Yezad. "Take it easy, Mr. Kapur. They are supposed to smash your glass, you don't have to do it yourself."

"Sorry, Yezad," he smiled feebly. "You handled them well. By the way, was Husain here when they came?"

"No, he'd already left on deliveries."

"Good. Don't mention Shiv Sena, poor chap will panic. Once he returns, we'll lock up."

"Why do that? They'll think we are frightened of them."

Mr. Kapur turned fiercely. "The man isn't born who can frighten me. My mood is ruined, that's all." He sat behind his desk and continued, "If I'd been present, I could have settled those low-lifes." He raised a fist. "Told them where to go. When are they coming back?"

"They wouldn't make an appointment. I said you were usually here in the morning."

Mr. Kapur frowned, and agreed to let the shop stay open. He spent the afternoon fulminating, cursing the Shiv Sena and the blight it had brought upon the city. There was a venom and bitterness Yezad had not seen before, and he felt hopeful – the strategy seemed to be working.

By evening, Mr. Kapur had calmed down considerably. He stopped by Yezad's desk and, playing perfect copy-book cricket, presented an imaginary straight bat on the front foot. "There are four options," he said.

"Four? They gave us two."

"Four," he repeated. "Change the name; don't change and pay the crooks; don't change and complain to the police; and finally, ignore them and see what happens."

Yezad said there was a fifth option: "The decision you once made – to run in the election. You'd get to know important people, make contacts with police and politicians. You could tackle the root of the problem from within the system."

"If it were possible, I would do it, I told you before," said Mr. Kapur heatedly, then lifted his hands and took a deep breath, as though reminding himself of his doctor's advice. "Have you ever seen a banyan tree, Yezad?"

He nodded.

"You know how it grows? Its long branches send down

aerial roots that go deep, become columns to support the branches that grow even larger while the roots spread over acres and acres."

"Yes, I've seen pictures. So what's the connection?"

"A municipal councillor tackling corruption is like a penknife trying to dig up a banyan tree."

Yezad could think of arguments to dispute the analogy, but Mr. Kapur shook his head sadly. "Forget it, Yezad," he sighed, "only four options," and slumped in his chair.

Next moment, he sat up with determination. "I'll wait: let the bastards come to me. For all we know, they dropped by at random, hoping to grab some cash from a frightened little shopkeeper."

The decision to be indecisive put Mr. Kapur in better spirits, and when they wished each other goodnight he volleyed with an invisible tennis racquet. Patting Yezad on the shoulder, he said he felt convinced the scum would not show up again.

Yezad wished he could assure him that they would.

16

S IPPING TEA WITH VILAS and the two actors in Merwan Irani's restaurant, Yezad listened while they discussed and looked over the script. The constant bustle and clatter of waiters and crockery filled the room, along with the pungent smell of bhajias frying.

Vilas had predicted correctly, thought Yezad – Gautam and Bhaskar did regard the Kapur project (as they called it) to be a fascinating experiment in theatre. Nothing so unusual had ever come their way during the normal pursuit of their hobby, they said.

In chawls and community halls, and in the narrow streets and gullies of Bombay, their talents were confined to one-act plays, short dramas concerned with serious social issues: Bride-Burning and Dowry Deaths, Menace of Communalism, Ugliness of Alcoholism, Evil of Wife Abuse, Tragedy of Gambling. There was humour too, about political buffoonery, the buying and selling of members of parliament, legislation guaranteeing the right of students to cheat in examinations, and the absurdities of the ration-card system.

They recalled, for Vilas and Yezad's benefit, a particularly successful performance about the Minister for Telecommunications, whose house had recently been raided by the Central Bureau of Investigation. The puja room had yielded two trunks and twenty-two suitcases, crammed with cash and arrayed behind the shrine of Laxmi.

"We composed that skit directly from newspaper headlines," said Bhaskar, pushing his Gandhiji glasses up the bridge of his nose. "All we had to do was add some jokes about the Minister defending himself. Saying that charges of corruption against him were baseless, the Goddess of Wealth had herself multiplied his meagre ministerial earnings because she thought he was doing a good job in government."

The young men enacted part of the skit: the Minister of Telecommunications and Laxmi conversing on cellphones, where the Goddess gave him financial advice; sometimes she counselled him by appearing on a special TV channel via satellite – All Laxmi, All the Time.

"They loved that play in every chawl," said Bhaskar, as Vilas and Yezad laughed heartily. "But the Kapur project will be like street theatre moving indoors." The doubt on Yezad's face prompted him to explain: "On the pavement there is no announcement. We start arguing, fighting, acting drunk, as though real life were unfolding. People stop to listen, a crowd gathers."

"Yes, but there's a difference," objected Gautam. "Sooner or later our street audience knows it is exactly that – an audience, watching us perform a naatak. For Mr. Kapur there'll be no one."

"I beg to differ," said Bhaskar. "I would say he himself will be both audience and actor, except he'll be unaware of it."

"An actor without awareness is a wooden puppet," declared Gautam grandly, believing he had scored a decisive point.

"In a culture where destiny is embraced as the paramount force, we are all puppets," said Bhaskar with equal grandness.

Yezad grew impatient, wishing they would stop sounding their own theatrical trumpets. The way they were carrying on, they might rise any moment to strike a stance with chest thrust out, chin high, sword arm aloft, declaiming "Khabardaar!" in the style of a Chanjibhai Cheecheepopo.

"We're not arguing destiny versus free will," said Gautam. "Stick to the point."

"It's all interconnected," said Bhaskar. "You're hung up on conventional ideas – as irrelevant as the proscenium arch."

"Nonsense, the proscenium arch is still absolutely vital. It has merely turned into the proscenium pavement, which—"

"That's enough, Mr. Bhaskar Olivier and Mr. Gautam Gielgud," said Vilas. "Yezad and I have to return to work in fifteen minutes."

His intervention allowed Yezad to describe what had happened thus far with Mr. Kapur. He took pains to emphasize he was fond of his employer, and that their little drama was intended only to nudge Mr. Kapur towards something he had always wanted to do – run in the election.

"In a way, it's like one of your plays about a social issue," said Vilas. "You could name it the Menace of Shiv Sena."

"True," said Gautam. "Basically, there's a call to action for Mr. Kapur, and an unstated moral: that evil must not be ignored by those able to oppose it."

"Look who's being rigid now. How the hell can you say—"

"Hai, stop it," said Vilas. "The play's the thing – Yezad's play. Pay attention."

"I think it's a great idea, using this Bombay-Mumbai name tax to motivate Mr. Kapur," said Bhaskar.

"Thank you," said Vilas. "You have to remember, though, it's not a question of straightforward intimidation. Extracting money is easy. Your assignment is to extract a crusade."

"Understood," said Gautam. "Basically, Mr. Kapur needs to experience an epiphany. So we must convey more than just present danger to him and his shop. We must transcend the here and now, move beyond this bank and shoal of time, and let him glimpse the horrors of a society where the best lack all conviction while the worst are full of passionate intensity."

The quotations were flying thick and fast as they got down to details: the visit would be in three days, in the morning, when Mr. Kapur would be alone at the shop. Yezad promised to stay away, meeting with the sports director of Don Bosco High School.

"Perfect," said Gautam.

"If I may take the liberty of summarizing," said Bhaskar, anxious not to lose his audience share. "Our objective is to rekindle Mr. Kapur's noble urges. We must move him beyond catharsis, beyond pity and terror, to a state of engagement – into the arena of epic realism, where the man of action . . ."

Yezad stopped listening. He felt he'd get a headache if they didn't end their jabbering.

"You two talk as though theatre is an exact science," said Vilas.

"Ah, the Vilasian doctrine of eternal scepticism," said Gautam. "If Brecht had yielded to such pessimism, where would we be today?"

"But why make it sound so complicated?" said Vilas. "All we're doing is deceiving Mr. Kapur for a good purpose."

"Well, I've told you what the Shiv Sainiks are supposed to look like," said Yezad, getting back to the subject. "And what their demands are. Anything else you need?"

The actors said they had all their entrances and exits, but they needed more tea.

Laughing, declining the offer of another cup, Yezad and Vilas left the restaurant while the two continued to argue and debate the future of the theatre.

"Solid talkers, aren't they?" said Yezad outside. He gave his hair a vigorous rub, as though to brush away the surfeit of words.

"Their whole group is like that. Amusing for a few minutes, then unbearable."

They halted, having arrived at Bombay Sporting, and Yezad stood gazing at the pavement. "Now what's wrong?" asked Vilas.

"I'm not sure. This plot with the actors . . . I'm thinking of Mr. Kapur's high blood pressure."

"Look, if you have a doubt, I can tell Gautam and Bhaskar to cancel—"

"No, don't do that," said Yezad, kicking an empty cigarette packet over the kerb and into the gutter. "I just hope Gautam and Bhaskar are dependable people."

"Dependable they are. My worry is about getting more than we bargained for."

Later that week, after his morning meeting with the sports director of Don Bosco High School, Yezad could barely keep from running into Mr. Kapur's office. But he sat at his desk and pretended to get on with work. Better to let Mr. Kapur come to him with the news.

He watched the intermittent flash of the red bulb in the window, the rising and falling bat. From the corner of his eye, it was as though some large, prehistoric insect were hovering in the window, while the reindeer acquired a troglodytic aspect. Put cudgels in their hooves and they would look like a bunch of goondas closing in on their victim: the man in red, who had no inkling that his brains were about to be bashed out . . .

The hand on his shoulder startled him, interrupting his gory daydream. "What are you so engrossed in?" asked Mr. Kapur.

"Sorry, didn't see you – I'm working on the Don Bosco quotation."

"Good." Mr. Kapur toyed with the large manila envelope in his hands, and dropped it on Yezad's desk.

"What's this?"

"Your two friends came in the morning."

"Friends?"

"Our friends, I should say – those bastards, Balaji and Gopinath, and their two thin moustaches." Looking around for the peon, he lowered his voice, "I took them into my office, so they wouldn't frighten Husain."

Then he tapped the envelope he was carrying. "This is for them. I took it from the suitcase – thirty-five thousand."

Yezad looked inside briefly, his face registering amazement, horror, and despair in quick succession.

"Yes, I was also surprised," said Mr. Kapur. "I didn't think they would return."

"But . . ." Yezad stood up, his voice shaking. "But that's crazy! You're handing over the money, just like that!"

"Enough lecturing! What are you trying to do, get my throat slit? My shop turned into a pile of ashes?"

He walked away to his office, and Husain followed with promises of hot tea. "Is something wrong, sahab?"

"Just business problem, Husain, you don't worry."

The peon went into the storeroom and put the kettle on to make a fresh brew. He called out minutes later, "Chai ready, sahab."

"I don't want any," answered Mr. Kapur.

Deflated, Husain returned to his stool in the back and perched upon it like a wounded bird. Mr. Kapur relented in moments.

The peon carried in the cup and saucer, set it on the desk, and withdrew to linger by the office door. He was attentive to every sound from within: Mr. Kapur blowing on his tea, sipping, exhaling.

The final sip was signalled by a gurgly slurp, following which Mr. Kapur emerged with the empty cup. His free hand played a tennis stroke, concentrating on the follow-through.

"Sorry for yelling, Yezad."

"That's okay, I had no business—"

"Forget it." Praising Husain for the tea, he beckoned to Yezad to follow him. The peon watched with satisfaction as they went into the office together: things were back to normal, his kettle had done its magic. He took up the duster.

Its energetic flapping could be heard inside the cubicle, and Mr. Kapur smiled at the sound before continuing, "You think I'm not upset? The idea of being terrorized by these low-lifes, gangsters posing as political parties – it makes me mad!" Then, as though remembering his blood pressure, he passed his hand over his face and added softly, "Sometimes it makes me want to weep."

Yezad swallowed. "Don't take it personally, these people are . . . you know . . . not worth it."

Mr. Kapur wiped the sweat from his neck and forehead; the air-conditioner was off. True to his word, he hadn't used it

335

since the day he swore to accept Bombay as she was. "You know what upset me most? Their arrogance: nothing will stand in their way, they seemed to say, now it is their kingdom. They are taking what they want – like a conquering army."

He stood up to stretch. "And poor Bombay has no champion to defend her. Unhappy city, that has no heroes."

Yezad went to the bathroom, plucked the small mirror off its hook, and brought it to the office. He held it before Mr. Kapur.

"What are you doing?"

"Showing you a hero."

Mr. Kapur smiled uncertainly.

Yezad persisted. "A hero who can save Bombay if he runs in the next election."

"Are you hounding me again?"

"Yes, I find it ridiculous, two skinny vegetarians bullying the Bombay Sporting Goods Emporium."

"Don't be fooled by their appearance. Skinny they may be, but these Baji Raos and Bhaji Khaos are descendants of Marathas, tough as nails – tough as that other spinach-eater, Popeye."

They laughed a little, and Mr. Kapur continued in a serious tone, "My business friends have dealt with similar situations. They all advise pay up and keep quiet."

Yezad stared at the desk, his spirit crushed. The plan had failed. Failed utterly. Nothing left to say or do. He pushed the envelope towards Mr. Kapur – a reminder to put it in a safe place.

Mr. Kapur slid it back. "Keep it in your drawer till they come to collect."

"Better if you gave it yourself."

"Bad idea. I might be tempted to spit in their faces." He picked up the mirror. "Please put this back in the bathroom."

Passing it across the desk, he hesitated and called Yezad to his side. "Look."

Yezad glanced over his employer's shoulder: they were both reflected in the mirror.

"See that?" said Mr. Kapur. "The faces of ordinary family men, not heroes."

⌒

How dare the actors depart from the agreed-upon plan, demanded Yezad, did they presume to understand Mr. Kapur better than he who had worked with the man for fifteen years? Now they had only succeeded in creating a bigger mess for him, more complication and confusion.

"Calm down," said Vilas. "I met Gautam and Bhaskar this morning. They followed our plan to the letter."

"So why has Mr. Kapur got the money packed and ready?"

Vilas patted the step beside him. "Did you expect an instant conversion? An overnight crusade?"

"I didn't expect instant capitulation either. One simple request I made to you – lodge a complaint with Shiv Sena about Santa Claus. That was all I wanted, nothing else."

"Yes, all you wanted was to play with fire."

Yezad looked at him scornfully. "Instead you bring a pair of bloody fake actors. They and their dramatic epiphany! Where is it? Where is Mr. Kapur's revelation, his clarity of vision?"

Vilas pretended to check his pockets. Yezad did not laugh.

"It will take time," he consoled him. "Only in novels do you get instant results."

"As if things weren't bad enough, now I have to be responsible for that envelope stuffed with thirty-five thousand rupees. I've got to keep it safe for two imaginary Shiv Sainiks who will never show up."

"Actually, Yezad, the money gives you an excuse to keep reminding Mr. Kapur of his duty. If our two thespians have planted the seed, your prompting could make it grow."

"And should I use a stage whisper?" asked Yezad savagely.

"Don't be upset. Why not hope for the best?"

Yezad thumped down the three steps and walked away, his head throbbing. By the time he turned the corner, he felt all his strength had drained from him. He was conscious of dragging his feet. How annoyed his mother used to get when he did it as a child. Don't walk khassar-khassar, she would scold, lift your feet.

He realized he was taking the long way to the station, past Wadiaji fire-temple. Well, the walk would do him good. What was the point of rushing home to those two wretched rooms? They would do nothing for his pounding headache, he needed peace and quiet.

Nearing the fire-temple, he glanced through the gate at the compound, and the little garden at its centre. He found himself envying those able to enjoy the serenity within. So could he, he reminded himself – all he had to do was put on a prayer cap and enter. But it would be dishonest, when he wasn't religious, hadn't even said the brief kusti prayers in twenty years. On the other hand, he still wore his sudra – nothing more pleasant against the skin than soft mulmul. And every morning after his bath he did wrap the kusti around his waist, albeit haphazardly. But it was from force of habit. And to keep Roxana happy.

On the other hand, there was no rule that he had to be religious to enter the fire-temple. The sign said Admittance For Parsis Only – he was one, and entitled to go inside.

Should he? What would he do, once within its cool, hushed interior? He hesitated at the little sandalwood shop.

"Hallo, uncle." A young boy was behind the counter this evening. "Want to buy sukhad, uncle? It's genuine Malbari."

Then Yezad saw the older man on a stool below the level of the counter. Training his son in the business. Would there be a business when the boy became a man, wondered Yezad, the way the Parsis were dwindling in Bombay, and the way people like himself treated the faith? And the sandalwood trees fast disappearing, thanks to bandits and smugglers like Veerappan . . .

"How much, uncle?" asked the youngster eagerly.

Yezad smiled. "Five rupees?"

"Sure." The boy selected a sliver of the fragrant wood, handed it over with both hands, and took the money.

"Thank you." Yezad held the piece reverently. He was tempted to lift it to his nose but remembered, through the mist of years, being told it was impolite to sniff the sandalwood that was for Dadaji, you had to be patient till you were inside, where you were free to enjoy the fragrance from the sacred fire.

Turning to go, he hesitated. "Can I borrow a cap?"

The boy glanced at his father and received a nod. He placed a box of prayer caps on the counter, of various sizes, mostly black, some grimier than others with hair oil and pomade.

Yezad looked queasily through the lot to find one that wasn't quite so unappetizing. A maroon specimen at the bottom of the box seemed clean. Probably not popular, he thought, because of the colour. The prayer cap his mother had bought for his navjote ceremony had been this very shade of maroon. He was seven then – and how proud the family was that he had mastered the prayers already. Others had to wait till nine or eleven.

He located the seam of the cap, knowing that it went to the back, and covered his head. "I'll return it in a few minutes."

"It's okay, uncle, you can pray as long as you like."

Yezad started to reply, "I'm not going to . . . ," and stopped. "Thank you," he said, and made his way through the compound to the veranda for ablutions.

He washed his hands and face, dried them with his handkerchief, and sat down to remove his shoes, eager to proceed inside to the tranquil room with the fire. Standing in his socks, he kicked his shoes under the bench.

But as he climbed the steps past the fluted columns, a sense of discomfort gnawed at him. He halted – it didn't feel right to go in without first doing his kusti. The training from decades ago forced him back to the veranda.

Then he realized he didn't know which direction to face. No one else was praying from whom he could take the cue. He recollected it had something to do with the sun; and it was evening, the sun had probably set by now, so . . .

At random he decided to face the parapet, and commenced untying the kusti's reef knots, glad no one could see him fumble. His fingers had lost the knack of working behind his back. He felt more comfortable when he came to the knots at the front.

And now, to his amazement, the words of Kem Na Mazda rose silently to his lips as though he'd been reciting the prayer all his life, morning and night, without missing a day. Phrase upon phrase, into the next section, through Ahura Mazda Khodai and manashni, gavashni, kunashni, into the final preparation for retying the kusti.

Slap-slap, slap-slap, he heard a pair of sapats behind him. They were getting closer. Very close now. And he felt a hand upon his shoulder. It was the elderly priest with the long white beard, the one who had caught him peering through the entrance.

The dustoorji smiled and wordlessly turned him around a hundred and eighty degrees. Yezad was mortified. He wondered how long the dustoorji had been watching. And had he seen him struggling with his kusti, tugging clumsily at the knots?

The dustoorji put a finger to his lips to counsel silence – the thread of prayer was not to be broken by profane speech and unnecessary explanation.

Yezad nodded. The dustoorji's hand, still resting on Yezad's shoulder, shifted to his nape, then ran firmly downwards to the small of his back.

Three times the dustoorji repeated the gesture along his back. Yezad felt as though he were physically removing something, pulling strands of stress out of his tortured being. Then, patting his shoulder again, the dustoorji continued on his way, slap-slap, slap-slap down the corridor.

Moved and confused, Yezad finished retying the kusti. Why had the dustoorji rubbed his back? He wondered if his problems were so obvious, his face harried, his brow clouded.

He went inside, his feet revelling in the luxury of the rich old Persian carpets as he padded through the vast hall. Surely it was at least six degrees cooler than the street.

He reached the end and paused outside the adjoining room, smaller and much dimmer than the hall he had just traversed. He felt the sudden urge to remove his socks as well. Peeling them off, he stuffed them into his trouser pocket and stepped into this room, which led to the sanctum. The sacred chamber, the place where the fire dwelt, demarcated by a marble threshold that the laity could not cross.

As a child, Yezad had been powerfully attracted to the sanctum. Not even all dustoorjis went into it, only those in a state of ritual purity. He had often fantasized about giving his parents the slip and running inside to stroke the huge silver afargaan that shone majestically on its pedestal, holding aloft the flames that rose and fell with the hours of the day. But it was forbidden. Just to approach the threshold, Dadaji's private place, had filled him with reverent fear – he worried he would stumble and fall, and a part of him, a hand or a finger, would accidentally cross the prohibited barrier, with some terrifying consequence . . .

A dozen feet from the sanctum's threshold, he sat on the carpeted floor and rubbed his hands over the lush carpet, enjoying its gentle prickle, smiling at his childhood self. The fire was only a glow of embers. Not much smoke, though the room was rich with sandalwood fragrance. Occasionally there was a loud crack as a spark flew towards the high dome.

How still it was, how restful. And the fire burning . . . burning continuously for almost a hundred and fifty years, since this atash-bahram was built . . . the same fire his parents had gazed upon, and his grandparents, and great-grandparents. The thought filled him with quiet, with reassurance.

Minutes passed. An old woman came in, her head covered by a scarf knotted tightly under her chin. She deposited a stick of sandalwood in the tray, knelt laboriously, then left. Yezad wondered if he too should make a move, it was getting late, Roxie would worry. He was reluctant to leave this place of tranquility. But he could always come again. Tomorrow, after work. He would leave promptly when the shop closed, not waste time with Mr. Kapur or Vilas, come here directly . . .

A dustoorji entered, gathered the sandalwood in the tray, and proceeded to the sanctum. He lowered the protective square of mulmul from his head to cover his nose and mouth – the fire must not be polluted with human breath. Yezad smiled, thinking of the long-ago jokes about priests and masked bandits.

The dustoorji halted at the threshold and turned to look at him. Yezad felt flustered, as though his thoughts had been read. The dustoorji pointed to his shirt and the fire, from one to the other.

Yezad looked: his stick of sandalwood was still in his pocket, the dustoorji was merely inquiring if he wanted to include it in this offering.

"Yes, thank you," he whispered, and handed it over.

Now the dustoorji stepped into the sanctum to perform the ceremony for the changing geh. Sunset, thought Yezad, and the fourth geh of the Zoroastrian day had commenced. He watched the ritual cleansing of the sanctum, the pedestal, the afargaan, the quiescent preparations before the offerings to the fire.

How calming, thought Yezad, to watch all this, to let the peace of the moment fill the room. Why did it have such a timeless quality? How comforting, to see the figure in the flowing white robe, see him moving, unhurried, employing the various silver utensils in the ceremony, performing the mystical gestures that were repeated five times each day, performed with an elegance that could come only with the cumulative grace of generations and centuries, so that it was encoded in blood and bone . . .

Now the dustoorji was ready to serve the fire. Expertly he tended the glowing embers, and flames began to lick at the tongs, growing to the soft murmur of prayers as he added the sandalwood collected from the tray.

And there, thought Yezad, with the rest, was his five-rupee piece as well, with all the other sticks carried here by hands like his. Which part of the fire, which tongue of flame was fed by his offering? Was the fire divisible in that way? Did it matter?

The dustoorji now moved to the conclusion of the ceremony. He approached the bell hanging in the corner of the sanctum and sounded the boi. At the first pure clang, loud and sudden, Yezad's heart skipped a beat. Then the peals rang out in a glorious chain, filling the sanctum and the dome, the dark room and the hall, proclaiming the new geh to the entire temple. It was ringing out life, thought Yezad, it was ringing hope, and his heart sang with the bell.

Then there was silence. The dustoorji, with a final obeisance to the fire, gathered ash in a silver scoop and offered it to Yezad. He took a pinch for his forehead and throat. The dustoorji touched his own forehead in Yezad's direction and disappeared.

Yezad approached the sanctum again. The fire was burning vigorously, the flames leaping with joy, and the room was a dance of light and shadow. He stood absorbed for a few moments, then felt it was churlish – churlish to refuse to bow before a sight so noble in its simple beauty. If he did not bend now, for this, what would he bend for?

He knelt; his forehead touched the marble threshold; he remained bowed for a long while.

In the vast hall he paused to pull on his socks before returning to the veranda to retrieve his shoes.

The evening had grown dark as he emerged from the fire-temple. He walked through the compound with his wealth of

343

repose, handed over the borrowed cap to the smiling boy at the sandalwood shop, and headed home.

❧

Roxana insisted, as she got into bed, that she could smell sandalwood fragrance on him.

"I went to the atash-bahram this evening," said Yezad.

"Why, suddenly?" She kept her voice casual. She knew her face was showing an excess of joy, and was glad the bedroom light was off.

"Had a very busy day, needed some quiet. And I remembered your suggestion."

"How was it?"

"Peaceful." He adjusted his pillow and added, "What I wouldn't give to have one corner of this flat as peaceful."

She smiled in the darkness, and summoned up the courage to inquire, "Did you . . . pray?"

"Of course not."

She didn't believe him.

THE DELAYED-ACTION EPIPHANY Yezad was awaiting failed to arrive. Every day he watched Mr. Kapur for some sign that what had been planned was working like a time-release capsule, gradually making its way through the digestive tract of his mind. And each day he was disappointed, for the boss came in, inspected his reindeer, and retired to his cubby-hole. He seemed pensive, and no longer invited Yezad inside at the end of the day.

Then one morning, with just over a week to Christmas, Mr. Kapur arrived unusually late, close to noon. Yezad asked what had delayed him.

"Delayed?" Mr. Kapur checked his watch. "You're right – look at the time. I didn't realize how long it would take by public transport. You see, I've finally sold my car."

"You came by train?"

"Taxi," said Mr. Kapur with a touch of embarrassment. "But the train is what I really wanted to take."

He described his strange adventure in detail: he'd gone to the station eager to become one of the millions who travelled like livestock upon the rails. Each time a train came in, he had pushed his way forward, and each time he was left behind on the platform. Once, he was at the very nucleus of the throng, certain that he would get on, but some centrifugal surge had elbowed him aside.

Yezad nodded. "That happens."

"After trying for over an hour I gave up. But I'll make another attempt tomorrow. I think it's a question of practice, like bowling a leg break." He looked regretfully at the unused ticket and chucked it in the dustbin, while Yezad asked why the sudden keenness on train travel.

345

"It's a philosophical decision – we talked about it once. I want to embrace everything my city has to offer. I want to mingle with her people, be part of that crush of bodies in the streets and trains and buses. Become one with the organic whole that is Bombay. That's where my redemption lies."

So much for Vilas's faith in his actors and in epic realism, thought Yezad. Poor Mr. Kapur, he was too far gone into the realm of fantasy. The realm of his rhetoric. Which he truly believed, and which, in the end, would accomplish nothing. That was the sad part.

"I ask myself why I was unsuccessful today. My spirit is one hundred per cent willing. Is my flesh slightly less? Still repulsed by body odour and dirty clothes and oily hair? Maybe. But I will overcome, I will take the train."

Yezad worried about his boss's blood pressure, and hoped he would tire of his train idea, come to his senses, and buy another car shortly.

The next day, however, Mr. Kapur dragged himself into the shop, dishevelled and limping. Husain ran to get him a chair, and Mr. Kapur flopped into it while Yezad relieved him of his attaché case. The peon poured tea in a saucer, which he held to his employer's mouth.

This irritated Mr. Kapur; he waved it away and took the cup. A few sips later, fortified, he commenced his tale: "You remember some months ago, I witnessed the miracle of a man being scooped up by passengers who were hanging outside the train, clinging by their fingers. They had gathered the runner into the safety of the compartment, making room for one more, though it was fully packed.

"Well, late last night, it occurred to me as I lay in bed that I could be the man on the platform. All I had to do was put my trust in my fellow Bombayites, and I would be able to get aboard.

"So this morning, when the train started moving, I moved alongside. It was easy at first, the speed was very slow. The men hanging in the door struggled to squeeze inside. Bit by bit

346

everyone seemed more secure, able to grip a handle or railing.

"Soon it would be my turn, and though I was out of breath, I raced to stay with the train. I held out my arm. Someone gestured. Was it a greeting or dismissal, I wondered, and reached up with both arms so they couldn't misunderstand, wouldn't think I was merely waving goodbye."

Mr. Kapur paused and gazed sorrowfully into his teacup. "They didn't help me, Yezad. Not one man held out his hand to grasp mine. They looked at me like I was some stranger. Yes, okay, I am a stranger. But I'm also their Bombay brother, am I not? And they just stared through me. Others seemed to find me amusing, turning to one another to laugh."

He drained his cup and gave it to Husain. "There was no miracle for me, Yezad. I tripped and fell as I neared the end of the platform. And then I took a taxi."

The rejection appeared to have broken his spirit. He sat in the doorway like an invalid waiting for his bed to be readied.

"I've been thinking," he whispered at last.

"Yes?" Yezad expected him to admit that selling the car was a mistake.

"On the way here in the taxi I asked myself, Why was I abandoned on the platform?"

Because the train was full, thought Yezad, and because they couldn't hear the romantic nonsense filling your head. "Hard to say," he answered.

"No, it's not. Just look at me – my clothes, my shoes, my hair. Go on, tell me what you think."

Yezad scrutinized the handiwork of Mr. Kapur's expensive hair stylist and moved his eyes downwards to the open collar of his fine linen shirt. Though smudged and crumpled from his railway adventure, there was no mistaking its quality; likewise his trousers with their perfect drape, cut from some lightweight blend of natural fibres. And finally there were his Italian loafers, whose supple leather gleamed with smug supremacy.

"Well?" said Mr. Kapur, getting impatient.

"Stylish, with a touch of class – that's my verdict."

"Exactly. And that's the problem. My whole appearance screams one thing: I am not one of you. For all that I have in common with the passengers, I might as well be from outer space. Why should their embrace carry me into the train when I'm doing my best to say, See me, so superior to you!"

Mr. Kapur swore to remedy this defect. From now on, he would buy his clothes not in air-conditioned department stores but at the pavement shops of Grant Road and Girgaum – kurta-pyjamas, or ill-fitting pants with crotches that wedged, and short-sleeved bushcoats that gripped the armpits. And no more socks and shoes, but chappals of the sort that would produce corns and calluses, allow the grime of Bombay to encrust his toenails.

"And never again am I going to Signor Valente's Salon. A pavement barber in Khetwadi will do the needful. After he hacks my hair, then we'll see if the train passengers pluck me off the platform or not."

"So when will you complete your transformation?" asked Yezad, unable to resist the taunt.

Mr. Kapur counted silently on his fingers. "In nine days. Right after Christmas." He rose and walked briskly towards his office, for the morning's dejection was already dissipating.

"By the way," said Yezad. "Sometimes even cheap clothes look good. Make sure it's a bad fit, before buying your new wardrobe."

But with Mr. Kapur's confidence regained, trying to needle him was like attempting to hurt a pincushion. "I will indeed," he said, then stopped, turned around, and stepped into the Christmas window.

17

Nightly, in chateau felicity, the row from the Munshi flat was audible from the ground floor to the rooftop. It commenced as soon as the handyman went home with his tool box, continuing through dinner, till he and his wife retired.

The quarrels surprised (and distressed) Jal, because when Edul had first started work on the ceiling, Manizeh was glad for her husband. It was no secret in the building that her proscription against using his skills in their own flat had always made her feel guilty.

But this job was of a magnitude quite unlike the little repairs Edul was used to muffing; it had been going on for days, and Manizeh had begun complaining that she missed him every evening. As time passed, her complaints grew sharply bitter: she might as well be a widow, her husband was never there with her.

Edul confided in Jal, assuring him there was no need to worry, he was parrying Manizeh's bitterness with humour, that as long as she could hear his hammer, she was the proud owner of a happy husband.

"All is well," he told Jal again and again.

But Jal suspected all was not as well as Edul pretended. His hunch was borne out on the day that full-scale hostilities ensued in the Munshi flat, at full volume.

"You think I haven't figured out what is going on upstairs?" shouted Manizeh. "You and that unmarried woman together! While that chhinaal's pandering brother goes out for a walk and leaves you with your tool box! How convenient!"

"Shh! Neighbours will hear!" pleaded Edul.

"Good, let them! Better than them laughing behind my back and saying her husband is making repairs for Coomy! Filthy woman, preying on a married man!"

"How can you be jealous of Coomy? Look at her, front and back she's completely flat. Your bum is so lovely, and your—"

"Speak softly, you fool! You want the neighbours to have a complete description? Just give them naked pictures of me, why not!"

Next evening, when Edul came to work on the ceiling, Jal could see that he had arrived swaggerless. The usually swinging tool box hung still as a broken clock's pendulum, and instead of his jaunty handyman style, he wore a sheepish smile. Following the hello, how are you, and his response of champion, there was an awkward silence.

"You must have heard my Manizeh last night," Edul attempted casually. "She was a little upset."

"Was she? No, we heard nothing. Is she all right now?"

"Champion. Just a little misunderstanding, women don't understand repairs and renovations."

He undid the clasp of the box and let the lid crash open. The tools clattered and clanged while he rummaged, his lips pursing to attempt a merry whistle. The tune emerged with some effort, and modulated into melancholy a few bars later.

This was the evening Jal had been awaiting eagerly, when Edul was to commence applying a new coat of plaster. But the handyman could not bring himself to it. His sack of plaster sat untouched by the front door.

The evening walk had to be renounced. Staying home, decided Jal, was the only way to silence Manizeh's charges of pandering. He wished he could clarify things for her, invite her to watch her Edoo at work, see for herself there was no questionable behaviour.

But he desisted – the nightly quarrels he heard while standing at the window made it clear that Manizeh was in no mood to be placated. To her anger she added a note of fatalism: such misfortune befalling their lives was no surprise – Edul had ventured into the house of unhappiness, the house that had destroyed families, killed two women, given birth to generations of sorrow. And the contagion had affected her husband.

Coomy told Jal to stop eavesdropping. "Isn't it strange how you can hear everything now? And when I talk to you, your ears have trouble understanding."

"It's easier from a distance," said Jal. "I can adjust the volume better."

He lamented that the couple used to be so lovey-dovey, and because of the broken ceiling their happy home was plunged into misery. Coomy noted it couldn't have been all that happy, or it wouldn't be affected by such a silly thing.

"Silly for you, not for Manizeh," said Jal. "She doesn't know the facts."

"Facts have nothing to do with it. People make up the facts they need. It's up to Edul to keep working or stop."

To Jal's relief, Edul kept working: on the ceiling, and at convincing Manizeh that she was mistaken. He admitted to her he was spending a lot of time upstairs, and enjoying the challenging work. This was no reason for his sweetie-pie to imagine dirty things, was it? Why couldn't she accept his manly hobby? Would she be happier if he took up embroidery or knitting? Was that what she wanted, a sissy?

The perseverance paid off; Manizeh relented; and the quarrels subsided. Now she began turning up at the job site for snap inspections, armed with some excuse or the other.

"Sorry to interrupt," she said to Jal, relieved to see her husband up a ladder and Coomy nowhere near. "Edoo, dear, do you want the fish fried tonight or in a sauce?"

"Tonight I want it fried," he answered, and winked. "Hot and sizzling I want it tonight."

Smothering her laugh, she looked at Jal, who pretended that his hearing aid was switched off.

Another time, she came to inquire about the ironing: the

blue shirt or the buff, which one would Edoo like?

"Blue shirt for tomorrow," answered her husband, then added, thinking they were alone, "And you can press my birthday suit tonight."

In panic Manizeh put a finger to her lips and motioned to where Coomy was standing, right outside the door. He covered his grinning mouth with a plaster-coated hand, as Coomy rolled her eyes and walked away, disgusted by their indecent behaviour.

Eight days after commencing the application of new plaster, Edul wiped his trowel clean and pronounced the drawing-room ready for habitation. He hailed Manizeh down the stairwell, and asked Jal to fetch Coomy from her room.

"Well?" he beamed. "What do you think?"

Though Jal and Coomy had been prepared for terrible results, they could not furnish a suitable response. They looked at the pockmarked ceiling covered with craters large and small, a domestic version of the lunar surface, and struggled to mask their dismay.

Manizeh jumped into the breach. "You know, Edoo, I can't believe you did this all by yourself." Turning to Jal and Coomy, she added, "Isn't he wonderful?"

"Good work, Edul," they managed to say. "We're so grateful."

"It's nothing," said Edul with a modest wave of his hand, though his eyes shone. "Sorry to have taken so long."

"Four weeks isn't long for such a beautiful job, I was expecting longer," said Coomy, while Manizeh glared at her.

"And now you can start on Pappa's room," said Jal.

But Edul informed them that he was first taking a break for three days. He and his wife went away hand in hand, Jal looking on like a happy father till Coomy shut the door.

After his little holiday, Edul began removing damaged plaster from the ceiling in Nariman's room. He made rapid progress, for Jal's hammering had been quite thorough. Now and again he paused in his whistling to marvel at the devastation wrought by the imaginary leak.

On the second day he said, "Son of a gun!" and summoned his clients to the room.

"You know the supporting beam across this ceiling?"

They nodded.

"Bad news. I've just discovered it's rotten."

"What?"

"Rotten," he repeated, enjoying the effect of his announcement. "R-o-t-t-e-n."

"Impossible!" said Jal, refusing to accept the spurious bombshell.

"Compose yourself, Jal my son. The news is shocking, but what can I do? I have to report honestly. See where it meets the third joist?"

"How can the wood rot so quickly?"

"Ah, but we don't know how long it's been wet. There could have been a slow leak for months before the plaster fell off."

"Impossible!"

Edul was puzzled. "Why do you keep saying that?"

"Because I know! Because—"

Worried that her brother might blurt something incriminating, Coomy intervened. "Let's suppose it's rotten. What happens next?"

"Why suppose? Are you doubting me? It is rotten. It must be replaced."

"No! Please don't touch it!"

"Stop acting like a child," said Coomy. "Let's consider it calmly. Edul, you're sure about this?"

"One thousand per cent."

"I see." She calculated: with the beam complication, there would be a further delay before Pappa returned. "Can you do the job?"

"I won't lie to you. It's a serious job. Could be dangerous if not done right. You want someone who works slowly, carefully."

"And that's you," she said, which made him smile.

"Please, just do the plastering and leave it!"

"Enough drama, Jal," said his sister.

"At least take a second opinion?"

"We handymen have a saying: Second opinion leads to a mountain of confusion."

"Makes sense," said Coomy.

"How does it make sense?" blustered Jal.

"Jal my son, relax, let me explain the method," said Edul. He proceeded to describe the steel posts he would employ, and the hydraulic jacks, with the load transferred off the joists by using surrogate supports. The thoroughness with which he detailed the task befitted a qualified engineer, a master craftsman with years of experience.

Jal missed some of it as he pulled out his earpiece, blew upon it, and reinserted it.

"The most important point is: I'm adding the steel girder parallel to the existing wood. At no time will the structure remain unsupported."

"Oh," said Coomy, relieved. "So we'll have two beams instead of one. You heard that, Jal? Two beams – even safer."

There were no more objections. It was agreed that Edul would go ahead.

WHEN JAL ARRIVED at Pleasant Villa, his heart beat a little faster to see Daisy at the bedside, with her violin. He tried to greet her, and almost caught her eye, but she swayed, her bow arm rose, and he ended up mouthing hello to her elbow.

His stepfather acknowledged him silently as he patted his shoulder and tiptoed to a chair. Adjusting his hearing aid to listen better to Daisy's music, he asked Roxana where Yezad was.

She whispered that he must have stopped at Wadiaji fire-temple on the way home from work.

Jal raised his brow. "Yezad? Fire-temple?"

She nodded. "Goes almost every day. Not to pray – he says the few minutes of peace and quiet help him."

He smiled and nodded. "Pappa's looking better too."

"He always brightens when Daisy comes."

"Shh," said Jehangir, "you're disturbing the music."

"Sorry, dikra," said Jal, and sat back. The violin, slow and evocative, drew him in as he listened. He felt the music speaking directly about things deep in his heart . . . those difficult emotions, impossible in speech. Sometimes, just for an instant, the sound seemed human, the instrument articulating words in a language he could almost understand . . .

The piece ended, they clapped, and Daisy said hello to Jal, apologizing for not greeting him when he came in.

"Oh, quite all right," he smiled bashfully.

"Splen splen splendid," murmured Nariman. "You must per perform it."

"That's my ambition – soloist with the BSO."

"Excuse me," said Jal. "What was the piece?"

"Beethoven's violin concerto," she replied.

"Number?"

"There is only one."

"And the part you were practising . . . which movement?"

"Second – the larghetto."

Daisy returned to telling Nariman about the difficulties of realizing her dream, and while she re-tuned, Jal's admiring eyes followed her every move. Roxana nudged him, "Go on, talk to her."

"Later," he whispered, retreating as the violin started again.

Then Yezad arrived, let himself in quietly with his latchkey, and saw Jal. He was anxious to hear about the ceiling, but waited till Nariman was asleep. After Daisy left, they retired to the back room.

"So what's the latest bulletin from Chateau Felicity?"

"A week ago, like Edul, I would have said champion. Now, I don't know any more." He delivered the news about the rotten beam, and looked anxiously from his face to hers.

"Not your fault," said Yezad. "Don't feel so guilty."

"But I'm the one always bringing you Edul's nonsense and—"

"Maybe the beam really is rotten," said Roxana. "How long will it take?"

"A year," said Yezad with a hollow laugh.

"Oh no, no," said Jal, "not that long."

He described Edul's plan to get equipment in place over the next few days, prepare for hoisting the steel girder. "Latest by the twenty-fourth, because he wants to use the Christmas holiday for the job. He says it shouldn't be left halfway, he'll work into the night if necessary, to finish it."

"Looks like a merry Christmas for you," said Yezad.

"Certainly won't be a silent night. And what about you, Jehangir? Are you going to hang up a stocking for Santa?"

"Yes," sighed Jehangir. "I'm fed up of arguing with Murad. He's driving me crazy, trying to make me believe it."

"But he's right," said Jal. "You're nine years old?"

"Yes," admitted Jehangir cautiously.

"There you are. Santa comes till ten. Your last chance."

"I'm not a small child, okay, Uncle? You can't fool me so easily."

Jal laughed, hugging him and shaking hands at the door with the others. He promised to bring news as soon as there was any. They shut the door and went to the balcony for the wave.

Roxana snuggled against her husband, enjoying the fragrance that sandalwood smoke had left in his clothes. "I think Jal really likes Daisy. Wouldn't it be nice if they—"

"Please," said Yezad. "Your family doesn't have a very good record in matchmaking."

Toying with his teacup, he sat at the dining table. She went to make dinner out of the odds and ends saved from the day before. He glanced at his father-in-law, hands and feet tossing helplessly beneath the sheet.

Like trapped animals struggling to break free. What a curse was sickness in old age. This damned Parkinson's, cruel as torture. If the new research in America would hurry up, something with foetal tissue, embryos . . . But there were groups protesting against it – they probably weren't living with Parkinson's or watching an old man's torment day after day. How nice the luxury, to argue about rights of the unborn, beginning of life, moment of death, all those sophisticated discussions. Empty talkers. Like Mr. Kapur . . . But no such luxury here. Should be a rule: Walk, first, through the fire, then philosophize . . .

Nariman groaned in his sleep, and Yezad broke off his rumination to go to the settee. "It's okay, chief," he touched his shoulder. "I'm sitting right here."

He returned to his teacup, not sure if Nariman had heard him. Strange trip, this journey towards death. No way of knowing how much longer for the chief . . . a year, two years? But Roxana was right, helping your elders through it – that was the only way to learn about it. And the trick was to remember it when your own time came . . .

Would he, he wondered? What folly made young people, even those in middle age, think they were immortal? How much better, their lives, if they could remember the end. Carrying your death with you every day would make it hard to waste time on unkindness and anger and bitterness, on anything petty. That was the secret: remembering your dying time, in order to keep the stupid and the ugly out of your living time.

He pushed back his chair quietly and took his cup and saucer to the kitchen. He rinsed them, wiped his hands, and returned to watch Nariman. Curious, he thought, how, if you knew a person long enough, he could elicit every kind of emotion from you, every possible reaction, envy, admiration, pity, irritation, fury, fondness, jealousy, love, disgust. But in the end all human beings became candidates for compassion, all of us, without exception . . . and if we could recognize this from the beginning, what a saving in pain and grief and misery . . .

The groans from the settee grew louder. He rose again, touched Nariman's shoulder again. Must be some way to help the chief.

The answer was easy: provide money for his medicines – and he didn't have any. Always came down to money, everything did.

There was that envelope in his desk at work, sitting uselessly for over a week now, waiting to be collected by imaginary Shiv Sena emissaries, while Mr. Kapur made his Santa Claus preparations. Would be Christmas in another week. If only he had the guts to spend from that envelope . . . instead of waiting – for what?

He had waited for Villie's Matka dream, and for Mr. Kapur's promised promotion. He had waited for Nariman's ankle to heal, and for the ceiling to be fixed, and for the actors to deliver an epiphany.

He had waited enough, he decided. In the end, he could only depend on himself. And the fire-temple – his sanctuary, in this meaningless world.

THE SANTA SUIT was delivered before noon on the twenty-third, and Mr. Kapur modelled it for Yezad and Husain.

"Very beautiful, sahab," said the peon, clapping his hands with unvarnished delight. "Lal colour looks so nice on you."

Mr. Kapur posed for the silent Yezad, who glanced at the cheap belt of black plastic, and gumboots of the type that smelled, which Murad and Jehangir used to wear in the monsoon till they rebelled.

"On the whole, quite good," was his verdict. "But your stomach needs fattening."

They looked around the shop and made a paunch by combining a pair of junior-size batting pads and boxing gloves. Then Mr. Kapur decided to don the rest of the ensemble, but the fluffy white beard and moustache made Husain flinch. He said to Yezad that sahab looked too fierce for his liking.

"Ho-ho-ho!" started Mr. Kapur. "Ho-ho-ho!" waving his arms frantically to make the wrist bells chime.

The peon whispered in Yezad's ear, "Why does sahab sound like something is paining?"

Yezad's chortles made Mr. Kapur ask what was so funny. The answer had him laughing too, increasing Husain's puzzlement.

"Aray, Husain miyan, that's not a noise of pain! It's the jolly laughter of Santa Claus!"

Husain seemed unconvinced but withheld further comment. In the afternoon he went to collect the sweets that had been ordered the previous day.

Mr. Kapur, still in the Santa suit, came up to Yezad and, peering into his face, asked why there were dark circles under his eyes. "Looks like you're not sleeping well."

"It's my father-in-law – he's staying with us for the time being. He talks and shouts in his sleep."

Yezad paused, then decided to keep going, to use this opportunity for prompting Mr. Kapur, as Vilas had called it. "Worrying about Shiv Sena also keeps me awake."

"Relax, Yezad, worrying won't help. Last night I had a brainwave. I've reconsidered the situation."

Yezad's heart leapt. Might the actors' effort still bear fruit?

"I have come to an important conclusion," began Mr. Kapur. "That Bombay is much more than a city. Bombay is a religion."

"Is this a promotion for the city? You used to say it was a beautiful woman."

Mr. Kapur laughed and cleared a corner on Yezad's desk to sit. "She is, Yezad. But now she has aged. And if she can accept her wrinkles with poise and dignity, so must I. For there is beauty too in such acceptance. This is going to be my holistic approach."

More like a hole-in-the-head approach, thought Yezad. "You won't do anything about the problems?"

"No. All her blemishes, her slums, her broken sewers, her corrupt and criminal politicians, her—".

"Hang on, Mr. Kapur. I don't think crime or corruption can be called a blemish. More a cancerous tumour. When a person has cancer in their body, they should bloody well fight it."

"Not in the holistic approach. Hating the cancer, attacking it with aggressive methods is futile. Holistically, you have to convince your tumour, with love and kindness, to change its malign nature to a benign one."

"And if the cancer won't listen?" said Yezad somewhat viciously. "She will die, won't she?"

"Now you mustn't be too literal with my beautiful-woman metaphor," chided Mr. Kapur.

"Am I? I was just applying it consistently. The young Bombay in your photographs, then the aging, the cancer—"

361

"Okay, forget the beautiful woman," said Mr. Kapur with a trace of irritation. "Remember I said Bombay is like a religion? Well, it's like Hinduism. I think."

"And how did you manage to work that out?"

"Hinduism has an all-accepting nature, agreed? I'm not talking about the fundamentalist, mosque-destroying fanatics, but the real Hinduism that has nurtured this country for thousands of years, welcoming all creeds and beliefs and dogmas and theologies, making them feel at home. Sometimes, when they are not looking, it absorbs them within itself. Even false gods are accommodated, and turned into true ones, adding a few more deities to its existing millions.

"The same way, Bombay makes room for everybody. Migrants, businessmen, perverts, politicians, holy men, gamblers, beggars, wherever they come from, whatever caste or class, the city welcomes them and turns them into Bombayites. So who am I to say these people belong here and those don't? Janata Party okay, Shiv Sena not okay, secular good, communal bad, BJP unacceptable, Congress lesser of evils?

"No, it's not up to us. Bombay opens her arms to everyone. What we think of as decay is really her maturity, and her constancy to her essential complex nature. How dare I dispute her Zeitgeist? If this is Bombay's Age of Chaos, how can I demand a Golden Age of Harmony? How can there be rule of law and democracy if this is the hour of a million mutinies?"

Yezad nodded, feeling his head would burst into a million pieces under Mr. Kapur's wild and unwieldy analogies.

Just then, Husain returned with the sweets, which made Mr. Kapur abandon the subject. He began examining the six large packages to make sure that everything he had ordered was there. Yezad remarked that judging by the quantity, the sweets must have cost a lot.

"I don't mind," said Mr. Kapur. "It's for a good occasion. If the Shiv Sena crooks can get thousands from us, why not some gifts for the children in our neighbourhood? Besides, they will learn about other communities and religions, about tolerance, no? They hear enough from Shiv Sena about intolerance."

And what about gifts for my children, thought Yezad bitterly, as they carried the packets into Mr. Kapur's office. Never mind gifts, what about necessities for my family?

"Which reminds me, Yezad. Have those crooks got their filthy hands on our money?"

"Not yet." He cursed the reminder – hardly an hour passed without his thinking about that wretched envelope. How long would it plague him in his desk? Till Mr. Kapur decided Shiv Sena weren't coming for it, and returned it to the suitcase. The end of a useless drama. Unless . . .

"Take a look at this, Yezad," said Mr. Kapur. It was a handwritten cardboard sign he'd made to hang outside. The letters were six inches high, green and red: COME, CHILDREN, MEET SANTA CLAUS! and below it, a Hindi version: AO, BACHCHAY, SANTA CLAUS KO MILO! Santa's hours were listed: 2 p.m. to 7 p.m. on December 24, and 10 a.m. to 1 p.m. on December 25.

"You're staying open on Christmas Day as well?"

"Not for business – for peace and goodwill. But you don't have to come, just enjoy the holiday. You too, Husain."

"Sahab, I want to come. Humko bhi mazaa ayega."

"Sure. Chalo, sign ko string lagaake fix karo."

Husain got the stepladder from the storeroom and tied the cardboard square to the bracket under the Bombay Sporting neon display. "Okay, sahab?"

"First class, we're all set."

Mr. Kapur played around for the rest of the afternoon, too excited to do any work, keeping on his costume while complaining that it was hot inside it. When he took it off at closing time, it was soaked with sweat.

"Hard work, being Santa," he joked, spreading the red jacket and trousers to dry on the counter. "I need a good rest tonight."

They locked up, and Husain escorted Mr. Kapur to the

kerb, waiting with him till he got into a taxi. He seemed happy that his kind sahab had emerged unchanged from inside the hairy-faced red monster.

Yezad said good night and walked down the footpath, jostled by the crowds of workers hurrying home. He yearned for the peace of the fire-temple. How fortunate that in the harsh desert this city had become, his oasis was so close by.

And today, he had brought his own prayer cap. He put his hand in his pocket and felt its reassuring velvet presence. Long unused, it was still soft against his fingers.

Eyes closed, Yezad sat by the sanctum, a prayer book open in his lap. The boi had been rung, the bell hung still, and the exuberant fire in the afargaan was starting to subside. The room returned to its comforting half-gloom.

He shut the prayer book and replaced it on the shelf. At the sanctum's marble threshold he bowed. His fingers took a generous pinch of ash to smear on his forehead and throat. Walking in reverse, he moved slowly away from the fire, out of the room.

On the veranda the white-bearded dustoorji was deep in conversation with another priest. Yezad imagined they were debating some profound matter – perhaps a problem of Gathic interpretation? How he would love to acquire that kind of knowledge. Would it be of help in making sense of this world, his world? Until he tried, he wouldn't know.

At the gate he slipped off his prayer cap and returned it to his pocket, then wiped off the ash. He made his way to Marine Lines station.

A few steps later he stopped, turned around, and strode briskly towards Bombay Sporting, taking a detour to avoid Vilas in case he was still writing letters outside the Book Mart. The keys were ready in his hand as he approached the shop. The door was opened swiftly – it was a smooth latch – and shut behind him.

He went inside without turning on the lights, able to see all that he needed to see. He passed the Santa costume draped over the counter, waiting for tomorrow. Selecting the right key by touch, he unlocked his desk, pulled out the drawer, removed the manila envelope, put it in his briefcase. He locked his desk, locked the door, and went home.

He said not a word to Roxana. He couldn't, not till his confusion cleared. The carefully considered act had only created more turmoil. And there was a tightness round his heart.

All evening, while Yezad grappled with the disarray in his mind, Murad and Jehangir eyed him with concern, keeping their distance. And Roxana, fearing a quarrel, wondered what was wrong again, after the calm she hoped had returned to bless their house.

WELL BEFORE TWO O'CLOCK the following afternoon, Mr. Kapur, reincarnated as Santa Claus, paced restlessly between the counters of Bombay Sporting. Now and again he startled Husain with an ebullient ho-ho-ho, or practised his wave, trying different styles to see which produced the most chimes. Just inside the door, where he would receive his visitors, the flashing bulb gave his chair an eerie red wash.

At last it was the appointed hour, and he sat with the sack full of sweets by his side. "Don't look so worried, Yezad, people will come."

"Oh yes, they'll come." Guilt must look like worry, he thought, trying to compose himself. The tightness in his chest from last night had troubled him all day, and he wondered if he should see a doctor.

After half an hour Mr. Kapur began pacing again. "Why is no one coming? Yesterday when I passed Akbarally's, it was packed with children. Look at me, Yezad. Am I inferior to the Akbarally's Santa?"

"You look wonderful. Problem is, they have a mailing list, and special invitations. My Jehangir also got one last week."

"Did you take him?"

"Of course not, he's too old for that. And if he wanted to meet Santa, I'd bring him here."

The response pleased Mr. Kapur. He tried to spot in the crowds rushing past a young child to whom he might wave, who might then ask to come inside.

Another half-hour passed, and the only sweets consumed were the ones eaten by Yezad. He kept unwrapping them, one after another, and crunching them down. As he fumbled with the wrappers, he realized his fingers were as unsteady as a chain-smoker's.

"No one wants my treats," said Mr. Kapur mournfully. "You might as well have them all. You and Husain take them home."

"Maybe the cardboard sign is the problem," said Yezad, putting back the sweet in his hand. "I wonder if people can read the message."

Mr. Kapur jumped at the excuse. "Of course. Why didn't I think of that? Husain can stand outside and direct people's attention to it."

The peon took his new assignment seriously. When a woman and her son paused to look in the window, he approached them with such alacrity, they shied away in alarm.

"Walk faster, baba, it's a crazy fellow," she said, looking around fearfully.

Wounded by the comment but undaunted, Husain selected another recipient for Kapur sahab's benefaction. A man and a little girl, probably his daughter, were stopping to examine shop displays. The child asked for something; the man smiled and shook his head, patting her cheek to console her.

They neared, and Husain got ready. He seemed determined that his quarry would not escape this time – a child would be provided for Kapur sahab. And when they passed, he pounced.

Grabbing the little girl's arm, he began supplicating the father. "Please come inside, bhai sahab! Free sweets milayga, your bachchi will enjoy!"

Perhaps the father thought it was an abduction attempt, or was annoyed at the aggressive solicitation. "Hai, sala!" he yelled. "Haath mut lagao!"

But Husain held on.

"Let us go or I'll break your head!"

As he made to strike Husain, Mr. Kapur decided it was time to rescue his peon. "Excuse me, sir!" he called from the entrance, pre-empting the blow. "Sorry for the inconvenience! We're just offering free sweets for Christmas."

Yezad went to the door too, ready to intervene if needed. But Mr. Kapur's words had reassured the parent. The child, however, looked at the red apparition and burst into tears. People were stopping to watch, unwilling to walk past what could be a unique altercation: Santa Claus versus the public.

"Rona nahi, my child," said Mr. Kapur, holding out a hand from which she flinched. "You understand English?"

"My daughter is in standard one, English medium," said the father haughtily, insulted by the question.

"Excellent," said Mr. Kapur. "So why are you crying, my little girl? You've never seen Santa Claus?"

The father said frostily, "We follow the Jain religion."

"That's good," said Mr. Kapur. "Myself, I am Hindu. But no harm in a bit of Christmas fun. And modern Santa Claus is secular, anyway."

Dragging his child who was now as fascinated as she was terrified, the man walked off while Mr. Kapur expounded on the virtues of a cosmopolitan society and the advantage of celebrating festivals of all faiths and religions. The crowd on the pavement heard him out, several people clapping in agreement. He gave them a wave, startling himself with the chimes, and returned inside, somewhat deflated.

"Oollu kay patthay!" he scolded Husain. "I said to inform people about Santa Claus. Not ghubrao them by snatching their children. Smile at them, be nice. As though you are inviting friends into your home. Jao, try again."

Husain returned to the pavement, worried about Kapur sahab's anger. Was the fierce-looking costume and beard changing his sweet nature?

Meanwhile, Yezad felt he needed to commiserate with Mr. Kapur: "New things take time to work."

"Santa Claus is not new," he said gloomily. "He is hundreds of years old."

They watched Husain have another go at enticing visitors. He grinned and bowed, indicated the sign, pointed at the man in red inside the shop. He mastered the art of communicating without intimidating, and they were rewarded with their first guests.

The boy was familiar with Santa etiquette. He went up to shake Mr. Kapur's hand and wordlessly endured the hug. The fond parents answered in an eager affirmative when their son was asked if he had been good this year.

Beaming, Mr. Kapur reached into his red sack and tried to engage the taciturn boy in conversation. In a burst of generosity he gave handfuls of sweets to the parents too.

A baffled Husain observed the ritual at the centre of his employer's elaborate preparations. His expression seemed to say it made no sense – sahab was giving away sweets to strangers who weren't interested in buying anything from the shop.

"Ho-ho-ho!" laughed Santa once more for the departing guests. "Merry Christmas, and see you next year!"

"Say thank you, Santa," instructed the parents. The boy ignored them, engrossed in his sweets as he skipped down the steps.

"That went well," said Mr. Kapur.

"Perfect," said Yezad from behind him, wishing the evening would come to an end. He wiped the sweat from his upper lip, dried the finger on his shirt sleeve, and reached into the sack for one more sweet.

"I think now it will get very busy," declared Mr. Kapur. "I feel it in my bones. Chalo, Husain, why are you staring at me like a buddhoo? Go outside, send in more bachchay with their ma-baap."

Though Mr. Kapur's bones were far from right, there was a trickle steady enough to warm his heart with a variety of experiences. Children who were seeing their first Santa gazed in fascination or turned away in horror. Others marched in and out like well-behaved robots. Those too old for Santa came for the free sweets with a mocking, jeering attitude. One boy kept repeating joyfully, "Father Christmas has bugs in his beard!"

The embarrassed mother explained: her son was mixing up Santa Claus with family jokes about a white-bearded priest whose facial hair was reputed to harbour insects.

The window lights were switched off at seven; Husain was told to stop recruiting visitors. In his office Mr. Kapur pried the beard and moustache from his face, wincing as the skin pulled. The reassuring clank of the steel shutters was heard outside. He sat to remove his gumboots, but his feet, encased in the hot rubber, had swollen. He managed to tug one boot off after a struggle.

While he wrestled with the other, Husain came in. "Ah, miyan bhai, can you help me? Bahut tight hai."

The peon knelt and grasped the boot's heel and toe as Mr. Kapur braced himself in the chair. The gumboot came off with a whoosh. He flexed his ankles, wiggled his toes, and slipped the aching feet into his comfortable Italian loafers. "Ready to leave, Yezad?"

They stepped outside, and while Yezad locked the shop, Mr. Kapur pointed to the signboard: "Look at that."

Rubbing a hand over his chest where the tightness persisted, Yezad stared at the sign. The neon lights said BOMBAY SPORTING GODS EMPORIUM – an o had blown. There was an o in each word, he thought uneasily, and yet this was the one that had gone dark.

"The electrician will be closed tomorrow," he said. "I'll have it checked day after."

"Absolutely. Spend the holiday with your family."

"Thanks, Mr. Kapur."

"Merry Christmas, Yezad."

18

AFTER MIDNIGHT, Yezad felt the tightness in his chest getting worse, and his forehead was dripping sweat. He rose cautiously, but the bed creaked and Roxana turned over.

"What's wrong, Yezdaa?"

"Nothing, just gas, I think. I'm going to drink ginger."

He left the kitchen dark and opened the refrigerator. Its light made him squint. There was one bottle of ginger on the door – he touched it: barely chilled.

His fingers made spoons clatter in the drawer before closing around the opener. He snapped the cap off, trying to catch it as it fell and rolled away under the table, then emptied the fizzing drink into a glass. Fresh bottle, he thought, and took a few sips. The effervescence continued to hiss in the dark.

His ginger burp was prompt in arriving, but he knew the relief he sought wasn't in this drink: it was not gas but the envelope – from the minute he'd brought it home it had turned into his biggest burden, squeezing the breath out of him. What had possessed him? Desperation, he knew. And he was still desperate, nothing had changed in twenty-four hours, the chief was still suffering, Roxana still driving herself to exhaustion, there wasn't enough to eat, and here was money to ease all the difficulties, if he would only open the envelope, start spending . . .

He heard bare feet approach the kitchen. Probably Roxana, to ask how he was feeling. The light went on. He shielded his eyes.

It was Murad, startled to find his father on the stool beside the stove. "Why are you sitting in the dark, Daddy?"

"The bulb is too bright." Pointing to the glass of ginger, he added, "Gas," and rubbed his chest. "What are you doing?"

"I've to put Jehangir's Christmas gift in his stocking."

His father narrowed his eyes. "How did you get the money for it?"

"By saving all my bus fare."

Yezad started to ask another stern question, then understood. He continued gently, "You should have told Mummy you were walking home, she was so anxious about you coming back late every day from school."

"I wanted to keep it secret. Surprise everyone on Christmas morning."

Yezad smiled. "I won't breathe a word." He took a sip from his ginger. "You must have planned this months ago."

Murad nodded. "Jehangir looks so sad all the time, worrying about everything. I wanted to cheer him up."

Yezad put his glass down. He rose from the stool and squeezed his son's shoulder.

Grinning, Murad opened the spice cabinet and reached behind the boxes and bottles to retrieve the hidden package. He sniffed the wrapping and made a face. "Smells like the Motilal masala shop."

"So what did you buy for Jehangir?"

"Three books – Enid Blyton." He shut the spice cabinet, and prepared to leave the kitchen. "Shall I keep the light on?"

"No."

The kitchen went dark again, and Murad knocked into something. "Hard to see," he whispered.

"Don't walk till your eyes adjust. Banging around, you'll wake up Jehangir and Grandpa."

He could hear his son's breathing, his eagerness to surprise his brother. Must have done something right, he felt, he and Roxana – but mostly Roxana – to have raised such a fine boy. Didn't show affection outwardly, the way Jehangla did, though he cared just as much.

"I can see clearly now," said Murad, and left the kitchen.

A few seconds later, Yezad followed his son. He did not want to miss the moment.

Noises by his bed told Jehangir his brother was approaching the stocking. Not really a stocking, just an old cloth shopping bag that Mummy had cut into the shape and put stitches around; the two handles were still attached. He wondered what was in his Christmas present.

He opened his eyes a sliver, waiting to catch Murad red-handed. He was moving very cautiously. Something rustled, Murad froze and looked directly at his pillow. Then Grandpa made a sound, and Murad almost fled to the balcony. But after murmuring a few words about Mr. Braganza, Grandpa was quiet, and Murad tried again to tuck the gift into the stocking.

Jehangir got ready to pounce. Now? He hesitated. He could see Murad's expression, the little smile that flickered. There was tenderness on his brother's face.

Suddenly he understood why Murad wanted him to believe in Santa Claus: not to make a fool of him, but because he wanted him to enjoy the story.

In a way, thought Jehangir, the Santa Claus story was like the Famous Five books. You knew none of it was real, but it let you imagine there was a better world somewhere. You could dream of a place where there was lots to eat, where children could have a midnight feast and raid the larder that was always full of sumptuous delicacies. A place where they organized picnics to the countryside and had adventures, where even the smugglers and thieves they caught were not too dangerous, just "nasty customers" who were "up to no good," as the kindly police inspector explained at the end of each book. A place where there were no beggars, no sickness, and no one died of starvation. And once a year a jolly fat man brought gifts for good children.

All this was what Murad wanted for him. To jump up in bed and say, I caught you, you can't trick me, would be so mean.

He shut his eyes tight, not moving a muscle. The package was stuffed into the stocking, and Murad tiptoed away to his balcony bed.

❧

In the dark kitchen Yezad picked up his glass of ginger again, wishing Roxana had been with him to see their sons. He was certain Jehangir had observed Murad, he knew from the way he'd relaxed and turned onto his back the moment Murad left the room. For days Jehangla had rejected the notion of Santa Claus. All he had had to do tonight was sit up in bed to prove his point. Instead he had let Murad stay and work the surprise.

He wanted to hug him, hug them both, tell them he loved them beyond measure, tell them how fortunate he was to have them for his sons, and how blessed they were to be brothers who cared about each other, and he wished their caring would never end, they would look out for each other all their lives. He wanted to wake Roxana, wake the chief, proclaim to everyone how he felt . . .

He drank some of the tepid ginger remaining in the glass, unable to reconcile this precious moment with the torment he had created for himself. The kitchen clock sounded once. Was it twelve-thirty, or one o'clock?

He strained to make out the position of the hands: one-thirty – and stared at the octagonal face, the glass door in its frame of dark polished wood, the brass pendulum catching just a gleam of light. He gazed at it, the clock that used to hang in the kitchen in Jehangir Mansion, the one remembrance of his childhood home, of his father . . .

As he looked, the clock swallowed up time. And he was back in that ground-floor flat, watching his father with the big chrome key in his hand, inserting it on the left, winding clockwise, then on the right, anti-clockwise. His father moving the hands through the hours, waiting for the bongs, setting the precise time, closing the glass door with a click after giving it a wipe. And the little boy that Yezad used to be was asking again to hear the story behind the engraving: *In gratitude for an exemplary display of courage and honesty in the course of duty*, the story of his father stranded in an exploding city with a fortune in cash . . .

The clock struck two, returning Yezad to the kitchen in Pleasant Villa. How comforting its ticking, reassuring, like a steady hand guiding the affairs of the universe. Like his father's hand that held his when he was little, leading him through the world of wonder and upheaval. And his father's words, always at the end of the story, *Remember your kusti prayers: manashni, gavashni, kunashni – good thoughts, good words, good deeds* . . .

He heard them in the ticking of the clock, and felt his heart constrict. His gaze followed the gleam of the pendulum for a few more moments. Then he closed his eyes, and decided: he would drop in at the shop in the morning.

Yes, he would wish Mr. Kapur a merry Christmas, and while Mr. Kapur was giving out sweets by the door he would replace the envelope in the drawer. Or he could go early, before anyone arrived.

He threw away the remaining ginger, ready to return to bed. He paused under the clock, running his hand over its face and patting the glass door.

The tightness in his chest had almost disappeared. He heard Nariman calling out in his sleep, and wished him good night in his thoughts. The bed creaked as he lay down.

"Yezdaa? How are you feeling?"

"Much better. Go to sleep now." He kissed her gently on the back.

❧

Up on one elbow, Jehangir listened to Grandpa having that same dream about Lucy singing their favourite song. Now he was asking her to step down, it was dangerous to stand up there. But he could only catch bits of Grandpa's dream. Like Daddy's badly working radio, where the sound came and went.

He turned the phrases over in his mind, storing them away with the other fragments he was saving. Some day, it would all fit together, and he would make sense of Grandpa's words, he was certain.

There was a commotion in the building – the ayah is singing on the terrace again! shouted someone. Looks like she is going to jump this time! – and Nariman froze with fear. Then he was possessed by a rage against Mr. Arjani, against himself, against Lucy, for subjecting herself and him to such misery.

He took a deep breath, tried to stay calm, as once more Mr. Arjani humbled himself by pleading for his assistance. And once more, for Lucy's sake, he agreed.

Yasmin was furious; he had expected she would be. But her anger, hurled at him like never before – like a fist, he felt – took him by surprise. Almost two months since the first drama on the terrace, she said. Two months the Arjanis had had, to send the crazy woman to a place where she would be safe without ruining the lives of other people. She forbade him to go to the rescue, it was none of his business.

But he climbed the stairs to the terrace. From the landing below, Yasmin reminded him to spare a thought for his honour, if he had any, and for his family. He turned, looked at her sadly, and kept climbing.

On the rooftop, things seemed to him almost identical to the last time. There was Lucy on the parapet, singing happily. There too were Mr. Arjani and his son crouching behind the water tank, their relief at seeing him almost palpable. And their fervent thanks again, which he disdained. He ordered them to leave the terrace. Overcome by a feeling of utter weariness, he coaxed Lucy into stepping down, returned her to the Arjanis, and went home.

He was expecting a storm like never before. Instead, he saw Yasmin sitting at the table, the silver thurible ready with hot coals for the evening loban.

Good, he thought, she was preparing to start her evening prayers, perhaps there wouldn't be another fight.

He noticed a stack of letters, cards, and photographs assembled next to the thurible and wondered what they were. Then he recognized them – Yasmin must have gone through his desk while he was on the terrace, ransacked the drawers.

"So you're back?" she said. "Now you can tell me why you have been saving this trash."

He remained silent.

"For all this time, you've said she is a nuisance, you're doing your best to be rid of her, trying to convince her to go away. So why keep all this? Were you lying to me? Answer me!"

His silence persisted.

"Be a man and admit it. Admit that you still have feelings for her."

"I no longer know what I have. Or for whom."

"Then you won't mind if I burn this." She picked up a handful of papers and dropped them on the hot coals in the thurible.

He wanted to rush to the table, rescue the letters, but he willed himself to remain in his chair. The pages began to smoulder, then burst into flame. More was added from the stack, photographs of Lucy, birthday cards, cards written for no particular reason, the little notes Lucy used to send on a whim – he watched them, the mementos of their halcyon days, fed one by one to the burning coals, and he saw them become ashes.

Yasmin went through the lot without another word. The flames died down, and he turned away.

This gesture of his rekindled Yasmin's earlier fury. "It's all a hoax! Her trick to get you up there. To flirt with you because I stopped you running after her every morning with your bottom waggling. For her this is a competition. To show that she controls my husband, makes him dance whenever she wants."

"Perhaps you are right. But what if you're wrong, and she does jump on the day I don't go?"

"Nonsense! People who really want to kill themselves never put on performances. There's nothing the matter with her head – working too smartly for her own good."

Then she lapsed into threats, swore she was leaving with all three children, he would never see his two-year-old daughter again. Rather than stay and be humiliated, she would starve to death with them before she suffered any more of his cruelty.

He could see that their mother's wild fury scared the children. Jal and Coomy were used to the fights, but this time they both burst into tears, as though they knew now that their mother, whom they believed strong, was really weak, trapped by her marriage, with nowhere to go. And he could feel their hatred towards him growing by the minute.

"You're a horrid man!" screamed Coomy. "Why are you treating Mamma so badly?"

Jal tried to quieten his sister, as she continued, "Just remember, God will punish you for what you're doing!"

His heart ached, but there was nothing he could say to them, and he sat with his head in his hands. He watched the children go to their mother, hug her, and lead her to bed.

In desperation, he went to see Lucy's family. It was Mrs. Braganza who came to the door, looked at him as though she'd met a ghost, and banged it shut. He kept ringing the bell. The door was opened again – by Mr. Braganza, who said he would call the police if he did not leave. Nariman began telling about Lucy, talking fast to describe the state she was in. He didn't get far; the door slammed. He kept talking till he realized there was no one listening on the other side.

Could Mr. Braganza really not care about what happened

378

to his own daughter? He tried to put himself and little Roxana in this situation, but found it impossible to imagine.

After a while people in Chateau Felicity paid almost no attention to Lucy. Hardly anyone gathered on the pavement or at their windows. He heard the talk in the building, that the occurrence was becoming routine: the ayah was a bit cracked, she liked to sing on the ledge once a week – and not even a different number each time, Khodai salaamat raakhay, but the same thing over and over – and then she came downstairs on Professor Vakeel's arm, that was all. Nothing worth making a big fuss about.

Like the Arjanis, everyone now took it for granted he would continue to do his duty, restore Lucy safely to earth and into their flat. No longer did a sense of danger surround the occasion. And, gradually, he began to feel the same. To accept things as they were was perhaps the best way.

One evening, when the message came, summoning him to the terrace, Yasmin said it was she who was going up today. She would talk to the madwoman face to face, see how crazy she really was.

He begged her not to. He tried impressing upon her how terribly distraught Lucy was behind her singing and her docile demeanour. But Yasmin said she would straighten out the woman once and for all, and nothing he said could dissuade her.

"Be careful, Mamma," cried Coomy. "The madwoman might hit you."

"Don't worry, my darling, I can hit back."

Nariman followed Yasmin up the stairs, keeping a few paces behind. When she got to the roof, he stopped in the shadow of the water tank.

Now what? He couldn't think for fear.

Dusk was falling, the evening was warm, still, without a breeze. A funnel of noise – car horns, screeching brakes –

379

reached the terrace like an intruder. In a dream, he watched Yasmin approach Lucy on the twilit parapet.

"Hey, ayah!" he heard her yell, her arms akimbo. "What's this nonsense? Get down from there and go to your kitchen. At once. Arjani seth is waiting for dinner!"

Frozen to the spot, he saw Lucy glance at Yasmin over her shoulder. She seemed not to recognize the woman shouting so rudely.

On the roof of the building across the road, a neon sign flashed red and blue, alternating the image of shoes with the manufacturer's slogan: Take the World in Your Stride.

He heard Yasmin speak again, and once more saw her met with a blank silence. He watched as though in a trance, while Yasmin gathered her skirt, stepped up on the parapet herself, and tapped Lucy roughly on the shoulder.

"Hey! Deaf or what?" she kept tapping the shoulder. "At least look at me when I speak to you."

He shook himself out of his stupor and crept forward. How to counsel reason, how to deal with two women on the ledge? Neon light bathed them in alternating blue and red.

"'We laughed then, we cried then,'" sang Lucy, brushing away the hand from her shoulder.

At last Yasmin had got some reaction. But this was not the kind she had sought. "Who do you think you are!" she yelled.

He watched in horror as she grabbed Lucy's arm with both hands, Lucy pulling away, trying to shake off her grasp, and the two women swaying dangerously on the ledge.

He ran towards them, his hands flying out to steady them, to hold them back. He did manage to take them both by their arms, but only for a second.

His grandfather screamed.

Jehangir sprang up on his elbow again, his heart pounding. He wondered what terror was stalking Grandpa in his dream. After a while he heard him sniffing. He got out of bed, careful about the noisy board, and asked in a whisper, "You need something, Grandpa?" He offered the spouted feeding cup. "Water?"

Grandpa shook his head, raising a hand to pat his face, and left it there. Jehangir felt it quiver against his cheek.

He clasped it with his own, and made a soft kissing sound. "I'll hold your hand, Grandpa, go to sleep."

HOW GOOD THE AIR FELT this morning, thought Yezad, taking a deep breath as he reached Bombay Sporting and let himself in with his key. Must be the December temperature, the slight drop.

Neither Mr. Kapur nor Husain had arrived, it was just coming up to nine. He put the envelope back in the drawer where it belonged, and locked the desk.

Whistling "White Christmas," he began turning on all the lights in the shop, including the one for the neon signboard. He brought the long handle from the back and stepped outside, enjoying the smoothness with which the shutters rose to let in the sunshine. Something special about this moment, the windows waking up, opening their big eyes. And how well-oiled Husain kept the gears.

As he finished and disengaged the handle, the peon arrived, salaamed, and waited morosely in the doorway. Yezad wondered if it was going to be one of his depression days. "Kapur sahab will soon come, he'll need chai."

"Why are you doing my job, sahab?" Husain asked with an injured air. "I can make chai and open the windows."

"Just for today, to help you," he placated him. "You will be very busy like yesterday, welcoming the children."

The reminder about his special assignment pleased Husain. He hurried to light the stove. Yezad switched on the display and decided to reposition the reindeer. While he crouched in the window, his back to the road, a knock on the pane startled him.

"Ho-ho-ho!" bellowed Mr. Kapur through the glass, looking immensely pleased to see him there. "You naughty boy!" He entered the shop and joined him in the window. "I thought you'd be home with your family."

"Came to see Santa Kapur in action again."

"Good. Great. I have a Christmas present for you. Had it ready yesterday, but in all the excitement I forgot."

They went to his office, and Mr. Kapur unlocked his desk to get the gift. Its wrapping paper had bells and holly.

Yezad smiled, examining both sides of the flat package that felt like a cardboard rectangle. "So what is it?"

"Open it, go on."

Yezad removed the paper and found a folder in which there were three cellophane sleeves. They held the three photographs of Hughes Road.

He looked at Mr. Kapur. "But . . . these are—"

"I hope you still like them."

"Yes, but I . . . they're so valuable, your collection . . ."

"But I want you to have them."

Yezad swallowed, running his finger along the edges. "Thank you, Vikram. It's too much, it's . . ."

"You're welcome, Yezad," said Mr. Kapur, putting an arm around him, relieving him of the need for words. "I'm so happy I could give you something meaningful. And now I must wear my costume."

While he got ready, Husain brought in two steaming cups, set them on the desk, and went to the front to prepare for visitors.

"Sahab, there are two people who want to talk to you."

Mr. Kapur clicked his tongue. "I'm not dressed yet. Didn't you show them the sign, Santa Claus begins at ten o'clock?"

"Sahab, they are two men, not children. I don't think they came for sweets."

"Then you should have said the shop is closed today."

"You want me to talk to them?" asked Yezad.

"But they mentioned Kapur sahab's name only," said Husain, hesitating.

"Okay, I'll see what they want." In his socks and partial

Santa outfit he went into the shop, followed by Yezad.

The visitors grinned, delighted by his attire. "Good morning, sir."

"What can I do for you?"

"Sorry for disturbing, sir, but we saw your signboard."

"Look," said Mr. Kapur, "in the first place, we open at ten. And in the second place, Santa Claus is giving free sweets to children only. I don't think you are children, are you?"

The young men smiled at the misunderstanding. "Not that sign, sir. Your shop sign. The one which is saying Bombay Sporting Goods Emporium."

"Sporting Gods, actually."

"Yes, sir," they smiled. "We saw O is out of order."

Mr. Kapur wondered if they were tradesmen soliciting work. "You want to fix my sign? How much will you charge?"

They smiled again. "No, no, sir, we are not electrical. We are coming from our local Shiv Sena shakha to kindly inform that sign should be saying Mumbai Sporting Goods Emporium, it's a new rule for—"

"Oh, that. Yes, I know all about that." Mr. Kapur's face had gone dark, and he glanced at Yezad as though to say, Here they are finally.

Blood drained from Yezad's face. What kind of crazy coincidence was this? He ran his cold hand over his mouth, trying to stay calm. At least the money was back in the drawer. Dizziness overcame him as he imagined Mr. Kapur asking for it, and him unable to produce it.

Meanwhile, Mr. Kapur's annoyance was making him hot in the red jacket. He unbuckled the wide black belt and flung it on a chair. The young men smiled, waiting patiently.

"I've been through that discussion already. If you've come to collect the money, why don't you say so?"

The two looked puzzled while he told Yezad to bring the envelope.

"But these are not the fellows who came the first time," whispered Yezad in his ear. "We shouldn't—"

"Just give it and get rid of them!"

Yezad unlocked his desk and passed the envelope to Mr. Kapur, who hurled it on the counter, towards the men.

"Here's the full payment. As arranged with Balaji and Gopinath."

"Please, sir, we are not understanding."

"Oh, you are not understanding?" he sneered. "Go and check with your shakha! What game are you two bastards trying to play?"

"Please, sir, do not be so abusive. We are not asking for money. We are just requesting to change your sign to Mumbai."

Yezad forcibly took Mr. Kapur aside, urging him not to lose his temper, it wouldn't help matters. Mr. Kapur brushed him away: enough was enough, he had reached his limit with these thugs.

"Thirty-five thousand is the price for special exemption! And I agreed to it, to keep Bombay!"

He picked up the envelope from the counter and thrust it at them, whacking one across the chest with it. Bewildered, they looked inside, and exchanged glances. "Sir, if you are wanting to give donation to Shiv Sena, that is fine. But shop name must definitely change to Mumbai."

"See that?" roared Mr. Kapur, snatching the envelope from their hands. "Donation! They want to have their cake and eat it too! Fucking crooks!"

"We are not crooks, sir. We are working most vigorously for social welfare, looking after interests of local people. We are working for upliftment of the poor and—"

"I'll work on your downliftment if you don't shut up! Your bogus history lecture doesn't interest me."

"Sir, you must not threaten us. We are simply stating the rule, your signboard must change. If this is not taking place in one week, it will be very bad."

Now Mr. Kapur advanced on them, shoving them back. The men staggered, and he shoved again, pushing them towards the door.

"You think you can scare me, you fucking grass-eating ghatis? You know who I am? I have drunk the milk of Punjab! Saalay bhonsdi kay bharve, I'll break your faces if you act smart with me!"

He kept pushing, till they were at the entrance. A final push, and the two went stumbling down the steps to the pavement.

"You will be sorry for your abusive behaviour!" they hissed.

Slamming shut the door, Mr. Kapur cursed them for spoiling his morning. He put the envelope back in Yezad's desk, then retrieved the black belt for his Santa suit and returned to the office with Yezad. Husain, quite shaken by the incident, followed them.

"Are you all right, sahab?"

"Yes, fine," said Mr. Kapur gruffly, the anger still afflicting his voice.

"More tea, sahab?"

"How much tea you want to give me? Tea doesn't solve every problem." He looked closely at Yezad, whose ashen face was just regaining colour. "Don't tell me even you are scared."

"Not scared. Worried. Maybe there's some mix-up at their shakha."

"Sahab, please . . ." Husain shuffled his feet, to indicate he wanted to speak. "Sahab, I wanted to say it's not good to fight with Shiv Sena. With them you can never win."

"I know about Shiv Sena. You needn't worry."

"No, sahab," he was in tears now. "You know when Babri Mosque was destroyed and all the riots were flaming, these bad people killed so many innocents, with my own eyes I saw it, sahab, they locked them in their houses and set fire to them, they attacked people with swords and axes . . ."

Mr. Kapur put an arm around the peon's shoulder. "It's okay, Husain miyan, you don't have to fear. They only attack poor people, weak people. Like all bullies, they are cowards at heart. Isn't that right, Yezad?"

"Yes, that is right," repeated Yezad, still in a daze.

Shaking his head, Husain left the office while Mr. Kapur asked Yezad to help him tie the wrist bells. Their tinkling began to restore his spirit.

They opened the entrance door cautiously to check if those characters were hanging around or if they had summoned reinforcements. But the street wore its normal air of benign frenzy, the footpaths packed with crowds, the road loud with traffic.

Soon it was ten o'clock, and Husain took his place on the pavement. The first visitors entered with their children, and Mr. Kapur's hearty ho-ho-ho's filled the shop again.

"GOOD MORNING, Coomy! Merry Christmas!"
Edul Munshi sailed past her into the passageway with a song on his lips: "I saw two ghatis come walk-ing up, come walk-ing up," he syncopated his modified carol. "I saw two ghatis come walk-ing up on Christmas day in the mor-ning."

"What nonsense are you singing?" Irritated and depressed this morning, Coomy was not willing to tolerate anyone's foolishness. Always, on Christmas, memories of her convent school, a happy time in her truncated childhood, haunted her, and she would have gladly renounced the pleasures of remembering, were it possible to get rid of the pain as well.

Six weeks before Christmas her school choir would start practising for the concert to which parents were invited. During the second week of December the tree went up. And decorating it was a special treat reserved for the girls in the choir. Like most non-Christian families, Coomy's parents too questioned from time to time if this school was the best place for their child. They were not worried about Jal, he was safe in Bharda New High School, but they wondered if there might not be too much of a Catholic flavour in Coomy's education, especially since there was so little Zoroastrian influence to countervail it. They felt their Parsi customs were seriously handicapped by the lack of any entertaining Santa Claus type of figure.

Then it was concert day. They went to hear Coomy sing, and those worries were temporarily forgotten. Afterwards, her father would declare the choir sounded beautiful, but his Coomy was the best and loudest of all. The first time this pleased her tremendously; the following year, as she learned more, she protested, "Pappa, my voice is supposed to blend with the choir! If you hear it, it means I'm singing badly!"

And her father, laughing, insisted that even if it were blended to perfection with a thousand voices he could still hear his little angel's voice. All this was during the happy years before he took to his bed and became, as their mother said, an angel himself.

Feeling fiercely protective of her good memories – the convent school, the choir, the Christmas tree, her father's delight – Coomy glared at Edul. She found his perversity, inflicted upon one of her favourite carols, an act of pure barbarism. "Your words make no sense," she told him.

"Oh yes, they do. You see, I've hired two ghatis from the ration shop to help me with the beam. They'll be coming at eleven o'clock." He sang again, "My gha-tis from the ra-tion shop, the ra-tion shop. My gha-tis from the ra-tion shop, on Christmas day in the mor-ning."

"Stop that!" she lashed out.

Behind her back, Jal tried to hush him with gestures. He too was tense this morning, for the raising of the beam weighed on his mind.

"How about this one? Hark, the han-dyman is wor-king! Glory to the new cei-ling!"

As Jal despaired about keeping the peace, the doorbell rang and Coomy left to answer it. He didn't like the way his sister was being teased; he understood how she was feeling today. But explaining to Edul would be almost impossible.

They heard her arguing with someone at the door, and went to see.

"Oh, there they are," said Edul. "My two ghatis from the ration shop."

"Yes," said Coomy. "I'm trying to tell them it's only nine o'clock, you wanted them at eleven."

"I'll explain it, my Marathi is much better than yours."

Edul started with a little scolding: "Tumee lok aykat nai! Bai tumhala kai saangte?"

That was as far as his vocabulary took him before he lapsed into a helpless medley of Hindi, Gujarati, and English, with the occasional Marathi word thrown in for flavour. "Asaala kasaala karte? Maine tumko explain kiya, na, eleven o'clock ao. Abhi jao, ration shop ko jao. Paisa banao, later vapis ao."

"It's the Issa Massih holiday, seth," they said. "No rations to carry today. We can help you with whatever you are doing."

Edul was weakening, and Coomy stepped in to insist that they leave. "I don't want them loitering in my house."

He drew her aside and cautioned against it: risky to send them back – what if they found other work and did not return? The entire schedule with the girder would be ruined.

The girder had sat in the passage under the ancestral portraits for more than a week, tripping Coomy up and generally annoying her by its presence. She did not relish the prospect of another week or two of the nuisance. The men were allowed to stay.

"But I won't pay you any extra," warned Edul.

"Oh, we don't want extra money. A little saucer of tea would earn you our sincere gratitude."

"What nerve!" said Coomy. "They think I'm running a tea-stall?"

Edul cajoled her into putting the kettle on, saying it was Christmas, and she should think of them as two wise men come to honour her ceiling. He clinched it by promising not to sing any more if she made tea.

But while she was in the kitchen Edul sang another modified carol to the men: "Away in a ration shop, you work as a team. Today you will carry for me this steel beam."

Sitting cross-legged on the floor, they listened intently without understanding a word. When he finished, there was loud applause.

Jal studied the two men and thought they looked familiar. He remembered: they were the same duo, many months ago, who had carried Pappa home after his fall into the ditch.

"I'm worried about this, Edul," he said. "Are you sure they are qualified for the work? They only know how to lift bags of grain on their head."

"Don't worry, Jal my son, I just need their brute strength. The skill and planning is supplied by yours truly."

The tea came, in tin mugs for the two labourers, and regular china for Edul, and was consumed noisily with slurps of appreciation. Then Edul led his team into Nariman's room. For the next couple of hours they could be heard preparing the supports for the beam-raising, securing the poles in place, and, at regular intervals, making sounds of mutual encouragement.

By noon, the posts and their braces were in position, lined up between the two facing walls. Jal examined them anxiously, and to set his mind at rest Edul demonstrated their worthiness by kicking a post and pushing his weight against it.

Half-expecting the assembly to tumble, Jal shielded his face, but it withstood the assault. "What happens now?"

"The main event." Edul led his men to where the steel girder was resting. "Chaal, Ganpat," he said, indicating one end of it, then turned to the other: "And what are you watching, Ganpat, haath lagao, take that side." He positioned himself in the middle.

"They both have the same name?" asked Jal.

Edul grinned. "I call all ghatis Ganpat."

The three men gripped the long dark steel and began manoeuvring the passageway into Nariman's room. The space was not wide enough for a straight entry; they moved forward and reversed a number of times, while Edul called out frantic instructions in his khichri of languages. "Ai baba! Assa nako ghay! This way, not that way, sunta hai kya. Sadanter idiot chhe, saalo."

Finally the men and the girder were in the room. Panting, they lowered it to the floor under the spot, twelve feet above, that was to be its final resting place.

"Okay, perfect," said Edul. Mopping the sweat from his brow, he turned to Jal and Coomy. "Now I must request you

391

both to leave the room, I need the area clear." But he gave them permission to watch from the passageway.

After checking each brace and post once more, he stood well back and told the men to proceed. Jal and Coomy held their breath as they lifted the girder to the first stage, four feet off the floor, and rested it on the intermediary supports.

They paused, refreshing their lungs before climbing the stepladders to lift it to eight feet. This was a little trickier, for the two men needed a sure footing. Edul had secured the ladders to prevent wobbling, but it was still a difficult move.

Standing on the fourth step, they picked the girder up cleanly and got it as high as their shoulders. But in shifting the weight on to the supports, one of the men staggered. His end of the girder missed its bracket.

"Hoi, careful!" shouted Edul. "Push higher! Jor lagao!"

The man recovered his balance and the girder was safe. He nodded to reassure Edul standing below.

"Assa kai, Ganpat!" he scolded. "No breakfast? No pao-bhaji?"

The last stage was the top of the two steel posts equipped with hydraulic jacks at their base. At Edul's signal they completed the task in one powerful movement.

"Sabaash!" Edul congratulated them, and the praise made the men taller with pleasure. They posed proudly with their hands on the beam.

Now Edul positioned a third ladder and went up to secure the steel. Four pairs of nuts and bolts were fastened at each end through pre-drilled holes, then everyone came down from their ladders. Edul said he would continue the work after lunch.

"Is it okay to leave it like this?" asked Coomy.

"Absolutely. It's solid as the tower of Pisa. I mean, the Eiffel Tower," he corrected himself, and delivered a series of vigorous kicks to the post.

He paid the men, adding a bakshis of ten rupees to the

agreed amount. "It's Christmas," he said to explain his impulse to Jal and Coomy.

The men were overwhelmed, and said as they were leaving that they'd be downstairs by the ration shop, in case there was more work.

Then Edul left too, promising to return from lunch in an hour, perhaps less, if Manizeh did not make a fuss.

∾

In the empty room Jal took the opportunity to inspect the ceiling, and saw something he hadn't noticed during all the excitement: a large gap, between the girder and the joists.

Hah, he thought, poor fellow had bungled, as usual. Thank God he'd spotted it before the whole thing was plastered over.

When Edul was back, he took him to task with relish. "Come here, Edul my son, look over there," he said, retaliating for the jibes he had suffered. "At least four inches between the beam and the ceiling."

"Jal my son," laughed Edul. "Let me show you. See these things at the bottom of the posts? They are jacks. You know what a jack is?"

"Of course."

"So I'll jack up both the posts, till the beam is tight against the ceiling."

Jal smiled foolishly, but Edul did not rub it in. "Your mistake is understandable," he said. "Why should you know about this equipment, you're not a handyman."

He began raising the two posts, alternating between them, a few strokes each to keep them even. The movement, in millimetres, was almost imperceptible.

Jal was bored after a while. Watching Edul scurry between two jacks had limited appeal. He went to take a nap.

Edul spent almost an hour before the girder was flush with the ceiling. Near the end he had to go up the ladder several times between strokes to ensure the rise was not excessive, or it would start to bow the ceiling.

Satisfied, he locked the jacks in place and admired his work. He felt like calling Manizeh upstairs so she could admire it too.

Then he noticed that on one side, the steel girder seemed to veer slightly away from the original wooden beam, meeting the wall at an angle. It should have been square.

He climbed the ladder to measure, and discovered it was off by three-quarters of an inch. Hardly noticeable. He put away the set square.

But the minor misalignment kept bothering him. Up he went once more, re-examined the anomaly, and changed his mind: he'd rectify it.

First, he had to lower the jacks a little, for the girder was too snug against the ceiling. When there was approximately an inch of clearance, he locked the jacks and climbed the ladder. Grasping the beam on the underside, he tugged.

It wouldn't budge. He tried again, without making a difference. Damn the swine, he thought. Only one thing for it – remove the bolts, make the correction, and refasten them.

His wrench dealt quickly with the four nuts, which he dropped in his pocket for safekeeping. Now to make the small adjustment. Then this job would be flawless.

Clutching the steel with his sweaty fingers, he exerted his strength, thought he felt it moving, and stopped to measure. No, still the same. He tried once more, going from silent abuse of the beam to cursing aloud.

"Shift, you bloody bastard!" he muttered softly. His hands were slippery, and he wiped them on his pants. "Son of a bitch, three-quarters is all I need from you!"

While he struggled with the girder, Coomy came and stood in the doorway. It was almost four o'clock. She had brought him tea and a slice of fruitcake.

"Oh sorry, Coomy!" he panted when he noticed her there. "Please excuse my language. The bugger is stuck."

"Maybe you should call the ghatis to help."

"No, I can manage. Just a small adjustment. See that gap?"

She entered the room to look, pausing below the ladder with her tray.

"I need to shift it a bit to my side. Is that Christmas cake? Great, give me a sec, I'll be down soon."

Grabbing the beam with intense hostility, he bellowed like a weightlifter and tugged it towards him.

"Careful!" said Coomy. "The post is moving!"

Her warning was too late. The beam had already lost its moorings. As it came crashing down, it swept Edul off the ladder. Coomy tried to dodge, but the glancing blow on the head was enough to break her skull. The girder came to rest across Edul's chest where he lay upon the floor.

∾

Awakened from his nap a few minutes earlier by Coomy for tea, Jal was still putting in his hearing aid when the post collapsed. It was not the noise but the tremor that signalled the accident. He felt his bed shake, and knew something terrible had happened. He ran to Nariman's room.

In the flat directly below, the crash was deafening. And the tremor, like a slight quake, was felt by Manizeh too. She tore up the stairs and began pounding her fist on the door.

He opened it, his face white as chalk. One look at him and she knew the truth but asked anyway, "Where is he? Is he okay?"

Jal was unable to answer. He lifted a hand to plead for something, not sure what – patience, courage, forgiveness?

She pushed past him into the passageway.

"Wait, Manizeh, please let me . . ."

She was already in the room, kneeling beside her husband, sobbing and holding his face. Her eyes riveted to his crushed chest, she screamed at Jal, "Call somebody! Doctor! Ambulance!"

He watched as she looked around and took in Coomy's fate, who had fallen not far from Edul, the blood in a small circle around her head. The two still bodies, the angle at which they lay, and the manner in which death had arranged their limbs, made them seem more intimate now than they had ever been in life, thought Jal.

At that moment the initial helplessness that had gripped him slowly released its hold. He felt calm, felt he knew exactly the things that would have to happen now, one after the other, all the inevitable tasks he would be required to perform. He would have to reflect, make decisions, act.

He looked at Manizeh's face. It was stupefied with shock. And something else, he felt, as her eyes kept returning to Coomy. Her torment was the most distressing thing in the room at that moment. She deserved better; to reassure her was his first duty.

"Tea, she came with tea," he urged her to believe. "And a slice of cake."

He found the shattered cup and saucer, and picked up the pieces. "See? This is what Coomy brought the tea in. And look, Manizeh, here is the wet place on the floor, look, where it splashed. Oh, and the fruitcake, over there."

By now, others had been drawn upstairs by the crash that had rung through the building like an explosion. They wandered in through the open door and were aghast, a few turning away in horror. Someone could be heard retching outside. Someone else telephoned for an ambulance.

It took a while to arrive, and when the attendants ran into the room, one of the neighbours began berating them that given the amount of time, any sign of life would have been extinguished by now. "Lucky for you they both died on the spot," he said.

"Why did you call us, in that case? Just call the police."

And, in what was seen as a callous addition of insult to

injury, the ambulancemen insisted on notifying the nearest police station. It was the law, they said.

The neighbours gathered in the flat went into a huddle. If the police were informed, there could be all kinds of complications and formalities, maybe even a postmortem, delaying the funeral beyond twenty-four hours from the time of death, which was undesirable within Zoroastrian rites.

"If you ask me, these fellows are hoping for an incentive," said someone.

"Well, let's give it to them and finish it. Tell them to forget they came here."

"Good idea. Hundred rupees will easily adjust their memories."

"But we still need proper papers, otherwise Doongerwadi is not going to accept the bodies."

Then Jal offered a suggestion that they found eminently sensible: appealing to Inspector Masalavala, who lived just across the road from Chateau Felicity.

Years ago, it was the inspector's father, the late Superintendent Masalavala, who had come to the family's rescue when Yasmin Vakeel and Lucy Braganza had fallen from the rooftop terrace. "No sense washing Parsi linen in public," had been his verdict, and he'd kept the matter as quiet as possible.

Despite the lower rank, the son proved to be equally resourceful. Inspector Masalavala listened sympathetically to the delegation that came to his residence, for he shared his father's philosophy. He even persuaded his neighbour, the retired Dr. Fitter, to help out, as he had done all those years ago in the Vakeel case.

They crossed the road and visited the scene of the accident together. Their entrance effected a miraculous change in the ambulancemen, whose officiousness vanished, replaced instantly by a new-found humility. They even attempted something like a salute for the police inspector.

Dr. Fitter examined the bodies, checked their pulses, and

said he would issue death certificates for both; there was no need for postmortems.

All routine now, thought Jal, as he watched numbly.

19

WITH AN ARM AROUND his brother-in-law Yezad said in a whisper, "I'm so sorry," then stepped aside for Roxana. She hugged Jal and began to cry.

Tears appeared in Jal's eyes too for the first time, as he found himself alone with them. The neighbours that had gathered earlier in the flat had departed, and all his grief, suppressed while he had been attending to practical matters, now found release. He was crying, he told them, as much at losing Coomy as at the thought that Coomy had lost out on life.

"That's what Pappa said," she sobbed. "When we gave him the news, he said how sad, that she died full of anger."

Jal nodded. He held her head against his chest and wept silently.

Then Roxana, deciding it was best to stay busy, suggested he should pack a small bag for the overnight vigil at the Tower of Silence. She went inside to get it started.

In their mother's room, which he and Coomy had been sharing, the one whose ceiling had been spared the hammer, she looked for Jal's things in his half of the space. Her eyes strayed to the other side. From a hook behind the door hung Coomy's floral-patterned nightgown. Her sensible shoes were under the bed. On the dressing table was a list of figures – household expenses she had been working on. Next to it, a sharpened pencil. The page had been kept in place by the weight of her prayer book. Roxana went closer to look; the Khordeh Avesta was open at the Aiwisruthrem Geh. So Coomy would have been reciting it yesterday, some time between sunset and midnight.

She began to cry uncontrollably. They heard it in the drawing-room and hurried to her. They saw her standing with Coomy's prayer book, and understood.

Not long afterwards the hearse arrived. They rode together to the Tower of Silence. The initial formalities, the ritual ablutions were completed for the funeral next afternoon, and the body, clad in white, was laid out on the marble slab in the prayer hall. For the moment, there was nothing more to do.

They sat on chairs that were lined along the wall in the dimly lit room. Now and again from the rear of the bungalow would be heard voices, and the clatter of utensils being washed and prepared for use in the funeral ceremonies. Then the noises faded; silence enveloped the bungalow.

Roxana left her chair to stand in the doorway, gazing out beyond the veranda. How lush was the foliage of the trees and the shrubbery, she thought, such a different world, up here, on top of the hill. And such tranquility, high above the dust and stink of the city.

The sound of insects began to punctuate the stillness as it got dark. Made the place even more serene, she felt. Her eyes tried to follow the path that led past the veranda and farther up the hill, where it disappeared in the twilight. The path along which Coomy's body will be carried tomorrow, she thought, up, to the Tower, and then the vultures will alight . . .

She went inside and glanced at Yezad. He nodded; it was time to leave. He bowed once more before the body, and stepped back. She lingered a moment longer to look upon the face. It was still uncovered; tomorrow, after the prayers, the sheet would be drawn over it.

Coomy's expression was so much softer now, she thought. She saw returned in it her childhood sister, the one who used to lavish affection upon her, who carried her around like a beloved doll. And tears streamed down her cheeks.

Yezad touched her elbow gently. He put his arm around her as she wiped her face and walked slowly to the door. Jal went out to the veranda with them.

They started down the path, then turned and waved to him. They walked down the hill shrouded in dusk and birdsong, the dense foliage looming above them like a huge dark umbrella.

In the taxi, Roxana waited till Yezad gave the driver directions for the quickest route home, then said, "I feel terrible. At a time like this, suddenly the ceiling came into my mind."

"Don't feel bad, I had the same thought. It's only natural."

"And even if it was fixed, and Pappa could go back, how would Jal ever manage all alone?"

"Perhaps it's our destiny to look after the chief."

He was silent the rest of the way, weary of his burdens. He couldn't carry them any longer. Now he would leave it in God's hands – whatever He willed would happen, as it did with everything anyway.

He asked the taxi driver to let them off outside the lane to Pleasant Villa. They walked the rest to save on the fare. While she went upstairs, he stopped at the chemist's to use the telephone, to let Mr. Kapur know he would not come to work the next day because of the funeral. But the telephone at the Kapur residence kept ringing.

He went home, and saw Roxana sitting on the bed with the boys, her arms around them. Murad had questions about the accident, about how Coomy Aunty had died, and Yezad and Roxana answered them as directly as they could.

"Will I go to the funeral?" asked Jehangir.

"Would you like to?"

He nodded.

"And Murad?"

He nodded too.

After dinner, Yezad went out to try Mr. Kapur's telephone again. Still no answer. He made three more attempts at suitable intervals till eleven o'clock, then gave up. He would have to go to Bombay Sporting in the morning and tell him in person.

Stuck to the door was a handwritten sign: *Due to Death in Family, Shop Will Be Closed Till Further Notice. Apologies For Inconvenience to Our Valued Customers.*

For a moment, the information disoriented Yezad – how did Mr. Kapur hear about Coomy's death? . . . and so good of him to consider me family . . .

His muddled thoughts grew more coherent. No, couldn't be for Coomy. But whose death, then? Another coincidence? Death in my family, death in Mr. Kapur's . . .

He reached for his keys, observing as he did that it wasn't the boss's handwriting on the notice. He decided to let himself in, telephone, find out who had passed away. He would give Mr. Kapur his condolences, and the news about the bereavement in his own family. He unlocked the deadbolt and put in the latchkey.

The latch turned, but the door wouldn't open. He tried again before noticing a padlock in the hasp at the foot of the door. He had been shut out. Why? Perhaps the person who wrote the sign put on the padlock, worried about security.

He returned his keys to his pocket and saw Husain approaching. The news would have to be explained to him.

"Salaam, sahab."

"Sorry, Husain, we cannot get in this morning."

The peon nodded, raising his hands in a mournful gesture towards the door and letting them fall lifeless. "My heart is breaking, sahab," he said, his voice a sob.

Yezad wondered why a death in Mr. Kapur's family would cause Husain such grief – the peon was in one of his over-wrought moods, kindness was needed. "Why waste your time here, Husain miyan? Go home, take rest. You'll still get paid. And we'll see Mr. Kapur when the shop reopens."

Husain looked at him, horrified. "What are you saying? We will never see Kapur sahab again!"

Yezad leaned against the door to fight the pavement as it spun and yawed around him. He lowered himself to the entrance step, almost tumbling with the effort. Husain steadied him, then sat beside him, crying.

"Tell me what happened," he urged the peon.

"What to tell? They killed him . . . two men." He shrugged, as though that were the full story.

Struggling to contain his own emotions, Yezad spoke gently to Husain, asking him specific questions about the men, what they said, was there a fight. He used Hindi now, as Mr. Kapur would have done, to encourage the peon to express himself more freely.

Husain started again with an effort. "I was outside on the footpath. I could hear sahab tell them shop was closed for business, only open for children. They laughed, that their business could be done better in a closed shop."

His face contorted with the strain of remembering. "They called him Punjoo – we will teach you a lesson, you Punjoo, they said, pushing him to the back of the shop. They hit him with blows in the stomach, and kicks. I tried to shout, but my voice wouldn't work. Suddenly, sahab picked up a cricket bat and threatened them – 'I'll knock your heads for a sixer,' he said."

The memory of his sahab having the upper hand made him brighten for an instant. But the description of Mr. Kapur, irrepressible, defiant to the last, played havoc with Yezad, and for a moment he forgot Husain's fragility. Then he composed himself again. "Phir kya hua, Husain?"

"The men got scared and ran behind the counter. But they took out knives. They circled around, one got behind him. Sahab cried out. Now I also screamed, suddenly my voice came back, and they ran away like dogs.

"Sahab fell to the floor, I rushed inside. At first I couldn't see the blood because of his red clothes. Then it began soaking the white border. 'Help me, Husain,' he said. 'Phone my wife.' So I did that, I heard Kapur bibi's voice, and I repeated what he said: Kapur sahab had accident, call ambulance, come quick."

Yezad nodded supportively, and Husain continued, "They took him to hospital, I also went, Kapur sahab told them he wanted me. I was holding his hand all the time till Kapur bibi came. They connected a tube to fill blood into his body from a bottle, because so much of his own blood had spilled. I told them if they needed more, they could take it out of my body. But they checked and said no, they needed same type."

He paused, and asked tearfully, "Why did hospital say no to my blood? Is it because mine is Muslim type and Kapur sahab's is Hindu?"

"No, no, Husain – absolutely not. When they talk of blood type, it's a medical thing, not religious. Your blood type can also be different from your own brother's. Kapur sahab's can be different from Kapur bibi's. Nothing to do with religion."

"Hanh, achha," he nodded, comforted by the explanation. Then he remembered where he had stopped. "In the evening, sahab's breath was gone, so they removed the blood tube."

He beat his hand upon his chest. "Such a good man! Why do they kill good people?"

Yezad wished he had the luxury, the simplicity to grieve like Husain. But he would have time to examine his own feelings later; right now, the peon needed him.

"How can we tell, Husain? It's the will of Allah." He put his arm around him, the way Mr. Kapur would have. "What about police?"

"Police?" Husain's scorn came clearly through his anguish. "They asked me questions, many questions. I told them everything. What the men looked like, what they said. They wrote it down. Must have been robbers, they said, and my shouting scared them away, no chance to steal.

"Their words could not make sense for me. I told them about Shiv Sena coming in the morning, and the big quarrel. I was scared to talk about that. But I wanted the police to catch the dogs who killed Kapur sahab." Husain paused, lost in his thoughts.

Yezad waited, then nudged him gently.

"They said it was not right to connect Shiv Sena, there was no evidence. One policeman laughed in a very bad way. He said, 'You Muslims, always trying to blame Shiv Sena.' He frightened me. 'I'm very sorry, police sahab,' I said with my hands joined. 'That's not my wish. Please punish the killers, whoever they are, I mention it only because you asked for everything.'"

Husain was shivering now, fussing with his chappal strap, shaking his head. Yezad patted his knee and told him he had been very brave.

"I must go now to Kapur bibi," he told the peon. "To express my sorrow, offer my help with the shop. You want to come with me?"

"She knows my sorrow. I'll stay here."

Yezad touched Husain's shoulder, then rose from the doorstep and started down the road. His mind was in turmoil now as he struggled with the news and tore blindly ahead, bumping into people, stumbling on the rubbled footpath.

Near Mr. Kapur's neighbourhood he stopped in a daze, trying to orient himself. He had to ask for directions to make sure he was turning into the correct lane. On the way there, he'd been able to think of nothing but his scheming with Vilas and the actors, blaming them, blaming himself for what had happened to Mr. Kapur . . . poor man, needlessly dead . . . no wonder he thought he was being double-crossed when the real Shiv Sainiks came . . . but who knew that they would? That was the problem, everyone dismissing the possibility of coincidence . . .

He entered the granite-faced lobby of the building and stared blankly at the listing on the wall. The watchman inquired who he was looking for, then told him the number of the flat. A high-speed elevator zoomed him to the sixteenth floor of the luxury tower.

The door of the Kapur residence was open, and he stood paralyzed in the corridor, wondering if he should ring the bell or walk in. The brass door-handle had the shape of a sitar. Inside, people were milling around. From a distance it would have resembled a big party in progress, he thought, but for their white clothing and the hum of hushed conversation . . .

More visitors arriving behind Yezad carried him along in their stream. He decided to pay his respects to Mrs. Kapur and leave quickly.

In the marble-tiled foyer he hesitated, debating which direction to go. The activity suggested Mrs. Kapur was in a room towards the right. He started off diffidently, aware that the crowd, probably family and close friends, was looking at him, wondering who he was. Someone greeted him and shook his hand.

"Such horrifying news," the man murmured. "What a shameful place of crime Bombay is becoming."

"Terrible," said Yezad, shaking his head. "Mrs. Kapur . . . ?"

"Yes, yes, please, in that room."

Yezad moved on, nodding to the people he passed in the hallway. He peered inside the room: yes, he had found Mrs. Kapur, there she was in a chair by the window.

But a phalanx of relatives surrounded her, and breaking through was difficult, he soon discovered. Each time he tried to get closer, someone outmanoeuvred him. He felt it would be unseemly to make a stronger effort, and waited for an opening.

Everyone seemed to be obsessed with being in physical contact with Mrs. Kapur, he noticed. As though their grief would be suspect unless they were clutching her fingers, stroking her hair, cupping her face. Poor woman . . . to suffer such a tragedy, and then to have to endure this . . .

He lingered behind a group he felt had already contributed more than their share of condolences. From their whispers, he gathered they were awaiting Mr. Kapur's body – it had been released by the police after forensic examination, and was expected to arrive shortly.

Then an excited voice on the balcony announced, "Yes, I think they're coming!" Something resembling a hearse had turned into the building gate.

Everyone flocked to the balcony to look. But it was a false alarm – just a furniture delivery van.

"Very sorry," said the man. "From up here, it's so difficult to see all the way down. I should get the binoculars from Vikram's study." He went off to find them.

But the distraction gave Yezad the opportunity to get next to Mrs. Kapur. Would she remember him? They had met years ago when she was still in the habit of dropping by at the shop.

"I am Yezad Chenoy," he started, "from Bombay Sporting—"

"Of course," she said, and took his hand. "Please sit down."

She gestured to the chair next to hers, which, owing to the balcony diversion, was empty. He sat on the edge, eschewing comfort as a mark of respect. Her composure was remarkable, he thought, especially in contrast to the others around her.

"It was such a shock," he said softly. "I saw the notice this morning when I went to the shop. Then Husain arrived and told me what happened."

"Poor Husain," said Mrs. Kapur. "He is very upset. Only an uneducated peon, but what a help yesterday. How lucky Vikram was in his employees. You know he was very fond of you, always praising you."

"It was an honour and pleasure for me to work with Mr. Kapur," he mumbled, his voice shaking. "If there is something I can do . . . regarding the shop . . . or anything else . . ."

"Thank you for coming, Yezad," she said.

"Not at all. I'm so sorry I won't be at the funeral. You see, my sister-in-law also died yesterday – an accident."

"I am sad to hear it. Of course I understand, family first."

He offered his hand again, then whispered, "One more thing, Mrs. Kapur . . ."

"Yes?"

He felt awkward, not sure how to tell her there was black money, undisclosed income hidden in the shop. "You see, in Mr. Kapur's office, there is a large suitcase."

She smiled conspiratorially. "It's quite safe. Thanks to Husain's screaming, the thieves ran away. I've brought it home."

"That's good," said Yezad, marvelling again at her calmness, her self-possession.

"I will let you know about the shop," she assured him. "Soon as I decide."

"If you need me in any capacity . . ."

"Yes, thank you."

He saw that the crowd keen on condoling was becoming impatient with his presence. A woman had squeezed her way behind his chair, and was rubbing the back of Mrs. Kapur's neck. Another had extended her arm to claim Mrs. Kapur's shoulder, fixing him with a half-hostile stare that compromised her mourning expression. It reminded him of a *National Geographic* photograph he had seen, of a Maori greeting-ritual grimace.

The women's fervour was unsettling. He shook hands with Mrs. Kapur and left, extricating himself carefully from the ever-growing cluster around her.

FROM FUNERAL TO UTHAMNA TO CHARAM, Yezad and Roxana saw Jal regularly for the four days of prayers and ceremonies. Each time he seemed more exhausted than the last. Then there was a gap during which they did not meet, and Roxana wondered if he was all right.

"He knows he's welcome to ask for any help," said Yezad.

Two evenings later Jal visited, confessing that the past week had tired him out, and he'd been staying home to rest, to think. He handed over some food in aluminium containers: so much extra at home, he explained, he hadn't yet reduced the Seva Sadan order from two persons to one.

The basket contained cutlets, mashed potatoes, a small bowl of gravy, and caramel custard. Roxana accepted it all eagerly, it would do nicely for dinner – the gravy thinned with a little water could stretch for five.

Then, talking about the last few days, Jal said that despite his fatigue, his nights at the Tower of Silence had been filled with the most peaceful sleep he'd ever experienced.

"I believe it," said Yezad. "A few years ago, I was there for my father. I swore I would sit with him till the sun came up. But Doongerwadi is a magical place. It took away the pain and sadness, left peace in its stead. Almost like angels and fareshtas came down to comfort me." He smiled at Roxana, to acknowledge he'd used her phrase, and continued, "Around three in the morning, I remember, I fell asleep. I slept as soundly as though my father's hand was stroking my head, rubbing my back, the way he would when I was a child."

"Exactly how I felt," said Jal. Then he told them that he had attended some prayers for Edul yesterday, as a gesture of reconciliation with Manizeh's family, who blamed him for

Edul's death. While offering his sandalwood to the fire, he'd had to pass the seated row of family members, and took the opportunity to nod and touch his forehead. Better to save the handshake and condolences for after.

"But when the prayers ended, they whisked Manizeh away. I went searching for her all around the fire-temple, and in the garden as well, but she was gone."

"I'm sure you'll get another chance," said Yezad. "Or you can make a condolence visit, she lives right below you."

"No, the flat is empty now, she's back at her parents' house. I hope they don't stay angry forever. A terrible thing, anger." He shook his head. "So many unhappy marriages in the world are dragged out in fights. And here, a perfect loving match is shattered. What is this absurd force called destiny?"

"Man proposes, God disposes," was Yezad's explanation. "We are not meant to understand everything. We just make ourselves miserable, trying to."

"You're right," said Jal. "By the way, tomorrow I'm planning to go and thank Inspector Masalavala for his help. And Dr. Fitter, for writing the death certificates."

"Good idea. Please convey our thanks as well."

Jal left before they sat down to dinner. Roxana began warming the food he'd brought, and the quantities distressed her. "So many cutlets – has he kept enough for himself?"

"I don't think he's planning to starve."

"Coomy used to do everything in the house. Must be so difficult for him."

"He's not a child, he'll be fine."

J AL RANG INSPECTOR MASALAVALA'S DOORBELL just after six-thirty the next evening. He wouldn't stay long, he decided, a few minutes to say how grateful he was, then on to Dr. Fitter's.

But when the servant opened the door, Jal saw that the doctor was in the front room with the inspector. They were comfortable in capacious rattan chairs, soft cushions tucked strategically behind them. On a glass-topped rattan table stood two drinks with ice cubes.

"Please don't get up," he said, and they were happy to comply, shaking his hand from the cosy depths of their chairs.

"I came to thank you, Inspector. For all your assistance last week. And later I was going to knock on your door, Doctor, to thank you as well."

"You can thank two birds with one knock," said Dr. Fitter.

"Please sit," said Inspector Masalavala. "I also wanted to show appreciation for our good doctor. Coming out of retirement at my request, eh?" He laughed. "So I invited him for a drink."

Inspector Masalavala was being modest, for it was more than a drink: he was treating Dr. Fitter to a double peg of Scotch from his treasured bottle of Johnnie Walker Blue Label. He asked if Jal would have one.

"No, thanks, I don't feel like drinking."

"I understand, I won't insist," said the inspector, quickly putting aside the bottle. "Something else? Cold drink?"

"No, nothing for me, honest. I just want to say how grateful I am. The whole family is, they send their thanks to you both."

"Not at all, not at all."

"Least we could do."

They picked up their glasses. "Salaamati," said Inspector Masalavala.

"Tandarosti," responded Dr. Fitter.

A short silence followed as they savoured their drinks, then the inspector said he was glad to have been able to help. "If we don't look after our own people in times of trouble, who will?"

"Agreed," said Dr. Fitter.

"But it was very kind of you," said Jal.

"Not at all, not at all."

They sipped the Scotch, praising its sterling qualities and nursing the glow of their good deed. Jal enjoyed watching the pleasure they took in the drinks. The doctor asked how Professor Vakeel was, and Jal said not very well.

"That's the problem with the damned Parkinson's," muttered the doctor. "Never gets better."

"Just before you came, Jal," said Inspector Masalavala, "we were chatting about the future of the Parsi community."

"Yes? The orthodox and reform argument?"

"That's only one part of it. The more crucial point is our dwindling birth rate, our men and women marrying non-Parsis, and the heavy migration to the West."

"Vultures and crematoriums, both will be redundant," declared Dr. Fitter, "if there are no Parsis to feed them. What's your opinion?"

"I'm not sure," said Jal, reluctant to be drawn into a debate over this explosive topic. "We've been a small community right from the beginning. But we've survived, and prospered."

"Those were different times, a different world," said Inspector Masalavala, not in a mood to tolerate optimism. "The experts in demographics are confident that fifty years hence, there will be no Parsis left."

"Extinct, like dinosaurs," said Dr. Fitter. "They'll have to study our bones, that's all."

Jal smiled. He liked the doctor despite the gruff personality and bluntness. His humour epitomized the Parsi spirit, he felt, the ability to laugh in the face of darkness.

"You will be named Jalosauras," said Dr. Fitter. "I will be Shapurjisauras. If they find my father's bones, we will have a Pestonjisauras with a pugree on his head. And our inspector here, who loves his Scotch, will be the powerful Whiskysauras, a magnum of Blue Label tucked under his arm. In the meantime, eat, drink, and be merry."

They laughed, the doctor and Jal, the latter realizing how good it was to do so again.

The inspector maintained his solemnness as he puzzled over why the idea of Parsi dinosaurs was funny. "I get very depressed when I think about these matters. The most frustrating thing is, we have the means to avert disaster."

"Really?" said the doctor.

"Take the falling birth rate. Our Parsi boys and girls don't want to get married unless they have their own flat. Which is next to impossible in Bombay, right? They don't want to sleep under the same roof as their mummy and daddy. Meanwhile, the other communities are doing it in the same room, never mind the same roof, separated by a plywood partition or a torn curtain. Our little lords and ladies want soundproofing and privacy. These Western ideas are harmful."

"Indeed," said Dr. Fitter. "The funny thing is, we used to pride ourselves on being Westernized, more advanced."

"Yes, but listen to my solution. If lack of privacy is holding up a marriage, Parsi Panchayat should pay to make modifications in the parents' flat. Take one corner and make it absolutely soundproof, so the couple can go in that room, enjoy, make as much noise as they like. And make lots of babies too."

"A mating room?" said Dr. Fitter. "You think young couples would go for it?"

"Worth trying. But privacy is not the only issue. There are lots of wealthy couples living alone in new flats who produce just one child. Two, if we're lucky. Parsis seem to be the only people in India who follow the family planning message. Rest of the country is breeding like rabbits."

413

"Well," said Dr. Fitter. "Your demographers will tell you, the more educated a community, the lower the birth rate."

"Then we need to fix that. I have two suggestions. First, our youth must be prohibited from going beyond a bachelor's degree. Give them cash incentives to study less. And those who want to do post-graduate studies, tell them they will get no funding from Panchayat unless they sign a contract to have as many children as the number of people over age fifty in their family. Maximum of seven – we don't want to spoil the health of our young women."

"I see," said Dr. Fitter. "But what about those who might have medical problems, inability to conceive?"

"That's no excuse," said the inspector. "Not these days, with in vitro fertilization and all those mind-boggling technologies that result in multiple births. We can produce six and seven Parsis in one shot, I'm telling you."

"Ah," said the doctor. "A very interesting proposition."

"Our community, our youth has to rediscover the joys of a large family," continued Inspector Masalavala, failing to notice the smiles exchanged by the doctor and Jal. "They have to realize what they are missing. The happy music of children's laughter filling the home, wife cooking huge hearty meals in the kitchen, clatter of pots and pans, the aromas of dhansak and dhandar."

"You will ensure in your plan," said the doctor, "that the evils that accompany large families do not creep in and ruin the joy and happiness."

"Yes, of course," assured the inspector. "What evils?"

"The usual – sickness, poverty."

"Oh, those. No, no, the Panchayat has enough money. No one will be sick or poor. The only things we have to worry about are notions of individualism. Poison. Pure poison, that's what these ideas are to the Parsi community."

"My dear fellow," sighed the doctor. "It's hard to stop the march of ideas."

"We have to try," said the inspector sternly. "They cause too much misery. Look at Edul Munshi's example. Crushed to death in his youth. Why? Because of his silly handyman hobby. If he had done his duty as a Parsi, had half-a-dozen children, he would have had no time to fool around with his tools. He'd still be alive."

"True," said Jal. So far, it was the only part of Inspector Masalavala's rant that made some sense.

"Same goes for your sister. I don't mean to upset you, Jal, but if she had married, she would have been in her husband's house, far from the steel beam that broke her skull."

"If, if, if," said Dr. Fitter. "If we are meant to die out, nothing will save us."

"Yes," said Inspector Masalavala. "But it will be a loss to the whole world. When a culture vanishes, humanity is the loser."

"Agreed," said Dr. Fitter. "So maybe we should bury a time capsule for posterity. To be opened in one thousand years. Containing recipes for dhansak, patra-ni-machhi, margi-na-farcha, and lagan-nu-custard."

Inspector Masalavala liked this suggestion, and it cheered him up. "How about including the Zend-Avesta, and words and music for Chhaiye Hamay Zarthosti?"

"Sure. And a few old issues of *Jam-e-Jamshed*."

"Also, some cassettes of Adi Marzban's radio comedies," said Jal. "Coomy used to love them."

"Complete instructions and explanations for all our rituals and ceremonies," said the inspector.

"Whatever you do, you mustn't forget a copy of our great Navsari epic," said the doctor.

"Which one is that?"

"'Ek Pila Ni Ladai.'"

Inspector Masalavala laughed, finally loosening up a little. "With an English translation," he said.

The three took a shot at it themselves, agreeing to "The Battle of the Chicken" for the poem's title. They tried hard to remember all the verses about the woman feuding with neighbours over the theft of her chicken, the confrontation that lasted fifty-four unforgettable days. Several stanzas were devoted to the dastardly way the dark deed was perpetrated, followed by her threats and curses: a string of horrible diseases for the thieves, should they so much as taste a morsel of the stolen bird. They had the most fun with the verses where the diseases were catalogued, an endless river of affliction, from typhoid, cholera, diphtheria, diarrhoea, dysentery, pyorrhoea, piles, and herpes, onwards to mumps, measles, madness, malaria, and, of course, chicken pox.

As the evening wore on, the three of them filled their imaginary time capsule with their favourite items, ancient and modern, serious and frivolous, sacred and profane, till they ran out of ideas.

Sighing, Inspector Masalavala poured more Scotch into the two empty glasses. "To think that we Parsis were the ones who built this beautiful city and made it prosper. And in a few more years, there won't be any of us left alive to tell the tale."

"Well, we are dying out, and Bombay is dying as well," said Dr. Fitter. "When the spirit departs, it isn't long before the body decays and disintegrates."

"That's beautiful," said Inspector Masalavala, discreetly touching the corner of his eye. "That makes sense. Makes me feel better."

"In the meantime, eat, drink, and be merry."

Then Mrs. Fitter arrived to call her husband home because dinner was ready.

"Fully ready or almost getting ready?" asked Dr. Fitter, for his Scotch was not quite finished.

"Fully ready and almost on the table," she said. "If you waste time the fish will get cold, Shapurji, and you will grumble non-stop."

She turned to them to complain, "This Parsi of mine is such a fussy fellow, you should hear him. You'd think he was still in his surgery, giving orders, instead of my retired dosaji."

"Okay, Tehmi, you've made enough malido of my honour for one evening," he said jovially. He drained his glass and struggled out of the deep rattan chair.

Jal was warmed by the banter of the old couple, the love they so obviously shared. He rose as well, to leave with them.

Mrs. Fitter scurried ahead while the two men lingered outside, looking through the dusk at the traffic and the people and the sky. Night had fallen on the city. But it was still as frenetic as ever. Vital, in its exuberance. Jal saw Dr. Fitter observe it all with satisfaction, nodding to himself, a slight smile playing on his lips, as though he were giving a patient good news. They shook hands before the doctor hurried away to his fish dinner.

Waiting at the kerb to cross the road, Jal looked at his watch. Almost eight-thirty. He had stayed much longer than he intended. But the company had been most enjoyable.

Strange, he thought, how Inspector Masalavala's deluge of pessimism could be deflected by Dr. Fitter's handful of words, his sly humour turning doom and gloom into something comic. He wished he had that ability to make sense of the world by using laughter, or at least using it like a shield against its constant assault. As for the inspector and his expert demographers, such despair was for fools – he needed to take only one look at Roxie and Yezad's family, at their sons, to know it. His nephews, he thought with pride.

THERE WAS NO NEWSPAPER to help Yezad pass the time. He had stopped it two days after Christmas, after the uncertainty about his next salary. The boys were at school, he was alone at the dining table. And yesterday had been Coomy's dusmoo prayers, which meant that Bombay Sporting had stayed closed for ten days already.

"Yezad, what will happen at the shop?" asked Roxana, overcome by the need to speak her anxiety. "Will they put you in charge now?"

He must stay calm for her sake, he resolved, not let her feel his worry about his job, whether there would even be one to go back to. "Mrs. Kapur needs time to recover first. Think about it – her husband murdered in the shop, without warning."

"You're right, ten days is nothing," she agreed. "It's just that when Jehangoo and Murad were putting on their uniforms . . ."

"What?"

"I felt they had lost weight."

"But, Roxie, they've always been skinny," he chuckled to feign amusement. "You know the game we used to play with them, counting their ribs, playing piano upon them."

She smiled, bolstered by the memory, and went to the kitchen, leaving her father's tea to cool for a bit in the feeding cup.

He wondered how much longer he could sustain this outward show of calm. But he had no choice – if he lost his grip, despair would overwhelm them. Reminding himself yet again that ultimately it was in the hands of God, he went to the balcony.

Shoulders slumped over the railing, elbows hanging, he stared at the street below. The parrot on the third floor across the road was hopping endlessly in its cage, shuffling from side to side, almost hurling itself against the bars. He winced. If it were his pet he would open the cage and let it go.

He couldn't bear to watch any more, and went inside. The feeding cup with tea was still on the table. He touched its side – cool enough now. About to call Roxana, he stopped himself.

"Ready, chief, for your tea?"

"Umm."

He sat on the edge of the settee and put the spout to Nariman's lips. It made a trickle at the corner of his mouth.

"Oops. Sorry, chief, it's a spout-and-a-half." He snatched the napkin beside the pillow and wiped Nariman's chin. The stubble, long and rough, grabbed the cloth. It was weeks since they had been able to afford the barber's services. "Good thing the growth is slow, chief. Or you'd have a full Karl Marx beard by now."

Nariman attempted a smile, and Yezad offered the feeding cup again. He got the hang of it, the angle that permitted a manageable flow. He tilted, Nariman swallowed. He realized this was the first time he had sat close to his father-in-law since his arrival months ago.

Though only a small cup, the tea took a while to finish. When the spout was drained, Nariman lifted his shaking hand and laid it over Yezad's. Their two hands held the cup together, trembling together.

Yezad knew he was saying thank you. He looked at the hand, the long fingers with nails due for cutting. The knuckles were like seaside pebbles exposed to the elements, the skin almost transparent, displaying the handiwork of time, the years endured.

"You're welcome, chief," he whispered, swallowing to clear his throat.

He returned the feeding cup to the kitchen, and Roxana thought he was bringing it to remind her.

"But it's empty," she said, looking inside, puzzled for just a fraction of a second before understanding: he had served Pappa. Her lip trembled.

"He drank it all," he said, and left the kitchen. On the way back he stopped at the dressing table to rummage in Roxana's small drawer till he found what he was looking for.

"Okay, chief, let's trim your nails." He lifted Nariman's hand from the bed, taking the thumb first. The tremor made his own hand shake, and the nail kept evading the clippers.

"Let's try something different." He sat sideways on the settee, crossing his leg so the knee was raised high. Upon this knee he placed his father-in-law's hand, then held it down with his own, the fingers spread out over his kneecap. With each snap of the clippers, hard yellow crescents shot across the room.

"There. How's that?"

"Excel excellent."

But the ends were rough, the brittle nails having broken in the clippers rather than been cut. He slid out the folding file and began smoothing the jagged ends, which made Nariman smile.

"Better now, isn't it?" said Yezad, checking the edges again.

"De-clawed. And ha ha harmless."

"Not you, chief. Not with that tongue you possess."

They laughed softly, and Yezad cast his eye across the floor, recovering many of the clippings in a scrap of old newspaper. "You know, chief, might as well do your toenails."

"Too much trub trub . . ."

"No trouble at all."

He moved the sheet aside from the legs and sat at his father-in-law's feet. The toenails were much harder, almost corneous. Like the beaks of tiny birds, he thought. He looked over his shoulder. A tear was running down Nariman's cheeks. He pretended he hadn't noticed, and squeezed the clippers.

He added the toe clippings to the newspaper square and wrapped it up. "Now we must do something about that beard, chief. I think you brought your razor with you, didn't you?"

It was in the suitcase, with the shaving brush and soap. But the blade was dull, it would scratch and nick, especially with this amount of stubble. He selected a new one from his own box and took his plastic mug to the kitchen for hot water.

"Shaving?" asked Roxana, glancing at the five o'clock shadow on her husband's cheeks.

He nodded and returned to the front room. He spread a towel over Nariman's chest and moistened his jowls, working up a vigorous lather to soften the stubble. Nariman made his lips disappear to let him brush under the nose.

"All set," said Yezad, and dipped the razor in the hot water. Starting at one ear, he stretched the skin to make it taut, his thumb having to pull quite a bit before it tightened. Nariman did his best to help, trying to twist his mouth sideways or puff his cheek.

Yezad was working under the chin when Roxana came into the room. She saw him leaning over Pappa, and panicked for a moment – was something wrong? Then she realized what he was doing. She put a hand over her mouth to keep silent.

He finished, and wiped off the leftover flecks from the nostrils and earlobes. Gathering up the shaving things, he turned. He saw her in the doorway, saw her eyes overflowing with gratitude so intense, he averted his own in guiltiness.

Just before dinnertime Jal arrived with another food package. "Lots extra again," he said cheerfully. "Hope you don't mind."

"No, it's very useful," said Roxana, though she was uncertain how Yezad might react to these deliveries.

Then Jal noticed Nariman spick and span, almost dapper, if being dapper in bed were possible. "Hello! Is that really you, Pappa?"

"Uncle, just feel this," urged Jehangir, squeezing his grand-father's chin. "So soft and smooth, like before."

Jal hesitated.

"Touch it, it feels so nice."

He leaned over from his chair and caressed the chin gently. "Jehangir's right. Better than my own shave."

Nariman smiled. "Yezad . . . res pon si ble for my trans . . ."

"Transformation? Yes?" He turned to Yezad, who looked away.

But Roxana was quick to praise, "Manicure, pedicure, facial, everything! Yezad gave Pappa the full beauty treatment!"

They laughed, and Murad joked that maybe Daddy should open up Monsieur Chenoy's Salon de Beauté.

"Learnt a little French, and see how big he talks," said Yezad with pride.

"You know, Daddy," said Jehangir pensively, "if you specialize in old people, you would have lots of customers. I'm sure there are many grandpas who . . . ," his voice trailed off.

Then Jal got up, overcome by emotion, and gave Yezad a hug. "You are such a good person. I cannot thank you enough."

"You don't have to thank me at all." Feeling uncomfortable, he eased himself out of Jal's arms.

Roxana asked her father if he would like one of the mutton patties that Jal had brought. He indicated no with a slight movement of his head, but whispered a need for the bedpan.

As she bent to get it, she noticed Yezad shrink in his chair, then rise and edge casually towards the balcony. Oh well, she smiled to herself, this was one thing he wouldn't help with.

∽

The man who came to deliver the note stared at the glass in Yezad's hand when he answered the door, at the dentures submerged in water. He looked at his mouth, as though trying to determine if there was room there for any more teeth.

422

Yezad, who had been scrubbing the dentures, laughed. "Not mine," he clarified for him. "I have my own, these are old father's."

"I was wondering," said the man. He remembered his errand and handed over the letter.

It was from Mrs. Kapur. Three weeks had passed since her husband's death. Yezad put the glass down and opened the envelope.

The servant waited till he finished reading. "Memsahab said to bring back your reply."

"Please say I will come tomorrow at ten o'clock as she wants. Should I write it down?"

"No, no, that much I can remember."

The servant left, and Roxana rejoiced at the news – it could only mean one thing. And Yezad would certainly get paid tomorrow. She hoped Mrs. Kapur would not deduct for the time the shop had been closed. "After all, you were willing to manage the place by yourself. At the most, she can cut one or two days for Coomy."

"Yes, we'll see."

A touch of fatigue in his restrained answer bothered her. "What's the matter, Yezdaa?"

"Nothing," he said, though he dreaded the thought of entering the shop again. He couldn't burden Roxana with it. That was now between God and himself.

20

W HEN YEZAD ARRIVED at the Bombay Sporting Goods
Emporium, the steel shutters were down though the
door was unlocked. The servant who had delivered Mrs.
Kapur's note the day before was inside. He pointed silently to
the office at the back.

As Yezad went around the counter, he could hear the air-
conditioner roaring, and the open door revealed Mrs. Kapur
in her husband's chair. He felt she occupied the seat as though
it had always been hers . . . come through her ordeal quite
unscathed . . . No, that was unkind, the human spirit was a
powerful thing, she was to be commended. Still, she did look
a bit too comfortable behind that desk, he thought. He envied
her appearance of well-being and strength.

"Good morning, Mr. Chenoy, please take a chair."

"Thank you." The other day she had called him Yezad, he
thought uneasily.

"I will come straight to the point. Bombay Sporting won't
be reopening."

He wondered why he experienced no shock, no surprise. If
anything, a strange sense of relief. He heard himself ask, "Are
you selling the shop?"

"Why? Would you like to buy it?" Her bright smile did not
obscure the message that it was none of his business.

He shook his head foolishly, and she proceeded, "Besides
the wages owing, I am giving you one month's extra salary."

She slid a slim envelope across the desk. He left it there,
reviewing the equation: fifteen years of dedicated service,
worth one month's pay to Mrs. Kapur.

"Please, take it," she said, misreading his stillness for reluctance. "I'm sure Vikram would have wanted you to."

"Thank you." He moved it closer to him on the desk. Was this it, should he get up now and pocket the envelope? He shifted to the chair's edge, ready to leave.

"By the way, Mr. Chenoy, you know the suitcase that used to be here?" she continued with the same bright smile.

"Yes?"

"Whenever Vikram mentioned it, he would praise you. He would say he never had to worry about a single rupee from the cash sales. Every evening you turned over all the money to him."

"What else would I do?"

She barked a laugh. "I could give you lots of examples. It's so difficult to find honest employees. If not for you, I'm sure the suitcase would be much smaller than it is."

And that's why she rewards me with a month's salary, he thought.

"Vikram used to call it our personal pension plan. My poor husband – he never got to enjoy it." She paused. "You know, some months ago he had this crazy idea of joining politics. He wanted to spend the suitcase for the election. I put my foot down."

"It must have disappointed him."

She shook her head. "My Vikram was like a child in many ways, wanting to try all sorts of silly things. I had to point out the problems. Sometimes I wonder how he ran the business without me."

"He was very good at it."

"Oh, that's nice of you – such a loyal employee. Which reminds me, do you know how much is in the suitcase?"

"No. I don't think even Mr. Kapur kept an exact figure."

She smiled. "He didn't, but I did. Every night he came home and told me the amount he had put in. We have a Punjabi saying: Bakshis can be a hundred thousand rupees, but accounts must be correct to the last paisa."

And what about black money and tax evasion, was there a saying for that, he felt like asking.

"Last night I counted the suitcase. And here is the problem. There's thirty-five thousand less than there should be."

So that's where this pleasant chat was leading, the smiling spider trying to weave a web for him. "Didn't Mr. Kapur tell you?" he asked politely.

"Tell me what?"

"About Shiv Sena. You know how they go to businesses, demanding their so-called donations for—"

"They've never bothered us," she interrupted sharply.

"They did this time." He told her of the Mumbai name-tax that Mr. Kapur had agreed to, to keep Bombay in his shop sign. "Which is why he took thirty-five thousand from the suitcase."

"I see. And did they provide a receipt for the payment?"

"That was the whole confusion on Christmas Day – two other fellows came, saying no exemption allowed. The first two never returned for the payment."

"Oh, I see, never returned. And what happened to the money?"

"It's still in my desk." He gestured behind him, towards the shop. "Unless the thieves stole it on Christmas Day."

Her eyes narrowed. "Nothing was touched, Mr. Chenoy, the thieves ran off when Husain screamed. By the way, I couldn't find the duplicate keys to your desk. Shall we look?"

He groped for the key ring in his pocket and they left the office. His hand was shaking as he unlocked his desk. He pulled open the drawer slowly, thinking of his father, of the clock in the kitchen, the question of honour and good name . . .

Without emotion he handed her the envelope. She bent down to peer, to see what else might be in the drawer.

"Better count it, Mrs. Kapur. Accounts must be correct to the last paisa, as you said."

"I still don't understand." Her tone was nakedly suspicious now, the hostility palpable. "Why was the money in your desk?"

"Mr. Kapur wanted me to deal with it. He said it made him sick to talk with the crooks."

"This whole business is very strange. Why did Vikram want an exemption instead of just changing the name? A new sign would have cost much less than thirty-five thousand."

"Mr. Kapur didn't calculate everything in terms of money," said Yezad, struggling to keep a level tone. "As you know, the name meant a lot to him. Bombay was the world to him."

She shook her head. "My Vikram was not so sentimental. Anyway, you should take your personal items from the desk, so you don't have to come again."

How little she knew her husband, he thought, as he opened the drawers, one by one, and sifted through the contents. There was not much of his in them. A few magazines, letters of appreciation from clients, Divali and New Year cards from business associates over the years.

Mrs. Kapur stood beside him to supervise, scrutinizing each article that went into his briefcase. She craned and shifted to keep things in view at all times.

Yezad did not rush, pretending to examine his files carefully, as though she weren't looking over his shoulder. But his mind was playing host to a childhood memory, come unbidden, of a servant, suspected of stealing . . . Henry, about fifteen, three or four years older than he, dismissed for some trivial reason. And Henry's father, full of shame, had come to take his son away. The boy's small trunk, rusting and dented, was ready by the back door, along with his skinny roll of bedding. But before they could leave, Henry had to empty the trunk and unroll the frayed, patched-up bedding for his employers, demonstrate that nothing was being smuggled out, while Henry's father, mortified, looked on . . .

And Yezad wondered if his own father was now watching his son's humiliation. He finished, pushed in the drawers, gave her the key.

"Thank you, Mr. Chenoy. On Vikram's behalf also I thank you. Now. Is there anything in the shop you would like to have for a souvenir? Something small, to keep in Vikram's memory?"

Perhaps she was trying to atone for her suspicions, he thought. He was about to refuse the offer, when he remembered.

"Actually, Mr. Kapur gave me a Christmas gift. I forgot to take it that day, in all the Shiv Sena commotion. Three photos of Hughes Road – he must have put them back in his desk for me."

"Oh, I know where they are, Mr. Chenoy. But those are very valuable."

He looked in her eyes. "Mr. Kapur gifted them to me," he repeated, keeping his voice steady. "On Christmas morning."

"I don't think it's possible. They are part of Vikram's collection. One of his hobbies. But I'll have to sell it – as a widow I have to be careful with money. Is there something else you'd like? Maybe that Santa Claus? Or a football?"

"No, thank you."

"Are you sure? Okay, bye-bye then."

Yezad's mind was blank as he left the shop. He touched the entrance keys in his pocket – she'd forgotten to take them back. He glanced behind him as he shut the door: no, she hadn't – both locks had been changed.

Walking along the kerb, he reached into his pocket again, fished out the keys, and dropped them in the gutter. Fifteen years. He heard the tinkle as they landed.

A scavenger sifting garbage nearby saw the keys fall, and dived to retrieve them. Scooping them out of the muck, he added them to a sack containing his metal collection.

Past the Jai Hind Book Mart, Yezad could hear his name being called. He pretended not to have heard, and kept walking. He did not stop till he reached Wadiaji fire-temple.

HE WENT THROUGH THE OLD HANDBAG with the broken zip in which Roxana kept important documents, receipts, medical information, the children's report cards. His high-school certificate, B.A. degree, sales and management diploma, and a fifteen-year-old version of his résumé were in there too.

He spread everything out on the dining table. He updated the résumé and made a handwritten copy. Roxana looked on encouragingly, admiring his penmanship.

"Lovely as ever, Yezdaa, your pearls on paper. With writing like yours, it's an advantage not to have it typed."

He smiled.

"I think you'll easily find a new job. Better than the old one." She kissed the top of his head and withdrew.

He finished the résumé and organized his briefcase, including in it the clients' letters of appreciation that he had brought back from Bombay Sporting. Then he went to the corner shop to get photocopies.

For three days he made the rounds of the major sports equipment outlets in the city. The managers and owners, aware of the misfortune befallen his previous place of employment, took his application sympathetically, promising to let him know if an opening came up. But Yezad couldn't help noticing their discomfort. They shook hands gingerly, as though they would prefer not to have contact with one so closely connected with a murder.

On the fourth day, he left in the morning at the usual time and walked to the fire-temple. His train pass had expired. He prayed for over two hours, then walked home. It was only one o'clock when he let himself in.

"Yezdaa? Back so soon?"

"There aren't any sports shops left to visit."

"Won't you look in other places?"

"What are you suggesting? That I'm lazy because I came home early today?"

"I was only wondering what your plan was."

"Don't wonder. All these people I've been to, they need time to offer me something. God will decide when it's my turn."

She left him alone, but later that afternoon asked if it would be all right for her to go out for a while, if he was staying in. "Jal wants me to sort out Coomy's clothes and shoes and things. He wants to donate them to the old people's home and the widows' chawl."

"Sure. Sooner the better – poor people can make use of it."

Before leaving, she gave her father the urinal without being asked. Her hissing told him what was required. He obliged by dribbling a few drops into it.

"Is that all, Pappa? Try again, so you won't need it till I get back."

Nariman groaned, tried again, managed a bit more. She drained it into the toilet and washed out the urinal. Reassuring Yezad that Pappa had been having a nice quiet day, she left.

Yezad paused for a while in the front room. He watched Nariman's fluttering hands, and his eyes, restless under closed lids. But it was his silence, grown almost complete in recent weeks, that saddened Yezad the most.

He went out to the balcony to lean at the railing, remembering his childish resentment of Nariman when he first came here four months ago. He thought about the times he had enjoyed with Nariman, his wit, his conversational vigour, ranging from a few telling words to a torrent of persuasion.

All down to a barely noticeable trickle. Like the fan of multiple speeds in the back room, down to just a slow swishing . . . In itself, that too was worth savouring, except that it foreshadowed the approaching stasis. End of all movement, all words . . .

He put the kettle on when the boys returned from school. He could tell that they enjoyed the novelty of their father being home at this odd hour, making their tea when he normally would be at work. He stayed with them while they drank it.

"Now to your books."

They went to the little desk in the back room, and he sat on the bed. The boys' foreheads shone with sweat. Not even the end of January, he thought, and the weather turning already. He asked what homework they had.

"I've got this French traduction," said Murad.

"I remember some of my French, if you need help."

"Merci, Pappa."

"What about Jehangla?"

"Arithmetic. But the sums are so stupid. This one says Mrs. Bolakani went to the market with Rs 100.00. She spent Rs 22.50 on eggs, Rs 14.00 on bread, Rs 36.75 on butter, and Rs 7.00 on onions. How many rupees were left when she came home?"

Yezad asked why it was stupid, and Jehangir said no one would buy so much butter all at once, Mrs. Bolakani did not have a good set of envelopes like Mummy's.

They laughed, and he squeezed their shoulders affectionately. Murad asked if he could have the fan on.

Jehangir frowned at his brother. "Mummy told you the electricity bill is very high when you use the fan."

"But I'm sweating so much, how can I remember all these French words?"

Yezad said they could have it on for ten minutes. He set the control to LOW, the only setting that worked, and the air came to life in the room.

By and by, Nariman's indistinct speech could be heard from the front room, drawing Yezad to his side. "How are you, chief?" He felt silly even as he asked the question. "Roxie's gone out, but we're all here."

Nariman's vocal efforts persisted, and Yezad returned to the boys. "I think Grandpa wants to say something. See if you understand."

The three lined up alongside the settee, and waited.

"Maybe he wants to do soo-soo?" suggested Yezad.

"No," said Jehangir. "For soo-soo you can make out he is saying 'bottle.' I think he needs to do kakka."

Yezad's heart sank. "Are you sure?" Leaning towards the pillow, he inquired gently, "Number two?"

Nariman groaned, and his relieved tone indicated an affirmative.

"Shall I get Villie Aunty?" asked Murad.

His father took a deep breath. "No. We don't need her."

His response stunned the boys. All they could think of was the absolute prohibition against touching the bed utensils, the many fights between their parents. Then approval for his decision showed on their faces.

"But I don't know how," said Jehangir. "It's more complicated than the bottle."

Murad nodded, the same went for him.

"We'll figure it out," said Yezad. "Can't be that difficult."

He lifted the sheet and pushed it aside to keep it from being soiled. The stale odour surrounding Nariman intensified. And this despite Roxie's never-ending efforts, he thought, to keep him fresh with sponge baths and talcum.

"Okay, Jehangla, when Murad and I raise Grandpa, you can slide in the bedpan. Ready?"

"Wait, I just remembered – Mummy always puts an extra plastic first."

The folded plastic was at the foot of the settee, tucked under the mattress. Jehangir shook it out.

"Ready?" asked their father. "Get set, go." Jehangir

432

slipped the plastic quickly over the white sheet, then placed the bedpan under his grandfather.

"Excellent," said Yezad, as he and Murad lowered him. "Feels all right, chief?"

Nariman acknowledged it with a sigh of relief, and they stood back.

How did Roxana do it by herself, wondered Yezad, the lifting, the plastic, the bedpan, day after day? And instead of praising her strength, what had he done but rage and complain. She had needed his help, and all he could spew were his pathetic harangues. The mornings, the evenings and nights, his bitter frustration countered by her patience . . .

Overcome with shame, he barely noticed the smell of the bedpan, his fastidious nose uncomplaining.

Jehangir's hand crept into his father's. "Daddy, will you find a job soon?"

"God is great. If He wants me to, I'm sure I will."

The boys looked away shyly, not accustomed to this new way of talking. Moments passed in silence broken only by Nariman's groans and sighs.

"I know what," said Yezad. "Tomorrow is a holiday. Why don't you both come with me to fire-temple in the morning? You can pray to God, ask Him to help us."

They nodded, feeling a little embarrassed. Such words used to come from Coomy Aunty, never from their father.

"I think Grandpa has finished," said Murad.

"Ya ya yes."

They lifted him slightly while Jehangir withdrew the bedpan and put on the lid. From under the sofa he picked up a basket filled with small squares cut out of old sudras and pyjamas. "To wipe Grandpa's bum – Mummy said paper rolls are too expensive."

Yezad blenched but took the basket from him. Then the front door opened, and Roxana was home.

"Oh Pappa, no!" she cried from the hallway where the smell reached her. "Did you spoil the bed?"

433

She entered the front room, saw them around the settee, the rags in Yezad's hand, and understood. "Thank you," she whispered, relieving him of the basket. "I'll do that."

"Thank Jehangir and Murad. Without them I could have done nothing."

She smiled, and her eyes struggled to keep back the tears.

"I don't know how you manage alone," said Yezad.

"It isn't hard. With practice I've got used to it."

Not practice, he thought, love and devotion. Must be some truth in the saying that love could move mountains, it certainly let Roxana lift her father.

"Open that parcel, Yezdaa, see what Jal sent for you."

He unwrapped the newspapered package and found a small silver thurible. Its exquisite shape replicated the huge five-foot afargaan in Wadiaji fire-temple. The round plate on top, where incense had been burned, was charred by coals.

He hefted the little afargaan in his hand and looked questioningly at Roxana.

"Mamma's," she replied. "Don't you recognize it? We used to see Coomy with it during her evening prayers, taking the loban through the house."

"Yes, I remember."

"Jal thought you might like it. Look, he even sent this packet of loban."

He opened the plastic bag and sniffed the frankincense. He liked the afargaan, the shape, its feel in his hand, its lustre.

NEXT MORNING, after breakfast Yezad reminded the boys about the fire-temple. Murad refused, saying it was not Navroze or Khordad Sal. "Feels funny, going just like that. It's not even exam time."

"You don't need a special occasion. God is ready to listen three hundred and sixty-five days."

"Three sixty-six in a leap year," said Jehangir. It had been a long time since he'd been out with his father, and he was eager to start. Reluctantly, Murad changed from his wear-at-home clothes into something better.

The streets were quiet as they walked to the fire-temple; shops and offices were closed for Republic Day. From time to time a car went by filled with people waving little paper flags. The boys said it would be nice to come out in the evening, after dusk, to see the illuminations.

Jehangir slipped his hand into his father's and synchronized his stride to match. Every few steps, he took an extra skip to keep pace. Murad walked slightly ahead, independent for a while, before slowing down. When he drew alongside, his father took his hand as well and began to whistle.

Looking up, Jehangir wondered which song it would turn into, but his father kept whistling cheerful phrases, like a bird. Then he began a tune, the *Laurel and Hardy* theme, and Murad waddled podgily, with his stomach thrust out.

They soon reached the sandalwood shop, and the man, who knew Yezad as a regular now, said hello as he reached into the box of sticks: "Three today?"

Yezad shook his head, joking to cover his embarrassment, "One family, one sukhad."

The man smiled. "Your sons?"

He nodded.

They put on their prayer caps and headed towards the veranda for ablutions. At the washing parapet Yezad opened the lid of the haando and lowered the silver karasio in it. Hitting the side accidentally, it rang like a bell. His arm disappeared to his shoulder before the karasio reached water. "Almost empty," he whispered.

"This haando is so big, Jehangir could swim in it," said Murad.

"As if I'm that short."

He poured water over his sons' hands, then washed his own. They shared his handkerchief to dry. "Once you start your kusti, no more chit-chat and jokes, okay?"

"Why not?" asked Murad.

"Because you're talking to God when you pray. And it's rude to interrupt."

Murad made a face behind his father's back to let Jehangir know he was only humouring Daddy, he didn't believe any of this. They pulled out their shirts, tucked the tails under their chins, and began untying their kustis.

Yezad kept an eye on them so they wouldn't skip any part of the sequence. From the corners of their eyes they watched their father, fascinated by his new skill with the nine-foot kusti. It was so elegant in his fingers, so graceful, the way he tied the knots, even the blind ones behind his back.

Leaving their shoes beneath the bench, they went inside, into the tranquil hush, where the fire was a glow of embers. Yezad knelt at the sanctum, and the boys followed. From his shirt pocket he drew out the sandalwood, hesitated, took Murad's hand and put it on the offering, reached for Jehangir's and did the same. Three hands placed it in the silver tray.

Still kneeling, he gathered a pinch of ash, smeared some on their foreheads and the rest on his own. Holding their shoulders, he pressed down. They understood they must bow to the fire, and bent till their brows touched the marble threshold.

Between them, he lowered his own head . . . O Dada

Ormuzd, bless my sons, keep them healthy and honest, look after all our family according to Your will, help me do what is Your will . . .

He rose, and the boys rose with him. They began backing away from the fire, but it became a race between the two to see who was faster in reverse. They almost slammed into a priest.

It was the old dustoorji, the tall, thin one with the long white beard, who had spoken to Yezad that first time. He took the boys' hands into his and inquired with a twinkle in his eye, "Did you recite everything properly? No gaapcha in your prayers, hanh?"

They nodded shyly.

Laughing, the dustoorji said to Yezad, "It always makes me happy to see young people here." He continued inside to fulfil his duties to the fire.

They returned to the veranda and retrieved their shoes, where Murad observed that if this dustoorji was fat and wore red robes, he could easily look like Santa Claus.

"And if Santa Claus lost some weight," said Yezad, "and wore white clothes, he would look like the dustoorji."

"You know what I was worried about, Daddy?"

"What, Jehangla?"

"That someone would steal our shoes while we were inside."

Yezad said he didn't think that was likely in a fire-temple. He asked if they had enjoyed the visit.

They answered yes. "But it would be more fun if we could enter where the big afargaan is, and put sandalwood ourselves on the fire," said Murad.

"I used to think the same when I was your age."

BUTTER, JAM, BISCUITS, cheese, bottles of chutney and achaar, and two packets of sev-ganthia tumbled out of the large parcel of provisions. In a separate bag there were oranges and a bunch of green grapes. Murad and Jehangir unpacked it all eagerly, arraying the food on the dining table, their eyes glittering as they examined the labels.

Their pleasure fuelled Yezad's unhappiness. He guessed Roxana had told Jal that Bombay Sporting no longer needed him. And here he was, come to spread his largesse. "We have not yet registered as a charity."

Jal pressed his finger to his earpiece, and Roxana hoped he hadn't heard.

But he had caught the last bit. "I brought it with love," he protested, adjusting the setting. "If you use such a word for my gift, how harshly must you think about me and Coomy."

Then he was penitent. "We deserve it. For shifting Pappa here." He lowered his voice so Nariman wouldn't overhear.

"Now that was a gift-and-a-half. The kind that changes people's lives forever."

"Please let's not argue," said Roxana, indicating the settee.

Jal sat still with his hands in his lap. "Your anger is justified. It was a terrible thing she – we did."

"She: you were right the first time," said Yezad.

"But I let her. I let her convince me. I should have stopped her."

"Could you have?"

He thought for a moment. "No, I don't think so. She believed Pappa was responsible for . . ." He shook his head, reminding himself not to think of those unfortunate years. "How much better forgiveness would have been."

"Poor Coomy," said Roxana. "Too late for her."

He nodded sadly. "You know, I was doing a little cleaning in the drawing-room yesterday, putting away some knick-knacks in the showcase. And it reminded me of Pappa's birthday party. I thought to myself, that was the last time we were all in that room together."

"It was a nice party," said Yezad.

"I think Coomy also enjoyed herself," said Jal.

They assured him she had. "Everyone had a good time. And such a tasty dinner she cooked."

"Yes, she loved to cook. And I was thinking yesterday, Why couldn't we have had more happy times together? It was possible to – it is possible, we don't have to continue in the same way, believe me. And regarding Pappa, I . . ."

They remained silent till he started again. "Believe me, I'll make things right between us. Please have patience a little longer. Two more weeks."

Jal kept his promise, returning a fortnight later to announce he had good news. They watched as he tore open a fresh pack of Longlife Batteries and inserted the two cells in his hearing aid. Snapping the cover shut, he turned on the switch and adjusted the volume.

"Let me guess," said Yezad. "You've found someone with a miracle cure for Nariman."

The sarcasm bounced harmlessly off Jal, prompting only a little smile. "Sorry, Yezad, there isn't a cure for Parkinson's disease yet. My plan is entirely practical. Provided you both agree, and like it enough to cooperate."

"You hear that, Roxie? Needs our cooperation."

She pressed her lips together and wished Yezad would hear Jal out without baiting him.

But Jal's composure was undisturbed. His voice stayed soft, so as not to disturb Nariman. "You remember I came here one day, fed up with Coomy? And you were so kind, you said if you had a big flat like Chateau Felicity, you would let me live with you?"

Yezad's heart sank. Surely Jal didn't want to—! He waited tensely, nodding, yes, he remembered the evening.

"That's what gave me the idea. Suddenly I realized – I have a big flat! This one is too small for you, even if Pappa were not here. And that one is huge for me alone."

Yezad nodded again, guardedly.

The solution, said Jal, was for the whole family, along with Pappa, to move into Chateau Felicity. It would be the best thing for all of them. Also a way to honour Coomy's memory – something good at last after years of unhappiness. From up there, he said, possessed of the knowledge and wisdom that came with dying, Coomy would surely approve.

"Didn't I tell you?" said Yezad. "Didn't I say we could rely on Jal? Happily ever after – inside a ruin."

Jal laughed, refusing to take offence. Of course the flat was in terrible shape, unmaintained for decades. And neither he nor they had the money to fix it up.

"Glad you realize it," said Yezad.

"But that's where this flat comes in. Small though it is, it's worth a lot because of the location. We can get at least forty lakhs."

"Sweet dreams."

"No, it's the going rate. I've checked with some brokers."

"Without a word to me, you get my flat appraised?"

"Sorry, Yezad, I had to, to make sure my plan would work. I didn't want to come with half-baked ideas."

Yezad abandoned his pique. "Forty lakhs is a serious figure?"

"Minimum."

"Almost ten times what Pappa paid," said Roxana in awe.

Some of that money, explained Jal, could be used to repair Chateau Felicity, the rest could be invested. "Even in fixed deposits, the interest will be enough for you, and enough for Pappa's expenses – nurse, medicine, proper hospital-type bed.

I don't need a single paisa from it. All I want is you to come and make your home there."

"Castles in the air. Talking like our problems will disappear tomorrow. Even if we want to move, finding a serious buyer will take months."

Jal coughed. "Actually, I've got someone."

This time Yezad was genuinely outraged. "I don't believe this fellow! Getting an appraisal is one thing, but to line up a buyer without asking us? Have you also hired a moving company? Maybe the lorry is waiting outside for our furniture."

Roxana hushed him, that Pappa would hear. Jal said please not to be upset, one of the brokers he'd met at the share bazaar just happened to mention the buyer when he was making inquiries.

After a few moments of sulking, Yezad asked, feigning indifference, "Who's this buyer?"

"A diamond merchant from Surat. His son is getting married."

Yezad mulled over the idea and came up with his next objection: "Let's suppose your diamond merchant is serious. This will be a black-money deal, correct? So how can we trust him to give us the cash? And where will we live while the repairs are done to the big flat?"

Once again, Jal had the answers. "The system is: half in advance, half when you vacate. You'll get twenty lakhs first, then we have a month for repairs, after which you move."

Yezad smiled. "You know the biggest flaw in your plan? The repairs. They will cost so much, there'll be nothing left to invest. We'll be exactly where we started, no money for Pappa, me without a job. In fact it will be worse, we'll have that huge flat to take care of."

Jal got up to reach inside his trouser pocket. He extracted an envelope folded in half and handed it to Yezad.

On three typewritten pages was a detailed estimate and work order, binding for sixty days, written up by the very reputable firm of Hafiz Lakdavala & Sons. It was a list of all repairs necessary to make the Chateau Felicity flat a comfortable home.

As Yezad read, with Roxana looking over his shoulder, he realized Jal was right, the numbers could hardly be disputed. But he went through the pages, item by item: new toilets, new bathrooms, hot-water geysers, tiles, faucets, electrical work, painting, kitchen flooring and cabinets, replacement of broken windows, etc., etc. . . .

He disputed whatever he could. Even when he knew the answers, he raised his queries. Jal patiently explained away the doubts. "So you see, roughly ten lakhs will take care of renovations. Thirty lakhs to invest."

Yezad arrived at the final item, and thought he was on to something; here was a figure that threw into question the reliability of the entire estimate.

"This is nonsense, even a layman like me knows it. How can they repair such serious damage for so little? With the beam rotten and everything?"

Jal got up to read the line where Yezad's finger was pointing. "You mean the ceiling. It's the easiest of the jobs. Just surface plastering."

"Don't talk rubbish, you sound like poor Edul. Have you taken over his handyman mania?"

Jal looked at his stepfather on the settee, then stared into his lap and squared his shoulders. "I know it because I'm responsible for it."

"Listen, Jal," said Yezad wearily. "You must stop blaming yourself for every bad thing that happens."

"I was the one," Jal repeated. "I borrowed Edul's hammer, climbed on a stool, and broke the plaster."

Roxana and Yezad gaped. But Jal kept nodding, saying yes, that was exactly what he'd done.

"Coomy's idea, wasn't it," said Yezad dully.

Jal ignored the comment, reiterating that he was the one who had climbed up and wielded the hammer.

"But why did she want to do that?" asked Roxana, desperate to hear some reason less vindictive than the truth.

"To avoid looking after Pappa." The answer's blunt honesty left them mute for what felt like minutes, until Jal spoke again. "Now at least you understand the ceiling is solid, Edul was mistaken, the beam isn't rotting."

After such a confession, there was not much left to say. He prepared to leave. "Whatever you decide, I'm glad I had a chance . . . to tell you."

They walked him to the door, uttering their goodbyes in a daze. They shut the door and went inside.

But within moments the bell rang again. It was Jal again.

"Sorry. I forgot a very important fact you should know: if you agree to the plan, we'll go to the landlord and add your names to the flat. I want you to feel completely secure, not feel you are just guests in Chateau Felicity."

The offer moved Yezad as profoundly as the confession had stunned. He muttered something about taking a couple of days to think, to talk it over.

"Take long as you like. If the diamond merchant goes elsewhere, there'll be other buyers. A location like Pleasant Villa is in high demand."

Shaking their hands, he said good night once more.

Yezad put the grate on the stove and arranged three lumps of coal on it. When they were red hot he transferred them with tongs into the small round bowl of Coomy's afargaan.

Roxana's heart was light as she took dinner plates to the table. The day she had brought the afargaan home, she had polished it with Silvo and left it on the shelf outside the kitchen where he would see it. Now the fragrance of frankincense would soon fill the rooms, she thought, the smoke would carry the grace of God . . .

As she returned with four glasses, she could hear her father trying to speak. In the sounds he made she heard her name.

"Yes, Pappa?" She bent closer.

Do not, my child. Do not do not do not.

"What, Pappa? Do not what?"

Inasmuch as. Inasmuch. Do not.

He kept clamouring for her attention. She felt it best to not make too much of it. But he got louder, his appeals more frantic.

She went to his side again and stroked his hand to soothe him. "Come here, Jehangoo, sit with Grandpa for a few minutes."

Jehangir began reading to him from his history text: "'Shivaji was born in 1627, and was the founder of the Maratha kingdom. He respected the beliefs of all communities, and protected their places of worship. In a time of religious savagery, Shivaji practised true religious tolerance.'"

Nariman would not be calmed. Jehangir leaned over and held his stubbled chin. Instead of chortling as usual, his grandfather got annoyed.

"Try something else," said Roxana.

"Okay, okay," said Jehangir. He stroked his grandfather's head and sang, "'I am a teapot, short and stout.'" He put his thumbs to his mouth to hoot like an owl.

"Nothing works," he said to his mother, getting frustrated. "And you always call me, you never tell Murad to do anything."

"Because Grandpa enjoys your company."

"It's all right, Jehangla," said his father, entering with the afargaan and incense packet. "After my kusti, I'll do loban and pray. That will calm his spirit, get rid of whatever bad thoughts are plaguing him."

Roxana was a little doubtful, reminding Yezad that Pappa had never been one for prayer, he had abandoned even the perfunctory observations because of the way his parents had treated Lucy. "He used to call it the religion of bigots. He hasn't stepped inside a fire-temple in forty years."

"That doesn't matter. It's never too late – look at my

example. Besides, belief is not essential. The prayer sound itself will bring him peace and tranquility."

She withdrew, reluctant to discourage him any further. She did not want to jeopardize the faith in prayer that had descended like a blessing upon him and their house.

Standing at the foot of the settee, Yezad started his kusti. Instead of the usual silent recitation, he chanted aloud, "Kem na mazda! Mavaite payum dadat, hyat ma dregvao!"

By the time he finished the segment, Nariman seemed quieter. Giving Roxana a triumphant glance, he picked up the afargaan, dipped his hand in the incense packet, and gathered a little in his fingers before proceeding to the front door.

She hurried ahead of him to open it. His fingers released a trace of the gritty powder onto the coals, and at once, with a crackle, a cloud of white fragrant smoke filled the doorway. He lifted the afargaan high, gliding it around in an arc, the way he remembered his father doing.

Next, he presented the afargaan to Roxana. Covering her head, she passed her fingers through the smoke, fanning it gently to bathe her face. She stroked the sides of the afargaan and clasped her hands together.

"It's like angels and fareshtas floating through our house," she murmured happily.

He carried the afargaan to the balcony for Jehangir and Murad. They looked up with a blank smile. He couldn't speak, wouldn't break his thread of prayer, but made sounds through clenched teeth that made them laugh. He got annoyed. Their mother showed them the proper way to respect the fire.

Then he went into the front room, visiting every corner and circling around the settee. The incense made Nariman uncomfortable; he coughed and his hands seemed to want to push the smoke away from him.

Yezad scattered a final pinch of loban and pulled up a chair beside the settee to recite the Sarosh Baaj. "Khshnaothra Ahurahe Mazdao! Ashem vohu vahishtem asti," he began, searching for the right pitch.

445

Nariman responded with a whimpering sound. Roxana watched as the tremble in his hands grew a little. "Pappa doesn't like it," she mouthed to Yezad.

He gestured back to be patient. "Pa name Yazdan Ahuramazda Khodai!" he sang. "Awazuni gorje khoreh awazayad!"

But the longer he prayed, trying to imitate the sonorous cantillation of dustoorjis he heard in the fire-temple, the greater became the agitation on the settee. Nariman continued with his same indistinct words, over and over.

"I wish Pappa would calm down," said Roxana, appealing to Yezad again. "Can't you see it's bothering him? Be a little softer!"

"Shushum-hmm-quiesh-hmm-hmm!" he answered, admonishing her interruptions through clenched teeth. Behind their father's chair, the boys grinned at the sounds, not daring to laugh aloud.

"Fravarane Mazdayasno Zarathushtrish!"

No no no! pleaded Nariman.

Roxana couldn't bear it any longer. She put the pot back on the stove and asked Jehangir to go and get Daisy. He said he didn't want to go anywhere. Not to Daisy Aunty, and not to Jal Uncle's house either, it was always so sad and gloomy there.

"A house isn't sad or gloomy," said his mother, "that depends on the people who live in it. Anyway, we haven't decided about moving." But he continued to sulk, and she asked Murad to go instead.

For an instant, Roxana cast a critical eye upon the housecoat Daisy had wrapped hastily around herself. Then she welcomed her, apologizing for the bother, explaining that Pappa was in such a state this evening.

"No bother. He's my most devoted audience."

"Hmm-shtopsh-hmm-hmm!" Yezad turned fiercely on all the profane chit-chat.

Roxana whispered to Daisy not to mind him, so she tuned the violin and began a soothing rendition of Schubert's Serenade. Yezad disregarded the competition for the first few bars, then ratcheted up his volume.

"Ahunem vairim tanum paiti!"

Daisy allowed more pressure on the bow, and the sound-board responded with greater amplification.

"Yasnemcha vahmemcha aojascha zavarecha afrinami!" continued Yezad.

Nariman wept.

Daisy switched to the chaconne from Bach's D Minor Partita; Yezad vigorously commenced Ahmai Raescha.

"Why is nothing helping Pappa?" wondered Roxana in anguish.

A glorious cascade of sound from the violin momentarily drowned the prayer. Louder yet came the response: "Hazanghrem baeshazanam, baevare baeshazanam!"

Jehangir tapped Daisy on the back. Face squished against the chin-rest, she looked down at him questioningly.

"Aunty, do you know 'One Day When We Were Young'? It's Grandpa's favourite."

The violin paused. "Hum it for me," she commanded.

He attempted the tune; the hint of it sufficed to remind her of the song from *The Great Waltz*. She abandoned the cha-conne.

While she played, the sash of her housecoat came undone but the music did not stop. Roxana frowned a little, glancing at her husband to check if he was looking at Daisy's petticoat. But his eyes were closed as he reached the concluding section: "Kerfeh mozd gunah guzareshnra kunam!"

After several repetitions of the verse and refrain, Nariman's sobs subsided. Roxana wiped away the tears, and he drifted towards sleep.

Winding up with a final Ashem Vohu, Yezad opened his eyes. He held out his hands towards the settee to indicate the calm that the vibrations of his praying had wrought. Daisy put the violin in its case and, turning away from him, retied the sash firmly around her housecoat.

∾

Yezad lay on his back for a long time, staring at the ceiling in the dark. "Roxana? Are you awake?"

"Umm."

He reached for her hand under the sheet and said he'd decided: they would go to live with Jal in Chateau Felicity.

She was wide awake now. "So you think Jal's idea will work?"

The darkness hid her expression, but he could feel its delight in her fingers. "I prefer to think of it as God's plan. If He wants us in Chateau Felicity, He will make it work."

She snuggled closer, and her fingers tightened round his hand, clasping it more firmly, as though she were afraid of losing it. Then, sighing, she said that when she looked back over all the events that had led them to this evening, it was almost proof of divine power in the universe, with Pappa's broken ankle the start of everything.

THE DIAMOND MERCHANT from Surat, Mr. Hiralal, came with Jal the following Sunday to be introduced to Yezad and Roxana. He was soft-spoken, with simple clothes and simple habits despite his wealth. He expressed sympathy for Nariman, who was asleep. They liked him instantly.

While being shown around the flat, Mr. Hiralal gave the impression that the walls and ceilings, bricks and mortar, were all he noticed, and the shabbiness attesting to the tenants' straitened circumstances was as good as invisible.

"So lovely is your flat," he assured them. "Just like your respected brother described. For my son it will be perfect."

Roxana asked if he would take some tea. His affirmative emerged eagerly. After sipping from his cup and praising the blend, he apologized for the clandestine manner in which they were forced to transact their business.

"So nice it would be, if I could write a cheque for you. But government regulations force us into different procedures. Black money is so much a part of our white economy, a tumour in the centre of the brain – try to remove it and you kill the patient."

They turned to the matter of the first instalment of twenty lakhs. "Maybe it is better in four batches of five lakhs each."

"Why?" asked Yezad, at once suspicious, and giving Jal a questioning glance. But Jal's expression was unaltered.

"One batch only is your preference? You know what twenty lakhs of cash in hundred-rupee notes will be like?"

"A whole heap of money," said Yezad with a worldly smile, gesturing to indicate a pile of a vague size.

Mr. Hiralal smiled back. "You're right. It is a lot. It fills up a thirty-two-inch VIP suitcase."

Yezad laughed nervously, remembering Mr. Kapur. "Maybe a suitcase should replace the Ashoka pillar as the national emblem. It should be embossed on all our coins."

Mr. Hiralal nodded at the joke: "This is a great country, I love it very much. Now, I can bring the cash for you in a suitcase, but how will you look after it?"

"I'll put it under my bed."

The diamond merchant smiled again and turned to Jal. "You Parsis with your sense of humour. So wonderful. When I was in Baroda college, Parsis were my best friends. So much fun we had."

He advised Yezad to rent lockers in bank vaults: "In different areas, and different banks. In your name, in your respected wife's name, your children's names. And whenever you are ready I will give you a batch, in a small bag – carry-on luggage size. Less suspicious and easier to handle."

"Sounds like a spy movie," said Yezad.

"Oh, we have to do better than that. Income tax department has seen all those movies."

They laughed, then arranged to meet in a different location for each transfer of money. "Any trouble for you will be trouble for me," said Mr. Hiralal. "Let's do the first one at Willingdon Club. Very safe, I'm a member there. Second time we go to your respected brother-in-law's house. Is that all right, Mr. Contractor?"

"I will be honoured," said Jal.

For the third batch Yezad would visit the diamond merchant's office. The last one would be delivered here, to Pleasant Villa.

"Not a word to anyone," Yezad warned Roxana and the boys. "Not in the building, or to friends in school."

"Why?" asked Murad. "Are we committing a crime?"

"Our government makes such crazy laws, people are forced to break them," he explained half-heartedly.

450

"Mahatma Gandhi said it's our duty to break bad laws," said Murad. "He said they should be broken openly."

"We just want to go to Chateau Felicity, okay? Not to jail with Mr. Hiralal. So keep your mouth shut."

Over the next four days, the money was stashed away in the rented bank lockers, and Hafiz Lakdavala & Sons were ready to commence work at Chateau Felicity. They were happy to proceed on a cash basis. The tasks needed to be arranged in order of priority; in thirty days, enough would have to be readied to allow the Chenoy family to vacate Pleasant Villa for Mr. Hiralal.

In her imagination, Roxana could already see the flat renovated and refurbished. She began allocating rooms: her parents' room with attached bathroom for herself and Yezad, her former room for Jehangoo, Coomy's for Murad – the two could share the bathroom in the passageway. And Jal was happy where he was.

"Yes, that sounds fine," said Yezad, preoccupied with his list of repairs.

Nariman tried to speak, appearing quite agitated by what was going on around him. Please, he murmured, please, and Roxana comforted him, "Yes, Pappa, don't worry, of course you will get your old room back."

She continued to muse, imagining fresh paint for the walls and rearranging the furniture. The furniture, she said, especially the beds, needed to be refinished. And she remembered that in the drawing-room one of the four matching lightshades had a crack. Also, some crystals were missing from the dining-room chandeliers. "Maybe we can find them at an antique shop in Chor Bazaar."

"First things first, Roxie! There's only one month to complete the repairs, and you're worried about a cracked light shade?"

"Yes, you're right, Yezdaa. I'm just so excited."

Once the work got underway, they went to select fixtures for the bathrooms and pick out the tiles. At the Cera dealer they examined basins, toilets, and a variety of faucets and shower heads. "It's like a dream," she kept repeating. "Most families in Bombay spend their whole lives in a one-room-and-kitchen. We're actually going to a big renovated flat. I worry I'll wake up, the dream will end."

He too was awed by their sudden change of fortune but had less difficulty accepting it because he knew God was firmly in control. Her exhilaration amused him. But at Restile Ceramics he had to stop her from looking so eager about the vitrified floor tiles. The salesman was lurking like a vulture, he whispered, and the price would shoot up.

Next, they began comparing brands and features for kitchen appliances. Roxana liked the Maharaja line of Turbo Mixie, Juicer, and Toaster. Yezad was adamant that the refrigerator be a Godrej, a venerable Parsi product. As for air-conditioning, they would have two Voltas window units, one each for the dining room and drawing-room. More could be added later, for the bedrooms.

During the renovation Yezad developed a new routine. After Wadiaji fire-temple in the morning, he went to Chateau Felicity. To keep an eye on things, he said. He came home for lunch, had a nap, and returned to the site, staying till the workmen left for the day. Then it was Aslaji agiary, where he spent at least an hour before the fire. He prayed with the Avesta open in his hands, though many sections had now been committed to memory.

At Chateau Felicity, whenever they saw Yezad, the workmen nudged one another and joked that the inspector had arrived. Each day there was at least one minor crisis with the labourers or tradesmen: internal quarrels, injuries, material delivered late, wrong items sent. Yezad tried, often without success, not to lose his temper with them.

Fortunately, Jal was usually present, and seemed to know how to sort things out, or at least smooth them over. Much of the time he managed to divert Yezad on an errand.

Sometimes, Yezad carried his irritation home with him, grumbling and fretting before Roxana. "These idiots don't know what they are doing. And Jal is a softie, being a gentleman with people who only understand tough talk."

"Calm down, Yezdaa. If something is wrong, tell Mr. Lakdavala – don't argue with the workers. You're getting upset about too many little things."

"If you ignore little things, they become big problems."

Once a week she went with him to see how the repairs were proceeding, when a representative of Hafiz Lakdavala & Sons was available to discuss any changes to the original specifications. She relished this weekly witnessing of progress in the sprucing up of their new home.

"Looks lovely, doesn't it?" she said to Yezad.

He nodded, keeping an eye on kitchen cabinets being unloaded, ready to yell if he saw any carelessness.

"Are you happy, Yezdaa?"

He nodded again.

At the appropriate time, she took the boys to see their rooms and select the colours for the walls. Yezad stayed home that day, to look after Nariman.

The bustle and noise of the workmen in Chateau Felicity fascinated Murad. He wandered about the flat, exploring the pile of materials and picking up tools to examine.

Jehangir was subdued. He watched his brother without tagging behind as he normally would have.

"What's wrong, Jehangoo?" said his mother when they returned home. "Why so sad?"

"I'm not sad." But after the prompt denial he added that all this hard work seemed like such a lot of trouble, just to go and live there. "Why do we have to? Our Pleasant Villa is so nice."

His parents laughed as though he had intended a joke.

He persisted with more objections, and Yezad understood

453

his son's uneasiness. "Think of it, Jehangla, such a beautiful big flat. Lots of space for us."

"There's enough space here, we all fit inside here."

"But see how crammed it is," said his mother. "No proper bed for you or Murad, and poor Grandpa stuck on the settee."

"He likes it, and I like sleeping beside him. And Murad likes his tent."

His mother tried again, "Remember the room I showed you? All yours. You'll have your own cupboard, your own desk, bookshelf. You can put up your drawings and pictures, whatever you like. You'll live like the Famous Five."

"Enid Blyton is rubbish," said Jehangir quietly.

There was silence. His father looked at him with delight. "That is correct, Jehangla. But having your own room is still a nice thing. And now, young man, decide what colour you want."

He liked being called young man. His father had never said that before, he thought, as he pretended to examine the paint chips they had brought back with them.

Murad was quite definite about his choice: he wanted pale green walls. But Jehangir seemed overwhelmed by the responsibility. He struggled to make a selection from the limitless palette spread out on the teapoy, then gave up. "You choose for me, Mummy."

She picked a cheerful yellow and asked if he liked it.

"It's beautiful," he said without emotion.

An elegant new brass plate, large enough to accommodate everyone, was ordered for the front door. Jal suggested the names should be engraved in alphabetical order:

Mr. & Mrs. Yezad Chenoy
Mr. Jal Contractor
Mr. Nariman Vakeel

ON MOVING DAY, four weeks after the renovations had begun, Jal came with an ambulance to take his stepfather home. A hospital ayah had been hired; she was waiting at Chateau Felicity to receive the patient. Roxana said it was such a load off her mind on this hectic day, knowing that Pappa was safe.

"But how will the ayah know what Grandpa means?" asked Jehangir. "Will she understand the sound of his words?"

"She will learn. And in the beginning, we can explain it to her."

While the ambulancemen were getting ready with the stretcher, Daisy came upstairs to say goodbye to Nariman. "It's been a pleasure, Professor. Thank you for tolerating my practice, all my mistakes."

Nariman smiled and murmured something. She leaned closer to hear, laughed, and shook his hand.

"What did Pappa say?" asked Roxana.

"He wants a farewell concert."

They laughed again, then Roxana and Yezad walked her to the landing. "I don't know what we'll do without you, Daisy," she said. "We won't be able to get you every time Pappa needs you."

Daisy nodded sympathetically.

"There's an excellent radiogram there," Yezad reminded them, "with lots of records. We'll play those for him."

"And if the records don't help," said Daisy slyly, "you can always recite your prayers." She waited on the landing and waved to Nariman as the attendants went past with the stretcher.

Soon after the ambulance left, the movers arrived. The boxes containing the good dishes, the rose bowl, the porcelain were identified for them, and they began carrying the furniture out. Yezad stationed himself on the footpath to watch over the lorry; he had been warned by the helpful Mr. Hiralal that it was common for things to disappear during loading.

Murad stayed upstairs to help his mother with the bathroom and kitchen last-minute packing. Jehangir went downstairs. Listless, he stood beside his father and watched as their belongings were swallowed up in the dark bowels of the lorry.

Late in the afternoon the movers were ready to leave. Yezad gave them instructions not to unload till he arrived, then returned upstairs with Jehangir.

He found Roxana and Murad standing in the middle of the empty front room. "I've checked everything," she said in a small voice. "Shall we go now?"

"I'll take a look as well. Coming?" Yezad asked Jehangir.

He shook his head and went to the balcony. Yezad watched him lean on the railing, crying.

"What is it, Jehangla?"

"I'm feeling very sad."

Yezad put his arm around him. "It's always sad when something ends. I felt the same when I had to leave Jehangir Mansion. But without ending the old, you cannot begin the new."

"I don't want the new, I like the old."

"That doesn't make sense, Jehangla. It's like saying you don't want to end the fifth standard. How would you get to the sixth? You want to spend your whole life with Miss Alvarez?"

Jehangir smiled through his tears – it seemed a very pleasant prospect, but he couldn't say this aloud to his father. He kept staring at the road.

Yezad waited, feeling dishonest, not believing any of the sensible words he'd uttered. The same dilemma tormented him. He wanted his sons to become men, but he loved the little boys he could carry on his shoulders; he, too, wanted to conquer time.

He took Jehangir's hand. "Come on, let's look together, one last time."

They went to the back room, their footsteps echoing sharply in the vacant space. Jehangir was wide-eyed, as though trying to imprint permanent images. In the kitchen he caressed the brass taps. He visited the bathroom and the toilet.

"If I want to see it again, will Mr. Hiralal let me?"

"He seems like a nice man," said Yezad. "I'm sure he will."

They returned to the balcony, and Jehangir whistled to the parrot across the road. "Bye bye, parrot sweetie."

The bird, locked in its frenzy of side-to-side hopping, did not answer. Jehangir tried again, and Yezad added his whistle to entice a response. The parrot ignored them both.

Villie Cardmaster was waiting at her door when they emerged from the empty flat. She hugged the boys, then offered her hand to Yezad. He gave it a quick reluctant shake and started down the stairs as she put her arms around Roxana.

From the landing below, he could hear them thanking each other for being such good neighbours, and Villie saying she would miss them dearly, it would be very quiet now on the third floor.

"Hurry up, Roxana!" he called between the banisters. "The lorry is waiting there for us."

They took a taxi, and Murad insisted on sitting next to the driver. The latter leaned towards him to reach the meter outside, and Murad offered to do it.

"Hanh, baba, you do it," the driver said good-humouredly.

457

Murad tilted the lever and pushed down the flag to start it ticking. "Very good, baba," said the driver.

They turned to look at the building. Roxana said, a little wistfully, that it was a nice flat even though it was tiny, and they had always been happy in it.

"Except for this last year," said Yezad.

"Yes." She thought for a moment. "Never mind, from now on life will be wonderful, in our big new house."

"Not new for you, Mummy," said Murad. "You're going back to your old house."

"But I have my whole family with me this time. That makes it new. And this time it will be a very happy place."

"Will I have to sleep in my own room tonight?" asked Jehangir.

"No," she reassured him, reading his thoughts. "You and Murad have to share, till all the repairs are finished."

He smiled and reached to the front seat to give his brother a poke.

"Are you happy, Jehangoo?" she asked.

He gave a tiny nod.

While the taxi waited at the kerb for a break in the traffic, they heard violin music. Roxana gazed at Pleasant Villa, at the wrought-iron balconies, the entrance arch, the old stone steps she had climbed countless times. A bird, perched on the ground-floor window, was chirping diligently.

Good omens, she thought.

The taxi began to move, and Jehangir turned for one last look. Then a moth floated lazily out from the darkened interior of the stairwell. He watched it fly straight towards the bird's open beak.

EPILOGUE

～

FIVE YEARS LATER

D ADDY AND MURAD had another fight today. They quarrel almost every day now. This one started when Murad returned from the barber shop in the afternoon, his hair styled *en brosse*.

"Does it have to be so short?" said Daddy. "Makes you look like a skinhead thug."

Mummy tried to avert an argument, laughing nervously, that wasn't it funny, a generation ago parents got upset because boys were keeping their hair too long. "How times change. Remember your college ID photo, Yezdaa? Hair to your shoulders!"

"Don't exaggerate, it was just a bit overgrown. Anyway, all the holy prophets had long hair – Zarathustra, Moses, Jesus. Why can't your son learn to resemble a normal human being?"

Murad kept smiling, pretending it was only a joke. At times, this tactic works; Daddy criticizes, then returns to the book he is reading or to his prayers. But it can also make him fly into a rage, that he is not a barking dog to be ignored, he will be heard and heeded.

In the case of the haircut, though, the long and the short of it was forgotten, and the fight took a different turn. Murad ventured much too near the drawing-room corner that Daddy has lately claimed as his prayer area.

Here, set up on a cabinet, are framed pictures of Zarathustra and the Udvada fire-temple, along with a silver model of the Asho Farohvar, photographs of the ancient remnants of the Persian Empire, the ruins at Persepolis, palaces, fire altars, and royal tombs of the Achaemenian and Sassanian dynasties. The arrangement of items is in a rough semicircle

461

that keeps growing. His latest acquisition is a miniature afargaan, plastic, with a tiny electric fire. Its filament flickers day and night at the centre of the semicircle.

This is the same glass-fronted cabinet that used to be filled with toys and knick-knacks. And the two clockwork monkeys, the drummer and the boozer, which were the cause of the fight when we had come for Grandpa's birthday party, years ago – at least six or seven, I think.

After Coomy Aunty died, Jal Uncle donated the toy collection to the Bandra orphanage. The cabinet stood empty for many months till Daddy took it over. Now his prayer books are inside, as well as his collection of additional holy items for which there is no room in the semicircle.

"Stop!" he shouted, as Murad wandered absently towards the cabinet.

There was real panic in his voice, and Murad froze. "What's wrong?"

Jal Uncle came out of his room, looking worried. He has a new high-tech hearing aid. You can hardly see it in his ear. Sometimes, he tries to make peace between Daddy and Murad, but he's been accused by Daddy of interfering in private family matters, and rarely opens his mouth these days.

Mummy complains to Daddy that it's not fair, first it was Coomy who used to shut poor Jal up, now he is doing the same. He replies that Jal is free to talk about anything except this one topic.

So Jal Uncle stood outside the drawing-room, quite miserable. The old habit of fiddling with his antique hearing aid made him touch his ear even though the new one needs no adjustment. Then he returned to his room while the argument continued.

"How many times must I explain to you?" said Daddy through gritted teeth.

"Explain what?" Murad was genuinely mystified.

"You are in the prayer space in your impure state. After a haircut, you are unclean till you shower and wash your head."

"That's idiotic. I'm not even touching your holy cabinet."

"Fifteen feet away, I told you! The minimum distance!"

"Calm down, Yezdaa," pleaded Mummy. "He'll remember next time."

"This is the twenty-first century," said Murad, "and you still believe such nonsense. It's sad."

"Fine, be sad," said Daddy.

"No, please don't say that, Yezad," implored Mummy. "I don't want anyone to be sad."

When Daddy reaches a certain stage of excitement, Murad enjoys baiting him. He no longer fears Daddy's temper, the way we used to as children.

"How did you get the exact figure? Did Zoroaster whisper it in your ear?"

"Your son is a wit-and-a-half, isn't he? Don't use Zoroaster, that's a Greek perversion of our prophet's name, say Zarathustra. And before you mock me, read the scriptures: Vendidaad, fargard XVII, explains the distance."

"Sorry, Daddy, I don't have the leisure to read all this interesting stuff. It's hard enough to finish my college work."

For the last few years, ever since we left Pleasant Villa, Daddy has been reading nothing but religious books, as though making up for lost time. In addition to the holy cabinet, my parents' bedroom has filled up with volumes about Parsi history and Zoroastrianism, various translations of the Zend-Avesta, interpretations of the Gathas, commentaries, books by Zaehner, Spiegel, Darukhanawala, Dabu, Boyce, Dhalla, Hinnells, Karaka, and many, many more. Some of them used to be in a bookcase that belonged to Grandpa's father. His name is inscribed in them on bookplates: *Marazban Vakeel*. But Daddy has been purchasing as well, in great quantities. Mummy suggested once there was no need to buy every single book, there were libraries to borrow from. She gave in because he kept complaining his spirit was being denied basic bread and water.

But the jibe, about leisure to read, hurt Daddy. He has not

worked since Bombay Sporting shut down. It did reopen later with a new name: Shivaji Sports Equipment, and the owner's wife never asked him to come back. The investments from the sale of Pleasant Villa used to provide just enough money to run the household and to meet Grandpa's expenses. Mummy had made up a new budget, with new envelopes. But after Grandpa died, she got rid of all the envelopes, she said we could be more relaxed now about spending. She doesn't mind that Daddy isn't working.

By and large, his fervent embrace of religion makes her happy. She agrees with him that the entire chain of events, starting with Grandpa's accident and ending with Mr. Kapur's murder, was God's way of bringing him to prayer.

Wounded by Murad's taunt, however, Daddy turned to her, his expression a child's who has been slapped without warning. And when Mummy sees him like this she behaves like a protective mother. She tried to shoo Murad away to the shower.

But he was not yet ready to end the argument. "I'm confused – I don't know how far exactly the fifteen feet extend."

"I've told you, this sofa is the boundary."

"That's a rough estimate, Daddy. You'll only achieve approximate purity. I think we should take a measurement and draw a line on the floor, so we all know how far to go."

Daddy appealed again to Mummy: "Our faith is a subject of ridicule for your son."

"What if an impure fly or mosquito or cockroach violates the sofa boundary? Do you check if they've showered? Maybe you should enclose your cabinet in a bubble."

"Enough!" Daddy dragged him by the arm to the other end of the room. "You approach that side again in your unclean condition and I'll break your legs!"

Murad laughed, "You're getting hysterical now," and I wished he would stop.

"Go for your shower," said Mummy quietly, and he left the room. He still listens to her when she uses the tone that would warn us, when we were small, if we were about to cross the limit of what was acceptable.

Meanwhile, Daddy said his chest pains were back, and asked for the angina medicine. He bewailed the fact that in his anger he had grabbed that saitaan's arm, the contact had made him unclean in the bargain. Now he too would need a full shower.

My father has emerged from the bathroom, and is doing his kusti by the cabinet. His expression is always very intense when he prays. He finishes tying the knots and sits with his prayer book before the electric afargaan, in the wooden chair no one else is allowed to use. He sits as though he is carrying a secret burden, whose weight is crushing him. He frowns a lot, his face contorting in pain. He doesn't just close his eyes, he clenches the eyelids shut, the cheeks rising, the brows pressing downwards to squeeze out whatever it is that haunts him. His Avesta recitations – the various Yashts, Gehs, Nyaishes, depending on the hour – are like a rebuttal, a protest. He is locked in a struggle.

Seeing my father like this, I think of him as he used to be, so jovial. Nowadays he hardly smiles, let alone laughs. And he never whistles, never joins in with songs on the radio. The last time I heard him sing was for Grandpa, the night before he died. And the radio is seldom played – only while Daddy is out of the house. When he is home, he's either praying or reading, and says the music disturbs him.

Mummy watches from the passageway, smiling contentedly, for things are back to normal after the haircut argument. She is pleased to see him at prayer, happy to arrange her routine around his requirements. The housework, the servant's comings and goings all revolve around Daddy's prayer schedule.

But there are times I've noticed her wringing her hands, looking worried when he prays on and on. Those must be her moments of doubt. I'm sure she wishes he wouldn't go to such extremes, and occasionally she voices her anguish in my presence: "If only Dada Ormuzd could help me understand! Why must prayer and religion lead to so many fights between father and son? Is that His will?"

When my father sits by himself, gazing out the window or pretending to read, I have seen her go to his side and put her hand on his shoulder. I have heard her ask him tenderly, "What is it, Yezdaa, is something worrying you?"

His answer is always the same: "Nothing, Roxie, I'm fine." Then he pats the hand on his shoulder, kisses it.

She strokes his hair. "Are you happy, Yezdaa?"

He smiles a sad, melancholy smile. "As happy as a soldier of Dada Ormuzd can be, fighting against Ahriman."

This type of vague answer with a spiritual flavour is his way of avoiding serious conversation. But she'll never be able to bring herself to say he should pray less. That, to her, would be blasphemous. So she blames his extremes, his new beliefs and practices on his new friends in the societies he has joined.

The League of Orthodox Parsis and the Association for Zarathustrian Education meet once a week. He returns from their sessions to tell us in detail about the agenda considered and the action taken, the petitions circulated and injunctions filed, the campaigns to be waged against films or publications that have given offence. All this provides more fodder for Murad.

Yesterday, Daddy told us over dinner that the League had discussed the 1818 case of a Parsi bigamist – married a non-Parsi woman in Calcutta, then moved to Bombay and married a Parsi. "For his crime he was excommunicated by the Panchayat," said Daddy, raising his hand to signify the gravity of the punishment. "And his father was told to disown him or he, too, would be."

"That doesn't seem fair," said Mummy. "Why excommunicate the father?"

"Why not? I wouldn't want to be known as the father of

such a scoundrel. But the bigamist reacted by insulting the high priests and the Panchayat, who went to court against him. Then things became so serious, he got scared, and asked to make a formal apology to end the matter. An Anjuman was called, where he had to confess his crime and humiliate himself by taking a pair of shoes, one in each hand, and striking his head five times with them. Right before the assembly."

"Were they brand-new shoes or old dirty shoes?" asked Murad.

"That wasn't noted in the Panchayat records. The point is, our committee members have agreed unanimously to challenge the Reformist propaganda – we will campaign to reintroduce a strict policy of excommunication. Parsi men and women who have relations with non-Parsis, in or out of marriage, will suffer the consequences. Excommunication will be reversed if they repent publicly with the shoe punishment."

There was silence around the dining table for almost a minute. Jal Uncle fiddled with his hearing aid, looking as though he wanted to speak but dared not. Most of his day he spends in his room, only joining us for meals. He no longer goes to the share bazaar. Sometimes, when Daddy is out, he will sit in the drawing-room to read the newspaper. He tries to keep to himself as much as possible.

He and I began to laugh now because Murad ducked under the dining table, emerged with his slippers, and started hitting the top of his head with them. Mummy pressed her lips tightly together, doing her best to smother her amusement. But her face could remain straight for no more than a few seconds.

For Daddy, hers was the ultimate betrayal. "Purity and pollution is not a laughing matter. Your son behaves like a jackass and you encourage him."

"I'm not laughing at you, Yezdaa," she soothed him. "I'm laughing at this clown."

"Just practising, Daddy, in case I have to take the punishment someday."

Murad's jokes are like the ones Daddy himself used to

crack when we were small. I remember once, long ago, we'd all gone to fire-temple on Khordad Sal, and after we came home Daddy had imitated a man we'd seen sliding along the walls of the main hall, kissing every photo-frame and portrait his lips could reach. And I also remember conversations Daddy and Grandpa would have, about the silliness of slavishly following conventions and traditions.

Grandpa died a year after we moved to Chateau Felicity. I think it was very lonely for him to have his own room again. In Pleasant Villa, in the front room, there was always someone near his settee.

At first we made an effort to keep him company, sitting by his side, talking to him and to one another. Sometimes I took my homework to his room. But it was not the same. Especially with a hospital ayah who did everything for him. The day he overheard Jal Uncle and my parents having a discussion about hiring her full-time, he became very upset. He began to cry, No ayah! Please, no ayah! I don't think they understood.

Her name was Rekha. Mummy explained her duties and demonstrated exactly how she wanted things done, in the hygienic manner to which she and Grandpa were accustomed. Rekha followed the instructions when she was being watched. But Mummy often caught her skipping steps if she came upon her without warning. Usually, it was the urinal – she would not rinse it clean each time Grandpa used it. I remember, once, Mummy found her proceeding to fetch Grandpa's soup from the kitchen after emptying the bedpan, not bothering to wash twice with soap and water.

"Your toilet hands you use to carry food?" shouted Mummy. "Not even once did you apply sabun!"

"Aray, bai, I forgot this time."

"I've seen you lots of times, taking shortcuts!"

Rekha's way with Grandpa bordered on roughness in things like turning him, changing the sheets, plumping the pillows. Her brisk manner of wielding the cloth during sponge baths made Mummy wince. She often took it away from Rekha and finished the sponging herself.

When Grandpa's mouth was scalded with hot tea from the feeding cup, it was the last straw. His scream made Mummy run to his room. I went too. Rekha pretended he had yelled in his sleep, there was nothing wrong. But Mummy noticed the unusual way Grandpa's mouth was hanging open. She went closer and examined it, saw the red beginning of blisters, smelled tea on his breath, and discovered the hot feeding cup hidden behind bottles on the dressing table.

Rekha was sent packing. She had lasted two months. It took a few days to find someone new, during which Mummy and I looked after Grandpa again. He seemed more at peace then.

The replacement was a wardboy in his thirties, a gentle fellow called Mahesh. Mummy especially liked the delicate way he applied ointment to the two bedsores on Grandpa's lower back, one on either side of the spine where the big bone, which Dr. Tarapore called the ilium, protruded. The sores had formed during Rekha's employment, and Mummy blamed herself for trusting that careless woman to do the work.

By the time Grandpa died, his back was covered with sores. Some were horrible, big and deep. Every time I looked at them, I felt a sharp pain in my back. The smell of pus and the sulpha ointment was always in the room. Grandpa didn't make a sound despite the agony he was going through. I wished he would scream. To see him lie quietly was more sad. Could he feel nothing?

Months passed under Mahesh's care. Grandpa continued to shrink. And when Dr. Tarapore told us the inevitable was perhaps a day away, two at best, I remembered the promise.

I reminded my parents. Mummy couldn't concentrate on what I was trying to say. She appreciated the doctor's well-meaning attempt to prepare her, but now that the end was approaching, she was too distressed to listen to me. "Please, Jehangoo, ask Daddy, I don't know what to do."

My father's opinion was that the promise wasn't a serious one, more like a joke between Grandpa and the violinist, and it wouldn't be fair to expect Daisy to keep it. Jal Uncle felt the same way.

"I think Grandpa was very serious," I said. "So was Daisy Aunty. They even shook hands to make the promise."

"But, Jehangla, look at Grandpa – he's almost unconscious. How will it help, whether she comes or not?"

I kept pestering my father all day because I felt it was extremely important. In the evening he got fed up with me. "Fine," he said. "You go and tell her if you want to. I can't leave Mummy and Grandpa alone at a time like this."

I walked to Pleasant Villa. It was faster than waiting for a bus, as they would be packed at this hour and the driver wouldn't have stopped.

This was my first visit to Pleasant Villa since we'd moved. The entrance steps seemed smaller. I remember the sadness that came over me as I went in, thinking about our old flat upstairs, how it might look now, what kind of furniture Mr. Hiralal had put in the rooms. I knocked on Daisy Aunty's door.

There was no sound of practising inside. I knocked several times, and just when I was giving up, Villie Aunty climbed the three steps and entered the building with her shopping basket.

"Hello, Jehangirji! What are you doing here?"

"I came for Daisy Aunty."

I could see her wondering why, but instead of inquiring she asked, "How is everyone?"

"Fine, thank you," I said quickly, knocking again.

"She went out with her violin," Villie Aunty volunteered. "I met her as I was going to the market."

"Do you know where?"

"Max Mueller Bhavan is what she said, for rehearsal."

I knew where that was: near Regal cinema. Should I go? Daddy had given me permission only as far as Pleasant Villa. But waiting till next day could mean Grandpa dying without the promise being kept.

This time I took the bus, the distance was too much to walk. I pushed myself onto the 123 bus. A half-hour later I got off where it turned the traffic circle past the museum.

Crossing the road took a long time, the cars kept coming, no one was obeying the traffic signals. When there was a jam I managed to run through to Max Mueller Bhavan.

Inside the building I wondered where to go. The office was empty, everyone had left because it was after six. But I heard music, many violins playing together, and I followed the sound.

It led me to where they were practising. I opened the door and peeked. The hall was dark and empty though the stage was lit, and Daisy Aunty was sitting in the first chair on the stage, next to the conductor. The music went on and on, no one could see me. I was not sure what I should do.

I waited. At one point all the instruments became silent except for the two cellos. The music was so sad, I felt my heart would break.

Suddenly, the conductor waved his baton from side to side like a windshield wiper, as though it was saying, Stop that! Cancel that! Everyone went quiet. He began to discuss something. Daisy Aunty pointed to the page on her music stand. Checking in his own book, the conductor hummed and moved his hands funnily. "Molto sostenuto," he said, and the orchestra nodded.

This was my chance, before they restarted. As I hurried towards the front I stumbled into a chair. It fell over. The entire stage looked startled, and the conductor said, "Yes? What is it?"

Then Daisy Aunty, who was peering into the darkness like everyone else, rose and came to the edge of the stage. "Jehangir? Is that you?"

"Yes, Aunty," I answered softly.

"Come closer. Are you crying?"

I hadn't realized I was. It must have begun while I was waiting in the dark. I quickly wiped my eyes. She got down on her haunches so her face came closer to mine – I was still quite short then, though now I've grown taller than her. She held the violin and bow together in her left hand and grasped my shoulder with the right. I liked her hand, her strong fingers made me feel better.

"What's wrong, Jehangir? Your parents know you're here?"

I shook my head and told her why I'd gone to Pleasant Villa. Her face became sad as I repeated Dr. Tarapore's words about Grandpa.

"To be honest, I had completely forgotten the promise."

I started to turn away.

"Wait, I'm glad you came. Give me a minute."

She spoke to the conductor and vanished to the side of the stage, then reappeared with the case for her violin and bow. I wondered if she was going to leap down from the stage. It was so high, and she was wearing high heels. But she went to one corner where there were steps I hadn't seen. She descended into the hall, waving to the conductor: "See you tomorrow, everybody."

She walked very fast. I half-ran to keep up. She called a taxi, and since I only had bus fare, I let her know. She smiled, telling me there was enough in her purse, and gave the driver the address for Pleasant Villa.

"But, Aunty, we don't live there any more!" I assumed she had forgotten in a moment of absentmindedness.

"I know. But I've to change my clothes first."

My eyes discreetly scrutinized her outfit: a pair of light brown pants and a pale yellow blouse with long sleeves that she had rolled up to her elbows. Worried about not getting to Grandpa quickly, I assured her that her clothes looked very nice, there was no need to change.

"Thank you. But they are not suitable for the occasion."

She asked the driver to wait, and we went inside. I sat in the front room while she disappeared to the back. There were lots of music books in the room, three music stands at different heights, two extra violins. It was an untidy room, but I felt comforted in it.

In a few minutes, I heard the sound of Daisy Aunty's heels approaching, tick-tocking like a very loud clock, and I turned to look. I will never forget what she was wearing: a long black skirt, very beautiful, and a black long-sleeved blouse with something in the cloth that made it twinkle like stars. Her shoes were black too. A string of pearls clung to her neck.

I recognized these clothes, she would dress in them for the big important concerts of the Bombay Symphony Orchestra. I used to see her from our old balcony upstairs, when she would step outside with her violin case and call a taxi. I always thought she looked gorgeous, like a picture in a magazine.

And now she had dressed the same way for Grandpa. She was the most wonderful lady I'd ever met. My throat felt like it was choking. We got back in the taxi, and she told the driver to take us fast to Chateau Felicity.

The door opened with a frown, Daddy was looking quite upset. "Where have you been? At a time like this, making us worry."

Then he saw Daisy Aunty standing to the side. Her lovely clothes had a calming effect on him, and he asked her to please come in. "I'm so sorry. Has he dragged you away from an important performance?"

"But this is the performance," she said. "Shall we go inside?"

We went to Grandpa's room, where everyone was gathered. Mummy sat by the bed, holding his hand. It barely shook now. Jal Uncle and Murad were standing behind her chair. Mahesh waited in the corner on his stool, fidgeting, wishing there was some work he could do for his patient.

Mummy looked over her shoulder and, seeing Daisy Aunty, began to apologize like Daddy for my inconsiderateness.

"Please, I promised," was all she said.

"Oh Daisy! Poor Pappa – I don't think he can even see you."

"That doesn't matter." While she moved to the side and tuned the violin softly, I could see Jal Uncle looking at her, wanting to go up to her but feeling awkward.

Then she approached the foot of the white hospital bed, glittering in her black clothes. I remember that she bowed solemnly to Grandpa before starting. Mahesh watched with great interest; he must never have had a patient for whom a splendidly dressed woman had played the violin. Daddy said in my ear it was the Serenade by Schubert. I knew that; she had played it before, many times, for Grandpa. Her eyes were closed. I kept mine open, I wanted to see and hear everything around me.

Maybe it was the mood in the room, but I don't think she'd ever played more beautifully in front of us. I looked at Grandpa, and felt he could hear the music, because his face had a contented expression.

Then Daisy Aunty began the Brahms "Lullaby," which Grandpa loved so much. Daddy whispered that he used to sing this tune for Murad and me when we were babies, he said it was also a Bing Crosby song that his father would sing to him. He hummed the words under his breath, "'Lullaby and good night . . .'"

Daisy Aunty heard it, and turned sharply. I thought she would be annoyed, but she said, "Sing it louder."

And Daddy stood up and sang it, and I saw tears running down his cheeks too, like Mummy's. "Excuse me," he said at the end of the piece, and took out his handkerchief.

Daisy Aunty played for over an hour, till Dr. Tarapore arrived, as he had promised that morning. She ended with Grandpa's favourite song, "One Day When We Were Young." When she finished she stood quietly for a moment, bowed again, then put away her violin.

There was a hush in the room. It lasted till Doctor said he wanted to check Grandpa, see if there was anything more he could do to make him comfortable. He took the blood pressure, as though, like Mahesh in the corner, he too needed something to occupy him. The wrap around Grandpa's arm puffed up as the rubber bulb was pumped. The column of mercury rose, dancing up and down. Then the air was let out, and Doctor murmured to Mummy that the professor was resting quite peacefully.

He sat with us for a few minutes, speaking some words to Jal Uncle and Daddy, patting Murad and me on the back, giving us cheerful smiles. Then he packed his bag and shook hands with everyone, including Mahesh in the corner. The last thing he did was to take Grandpa's hand in both of his and whisper, "Good night, Professor."

After Daddy had seen him to the door, Daisy Aunty said she had a bit of good news to share. She spoke as though she was addressing Grandpa and he was listening. He was right, she said, she was going to get her wish, and would be performing the Beethoven concerto with the BSO later that year, at the NCPA.

My parents congratulated her. Jal Uncle edged forward as though he would shake her hand, then held back shyly.

She told us the date and took out some passes from her purse. Looking around to count us, she separated five from the wad. Now Jal Uncle went closer, to receive them from her hand. He said he would attend, definitely, and put the passes safely in his pocket.

Daisy Aunty clicked her purse shut, kissed Grandpa's cheek, and left.

Very early the next morning, Daddy came to wake me. Grandpa had died a short while ago. "Come," he said.

The sun was just rising as we passed the window. I slowed down to see the colour of the dawn sky. Not yet cerulean, I thought. Daddy's hand on my shoulder drew me along. Murad was up already, he was with Mummy in Grandpa's room.

The clock in the passageway struck six. I stood at the foot of the bed and looked at Grandpa. A small oil lamp had been lit on the table beside his head. It was strange to see his hands and feet absolutely still. For as long as I could remember, they had always trembled.

"Come," said Daddy again, and led me next to the pillow.

I kept moving my eyes away from Grandpa's face. On the other side of the bed sat Mummy, crying silently with her hands joined as though she was praying. Murad and Jal Uncle left the room now, and Daddy told me to give Grandpa a kiss, I wouldn't be allowed to touch him later, after the prayer ceremonies began. I asked if Murad had kissed him.

Mummy nodded from across the bed to encourage me. I leaned forward, a little scared, and, without putting my arms around him as I used to, kissed him quickly. It did not feel like I was kissing Grandpa.

And suddenly I understood what dying meant. Nothing would ever be the same, Grandpa was gone forever. I began to cry.

Daddy held my arm and led me away from the bed. I squirmed in his grasp as though to escape, but I didn't know where else I wanted to be. Mummy held out her hand and I ran into her arms. She said that Grandpa was happy now, no more pain or sickness for him.

Her crying made her choke on the words, and Daddy gently patted her back. He lifted my face from where it was buried in her shoulder, and hugged us both together, Mummy and me.

He led me closer again, right next to Grandpa. He told me to look at the face, see how serene was the expression on it.

I looked. I wasn't sure what I saw. A little later, the hearse arrived from the Tower of Silence.

After the funeral and four days of ceremonies, after Mummy finished the vigil and came home from Doongerwadi, she no longer cried – as though it didn't matter to her any more that Grandpa was dead. I remember how much I resented that.

Then the rented hospital bed was sent back, the urinal and bedpan scrubbed and put away in storage. Bit by bit, all signs of Grandpa began to vanish.

Mummy told me I, too, should stop crying now, or it would make Grandpa's soul unhappy. "Think of the good memories, Jehangoo. Remember the first day when Grandpa came to us by ambulance?"

I nodded.

"And you fed him lunch, doing aeroplanes with the spoon?"

I tried my best to smile.

"He used to have so much fun playing with you, no? How he laughed at your aeroplane noises."

"I spilled some food on his shirt. You scolded me."

"Yes, I had to, I'm your mother. But it was beautiful to see you feeding Grandpa. And how you and Murad used to stroke his bald head and squeeze his chin."

My fingers still remember the feel of Grandpa's jujube chin. It was such a unique sensation, the combination of tiny stubble and rubbery skin.

Mummy kept trying to cheer me up, and I kept nodding. But next day, while I was growing used to the absence of the white bed in Grandpa's room, all his medicine bottles were taken away from his dressing table, for donation to the charity hospital.

"Why can't you leave Grandpa's things alone?" I protested.

"Grandpa is in heaven, Jehangla," said Daddy. "He doesn't need them any more. Dada Ormuzd is providing for him now. Clothes, ice cream, pudding, everything." And Mummy smiled, agreeing with this jolly idea of God's tailoring and catering services.

I think I scowled back at them. I knew they were trying to be humorous to make me feel better, but I wasn't in the mood for it.

Grandpa's smell stayed in his room though his things were gone. I went there often. After a few days even that disappeared.

When Jal Uncle reminded us of Daisy Aunty's concert with the Bombay Symphony Orchestra, Mummy said it was only three months since Grandpa's funeral and she did not feel right about going. Daddy said he felt the same way.

I disagreed, saying they had encouraged me to think happy thoughts, and here was something nice we could enjoy, the music that Grandpa liked the most. What sense did it make to waste the passes Daisy Aunty had given us?

They tried to explain the convention of mourning, the observance of social proprieties, the expectations of the community. I refused to accept any of it.

Eventually, Mummy said that she and Daddy weren't going, that was final. And Jal Uncle and Murad and I could do as we wished.

Now that the responsibility for the decision was on my shoulders, I no longer felt so confident. All through the week I kept agonizing over it, wondering what Grandpa would have wanted me to do.

On Friday morning, the day of the concert, I made up my mind. Before leaving for school I told Jal Uncle I wanted to go.

So we went, just the two of us. That evening he wore his best suit and tie. I ironed a long-sleeved shirt and long pants for myself. It was an enormous auditorium, much bigger than Max Mueller Bhavan, where I had seen the orchestra practising. The sign told me what NCPA meant: National Centre for the Performing Arts. It seemed such an important place, I was almost reluctant to enter.

The foyer was crowded with beautifully dressed people. Some women's saris looked more expensive than Mummy's wedding sari. I smelled perfume, and it reminded me of Miss Alvarez, though hers was much nicer, it didn't feel like a headache the way this did. Jal Uncle and I were very alone in the excitement around us. Everyone except us seemed to know everybody else.

But once the bell rang and we were in our seats, the lights dimmed and I didn't care about other people because the orchestra came out to the stage, then Daisy Aunty came out with the conductor, and I knew her – the most important person there. She was wearing the beautiful black clothes she had worn for Grandpa.

Taking her position to the left of the conductor, she put the violin under her chin and checked its tuning. The conductor signalled to the orchestra, and all the instruments played one note. He seemed satisfied with the sound. Raising his baton, he nodded at Daisy Aunty. The concert began.

I felt a great surge of pride when her solo part entered the score. For me, that was the most thrilling moment of the concerto. I'm sure Jal Uncle and I clapped more loudly than anyone in the auditorium.

At the end of the concert, after the encore, Jal Uncle suggested saying hello. We were swept up the aisle along with the rest of the audience, out into the foyer. There, we followed the corridor to get behind the stage.

People had surrounded Daisy Aunty, saying congratulations, a magnificent interpretation, so fresh and energetic. Some of them gave her flowers. We stood back, and waited our turn.

Then she saw us, and broke through the crowd to shake Jal Uncle's hand and give me a hug. "Did you enjoy it?" she asked.

I nodded, smiling, though I wanted to say something, not stay dumb like a shy little boy. I also wanted to tell her that I was feeling good for the first time since Grandpa died.

Meanwhile, Jal Uncle managed to murmur that the concert was wonderful, before becoming tongue-tied again. He too kept smiling, gazing with admiration at Daisy Aunty.

"It was very nice of you to come," she said, and prepared to return to her fans.

It was now or never. "Not at all," I said, "the pleasure was all mine."

Daisy Aunty beamed; I could see she was delighted with my answer. Now she and Jal Uncle talked a little more. She asked him if he would like to go to another concert – she had passes for something called the Bolshoi Ballet. He said yes at once.

I was disappointed she didn't invite me, but I knew it would be better for the two of them to be alone. I was sure Mummy would also like that.

Then, as she was getting ready to leave us, she stopped suddenly and came closer. "You know, just before I came out on stage this evening, I was thinking of Professor Vakeel. I was imagining him in the audience."

I wanted to say that I too had been thinking of Grandpa. But I think she already knew that.

DADDY HAS CAUGHT MURAD kissing a girl in the stair-well. He comes in grim-faced and announces it to Mummy, whose first concern is if it's someone from the building, anyone we know.

"She is a non-Parsi," he answers in a doom-laden voice, and leaves the room. Mummy hurries after him, inquiring anxiously if words were exchanged downstairs, how did it end, does he need his angina medicine?

"I would not give a parjaat girl the satisfaction of seeing me argue with my son. At least he had the shame to leave, the moment he saw me. But just wait till he's home."

The threat, and his tone, makes Mummy fear that a big fight is looming. She spends the next hour in the kitchen, cutting and chopping, preparing dinner, fretting, shaking her head, till the doorbell rings. She wipes her hands and rushes to the drawing-room, father and son must not be left alone.

As she goes in, Jal Uncle puts down his newspaper and returns to his room. I can see Mummy wanting to tell him, Stay, it's your house too, but she thinks better of it.

"So what do you have to say?" begins Daddy as Murad enters.

"About what?" he asks innocently.

"That girl. Who is she?"

"Oh, you mean Anjali – she's in my college. We were just waiting for some friends."

"So you always kiss girls when you're waiting for friends?"

Then Daddy stops himself and lowers his voice. He sits on the sofa, asks Murad to sit in the chair opposite. "I don't want us to shout at each other. This is very serious, please listen carefully. This friendship of yours . . ."

He pauses to clear his throat, searching for words. "Your relationship with this girl is not possible."

"What relationship?" laughs Murad. "We're just friends, I told you."

"A girl you kiss in that way cannot be just a friend. Either she's your girlfriend, which is unacceptable, or you're having your fun with her, which is even more unacceptable."

"We're both having fun."

Daddy clutches his forehead. "A child thinks playing with matches is fun. But we still have to stop it. This will go nowhere, it cannot have a happy ending."

"We're not thinking in those terms, okay?"

"You see?" he appeals to Mummy. "He listens to nothing. From the trivial to the most significant matters of life, he listens to not a word."

He turns to Murad again. "I'm warning you, in this there can be no compromise. The rules, the laws of our religion are absolute, this Maharashtrian cannot be your girlfriend."

"It's just prejudice," says Murad.

"Nothing of the sort. My best friend was a Maharashtrian, Vilas Rane, the letter writer. Remember, he used to give me picture books for you when you were little? You can have any friends you like, any race or religion, but for a serious relationship, for marriage, the rules are different."

"Why?"

"Because we are a pure Persian race, a unique contribution to this planet, and mixed marriages will destroy that."

"You think you're superior?"

"Inferior or superior is not the question. Purity is a virtue worth preserving."

Now Murad appeals to Mummy. "See? It proves he's a bigot. Hitler had the same kind of ideas about purity, and look what happened."

Daddy loses his temper. More because he is hurt than because of Murad's obstinacy. He shouts and bangs his fist on the teapoy, complains his chest pains are returning, then leans

482

back exhausted, muttering under his breath – how can two boys be so different, look at Jehangla, obedient, hard-working, caring, and look at this fellow, also my son but behaving like a total ruffian, what kind of person calls his father by the name of the greatest monster of the twentieth century?

"Yes, really, Murad," says Mummy. "That's shameful. You should not call your father Hitler."

"I didn't. Don't you listen? I said he had the same kind of ideas about purity."

Daddy is not interested in semantics. "Just to show you the contrast, I suggest you consider what your Maharashtrian friend was doing with you under the stairwell. A Parsi girl would never behave in such a way."

"That's pathetic," snaps Murad, and goes to his room. "You can keep ranting."

I remain in the drawing-room with my face down in my book. I feel like telling my father that he is mistaken. Farah Arjani, who lives on the ground floor, is the great-granddaughter of the late Mr. Arjani, the one who had the feud with Grandpa's father. She and I were alone in the lift last week. We were laughing about something, and I teased her, she shoved me, I shoved back, and soon we were holding each other tight, pretending to fight, pressing against each other and kissing, and I squeezed her breast. If the lift doors hadn't opened, she would have let me slip my hand inside her T-shirt.

Mummy tries to reason with Daddy. "What Murad is doing is only natural, Yezdaa. Next week he'll be eighteen complete, nineteen running. How long can we treat him like a boy?"

"Till he behaves like a man. Till he understands his duties as a Zarathushtrian."

She clasps her hands together and looks towards the holy cabinet, at the flickering filament in the plastic afargaan, as though seeking divine intervention. "I just had a great idea, Yezad. About your friend the letter-writer."

483

"What idea?"

"It's difficult for you and Murad to talk calmly. He says silly things, you get angry, and it turns into a fight."

"Is that my fault?"

"No, it's not. But why don't you write him a nice long letter? Explain everything logically? Our son is sensible, and you always say there is a scientific basis to our religious laws, so show him that. And you could ask your friend to help you write it, he's a professional."

"Are you mad?" says Daddy, highly insulted. "First of all, that old life of mine is finished, I don't want to renew contact with Vilas. Second of all, he wrote for illiterates. For unschooled labourers who never learned their ABC or Ka Kha Ga. He was not some Shakespeare who could compose a letter to melt your son's uncaring heart. And third of all, if a father cannot talk to his son face to face and has to write letters, he might as well forget his son."

Mummy winces, and looks again towards the prayer cabinet.

Jal Uncle, careful to stay away from this huge argument, has kept busy cleaning out the cupboards in the spare room, sorting out items for donation to a charity drive that Daisy and the BSO have initiated. Now he brings some things to show us, and I get the feeling he is trying a diversionary tactic.

But he is very emotional as he opens a small box. "Look what I found," he says, and we crowd around him.

Inside, there are two pairs of gold cufflinks and two sets of shirt studs. There is a note with them: *For Murad and Jehangir, on their wedding.*

"That's Coomy's handwriting!" says Mummy.

"Yes," says Jal Uncle. "You know how methodical she was. And these buttons – they belonged to our father, to Palonji Pappa. Seems like Coomy saved them for the boys."

My mother has tears in her eyes now, and wipes them away quickly. The discovery of Coomy Aunty's box is confusing. And makes me feel sad. What am I to think now? There were such few hints from her about her feelings towards Murad and me.

"Put them in a safe place, Jal," says my father. "We'll honour Coomy's wish when the happy day arrives. What else have you got there?"

Jal Uncle shows us a stack of holy pictures he found in one of the cupboards: Sai Baba, Virgin Mary, a Crucifixion, Haji Malang, several Zarathustras, Our Lady of Fatima, Buddha.

"Where did these come from?" asks Daddy.

"I remember seeing them as a child," says Jal Uncle. "They used to hang all over the flat. You know how, in those days, it was usual for most Parsis to keep tokens of every religion. Pappa took them down after Mamma and Lucy died."

Daddy examines the pictures, some in frames and some yellow and curling. There are dates on the framing boards of several, I notice, going as far back as 1869.

While on the subject, Jal Uncle mentions the dour portraits of Grandpa's ancestors hanging in the long passage. "I'm not particularly attached to those gloomy faces," he jokes. "If you want to use the frames for something else, feel free."

"No," says Daddy. "They are the elders and achievers of the community, the stalwarts. If there were more of them alive today, the Parsi komm wouldn't be in such dire straits. They must stay as an inspiration to us all. Especially to the boys."

"And the holy pictures?"

My father wants time to decide about them.

Because it will be Murad's eighteenth birthday in two weeks, Mummy plans to make it special. She suggests inviting a dozen of his college friends for a little party from five o'clock to seven o'clock. Dinner would be restricted to eight people: our family and three of his closest friends – my father doesn't like big crowds.

"Just make sure that the Maharashtrian girl is not one of the three," said Daddy when he heard about the plan.

"She is," said Murad at once. "Anjali will stay for dinner."

And the fighting begins again.

My father resorts to preaching what he has assimilated from the meetings and discussions of his religious societies, citing scripture, quoting commentaries by high priests. I've heard it so often, I could rattle it off by heart.

"You're becoming more and more fanatical," says Murad. "I don't understand what's changing you, Daddy."

"You will, as you get older. It's a spiritual evolution. You will reach a stage in your life when you too thirst for spirituality."

This makes no impression on Murad. He says that perhaps the League of Orthodox Parsis could invent a Purity Detector, along the lines of the airport metal detector, which would go beep-beep-beep when an impure person walked through.

"You think the question of purity, the life and death of our community, is a joking matter?"

"I think bigotry is certainly to be laughed at."

"Don't throw words around. It's a modern trend to call people names if you don't agree with them."

"What do you have against my friend?"

"We've been through that. I know where your friendship is going with that girl, and I won't tolerate it in my house. If she comes to dinner, it will make me sick. I will vomit on the dining table, I'm warning you."

Murad says to Daddy that his ideas make him feel like vomiting too, and between the two of them they could launch his birthday party on a sea of vomit.

"Stop it, Murad!" cried Mummy. "Don't say such disgusting things!"

"He started it. He's using religion like a weapon. Do you know the obsession with purity is creating lunatics in our community? I'm never going to accept these crazy ideas."

"Shameless rascal! Calling his father a lunatic! That's it, I'm leaving, I'm going to fire-temple, I cannot look at his face any more!"

"Why don't you set up a little tent in the main hall? You could live inside it, the amount of time you spend there."

"Hear that? Your son wants to turn me out of the house!"

"He's cracking a silly joke, Yezdaa. Aren't you, Murad."

"No, I'm serious, I'm planning to go to Pleasant Villa and borrow Villie Aunty's big tablecloth for Daddy."

"Oh, Villie was so helpful to us," laments Mummy upon being reminded. "And we never did thank her properly. Never even told her we were moving, till the very last minute. I'm so ashamed."

"She should be the one to feel ashamed," says Daddy vehemently, astonishing all of us. "She tempted me with Matka and made me gamble, something I'd never done in my life."

This is more than even Mummy can take. Without a word she leaves the room.

On the Zoroastrian calendar, which we follow for prayers and religious ceremonies, the roj for Murad's birthday falls four days earlier. To mark this day, Mummy has ordered sweetmeats from Parsi Dairy Farm. The servant, Sunita, who comes to clean every morning, is sent to buy flowers: toruns to hang in the doorways. And Mummy cooks ravo for breakfast, seasoned with cardamom, nutmeg, and cinnamon and garnished with lots of raisins and blanched almonds. The kitchen smells delicious this morning.

"Why are you celebrating his birthday twice?" asks Daddy.

"Because it's his eighteenth – you know that."

"Two treats for a boy who does not deserve even one," he remarks, and she makes a disapproving face at him.

When I return from school in the afternoon, Mummy wants me to go to the building across the road and deliver two sweetmeat boxes: one to Dr. Fitter, the other to Inspector Masalavala.

I put up a mild protest: I hardly know them, she should have sent the mithai with Sunita in the morning. Their names, of course, are familiar to me; I know they were very helpful after Coomy Aunty's accident. And I've also heard the stories about the doctor and the inspector's father intervening on Grandpa's behalf, when Lucy and my grandmother died.

"Sending a servant is not the same," explains Mummy. "It shows more respect when a family member presents the mithai."

So I take the boxes of jalebi on a tray, covered by a cloth embroidered with peacocks in its four corners. First I stop at Inspector Masalavala's flat. He is not home, his servant informs me at the door, and following Mummy's instructions, I ask for Mrs. Masalavala.

"Yes?" she appears suddenly, as though she has been listening in the next room. "Who is it?"

"Jehangir," I say, "Roxana Chenoy's son, from Chateau Felicity." I point over my shoulder, hoping that will help identify me. "Nariman Vakeel's grandson."

"Oh yes yes yes, I recognize you," she says to my relief.

I put my hand under the cloth and slide one box out. "Mummy has sent mithai for Inspector and you. It's my brother's roj birthday – his eighteenth."

"Oh yes yes yes, how nice. Please say happy birthday to him from us. And say thank you to your mummy." She takes the box as though it were her due, seeing me off briskly.

Glad that it was short, I go to the flat opposite the Masalavalas', hoping for a similar swift exit. But Dr. Fitter, who opens the door, interrupts my introduction and, with a broad smile, takes me by the arm.

"Of course I know who you are, young man. Come in, come in for a minute. Tehmi! Tehmi!"

Mrs. Fitter answers from inside: "Now what is it, Shapurji, how will I get your dinner ready if you keep bothering me?"

Scolding away, she comes to the veranda, walking with a heavy stoop. In her hand is a knife she has been using to chop something, I can see green specks upon the blade. "Hullo? Nariman's grandson is here, and you don't even tell me?"

She puts the knife down on the teapoy, wipes her hands on her skirt, and pinches my cheek. I smell coriander, fragrant on her fingers. Then I uncover the tray and hand over the jalebi, delivering Mummy's message.

"Murad eighteen already!" she says, taking the tray from me. "How wonderful! And you are?"

"Fourteen," I answer, "fifteen running."

Dr. Fitter smiles. "The new generation, ready to rule the world. And you will make it a much better place, I hope? Sit, tell me which school you go to."

He chats with me for a while as Mrs. Fitter disappears with the mithai. I am anxious about the tray – will she remember to bring it back? Meanwhile, Dr. Fitter declares how good it is that our family is living in Professor Vakeel's flat.

"For much too long there was an emptiness in that house. An absence . . . Your grandfather, he had a very unfortunate life. I still remember the day he came downstairs to speak to his girlfriend – the day he was wearing only a towel around his waist."

Dr. Fitter chuckles at the memory. I nod knowingly and try to prompt him to talk some more: "My parents always say you were so kind to help my grandfather."

He shakes his head to dismiss the thanks. "The least we could do, Superintendent Masalavala and I. And even then, even without a police case, how many rumours were flying – was it double murder, was it double suicide, was it pure accident?"

I feel as though the colour is leaving my face, and hope he doesn't notice. "Rumours are always on the human agenda," I remark smartly, grateful for the words.

Dr. Fitter laughs. "Just the kind of thing Professor Vakeel would say. Of course, you can't blame people, it did look suspicious."

Mrs. Fitter returns for the knife she has left behind, and

overhears. "What are you doing, Shapurji," she reproaches him. "These are not matters to discuss with a little boy."

"Fifteen running is not a little boy, Tehmi. And your grandmother – what was her name?"

"Yasmin."

"Right – her dying words made it even more complicated."

I hold my breath. "Did you hear her yourself?"

"Of course I did. I remember it like yesterday, me rushing outside when the two of them fell, then Masalavala hurrying over . . . And the Catholic lady – what was her name?"

"Lucy."

"Right. She died instantly. But your grandmother was conscious, managing to speak a little. And all the confusion was due to one word in her sentence: did she say 'he' or 'we'?"

"What do you think she said?" I inquire meekly.

"Oh, I know what she said. She said, 'What did we do!' But there were other people gathered around. Some of them heard, 'What did he do!' and they claimed it incriminated Nariman."

Dr. Fitter gestures to indicate he doesn't believe it. "People don't bother to think clearly. A last cry of regret, about their miserable marriage, their wasted lives – that's what it was."

"But what made them fall?" I ask.

"All I know is, Nariman and Yasmin and Lucy followed their destinies as they were engraved on their foreheads. That's all. All there ever is."

Mrs. Fitter brings back the tray with a small mound of sugar on it. I thank her and cover it with the peacock cloth. They both come to see me to the door, making me promise to visit again.

I return the tray to Mummy in the kitchen, who is delighted to find the sugar that acknowledges the mithai. "Was it Mrs. Fitter?" she inquires, and I confirm her guess with a nod.

I go to my room and lie on the bed. I think of all the things

I've heard, over the years, about Grandpa and Lucy and my grandmother. And the picture is still not complete. Like some strange jigsaw puzzle of indefinite size. Each time I think it's done, I find a few more pieces. And its form changes again, ever so slightly.

My old jigsaws, including the beautiful Lake Como puzzle, are still on my shelf. And my Enid Blyton books, though I can't bear to even open them. I wonder what it was about them that so fascinated me. They seem like a waste of time now.

Jumping off the bed, I gather the whole lot in a box and carry it to the passageway where Jal Uncle has stacked the clothes, shoes, crockery to be donated to Daisy Aunty's BSO charity drive. My contribution of books and jigsaws goes on top of the pile.

There is only one puzzle worth struggling with now.

My father has at last decided about the holy pictures. He must have consulted his Orthodox League friends. He returned this afternoon from the meeting and said that all the non-Zarathusti images must go – in a Zarathusti home, they interfere with the vibrations of Avesta prayers.

"It's no wonder there is so much quarrel and fighting in this house. Once the pictures are gone, my prayers will be more efficacious. Understanding will come to Murad."

He said they should be disposed of properly, in keeping with the Zarathustrian tradition of respect for all religions, which, he explained to me, went way back to Cyrus the Great, the founder of the Achaemenian dynasty, who set the example when he conquered Babylon, liberated the Jews who were there in captivity, and even helped them rebuild their Temple, earning him the title of God's Anointed in the Hebrew Bible.

"We'll make a packet of the pictures, along with flowers, and offer it to the sea, to Avan Yazat, for safekeeping."

He sent me to buy the flowers – a garland, he specified. He wrapped the holy pictures in brown paper and looped the garland around the packet, a ribbon of marigolds.

I went with him to Chowpatty. We walked till we reached the firm wet sand and the shimmering water. A mild foamy surf teased our feet. The tide was going out, the waves were spent. And the gulls were loud, wondering if we'd brought anything edible.

My father touched the packet to his forehead and asked me to do the same. Then he tossed it into the sea, into the protecting arms of Avan Yazat.

We sat on the sand for a while, looking out to the horizon, where the sun was slowly slipping into the water. We sat in silence, Daddy with his secret burdens and me with my countless questions about him locked in my head. I wanted to tell him I still loved him, but couldn't understand the new person he had become, I much preferred the father who made jokes, who could be funny and sarcastic, who could be angry one minute and laughing the next, as loving as he was headstrong, and able to stand up without clutching at religiousness for support. I wanted to ask him about his childhood in Jehangir Mansion, and to hear again the stories he used to tell about the neighbours, and the friends he played cricket with, and his teachers at St. Xavier's, especially the Gujarati master they called Ayo, and the Madrasi one with the funny pronunciations whom they had nicknamed Vada.

There was so much I wanted to ask and tell my father, all the things that filled my head whenever I was alone. But with him beside me, they remained frozen on my tongue.

Some children scampered past, raising sand with their feet. A sugar-cane vendor stopped to tempt us. He moved on when my father shook his head.

"Shall we go? The sun has set – time for the Aiwisruthrem Geh. I must recite it before dinner."

I checked the receding waves for the packet of holy pictures and flowers. It was nowhere in sight. We walked across the beach towards the road. I liked the sinking feeling, the labour of trudging in the soft sand.

Daddy has passed the menstruation laws. At least, that's what Murad calls them.

The decree states that Mummy must not enter the drawing-room at all while she has her period. She will sleep in the spare bedroom on those days, and avoid the kitchen. The cook will take her meals to her.

The servant, Sunita, who comes half-a-day to sweep and dust, wash the dishes, clean the bathrooms, will not enter the house during her time of the month. It's Mummy's job to monitor Sunita's cycle, which she finds very awkward.

"He's gone over the edge," says Murad. "Deep into the abyss of religion."

Daddy ignores him and goes to his room, his instructions complete. Mummy follows, trying to reason with him. "You've never believed in these things. Why start now?"

"Because it's the right path. It is standard procedure in an orthodox household."

"Orthodox households I know all about, Yezad – my mother's family followed those same practices. But you and I have never lived like that."

"I was ignorant before. Now I have studied the religion, attended the lectures of learned men."

They don't know I am listening to their conversation. As always, I see and hear everything. Sometimes it becomes so depressing, I wish I could turn a deaf ear to it.

My father promises to throw Murad out of the house if he does not live by his rules. My mother says not to make threats he wouldn't carry through.

"Just watch me," he replies. "If your son won't stop his nonsense with that girl, he and you will both find out."

She cries that it's easy for him to say such horrid things. "But I'm his mother. I carried him inside me for nine months and brought him into the world with the pain of childbirth. You might as well kill me if you are going to throw my child out of the house."

Jal Uncle intervenes and makes matters worse. He offers to let Murad stay in his part of the flat, in his room, out of his father's way, till things settle down, the crisis blows over, and Yezad and Murad learn to get along.

"Is this why you asked us to come and live here?" shouts my father. "So you can interfere in our life? So you can have the pleasure of driving a wedge between father and son?"

Jal Uncle tries to point to the illogic of his accusation. "I'm doing just the opposite, Yezad. You want to chuck him out, I am saying I'll keep him safe for you, till you and he are ready to be friends again."

"Mind your own business," says my father, and goes to prepare the coals for the evening loban.

My mother grieves by herself about the ceaseless quarrelling and bitterness that has taken hold. She confides in me that Grandpa, during those last days at Pleasant Villa, had tried to warn her not to move to Chateau Felicity, into his house of unhappiness. She is sure of it now, certain that that was what Grandpa had tried to tell her, and she did not heed him.

Daddy is dismissive, saying a house is only bricks and mortar, it is up to us to be unhappy or happy in it.

But my mother isn't convinced: "Learn from this, Jehangoo. Listen to the advice of elders. When we grow up, we think we know everything. We assume old people are not right in their heads. Too much pride we acquire with our years. And then it brings us down."

My mother repeats this regret over and over. Her conscience hurts, she says, because she did not do everything she could for Grandpa.

When my father overhears, he gets very annoyed. He says she is addicted to melodrama, deliberately distorting the events of five years ago, when she was a virtual slave to her father. "If anything, you went to the other extreme, neglecting the rest of us because of him."

The accusation leaves her aghast. "Is that how you feel?" She turns to me. "I neglected you?"

I shake my head, and Daddy says, "Don't ask Jehangir, he was too young then to understand what was going on."

"I was nine years old, I understood everything."

"Sure. You don't even remember half of it."

"Ask me anything," I challenge him. "I remember exactly what happened."

"Ah, we all think we do," says Daddy.

But Mummy is certain that Grandpa would have lived longer and been happier if she had continued to care for him instead of hiring strangers. "The proof is in the bedsores. For almost a year I washed Pappa and kept him clean and dry, and he was fine. Soon as the ayah and wardboy came, the bedsores appeared."

"Nonsense," argues Daddy. "In bed for so long, he would have got sores no matter who was nursing him. Just coincidence."

"You say there is no such thing as coincidence," she points out. "You call it another word for the Hand of God."

He waves her away. Then she pleads again for Murad and Anjali, begs Daddy to let her come to dinner, gives the example of Grandpa and Lucy, and how it led to lifelong strife and misery for so many. The stronger the attempt to separate them, the more stubborn they could become. "For all you know, they'll make new friends and this will fizzle out."

"And what if it doesn't?" asks my father. "What if it becomes more serious? One more nail in the coffin of the Parsi komm. And you will be responsible for hammering it in."

A compromise has been reached. Daddy agrees to let Anjali come to the birthday dinner, provided there is a special rearrangement of the furniture in the drawing-room. It must be deployed to form a barricade at the appropriate distance from the prayer cabinet.

This takes care of Daddy's main worry, that someone might pollute the prayer space. Tomorrow, Murad and I will move the sofa, chairs, and tables to erect this *cordon sanitaire*, as my brother calls it.

Jal Uncle says to me, "Wouldn't it be nice if Daisy also came for dinner?"

Taking the hint, I mention it to Mummy, and she agrees right away. I think she is still hoping they'll start chirping like two lovebirds, though Jal Uncle has been content just to go to concerts with Daisy Aunty and leave it at that.

Yesterday, Mummy ordered more boxes of sweetmeats from Parsi Dairy Farm: jalebi, sooterfeni, burfi, malai-na-khaja. They will be delivered tomorrow morning – the English calendar birthday. She wanted to send a box for Villie Aunty too, but Daddy said that that old life was finished, there was no need to keep in touch with people in Pleasant Villa any more.

We assemble near the prayer cabinet. The floor, prepared by Mummy early in the morning, is decorated with chalk patterns. She has used a fish motif stencil because fish are auspicious. They are of white chalk powder, their eyes are imprinted in red.

Jal Uncle waits by the record player for his cue. At a signal from Daddy he starts the "Happy Birthday" song, an instrumental version. We provide the lyrics. Mummy enters the drawing-room with the round silver tray that holds everything she will need for the ceremony. She sets it down on the table and motions to Murad to come forward.

"With your right foot," she reminds him.

Murad steps gingerly into the chalk patterns, his feet among the fish, and smiles at us. And while we sing to him, there he stands in his prayer cap, borne aloft on the backs of the fish who oblige because it is his birthday.

From the silver tray Mummy picks up the garland of roses, lilies, and jasmine. Murad lowers his head so she can slip it round his neck. Next, she places in his hand all the symbols of good luck and prosperity: betel leaves and betel-nuts, dates, flowers, a coconut. She dips her thumb in the little silver cup of vermilion and applies the paste to his forehead in a long vertical teelo. Finally, she takes grains of rice in her palm and presses them against the teelo, making a few stick to his forehead. She takes more rice and sprinkles it over him, her hands moving in a lovely arc that could be part of a dance.

She holds him in a long hug, whispering things in his ear that I can't hear. The rest of us are still singing. Then she steps back, and it's Daddy's turn.

He goes to the silver tray, gathers rice in his hands, and sprinkles it too. There is a new wristwatch in the tray, Murad's birthday gift. Mummy has left it for Daddy. We wait, wondering how he will deal with it. She puts her fingers over her mouth to hide her anxiety.

He reaches for the box, hesitates, leaves it in the tray, and takes Murad's left wrist. He unbuckles the strap of the old watch and puts it aside, then picks up the new one from the tray. It has a metal band, and he passes it gently over Murad's bunched fingers, settling the dial on the wrist before turning his hand over to snap shut the clasp.

Still keeping Murad's hand in his, Daddy finally looks into his face. For a few moments they hold each other's unwavering gaze. Now Daddy places his right hand on Murad's head, over the prayer cap, and I think he is saying a prayer. Murad waits without rolling his eyes or displaying any sign of impatience.

Then Daddy relieves him of the flowers and betel leaves and nuts, returns them to the tray, and hugs him. Murad responds by putting his arms around Daddy.

Jal Uncle and I have stopped singing, feeling silly about repeating the verse more than three times; besides, the record has ended. We can hear Daddy whispering, "Happy birthday, my son. Live a long, healthy, wealthy life, and lots of happiness."

Mummy starts bustling around to hide the fact that she is crying. She tells me it's my turn to wish my brother, as Jal Uncle steps aside after presenting Murad with an envelope. It contains one hundred and one rupees. I know, because he sent me to the bank yesterday to fetch crisp new notes.

I go up to Murad, to the edge of the chalk fish, and pause, not sure if he will like me hugging him. So I give him my hand: "Happy birthday, Murad."

He takes my hand, then yanks it towards him. As I lose my balance, he puts out his arm to keep me from falling and hugs me. We both laugh at the trick.

"Come on, everybody," Mummy hurries us, "the sev is ready, let's eat it fresh before it sticks to the bottom of the pot."

Murad shows Jal Uncle the new watch as we go to the dining room. I linger behind, observing Daddy lost in thought on the sofa. Mummy stops beside him. He looks up and smiles sadly.

"Yezdaa? Is something wrong?"

He shakes his head and gives her another small smile.

"And, Yezdaa, the kitchen clock needs winding."

"Later," he answers. "Or you can ask Murad."

THE AFTERNOON PARTY IS OVER, Murad's friends have left, but it is not yet time for the dinner.

I sit in the drawing-room, looking beyond the special barricade of furniture, at the prayer cabinet in its protected corner. I imagine it full of toys and knick-knacks as it once was, the sad fragments of Coomy Aunty and Jal Uncle's unhappy childhood. Now it is filled with Daddy's holy items. And he is just as unhappy.

Jal Uncle is in his room, getting ready. He has been excited all day because Daisy Aunty is coming to dinner – she accepted the invitation the moment Mummy made it on the telephone.

To my surprise, Mummy is putting out the rose bowl and the porcelain shepherdess in the drawing-room. The dining table is set with the good china that Grandpa gave to her and Daddy on their wedding. She comes in with a vase, strokes the shepherdess, runs her fingers along the scalloped rim of the rose bowl.

"All these things were gifts from Grandpa," she smiles. "Aren't they gorgeous?"

I nod. It reminds me of the time long ago when Grandpa came to live with us in Pleasant Villa. And how my world suddenly became a much bigger place, much more complicated, and painful. I think of Grandpa sleeping on the settee beside me, holding my hand to comfort me. And later, me holding his when he had bad dreams. I think of the violin music we enjoyed. And the words he taught me, the stories he told, to describe and understand the world.

"Remember what Grandpa said to us one day?" continues my mother. "To take pleasure in these beautiful things, to defeat the sadness and sorrow of life?"

I feel she is seeking approval for her decision to use the

good china today. So I nod again. I try to recall an earlier time, before Grandpa arrived, a time when the world was so safe and small and manageable – my parents were in charge of it, and nothing could go wrong.

"Can you help me for a minute in the kitchen, Jehangoo?" she calls on her way out of the drawing-room.

"Yes," I answer, but stay in my chair. I wonder what lies ahead for our family in this house, my grandfather's house, in this world that is more confusing than ever. I think of Daddy, who makes me feel that my real father is gone, replaced by this non-stop-praying stranger.

My mother, hurrying as always, brings in more things from the kitchen. My face must have a faraway expression, for she comes closer, her hand reaching out towards my shoulder. She hesitates, leaving the gesture incomplete. I can sense her fingers an inch away.

Then she lets them settle lightly on my arm. "What is it, Jehangoo? Aren't you happy?"

"Yes," I say. "Yes, I'm happy."

Simply Fresh

RubyTuesday

Simply Fresh

CASUAL DINING AT HOME

BY JEFF MORGAN

PHOTOGRAPHS BY
BEALL + THOMAS

Andrews McMeel
Publishing, LLC
Kansas City • Sydney • London

Andrews McMeel Publishing, LLC
an Andrews McMeel Universal company
1130 Walnut Street, Kansas City, Missouri 64106

www.andrewsmcmeel.com

www.rubytuesday.com

11 12 13 14 15 SDB 10 9 8 7 6 5 4 3 2 1

ISBN: 978-1-4494-0826-8

Library of Congress Control Number: 2011921499

Packaged and designed by Jennifer Barry Design, Fairfax, California
Layout production: Kristen Hall
Photography: beall + thomas, Kreis Beall and Heather Anne Thomas
Food styling: Michael Pederson
Prop styling: Lynda White and Jeff Wood

ATTENTION: SCHOOLS AND BUSINESSES
Andrews McMeel books are available at quantity discounts with bulk purchase for educational, business, or sales promotional use. For information, please e-mail the Andrews McMeel Publishing Special Sales Department:
specialsales@amuniversal.com

Table of Contents

FOREWORD BY SANDY BEALL   ix

INTRODUCTION   xi

DRINKS   1

APPETIZERS & SIDE DISHES   19

BRUNCH   49

SALADS & SOUPS   69

PASTA   93

SEAFOOD   109

BEEF, PORK, & POULTRY   127

DESSERTS   165

BASICS   191

ACKNOWLEDGMENTS   198

INDEX   199

Foreword

This is a book about fresh, simple, great-tasting food and how to prepare it, but it's also a book about connecting and sharing, because food lets us do that. Being with family and friends, talking and listening, telling each other about our lives and understanding more about what's important—those things happen at mealtimes. Food brings people together in meaningful ways.

My wife, Kreis, and I discovered soon after we were married that we loved to create menus, shop for ingredients, cook together, select a few bottles of wine, and then gather our friends and family for a simple supper, a summer lunch on the terrace, or brunch before a game. We learned to use whatever was at hand, to mix and match china and put out the silver from our grandparents, cover the table with an heirloom quilt and cut flowers from the yard to create a special setting for a special, simple meal. We came to realize we could do it inexpensively, and that it's fun!

That was more than 30 years ago, just about the same time I opened the very first Ruby Tuesday. And as I look back on the growth of our company from one restaurant to nearly a thousand, I realize that a big reason for our success is the love of making and sharing fresh, full-of-flavor dishes, prepared with the very best ingredients, never fancy for fancy's sake, always generously served with gracious hospitality. Restaurants like ours are casual, welcoming places where people know they can meet a friend, have a date, take time to sit down with their family, and get the kind of food and drinks they know and love.

The pages ahead show you how to prepare many of our most popular dishes, and along with that, they include some new takes on classic American food. They also help you make handcrafted drinks and give you the confidence to pair wine with food without fear. Jeff Morgan has done a great job of adapting the work of our culinary team to steps you can follow at home. The recipes are simple to prepare, fun to serve, and meant to encourage you to gather your friends and family for simple, fresh meals and precious times together. Our mission at Ruby Tuesday is to make people happy, and I hope Simply Fresh will help you do that, too.

—Sandy Beall, founder, Ruby Tuesday restaurants

Introduction

Soon after I began writing this book, I came to appreciate how Ruby Tuesday founder Sandy Beall's commitment to fresh, wholesome ingredients extends to the people who work with him, particularly his team of talented chefs. These culinary artists source their menu items from farmers who place a premium on agricultural sustainability. Whenever possible, meat and poultry come from animals that have not been treated with hormones, antibiotics, or other drugs. Fresh eggs are from cage-free hens, and, in general, a preference is maintained for livestock raised in a humane manner. Knowing this has given me great confidence in Ruby Tuesday. It has provided me with a sense of discovery and delight at seeing a large restaurant chain with a genuine concern for food integrity.

Ultimately—in addition to providing tasty meals—Ruby Tuesday's mission is to help care for our planet and serve food with no artificial trans fats, MSG, high-fructose corn syrup, or other ingredients that can have a negative impact on our bodies or the environment. It's no wonder that the menu also includes organic greens, fresh, seasonal local produce, and sustainable seafood.

The title, Simply Fresh, says a lot about what's in these pages. The recipes are uncomplicated and generally feature ingredients that are budget friendly. And every dish is rooted in the kind of fresh, wholesome food used in the restaurants.

I have tried to highlight the equally fresh, vibrant flavors featured at Ruby Tuesday, where you'll find the menu retains a contemporary style that honors America's culinary diversity without losing sight of its traditions. It is a culinary philosophy I am honored to share with you.

As a result, Simply Fresh offers a wide variety of recipes to please a broad audience. American standards like slow-cooked baby back ribs, classic burgers, and fried chicken with gravy are here in all their homespun glory. But readers will also find more esoteric fare, such as Crab Cakes with Corn and Pineapple Chutney or Cowboy Sirloin with Red Chili Rub, Caramelized Onions, and Blue Cheese Butter.

Where there's great food, there should be something fun to drink, as well. To that end, I've included recipes for a number of Ruby Tuesday's most popular bar drinks, along with advice for making mixed drinks at home like a pro. Over the years, Ruby Tuesday has created a wine list with an exciting international selection to suit every dish and every diner. With this in mind, the book presents simple guidelines for selecting and pairing wine with food, whether you're entertaining at home or eating out. Plus, nearly every recipe includes a suggested wine pairing.

The flavors on your dinner plate begin in the farms, fields, and waters that provide us with exceptional bounty. Knowing how to select fresh ingredients and what to do with them in your own kitchen should be easy and fun. Throughout the book, you'll find tips and techniques that Ruby Tuesday's executive chefs have generously shared with me. They will guide you in the kitchen, at the market, and when you entertain.

Many of my best memories are associated with home-cooked meals. Thanks to Ruby Tuesday, we can all enjoy this easy-to-follow guide to casual dining at home.

—Jeff Morgan

Drinks

Simple Syrup	8
Strawberry Lemonade	8
Tropical Sunrise	9
Arnold Palmer	9
Ruby Relaxer	11
Cosmopolitan	11
Sangria	12
Ultimate Mojito	15
Ultimate Margarita	15
Cajun Mary	16

Drinks
Great meals are often served with memorable drinks. A cocktail can stimulate both the palate and conversation, and the classic starters featured here are among the many mixed drinks served at Ruby Tuesday. Beer can double as an opener and be served throughout the meal, as can wine. In this chapter, you will find recipes for mixed drinks with and without alcohol, short primers on wine and beer, and suggestions for pairing your favorite foods with drinks that complement them.

FOOD AND WINE: A PERFECT MATCH
Why do food and wine taste so good together? The reason is simple. All wines are blessed with natural acidity from wine grapes. That acidity, which leaves a fresh taste in our mouths, balances the natural fats and oils found in just about everything we eat, from salads and seafood to steaks.

Of course, wine offers us much more than fresh acidity. It's filled with flavor, too. But flavor doesn't necessarily provide us with the key to food-and-wine pairing. What counts most is the style of what's in our glass and on our plate.

A MATTER OF STYLE: RED AND WHITE WINES
We use terms such as full-bodied and rich to describe style. At the most basic level, food-and-wine pairing boils down to this: similarly styled wine and food often pair well together. That's why we enjoy a full-bodied Cabernet Sauvignon with a rich, juicy steak and a light-bodied Chardonnay with a delicate fillet of sole.

If you remember only one thing about wine style, it should be this: red wines tend to be lower in acidity and more full bodied; white wines are often higher in acidity and more light bodied. If you can define the style of what you are eating with simple words like rich or light, you can easily figure out what kind of wine to drink with it.

The "Right" Wine

There is a lot of middle ground here, and that's good news. It gives you many options. The most versatile wines are medium bodied; that is, they offer modest acidity and body. And they work best with dishes that incorporate both heavy and lighter elements, like light-textured chicken smothered in a rich cream sauce. Medium-bodied wines come in all colors—red, white, and rosé—and they match up with nearly every meal. Throughout this book, you'll find a broad array of wine recommendations designed to help you make your own pairing decisions with the ease of a pro.

A Perfect Match

In truth, many perfect food-and-wine matches exist, and you'll know them when you taste them. What's most important is to remain open to new flavors and possibilities. It's fun to discover a wine you've never drunk before or a pairing that's surprisingly good. Sure, some wines taste better than others, but any wine that makes mealtime more enjoyable is one worth drinking!

Wine Varietals: Red, White, and Rosé

Many of the wines served at Ruby Tuesday are labeled with their varietal name. This refers to the grape (or grapes) used to make them. For example, Cabernet Sauvignon is a red grape grown throughout many of the world's wine regions. Chardonnay is a white grape. It's as simple as that.

Varietal labeling is most common in wines from the New World, which includes North and South America, Australia, and New Zealand. In Europe, a different labeling practice prevails. France, Spain, and Italy, for example, have long referred to their wines by region. Each wine region is known to produce wines from distinct grape varieties, and it is considered unnecessary

Simple Tips for Food-and-Wine Pairing

It's hard to argue about matters of taste. So don't be afraid to drink whatever tastes good to you. Nonetheless, the following tips can help you select the best wine for dinner tonight:

1. Look for foods and wines that share similar characteristics. Are they rich or light?

2. White wines are often more light bodied than red wines. Pair white wines with lighter fare, like salads and fish.

3. Red wines are often more full bodied than white wines. Pair them with richer foods, like red meats or stews.

4. Dry rosé (pink) wines resemble both white wines and red wines. That makes them pair well with most anything. Drink them chilled.

5. Hot, spicy foods go best with chilled white wines, both still and sparkling.

6. Remember that exceptions to the rules abound. That's what makes food-and-wine pairing fun.

7. When in doubt, open a beer! (For more about beer, see page 7.)

BARTENDER'S TIP: *Basic Bar Tools and Muddling*

It's helpful to have a few basic bar tools on hand when making mixed drinks. A 24-ounce stainless-steel cocktail shaker simplifies chilling a beverage quickly by shaking it vigorously with ice. A cocktail strainer allows you to strain a chilled cocktail into a glass. (Use a small fine-mesh sieve as a substitute.) A double-ended jigger, typically with a 1-ounce cup on one end (for measuring a jigger, or shot) and a ½-ounce cup on the opposite end (for the less-potent pony shot), helps measure ingredients.

Some recipes call for muddling, a mixology term that means to mash or crush. Muddling helps release flavors and aromas from fruits and herbs. For this step, professionals and home aficionados use a tool called a muddler, a flat-ended wooden or stainless-steel baton that acts as a pestle. If you don't have a muddler, the handle of a long wooden spoon is a good substitute.

TOOLS

24-ounce stainless-steel cocktail shaker
Double-ended jigger
Muddler
Cocktail strainer

1 Place any herbs or fruits called for in the cocktail recipe in the shaker, along with any liquid specified.

2 Using a muddler or the handle of a long wooden spoon, press the fruits or herbs against the side of the shaker several times to release the juices and/or aromas. Add the remaining ingredients, cover the shaker, and shake the cocktail vigorously to mix and chill, then pour through the strainer into a glass.

to list the varietal on the bottle. Although Old World producers continue to identify their wines by region, an increasing number of them now show the varietal composition on the label, as well.

In addition to Cabernet Sauvignon, other well-known red varietals include Pinot Noir, Zinfandel, Malbec, Merlot, Cabernet Franc, and Syrah. Along with Chardonnay, Pinot Grigio, Sauvignon Blanc, Riesling, Viognier, and Gewürztraminer are among the best-known whites.

Rosé—or pink wine—can be made from any red grape variety. Normally, red wine is colored by the pigments found in red grape skins. But rosé's short skin maceration during fermentation causes the wine to turn a pale pink. Not surprisingly, rosé drinks a little like a red wine and a white wine. Like white wine, it should be drunk chilled.

The many wine varietals available today offer a wide selection of flavors and styles sure to please many tastes. It's okay to be daring when choosing a wine for dinner. The odds of finding something good are in your favor.

BEER BASICS

Beer offers many of the same taste impressions that wine does. Its bright acidity refreshes the palate, and it is produced in various styles. Some beers are pale and light textured; others are darker and richer.

Most beers can be classified as lagers or ales. These titles refer to the method of fermentation and the type of yeast used. But all you really need to know is that lagers are lighter bodied than ales. Stout, also known as porter, is another kind of beer named, in part, because it is even richer than many types of ale. It is usually dark colored with hints of coffee or chocolate, flavors that may come from the dark-roasted grain used to make it.

It helps to know a little about these different beer styles. Looking for a fresh, light beer after a hard day at work? Then maybe a lager will do the trick. Or, maybe you want to settle in with something showing more richness. In that case, ale would be appropriate.

At Ruby Tuesday, we serve a diverse selection of beers produced by many of the finest breweries in the United States and abroad. You can do the same thing at home. Instead of purchasing only one kind of beer, split up a six-pack with two different styles, one dark and one light. You can even choose different labels within the styles. It's a good way to have something on hand to suit everyone and to explore new brands.

Of course, beer's most distinctive characteristic is its bubbles, the result of naturally occurring carbon dioxide formed during fermentation. The bubbles are what give beer its freshness. Beer is much lower in alcohol than wine. Most beers hover between 4 and 6 percent alcohol; wines contain at least twice that amount.

Sometimes nothing seems so satisfying as a cold beer with a simple appetizer like Guacamole (page 25). Certainly, beer partners well with any of our burgers (pages 130 to 134). And your favorite brew might be just the ticket to accompany Fork-Tender Baby Back Ribs (page 137). Indeed, the possibilities are endless. For more ideas on pairing beer with food, see Simple Tips for Food-and-Wine Pairing on page 4. What works for wine, works for beer.

SIMPLE SYRUP

MAKES ABOUT 1½ CUPS

This standard syrup is commonly used to sweeten homemade drinks, such as the Sangria (page 12), Ultimate Mojito (page 15), and Ultimate Margarita (page 15) in this chapter. With only two ingredients and 5 minutes prep time, it is as easy to make as its name suggests. It is also available commercially, often stocked among the fruit syrups used for making drinks in the supermarket or liquor store. But the low cost of a cup of sugar makes this recipe more than worth the home effort.

1 cup water
1 cup sugar

In a small saucepan, combine the water and sugar and bring to a boil over medium-high heat, stirring occasionally, for 3 to 4 minutes, until the sugar has dissolved. Remove from the heat and let cool to room temperature.

Use immediately, or refrigerate in a glass jar or plastic container with a tight-fitting lid for up to 2 weeks.

STRAWBERRY LEMONADE

SERVES 1

Tangy yet still sweet—that's the refreshing beauty of lemonade. Mixed like a cocktail, this version includes strawberry syrup, which can be found among the fruit syrups in your local supermarket's beverage aisle. Feel free to substitute an alternative syrup, such as pomegranate, cherry, or cassis. Or, if you are a purist, you can forgo the fruit syrup altogether. If you do, add a little more simple syrup to taste (1 to 1½ ounces), or your lemonade may be a tad too tart.

Ice cubes
Juice of 2 lemons (about 1½ ounces)
¾ ounce simple syrup (left)
¾ ounce strawberry syrup
6 ounces water
¾ ounce club soda or sparkling water
1 lemon wedge
2 strawberry slices

Fill a cocktail shaker one-third full with ice cubes. Add the lemon juice, simple syrup, strawberry syrup, water, and club soda, cover the shaker, and shake steadily for 3 to 5 seconds. Pour everything in the shaker (including the ice) into a tall tumbler (about 14 ounces). Garnish with the lemon wedge and strawberry slices.

TROPICAL SUNRISE

SERVES 1

Watch a red sun rise in your glass as this colorful, nonalcoholic drink serves up a tropical taste adventure.

Ice cubes
3 ounces pineapple juice
2 ounces freshly squeezed orange juice
2 ounces mango juice
$\frac{1}{2}$ ounce grenadine
1 maraschino cherry

Fill a cocktail shaker half full with ice cubes. Add the 3 fruit juices, cover the shaker, and shake steadily for about 3 seconds. Pour everything in the shaker (including the ice) into a tall tumbler (about 14 ounces). Carefully pour the grenadine in a circle around the inside edge of the glass. It should sink straight to the bottom and then slowly rise up through the drink. Garnish with the cherry.

ARNOLD PALMER

SERVES 1

Here is a nonalcoholic, not-too-sweet refresher with a zippy citrus kick. Anyone with a sweet tooth can add more syrup to taste.

Ice cubes
4 to 6 ounces unsweetened black tea
   (such as English breakfast)
$1\frac{1}{2}$ ounces simple syrup (opposite page)
1 ounce freshly squeezed lemon juice
1 ounce freshly squeezed orange juice
1 lemon wedge

Fill a cocktail shaker half full with ice cubes. Add the tea, simple syrup, lemon juice, and orange juice. Cover the shaker and shake for about 2 seconds. Pour everything in the shaker (including the ice) into a tall tumbler (about 14 ounces). Add more ice, if desired. Garnish with the lemon wedge.

RUBY RELAXER

This juicy, fruity drink will wash away all the cares of the day.

Ice cubes
2 ounces cranberry juice
2 ounces pineapple juice
¾ ounce Peachtree schnapps
¾ ounce light rum
¾ ounce vodka
½ ounce grenadine
1 orange wedge
1 maraschino cherry

Fill a cocktail shaker half full with ice. Add the cranberry juice, pine-apple juice, schnapps, rum, vodka, and grenadine. Squeeze the juice from the orange wedge into the shaker, then drop in the spent wedge. Using a long-handled cocktail spoon or wooden spoon, stir gently to mix well. Pour everything from the shaker (including the ice) into a tall tumbler (about 14 ounces). Garnish with the cherry.

COSMOPOLITAN

This pretty, rose-colored cocktail sits high in a long-stemmed martini glass. Sip it with elegance and style.

Ice cubes
1 ounce cranberry juice
¼ ounce freshly squeezed lime juice
¼ ounce simple syrup (page 8)
1 ounce triple sec
1½ ounces Absolut Citron vodka
1 thin lime slice

Fill a cocktail shaker half full with ice cubes. Add the cranberry juice, lime juice, simple syrup, triple sec, and vodka, cover the shaker, and shake steadily for about 5 seconds. Strain the liquid through a cocktail strainer or fine-mesh sieve into a long-stemmed martini glass. Garnish with the lime slice.

Left: Ruby Relaxer

SANGRIA

Americans have come to like this festive Spanish wine punch for its fruity flavors and impressive versatility. It can stand in for cocktails or a dinner beverage and fits in at both picnics and more formal affairs. For the best result, use fruit-forward wines, white or red. And feel free to experiment with fruits other than those suggested here. With sangria, anything goes!

Ice cubes
1 (750-milliliter) bottle red or white wine
5 ounces simple syrup (page 8)
Juice of 1 lime
4 ounces vodka
1 orange, cut into 10 to 12 wedges
1 apple, cut into 10 to 12 wedges
Club soda or favorite citrus-flavored soft drink
    (such as Sprite or 7 Up)

Fill a large water glass (about 15 ounces) with ice cubes, then pour the ice cubes into a large pitcher (about 2 quarts). Add the wine, simple syrup, lime juice, and vodka. Stir gently to mix. Add half of the orange and apple wedges and let sit for 5 minutes.

For each serving, fill a 10- to 12-ounce wineglass half full with ice cubes. Pour in enough of the wine mixture to fill the glass about three-fourths full. Add an orange and/or apple wedge and top off the glass with club soda.

ULTIMATE MOJITO

SERVES 1

With its mix of tart lime juice, cooling mint, racy rum, and a splash of effervescence, this refreshing cocktail is sure to brighten every festive occasion.

8 to 10 fresh mint leaves, plus 1 sprig
½ ounce simple syrup (page 8)
Juice of ½ lime
2 ounces light rum
Ice cubes
2 ounces club soda or sparkling water
1 thin lime slice, split halfway

In a cocktail shaker, combine the mint leaves, simple syrup, and lime juice. Using a muddler or the handle of a long wooden spoon, crush the leaves. Add the rum and fill the cocktail shaker about two-thirds full with ice cubes. Cover the shaker and shake steadily for 5 to 10 seconds. Fill a tall tumbler (about 14 ounces) two-thirds full with ice cubes. Strain the liquid through a cocktail strainer or fine-mesh sieve into the tumbler. Add the club soda and stir to mix. Garnish with the mint sprig and with the lime slice, balancing it on the glass rim.

ULTIMATE MARGARITA

SERVES 1

Here's a cool, bright-tasting margarita topped with a spicy hint of Grand Marnier. It's especially enticing when served with Guacamole (page 25).

1 teaspoon salt
1 lime wedge
Ice cubes
1 ounce simple syrup (page 8)
1 ounce freshly squeezed lemon juice
2 ounces freshly squeezed lime juice
1½ ounces tequila
½ ounce triple sec
½ ounce Grand Marnier

Sprinkle the salt onto a small, flat plate in a circle about the same circumference as a tall tumbler (14 ounces). Run the lime wedge around the edge of the tumbler, and dip the moistened edge into the salt to coat it. Set the glass aside upright.

Fill a cocktail shaker half full with ice cubes. Add the simple syrup, lemon juice, lime juice, tequila, and triple sec. Cover the shaker and shake steadily for about 5 seconds. Fill the tumbler half full with ice cubes. Strain the liquid through a cocktail strainer or fine-mesh sieve into the tumbler. Top with more ice as needed to nearly fill the glass. Pour the Grand Marnier over the ice.

Left: Ultimate Mojito

Cajun Mary

This spicy Cajun Mary turns on the heat while it chills you down. Brunch is the classic call for this wake-up drink, which will inspire both conversation as well as your appetite.

4 cups tomato juice
2 tablespoons freshly squeezed lemon juice
1 teaspoon Worcestershire sauce
1 teaspoon prepared horseradish
½ teaspoon red Tabasco sauce
½ teaspoon green Tabasco sauce
½ teaspoon cayenne pepper
1 teaspoon paprika
1 teaspoon dried oregano
Ice cubes
4 ounces vodka
4 lemon wedges
4 small, inner celery stalks with leaves attached
    (optional)

Pour the tomato juice into a large pitcher. Stir in the lemon juice, Worcestershire sauce, horseradish, the Tabasco sauces, cayenne pepper, paprika, and oregano.

Fill 4 tall tumblers (each about 14 ounces) about one-third full with ice cubes. Add some of the tomato juice mixture to each glass, leaving enough room for the vodka.

Add 1 ounce vodka to each glass and stir. Garnish each glass with a lemon wedge and a celery stalk.

Appetizers & Side Dishes

Pico de Gallo and Homemade Tortilla Chips 22

Spinach and Artichoke Dip 23

Guacamole 25

Blue Cheese Dip 26

Chicken Wings Three Ways:
Fire, Boston Barbecue, and Asian Sesame 27

Thai Phoon Shrimp 31

California Club Quesadilla 32

Roasted Brussels Sprouts with Bacon 35

Broccoli with Lemon and Olive Oil Drizzle 36

Sautéed Carrots with
Cumin Seeds and Cilantro 36

Wilted Spinach with Bacon and Garlic 37

Creamy Mashed Cauliflower 37

Asparagus with Olive Oil and
Parmesan Cheese 39

Corn and Edamame Succotash 40

Sautéed Baby Bella Mushrooms with
Garlic and Rosemary 41

Polenta 42

Brown Rice Pilaf 42

White Cheddar Mashed Potatoes 45

Herbed Panfried Potatoes 46

Oven-Roasted Potato "Fries" with Rosemary 46

Appetizers & Side Dishes

Appetizers set the tone for every meal and offer us a chance to taste without overindulging. Many of the recipes presented here can be eaten without utensils, making them easy to eat in a casual setting like a living room or backyard.

You can scoop up dips such as Pico de Gallo (page 22) and Guacamole (page 25) with warm homemade tortilla chips. Raw vegetables, such as carrot or celery sticks, are good for dipping into Blue Cheese Dip (page 26) or creamy Spinach and Artichoke Dip (page 23). Thai Phoon Shrimp (page 31), another finger food, is a serious crowd-pleaser at the restaurant. It's served with its own spicy dipping sauce. And you'll find three different ways to prepare chicken wings (page 27), which can also double as a main course if you eat enough of them! Just remember to supply plenty of napkins.

You'll also discover a wide range of side dishes in this chapter. Some of them, such as White Cheddar Mashed Potatoes (page 45) and Corn and Edamame Succotash (page 40), are inspired by the popular Ruby Tuesday menu section titled Signature Sides. Others, such as Broccoli with Lemon and Olive Oil Drizzle (page 36), would also make a fine first course, replacing a light salad, for example.

Mix and match the side dishes with one another for a simple supper, or put them alongside one of the more substantial dishes in the chapters that follow. There's no right or wrong pairing, although suggestions are offered along the way. You'll find these recipes easy to prepare and designed to maximize free time for socializing with friends and family.

Pico de Gallo and Homemade Tortilla Chips

With its bright, fresh flavors, this traditional Mexican salsa is a versatile addition to snacks or meals. Enjoy it on its own as a dip with tortilla chips, as it is presented here, or serve it alongside fish, meat, or rice dishes. We also use it as a condiment for our California Club Quesadilla (page 32) and to spice up our Guacamole (page 25). This version delivers some heat, but it shouldn't set off any fire alarms. For more kick, double the amount of cayenne pepper. Adding diced watermelon or mango is a way to offer even more interesting flavors.

If you don't feel like making your own tortilla chips, substitute commercially made chips. Fresh-fried homemade chips are easy to make, however, and are guaranteed to earn you brownie points with your friends and family. They are lighter than the store-bought version and offer just the right blend of softness and crunch. For maximum flavor, serve them warm.

Pico de Gallo

2 cups diced fresh tomatoes (about 4 medium tomatoes)
½ cup minced onion
¼ cup diced green bell pepper
¼ cup firmly packed minced fresh cilantro
1 tablespoon minced jalapeño chile
1 clove garlic, minced
½ teaspoon salt
⅛ teaspoon cayenne pepper
1 tablespoon freshly squeezed lime juice

Tortilla Chips

Canola oil, for frying
8 (6- to 8-inch) corn tortillas
Salt

To make the Pico de Gallo, in a medium bowl, combine all of the ingredients and mix thoroughly with a wooden spoon. If you are serving right away, set aside at room temperature. Or, cover and refrigerate for up to 3 days.

To fry the chips, pour the canola oil to a depth of ½ inch into a large, heavy skillet over medium-high heat. Heat for about 5 minutes, or until the oil begins to shimmer. While the oil is heating, cut each tortilla into 8 pie-shaped wedges. Line a large baking pan with 2 or 3 layers of paper towels.

When the oil is ready, decrease the heat to medium. Using a slotted spoon, gently place as many tortilla wedges into the pan as will fit without overlapping one another. Fry the wedges for 2 minutes, then, using the slotted spoon, flip them over and fry for another 2 minutes, or until golden brown on both sides. Using the slotted spoon, transfer the chips to the prepared baking pan and sprinkle lightly with salt. Repeat with the remaining tortilla wedges.

Transfer the salsa to a small serving bowl, and set the bowl in the middle of a large platter. Arrange the chips on the platter around the salsa. Invite diners to scoop up the salsa with the chips.

Tips on How to Follow a Recipe

The most important ingredient for success in the kitchen is organization. With this in mind, always read all the way through a recipe, both the ingredients list and the instructions, before you begin to prepare it. Next, survey your pantry and refrigerator and make a list of any ingredients you'll need to purchase to complete the dish. Then, check to see that you have all the kitchen equipment you'll need. (The recipes in this book are designed for basic kitchen utensils and cookware.)

Before you start to cook, line up all the required ingredients and ready them as indicated. Ingredients and various cooking techniques are listed in the order in which they will be used. If chopping or other preparation is required ahead of time, it is stated in the ingredients list or at the appropriate moment in the instructions.

SPINACH AND ARTICHOKE DIP

A classic American appetizer, this hearty, warm dip is loaded with creamy spinach and chopped artichoke hearts and topped with toasty Parmesan cheese. If you want to serve the dip to company, you can make it in advance, let it cool to room temperature, then cover and refrigerate it for up to 24 hours. Reheat it in the microwave before serving. It pairs well with just about any beverage, too, from mixed drinks and beer to Sangria (page 12) and most wines.

1 teaspoon canola oil
2 (14-ounce) cans artichoke hearts in water
1 pound baby spinach leaves
2 teaspoons Tabasco sauce
3 tablespoons unsalted butter
½ onion, finely chopped
2 cloves garlic, minced
2 tablespoons all-purpose flour
1 cup heavy cream
¾ teaspoon salt
1 cup sour cream
1¼ cups freshly grated Parmesan cheese
Tortilla chips, homemade (page 22) or store-bought

Preheat the oven to 350°F. Grease an 8-inch square broiler-proof baking dish with the canola oil.

Drain the artichokes well. Chop coarsely and set aside.

Rinse the spinach leaves in a colander, but do not dry them. Place the wet spinach in a medium pot, place the pot over medium-high heat, and cook, stirring occasionally, for about 3 minutes, or until completely wilted.

Drain the spinach in a colander. When it is cool enough to handle, squeeze out the excess liquid with your hands until the leaves are fairly dry. Coarsely chop the spinach. In a large bowl, using a large spoon, stir together the spinach, artichoke hearts, and Tabasco sauce. Set aside.

In a large skillet, melt the butter over medium-high heat. Add the onion and sauté for about 3 minutes, or until translucent. Add the garlic and sauté for about 30 seconds, or until fragrant. Decrease the heat to medium, whisk in the flour, add the cream, and cook, continuing to whisk to prevent lumps from forming, for 4 to 5 minutes, until creamy smooth. Add the salt and sour cream and stir to mix well. Add the spinach-artichoke mixture and 1 cup of the Parmesan cheese and stir until all the ingredients are thoroughly blended. Remove from the heat.

Transfer the mixture to the prepared baking dish, spreading it evenly in the dish. Bake for 25 to 30 minutes, until the mixture bubbles. Remove from the oven and sprinkle the remaining ¼ cup cheese evenly over the top. Turn the oven to broil. Place the baking dish on the top rack of the oven and broil for about 3 minutes, or until the surface of the dip turns light brown.

Remove from the oven and let firm up for 10 to 15 minutes before serving. The dip will still be quite warm when served. Serve with the tortilla chips.

GUACAMOLE

This creamy avocado dip makes a fine shared appetizer. Be sure to use avocados that are ripe and reasonably soft; they should yield to gentle pressure when squeezed. The recipe produces a mildly spicy dip. You can increase the heat by doubling the amount of red pepper flakes. Tangy Pico de Gallo adds a fresh touch and festive color.

3 medium ripe avocados
¼ teaspoon salt
½ cup Pico de Gallo (page 22)
½ teaspoon red pepper flakes
Tortilla chips, homemade (page 22) or store-bought

Cut each avocado in half and remove the pit. Use a tablespoon to scoop out the flesh into a medium bowl. Using a potato masher or a fork, mash the avocado until it has a creamy, smooth consistency. (If you prefer it to be chunky, mash it less.) Add the salt, Pico de Gallo, and red pepper flakes and mix thoroughly with a spoon or fork.

Transfer the avocado dip to a small serving bowl, and set the bowl in the middle of a large platter. Arrange the chips on the platter around the dip. Invite diners to scoop up the dip with the chips.

CHEF'S TIP: *Removing an Avocado Pit*

1 Using a large, sharp knife, cut the avocado in half lengthwise, cutting down to and around the pit. Gently twist the halves in opposite directions to separate them.

2 Hold the half with the pit in your nondominant hand. With your dominant hand, strike the pit soundly in the middle with the heel of the knife blade, lodging it firmly in the pit, then twist the knife clockwise, lifting out the pit as you twist.

Blue Cheese Dip

This creamy dip cools down the heat from our Fire Wings (page 27) and also adds a fresh, tangy flavor to anything else that can be dipped, such as chips or celery, carrot, or jicama sticks.

1 (8-ounce) package cream cheese,
    at room temperature
1 cup crumbled blue cheese
¼ cup sour cream
¼ cup mayonnaise
1 clove garlic, minced
¼ teaspoon salt

In a medium bowl, combine all of the ingredients. Using a handheld mixer, beat on medium speed until smooth and creamy. Or, combine all of the ingredients in a food processor and pulse until the mixture is smooth and creamy.

Transfer to a single large serving bowl or individual serving bowls and serve. If not serving the dip right away, transfer it to an airtight container and refrigerate for up to 24 hours. Remove from the refrigerator about 20 minutes before serving and stir gently a few times.

GAME DAY: *Dips and Chips!*

All of the dips in this chapter will make perfect snacks for watching the Big Game, whether it is family on the guest list or a slew of friends. Just make sure you've got enough chips available. Home-made tortilla chips (page 22) are terrific, but store-bought varieties of any kind will work fine, as long as they are sturdy enough for dipping. Needless to say, dips and chips can lead to a powerful thirst. Cold beer and a batch of freshly made Sangria (page 12) will come in handy.

Chicken Wings Three Ways:
Fire, Boston Barbecue, and Asian Sesame   Serves 4 to 6 as an appetizer; 3 to 4 as a main course

At the restaurant, we make chicken wings in different ways, each defined by the sauce that is used to marinate the wings. Here, you'll find recipes for three popular sauces. The Fire Wing Sauce calls for chile in three different forms: sauce, flakes, and ground. The Boston Barbecue Sauce calls for beer, which is boiled to remove all but trace elements of alcohol before it is mixed with a smoky barbecue sauce. Finally, the Asian Sesame Sauce calls for two types of rich, dark toasted sesame oil (look for them in the Asian specialties section of the supermarket) and a cupboard of aromatic seasonings. Typically, we serve chicken wings alongside Blue Cheese Dip (page 26) and celery sticks. Make the dip while the wings are marinating.

Chicken wings are great as an appetizer, but they are also delicious as a main course. Double the recipe for extra-hungry guests or for a large party. And remember that this is finger food, so make sure you have plenty of napkins on hand. At the table, pour cold beer, Sangria (page 12), or iced tea. A chilled white wine is also an excellent match.

Fire Wing Sauce
1/2 cup hot sauce (such as Frank's or Crystal)

2 tablespoons canola oil

2 cloves garlic, minced

2 teaspoons granulated onion

1 tablespoon brown sugar

1 teaspoon red pepper flakes

1/2 teaspoon chipotle chili flakes (see page 81) or additional red pepper flakes

1/2 teaspoon cayenne pepper

Boston Barbecue Sauce
1/2 cup lager or other beer (such as Samuel Adams Boston lager)

2 cups barbecue sauce, homemade (page 196) or store-bought

2 tablespoons A.1. Steak Sauce

Asian Sesame Sauce
1 cup toasted sesame oil

2 tablespoons toasted sesame chili oil

1/3 cup tamari or soy sauce

1/4 cup rice vinegar

1/4 cup hoisin sauce

2 teaspoons ground ginger

1 teaspoon granulated garlic powder

1 teaspoon ground allspice

1/2 teaspoon cayenne pepper

4 pounds chicken wings (about 2 dozen wings)

1 tablespoon canola oil

About 3 cups Blue Cheese Dip (page 26) and celery sticks (optional)

(recipe continued on page 28)

CHICKEN WINGS THREE WAYS (continued)

First, choose a sauce. If making the Fire Wing Sauce, whisk together all of the ingredients in a large bowl until well blended. Set aside.

If making the Boston Barbecue Sauce, in a small saucepan, bring the beer to a boil over high heat. Remove from the heat, pour into a large, heatproof bowl, add the barbecue sauce and the A.1. sauce, and whisk until well blended. Set aside.

If making the Asian Sesame sauce, whisk together all of the ingredients in a large bowl and set aside.

To prepare the wings, using a sharp knife, remove and discard the wing tips. Cut between the remaining 2 joints of each wing to separate them, then place all of the wing pieces in the sauce. Using your hands, mix the wings with the sauce until each piece is evenly coated. Cover the bowl with plastic wrap, or transfer the wings and sauce to 1 or 2 large, resealable plastic bags. Alternatively, you can pour the wings and sauce into the plastic bag(s), seal the bag(s), and massage the wings in the bag(s). It's certainly less messy. Refrigerate for 1½ to 2 hours.

Preheat the oven to 400°F. Lightly coat a large baking pan with the canola oil. Place the marinated chicken wings in a single layer in the prepared pan. (Discard any leftover marinade.)

Bake the wings for 30 minutes. Turn the oven to broil, move the wings to the top oven rack, and broil for 5 minutes. Watch closely to make sure the wings do not burn or blacken. Remove the pan from the oven and flip the wings. Return the pan to the top oven rack and broil for about 5 minutes more, or until crisp and golden brown on top.

Arrange the hot wings on a large platter. Pass the dip and the celery sticks at the table.

Right: Chicken Fire Wings with Blue Cheese Dip

THAI PHOON SHRIMP

SERVES 4 TO 6

Panko gives these shrimp a light, crunchy exterior, while their interiors remain sweet and meaty. Seasoned with a Thai-inspired mix of spices, the shrimp pack enough power (in the form of heat) to borrow their name from an Asian storm. Panko is Japanese bread crumbs. The flakes are coarser and larger than regular bread crumbs and produce a lighter, crunchier coating. Panko is stocked in many supermarkets. If you cannot find it, regular bread crumbs can be substituted.

To tame the heat and refresh your palate, drink something cool. A cold light-bodied lager is a fine match. Many chilled white wines make good pairings, too. Try a buttery Chardonnay, an herbal Sauvignon Blanc, or a fruity Riesling. These shrimp also marry well with a number of mixed drinks (see pages 8 to 16)—the fruitier the better!

Chipotle Aioli (page 194)
¾ cup all-purpose flour
¾ teaspoon paprika
1 teaspoon ground turmeric
¾ teaspoon cayenne pepper
1½ teaspoons salt
3 eggs
⅓ cup milk
1½ cups panko bread crumbs
Canola or vegetable oil, for frying
15 to 20 medium shrimp (about 1 pound),
    peeled and deveined

Prepare the aioli, cover, and refrigerate.

In a medium bowl, whisk together the flour, paprika, turmeric, cayenne pepper, and salt. In a second medium bowl, whisk together the eggs and milk. Place the bread crumbs in a third bowl.

Pour the canola oil to a depth of 1 inch into a large, heavy skillet over high heat. Heat for about 5 minutes, or until the oil begins to shimmer. While the oil is heating, dredge the shrimp, several at a time, in the spiced flour mix, shaking off the excess. Dip them into the egg-milk mixture, allowing the excess to drip off into the bowl, and then dredge them in the bread crumbs, coating them evenly. Dip the shrimp into the egg-milk mixture a second time, and then coat them once more with the bread crumbs. As the shrimp are ready, set them aside on a large platter or tray.

When the oil is ready, working in batches to avoid crowding, carefully place the shrimp in the hot oil to avoid splattering and fry for about 3 minutes, or until golden brown on the bottom. Using tongs or a slotted spoon, turn the shrimp over and fry for 2 to 3 minutes more, until both sides are golden. Using the tongs or spoon, transfer the shrimp to paper towels to drain. Repeat until all of the shrimp are fried.

Arrange the shrimp on a serving plate and place the aioli on the side for dipping. Serve right away.

CALIFORNIA CLUB QUESADILLA

Quesadillas are Mexican-style pizzas. The cheese is the main attraction; it highlights the supporting cast of other ingredients—in this case, chicken, avocado, bacon, and tomato—all framed by two toasty fried corn tortillas. This is a great recipe for using up leftover chicken. But if you don't have any in the refrigerator, you can pick up a boneless, skinless chicken breast at the market and quickly cook it on the stovetop.

Usually eaten as appetizers, quesadillas can also be a satisfying main course following a light salad, such as Mixed Baby Greens with Mustard Vinaigrette (page 72). Probably the best beverage choice is a cold beer, preferably a light lager. But iced tea or lemonade would make a fine option, as well.

1 boneless, skinless raw chicken breast, or
    ¾ cup cubed cooked chicken (¼- to ½-inch cubes)
Salt
3 tablespoons canola oil, plus 1 tablespoon,
    if cooking chicken
4 slices bacon, cut in half crosswise
4 (8-inch) white corn tortillas
1 cup grated Cheddar cheese
2 medium tomatoes, sliced
3 green onions, white part only, thinly sliced
1 medium ripe avocado, pitted (see Chef's Tip, page 25),
    then peeled and sliced
2 tablespoons minced fresh cilantro
1 cup grated Swiss cheese
Sour cream, for garnish
Pico de Gallo (page 22), for garnish

If you are cooking the chicken breast, cut it into ¼-to-½-inch cubes and lightly salt them. In a small skillet, heat the 1 tablespoon canola oil over medium-high heat. Place the chicken in the pan and cook, stirring occasionally, for about 2 minutes. Flip the chicken pieces and continue to cook, stirring occasionally, for about 2 minutes more, or until all the pieces are cooked through. Remove from the heat and set aside.

In a medium skillet, cook the bacon over medium-high heat, turning once, for about 2 minutes on each side, or until it starts to crisp. Transfer to paper towels to drain and reserve. Discard the drippings.

For ease of assembly, lay out all of the ingredients except the tortillas on a large, flat platter or other flat surface. Place 2 tortillas on a clean countertop. Layer on top, in the following order and dividing the ingredients evenly between the tortillas, the Cheddar cheese, chicken, tomatoes, green onions, avocado, bacon, cilantro, and finally the Swiss cheese. Lay a second tortilla on top of each stack of layered ingredients. Using your palm, gently but firmly press down on each quesadilla, making sure the edges of the top and bottom tortillas touch.

In a large skillet, heat the 3 tablespoons canola oil over medium-high heat until it begins to shimmer. Carefully place 1 quesadilla into the hot oil. Pressing down gently on the top tortilla now and then with a spatula, cook for about 2 minutes, or until the bottom is golden brown. Using the spatula, carefully flip the quesadilla over and continue to cook, gently applying pressure to the top tortilla as before, for about 2 minutes more, or until the bottom is golden brown. Using the spatula, transfer the quesadilla to a paper towel to drain. Repeat with the second quesadilla.

Set each quesadilla on its own plate and cut into quarters. Garnish each quesadilla with a dollop each of the sour cream and the salsa. Serve hot.

ROASTED BRUSSELS SPROUTS WITH BACON

We admit that bacon makes Brussels sprouts taste better. But these Brussels sprouts have their own sweet, earthy charm, too. When roasted in the oven with bacon, the results are stunning.

3 slices bacon, cut crosswise into
    ¼-inch-wide strips
½ medium onion, coarsely chopped
3 cloves garlic, minced
1 tablespoon olive oil
2 pounds Brussels sprouts, bottoms trimmed and
    halved lengthwise
Salt and freshly ground black pepper

Preheat the oven to 400°F.

In a large ovenproof skillet, cook the bacon over medium-high heat, stirring occasionally to prevent burning, for 2 to 3 minutes, until it begins to crisp. Decrease the heat to medium, add the onion, and sauté for about 3 minutes, or until translucent. Add the garlic and sauté, stirring occasionally, for about 30 seconds, or until fragrant.

Add the olive oil and Brussels sprouts and stir gently to coat the sprouts with the oil. Season with salt and pepper. (Go easy on the salt; the bacon will already have added saltiness. You can adjust the seasoning after the Brussels sprouts have cooked.) Place the pan in the oven and bake for about 25 minutes, or until the sprouts are golden brown and can be easily pierced with a fork.

Transfer to a serving bowl and serve right away.

BROCCOLI WITH LEMON AND OLIVE OIL DRIZZLE

SERVES 4 TO 6

What can be more satisfying than something that is healthy and tastes good, too? Despite its wealth of vitamins and minerals, broccoli has been maligned by generations of children and adults. But dressed simply in olive oil with a little lemon juice and salt, this broccoli dish takes on a fresh array of flavors that will leave no leftovers on the table.

1 pound broccoli florets
4 tablespoons extra-virgin olive oil
1 tablespoon freshly squeezed lemon juice
1/4 teaspoon coarse salt
Freshly ground black pepper

Pour water to a depth of 1 inch into a large pot, and place a steamer basket in the pot. The bottom of the basket should not touch the water. Place the broccoli in the basket and bring the water to a boil over high heat. Cover and steam for about 7 minutes, or until just tender and still bright green. Alternatively, fill a large pot three-fourths full with water and bring to a boil over high heat. Add the broccoli, lower the heat to medium, and cook for about 5 minutes, or until just tender and still bright green. (Overcooked broccoli turns a faded, dull green, signaling that it has lost both flavor and nutrients.)

If steaming, lift out the basket. If boiling, drain the broccoli in a colander. Arrange the florets on a large platter or in a large serving bowl. Drizzle with the olive oil and lemon juice and sprinkle with the salt. Toss gently to coat evenly. Top with a few grinds of pepper and serve.

SAUTÉED CARROTS WITH CUMIN SEEDS AND CILANTRO

SERVES 4

Sweet, buttery carrots are enhanced by cumin and cilantro in this terrific side dish that complements any number of entrées featured in this book. Most noteworthy are Pork Loin with Rosemary-Garlic Rub (page 150) and Cajun-Spiced Tilapia (page 123).

1 pound medium carrots, peeled and cut into
    1/4-inch-thick rounds
1 tablespoon unsalted butter
1 teaspoon cumin seeds
1/8 teaspoon salt
2 tablespoons minced fresh cilantro

Fill a medium pot two-thirds full with lightly salted water and bring to a boil over high heat. Add the carrots and cook for about 5 minutes, or until barely tender. Drain in a colander and rinse with cold running water to stop the cooking. Set aside.

In a medium skillet, melt the butter over medium heat. Add the cumin seeds and sauté for about 1 minute, or until the seeds are fragrant and turn dark brown. Add the carrots and salt and stir to coat the carrots thoroughly with the butter and cumin seeds. Cover and continue to cook for 8 to 10 minutes, until the carrots can be easily pierced with a fork.

Remove the pan from the heat and stir in the cilantro. Transfer the carrots to a serving bowl or platter and serve at once.

Wilted Spinach with Bacon and Garlic

SERVES 4

Spinach is loaded with vitamins and minerals. It's a rich source of beta carotene and is blessed with generous amounts of vitamins B, C, E, and K and with calcium and iron. Bacon gives this decidedly healthy dish a smoky, sweet edge—and just a touch of decadence!

1 pound baby spinach
1 tablespoon extra-virgin olive oil
3 slices bacon, cut crosswise into ¼-inch-wide strips
3 cloves garlic, minced
¼ teaspoon salt
Freshly ground black pepper

Rinse the spinach leaves in a colander, but do not dry them. Set aside.

In a large skillet, heat the olive oil over medium-high heat. Add the bacon and cook, stirring occasionally, for about 3 minutes, or until crisp. Add the garlic and sauté for about 30 seconds, or until fragrant. Add the wet spinach leaves, in batches if necessary, and sauté for about 2 minutes, or until the leaves are wilted but not overcooked. (The leaves should remain a vivid green.) Add the salt and stir to mix thoroughly.

Using a slotted spoon, transfer the spinach to a serving bowl. Garnish with pepper and serve immediately.

Creamy Mashed Cauliflower

SERVES 4 TO 5

Take a break from mashed potatoes with this light, creamy, satisfying cauliflower purée. It's different but still seems familiar. We call it comfort food with a twist.

1 head cauliflower, cut into small florets
2 tablespoons unsalted butter
1 cup heavy cream
¼ teaspoon salt

In a medium saucepan, combine the cauliflower with cold water to cover and bring to a boil over high heat. Decrease the heat to medium-high and simmer for about 8 minutes, or until the cauliflower is tender.

Drain the cauliflower in a colander, reserving ½ cup of the cooking water. Return the warm, empty saucepan to the stovetop over an unlit burner. Place the butter in the pan.

Transfer the warm cauliflower to a blender or food processor, add about half of the cream, and process to a smooth purée, adding some of the reserved cooking water if necessary to achieve the desired consistency. (If using a blender, you will probably need to work in batches.) Return the purée to the saucepan with the butter, add the remaining cream and the salt, and stir to combine.

Turn on the burner to medium-low and heat the purée, stirring frequently, for about 5 minutes, or until it thickens. Transfer to a serving bowl and serve right away.

Asparagus with Olive Oil and Parmesan Cheese

Cooking doesn't get much easier! Salty, nutty Parmesan cheese—not grated, but shaved into thin slices—makes a fine companion for these simply cooked asparagus spears. The only other ingredients are fruity olive oil, a little coarse salt, and some freshly ground pepper. The finished dish makes a good side dish or first course, served warm, cold, or at room temperature.

Wine and asparagus make good partners, provided you pick the right wine. Asparagus (and artichokes, too) seem to make wine taste oddly sweet. That's why it's a good idea to drink bright, zippy whites like Sauvignon Blanc or Riesling with this dish. They have the freshness—or the sweetness, as it may be—to retain their character in the face of this wine-challenged vegetable. Beer is also a good match with asparagus.

1 pound asparagus spears
3 tablespoons extra-virgin olive oil
2 pinches of coarse salt
8 thinly shaved slices Parmesan cheese
    (about 1 inch square)
Freshly ground black pepper

Trim off the tough stem end from each asparagus spear, usually 1 to 2 inches. (The tough portion will be paler and visibly fibrous.) Pour water to a depth of 1 inch into a large skillet and bring to a boil over high heat. Lay the spears in the boiling water, cover, and cook for 3 to 5 minutes, until tender enough to be easily pierced with a fork. Drain in a colander and rinse with cold running water to stop the cooking and set the vivid green color.

Pat the spears dry with paper towels and lay them on a large serving plate. Drizzle with the olive oil, sprinkle with the salt, and garnish with the Parmesan. Top with a few grinds of pepper.

Corn and Edamame Succotash

This American standard has been enjoyed in various forms for much of our nation's history. It is traditionally made with corn and lima beans, but our version features edamame, green soybeans harvested early in the growing season. To retain freshness, the soybeans are typically parboiled soon after harvesting and then frozen. They are widely available in most supermarkets, both shelled and in the pod. You can substitute lima beans, if you like.

Highlighted by flecks of yellow, green, and red, this succotash makes a pretty presentation on any dinner plate. Enjoy it as an alternative to rice and as a versatile accompaniment to many of the main dishes featured in this book, such as Fork-Tender Baby Back Ribs (page 137) and Buttermilk Fried Chicken with Mushroom Gravy (page 153).

1 cup frozen shelled edamame
1 tablespoon canola oil
1 slice bacon, finely diced
¼ cup diced onion
2 cloves garlic, minced
½ red bell pepper, seeded and diced (about ¾ cup)
3 cups yellow corn kernels (from about 5 ears)
1 teaspoon dried tarragon
¼ teaspoon salt
½ cup water
½ cup heavy cream
Freshly ground black pepper

Fill a large saucepan half full with lightly salted water and bring to a boil over high heat. Add the *edamame*, bring the water back to a boil, and blanch the beans for 3 minutes. Drain and rinse with cold running water to stop the cooking. Set aside.

In a large skillet, heat the oil over medium-high heat. Add the bacon and cook, stirring occasionally, for about 2 minutes, or until crisp. Decrease the heat to medium, add the onion and garlic, and sauté, stirring occasionally, for about 2 minutes, or until the onion is translucent. Add the bell pepper and continue to cook, shaking the pan or stirring frequently to prevent burning, for about 2 minutes more, or until the pepper softens. Stir in the corn, *edamame*, tarragon, and salt. Add the water, raise the heat to medium-high, and continue to cook, stirring occasionally, for about 5 minutes, or until most of the liquid has evaporated. Add the cream and simmer for 3 to 4 minutes, until thick.

Transfer to a serving bowl and garnish with pepper. Serve immediately, or cover and set aside for up to 2 hours, then serve at room temperature or reheat over medium heat. Or, refrigerate for up to 24 hours, then serve at room temperature or reheat before serving.

Sautéed Baby Bella Mushrooms with Garlic and Rosemary

These herbed mushrooms are easy to prepare and will add an earthy freshness when served alongside many of the chicken and meat main courses in this book. They also pair nicely with meaty fish such as Soy-Sesame Tuna Steaks (page 125) and Asian Glazed Salmon (page 124).

Baby bella is another name for the common small, brown mushrooms also known as crimini (or cremini) or Italian brown mushrooms. They grow up to become large, brown portobellos. Use either brown mushrooms or common white button mushrooms, depending on availability and preference. Dried rosemary is called for here, but you can also use just about any other dried herb, such as thyme, oregano, or tarragon, with excellent results.

1 tablespoon extra-virgin olive oil
1 large shallot, minced (about ¼ cup)
3 cloves garlic, minced
1 pound baby bella mushrooms, sliced
1 teaspoon dried rosemary
¼ teaspoon salt, plus additional for seasoning
2 to 3 tablespoons water
Freshly ground black pepper

In a large skillet, heat the olive oil over medium heat. Add the shallot and sauté for about 2 minutes, or until translucent. Add the garlic and sauté for about 30 seconds, or until fragrant. Add the mushrooms and stir to coat evenly with the oil. Stir in the rosemary, the ¼ teaspoon salt, and just enough of the water to prevent burning, mixing thoroughly. Cover the pan and cook, stirring occasionally, for about 5 minutes, or until the mushrooms have softened.

Uncover the pan, raise the heat to medium-high, and continue to cook for about 5 minutes, or until all of the liquid evaporates. Season with salt and pepper.

Transfer to a serving dish and serve at once.

POLENTA

SERVES 4 TO 6

Quick and easy to prepare, this smooth cornmeal porridge makes a great substitute for rice or potatoes on a dinner plate, where it readily soaks up gravy or pan juices. You can buy instant polenta that cooks in about 5 minutes. But regular polenta cooks quickly too, in about 10 minutes, and tastes better.

For a softer texture, serve the polenta within a few minutes of removing it from the heat. If it is allowed to sit in a serving dish for 5 to 10 minutes, it will stiffen—an equally enjoyable way to eat it. Enjoy it either way, depending on your preference.

5 cups water
1 teaspoon salt
1 cup polenta
1/2 cup heavy cream
2 tablespoons unsalted butter
1/2 cup freshly grated Parmesan cheese
Freshly ground black pepper

In a large saucepan, combine the water and salt and bring to a boil over high heat. Add the polenta in a slow, steady stream while whisking constantly. Decrease the heat to medium-low and simmer for 5 minutes, stirring occasionally with a wooden spoon.

Pour in the cream and stir to mix. Continue to cook, stirring occasionally, for about 5 minutes, or until all the liquid is absorbed. Remove from the heat, add the butter and cheese, and stir until thoroughly incorporated.

Pour the polenta into a heat-resistant glass baking dish or bowl. Allow it to settle for at least a few minutes before serving. Garnish with a few grinds of pepper.

BROWN RICE PILAF

SERVES 4 TO 6

This is a good-for-you rice pilaf. The brown rice is high in fiber and has a nutty quality, here punctuated by pleasing herbal notes, mostly from the celery, bell pepper, and oregano. Serve it alongside almost any dish complemented by rice, such as Soy-Sesame Tuna Steaks (page 125), Baked Halibut with Chili-Lime Butter (page 118), or Chicken Fresco with Parmesan Cream Sauce and Roasted Tomatoes (page 162).

Remember that brown rice takes twice as long to cook as white rice (about 40 minutes versus 20 minutes).

1 tablespoon extra-virgin olive oil
1 cup finely diced onion
2 celery stalks, finely diced
1/2 cup finely diced red bell pepper
1 cup brown rice
1 teaspoon dried oregano
2 1/2 cups water
1/2 teaspoon salt

In a medium saucepan, heat the olive oil over medium-high heat. Add the onion and celery and sauté, stirring occasionally, for about 3 minutes, or until the onion is translucent. Add the bell pepper and continue to sauté, stirring occasionally, for about 1 minute, or until it begins to turn orange. Add the rice and oregano and stir to mix well. Cook, continuing to stir now and then to prevent burning, for about 3 minutes, or until the rice begins to toast and become fragrant.

Add the water and salt, raise the heat to high, and bring to a boil. Decrease the heat to low, cover, and cook for about 40 minutes, or until all of the water has been absorbed and the rice is tender.

Remove from the heat and, using a fork or spoon, fluff the rice to mix all of the ingredients evenly. Serve immediately, or re-cover to keep warm and set aside for up to 30 minutes before serving.

Right: Brown Rice Pilaf

White Cheddar Mashed Potatoes

These tasty spuds, which are spiked with Cheddar cheese and rely more on olive oil than butter, make an excellent stand-in for standard mashed potatoes. Olive oil has a dual role in this recipe: It contributes a subtle fruitiness and creamy texture and is also healthier.

3 pounds white new potatoes, unpeeled, quartered
½ cup extra-virgin olive oil, plus additional
    for drizzling
½ teaspoon salt, plus additional for seasoning
2 tablespoons unsalted butter, at room temperature
½ pound aged white Cheddar cheese, grated
    (about 2 cups)
Freshly ground black pepper

In a large pot, combine the potatoes with cold water to cover and bring to a boil over high heat. Decrease the heat to medium and cook for 10 to 12 minutes, until tender.

Drain the potatoes in a colander and return them to the pot. Add ¼ cup of the olive oil and mash with a potato masher until incorporated. Add the remaining ¼ cup olive oil and continue to mash until fairly smooth. (Don't worry if they are slightly lumpy.) Add the ½ teaspoon salt and the butter and mash until the butter melts. Add half of the cheese and mash to mix well. Add the rest of the cheese and continue to mash until the cheese is thoroughly combined. Taste and adjust the seasoning with salt.

Transfer the potatoes to a serving bowl, drizzle a small amount of olive oil over the top, and garnish with pepper. Pass additional olive oil and pepper at the table for diners to add as desired. Or, cover to keep warm and set aside for up to 30 minutes before serving, then serve as described.

HERBED PANFRIED POTATOES

SERVES 4

These panfried potatoes are so good on their own, you won't even want to reach for the ketchup bottle. A sophisticated version of home fries, they are terrific with eggs for breakfast or brunch. Paprika gives them just a trace of heat, as well as an alluring orange tint. If you're entertaining guests, cook these potatoes in advance and reheat them on the stovetop prior to serving. They'll taste even better than freshly cooked.

5 white or red potatoes, about 2 pounds total,
    peeled and cut into 1-inch cubes
5 tablespoons extra-virgin olive oil
½ medium onion, diced
½ teaspoon paprika
1 teaspoon dried oregano
½ teaspoon salt, plus additional for seasoning
Freshly ground black pepper

Fill a large pot half full with lightly salted water and bring to a boil over high heat. Add the potatoes, bring the water back to a boil, decrease the heat to medium-high, and cook for about 10 minutes, or until the potatoes can be easily pierced with a fork. Drain in a colander and rinse under cold running water to stop the cooking. Set aside.

In a large skillet, heat 3 tablespoons of the olive oil over medium-high heat. Add the onion and sauté for about 3 minutes, or until translucent. Push the onion to the side of the pan and add the remaining 2 tablespoons olive oil and the potatoes. Sprinkle the potatoes with the paprika, oregano, and the ½ teaspoon salt and mix gently with the onion. Decrease the heat to medium and cook for about 5 minutes, or until golden brown on the bottom. Using a large spatula, flip the potatoes over and cook for 3 to 5 minutes more, until they are golden and crisp on both sides.

Season with salt and pepper, transfer to a serving dish, and serve right away.

OVEN-ROASTED POTATO "FRIES" WITH ROSEMARY

SERVES 4

Without a commercial fryer, it's not easy to make French fries at home. But you can make these tasty, toasty, and equally satisfying oven "fries." Just the smell of these potatoes cooking will make you hungry! Serve them with any number of dishes featured in this book, including burgers (pages 130 to 134) or Pork Loin with Rosemary-Garlic Rub (page 150). They are especially delicious with omelets (pages 65 to 66). Dijon mustard makes a good condiment.

5 tablespoons extra-virgin olive oil
3 pounds large red potatoes, unpeeled, cut
    into ⅛-inch-thick rounds
1 tablespoon dried rosemary
Salt and freshly ground black pepper

Preheat the oven to 400°F. Coat a large roasting pan with 2 tablespoons of the olive oil.

Arrange the potato slices in long rows, each slice slightly overlapping the next one, in the prepared pan. Drizzle the remaining 3 tablespoons olive oil evenly over the potatoes, then dust the potatoes with the rosemary. Season with salt and pepper.

Bake the potatoes for about 30 minutes, or until they are golden brown and crisp around the edges but still soft in the middle. Serve hot.

Right: Oven-Roasted Potato "Fries" with Rosemary

Brunch

Buttermilk Biscuits   53

French Toast with Rolled Oats
and Coriander   54

Crêpes: Sweet and Savory
Apple-Cranberry Crêpes with Whipped Cream
   and Maple Syrup
Crabmeat Crêpes with Hollandaise Sauce   57

Steak and Eggs Benedict   60

Poached Eggs Benedict with Smoked Salmon   62

Western Frittata with Green and
Red Peppers, Ham, and Cheese   63

Apple and Cheese Omelet   65

Spinach, Mushroom, and Feta Cheese Omelet   66

Brunch

The word brunch says it all. It's not quite breakfast, and it's not quite lunch. But it can easily stand in for either, which is why we often enjoy it on days when we sleep in. On lazy mornings, we're not quite ready for lunch, but we're hungry enough to eat it anyway!

It's no surprise that eggs—perfectly suited to meals at any time of day—are at the heart of our brunch repertoire. They are part of an American breakfast tradition, but they are also ideal for more adventurous fare that's still easy to prepare. This includes omelets and frittatas, which you'll find here, along with poached and scrambled eggs—both dressed in a lush hollandaise sauce. If you crave additional protein, you'll be happy to find steak and smoked salmon on the menu, too. Homemade biscuits (page 53) and crêpes (page 57) are also among our brunch offerings, as well as a dazzling version of French toast made with rolled oats and flavored with coriander (page 54).

When it comes to choosing beverages, brunch is on a par with lunch. At Ruby Tuesday, we serve a wide range of mixed fruit drinks. See the Drinks chapter (page 1) for some our most popular offerings. Cocktails and wine punches, such as the Ruby Relaxer (page 11), Sangria (page 12), and Cajun Mary (page 16), are also excellent options for a weekend brunch.

Of course, beer and wine pair well with any meal of substance. For a festive choice, pour glasses of sparkling wine, because sleeping in is cause enough for celebration. Add a home-cooked meal with friends and family to your late-morning start and you'll wonder why you don't host a brunch every weekend.

CRÊPES: SWEET AND SAVORY
APPLE-CRANBERRY CRÊPES WITH WHIPPED CREAM AND MAPLE SYRUP
CRABMEAT CRÊPES WITH HOLLANDAISE SAUCE

MAKES 8 TO 10 FILLED CRÊPES; SERVES 4 OR 5 AS A MAIN COURSE OR 8 OR 10 AS AN APPETIZER

Crêpes are so delicious that it's no surprise the French never embraced flapjacks! These superthin French-style pancakes can be stuffed with many different fillings. Here, we feature just two: a sweet mix of apple and cranberry and a savory crabmeat.

The batter recipe yields enough crêpes for only one filling recipe. If you are inspired to make both fillings—to host a crêpe party, for example— you'll need to make a double batch of the batter. If possible, use a nonstick pan for cooking the crêpes. You won't need to use oil or butter, and the crêpes will turn out especially light and airy. If using a regular skillet, you will need to grease it with a small amount of canola oil to prevent the crêpes from sticking.

Enjoy the crabmeat crêpes with a glass of sparkling wine or a crisp white, such as Pinot Grigio, Sauvignon Blanc, or Chardonnay. The sweeter fruit-filled crêpes also pair nicely with sparkling wines, as well as fruit juices and other breakfast drinks.

CRÊPE BATTER
2 eggs

1 cup all-purpose flour

2 tablespoons unsalted butter, melted

½ cup milk

½ cup water

¼ teaspoon salt

APPLE-CRANBERRY FILLING
4 tablespoons unsalted butter

3 Granny Smith apples, peeled and finely diced

¾ cup dried cranberries, coarsely chopped

½ teaspoon ground cinnamon

3 tablespoons brown sugar

1 cup heavy cream

Maple syrup, for serving

CRABMEAT FILLING
2 tablespoons unsalted butter

1 cup finely chopped onion

1 celery stalk, minced

2 cups sliced button mushrooms

1 teaspoon dried tarragon

½ teaspoon salt

1 tablespoon freshly squeezed lemon juice

½ cup white wine

½ cup heavy cream

1 pound fresh jumbo lump crabmeat, cartilage and shell bits removed (about 3 cups)

Freshly ground black pepper

About 1 cup hollandaise sauce (page 59), or more as desired

(recipe continued on page 58)

CRÊPES: SWEET AND SAVORY (continued)

To make the batter, in a blender or food processor, combine the eggs and flour and pulse for 10 seconds. Add the melted butter, milk, water, and salt and pulse for 10 seconds more. Scrape down the sides of the beaker or bowl with a rubber spatula to bring all the batter back to the bottom and process for another 10 seconds. Cover and refrigerate the batter for 1 hour.

Choose a filling to make. To make the apple-cranberry filling, in a medium skillet, melt the butter over medium heat. Add the apples, cranberries, and cinnamon and stir to coat the apples and cranberries thoroughly with the butter. Decrease the heat to low and sauté the apples, stirring frequently, for about 15 minutes, or until they start to soften and caramelize. Sprinkle in the brown sugar, mix thoroughly, and continue to sauté, stirring frequently, for about 10 minutes more, or until the apples are soft and all the ingredients are well integrated. Remove from the heat, cover, and set aside until ready to use.

To make the crabmeat filling, in a large skillet, melt the butter over medium-high heat. Add the onion and celery and sauté for about 4 minutes, or until the onion is translucent. Add the mushrooms and sauté for about 5 minutes, or until the mushrooms soften. Decrease the heat to medium, add the tarragon, salt, lemon juice, and white wine, and simmer for 2 to 3 minutes, until the wine has reduced by half. Stir in the cream and simmer for about 3 minutes, or until the sauce has thickened. Add the crabmeat, stir to mix well, and simmer for about 2 minutes, or until the crabmeat is warmed through. Remove from the heat, cover, and set aside until ready to use.

Make the hollandaise sauce as directed and set aside over the pan of hot water.

To cook the crêpes, first cut 8 to 10 pieces of waxed paper 6 to 8 inches square—or nearly as wide as the crêpes will be—and set them aside.

Place a nonstick 10-inch skillet over medium heat. When it is hot, carefully pour 1/4 cup of the batter into the pan and immediately tilt and swirl the pan so that the batter fully and evenly coats the bottom. Cook for 20 to 30 seconds, until small bubbles appear in the middle of the surface. Loosen the edges with a spatula, grasp the edge with your fingers, and flip the crêpe. Cook the second side for 10 to 15 seconds, until lightly browned and just set. Slide the crêpe onto a large plate. Place a square of waxed paper on top. Repeat with the remaining batter, stacking the crêpes, with squares of waxed paper in between, as you go. You should have 8 to 10 crêpes in all.

Now, fill and serve the crêpes. If using the apple-cranberry filling, reheat over medium heat. Meanwhile, in a medium bowl, using an electric mixer on medium speed, whip the cream for about 1 minute, or until it thickens just enough to form small peaks. Lay a crêpe flat on a large plate and place about 2 tablespoons of the hot apple filling in the middle. Fold one edge of the crêpe over the filling and roll the crêpe into a cylinder, then place, seam down, on an individual plate. Repeat with the remaining crêpes. Place a large dollop of whipped cream on or at the base of each crêpe. Serve with maple syrup on the side.

If using the crab filling, first reheat the hollandaise sauce by bringing the water in the saucepan to a simmer, then whisking a little hot water (3 to 4 tablespoons) into the sauce to return it to a smooth, liquid consistency. Lay a crêpe flat on a large plate and place about 1/4 cup of the filling in the middle. Fold one edge of the crêpe over the filling and roll the crêpe into a cylinder, then place, seam down, on an individual plate. Repeat with the remaining crêpes. Top each crêpe with 2 tablespoons hollandaise, or more if desired, and finish with a little pepper.

Chef's Tip: *Making Hollandaise Sauce*

This creamy, egg-based sauce is traditionally used to dress up egg dishes, such as Poached Eggs Benedict with Smoked Salmon (page 62) and Steak and Eggs Benedict (page 60). It also dresses our savory crabmeat-filled crêpes (page 57).

4 egg yolks
1 tablespoon freshly squeezed lemon juice
½ cup unsalted butter, melted
Pinch of cayenne pepper
Pinch of salt

1 In a heatproof bowl or the top of a double boiler, whisk together the egg yolks and lemon juice for about 1 minute, or until emulsified.

2 Place the bowl over (not touching) simmering water in a saucepan and continue to whisk rapidly. Do not let the eggs get too hot, or they will begin to scramble.

3 Slowly drizzle in the melted butter and continue to whisk until the sauce thickens and doubles in volume. Turn off the heat and whisk in the cayenne pepper and salt. Serve at once, or set aside over the hot water until ready to use. You should have about 2 cups; serves 4 to 6.

STEAK AND EGGS BENEDICT

Steak and eggs find their apogee in this mini-tower of great taste. The tomato and greens are warmed by slices of panfried steak and topped with Cheddar cheese–laced scrambled eggs. Rich, lemony hollandaise drenches it all. We call for tenderloin here, which is indeed tender but also pricey. Feel free to try other beef cuts to hold down costs.

This recipe is not hard to make, but it requires a little extra coordination in the kitchen. Having someone to help out will not only make things easier, but also more fun. Start with the hollandaise, next cook the steak, and finish with the eggs, and then assemble the elements.

Brunch leaves open myriad drinks possibilities, from coffee and juice to all manner of mixed drinks (pages 8 to 16). Bubbles are also appropriate; they perk up the body as well as the palate. Full-bodied ale or a lighter sparkling wine would be an excellent selection in your glass.

Hollandaise sauce (page 59)
2 beef tenderloin steaks, each about ½ pound
    and 1 inch thick
Salt and freshly ground black pepper
1 tablespoon canola oil
4 eggs
1 tablespoon extra-virgin olive oil
1 cup grated Cheddar cheese
4 English muffins, split
4 to 8 leaves butter lettuce, or 1 cup loosely packed
    mixed baby greens
4 tomato slices

Make the sauce as directed and set aside over the pan of hot water.

Cut the steaks in half horizontally to make steaks each ½ inch thick. Season the meat on both sides with salt and pepper. In a medium skillet, heat the canola oil over high heat. When the oil begins to shimmer, add the steaks and panfry, turning once, for about 2 minutes on each side for medium-rare. Transfer the steaks to a plate. Tent with aluminum foil and set aside.

In a medium bowl, whisk the eggs until blended. Rinse and wipe the skillet, place over medium heat, and add the olive oil. When the oil begins to shimmer, add the eggs and let them firm up somewhat in the pan, mixing now and then with a wooden spoon, for about 2 minutes, or until they are fluffy. Before they become completely solid, sprinkle in the cheese and mix well.

While the eggs are cooking, toast the English muffins and place, cut sides up, on individual plates. To reheat the sauce, bring the water in the saucepan to a simmer, then whisk a little hot water (3 to 4 tablespoons) into the sauce to return it to a smooth, liquid consistency.

Cut each steak across the grain into 3 or 4 slices, each about ¼ inch thick. Place 1 or 2 lettuce leaves or evenly divide the baby greens on each pair of muffin halves. Place a tomato slice on top of each serving of greens. Set the steak slices on top of the tomatoes. Evenly divide the eggs among the servings, placing them on top of the steak. Pour a generous portion of the sauce over the eggs, and top each serving with a few grinds of pepper. Serve at once.

POACHED EGGS BENEDICT WITH SMOKED SALMON SERVES 4

This is a richly satisfying dish. It features a generous serving of creamy sauce over warm, soft egg yolks that run slowly across the smoked salmon. If you have never poached an egg, you will be happy to learn that poaching eggs is as easy as frying them. On the side, Herbed Panfried Potatoes (page 46) and/or Broccoli with Lemon and Olive Oil Drizzle (page 36) would make fine additions. For ease in the kitchen, make these side dishes in advance. Keep them warm or reheat in a microwave before serving.

Sparkling wine, a cold beer, Sangria (page 12), or a Cajun Mary (page 16) would handily slake your late-morning or early-afternoon thirst.

Hollandaise Sauce (page 59)
1 tablespoon white wine vinegar or cider vinegar
8 eggs
4 English muffins, split
2 tablespoons unsalted butter, at room temperature.
8 slices smoked salmon (about ½ pound total)
Freshly ground black pepper

Make the sauce as directed and set aside over the pan of hot water.

Pour water to a depth of 1½ inches into a large, wide, deep-sided skillet. Add the vinegar and bring to a boil over high heat. Decrease the heat to medium to maintain a strong simmer. Gently crack the eggs into the simmering water and cook for 3 minutes for runny yolks.

While the eggs are cooking, toast the English muffins, lightly butter each half, and place them, buttered side up, on individual plates. Lay 1 salmon slice, folded in half, on each muffin half.

When the eggs are ready, using a slotted spoon, remove them, one at a time, from the water and place an egg on top of each salmon slice.

To reheat the sauce, bring the water in the saucepan to a simmer, then whisk a little hot water (3 to 4 tablespoons) into the sauce to return it to a smooth, liquid consistency. Drizzle the sauce liberally over the eggs. Top each serving with a grind or two of pepper and serve right away.

Western Frittata with Green and Red Peppers, Ham, and Cheese SERVES 4

This is a Western omelet with Italian flair. The ham is Italian prosciutto, a dry-cured delicacy that is sweeter and richer than boiled ham. And the cheese is Italian Fontina, a mild cow's milk cheese that brings a hint of nuttiness to the mix. Both prosciutto and Italian Fontina are fairly easy to locate in well-provisioned supermarkets. But if you can't find prosciutto, any ham will suffice. In the absence of Italian Fontina, look for Danish Fontina—a similar but milder cheese. Or, you can experiment with any cheese you like.

You'll discover that this frittata is really an omelet that's finished under the broiler. Here, the ham and cheese sit atop a colorful layer of green and red peppers. And the broiler's flame toasts the cheese to create a crispy topping that will have your guests clamoring for more!

2 tablespoons extra-virgin olive oil
1 cup diced onion
1 green bell pepper, seeded and diced
1 red bell pepper, seeded and diced
8 eggs
6 thin slices prosciutto (about 3 ounces total),
    each pulled into 4 or 5 pieces by hand
¼ pound Italian Fontina cheese, thinly sliced
Freshly ground black pepper

In a large broiler-proof skillet, heat the olive oil over medium heat. When the oil begins to shimmer, add the onion and sauté for about 3 minutes, or until translucent. Add the bell peppers and cook, stirring occasionally, for about 10 minutes, or until they soften.

While the peppers are cooking, in a large bowl, beat the eggs with a whisk or a fork until blended. When the peppers are ready, push the onion and peppers to the side of the pan and decrease the heat to medium-low. Pour in the eggs and, using a wooden spoon or a spatula, spread the onion mixture evenly throughout the eggs. Distribute the prosciutto pieces evenly across the surface of the uncooked eggs, then lay the cheese slices on top of the prosciutto.

Cook for 5 to 7 minutes, until the eggs have set on the bottom. The top of the eggs should still be runny. Meanwhile, preheat the broiler.

When the eggs are ready, transfer the skillet to the top rack in the oven and broil for 3 to 4 minutes, until the cheese has melted and is just beginning to turn golden.

Remove the pan from the oven and cut the frittata into quarters. Top with a few grinds of pepper and serve at once.

Apple and Cheese Omelet

Serves 4

Fruit and cheese always taste good together. So it's no wonder that apples and cheese make perfect bedfellows in an omelet. Use a tart Granny Smith or McIntosh apple for the best results. Pour a rich lager or a fruity wine, such as Riesling or Chardonnay, at the table.

2 tablespoons extra-virgin olive oil
1 apple, halved and sliced
8 eggs
¼ pound Gruyère or Swiss cheese, sliced or grated
1 teaspoon dried thyme

In a medium skillet, heat the olive oil over medium heat. When the oil begins to shimmer, add the apple slices and cook, stirring occasionally, for about 2 minutes, or until they start to soften. Using a spatula, flip the slices and cook for another minute or two, until they are soft and just beginning to brown.

While the apple is cooking, in a large bowl, beat the eggs with a whisk or fork until blended. Then, when the apple is ready, push the apple slices to the side of the pan and decrease the heat to low. Pour the eggs into the pan and, using a wooden spoon or a spatula, spread the apples evenly throughout the eggs. Distribute the cheese evenly across the surface of the uncooked eggs. Sprinkle the thyme evenly over the cheese.

Cover the pan and cook for 15 to 20 minutes, until the eggs are firm. Cooking time will vary depending on the size of your pan and how thick the omelet is. A larger pan will cook faster, because the omelet will be thinner.

Remove the pan from the heat and cut the omelet into quarters. Serve at once.

Omelets

Omelets are simple to make and just about everyone likes them. They can be cooked many ways, and countless ingredients can be added to them, from vegetables to fruits to meats. Some are savory, like Western Frittata with Green and Red Peppers, Ham, and Cheese (page 63) and Spinach, Mushroom, and Feta Cheese Omelet (page 66), and some incorporate sweetness, such as Apple and Cheese Omelet (left).

The omelets featured here adapt well to home entertaining. Once the ingredients are in the pan, they require little attention. That means you can focus more on your guests and less on the stovetop!

One omelet will easily serve four hungry diners. But you can also stretch these omelets to feed five or six. If you do the latter, you'll want to provide a substantial side dish, such as Oven-Roasted Potato "Fries" with Rosemary or Herbed Panfried Potatoes (page 46). Cook side dishes in advance and keep them warm in the oven or covered on the countertop until serving.

You don't need to confine these omelets to brunch menus. Feel free to serve them for lunch or dinner, too. And while they taste great with a cup of steaming coffee, they also can be enjoyed with fruit juices, beer, mixed drinks like Sangria (page 12), Cajun Mary (page 16), or sparkling and still wines—red, white, or rosé.

Spinach, Mushroom, and Feta Cheese Omelet

Topped with thyme and tangy feta cheese, this is not your average omelet. The feta, traditionally made with sheep's or goat's milk or a mixture, offers a bright note that perks up the palate. Antioxidant-rich spinach and meaty mushrooms also add character. Easy to prepare, this rustic dish still delivers a fair measure of refinement. For brunch or dinner, try it with a side dish like Oven-Roasted Potato "Fries" with Rosemary (page 46) or Brown Rice Pilaf (page 42). And because eggs are versatile at the table, it's no surprise that this omelet marries well with both red and white wines.

1 tablespoon extra-virgin olive oil
2 cloves garlic, minced
¼ pound crimini or button mushrooms, sliced
¼ pound baby spinach
8 eggs
½ cup crumbled feta cheese
2 teaspoons dried thyme
Freshly ground black pepper

In a large skillet, heat the olive oil over medium heat. Add the garlic and sauté for about 1 minute, or until it begins to brown. (If the garlic begins to turn dark and smoke, add a few tablespoons of water.) Add the mushrooms and stir to coat well with the oil and sautéed garlic. Cover and cook, stirring occasionally to prevent burning, for about 5 minutes, or until the mushrooms soften. Uncover the pan and push the mushrooms to the side of the pan.

Raise the heat to medium-high and add the spinach. (It will pretty much fill the pan but will soon reduce significantly in volume.) Re-cover the pan and cook for about 2 minutes, or until the spinach wilts.

While the spinach is cooking, in a large bowl, beat the eggs with a whisk or fork until blended. Then, when the spinach is ready, using a wooden spoon, mix together the spinach and mushrooms, then push them to the side of the pan. Decrease the heat to low. Pour the eggs into the pan and, using a wooden spoon or a spatula, spread the spinach and mushroom mixture evenly throughout the eggs. Spread the feta cheese evenly across the surface of the uncooked eggs. Sprinkle the thyme over the cheese.

Cover the pan and cook for 20 to 25 minutes, until the eggs are firm on top. Cooking time will vary depending on the size of your pan and how thick the omelet is. A larger pan will cook faster, because the omelet will be thinner.

Remove the pan from the heat and cut the omelet into quarters. Top with a few grinds of pepper and serve at once.

Salads & Soups

Mixed Baby Greens with
Mustard Vinaigrette 72

Chinese Chicken Salad 74

Avocado and Shrimp Salad
with Creole Seasoning and
Avocado Ranch Dressing 75

Salmon and Spinach Salad with
Sesame-Peanut Dressing 77

Ham and Pea Salad with
Fresh Dill Ranch Dressing 78

Potato Salad with Chipotle Chile
and Bacon 81

Tomato Soup with Fresh Basil 82

Broccoli and Cheese Soup
with Parmesan Crostini 85

Minestrone Soup 86

Manhattan Clam Chowder 87

White Bean Chicken Chili 88

Tortilla Soup 90

Salads & Soups

Together, soup and salad make an excellent light meal. Enjoy them one after the other, or serve them at the same time. The recipes featured in this chapter are nutritious and easy to prepare. As a bonus, you'll find that leftover soup often tastes even better the day after it is made.

Some of the soups presented here offer more substance than might be expected from a bowl of soup. For example, White Bean Chicken Chili (page 88) and Tortilla Soup (page 91) will satisfy even the hungriest of diners.

The salads range from fresh and light, best illustrated by Mixed Baby Greens with Mustard Vinaigrette (page 72), to substantial, such as Chinese Chicken Salad (page 74) and Salmon and Spinach Salad with Sesame-Peanut Dressing (page 77), a tangy blend of crunchy cabbage and panfried chicken breast.

But salads don't have to include greens. Potato Salad with Chipotle Chile and Bacon (page 81) is a rich, full-flavored affair, and Ham and Pea Salad with Fresh Dill Ranch Dressing (page 78) is a creamy pasta salad. Both can be enjoyed warm or at room temperature, which makes them ideal for picnics or other casual outdoor events.

Each salad in this chapter sports its own unique dressing. The dressings are made simply. Most can be assembled at the base of a salad bowl within minutes. Once you've started making your own tasty salad dressings from scratch, you may never go back to store-bought dressing again.

Mixed Baby Greens with Mustard Vinaigrette

These greens are tossed with a sassy vinaigrette that serves up just the right blend of tangy vinegar and aromatic seasonings. The secret to the dressing is tarragon, which adds a distinctive flavor. If you don't have any tarragon on your shelf, you can substitute other herbs, such as dried thyme or rosemary. The shallot is optional, especially for cooks in a hurry.

Salads and wine are not typically recommended companions. The vinegar in a dressing can make a wine taste bitter. But any wine with good acidity, especially bubbly or white wines like Sauvignon Blanc or Pinot Grigio, will stand up well to most vinaigrettes. That said, if you're enjoying a glass of red wine when the salad is served, don't worry. The French have enjoyed red wine with their salads for a very long time. Why shouldn't we?

Vinaigrette

3 tablespoons extra-virgin olive oil
1 tablespoon white wine vinegar
1 teaspoon whole-grain mustard
½ teaspoon dried tarragon
1 small clove garlic, minced
1 tablespoon minced shallot (optional)
Pinch of coarse salt
Freshly ground black pepper

1 large ripe avocado
1 large tomato, cut into 8 wedges
½ pound mixed baby greens, washed and dried,
   or 1 medium head Bibb lettuce, leaves separated

To make the vinaigrette, in a large salad bowl, combine the olive oil, vinegar, mustard, tarragon, garlic, shallot, and salt. Season with pepper. Using a wooden spoon or a whisk, mix until emulsified.

Cut the avocado in half and remove the pit (see Chef's Tip, page 25). Using a paring knife, score each avocado half down to the peel, cutting parallel lines lengthwise ½ inch apart. Rotate the half 90 degrees and cut a second series of parallel lines perpendicular to the first series, to create squares. Using a large spoon, scoop the squares from each half into the vinaigrette in the bowl.

Add the tomato to the bowl and stir gently to coat the tomato and avocado with the vinaigrette. Add the greens and toss until they are evenly coated. Serve at once.

Chef's Tip: *Making Mustard Vinaigrette*

1 Assemble the ingredients for the vinaigrette on a countertop, then add them to the bottom of a large salad bowl.

2 Use a whisk or wooden spoon to blend the ingredients vigorously until the mixture emulsifies, or thickens slightly and remains blended. If you don't plan to use the vinaigrette immediately, make it in a medium bowl and cover with plastic wrap until ready to use.

CHINESE CHICKEN SALAD

This zippy salad serves up a fresh, lively array of flavors and textures. Sesame seeds and shredded cabbage provide a crisp touch, fresh lime juice imparts tartness, and cayenne pepper turns up the heat. The mixed greens are topped with sautéed chicken breast to make a perfect light lunch or dinner. If you're contemplating a glass of wine, enjoy a chilled white or rosé.

Two key ingredients here are easy to find but may not be familiar to everyone. One is toasted sesame oil, a rich, dark oil that adds a lushness to the mix. The other is Asian fish sauce, sometimes referred to as Thai or Vietnamese fish sauce. Despite the name, it is not fishy at all, but instead imparts a pleasing hint of nuttiness. Both toasted sesame oil and Asian fish sauce can be found in the Asian foods section of most well-stocked supermarkets.

DRESSING

2 tablespoons tamari or soy sauce
2 tablespoons rice vinegar
¼ cup toasted sesame oil
Juice of 1 lime (about 2 tablespoons)
1 tablespoon Asian fish sauce
1 clove garlic, minced
1 tablespoon peeled and grated fresh ginger
Pinch of cayenne pepper

3 cups firmly packed baby spinach
3 cups firmly packed mixed baby salad greens
3 cups thinly sliced green cabbage
½ cup coarsely chopped fresh cilantro
1 medium carrot, peeled and grated
5 green onions, white part only, sliced
3 boneless, skinless chicken breasts (about 1¼ pounds)
Salt and freshly ground black pepper
1 tablespoon canola oil
1 tablespoon toasted sesame oil
2 tablespoons sesame seeds, toasted (page 192)

To make the dressing, in a small bowl, combine all of the ingredients and mix thoroughly with a whisk or spoon. Set aside.

In a large bowl, combine the spinach, salad greens, cabbage, cilantro, carrot, and green onions and mix well. Set aside.

Season the chicken breasts on both sides with salt and black pepper. Cut the breasts lengthwise into 16 to 20 strips, each 1 inch wide. In a medium skillet, heat the canola oil and sesame oil over medium-high heat. When the oil begins to shimmer, place the chicken strips in the pan and sauté, turning once, for about 2 minutes on each side, or until golden brown on both sides and cooked through. Transfer to a plate.

Pour the dressing over the salad greens and toss to coat evenly. Divide the greens among 4 plates. Place 4 or 5 slices of chicken breast on top of each salad and garnish with the sesame seeds.

CHEFS' GARDEN

At Ruby Tuesday, we take our produce seriously. That's why we seek out the freshest possible fruits and vegetables from a broad range of purveyors nationwide. But we also work on a smaller scale. The chefs at our test kitchens in Maryville, Tennessee, cultivate their own garden, which provides them with ultrafresh ingredients for developing new recipes. In the spirit of sustainability and giving back, our kitchen team sells extra produce from the garden at local farmers' markets and donates the profits to charity.

Potato Salad with Chipotle Chile and Bacon

Here's a potato salad that will add bright color and great flavors to your meal. Red pepper and green onions offer visual contrast, while bacon and chipotle chili flakes add smoke and heat. This salad is a perfect side dish for burgers (pages 130 to 134), Fork-Tender Baby Back Ribs (page 137), Barbecue Grilled Chicken Breasts (page 156), or just about anything else cooked on the grill.

2 pounds medium red potatoes, unpeeled,
    cut into 1-inch cubes
3 slices bacon, cut crosswise into 1/4-inch-wide strips
1/2 teaspoon chipotle chili flakes or red pepper flakes
1 clove garlic, minced
1 cup mayonnaise, homemade (page 194) or store-bought
1 red bell pepper, seeded and diced
5 green onions, white and tender green parts, cut into
    1/4-inch-thick rounds
1/4 cup loosely packed, coarsely chopped fresh cilantro
Salt and freshly ground black pepper

Bring a large pot half full of lightly salted water to a boil over high heat. Add the potatoes, bring the water back to a boil, decrease the heat to medium-high, and cook the potatoes for about 10 minutes, or until the potatoes can be pierced easily with a fork. (Do not overcook, or they will become mushy.) Drain the potatoes in a colander and rinse briefly with cold running water to stop the cooking. Set aside.

In a small skillet, cook the bacon over medium-high heat, stirring occasionally, for 3 to 5 minutes, or until crisp. Using a slotted spoon, transfer the bacon pieces to a small bowl and set aside.

In a small bowl, use a fork or whisk to stir the chipotle chili flakes and garlic into the mayonnaise.

In a large serving bowl, combine the potatoes, bacon, bell pepper, green onions, and cilantro and stir gently to mix. Add the seasoned mayonnaise and toss and stir gently to coat all the ingredients evenly. Season with salt and pepper, then serve.

Chipotle Chili Flakes

Chipotle chiles are smoke-dried jalapeño chiles. They are deep brown and wrinkled, have a distinctively smoky, almost baconlike flavor, and carry a good bit of heat. The chiles are sold crushed into flakes, which are stocked on the spice shelves of most neighborhood supermarkets. If you can't find them, however, the more common red pepper flakes make an excellent substitute.

TOMATO SOUP WITH FRESH BASIL

This chunky, flavorful soup is perfect in summertime, when ripe tomatoes fresh off the vine are available. It also works year-round, however. Just use canned tomatoes when good-quality fresh ones are out of season.

The soup has a bright edge, which makes it refreshing and lively. Fresh basil—straight from the garden or from your local green grocer—adds a special touch. If you are looking for a wine to pour, think about the bright acidity from the tomatoes and the herbal notes from the basil. Not surprisingly, a bright, herbal wine such as Sauvignon Blanc would make a fine match. Among reds, look for something with equally good acidity, like Pinot Noir or Sangiovese.

4 pounds fresh, ripe tomatoes, or 2 (28-ounce) cans
    whole tomatoes with juice
2 tablespoons extra-virgin olive oil
1 medium onion, coarsely chopped
1 small carrot, peeled and diced
2 tablespoons all-purpose flour
2 cups chicken stock (page 193) or canned
    low-sodium broth
4 teaspoons chopped fresh basil, plus 1 teaspoon
    finely sliced
½ teaspoon dried thyme
1 teaspoon salt, plus additional for seasoning
1 cup half-and-half
Freshly ground black pepper

If using fresh tomatoes, with a paring knife, cut a shallow X in the blossom (smooth) end of each tomato. Bring a large pot three-fourths full of water to a boil. Working in 2 batches, add the tomatoes and leave for 30 to 40 seconds, until the skins are just beginning to loosen. Using a slotted spoon, transfer the tomatoes to a bowl and let them cool for a minute or two until you can hold them in your hands. Then, starting at the X on each tomato, peel off the skin. Coarsely chop the tomatoes, making sure you conserve the juice, and set aside. If using canned tomatoes, drain the tomatoes, reserving the juice. Chop the tomatoes coarsely and set the juice and the tomatoes aside.

In a Dutch oven or large soup pot, heat the olive oil over medium heat. Add the onion and carrot and sauté, stirring frequently, for 3 to 5 minutes, until tender. Add the flour and cook, stirring constantly, for about 30 seconds, or until well integrated. Add the tomatoes with their juice, the chicken stock, the chopped basil, the thyme, and the 1 teaspoon salt. Bring to a boil, decrease the heat to low, and simmer, stirring occasionally, for about 15 minutes, or until the chunks of tomato start to fall apart. Remove from the heat and let cool slightly.

In a food processor or blender, process the soup in batches until it is fairly smooth. (Don't worry about having an absolutely smooth soup. A coarse purée makes an interesting texture.) Return the puréed soup to the pot and stir in the half-and-half. Heat the soup over medium-high heat until it begins to bubble. Decrease the heat to medium-low and simmer for 3 to 5 minutes to integrate all of the flavors. Season with salt and pepper.

Ladle into soup bowls and garnish with the sliced basil. Serve at once.

Broccoli and Cheese Soup with Parmesan Crostini

This creamy soup takes everyday broccoli to a higher level. Bits of carrot add color, and two cheeses, Cheddar and Parmesan, give it richness. You'll also find some heat thanks to the cayenne pepper. If you prefer a milder version, use half as much cayenne. The warm, crunchy Parmesan crostini can be floated on top of the soup or served on the side.

For a light meal, serve this soup with a green salad and a glass of chilled Sauvignon Blanc, Pinot Grigio, or Chardonnay.

2 tablespoons unsalted butter
1 small onion, diced
1 celery stalk, diced
1 medium carrot, peeled and diced
1 clove garlic, minced
½ teaspoon salt
¼ teaspoon cayenne pepper
3 tablespoons all-purpose flour
3 cups chicken stock (page 193) or canned
    low-sodium chicken broth
6 cups broccoli florets (about ¾ pound)
½ cup heavy cream
¾ cup grated Cheddar cheese
¼ cup freshly grated Parmesan cheese
Freshly ground black pepper

Parmesan Crostini (optional)
12 slices baguette, each ½ inch thick
¼ cup extra-virgin olive oil
½ cup freshly grated Parmesan cheese
Freshly ground black pepper

Preheat the oven to 350°F.

In a Dutch oven or large soup pot, melt the butter over medium heat. Add the onion, celery, and carrot and cook, stirring occasionally, for about 5 minutes, or until soft. Add the garlic, salt, and cayenne pepper and sauté for about 30 seconds, or until fragrant. Add the flour and cook, stirring constantly, for about 45 seconds, or until well integrated with the vegetables. Slowly add the chicken stock while whisking occasionally. Bring to a boil, decrease the heat to medium-low, and simmer for about 5 minutes, or until thickened. Add the broccoli, bring to a gentle boil over medium-high heat, cover, and cook, stirring occasionally, for about 10 minutes, or until the broccoli is tender.

While the soup is cooking, begin making the crostini. Using a pastry brush, brush one side of each baguette slice with the olive oil. Arrange the slices, oiled side up, on a baking sheet, and sprinkle evenly with the Parmesan. Bake for 20 minutes, or until golden brown. Remove from the oven and grind a little black pepper over the tops. Keep warm.

When the soup is ready, remove from the heat and let cool slightly. In a food processor or blender, process the soup in batches until smooth. As each batch is ready, transfer it to a clean soup pot. When all of the soup has been puréed, reheat it gently until it begins to simmer. Stir in the cream, mixing thoroughly, then add both cheeses and stir until melted.

Ladle into soup bowls and garnish each serving with some pepper. Serve at once, with the crostini on the side or floating on top of the soup as a garnish.

Minestrone Soup

This hearty Italian vegetable soup will bring plenty of warmth and flavor to your home. Served with crusty country bread, an assortment of cheeses, and a salad of Mixed Baby Greens with Mustard Vinaigrette (page 72), it makes a marvelously simple, rustic meal. Add a bottle of red wine, such as a Sangiovese or Zinfandel, and you'll be hosting a festive dinner party that's easy and inexpensive to prepare.

We recommend using elbow macaroni, but any small, short pasta will do. Cook the pasta in advance so that it is ready to add to the bowls. Note that a piece of Parmesan cheese rind is called for in the ingredients list. The thick rind of this nutty aged cheese imparts a rich flavor to the simmering soup. If you don't have Parmesan rind on hand, the soup will still be delicious. Just add a bit more grated cheese when serving.

1 pound elbow macaroni
2 tablespoons extra-virgin olive oil
½ onion, diced
1 leek, white part only, thinly sliced
3 cloves garlic, minced
1 teaspoon dried thyme
1 teaspoon dried oregano
2 medium carrots, peeled and diced
2 celery stalks, coarsely chopped
1 medium white potato, diced
1 medium zucchini, diced
3 cups chopped kale
1 (14-ounce) can whole tomatoes, drained and
    coarsely chopped
6 cups chicken stock (page 193) or canned
    low-sodium chicken broth
1½ teaspoons salt

2-inch square Parmesan cheese rind (optional)
2 (15-ounce) cans cannellini or white kidney beans,
    drained and rinsed
6 to 8 tablespoons freshly grated Parmesan cheese
Freshly ground black pepper

To cook the macaroni, bring a 6-quart pot two-thirds full of lightly salted water to a boil over high heat. Add the pasta, decrease the heat to medium-high, and cook, stirring occasionally, for about 8 minutes, or until al dente. Drain the pasta in a colander, rinse with cold running water, and set aside.

In a large soup pot or Dutch oven, heat the olive oil over medium-high heat. Add the onion and sauté for about 3 minutes, or until transparent. Add the leek and sauté for 3 minutes more. Add the garlic and sauté for about 30 seconds, or until fragrant. Decrease the heat to medium-low, add the thyme and oregano, and stir well. Mix in the carrots, celery, potato, and zucchini and sauté, stirring constantly, for about 5 minutes, or until the vegetables begin to soften. Add the kale and sauté for 2 minutes more. Stir in the tomatoes and add the chicken stock, salt, and Parmesan cheese rind. Raise the heat to high and bring the soup to a boil. Decrease the heat to a simmer, cover, and cook, stirring occasionally, for about 30 minutes to integrate all of the flavors.

Place the beans in a medium bowl and mash them partially using a potato masher or a fork. Add ½ cup of the soup broth to the beans and stir to make a thick paste. Add the paste to the soup and stir to mix well. Cook for 5 minutes more. Remove and discard the cheese rind.

To serve, place about ½ cup of the macaroni in each soup bowl and ladle the hot soup over the macaroni. (Reserve the remaining macaroni for another use.) Garnish each serving with 1 tablespoon of the Parmesan cheese and grind pepper over the top. Serve at once.

TORTILLA SOUP

Freshly squeezed lime juice gives this zesty soup an exotic aroma. The soup is made with a rich chicken stock base and crowned with a quartet of toppings: homemade tortilla chips, cheese, avocado, and cilantro. Here, the cook adds the toppings, but you can also put them out on the table and let guests garnish their own soup.

Homemade tortilla chips are easy to make and add a pleasing crunch, but if you are short of time, you can use store-bought chips. Break them in half for ease of eating in the soup.

1 (14-ounce) can whole tomatoes, drained
½ cup loosely packed, coarsely chopped fresh cilantro,
    plus 6 to 8 teaspoons chopped for garnish
1 small jalapeño chile, seeded and minced
2 tablespoons canola oil, plus additional for frying
1 medium onion, coarsely chopped
3 cloves garlic, minced
¾ teaspoon ground cumin
1 teaspoon dried oregano
2 medium carrots, peeled and thinly sliced
1 medium white potato, cut into ½-inch cubes
1½ teaspoons salt, plus additional for seasoning
6 cups chicken stock (page 193) or canned low-sodium
    chicken broth
6 (6- to 8-inch) white or yellow corn tortillas,
    cut into 4 by ½-inch strips
2 large ripe avocados
1 cup grated Cheddar cheese
2 limes, quartered

In a blender or food processor, combine the tomatoes, ¼ cup of the cilantro, and the chile and process until a thick liquid forms. Discard any large pieces of tomato skin that might remain, and set the purée aside.

In a large soup pot or Dutch oven, heat the 2 tablespoons canola oil over medium-high heat. Add the onion and sauté for about 4 minutes, or until translucent. Add the garlic and cumin and sauté for about 30 seconds, or until fragrant. Decrease the heat to medium, add the oregano, carrots, and potato, and stir to coat evenly with the oil. Continue to cook, stirring occasionally, for about 5 minutes, or until softened. Add the puréed tomato mixture and the 1½ teaspoons salt, stir to mix well, and simmer for 2 minutes. Add the chicken stock and bring to a boil over high heat. Decrease the heat to a simmer, cover, and simmer for 30 minutes to blend the flavors.

While the soup is cooking, fry the tortilla strips. Pour the canola oil to a depth of 1 inch into a medium skillet and heat over high heat. When the oil begins to shimmer, add as many of the tortilla strips to the pan as possible without crowding and fry for about 2 minutes, or until crisp. Using tongs or a slotted spoon, transfer the strips to paper towels to drain, then salt lightly. Repeat with the remaining tortilla strips and reserve.

Cut the avocado in half and remove the pit (see Chef's Tip, page 25). Using a paring knife, score each avocado half down to the peel, cutting parallel lines lengthwise ½ inch apart. Rotate the half 90 degrees and cut a second series of parallel lines perpendicular to the first series, to create squares. Using a large spoon, scoop the squares from each half into a bowl.

To serve, ladle the soup into soup bowls. Divide the fried tortilla strips evenly among the servings, floating them on top of the soup. Place the cheese and then the avocado squares on top of the tortilla strips, dividing them both evenly. Garnish each serving with 1 teaspoon cilantro. At the side of each bowl, set a lime wedge for guests to squeeze into their soup.

Pasta

Lobster Carbonara with English Peas	96
Lemon Pasta with Parmesan and Herbs	98
Basil-Mint Pesto Pasta	99
Seafood Pasta with Andouille Sausage	101
Fettuccine with Roasted Red Pepper Sauce and Italian Sausage	102
Tomato, Basil, and Bocconcini Pasta Salad	103
Mac and Cheese	104
Mediterranean Pasta Salad	106
Spicy Sesame Noodles	107

Tomato, Basil, and Bocconcini Pasta Salad

Except for the pasta, this recipe requires no cooking. We recommend corkscrew-shaped fusilli pasta, which nicely traps the sauce in its twists and turns. But any other pasta will suffice. Bocconcini, soft, mild bite-sized mozzarella balls, make an easy addition to this festively colored dish. If you can't find bocconcini, use a large ball of fresh mozzarella and cut it into ½-inch cubes. This dish tastes equally good warm or at room temperature—perfect for picnics and other outdoor gatherings.

Drink a fresh white wine, such as Pinot Grigio or Sauvignon Blanc; a fruity rosé; or a lighter-styled red, like Pinot Noir, Malbec, or Sangiovese for an excellent pairing.

1 pound dried fusilli pasta
⅓ cup extra-virgin olive oil
¼ cup minced fresh basil
2 cups cherry tomatoes, halved crosswise
2 cloves garlic, minced
1 tablespoon freshly squeezed lemon juice
½ teaspoon salt, plus additional for seasoning
3 tablespoons freshly grated Parmesan cheese,
    plus additional for garnish (optional)
1 cup bocconcini
Freshly ground black pepper

Bring a 6-quart pot two-thirds full of lightly salted water to a boil over high heat. Add the pasta, decrease the heat to medium-high, and cook, stirring occasionally, for about 10 minutes, or until al dente.

While the pasta is cooking, in a bowl large enough to toss the pasta, combine the olive oil, basil, tomatoes, garlic, lemon juice, and the ½ teaspoon salt. Add 3 tablespoons of the boiling water from the pasta pot. Mix thoroughly and, using a potato masher or the back of a large wooden spoon, gently mash the tomatoes into the sauce. Add the 3 tablespoons Parmesan and the *bocconcini* and stir to mix well.

When the pasta is ready, drain it in a colander and shake it dry. Add the cooked pasta to the sauce and toss thoroughly to coat the noodles evenly. Season with salt and pepper.

Divide among 4 large plates or shallow bowls. Top each serving with a dusting of Parmesan. Serve warm or at room temperature.

How to Cook Pasta

Not all types of pasta cook in the same amount of time. Thicker noodles need more time than thinner noodles, for example. And fresh pasta cooks much faster than dried pasta. (All the pasta recipes in this book use dried pasta.) What's most important to remember is that overcooked noodles will be mushy.

In general, you need a 6-quart pot and 4 quarts of water to cook 1 pound dried pasta. A smaller pot might overflow, or crowd the noodles, causing them to stick together or cook unevenly. Bring the water to a boil over high heat. Add a pinch or two of salt to the water, then add the pasta. Do not cover the pot. Decrease the heat to medium-high—you want enough heat to maintain a modest boil—and stir the noodles occasionally as they cook.

Cook pasta until it is al dente, that is, tender but still with some resistance to the bite. Thicker noodles usually cook in about 10 minutes. Thinner noodles, such as angel hair or spaghetti, might take as few as 6 to 8 minutes. That's why it's important to taste the pasta for doneness as it gets toward the suggested cooking time. When it has finished cooking, drain it in a colander and shake it to release the excess moisture. Don't rinse pasta with running cold water unless you want to cool it down to room temperature quickly. A sauce won't easily adhere to dripping wet pasta, and the additional moisture will dilute the flavors in your dish.

MAC AND CHEESE

SERVES 4 TO 6

After eating this homemade macaroni and cheese, you'll never opt for a packaged version again. The top crust is fabulously crunchy, thanks to light-textured panko *bread crumbs. (If you can't find* panko, *available in most supermarkets, substitute regular bread crumbs.)*

Beneath the crunchy crust lie elbow noodles swimming in a rich, creamy sauce. For a special touch, garnish this dish with a few dashes of exotic, earthy truffle oil. Fortunately, truffle oil is not nearly as expensive as real truffles are. Pick up a small bottle at your local supermarket, and remember that a little goes a long way!

1 pound elbow macaroni
4½ tablespoons unsalted butter
2 cups grated Cheddar cheese
¾ cup freshly grated Parmesan cheese
¼ cup panko bread crumbs
2½ cups milk
4 tablespoons all-purpose flour
½ teaspoon salt
Freshly ground black pepper
Truffle oil, for garnish (optional)

Bring a 6-quart pot two-thirds full of lightly salted water to a boil over high heat. Add the macaroni, decrease the heat to medium-high, and cook, stirring occasionally, for about 5 minutes, or until just barely al dente. (Do not overcook the noodles or they will soften too much and lose their shape when baked.) Drain in a colander and rinse under cold running water to stop the cooking. Return the noodles to the pot in which they were cooked and set aside.

Preheat the oven to 350°F. Use the ½ tablespoon butter to grease a 9-inch square baking pan or a similarly sized broiler-proof gratin dish. Set the pan aside.

In a small bowl, stir together the Cheddar and ¼ cup of the Parmesan cheese. In another small bowl, combine the remaining ½ cup Parmesan and the bread crumbs. Set both mixtures aside.

In a medium pot, heat the milk over medium heat until small bubbles begin to form along the edge of the pan. Do not allow it to boil. Decrease the heat to low to keep the milk warm.

In another medium pot, melt the remaining 4 tablespoons butter over medium heat. Whisk in the flour, then cook, whisking frequently to prevent burning, for 3 to 5 minutes, until the mixture thickens and turns golden brown. Slowly add the warm milk in a steady stream while whisking constantly to prevent the lumps from forming. Once all of the milk has been added, whisk in the Cheddar-Parmesan cheese mixture. Remove the pot from the heat and continue to whisk until the cheeses are completely incorporated into the milk. The mixture will thicken while you are whisking.

Pour the cheese sauce over the noodles and mix well to coat evenly. Season with salt and pepper. Transfer the sauced macaroni to the prepared baking pan.

Bake for 15 minutes. Remove the dish from the oven and turn the oven to broil. Sprinkle the top of the macaroni with the bread crumb–Parmesan mixture. Return the macaroni to the oven, placing it on the top rack about 4 inches from the broiler. Broil for 3 to 5 minutes, until the top is golden brown.

Remove from the oven and spoon onto plates. Top each serving sparingly with truffle oil and serve at once.

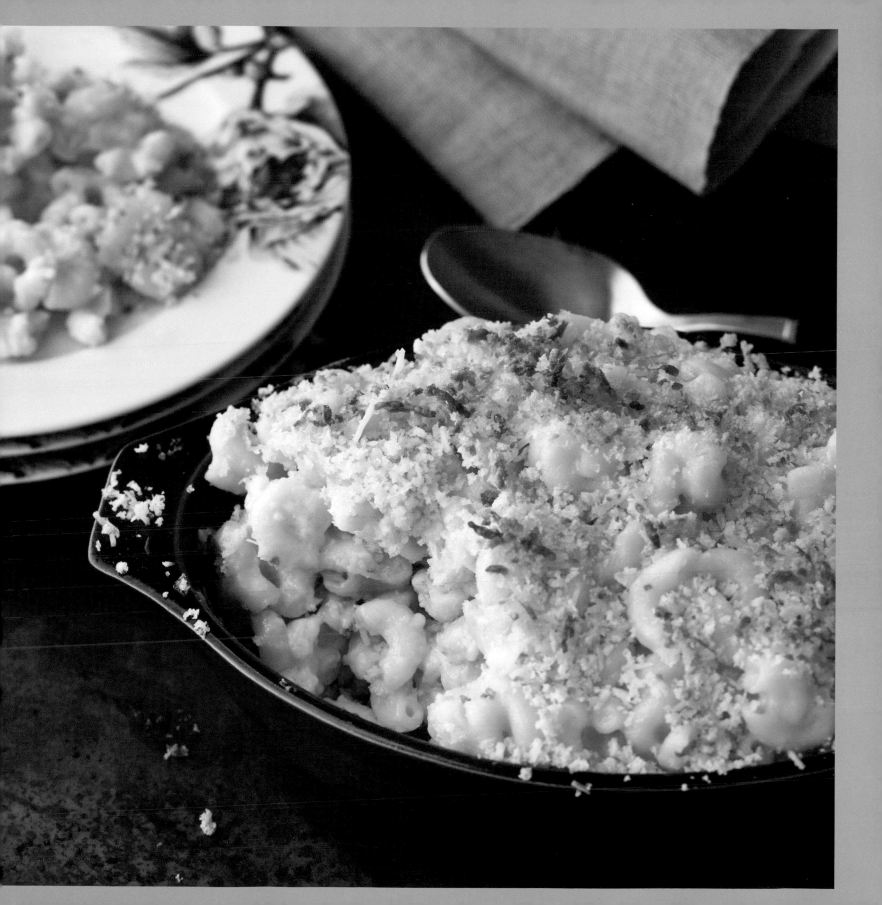

MEDITERRANEAN PASTA SALAD

Pasta can be refreshing, especially when it's served chilled or at room temperature. This pasta salad serves up the kind of flavors you might find on a visit to France's famous Côte d'Azur, where the hillsides are lushly planted with olive trees and herbs such as rosemary and thyme. Here, rosemary and basil provide an aromatic backdrop for roasted sweet red peppers and briny olives. You can easily roast your own peppers, or you can purchase them already prepared at the grocery store. Two tangy cheeses, feta and Parmesan, add an earthy richness.

Because it can be served warm or at room temperature, this dish is ideal for picnics, barbecues, and the like. For ease in the kitchen, cook the pasta up to 24 hours in advance and roast the peppers up to 3 days in advance, and refrigerate them both. The rest of the recipe takes only about 10 minutes to prepare.

Any chilled crisp white wine or rosé would make a perfect match here. So would lighter reds, such as Pinot Noir, Merlot, or Malbec.

1 pound dried linguine or other dried long pasta

⅓ cup extra-virgin olive oil

1 clove garlic, minced

1 tablespoon dried rosemary

¼ teaspoon salt, plus additional for seasoning

¼ cup freshly grated Parmesan cheese

4 to 6 red bell peppers, roasted, peeled, and seeded
   (page 193), or 2 cups store-bought roasted red peppers

2 cups firmly packed baby spinach, finely sliced

¼ cup firmly packed fresh basil leaves, finely sliced

¾ cup pitted Kalamata or similar small olives, halved

½ red onion, thinly sliced in crescents (about ½ cup)

½ cup crumbled feta cheese

Freshly ground black pepper

Bring a 6-quart pot two-thirds full of lightly salted water to a boil over high heat. Add the pasta, decrease the heat to medium-high, and cook, stirring occasionally, for about 10 minutes, or until al dente. Drain the pasta in a colander and shake it dry. Set aside if using within about 30 minutes, or refrigerate in a closed container for up to 24 hours.

In a bowl large enough to toss the pasta, combine the olive oil, garlic, rosemary, the ¼ teaspoon salt, and the Parmesan cheese. Add the pasta to the bowl and toss until the noodles are thoroughly coated. Cut the roasted peppers into strips 2 inches long and ½ inch wide. Add to the pasta along with the spinach, basil, olives, onion, and feta cheese. Toss again to blend thoroughly.

Season with salt and pepper. Divide among 4 large plates or shallow bowls and serve warm or at room temperature.

Spicy Sesame Noodles

These spicy noodles are brimming with Asian flavors and aromas. Ginger and earthy tamari (a thick, dark Japanese soy sauce) are keynote tastes, and dark toasted sesame oil (not to be confused with light, untoasted sesame oil) adds richness. The heat comes from chili-infused toasted sesame oil. Look for both toasted sesame oils with the other oils or with the Asian condiments in your supermarket.

Enjoy this dish at room temperature or chilled. It can be stored in the refrigerator for up to 24 hours before serving. For a terrific light lunch or dinner, start with a Mixed Green Salad with Mustard Vinaigrette (page 72) followed by the noodles. Add a touch of elegance with a chilled glass of rosé or white wine such as Sauvignon Blanc or Riesling. A cool, frothy ale would also be a good choice.

1 pound dried pasta (such as linguine or fettuccine)
3 tablespoons toasted sesame oil
1 tablespoon toasted sesame chili oil
6 tablespoons tamari or soy sauce
1 clove garlic, minced
½ teaspoon ground ginger
½ teaspoon ground allspice
12 to 14 ounces firm tofu, cut into ½-inch cubes
1 red bell pepper, seeded and cut in ¼-inch dice
4 green onions, white and tender green parts, thinly sliced
3 tablespoons sesame seeds, toasted (page 192)

Bring a 6-quart pot two-thirds full of lightly salted water to a boil over high heat. Add the pasta, decrease the heat to medium-high, and cook, stirring occasionally, for about 10 minutes, or until al dente.

While the pasta is cooking, prepare the sauce. In a bowl large enough to toss the pasta, combine the sesame oils, tamari, garlic, ginger, and allspice and stir to mix well. Add the tofu and toss to coat thoroughly.

When the pasta is ready, drain in a colander and rinse under cold running water. Shake the noodles dry, add them to the tofu-sesame sauce, and toss to coat evenly.

Add the bell pepper, green onions, and sesame seeds and toss to mix well. Divide among 4 large plates or shallow bowls and serve.

Seafood

Crab Cakes with Corn and
Pineapple Chutney   112

Scallops with Shallots, Parsley,
and White Wine Sauce   115

Grilled Lemon-Lime Shrimp with
Yogurt-Cilantro Dipping Sauce   117

Baked Halibut with Chili-Lime Butter   118

Baked Petrale Sole with
Fennel, Tomatoes, Potatoes, and Capers   121

Cajun-Spiced Tilapia   123

Asian Glazed Salmon   124

Soy-Sesame Tuna Steaks   125

Seafood

Fish is an excellent source of protein, vitamins, and minerals. It's also rich in omega-3 fatty acids, which have been found to decrease the risk of heart disease. As a result, the American Heart Association recommends eating fish at least twice a week. It's nice to know something that's so good for us tastes good, too! Even better, fish is easy to cook. Meaty salmon and halibut, for example, require only short stints on the stove or in the oven and readily take on the flavors of the spices or sauces with which they are cooked. You'll find similar results with Cajun-Spiced Tilapia (page 123), dredged in tangy Louisiana spices and then panfried for 10 minutes.

Fish also pairs beautifully with vegetables. Baked Petrale Sole with Fennel, Tomatoes, Potatoes, and Capers (page 121) blends the flavors of the fish and its accompaniments by steaming them together in a simple foil pouch.

You'll find outstanding shellfish recipes in this chapter, as well. Crab Cakes with Corn and Pineapple Chutney (page 112) can serve as an appetizer or a main course. And Scallops with Shallots, Parsley, and White Wine Sauce (page 115) will put Old World elegance on the dinner table with minimum fuss.

Thanks to the wonders of modern-day airfreight, fresh fish is easy to find almost everywhere. Many supermarkets offer a diverse selection, often under the supervision of an in-house fishmonger. Ask for what's freshest and don't worry too much about finding a particular variety. They are often interchangeable. That's why many of the recipes in this chapter also recommend fish substitutes not listed in the recipe title.

CRAB CAKES WITH CORN AND PINEAPPLE CHUTNEY

SERVES 4 AS A MAIN COURSE OR 6 AS AN APPETIZER

Crunchy on the outside and tender inside, these plump crab cakes rest on a bed of chutney that mixes sweet, smoky corn, tropical pineapple, and a colorful mix of red bell pepper, red onion, and parsley. Most fishmongers sell freshly cooked crabmeat picked from the shell, which makes this recipe easy to prepare. Panko, coarse, crisp Japanese bread crumbs, will ensure a flakier, lighter fry than regular bread crumbs, though the latter can be used in a pinch. Look for panko in well-stocked supermarkets and Asian groceries.

These crab cakes are wine friendly. Serve them with a chilled white such as Sauvignon Blanc or Chardonnay. A fruity Riesling would also make a fine match.

CHUTNEY

1 tablespoon canola oil
Kernels from 2 ears yellow corn (about 1½ cups)
2 tablespoons extra-virgin olive oil
¼ cup diced red bell pepper
1 tablespoon minced jalapeño chile
3 tablespoons minced red onion
1 cup diced fresh pineapple
2 teaspoons rice vinegar
½ teaspoon sugar
2 tablespoons coarsely chopped fresh flat-leaf parsley

CRAB CAKES

3 tablespoons finely chopped celery
3 tablespoons finely chopped red onion
3 tablespoons minced fresh cilantro
1 egg
¼ cup mayonnaise, homemade (page 194) or store-bought
1 tablespoon Dijon mustard
⅛ teaspoon cayenne pepper
1½ cups panko bread crumbs
1 pound fresh jumbo lump crabmeat, cartilage and shell bits removed (about 3 cups)
¼ teaspoon salt
⅛ teaspoon freshly ground black pepper
¼ cup canola oil

To make the chutney, in a medium skillet, heat the canola oil over medium heat. Add the corn kernels and sauté, shaking the pan frequently to prevent burning, for about 5 minutes, or until the kernels begin to turn golden brown. Transfer the kernels to a bowl. If some of the kernels have stuck on the pan bottom, dislodge them with a spatula and add to the bowl.

In the same pan, heat the olive oil over medium-low heat. Add the bell pepper, chile, and onion and sauté for about 2 minutes, or until the mixture has softened. Add the pineapple and return the corn kernels to the pan. Mix the ingredients together and cook, stirring occasionally, 3 to 4 minutes more, until the pineapple softens. Stir in the vinegar and sugar, then remove from the heat and stir in the parsley. Transfer the chutney to a bowl and set aside.

(recipe continued on page 114)

CRAB CAKES WITH CORN AND PINEAPPLE CHUTNEY (continued)

To make the crab cakes, preheat the oven to 350°F.

In a large bowl, combine the celery, onion, cilantro, egg, mayonnaise, Dijon mustard, and cayenne pepper. Use a wooden spoon to mix thoroughly. Add 1 cup of the *panko* and mix well. Add the crabmeat, salt, and pepper and mix well.

Using your hands, divide the crab mixture into 12 small balls each about 2 inches in diameter. With your palm, a fork, or a spatula, press gently on each ball to flatten slightly, forming little cakes each about 3 inches in diameter and 1 inch thick. Put the remaining ½ cup *panko* on a small plate or in a dish. Dip the tops and bottoms of each crab cake into the *panko* to coat lightly. Set the cakes aside on another plate.

In a large skillet, heat the canola oil over high heat. When the oil begins to shimmer, carefully place the crab cakes in the pan and cook, turning once, for about 2 minutes on each side, or until golden on both sides.

Transfer the browned cakes to a nonstick baking sheet. Bake for 15 minutes, or until cooked throughout.

To serve, place a tablespoon of chutney on each dinner plate and flatten it into a circle about 3½ to 4 inches in diameter. Set 1 crab cake on top of the chutney. Repeat with 2 or 3 cakes total on each plate. Use extra chutney to garnish the tops of the cakes, if desired. Serve immediately.

ENTERTAINING TIP: *Keep Them Bite Sized!*

Turn these crab cakes and other substantial dishes like omelets (pages 65 to 66) into bite-sized appetizers by simply making them smaller, then offer along with cocktails to guests before everyone sits down to eat. Use half as much crab mixture for each cake, for example, or cut the omelets into 2-inch squares. (If your guests are enjoying the cakes without dining utensils, the chutney that accompanies them is more practical as a garnish.) When serving finger food, remember to keep a steady supply of napkins on hand.

CAJUN-SPICED TILAPIA

Tilapia, a freshwater fish farmed throughout the world, is available in most fish markets. It is known for its tender, mild-tasting white flesh—perfect for taking on the flavors of whatever spice or sauce it is cooked with. This recipe is inspired by the cuisine of New Orleans, where paprika and cayenne pepper make a strong imprint on regional cooking.

It takes almost no time at all to prepare the spice mix, and the tilapia fillets cook in about 10 minutes. This kind of quick cooking makes this dish practical for home entertaining. Sautéed Carrots with Cumin Seeds and Cilantro (page 36), Wilted Spinach with Bacon and Garlic (page 37), or Brown Rice Pilaf (page 42) would all partner well on your guests' dinner plates. As with many side dishes, these can be made in advance and kept warm or warmed up prior to serving.

In your glass, the options are many. Rich, buttery Chardonnay or bright, crisp Sauvignon Blanc would add an interesting dimension to the menu. A cool, dry rosé would also be delicious. So, too, would a light, chilled lager beer.

SPICE MIX

1 cup all-purpose flour

1 tablespoon salt

2 teaspoons paprika

1 teaspoon dried oregano

½ teaspoon onion powder

½ teaspoon granulated garlic powder

½ teaspoon dried thyme

¼ teaspoon cayenne pepper

4 skinless tilapia fillets, 6 ounces each

Salt

2 tablespoons canola oil

1 cup white wine

2 tablespoons unsalted butter

1 lemon, quartered

To make the spice mix, in a medium bowl, combine all of the ingredients. Use a fork or a small whisk to mix well.

Lightly season the tilapia fillets on both sides with salt. Dredge the fillets thoroughly in the spice mix at least twice to make sure they are well coated with the mix. Shake off the excess and set them aside on a plate.

In a large skillet, heat the canola oil over medium-high heat. When the oil begins to shimmer, place the fillets in the pan and cook for about 5 minutes, or until the underside is reddish gold. Turn the fillets and cook for 3 to 5 minutes more, until the second side is a similar color. Transfer each fillet to a dinner plate.

Add the wine to the pan, bring to a boil, and boil for about 1 minute, scraping up any browned bits on the pan bottom with a wooden spoon. Decrease the heat to medium, add the butter, and stir the butter as it melts. When the butter has melted, spoon the pan sauce over the fillets.

Squeeze a lemon quarter over each fillet. Serve at once.

Asian Glazed Salmon

A sesame-peanut glaze gives this baked salmon its sweet and spicy kick. The heat comes from chili-infused toasted sesame oil. You can find it with the other oils or in the Asian condiments aisle at your supermarket. The latter is where you'll find the fruity hoisin sauce, too. This simple glaze, which is assembled quickly, infuses salmon fillets with intriguing Asian flavors. Brown Rice Pilaf (page 42) makes an excellent side dish. While the rice is cooking, make the salmon. The fish and rice will be ready at the same time.

Select a fruity white or red wine for this distinctive dish. Riesling, Chardonnay, Pinot Noir, and Zinfandel come to mind. Rosé would also be an excellent choice.

Glaze

2 tablespoons unsalted creamy peanut butter

2 tablespoons tamari or soy sauce

1 tablespoon toasted sesame oil

1 tablespoon toasted sesame chili oil

1 tablespoon hoisin sauce

1 tablespoon brown sugar

½ teaspoon ground ginger

½ teaspoon ground allspice

1 small clove garlic, minced or crushed

¼ cup water

½ teaspoon canola oil

4 skin-on salmon fillets, ½ pound each

Preheat the oven to 400°F.

To make the glaze, in a small saucepan, combine all of the ingredients. Whisk to blend well, then bring to a boil over high heat. Decrease the heat to medium and let the glaze simmer, stirring occasionally, for about 5 minutes, or until it thickens to a creamy, soft texture.

Lightly oil a baking dish or pan just large enough to hold the salmon fillets with the canola oil. Place the fillets, skin side down, in the prepared pan. Use a spoon or knife to coat the tops and sides of the fillets liberally with the glaze.

Bake the fillets for about 15 minutes, or until they are barely opaque at the center when tested with a knife but still moist.

Using a spatula, lift the fillets, one at a time, from the pan and place them on plates. Most of the skin, which can be discarded, will remain in the pan. Place a mound of the warm pilaf next to each salmon fillet and serve at once.

SOY-SESAME TUNA STEAKS

These meaty tuna steaks are coated with a briny, spiced marinade, fragrant cilantro, and a squeeze of tart lemon juice. If you can't find fresh tuna, substitute any meaty fish, such as mahimahi or swordfish. Enjoy the steaks with any number of the side dishes in Appetizers & Side Dishes (page 19). One of our favorite pairings is Corn and Edamame Succotash (page 40). The colorful display of yellow corn kernels, red pepper, and green edamame provides a pretty contrast to the dark-hued tuna. Brown Rice Pilaf (page 42) would also make a fine accompaniment.

Richly textured tuna goes well with both white and red wines. A full-bodied Chardonnay and a fine-tuned Pinot Noir are two excellent options.

¼ cup tamari or soy sauce

3 tablespoons toasted sesame oil

½ teaspoon ground ginger

⅛ teaspoon cayenne pepper

4 tuna steaks, ½ pound each

Canola oil, for searing

2 tablespoons minced fresh cilantro

Juice of ½ lemon

In a bowl or a baking dish large enough to hold the tuna steaks, stir together the tamari or soy sauce, sesame oil, ginger, and cayenne pepper. Place the tuna in the soy mixture, turn to coat both sides, and marinate at room temperature for about 30 minutes. Flip the steaks occasionally so that each side absorbs more of the marinade.

In a large skillet, pour the oil to a depth of ⅛ inch and heat over high heat. When the oil begins to shimmer, place the tuna steaks in the pan, decrease the heat to medium-high, and sear, turning once, for about 2 minutes on each side for medium-rare.

Transfer each tuna steak to a dinner plate. Garnish with the cilantro and lemon juice. If serving with a side dish, as suggested in the headnote, place a mound of it on each plate and lean the tuna up against it at an angle. Serve at once.

Beef, Pork, & Poultry

The Classic Burger   130

Brewmaster Burger   133

Avocado Turkey Burger   134

Fork-Tender Baby Back Ribs   137

Braised Short Ribs   139

Meat Loaf   140

Rib Eye with Garlic Brown Butter   142

Peppercorn Steaks with
Brandy Cream Sauce and Sautéed Mushrooms   145

Cowboy Sirloin with Red Chili Rub,
Caramelized Onions, and Blue Cheese Butter   146

Pork Chops with Fried Garlic
and Red Wine Gravy   149

Pork Loin with Rosemary-Garlic Rub   150

Buttermilk Fried Chicken
with Mushroom Gravy   153

Braised Chicken with Fresh Fennel,
Carrots, Zucchini, Potatoes, and Herbs   155

Barbecue Grilled Chicken Breasts   156

Chicken Broccoli Stir-Fry
with Lemon Butter and Brown Rice   159

Chicken Curry with Coconut Rice   160

Chicken Fresco with
Parmesan Cream Sauce and Roasted Tomatoes   162

Beef, Pork, & Poultry

A nice piece of meat makes nearly any meal seem special. The same can be said for chicken. Not only do meat and chicken taste good, but they are good for us, too. Plus, the proteins they contain smooth out the texture in red wines—an added bonus if you're enjoying a full-bodied Cabernet Sauvignon or a fruit-forward Malbec, for example.

In this chapter, we share dishes that have delighted literally millions of our customers over the years. You'll find great ways to cook burgers, steaks, and ribs and also discover a fresh take on yet another American classic, Meat Loaf (page 140).

While we celebrate meat, let's not forget versatile chicken. This moderately priced protein pairs beautifully with anything with which it's cooked. That's why we can enjoy it in so many different dishes around the world. Some of the following recipes, such as Barbecue Grilled Chicken Breasts (page 156) and Chicken Fresco with Parmesan Cream Sauce and Roasted Tomatoes (page 162), are inspired by popular standards at Ruby Tuesday. Others, like Braised Chicken with Fresh Fennel, Carrots, Zucchini, Potatoes, and Herbs (page 155) and Chicken Broccoli Stir-Fry with Lemon Butter (page 159), offer imaginative new tastes for your table.

Whether you're cooking for a special occasion or a casual family dinner, you'll find these meat and chicken recipes will ensure success in the kitchen. And because they are designed with convenience in mind, most of them are quick and easy to prepare. Just fire up the stove and get ready to feast on the ultimate in dining pleasure.

The Classic Burger

This burger is all about the beef. You can use any ground cut you like, but we recommend freshly ground beef chuck—the hamburger gold standard for most butchers. With about 20 percent fat content, chuck is still juicy and flavorful when it comes off the fire.

Roasted garlic mayonnaise (page 195) adds a special touch. But if you don't have time to make it from scratch, any top-notch commercial mayonnaise will yield excellent results, with or without the garlic.

And if you're enjoying your burgers with wine, look for a fruit-forward red like Zinfandel or Malbec. Rosé is a fine match for burgers, too. It has bright acidity and fruit flavors that can stand up to onion, mayonnaise, and ketchup. By extension, fruity Sangria (page 12) is also an excellent choice for your glass.

2 pounds ground beef (preferably chuck)

½ teaspoon salt

Freshly ground black pepper

1 teaspoon canola oil, if cooking on the stovetop

Roasted garlic mayonnaise (page 195) or mayonnaise (page 194), or store-bought, for spreading

4 hamburger buns (such as ciabatta, potato, or English muffin), split and toasted

4 to 8 leaves butter or other green leaf lettuce

4 tomato slices

4 onion slices

8 round dill pickle slices (optional)

Ketchup, for serving (optional)

Prepare an outdoor charcoal or gas grill for direct-heat grilling over medium-high heat. Or, have ready a large, heavy skillet.

Place the beef in a large bowl, sprinkle with the salt, and add several grinds of pepper. Using your hands, mix together thoroughly. Divide the meat into 4 equal portions. Gently shape each portion into a ball, then toss the ball back and forth between your hands a few times to eliminate any air pockets. Gently flatten each ball into a patty about 5 inches in diameter and 1 inch thick.

If not using an outdoor grill, coat the surface of the skillet with the canola oil and heat on the stovetop over medium-high heat. Place the patties on the grill rack or in the skillet and cook, turning once, for about 5 minutes on each side for medium-rare or about 7 minutes on each side for medium. Remove from the grill or pan.

Spread a dollop of mayonnaise on the bottom half of each bun. Place a leaf or two of lettuce on top of the mayonnaise. Set the burger on top of the lettuce. Layer 1 tomato slice, 1 onion slice, and 2 pickle slices on top of the burger. Cover with the top half of the bun. If desired, cut the burgers in half for ease of eating. Pass the ketchup at the table.

BURGERS

It's no accident that we take our burgers seriously. Nearly one out of every five diners at Ruby Tuesday orders one. That adds up to some 13 million burgers each year. A great burger should be plump, juicy, and flavor filled. At the restaurant, our burgers are prepared simply—seasoned only with salt and pepper—to showcase the rich, natural taste of the meat. They are typically dressed with roasted garlic mayonnaise, tomatoes, lettuce, onion slices, and dill pickles. We hold back on the ketchup, however, which is served on the side. Of course, we love ketchup as much as anyone, but we prefer to leave it up to our guests whether they want to add it. The same is true for mustard.

THE BEEF

The typical meat counter holds a few different types of ground beef. For burgers, your best bet is ground chuck, which usually has a 20 percent fat content. Fat helps carry the flavors along your palate and keeps the meat moist.

THE BUN

Almost as important as the burger is the bun it's served on. We like to frame our burgers in a special ciabatta bun. This Italian-style bread has more substance than the average hamburger bun. It's chewier and often seasoned with herbs. If you can't find ciabatta buns at your local bakery or supermarket, try potato buns or English muffins as an alternative to regular hamburger buns.

BEYOND THE CLASSIC BURGER

We've also included our popular Brewmaster Burger (page 133) in this section. It's dressed in barbecue sauce and topped with bacon. And anyone who is looking for a burger made without beef will be happy to discover our Avocado Turkey Burger (page 134).

At the restaurant, we serve burgers with French fries. But if you don't want to deep-fry a batch at home, try our Oven-Roasted Potato "Fries" with Rosemary (page 46) or Herbed Panfried Potatoes (page 46). They are easy to prepare and deliciously satisfying.

Tips for Backyard Barbecues

When hosting a casual backyard barbecue, the more you plan in advance, the more free time you'll have to enjoy with friends and family. The following tips will help ensure you're having as much fun as your guests.

1. Keep your grill clean. A clean grill helps prevent sticking and also discourages off flavors from carbon buildup on the rack.

2. Check your fuel source. It's no fun running out of propane gas or charcoal briquettes with hungry guests waiting to eat.

3. Prepare anything that needs grilling—burgers, chicken, steaks—before your guests arrive. Keep the items refrigerated until it's time to set them over the heat.

4. Ready any other dishes in advance, such as salads, side dishes, and desserts, and set them aside in a cool place or refrigerate them. It's a good idea to plan a menu that includes as many dishes as possible that require no heating. The less you need to worry about the temperature of your food, the easier your job will be. And if you're whipping up your own barbecue sauce (page 196), make it a day in advance.

5. If your party is on a hot summer day, make sure there is plenty of available shade. If it is an evening get-together, provide enough light to allow your guests to move about safely.

6. Have plenty of ice on hand and an ice chest for cold drinks. White wines need to be kept cold, and red wines should be stored out of the sun. Warm red wine will taste "hot," or alcoholic.

7. And speaking of alcohol, not everyone drinks it. Remember to provide plenty of nonalcoholic drinks as well.

8. With finger food, napkins are required. Don't be caught short!

Brewmaster Burger

This burger is topped with Cheddar cheese, bacon, and a smoky barbecue sauce spiked with lager beer. (Parents of minors should note that the beer is boiled briefly, which burns off most, though not all, of the alcohol.) The beer's natural acidity adds a subtle, tangy note. For the best results, use our homemade barbecue sauce.

At the restaurant, we don't typically top these burgers with bacon. But the bacon and the sauce are so good together that we've included it as an option. Pickles and onions add crunch and flavor. And if you have room on the bun for a slice of tomato, go for it! Of course, because you are using a tomato-based barbecue sauce, that tomato slice won't be missed.

A cold beer is the most obvious drink to enjoy with this burger. Fruity Sangria (page 12) would be an excellent choice, as well. On the wine list, look for such spicy, fruit-forward reds as Zinfandel and Malbec or for fresh, lively rosés.

½ cup lager (such as Samuel Adams Boston lager)

2 tablespoons A.1. Steak Sauce

2 cups barbecue sauce, homemade (page 196)
   or store-bought

4 slices bacon (optional)

2 pounds ground beef (preferably chuck)

½ teaspoon salt

Freshly ground black pepper

1 teaspoon canola oil, if cooking on the stovetop

4 Cheddar cheese slices

4 onion slices

4 hamburger buns (such as ciabatta, potato, or
   English muffin), split and toasted

4 tomato slices (optional)

8 round dill pickle slices

Prepare an outdoor charcoal or gas grill for direct-heat grilling over medium-high heat. Or, have ready a large, heavy skillet.

In a small saucepan, bring the beer to a boil over high heat, then remove from the heat. In a medium bowl, stir together the beer, A.1. sauce, and barbecue sauce. Set aside.

If using the bacon, in a medium skillet, cook the bacon over medium-high heat, turning once, for 4 to 5 minutes on each side, or until crisp. Transfer to paper towels to drain and reserve. Discard the drippings.

Place the beef in a large bowl, sprinkle with the salt, and add several grinds of pepper. Using your hands, mix together thoroughly. Divide the meat into 4 equal portions. Gently shape each portion into a ball, then toss the ball back and forth between your hands a few times to eliminate any air pockets. Gently flatten each ball into a patty about 5 inches in diameter and 1 inch thick.

If not using an outdoor grill, coat the surface of the skillet with the canola oil and heat on the stovetop over medium-high heat. Place the patties on the grill rack or in the skillet and cook, turning once, for about 5 minutes on each side for medium-rare or about 7 minutes on each side for medium. A minute or two before the burgers are ready, coat the top of each burger with a little of the barbecue sauce mixture. Lay a cheese slice on top of the sauce on each burger, and cover the grill or pan to melt the cheese. Remove from the grill or pan.

Place an onion slice on the bottom half of each bun, top with a tomato slice, and then with 2 pickle slices. Set the burger on top of the pickle slices. If using bacon, cut each bacon slice in half and lay 2 halves on top of each burger. Cover with the top half of the bun. If desired, cut the burgers in half for ease of eating. Pass the remaining barbecue sauce at the table.

Avocado Turkey Burger

It's a refreshing change to make burgers from meats other than beef. Turkey, in addition to being low in fat, has a mild flavor that can show off the other ingredients tucked into the bun. In this recipe, bacon adds a smoky note, and avocado and cheese contribute a full, rich taste. The easy-to-make garlic mayonnaise spices up everything nicely, though store-bought plain mayonnaise will work well, too.

Make these patties somewhat thinner than you would The Classic Burger (page 130). The ingredients pile up high on the bun, and you want to keep things manageable for easy eating.

Pale ale or other beers, Sangria (page 12), or a fruity white wine like Chenin Blanc or Riesling would nicely complement the burgers.

4 slices bacon

1½ pounds ground turkey

½ teaspoon salt

Freshly ground black pepper

1 teaspoon canola oil, if cooking on the stovetop

4 mild white cheese slices (such as Cheddar or Havarti)

Roasted garlic mayonnaise (page 195) or mayonnaise
　　(page 194), or store-bought, for spreading

4 hamburger buns (such as ciabatta, potato, or
　　English muffin), split and toasted

4 to 8 leaves butter or other green leaf lettuce

4 tomato slices

4 onion slices

1 medium ripe avocado, pitted (see Chef's Tips, page 25),
　　then cut into ¼-inch-thick slices and slices peeled

In a medium skillet, cook the bacon over medium-high heat, turning once, for 4 to 5 minutes on each side, or until crisp. Transfer to paper towels to drain and reserve. Discard the drippings.

Prepare an outdoor charcoal or gas grill for direct-heat grilling over medium-high heat. Or, have ready a large, heavy skillet.

Place the turkey in a large bowl, sprinkle with the salt, and add several grinds of pepper. Using your hands, mix together thoroughly. Divide the meat into 4 equal portions. Gently shape each portion into a ball, then toss the ball back and forth between your hands a few times to eliminate any air pockets. Gently flatten each ball into a patty about 5 inches in diameter and ½ inch thick.

If not using an outdoor grill, coat the surface of the skillet with the canola oil and heat on the stovetop over medium-high heat. Place the patties on the grill rack or in the skillet and cook, turning once, for 7 to 8 minutes on each side, until golden brown on the outside and completely white on the inside. Or, insert an instant-read thermometer into a burger; it should register 165°F. A minute or two before the burgers are ready, lay a slice of cheese on top each burger and cover the grill or pan to melt the cheese. Remove the burgers from the grill or pan.

Spread a dollop of mayonnaise on the bottom half of each bun. Place a leaf or two of lettuce on top of the mayonnaise. Top with a tomato slice, an onion slice, and 2 avocado slices. Place the burger on top of the avocado. Cut each bacon slice in half and lay 2 halves on top of each burger. Cover with the top half of the bun. If desired, cut the burgers in half for ease of eating.

Burger Bar

Not everyone likes the same toppings on their burgers. Nor does everyone like the same kind of bun. But it's easy to make everyone happy by setting out a variety of condiments and buns, and then letting your guests dress their own burgers as they like. Just make sure the condiments are displayed with easy access.

Arrange your condiments in small, attractive serving bowls to add a touch of class to a casual affair. If you're hosting a party, serving burgers without dressing them yourself will streamline assembly, as well. Here is a burger-bar display checklist:

A variety of buns and breads
Ketchup
Mustard
Mayonnaise, homemade
    (page 194) or store-bought
Barbecue sauce, homemade
    (page 196) or store-bought
Steak sauce (such as A.1.)

A variety of sliced cheeses
Lettuce leaves
Relish
Pickle slices
Tomato slices
Onion slices
Avocado slices
Cooked bacon slices

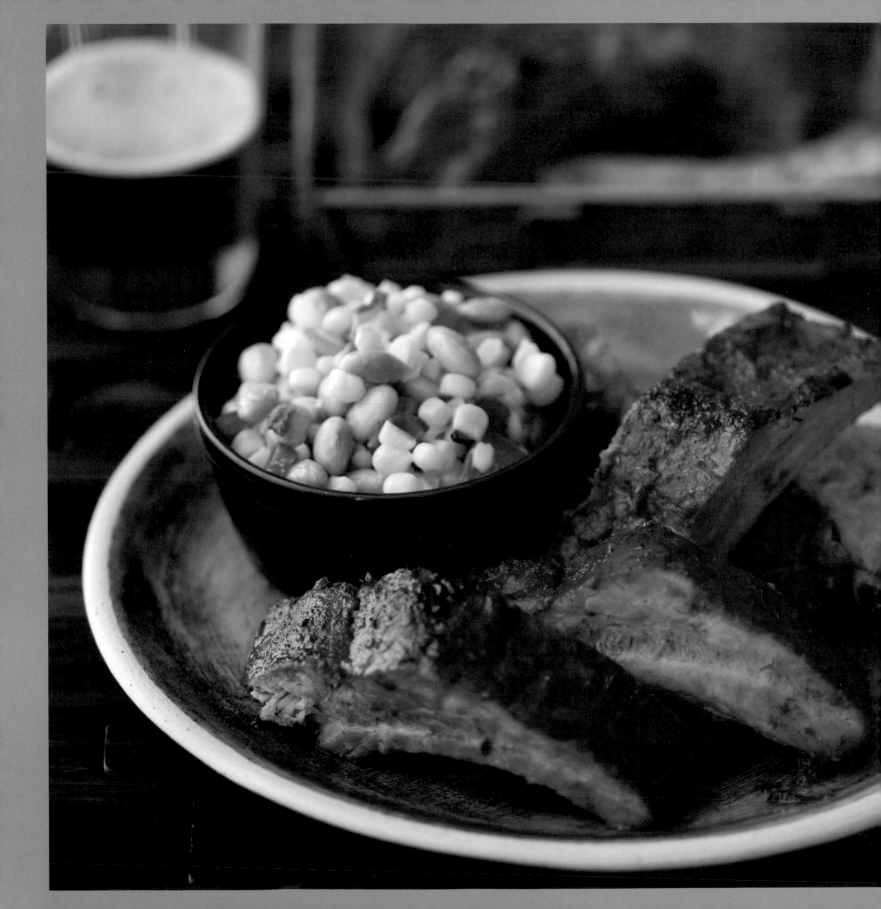

Chef's Tip: *Panfrying a Steak*

A heavy skillet—cast iron is the ideal material—distributes and maintains heat more evenly than a light pan. Use a little oil, preferably one with a high smoke point such as canola or peanut, to prevent initial sticking or burning. And don't crowd the steaks in the pan; you'll need room to flip them easily. Plus, the pan won't hold its heat properly if it's overloaded. Prior to serving, let the steaks sit away from the heat for 3 to 5 minutes. During this time, the juices, which will have been driven toward the center of the steak during cooking, will redistribute themselves throughout the meat, ensuring a juicier result. Also, remove the steaks from the pan a tad earlier than you might otherwise. The residual heat trapped in the steaks will continue to cook the meat.

1 In a heavy skillet, heat the oil over medium-high heat until it shimmers. Add the steaks to the pan without crowding them.

Flip the steaks every 2 or 3 minutes to seal in flavors without overcooking the surface. Cook to desired doneness, depending on the size and thickness of the steaks.

2 Transfer the steaks to a cutting board, plates, or a platter. Let rest for 3 to 5 minutes before serving.

Peppercorn Steaks with Brandy Cream Sauce and Sautéed Mushrooms

This American version of the classic French steak au poivre is punctuated by bright-edged peppercorns and draped in a lush, creamy sauce. The recipe calls for two kinds of peppercorns, black and the milder green. Green peppercorns are readily available on the spice rack at your supermarket. If you can't find them, substitute 1½ teaspoons black peppercorns for the 1 tablespoon green peppercorns.

When shopping for steak, note that sirloin steak is sometimes called New York steak. It is tender and best cooked medium-rare. Buttery mushrooms add luster to these steaks, which are guaranteed to please anyone with a craving for red meat. White Cheddar Mashed Potatoes (page 45) is the perfect side dish. A full-bodied red wine, such as Cabernet Sauvignon, completes the culinary tableau.

4 tablespoons unsalted butter

¾ pound crimini or button mushrooms, thinly sliced

1 tablespoon black peppercorns, coarsely crushed

1 tablespoon green peppercorns, coarsely crushed

4 boneless sirloin steaks, each about ½ pound
    and 1½ inches thick

Salt

2 tablespoons canola oil

2 tablespoons minced shallot

3 tablespoons brandy

1 cup heavy cream

Cook the mushrooms first. In a medium skillet, melt 2 tablespoons of the butter over medium heat. Add the mushrooms and sauté, stirring frequently to prevent burning, for about 10 minutes, or until tender. Remove from the heat, cover to keep warm, and set aside.

Put all of the peppercorns in a mortar and crush with a pestle. Alternatively, put all of the peppercorns in a resealable plastic bag, seal closed, and crush with a rolling pin or the flat side of a large knife blade. Spread the crushed peppercorns on a flat plate. (The black and green peppercorns should be mixed together well.) Season both sides of each steak with salt. One at a time, place the steaks on top of the crushed peppercorns, pressing down lightly so the peppercorns stick to the surface. Turn the steak over and repeat to coat the second side.

In a large skillet, heat the canola oil over high heat. When the oil begins to shimmer, place the steaks in the pan, decrease the heat to medium-high, and cook for a total of 4 to 5 minutes per side for medium-rare. Flip the steaks every 2 or 3 minutes for the best results (see Chef's Tip, page 143). When the steaks are almost ready, reheat the mushrooms over medium heat, stirring occasionally.

When the steaks are done, transfer them to a platter, tent with aluminum foil, and let rest for about 3 minutes. Decrease the heat to medium and add the remaining 2 tablespoons butter to the pan. Add the shallot and sauté for about 1 minute, or until fragrant. Add the brandy and stir to scrape up any browned bits from the pan bottom. Pour in the cream and mix well. Simmer the sauce for about 1 minute, or until thick enough to coat the back of a wooden spoon.

Place 1 steak on each dinner plate. Spoon the cream sauce over the steaks, then top with the sautéed mushrooms, dividing them evenly. Serve at once.

COWBOY SIRLOIN WITH RED CHILI RUB, CARAMELIZED ONIONS, AND BLUE CHEESE BUTTER

These buttery-soft steaks are coated with a spicy chili rub nicely tempered by blue cheese butter and served with a big spoonful of sweet, slow-cooked onions on the side. For the best results, use top sirloin or tenderloin steaks. (Tenderloin, also called filet mignon, will be pricier; it is the most tender of the sirloin cuts.)

Don't be concerned about the number of steps and numerous ingredients here. Quite frankly, this dish is easy to prepare. Just take it one step at a time. If you have friends coming for dinner, make the spice rub, blue cheese butter, onions, and any other side dishes in advance. (White Cheddar Mashed Potatoes, page 45, would be perfect on the side, for example.) You can quickly reheat the side dishes prior to serving. Prepare the steaks in advance, too, but cook them in short order after your guests have arrived.

The recipe calls for searing the meat on the stovetop and finishing it in the oven. But you can also cook the steaks on an outdoor grill, flipping them every 2 or 3 minutes until they are done. Total cooking time for medium-rare will be about 15 minutes.

Any full-bodied red wine makes an excellent match with this meal.

CHILI RUB

2 tablespoons chili powder
1 tablespoon brown sugar
1/2 teaspoon salt
1/2 teaspoon ground cumin
1/2 teaspoon granulated garlic powder
1/2 teaspoon ground coriander
1/2 teaspoon ground oregano
1/4 teaspoon cayenne pepper

BLUE CHEESE BUTTER

4 tablespoons unsalted butter, at room temperature
2 ounces blue cheese (such as Roquefort or Stilton), at room temperature

CARAMELIZED ONIONS

3 tablespoons extra-virgin olive oil
4 large yellow or white onions, thinly sliced
1 teaspoon sugar
1 tablespoon balsamic vinegar
1/2 teaspoon salt

4 top sirloin or tenderloin steaks, each 6 to 8 ounces and about 1 1/2 inches thick
2 tablespoons canola oil

To make the rub, in a medium bowl, combine all of the ingredients. Use a spoon or fork to mix thoroughly. Set aside.

To make the butter, in a medium bowl, use a fork to mash together the butter and blue cheese thoroughly until a creamy mixture forms. Scrape the mixture onto a sheet of plastic wrap and then roll it into a neat log, using the plastic wrap as a guide. Wrap securely in the plastic wrap, twist the ends closed, and refrigerate until ready to use. (The butter can be made up to 24 hours in advance; keep refrigerated until serving.)

To prepare the onions, in a large skillet, heat the oil over medium-high heat. Add the onions and, using a wooden spoon, stir them to separate the slices and coat them with the oil. Cover, decrease the heat to low, and continue to cook, stirring occasionally, for about 15 minutes, or until the onions have wilted.

Sprinkle the sugar over the onions and stir to mix. Add the vinegar and stir again. Add the salt and stir until all of the ingredients are well mixed. Continue to cook uncovered, stirring occasionally, for about 20 minutes, or until the onions are soft and golden. Remove from the heat, cover, and set aside. Shortly before serving, reheat the onions over low heat.

Lay the steaks on a flat work surface, such as a large cutting board, and trim off any large fat deposits. Spoon 1 teaspoon of the rub onto each steak. Using your hands, gently massage the rub into the surface of the meat. Flip each steak and do the same thing on the other side. Pour any rub remaining in the bowl onto the work surface. One at a time, stand each steak on its edge and coat the entire edge with the rub. Set the steaks aside for 15 to 30 minutes before cooking.

Preheat the oven to 475°F.

In a large ovenproof skillet, heat the canola oil over high heat. When the oil begins to shimmer, place the steaks in the pan and sear them, turning them once with tongs or a large fork, for 2 minutes on each side. Transfer the pan to the oven and roast the steaks for about 8 minutes, or until an instant-read thermometer inserted into the thickest part of a steak registers 140°F for medium-rare.

Remove the steaks from the oven and place 1 steak on each dinner plate. Cut 4 slices of blue cheese butter, each ¼ inch thick, and place 1 slice on each steak. (Leftover butter will make a delicious spread on bread.) Set a mound of warm onions next to each steak. Serve at once.

PORK CHOPS WITH FRIED GARLIC AND RED WINE GRAVY

This is a soulful dish, exquisite in its simplicity. Crunchy fried garlic tops these meaty chops, which are bathed in a no-frills red wine gravy. Not surprisingly, a glass of robust red wine, such as Cabernet Sauvignon, Merlot, or Zinfandel, will nicely round out your meal. Accompany the chops with Roasted Brussels Sprouts with Bacon (page 35) or Creamy Mashed Cauliflower (page 37). For ease of serving, cook the side dish first and then reheat just before the chops are ready.

4 bone-in pork chops, about ½ pound each
Salt and freshly ground black pepper
2 tablespoons extra-virgin olive oil
8 to 10 large cloves garlic, sliced crosswise
2 cups red wine
2 tablespoons unsalted butter

Trim off any excess fat from the pork chops. Season the chops on both sides with salt and pepper and set aside.

In a large skillet, heat the olive oil over medium heat. Add the garlic and sauté, being careful not to let it burn, for about 5 minutes, or until golden. Using a slotted spoon, transfer the garlic bits to a small bowl and set aside.

Raise the heat to medium-high and place the pork chops in the pan. Sear them, turning them once, for about 3 minutes on each side. Then continue to flip them every 2 to 3 minutes for 10 to 12 minutes total, until an instant-read thermometer inserted into the center of a chop away from bone registers 150°F. If the oil begins to smoke, decrease the heat slightly. Transfer the chops to a large plate and tent loosely with aluminum foil.

With the pan still over medium-high heat, pour in the wine, taking care not to splatter any of the hot oil. Use a wooden spoon to scrape up any browned bits from the pan bottom. Raise the heat to high and cook for 5 to 7 minutes, until the wine has reduced by half. Decrease the heat to medium-low, add the butter, and stir it occasionally until it has melted.

Place the pork chops on dinner plates. Pour the juices remaining in the plate that held the chops into the pan with the wine gravy and stir to mix. Garnish each chop with fried garlic bits, then generously drizzle the red wine gravy over the chops and—if desired—any side dishes. Serve at once.

Pork Loin with Rosemary-Garlic Rub

SERVES 6

Rosemary is the defining element in this simple, elegant recipe, imparting an herbal, earthy edge to the meat. Salt, a touch of freshly ground pepper, and fruity olive oil are the supporting cast. This is a versatile recipe that works well with many of the side dishes in this book. Among the best matches are Sautéed Carrots with Cumin Seeds and Cilantro (page 36), Creamy Mashed Cauliflower (page 37), Brown Rice Pilaf (page 42), White Cheddar Mashed Potatoes (page 45), and Oven-Roasted Potato "Fries" with Rosemary (page 46).

The pork is dressed with a wine sauce that can be made with red or white wine. Either color will turn a shade of light brown as it cooks. More important than the color of the wine is its natural acidity, which balances the richness of the pork. For the sauce, use ½ cup wine from a bottle of any good red or white, such as Pinot Noir or Chardonnay. Then drink the rest!

ROSEMARY-GARLIC RUB

4 cloves garlic, minced
1 tablespoon dried rosemary
2 tablespoons extra-virgin olive oil
¼ teaspoon salt
⅛ teaspoon freshly ground black pepper

1 boneless pork loin roast, 2 pounds
½ cup water
½ cup red or white wine
2 tablespoons unsalted butter

Preheat the oven to 450°F.

To make the rub, in a small bowl, combine all of the ingredients and mix with a spoon to form a thick paste.

Place a rack in a roasting pan just large enough to accommodate the roast. Place the pork loin, fat side up, on the rack. Spoon the rosemary-garlic rub over the top of the roast and spread it evenly (on the top only) with the back of the spoon or a knife. Pour the water into the bottom of the pan.

Place the pan in the oven and roast for 10 minutes. Decrease the oven temperature to 350°F and continue to roast for about 45 minutes, or until an instant-read thermometer inserted into the thickest part of the loin registers 150°F.

Remove the meat from the roasting pan but leave the juices in the pan. Place the roast on a large platter or cutting board and tent it with aluminum foil until ready to serve.

To make the wine sauce, place the roasting pan with the reserved juices on the stovetop over medium-high heat. Add the wine and, using a wooden spoon, stir to loosen any browned bits on the bottom of the pan. Bring the wine to a boil and boil for about 5 minutes, or until reduced by half. Decrease the heat to medium-low, add the butter, and stir occasionally until it melts. Transfer the sauce to a small pitcher or gravy boat.

Carve the roast into ½-inch-thick slices and divide among dinner plates. Drizzle each serving with some of the pan sauce.

CHICKEN BROCCOLI STIR-FRY WITH LEMON BUTTER AND BROWN RICE

This easy recipe takes very little time to prepare. The brown rice cooks the longest. With lemon and rosemary as key flavor elements, you'll find this refreshing dish becomes even more so when accompanied by a glass of cool, crisp white wine, such as Chardonnay or Pinot Grigio.

2 cups plus 3 tablespoons water

½ teaspoon salt, plus additional for seasoning

1 cup long-grain or short-grain brown rice

2 boneless, skinless chicken breasts, about ½ pound each, cut into ½-inch cubes

3 tablespoons extra-virgin olive oil

4 cups broccoli florets (about ½ pound)

10 cherry tomatoes, halved

1 tablespoon dried rosemary

4 cloves garlic, minced

¼ cup freshly squeezed lemon juice

3 tablespoons unsalted butter

Freshly ground black pepper

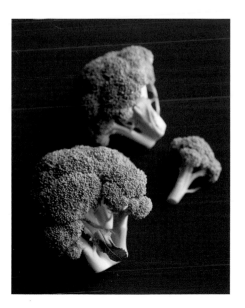

In a medium saucepan, combine 2 cups of the water and the ½ teaspoon salt and bring to a boil over high heat. Stir in the rice and return the liquid to a boil. Decrease the heat to low, cover, and cook for about 40 minutes, or until all of the water has been absorbed and the rice is tender. Remove from the heat and keep covered until ready to use.

While the rice is cooking, prepare the stir-fry. Season the chicken cubes with salt and set them aside. In a large skillet or wok, heat 1 tablespoon of the olive oil over medium-high heat. Add the broccoli and tomatoes and stir to coat evenly with the oil. Add 2 tablespoons of the water, cover, and cook for about 3 minutes, or until the tomatoes are soft and the broccoli is tender. Transfer the broccoli and tomatoes to a large bowl and reserve.

Add 1 tablespoon of the olive oil to the pan and raise the heat to medium-high. Stir in the chicken and rosemary, cover, and cook for 2 minutes. Flip the chicken pieces, re-cover, and cook for 3 to 4 minutes, until the chicken is cooked through. Transfer the chicken to the bowl with the broccoli and tomatoes.

Decrease the heat to medium and add the remaining 1 tablespoon olive oil to the pan. Add the garlic and cook, stirring occasionally to prevent burning, for about 1 minute, or until it is golden. Add the lemon juice and the remaining 1 tablespoon water. Add the butter and stir occasionally until it melts. Return the chicken, broccoli, and tomatoes to the pan, stir gently to mix well, and reheat for 1 minute. Remove from the heat and season with salt and pepper.

Place a mound of rice on each dinner plate. Divide the stir-fry among the plates, spooning it over the rice. Serve at once.

CHICKEN CURRY WITH COCONUT RICE

This delightfully fragrant dish features coconut rice made with creamy coconut milk, which can be found in most supermarkets. The curry itself is enhanced by the addition of tomatoes and cilantro. Don't be put off by the long list of ingredients in this recipe. Most of them are spices that are mixed together to make a seasoning paste for the chicken prior to cooking, and they can all be readily found on the spice rack at your local supermarket.

Anything made with curry calls for a cool, thirst-quenching beverage. A cold beer would do the trick nicely. But so would a chilled white wine, such as a steely Sauvignon Blanc, a full-bodied Chardonnay, or a fruity, sweeter Riesling.

CURRY

2 teaspoons ground coriander

1 teaspoon ground cumin

1/2 teaspoon ground turmeric

1/4 teaspoon cayenne pepper

3/4 teaspoon salt, plus additional for seasoning

1 cup plus 2 tablespoons water

1 whole chicken, about 4 pounds, cut into
   10 to 12 pieces and skin removed

2 tablespoons canola oil

1 medium onion, diced

2 cloves garlic, minced

1 teaspoon peeled and grated fresh ginger

2 medium tomatoes, diced

1 cup plain yogurt

2 teaspoons curry powder

Freshly ground black pepper

COCONUT RICE

1 (13- to 14-ounce) can unsweetened coconut milk

1 tablespoon unsalted butter

2 cups long-grain white rice

3 cups water

1/4 teaspoon salt

1 cinnamon stick

1/2 cup minced fresh cilantro

To make the curry, in a small bowl, stir together the coriander, cumin, turmeric, cayenne pepper, 1/4 teaspoon of the salt, and 2 tablespoons of the water to make a paste. Place the chicken pieces on a large platter, and spread the paste on the tops of the pieces. Let the chicken sit at room temperature for 30 minutes.

In a large, heavy skillet or Dutch oven, heat the canola oil over high heat. When the oil begins to shimmer, place the chicken pieces, paste side down, in the hot oil and sear for 3 to 4 minutes, until golden brown on the underside. Turn the chicken pieces over and sear on the second side for 2 to 3 minutes, until golden. (If your pan is too small to accommodate all of the chicken pieces without crowding, do this in 2 batches.) Remove the chicken from the pan and set it aside on a large serving plate.

Decrease the heat to medium, add the onion, and sauté for about 3 minutes, or until translucent. Add the garlic and ginger and sauté for about 30 seconds, or until fragrant. Add the tomatoes and stir to mix well. Add the yogurt, the remaining 1 cup water, and the remaining ½ teaspoon salt. Stir together all of the ingredients to mix thoroughly. Add the curry powder and stir to mix well. Return the chicken pieces to the skillet, making sure they are fully immersed in the sauce. Raise the heat to medium-high and bring to a gentle boil. Decrease the heat to medium, cover, and simmer, stirring occasionally, for 30 minutes. Uncover and simmer for 10 minutes more to thicken the sauce. Taste and adjust the seasoning with salt and season with black pepper. (If the curry is ready before the rice has finished cooking, remove from the heat and cover to keep warm.)

While the curry is cooking, prepare the rice. In a small saucepan, heat the coconut milk over medium heat, stirring to liquefy, for about 2 minutes, or until all of the solids have melted. Do not allow to boil. Remove from the heat.

In a 4-quart saucepan, melt the butter over medium-high heat. Add the rice and cook, stirring regularly to prevent burning, for about 5 minutes, or until the rice turns lightly golden. Add the water, the warm coconut milk, and the salt. Use a wooden spoon to incorporate any remaining coconut milk solids into the liquid. Add the cinnamon stick and bring the liquid to a boil. Decrease the heat to medium-low, cover, and cook for about 15 minutes, or until the liquid is completely absorbed and the rice is tender.

Remove the rice from the heat, discard the cinnamon stick, and fluff the grains with a fork. Place a large serving of rice in the middle of each dinner plate. Top the rice with the chicken and curry sauce. Garnish each serving with a generous sprinkling of cilantro and serve at once.

Chicken Fresco with Parmesan Cream Sauce and Roasted Tomatoes   Serves 4

These plump, juicy chicken breasts with their crisp, browned skin are blanketed in a rich Parmesan cream sauce. At the restaurant, we generally top the chicken with tomato slices. But here, we've prepared herb-roasted tomatoes—cooked at the same time as the chicken—in a classic Mediterranean style. For the best results, make the dish in the summertime, when garden-fresh tomatoes are in the market, or look for good-quality locally grown greenhouse tomatoes the rest of the year.

As a side dish, consider serving Asparagus with Olive Oil and Parmesan Cheese (page 39), Corn and Edamame Succotash (page 40), or Brown Rice Pilaf (page 42). In your wineglass, many white or red wines will serve you well. Look for a wine with good acidity, such as Pinot Grigio, Sangiovese, or Zinfandel.

2 large tomatoes, halved crosswise
Salt and freshly ground black pepper
1 tablespoon plus 2 teaspoons extra-virgin olive oil
1 teaspoon dried oregano
1 teaspoon freshly grated Parmesan cheese
4 boneless, skin-on chicken breasts, 6 to 8 ounces each

Sauce
2 tablespoons unsalted butter
2 tablespoons minced shallot
1 tablespoon all-purpose flour
1 cup white wine
1/2 cup heavy cream
1/8 teaspoon salt
2 tablespoons freshly grated Parmesan cheese

Chopped fresh flat-leaf parsley, for garnish (optional)

Preheat the oven to 400°F.

Season the cut surface of each tomato half with salt and pepper. Drizzle the 2 teaspoons olive oil evenly over the seasoned surfaces, then sprinkle evenly with the oregano and Parmesan. Place the tomatoes, seasoned surface up, in a 9-inch square baking pan or dish and set aside.

Season the chicken breasts on both sides with salt and pepper. In a large ovenproof skillet, heat the remaining 1 tablespoon olive oil over high heat. When the oil begins to shimmer, place the chicken breasts, skin side down, in the pan. Decrease the heat to medium-high and sear for 4 to 5 minutes, until the skin is browned and crisp.

Place the pan with the chicken and the pan with the tomatoes in the oven and bake for about 15 minutes, or until the chicken is opaque throughout and the tops of the tomatoes are golden brown. Remove both pans from the oven and tent them with aluminum foil until ready to use.

While the chicken and tomatoes are in the oven, make the sauce. In a medium saucepan, melt the butter over medium heat. Add the shallot and sauté for 1 minute, or until translucent. Decrease the heat to medium-low and, using a wooden spoon, stir in the flour. Cook, stirring constantly, for about 15 seconds, or until the mixture thickens. Slowly add the wine while whisking constantly, then raise the heat to high and bring to a boil. Decrease the heat to medium and simmer, stirring frequently, for about 3 minutes, or until the sauce is very thick. Stir in the cream and salt and continue to simmer for about 1 minute, or until the sauce has thickened enough to coat the spoon. Add the Parmesan cheese and stir to mix well. Remove from the heat.

Place a warm chicken breast, skin side up, and a roasted tomato half on each dinner plate. Spoon a generous serving of the sauce over each breast, sprinkle with parsley, and serve at once.

Desserts

HAZELNUT CHOCOLATE CHUNK COOKIES 168

MACADAMIA NUT AND
WHITE CHOCOLATE CHIP COOKIES 170

LEMON ZABAGLIONE 171

PEACH CRISP 173

OLD-FASHIONED APPLE PIE 174

CHEESECAKE WITH FRESH RASPBERRY SAUCE 177

PECAN CARROT CAKE WITH
VANILLA BUTTER CREAM ICING 179

ITALIAN CREAM CAKE 180

STRAWBERRY ANGEL FOOD CAKE 185

GINGER CRÈME BRÛLÉE 186

CHOCOLATE SOUFFLÉ 187

CHOCOLATE ALMOND TORTE WITH
FRESH STRAWBERRIES AND WHIPPED CREAM 188

Desserts

Every meal unfolds like a story, with a beginning, a middle, and an end. And we all love a sweet ending. No matter how much we have indulged, we always have room for dessert.

Sometimes just a few bites will suffice. That's when cookies are best. And what could be better than Hazelnut Chocolate Chunk Cookies (page 168) or Macadamia Nut and White Chocolate Chip Cookies (page 170)? Looking for something more filling? Lemon Zabaglione (page 171) and Ginger Crème Brûlée (page 186)—on their own or served with the cookies—should do the trick.

In this chapter, fresh fruits are featured, transformed into a lively Peach Crisp (page 173) or a fine Old-Fashioned Apple Pie (page 174). And anyone looking for a rich, soft, satisfying cake will find some excellent candidates here: Italian Cream Cake (page 180), Pecan Carrot Cake with Vanilla Buttercream Icing (page 179), and Chocolate Almond Torte with Fresh Strawberries and Whipped Cream (page 188). In addition, Strawberry Angel Food Cake (page 185) will satisfy your sweet tooth with a lighter touch.

There is a sweet treat for everyone and every meal in the pages that follow. Enjoy these desserts in the spirit of celebration.

Hazelnut Chocolate Chunk Cookies

If you like chocolate chip cookies, you will definitely like these. Chocolate chunks are just what they sound like: big chips. But if you can't find chunks, regular chips will do. Toasting hazelnuts (also known as filberts) intensifies their flavor, and it is easy to do on your stovetop in just minutes. These cookies are an excellent addition to the menu for any casual party or to your kitchen cookie jar.

1 cup hazelnuts
2¼ cups all-purpose flour
1 teaspoon baking soda
½ teaspoon salt
1 cup (8 ounces/2 sticks) unsalted butter,
    at room temperature
¾ cup granulated sugar
½ cup firmly packed brown sugar
2 eggs
½ teaspoon vanilla extract
2½ cups semisweet chocolate chunks or chips

Preheat the oven to 350°F.

Toast the hazelnuts as directed on page 192. Lay a paper towel on a flat work surface. When the nuts are ready, transfer them to the towel in a single layer. Cover with a second paper towel and, using your palm, roll the hot nuts between the towels to remove most of their skins. Discard the skins and the towels and place the hazelnuts in a resealable plastic bag. Using a rolling pin, gently crush the nuts into large chunks. Set aside.

In a medium bowl, whisk together the flour, baking soda, and salt to blend thoroughly. Set aside.

In a large bowl, using an electric mixer on medium-high speed, beat together the butter, granulated sugar, and brown sugar until the mixture is smooth and fluffy. Add the eggs and vanilla and continue to beat for another minute. On low speed, add the flour mixture and beat until thoroughly blended. Using a wooden spoon, gently stir in the hazelnuts and chocolate chunks. The dough will noticeably thicken.

Have ready 2 nonstick baking sheets. Scoop out a tablespoon of the dough and place it on a baking sheet. Do not flatten the mound. Repeat with the rest of the dough, spacing the mounds about 1½ inches apart.

Bake the cookies for 10 to 12 minutes, until the edges are golden brown and the centers are fairly firm to the touch. Remove from the oven and let the cookies cool on the pans for a few minutes to firm up, then transfer them to the racks and let cool completely. Store in an airtight container at room temperature for up to 3 days.

Right: Macadamia Nut and White Chocolate Chip Cookies
and Hazelnut Chocolate Chunk Cookies

MACADAMIA NUT AND WHITE CHOCOLATE CHIP COOKIES

MAKES ABOUT 30 COOKIES

At Ruby Tuesday, our cookies are baked fresh daily. It's a bit like having a local bakery in each of our kitchens. For these scrumptious cookies, we use white chocolate to serve up a rich vanilla flavor and macadamia nuts for an exotic touch. The cookies are crunchy on the edges and chewy at the center. Serve them for dessert or keep them on hand for a midday snack.

2½ cups all-purpose flour
1 teaspoon baking soda
½ teaspoon salt
1 cup (8 ounces/2 sticks) unsalted butter,
    at room temperature
¾ cup firmly packed brown sugar
½ cup granulated sugar
2 eggs
2 teaspoons vanilla extract
1½ cups white chocolate chips
1½ cups coarsely chopped macadamia nuts

Preheat the oven to 350°F.

In a medium bowl, whisk together the flour, baking soda, and salt. Set aside.

In a large bowl, using an electric mixer on medium-high speed, beat together the butter, brown sugar, and granulated sugar until the mixture is smooth and fluffy. Add the eggs and vanilla and continue to beat for another minute. On low speed, add the flour mixture and beat until thoroughly blended. Using a wooden spoon, gently stir in the white chocolate chips and macadamia nuts.

Have ready 2 nonstick baking sheets. Scoop out a tablespoon of the dough and place it on a baking sheet. Do not flatten the mound. Repeat with the rest of the dough, spacing the mounds about 1½ inches apart.

Bake the cookies for 10 to 12 minutes, until the edges are golden brown and the centers are slightly firm to the touch. Remove from the oven and let the cookies cool on the pans for a few minutes to firm up, then transfer them to the racks and let cool completely. Store in an airtight container at room temperature for up to 3 days.

LEMON ZABAGLIONE

This frothy lemon custard, topped with a dollop of whipped cream, provides the perfect light finish to a meal. Serve it in stemmed wineglasses for a simple yet elegant presentation.

4 egg yolks
½ cup sugar
⅓ cup sweet wine (such as Marsala or tawny port)
Finely minced zest of 1 lemon
1 tablespoon freshly squeezed lemon juice
Whipped cream, homemade (page 192) or store-bought,
    for serving
Fresh berries (such as blueberries or blackberries),
    for serving (optional)

Pour water to a depth of 2 inches into the bottom of a double boiler or a saucepan large enough to rest a medium stainless-steel bowl in its rim. Bring to a boil over high heat. Decrease the heat to a simmer.

In the top pan of the double boiler or in the stainless-steel bowl, whisk together the egg yolks, sugar, wine, lemon zest, and lemon juice. Place the pan or bowl over (not touching) the simmering water and whisk fairly continuously for about 10 minutes, or until the mixture thickens and doubles in volume. Using a rubber spatula, occasionally scrape the mixture from the sides of the bowl. To prevent the eggs from scrambling, lift the bowl off the steam occasionally while whisking.

When the mixture is ready, remove the bowl from the heat and whisk about 5 times to cool it slightly. Evenly divide the custard among 4 medium wineglasses. The custard should fill the glasses from one-third to one-half full, depending on their size. (If you don't have stemmed wineglasses, use any 10- to 12-ounce tumblers.) When all of the custard is in the glasses, use a paper towel to wipe away any custard spills on the upper part of the glasses. Cover each glass with plastic wrap and refrigerate for at least 1 hour or up to 12 hours.

Just before serving, top each custard with a dollop of whipped cream and 2 or 3 berries.

PEACH CRISP

A sweet, crumbly topping infused with cinnamon frames this summer-friendly crisp. Make it with ripe, juicy, freshly picked peaches from a nearby farm or farmers' market for the best results. This dessert is delicious on its own. But a scoop of cool, rich vanilla ice cream alongside is a welcome addition.

FILLING

8 medium yellow peaches, pitted and cut into
    1-inch cubes
¼ cup granulated sugar
¼ teaspoon ground cinnamon
⅛ teaspoon ground nutmeg
1 teaspoon freshly squeezed lemon juice
2 teaspoons cornstarch

TOPPING

½ cup (4 ounces/1 stick) unsalted butter,
    at room temperature
½ cup firmly packed brown sugar
¼ cup granulated sugar
½ teaspoon ground cinnamon
1 teaspoon vanilla extract
1 cup all-purpose flour

Vanilla ice cream, for serving (optional)

Preheat the oven to 425°F.

To make the filling, in a large bowl, combine the peaches, granulated sugar, cinnamon, nutmeg, lemon juice, and cornstarch. Using 2 wooden spoons, toss to coat the peaches evenly with the other ingredients. Pour the peaches into an 8-inch square baking dish and spread them evenly. Set aside.

To make the topping, in another large bowl, using an electric mixer on medium-high speed, beat together the butter, brown sugar, granulated sugar, cinnamon, and vanilla until creamy. Add the flour and mix with a wooden spoon until thoroughly combined and the mixture is crumbly.

Using a large spoon, distribute the butter-flour mixture evenly across the top of the peaches. Bake the crisp for about 20 minutes, or until the top is golden brown and crunchy. Remove from the oven and serve hot, warm, or at room temperature. Spoon the crisp into individual bowls and accompany with ice cream.

OLD-FASHIONED APPLE PIE

This quintessential American dessert is blessed with a light, flaky crust that frames a bright-tasting apple filling. For the best results, use tart Granny Smith apples or other apples with good acidity, such as McIntosh or Fuji. You'll discover here that it's not hard to make a terrific crust from scratch. Bake this pie in the late afternoon and enjoy it—still warm from the oven—for dinner.

CRUST

2½ cups all-purpose flour, plus additional for dusting

2 teaspoons sugar

1 teaspoon salt

1 cup (8 ounces/2 sticks) unsalted butter, chilled

6 tablespoons ice water

FILLING

2 cups sugar

½ teaspoon ground cinnamon

¼ teaspoon ground nutmeg

5 or 6 Granny Smith apples

2 tablespoons freshly squeezed lemon juice

1 tablespoon cornstarch

2 tablespoons unsalted butter, cut into small pieces

To make the crust, in a food processor, combine the flour, sugar, and salt and pulse for about 10 seconds to mix well. Cut the butter into 14 to 16 pieces (7 or 8 pieces per stick). Feed the pieces, one at a time, into the food processor while continuing to pulse. After all of the butter has been added, continue to pulse until the mixture appears crumbly. Mixing in the butter should take a total of 30 to 45 seconds.

Pour the contents of the processor into a large bowl. Drizzle the ice water over the top and mix with a wooden spoon until evenly moistened. (The mixture will become very moist and doughlike.) Gather the dough into a ball, wrap it in plastic wrap, and refrigerate for at least 30 minutes or up to 24 hours. (To save time, you can put the dough in the freezer for 10 minutes.)

While the dough is in the refrigerator, make the filling. In a large bowl, stir together the sugar, cinnamon, and nutmeg to mix well. Peel and core the apples, then cut them into ½-inch-thick slices. Add the apples to the bowl. Using 2 wooden spoons or your hands, toss the apple slices with the sugar mixture to coat evenly. Add the lemon juice and cornstarch and toss to mix well. Cover the bowl with plastic wrap and refrigerate until you have finished making the pie crust.

Preheat the oven to 450°F.

Dust a work surface with a handful of flour to prevent sticking. Remove the dough from the refrigerator, unwrap it, and cut it in half. Coat both halves lightly with flour from the work surface and set half aside. Using your palm, flatten the other half into a pancake shape about 1 inch thick. Roll out the dough into a round about 12 inches in diameter and ¼ inch thick, dusting the dough with additional flour if needed to prevent sticking. Carefully transfer the round to a 10-inch glass or metal pie pan, and press it firmly into the bottom and up the sides. About 1 inch of dough should overhang the rim of the pan. Roll out the remaining dough half the same way and leave it on the floured surface.

Spoon the apple filling into the crust-lined pan, mounding it a little higher in the center than at the edges. Pour any juices remaining in the bottom of the bowl over the apple slices. Distribute the butter pieces evenly over the apples.

Carefully drape the second dough round over the apple filling, making sure to center it. If necessary, use kitchen scissors or a sharp knife to trim the edge of the top and bottom crusts, leaving a ¾-inch overhang.

Fold the overhang under so it is even with the rim of the pan, then crimp or flute the edge attractively. Cut 4 or 5 vents, each 2 inches long, in the top crust to allow steam to escape.

Bake the pie for 10 minutes. Decrease the oven temperature to 350°F and continue to bake for about 50 minutes, or until the crust is golden and the edges are a darker golden brown. Let cool on a wire rack. Serve warm or at room temperature.

CHEESECAKE WITH FRESH RASPBERRY SAUCE

With its chiffonlike texture, this creamy-smooth cheesecake is a refreshing dessert. The raspberry sauce adds a colorful, fruity touch. Don't be put off by the fact that the recipe has three components: the crust, the filling, and the sauce. None of them is difficult to make, and the sauce is prepared quickly while the cake cools in the refrigerator.

CRUST
½ cup (4 ounces/1 stick) plus 1 tablespoon
    unsalted butter
15 whole graham crackers, broken into squares
¼ cup sugar

FILLING
2¼ pounds cream cheese, at room temperature
½ pound mascarpone cheese, at room temperature
1¼ cups sugar
2 eggs
¾ teaspoon salt
2 teaspoons vanilla extract

RASPBERRY SAUCE
2½ cups fresh raspberries, plus additional for garnish
¼ cup sugar
1 teaspoon freshly squeezed lemon juice

To make the crust, preheat the oven to 325°F. Grease the bottom and sides of a 9-inch springform pan with the 1 tablespoon butter.

In a food processor or blender, pulse the graham crackers until they form coarse crumbs. Scrape down the sides of the processor or shake the blender as needed to pulse them evenly. Add the sugar and process until the crumbs are finely ground.

In a small saucepan, melt the remaining ½ cup butter over low heat. Pour the butter into the crumbs in a steady stream while you continue to pulse. Stop to scrape down the sides or bottom of the bowl or beaker as needed. To test if the mixture is ready, squeeze a bit of it in your hand; it should feel moist and firm.

Pour the crumb mixture onto the bottom of the prepared springform pan. Pat and press the crust firmly and evenly onto the bottom and about 1 inch up the sides of the pan.

Bake the crust for 5 to 7 minutes, until it is golden brown. Let cool on a wire rack for about 10 minutes, or until cooled to room temperature. Decrease the oven temperature to 300°F.

To make the filling, in a large bowl, using an electric mixer on medium-high speed, beat together the cream cheese and mascarpone for about 1 minute, or until soft and fluffy. Scrape down the sides of the bowl with a rubber spatula as needed. Add the sugar in a steady stream and continue beating. Add the eggs, one at a time, beating well after each addition. Continue to scrape down the sides of the bowl as needed. Add the salt and vanilla and beat for about 1 minute, or until well blended. Set aside.

(recipe continued on page 178)

CHEESECAKE WITH FRESH RASPBERRY SAUCE (*continued*)

When the crust has cooled, wrap the bottom and sides of the spring-form pan with heavy-duty aluminum foil. This will ensure that no water will seep into the crust while the cheesecake bakes in a water bath. Pour the cream cheese mixture into the crust and smooth the top with the rubber spatula. Place the wrapped springform pan into a baking pan, and pour warm water into the baking pan to reach halfway up the sides of the springform pan.

Carefully transfer the baking pan to the oven and bake the cake for 1¼ hours, or until the surface is pale gold and the top has risen nearly to the rim of the pan. The cake should jiggle slightly when the pan is moved.

When the cake is done, turn off the oven and leave the oven door slightly ajar. Let the cake rest in the oven for 1 hour. Then remove the cake from the water bath, discard the foil from around the bottom and sides, and place the cake in the refrigerator for 4 hours, or until well chilled.

Meanwhile, make the sauce. In the blender or food processor, combine all of the ingredients and process until smooth. Strain the purée through a fine-mesh sieve into a medium saucepan. Press on the contents of the sieve with the rubber spatula to force as much liquid through the sieve as possible. Discard any solids caught in the sieve.

Place the pan over medium-low heat and bring the purée to a simmer. Decrease the heat to low and continue to simmer, stirring occasionally, for about 5 minutes, or until the liquid begins to thicken. Remove from the heat. The sauce can be served warm or at room temperature.

To serve, unclip and lift away the pan sides, then slide the cheesecake off the bottom of the pan onto a flat plate or other flat serving surface. Slice the cake and top each slice with a tablespoon of the raspberry sauce and a scattering of raspberries.

CHEF'S TIP: *Frosting Layer Cakes*

Let the cake layers cool completely before you frost them. If both cake layers have a rounded top, use a long, sharp knife to slice off the rounded top of one of them to give it a flat surface. This will be the bottom layer.

1 Place the bottom layer on a plate. Using a rubber spatula, scoop about one-third of the icing onto the layer. Then, using an offset spatula (or the rubber spatula), spread the icing evenly over the surface in a layer about ⅓ inch thick.

2 Gently place the second layer, rounded side up, on top of the iced bottom layer.

3 Scoop more icing on top of the cake. Using the offset spatula (or the rubber spatula), spread the icing in broad strokes over the top and then the sides of the cake to cover completely.

4 Still using the spatula, and adding any remaining icing, go over the top again to create an attractive finish.

1

3

2

4

STRAWBERRY ANGEL FOOD CAKE

SERVES 8

This summertime classic combines sweet, ripe strawberries, creamy whipped cream, and light, fluffy angel food cake—perfect for picnics and parties.

Superfine (or ultrafine) sugar is a fine-grained sugar commonly used in baking. As its name implies, it dissolves quickly and keeps this angel food cake light textured. Look for it in the baking aisle of your local supermarket.

1½ cups plus 1 tablespoon superfine sugar
1 cup cake flour
12 egg whites
1 teaspoon cream of tartar
¼ teaspoon salt
2 teaspoons vanilla extract
1 pound fresh strawberries (about 3½ cups)
Whipped cream, homemade (page 192) or
    store-bought, for garnish

Position an oven rack on the second rung from the bottom and preheat the oven to 325°F.

In a small or medium bowl, whisk together ¾ cup of the sugar and the cake flour. Set aside.

In a large bowl, using an electric mixer on medium-high speed, beat the egg whites for about 30 seconds, or until frothy. Add the cream of tartar and salt and continue beating for about 2 minutes, or until soft peaks form. Add another ¾ cup sugar in 2- or 3-tablespoon increments and continue beating for about 1 minute, or until stiff peaks form. Add the vanilla and beat for 10 seconds more to combine thoroughly.

Sift ¼ cup of the flour-sugar mixture into the egg whites and fold it in gently with a rubber spatula. Repeat with the remaining flour-sugar mixture, ¼ cup at a time, folding after each addition just until combined.

Spoon the batter into an ungreased nonstick 9-inch tube pan. Smooth the top with the spatula. Place the pan on the second-from-the-bottom rack and bake for about 30 minutes, or until a toothpick inserted near the center of the cake comes out clean and the top springs back when lightly pressed.

Remove the cake from the oven and let cool upside down (but still in the pan) on a wire rack for 1 hour. When cool, gently run a knife along the inside edge of the pan to loosen the cake sides, then invert the pan and tap the bottom to release the cake from the pan. Turn the cake right side up on a platter.

About 1 hour before serving, hull and slice the strawberries, place them in a medium bowl, and sprinkle with the remaining 1 tablespoon sugar. Mix gently and let the strawberries sit at room temperature.

To serve, lay a slice of cake on its side on each dessert plate, spoon 2 tablespoons of the strawberries on the cake, and garnish with a large dollop of whipped cream.

GINGER CRÈME BRÛLÉE

A sweet, crunchy topping and a velvety, soft interior are the hallmarks of a great crème brûlée. This one's got an added ginger spice note, which makes it especially seductive. For a dinner party, bake the custards in advance and store in the refrigerator. Then, just before serving, slip the ramekins under the broiler for a couple of minutes to caramelize the tops.

3 cups heavy cream
2 tablespoons peeled and grated fresh ginger
8 egg yolks
1 cup plus 6 teaspoons sugar

Preheat the oven to 325°F.

In a small saucepan, combine the cream and ginger over medium heat. Bring to a simmer, but do not allow to boil. Remove from the heat and let cool for 15 minutes.

While the cream is cooling, in a large bowl, whisk together the egg yolks and 1 cup of the sugar for about 1 minute, or until pale yellow and smooth. When the cream mixture has cooled, strain it through a fine-mesh sieve into a small bowl. Slowly pour the cream mixture into the egg-sugar mixture while gently whisking.

Divide the custard evenly among six ¾-cup broiler-proof ramekins, using a paper towel to clean up any custard spilled along the rims. Place the ramekins in a shallow baking dish, and pour warm water into the baking dish to reach halfway up the sides of the ramekins.

Carefully place the baking dish in the oven and bake for about 35 minutes, or until the custards are firm. Remove the ramekins from the water bath and let cool at room temperature for up to 2 hours, or let cool to room temperature and then refrigerate, uncovered, for up to 8 hours.

When ready to serve, preheat the broiler. Transfer the ramekins to a baking sheet and sprinkle each one evenly with 1 teaspoon of the remaining sugar. Place the baking sheet on the top rack of the oven 2 to 3 inches from the heat source, lining the ramekins up directly under the heat source. Broil for 1 to 2 minutes, until the tops are golden brown. Carefully monitor the ramekins to avoid burning the tops (you can leave the oven door slightly ajar to make watching easier). Serve at once.

CHOCOLATE SOUFFLÉ

Light and airy on top, dark and soft on the inside, these chocolate desserts are plenty sweet but not cloying or heavy. They are also easy to make. Just remember that with soufflés, timing is everything. They are best when eaten hot from the oven.

A tip for home entertaining and general ease in the kitchen: Make the batter and fill the ramekins up to 4 hours in advance, then refrigerate them. Remove from the refrigerator about 10 minutes before you are ready to bake, then bake as directed.

1 cup (8 ounces/2 sticks) plus 2 tablespoons unsalted butter, at room temperature
¼ cup plus 6 teaspoons all-purpose flour
1½ teaspoons baking powder
9 ounces bittersweet chocolate, coarsely chopped
⅓ cup granulated sugar
5 eggs
Confectioners' sugar, for dusting

Preheat the oven to 400°F. Grease six ¾-cup ramekins with the 2 tablespoons butter. Sprinkle each ramekin with 1 teaspoon of the flour, then tilt and shake the ramekin to coat evenly. Turn the ramekins upside down and tap gently to remove any excess flour.

In a small bowl, whisk together the remaining ¼ cup flour and the baking powder. Set aside.

Pour water to a depth of 2 inches into the bottom of a double boiler or a saucepan large enough to rest a medium stainless-steel bowl in its rim. Bring to a low simmer over medium-high heat, then decrease the heat to maintain a low simmer.

Place the chocolate in the top pan of the double boiler or in the stainless-steel bowl, and place the pan or bowl over (not touching) the simmering water. Heat the chocolate, stirring occasionally, for about 5 minutes, or until it has melted.

Remove the pan from the heat, but leave the chocolate in the pan or bowl over the hot water to keep it fluid.

While the chocolate is melting, in a large bowl, using an electric mixer on medium speed, beat together the remaining 1 cup butter and the granulated sugar for 1 to 2 minutes, until pale yellow. Add the eggs, one at a time, mixing well after each addition until thoroughly combined. Add the reserved flour mixture to the egg mixture and beat until combined. The batter will be a bit lumpy, but it will smooth out as the chocolate is added.

Slowly whisk the melted chocolate into the batter for about 1 minute, or until all of the ingredients are thoroughly blended.

Using a large spoon, fill each ramekin three-fourths full with the batter, then smooth the top with the rubber spatula. Gently tap the bottom of each filled ramekin on the countertop to help settle the batter.

Place the ramekins on a baking sheet and bake for about 15 minutes, or until the soufflés have risen ½ inch above the rim of the ramekins. The tops will have split a bit and should be fairly crunchy.

Remove the soufflés from the oven and let cool for 5 minutes. Use a fine-mesh sieve or a small spoon to dust the tops with confectioners' sugar. Serve at once.

CHOCOLATE ALMOND TORTE WITH
FRESH STRAWBERRIES AND WHIPPED CREAM

Chocolate lovers will be especially pleased with this dark, rich flourless cake. The almonds add a pleasing crunch, and the cake is enhanced by fresh strawberries and silky smooth whipped cream. For maximum pleasure, make the whipped cream. It's quick and simple to do, and it will taste much better than most store-bought versions.

½ cup (4 ounces/1 stick) plus 1 tablespoon
    unsalted butter

1 cup almonds

8 ounces semisweet or bittersweet chocolate, coarsely
    chopped

½ teaspoon almond extract

5 eggs, separated

1 cup granulated sugar

1 tablespoon confectioners' sugar

1½ to 2 cups whipped cream, homemade (page 192)
    or store-bought

2 cups sliced fresh strawberries

Preheat the oven to 350°F. Grease the bottom and sides of a 9-inch springform cake pan with the 1 tablespoon butter. Line the bottom of the pan with a round of parchment paper. (You can find parchment paper cut to fit 9-inch pans at many well-stocked supermarkets, or trim a larger piece to fit.)

Using a food processor or blender, pulse the almonds until a coarse powder forms. The powder should retain some crunch. Set aside.

In a small saucepan, combine the chocolate and the remaining ½ cup butter, place over low heat, and heat, stirring frequently to prevent burning, until melted. Stir in the almond extract. Keep the mixture warm over very low heat (just hot enough to keep the mixture fluid) until ready to use.

In a medium bowl, using an electric mixer on medium-high speed, beat the egg yolks until blended. Add ½ cup of the granulated sugar in a slow, steady stream and beat for about 1 minute, or until the sugar is well incorporated and the mixture is thick and pale yellow. Set aside.

In a large bowl, using the electric mixer fitted with clean beaters, beat the egg whites on medium-high speed until they are foamy. Slowly add the remaining ½ cup granulated sugar and continue to beat for about 1 minute, or until soft, slightly stiff peaks form. Using a rubber spatula, gently fold the egg yolk mixture into the egg whites. Add the ground almonds and stir gently to mix well. Pour in the melted chocolate and stir until the color is uniform throughout.

Pour the batter into the prepared cake pan. Bake for about 30 minutes, or until a toothpick inserted into the center of the cake comes out clean. Let cool in the pan on a wire rack to room temperature.

Unclip and lift away the pan sides, then gently turn the cake upside down onto a platter. Carefully remove the bottom of the baking pan, and peel off the parchment paper. Use a fine-mesh sieve to dust the top of the cake with the confectioners' sugar.

To serve, cut the cake into wedges. Liberally top each serving with a dollop of whipped cream and the strawberries.

Basics

Every cook benefits from knowing a few basic recipes and techniques. In the previous pages, we have highlighted some of these basics, such as making a hollandaise sauce or frosting a cake. In this chapter, we are including recipes and techniques that are used to prepare many dishes throughout the book. Possibly the most useful of them all is chicken stock (page 193). You can make it from cooked or raw chicken and then freeze it for later use. It makes a terrific soup base and is used in gravies and sauces, to cook rice, and in other preparations.

Also in this chapter, you'll find a method for toasting nuts and seeds (page 192), a simple procedure that will boost the flavor of dishes as diverse as Spicy Sesame Noodles (page 107) and Hazelnut Chocolate Chunk Cookies (page 168).

Our versatile barbecue sauce (page 196), which is featured in recipes for burgers, chicken, and ribs, is here, too. So are four different versions of mayonnaise (pages 194 to 195), all of which will make it hard for you to go back to commercial brands that pale by comparison. On the sweet side, nothing may be as delicious as home-made whipped cream (page 192)—another "simply fresh" improvement on what you can buy at the store.

Make these basic recipes and techniques part of your standard kitchen repertoire and your daily meals will be greatly enhanced.

WHIPPED CREAM

Homemade whipped cream is richer and thicker than commercial whipped cream. For a lighter texture, substitute confectioners' sugar for the granulated sugar. Or, for a different flavor, use maple syrup in place of sugar.

1 cup heavy cream, chilled
2 teaspoons sugar

In a deep bowl, combine the cream and sugar. Using a whisk or an electric mixer on medium-high speed, beat the cream until soft peaks form.

Use immediately, or cover and refrigerate for up to 2 hours.

TOASTING NUTS AND SEEDS

Toasting nuts or seeds intensifies their aroma and heightens their crunchiness. This technique is easy, calling for nothing more than a small skillet and the stovetop. You'll need to keep an eye on the pan, however. Once the nuts or seeds begin to reach the right temperature, they can quickly burn if you don't remove them from the heat promptly.

Place the nuts or seeds in a small, dry skillet over medium heat and toast, stirring with a wooden spoon or shaking the pan regularly, for 3 to 4 minutes for seeds and small nuts or 8 to 10 minutes for larger nuts, or until they are fragrant and begin to take on color. Immediately pour onto a plate to cool.

ROASTED RED PEPPERS

Roasted red bell peppers are used in Fettuccine with Roasted Red Pepper Sauce and Italian Sausage (page 102) and Mediterranean Pasta Salad (page 106). They require little effort to prepare—so little that you'll wonder why you don't prepare them more often. You can also serve them on their own as an appetizer: drizzle them with extra-virgin olive oil and garnish with a little coarse salt and freshly ground black pepper.

Preheat the oven to 400°F. Place the peppers in a baking dish or roasting pan. (It is a good idea to roast a big batch so you have them on hand.) Roast for 20 to 30 minutes, until the tops of the peppers begin to change color from red to black. Remove from the oven and let cool.

To remove the skins and seeds, pull the peppers partially apart under cold running water, and use your fingers to peel off the skins and rub the seeds away. Then pull the peppers into halves or quarters and pat dry with a paper towel.

If you are using the peppers within 30 minutes or so, set them aside in a medium bowl. Alternatively, store them in an airtight container in the refrigerator for up to 3 days. (They will release liquid during this time. Discard the liquid before using.)

CHICKEN STOCK   MAKES ABOUT 2½ QUARTS

Chicken stock is an important flavor enhancer. It is the foundation for nearly all of the soup recipes in this book. It can also be used to make gravy (see Buttermilk Fried Chicken with Mushroom Gravy, page 153), and in place of water for richer, more flavorful rice. Best of all, chicken stock is easy to make.

Leftover chicken and chicken bones from a roast chicken will produce an excellent stock. You can also use raw chicken parts, which will yield a slightly more intensely flavored stock. Leftovers are more practical, however. Just make a little stock each time you roast a chicken and freeze it until needed.

Commercially made chicken broth, preferably one marked reduced or low sodium, can stand in for homemade stock. But remember, this recipe delivers a lot of flavor with little effort.

2 to 3 pounds cooked chicken carcass or
    raw chicken parts (such as backs, wings, and necks)
1 onion, coarsely chopped
1 large carrot, peeled and coarsely chopped
4 cloves garlic
½ teaspoon dried thyme
1 bay leaf
1 teaspoon salt
3 quarts water

In a large pot, combine all of the ingredients and bring to a boil over high heat. Decrease the heat to low and simmer uncovered, skimming off any foam that forms on the surface, for 1½ hours.

Remove from the heat and strain the stock through a fine-mesh sieve into a clean container. Discard the solids and let the stock cool to room temperature. Cover and refrigerate until the fat congeals on the surface. Remove and discard the fat, then use the stock at once, or cover and refrigerate for up to 3 days or freeze for up to 3 months.

Mayonnaise Four Ways

Mayonnaise is ubiquitous in our dining culture, yet many of us think of it as nothing more than a sandwich spread. It also makes a fine dipping sauce for vegetables, fish, and meats. The addition of garlic to make aioli or of garlic and chili flakes to make chili aioli contributes extra layers of flavor. Mayonnaise also acts as a tasty binding agent for crab cakes (page 112).

Homemade mayonnaise has a freshness and flavor intensity rarely found in commercial mayonnaise. You can make it with any kind of oil, but we recommend a blend of olive oil and canola oil. The olive oil adds a rich, fruity component and the canola oil delivers lightness. Commercial mayonnaise is generally slightly sweet because of the addition of sugar or honey. Look for commercial brands that are low in sugar or honey for a more savory flavor. And if you are substituting commercial mayonnaise for homemade mayonnaise in the recipes in this book, keep the sweetness in mind. When you use commercial mayonnaise as a sandwich spread, such as for our burgers (pages 130 to 134), your palate will hardly notice the difference because the combination is so familiar. But if you use it for a dipping sauce like aioli, the sweetness will be noticeable.

Unlike commercial mayonnaise, homemade mayonnaise is made with raw eggs. Most eggs are produced under sanitary conditions, but the threat of salmonella is a real—albeit unlikely—one, particularly for small children, pregnant women, older individuals, or people with a compromised immune system. Anyone concerned about salmonella should use a minimally sweetened commercial mayonnaise. Otherwise, organically produced eggs from cage-free chickens will be your best option when making your own mayonnaise.

Making mayonnaise at home requires only 5 to 10 minutes. For the best results, have the egg yolk at room temperature. Cold eggs do not emulsify well.

Mayonnaise

1 egg yolk, at room temperature
1 teaspoon Dijon mustard
Pinch of salt, plus additional for seasoning
½ cup extra-virgin olive oil
⅔ cup canola oil

In a medium bowl, whisk together the egg yolk, mustard, and salt until well blended. Combine the oils in a liquid measuring cup. Add the oils to the bowl in a fine, slow drizzle, a small amount at a time, whisking constantly until the mixture emulsifies and then thickens, forming a sauce. Once the mixture emulsifies, the oils can be added slightly faster. Alternatively, in a food processor or blender, combine the egg yolk, mustard, and salt and pulse until well blended. With the machine running, add the oils in a slow, steady stream and process until a thick, emulsified sauce forms. Taste and adjust the seasoning with salt.

Use immediately, or cover and refrigerate for up to 2 days.

Aioli and Chipotle Aioli

French cooks make a garlic-flavored mayonnaise known as aioli, but similar garlic mayonnaises are enjoyed around the Mediterranean. Although aioli is traditionally used as a dipping sauce, it also doubles nicely as a sandwich spread. The minced garlic adds a tangy, fresh quality to the mayonnaise. For a spicer sauce, add chipotle chili flakes along with the garlic.

1 clove garlic, finely minced
1½ cups mayonnaise, homemade (above) or store-bought
½ teaspoon chipotle chili flakes (see page 81) or
    red pepper flakes (optional)

For aioli, in a medium bowl, stir or whisk the garlic into the mayonnaise. For chipotle aioli, whisk in the chili flakes with the garlic.

Use immediately, or cover and refrigerate for up to 2 days.

ROASTED GARLIC MAYONNAISE

Roasting garlic gives it a soft, nutty sweetness. Despite the fact that this recipe calls for a whole head of garlic, the resulting mayonnaise is milder and more subtle than aioli (opposite page) made with a single clove of raw garlic. Roasting garlic is an easy kitchen technique, and soft, creamy cloves are also delicious spread directly on bread or toast—without the mayonnaise!

1 medium head garlic
1 teaspoon extra-virgin olive oil
1½ cups mayonnaise, homemade (opposite page) or
    store-bought

Preheat the oven to 400°F.

Rub off any loose, papery skin from the garlic head. Using a sharp knife, cut off the top one-third of the head (the pointed part) to reveal the tops of the cloves. Wrap the garlic head in aluminum foil, leaving the top open, and place in a small baking pan. Drizzle the exposed garlic with the olive oil.

Roast for about 45 minutes, or until the top is golden and the garlic is tender. Remove from the oven, let cool for about 5 minutes, and then remove the foil. (The garlic can be roasted up to 1 week in advance. Store the whole head, wrapped in the foil, in the refrigerator.)

Turn the head upside down and squeeze as much of the soft garlic as you can directly into the mayonnaise. Use a fork to stir the cloves into the mayonnaise. It's okay to leave chunks of the soft, sweet cloves intact.

Use immediately, or cover and refrigerate for up to 2 days.

BARBECUE SAUCE

MAKES ABOUT 2 CUPS

You can find many good commercial barbecue sauces on store shelves today. But this quickly prepared, homemade version delivers exceptional taste, plus you'll be proud that you made it yourself! It boosts the flavor of a number of dishes in this book, including Brewmaster Burger (page 133), Fork-Tender Baby Back Ribs (page 137), Meat Loaf (page 140), and Barbecue Grilled Chicken Breasts (page 156). So, just simmer and then slather away!

1½ cups tomato sauce
½ cup ketchup
¼ cup white wine vinegar
2 teaspoons hickory liquid smoke
3 tablespoons brown sugar
2 tablespoons Worcestershire sauce
½ teaspoon mustard powder
½ teaspoon ground cumin
½ teaspoon cayenne pepper
½ teaspoon granulated garlic powder
½ teaspoon onion powder
½ teaspoon salt

In a medium saucepan, combine all of the ingredients over medium heat and bring to a boil, stirring occasionally to prevent scorching. Decrease the heat to low and simmer, stirring occasionally, for 10 minutes to blend the flavors.

Use immediately, or let cool, cover, and refrigerate for up to 5 days.

ACKNOWLEDGMENTS

Every book is a team effort, and this one is no exception. Without the support and assistance of many talented individuals, this book could never have been written. First and foremost, I would like to thank Ruby Tuesday founder Sandy Beall for entrusting me with the task of representing his vision in these pages. I would also like to thank Sandy's son, Sam (who runs the family's other fine-dining establishment and resort, Blackberry Farm), for introducing me to Sandy.

Getting started was aided by Ruby Tuesday CMO Mark Young, who understood that time was of the essence and got us on the fast track to publication. Part of his strategy was calling on Rick Johnson—who I now know can move mountains—to assist in this endeavor.

Of course, no cookbook would have been possible without the ongoing participation of Ruby Tuesday's talented chefs, led by executive chef Peter Glander. These dedicated culinary artists have brought Ruby Tuesday to a new level of creativity and excellence that I hope is evident in these pages. But even great chefs need someone to test cookbook recipes for use in a home kitchen. That task fell to my longtime cookbook collaborator and wife, Jodie Morgan, without whom I probably couldn't do much of anything.

And as you peruse the recipes, you are certain to be impressed by Heather Anne Thomas's exquisite photographs. They provide an ongoing source of inspiration for anyone interested in cooking and eating well. Thanks must also be extended to food stylist Michael Pederson, prop stylists Lynda White and Jeff Wood, and photography assistant Zane Jernigan.

Additionally, I have been blessed with amazing editorial support. Initial thanks go to Kirsty Melville, president of the book division of Andrews McMeel Publishing. Her early enthusiasm and her ability to get things done were critical to the creation of the book. Designer Jennifer Barry has not only given the book a beautiful look, but also managed the project and kept us all on track. And every writer should have the good fortune to work with a copy editor as talented and thorough as Sharon Silva.

Finally, I would like to express my deepest appreciation to Carole Bidnick, my literary agent, who is always there to guide me. With her East Coast savvy and her West Coast sensitivity, I couldn't possibly ask for a better advocate.

— Jeff Morgan

INDEX

A

Aioli, 194
  Chipotle Aioli, 194
Almonds
  Chocolate Almond Torte with Fresh
    Strawberries and Whipped Cream, 188
  toasting, 192
Angel Food Cake, Strawberry, 185
Appetizers
  Pico de Gallo and Homemade Tortilla Chips, 22
  Spinach and Artichoke Dip, 23
  Guacamole, 25
  Blue Cheese Dip, 26
  Chicken Wings Three Ways:
    Fire, Boston Barbecue, and Asian Sesame, 27
  Thai Phoon Shrimp, 31
  California Club Quesadilla, 32
Apples
  Apple and Cheese Omelet, 65
  Old-Fashioned Apple Pie, 174–75
  Sangria, 12
  Sweet and Savory Apple-Cranberry Crêpes
    with Whipped Cream and Maple Syrup,
    57–58
Arnold Palmer, 9
Artichoke and Spinach Dip, 23
Asian Glazed Salmon, 124
Asian Sesame Sauce, 27–28
Asparagus with Olive Oil and Parmesan
    Cheese, 39
Avocados
  Avocado and Shrimp Salad with Creole
    Seasoning and Avocado Ranch Dressing, 75
  Avocado Turkey Burger, 134
  California Club Quesadilla, 32
  Guacamole, 25
  Mixed Baby Greens with Mustard Vinaigrette, 72
  removing pit from, 25
  Tortilla Soup, 91

B

Bacon
  California Club Quesadilla, 32
  Potato Salad with Chipotle Chile and Bacon, 81
  Roasted Brussels Sprouts with Bacon, 35
  Wilted Spinach with Bacon and Garlic, 37
Baked Halibut with Chili-Lime Butter, 118
Baked Petrale Sole with Fennel, Tomatoes,
    Potatoes, and Capers, 121
Barbecue Grilled Chicken Breasts, 156
Barbecue Sauce, 196
Barbecue tips, 132
Bar tools, 6
Basil
  Basil-Mint Pesto Pasta, 99
  Mediterranean Pasta Salad, 106
  Tomato, Basil, and Bocconcini Pasta Salad, 103
Beans
  Corn and Edamame Succotash, 40
  Minestrone Soup, 86
  White Bean Chicken Chili, 88
Beef
  Braised Short Ribs, 139
  Brewmaster Burger, 133
  The Classic Burger, 130
  Cowboy Sirloin with Red Chili Rub, Caramel-
    ized Onions, and Blue Cheese Butter, 146–47
  Meat Loaf, 140
  Peppercorn Steaks with Brandy Cream Sauce
    and Sautéed Mushrooms, 145
  Rib Eye with Garlic Brown Butter, 142
  Steak and Eggs Benedict, 60
  steaks, panfrying, 143
Beer
  alcohol content of, 7
  Boston Barbecue Sauce, 27–28
  Brewmaster Burger, 133
  pairing food and, 7
  styles of, 7

Bell peppers
  Brown Rice Pilaf, 42
  Corn and Edamame Succotash, 40
  Fettuccine with Roasted Red Pepper Sauce and
    Italian Sausage, 102
  Mediterranean Pasta Salad, 106
  Pico de Gallo, 22
  roasting, 193
  Spicy Sesame Noodles, 107
  Western Frittata with Green and Red Peppers,
    Ham, and Cheese, 63
Biscuits, Buttermilk, 53
Blue cheese
  Blue Cheese Butter, 146–47
  Blue Cheese Dip, 26
Boston Barbecue Sauce, 27–28
Braised Chicken with Fresh Fennel, Carrots,
    Zucchini, Potatoes, and Herbs, 155
Braised Short Ribs, 139
Bread. See also Burgers; English muffins
  French Toast with Rolled Oats and
    Coriander, 54
  Parmesan Crostini, 85
Brewmaster Burger, 133
Broccoli
  Broccoli and Cheese Soup with Parmesan
    Crostini, 85
  Broccoli with Lemon and Olive Oil Drizzle, 36
  Chicken Broccoli Stir-Fry with Lemon Butter
    and Brown Rice, 159
Brown Rice Pilaf, 42
Brussels Sprouts, Roasted, with Bacon, 35
Burgers
  Avocado Turkey Burger, 134
  Brewmaster Burger, 133
  The Classic Burger, 130
  tips for, 131
  toppings for, 135

Butter
    Blue Cheese Butter, 146–47
    Chili-Lime Butter, 118
Buttermilk
    Buttermilk Biscuits, 53
    Buttermilk Fried Chicken with Mushroom
      Gravy, 153

C

Cabbage
    Chinese Chicken Salad, 74
Cajun Mary, 16
Cajun-Spiced Tilapia, 123
Cakes
    Cheesecake with Fresh Raspberry Sauce, 177–78
    Chocolate Almond Torte with Fresh
      Strawberries and Whipped Cream, 188
    frosting layer, 183
    Italian Cream Cake, 180–82
    Pecan Carrot Cake with Vanilla Buttercream
      Icing, 179
    Strawberry Angel Food Cake, 185
California Club Quesadilla, 32
Caramelized Onions, 146–47
Carrots
    Braised Chicken with Fresh Fennel, Carrots,
      Zucchini, Potatoes, and Herbs, 155
    Pecan Carrot Cake with Vanilla Buttercream
      Icing, 179
    Sautéed Carrots with Cumin Seeds and
      Cilantro, 36
Cauliflower, Creamy Mashed, 37
Cheese
    Apple and Cheese Omelet, 65
    Asparagus with Olive Oil and Parmesan
      Cheese, 39
    Avocado Turkey Burger, 134
    Blue Cheese Butter, 146–47
    Blue Cheese Dip, 26
    Brewmaster Burger, 133
    Broccoli and Cheese Soup with Parmesan
      Crostini, 85
    California Club Quesadilla, 32
    Cheesecake with Fresh Raspberry Sauce, 177–78

Italian Cream Cake, 180–82
Lemon Pasta with Parmesan and Herbs, 98
Lobster Carbonara with English Peas, 96–98
Mac and Cheese, 104
Mediterranean Pasta Salad, 106
Parmesan, 95
Parmesan Cream Sauce, 162
Polenta, 42
Spinach, Mushroom, and Feta Cheese
    Omelet, 66
Steak and Eggs Benedict, 60
Tomato, Basil, and Bocconcini Pasta Salad, 103
Tortilla Soup, 91
Western Frittata with Green and Red Peppers,
    Ham, and Cheese, 63
White Cheddar Mashed Potatoes, 45
Chicken
    Barbecue Grilled Chicken Breasts, 156
    Braised Chicken with Fresh Fennel, Carrots,
      Zucchini, Potatoes, and Herbs, 155
    Buttermilk Fried Chicken with Mushroom
      Gravy, 153
    California Club Quesadilla, 32
    Chicken Broccoli Stir-Fry with Lemon Butter
      and Brown Rice, 159
    Chicken Curry with Coconut Rice, 160–61
    Chicken Fresco with Parmesan Cream Sauce
      and Roasted Tomatoes, 162
    Chicken Stock, 193
    Chicken Wings Three Ways, 27–28
    Chinese Chicken Salad, 74
    frying, 154
    White Bean Chicken Chili, 88
Chili, White Bean Chicken, 88
Chili-Lime Butter, 118
Chinese Chicken Salad, 74
Chipotle chiles
    Chipotle Aioli, 194
    flakes, 81
    Potato Salad with Chipotle Chile and Bacon, 81
Chips, Homemade Tortilla, 22
Chocolate
    Chocolate Almond Torte with Fresh
      Strawberries and Whipped Cream, 188

Chocolate Soufflé, 187
    Hazelnut Chocolate Chunk Cookies, 168
Chowder, Manhattan Clam, 87
Chutney, Corn and Pineapple, 112–14
Clam Chowder, Manhattan Clam, 87
The Classic Burger, 130
Coconut
    Chicken Curry with Coconut Rice, 160–61
    Italian Cream Cake, 180–82
Cookies
    Hazelnut Chocolate Chunk Cookies, 168
    Macadamia Nut and White Chocolate Chip
      Cookies, 170
Corn
    Corn and Edamame Succotash, 40
    Crab Cakes with Corn and Pineapple Chutney,
      112–14
Cosmopolitan, 11
Cowboy Sirloin with Red Chili Rub, Caramelized
    Onions, and Blue Cheese Butter, 146–47
Crab
    Crab Cakes with Corn and Pineapple Chutney,
      112–14
    Crabmeat Crêpes with Hollandaise Sauce,
      57–58
Cranberries
    Cosmopolitan, 11
    Ruby Relaxer, 11
    Sweet and Savory Apple-Cranberry Crêpes with
      Whipped Cream and Maple Syrup, 57–58
Cream, Whipped, 192
Creamy Mashed Cauliflower, 37
Crème Brûlée, Ginger, 186
Crêpes
    Crabmeat Crêpes with Hollandaise Sauce, 57–58
    Sweet and Savory Apple-Cranberry Crêpes with
      Whipped Cream and Maple Syrup, 57–58
Crisp, Peach, 173
Crostini, Parmesan, 85
Curry, Chicken, with Coconut Rice, 160–61

D

Desserts
    Cheesecake with Fresh Raspberry Sauce, 177–78

Chocolate Almond Torte with Fresh
Strawberries and Whipped Cream, 188
Chocolate Soufflé, 187
Ginger Crème Brûlée, 186
Hazelnut Chocolate Chunk Cookies, 168
Italian Cream Cake, 180–82
Lemon Zabaglione, 171
Macadamia Nut and White Chocolate Chip
Cookies, 170
Peach Crisp, 173
Pecan Carrot Cake with Vanilla Buttercream
Icing, 179
Strawberry Angel Food Cake, 185
Dill Ranch Dressing, 78
Dips
Blue Cheese Dip, 26
Guacamole, 25
Spinach and Artichoke Dip, 23
Drinks. *See also* Beer; Wine
Arnold Palmer, 9
Cosmopolitan, 11
equipment for, 6
Ruby Relaxer, 11
Sangria, 12
Strawberry Lemonade, 8
Tropical Sunrise, 9
Ultimate Margarita, 15
Ultimate Mojito, 15

E

Edamame and Corn Succotash, 40
Eggs
Apple and Cheese Omelet, 65
Chocolate Soufflé, 187
Ginger Crème Brûlée, 186
Lemon Zabaglione, 171
Poached Eggs Benedict with Smoked
Salmon, 62
Spinach, Mushroom, and Feta Cheese
Omelet, 66
Steak and Eggs Benedict, 60
Strawberry Angel Food Cake, 185
Western Frittata with Green and Red Peppers,
Ham, and Cheese, 63
English muffins

Poached Eggs Benedict with Smoked
Salmon, 62
Steak and Eggs Benedict, 60

F

Fennel
Baked Petrale Sole with Fennel, Tomatoes,
Potatoes, and Capers, 121
Braised Chicken with Fresh Fennel, Carrots,
Zucchini, Potatoes, and Herbs, 155
Fettuccine with Roasted Red Pepper Sauce and
Italian Sausage, 102
Fire Wing Sauce, 27–28
Fish
Asian Glazed Salmon, 124
Baked Halibut with Chili-Lime Butter, 118
Baked Petrale Sole with Fennel, Tomatoes,
Potatoes, and Capers, 121
Cajun-Spiced Tilapia, 123
in foil cooking pouch, 122
nutrition and, 111
Poached Eggs Benedict with Smoked Salmon,
62
Salmon and Spinach Salad with Sesame-Peanut
Dressing, 77
Seafood Pasta with Andouille Sausage, 101
Soy-Sesame Tuna Steaks, 125
substituting, 111
Fork-Tender Baby Back Ribs, 137–38
French Toast with Rolled Oats and Coriander, 54
Frittata, Western, with Green and Red Peppers,
Ham, and Cheese, 63

G

Garlic
Aioli, 194
Chipotle Aioli, 194
Garlic-Rosemary Rub, 150
Pork Chops with Fried Garlic and Red Wine
Gravy, 149
Rib Eye with Garlic Brown Butter, 142
Roasted Garlic Mayonnaise, 195
Sautéed Baby Bella Mushrooms with Garlic
and Rosemary, 41

Wilted Spinach with Bacon and Garlic, 37
Ginger Crème Brûlée, 186
Grand Marnier
Ultimate Margarita, 15
Gravy
Mushroom Gravy, 153
Red Wine Gravy, 149
Grilled Lemon-Lime Shrimp with Yogurt-Cilantro
Dipping Sauce, 117
Guacamole, 25

H

Halibut
Baked Halibut with Chili-Lime Butter, 118
Seafood Pasta with Andouille Sausage, 101
Ham
Ham and Pea Salad with Fresh Dill Ranch
Dressing, 78
Western Frittata with Green and Red Peppers,
Ham, and Cheese, 63
Hazelnuts
Hazelnut Chocolate Chunk Cookies, 168
toasting, 192
Herbed Panfried Potatoes, 46
Hollandaise Sauce, 59
Homemade Tortilla Chips, 22

I

Icing, Vanilla Buttercream, 179
Italian Cream Cake, 180–82

K

Kale
Minestrone Soup, 86

L

Lemons
Arnold Palmer, 9
Broccoli with Lemon and Olive Oil Drizzle, 36
Grilled Lemon-Lime Shrimp with
Yogurt-Cilantro Dipping Sauce, 117
Lemon Pasta with Parmesan and Herbs, 98
Lemon Zabaglione, 171

Lemons (*continued*)
Strawberry Lemonade, 8
Ultimate Margarita, 15
Limes
Chili-Lime Butter, 118
Grilled Lemon-Lime Shrimp with
Yogurt-Cilantro Dipping Sauce, 117
Sangria, 12
Ultimate Margarita, 15
Ultimate Mojito, 15
Lobster
Lobster Carbonara with English Peas, 96–98
tail, removing meat from, 96

M
Macadamia Nut and White Chocolate Chip
Cookies, 170
Mac and Cheese, 104
Mango juice
Tropical Sunrise, 9
Manhattan Clam Chowder, 87
Margarita, Ultimate, 15
Mayonnaise, 194
Aioli, 194
Chipotle Aioli, 194
Roasted Garlic Mayonnaise, 195
Meat Loaf, 140
Mediterranean Pasta Salad, 106
Minestrone Soup, 86
Mint
Basil-Mint Pesto Pasta, 99
Ultimate Mojito, 15
Mixed Baby Greens with Mustard Vinaigrette, 72
Mojito, Ultimate, 15
Muddling, 6
Mushrooms
Buttermilk Fried Chicken with Mushroom
Gravy, 153
Peppercorn Steaks with Brandy Cream Sauce
and Sautéed Mushrooms, 145
Sautéed Baby Bella Mushrooms with Garlic and
Rosemary, 41
Spinach, Mushroom, and Feta Cheese
Omelet, 66
Mustard Vinaigrette, 72

N
Nuts, toasting, 192. *See also individual nuts*

O
Oats, Rolled, French Toast with Coriander and, 54
Old-Fashioned Apple Pie, 174–75
Olives
Mediterranean Pasta Salad, 106
Omelets
Apple and Cheese Omelet, 65
making, 65
Spinach, Mushroom, and Feta Cheese Omelet, 66
Onions, Caramelized, 146–47
Oranges
Arnold Palmer, 9
Sangria, 12
Tropical Sunrise, 9
Oven-Roasted Potato "Fries" with Rosemary, 46

P
Parmesan cheese, 95
Asparagus with Olive Oil and Parmesan
Cheese, 39
Lemon Pasta with Parmesan and Herbs, 98
Lobster Carbonara with English Peas, 96–98
Mac and Cheese, 104
Parmesan Cream Sauce, 162
Parmesan Crostini, 85
Pasta
Basil-Mint Pesto Pasta, 99
cooking, 103
Fettuccine with Roasted Red Pepper Sauce and
Italian Sausage, 102
Ham and Pea Salad with Fresh Dill Ranch
Dressing, 78
Lemon Pasta with Parmesan and Herbs, 98
Lobster Carbonara with English Peas, 96–98
Mac and Cheese, 104
Mediterranean Pasta Salad, 106
Minestrone Soup, 86
party, 99
Seafood Pasta with Andouille Sausage, 101
Spicy Sesame Noodles, 107
Tomato, Basil, and Bocconcini Pasta Salad, 103
Peach Crisp, 173

Peanuts
Asian Glazed Salmon, 124
Salmon and Spinach Salad with Sesame-Peanut
Dressing, 77
toasting, 192
Peas
Ham and Pea Salad with Fresh Dill Ranch
Dressing, 78
Lobster Carbonara with English Peas, 96–98
Pecan Carrot Cake with Vanilla Buttercream
Icing, 179
Peppercorn Steaks with Brandy Cream Sauce and
Sautéed Mushrooms, 145
Pesto Pasta, Basil-Mint, 99
Petrale Sole, Baked, with Fennel, Tomatoes,
Potatoes, and Capers, 121
Pico de Gallo, 22
Pie, Old-Fashioned Apple, 174–75
Pilaf, Brown Rice, 42
Pineapple
Crab Cakes with Corn and Pineapple Chutney,
112–14
Pecan Carrot Cake with Vanilla Buttercream
Icing, 179
Ruby Relaxer, 11
Tropical Sunrise, 9
Poached Eggs Benedict with Smoked Salmon, 62
Polenta, 42
Pork
Fork-Tender Baby Back Ribs, 137–38
Meat Loaf, 140
Pork Chops with Fried Garlic and Red Wine
Gravy, 149
Pork Loin with Rosemary-Garlic Rub, 150
Potatoes
Baked Petrale Sole with Fennel, Tomatoes,
Potatoes, and Capers, 121
Braised Chicken with Fresh Fennel, Carrots,
Zucchini, Potatoes, and Herbs, 155
Herbed Panfried Potatoes, 46
Manhattan Clam Chowder, 87
Minestrone Soup, 86
Oven-Roasted Potato "Fries" with Rosemary, 46
Potato Salad with Chipotle Chile and
Bacon, 81

Potatoes (*continued*)
    White Cheddar Mashed Potatoes, 45
Prosciutto. *See* Ham

Q
Quesadilla, California Club, 32

R
Raspberry Sauce, 177–78
Red Wine Gravy, 149
Rib Eye with Garlic Brown Butter, 142
Ribs
    Braised Short Ribs, 139
    Fork-Tender Baby Back Ribs, 137–38
    tips for, 138
Rice
    Brown Rice Pilaf, 42
    Chicken Broccoli Stir-Fry with Lemon Butter
        and Brown Rice, 159
    Chicken Curry with Coconut Rice, 160–61
Roasted Brussels Sprouts with Bacon, 35
Roasted Garlic Mayonnaise, 195
Ruby Relaxer, 11
Rum
    Ruby Relaxer, 11
    Ultimate Mojito, 15

S
Salad dressings
    Avocado Ranch Dressing, 75
    Dill Ranch Dressing, 78
    Mustard Vinaigrette, 72
    Sesame-Peanut Dressing, 77
Salads
    Avocado and Shrimp Salad with Creole
        Seasoning and Avocado Ranch Dressing, 75
    Chinese Chicken Salad, 74
    Ham and Pea Salad with Fresh Dill Ranch
        Dressing, 78
    Mediterranean Pasta Salad, 106
    Mixed Baby Greens with Mustard Vinaigrette, 72
    Potato Salad with Chipotle Chile and
        Bacon, 81
    Salmon and Spinach Salad with Sesame-Peanut
        Dressing, 77

Tomato, Basil, and Bocconcini Pasta Salad, 103
Salmon
    Asian Glazed Salmon, 124
    Poached Eggs Benedict with Smoked
        Salmon, 62
    Salmon and Spinach Salad with Sesame-Peanut
        Dressing, 77
Salsas. *See* Sauces and salsas
Sangria, 12
Sauces and salsas
    Asian Sesame Sauce, 27–28
    Barbecue Sauce, 196
    Basil-Mint Pesto, 99
    Boston Barbecue Sauce, 27–28
    Fire Wing Sauce, 27–28
    Hollandaise Sauce, 59
    Parmesan Cream Sauce, 162
    Pico de Gallo, 22
    Raspberry Sauce, 177–78
    Roasted Red Pepper Sauce, 102
    Yogurt-Cilantro Dipping Sauce, 117
Sausage
    Fettuccine with Roasted Red Pepper Sauce
        and Italian Sausage, 102
    Seafood Pasta with Andouille Sausage,
        101
Sautéed Baby Bella Mushrooms with Garlic
    and Rosemary, 41
Sautéed Carrots with Cumin Seeds and
    Cilantro, 36
Scallops
    Scallops with Shallots, Parsley, and White
        Wine Sauce, 115
    Seafood Pasta with Andouille Sausage, 101
Schnapps
    Ruby Relaxer, 11
Seafood Pasta with Andouille Sausage, 101
Seeds, toasting, 192
Sesame oil
    Asian Sesame Sauce, 27–28
    Sesame-Peanut Dressing, 77
    Soy-Sesame Tuna Steaks, 125
    Spicy Sesame Noodles, 107
Shopping tips, 78

Shrimp
    Avocado and Shrimp Salad with Creole
        Seasoning and Avocado Ranch Dressing, 75
    Grilled Lemon-Lime Shrimp with
        Yogurt-Cilantro Dipping Sauce, 117
    Seafood Pasta with Andouille Sausage, 101
    Thai Phoon Shrimp, 31
Simple Syrup, 8
Side Dishes
    Roasted Brussels Sprouts with Bacon, 35
    Broccoli with Lemon and Olive Oil Drizzle, 36
    Sautéed Carrots with
        Cumin Seeds and Cilantro, 36
    Wilted Spinach with Bacon and Garlic, 37
    Creamy Mashed Cauliflower, 37
    Asparagus with Olive Oil and
        Parmesan Cheese, 39
    Corn and Edamame Succotash, 40
    Sautéed Baby Bella Mushrooms with
        Garlic and Rosemary, 41
    Polenta, 42
    Brown Rice Pilaf, 42
    White Cheddar Mashed Potatoes, 45
    Herbed Panfried Potatoes, 46
    Oven-Roasted Potato "Fries" with Rosemary, 46
Soufflé, Chocolate, 187
Soups
    Broccoli and Cheese Soup with Parmesan
        Crostini, 85
    Manhattan Clam Chowder, 87
    Minestrone Soup, 86
    Tomato Soup with Fresh Basil, 82
    Tortilla Soup, 91
Soy-Sesame Tuna Steaks, 125
Spicy Sesame Noodles, 107
Spinach
    Chinese Chicken Salad, 74
    Mediterranean Pasta Salad, 106
    Salmon and Spinach Salad with Sesame-Peanut
        Dressing, 77
    Spinach and Artichoke Dip, 23
    Spinach, Mushroom, and Feta Cheese
        Omelet, 66
    Wilted Spinach with Bacon and Garlic, 37

Steaks
    Cowboy Sirloin with Red Chili Rub, Caramelized
        Onions, and Blue Cheese Butter, 146–47
    panfrying, 143
    Peppercorn Steaks with Brandy Cream Sauce
        and Sautéed Mushrooms, 145
    Rib Eye with Garlic Brown Butter, 142
    Steak and Eggs Benedict, 60
Stock, Chicken, 193
Strawberries
    Chocolate Almond Torte with Fresh
        Strawberries and Whipped Cream, 188
    Strawberry Angel Food Cake, 185
    Strawberry Lemonade, 8
Succotash, Corn and Edamame, 40
Sweet and Savory Apple-Cranberry Crêpes with
    Whipped Cream and Maple Syrup, 57–58
Syrup, Simple, 8

T
Tea
    Arnold Palmer, 9
Tequila
    Ultimate Margarita, 15
Thai Phoon Shrimp, 31
Tilapia, Cajun-Spiced, 123
Tofu
    Spicy Sesame Noodles, 107
Tomatoes
    Avocado and Shrimp Salad with Creole
        Seasoning and Avocado Ranch Dressing, 75
    Baked Petrale Sole with Fennel, Tomatoes,
        Potatoes, and Capers, 121
    Barbecue Sauce, 196
    Cajun Mary, 16
    Chicken Broccoli Stir-Fry with Lemon Butter
        and Brown Rice, 159
    Chicken Fresco with Parmesan Cream Sauce
        and Roasted Tomatoes, 162
    Manhattan Clam Chowder, 87
    Minestrone Soup, 86
    Mixed Baby Greens with Mustard Vinaigrette, 72
    Pico de Gallo, 22
    Seafood Pasta with Andouille Sausage, 101

Tomato, Basil, and Bocconcini Pasta Salad, 103
Tomato Soup with Fresh Basil, 82
Tortilla Soup, 91
Tortillas
    California Club Quesadilla, 32
    Homemade Tortilla Chips, 22
    Tortilla Soup, 91
Triple sec
    Cosmopolitan, 11
    Ultimate Margarita, 15
Tropical Sunrise, 9
Tuna Steaks, Soy-Sesame, 125
Turkey Burger, Avocado, 134

U
Ultimate Margarita, 15
Ultimate Mojito, 15

V
Vanilla Buttercream Icing, 179
Veal
    Meat Loaf, 140
Vinaigrettes. *See* Salad dressings
Vodka
    Cajun Mary, 16
    Cosmopolitan, 11
    Ruby Relaxer, 11
    Sangria, 12

W
Walnuts
    Italian Cream Cake, 180–82
    toasting, 192
Western Frittata with Green and Red Peppers,
    Ham, and Cheese, 63
Whipped Cream, 192
White Bean Chicken Chili, 88
White Cheddar Mashed Potatoes, 45
White Chocolate Chip and Macadamia Nut
    Cookies, 170
Wilted Spinach with Bacon and Garlic, 37
Wine
    Lemon Zabaglione, 171
    pairing food and, 3–4

Red Wine Gravy, 149
Sangria, 12
varietals, 4, 7

Y
Yogurt-Cilantro Dipping Sauce, 117

Z
Zabaglione, Lemon, 171
Zucchini
    Braised Chicken with Fresh Fennel, Carrots,
        Zucchini, Potatoes, and Herbs, 155
    Minestrone Soup, 86